WILBUR SMITH

BIRDS OF PREY

MACMILLAN

First published 1997 by Macmillan

an imprint of Macmillan Publishers Ltd
25 Eccleston Place, London SW1W 9NF
and Basingstoke

Associated companies throughout the world

ISBN 0 333 65330 0

1 3 5 7 9 8 6 4 2

A CIP catalogue record for this book is available from
the British Library

Typeset by CentraCet, Cambridge
Printed by Mackays of Chatham plc, Chatham, Kent

This book is for Danielle Antoinette.
For thirty years your love has been my shield;
your strength and courage have been my sword.

Author's Note

Although this story is set in the mid-seventeenth century, the galleons and caravels in which my characters find themselves are more usually associated with the sixteenth century. Seventeenth-century ships often bore a strong resemblance to those of the sixteenth century, but as their names may be unfamiliar to the general reader, I have used the better-known, if anachronistic, terms to convey an accessible impression of their appearance. Also, for the sake of clarity, I have simplified terminology in respect of firearms and, as it exists as such in common idiom, I have occasionally used the word 'cannon' as a generic.

The boy clutched at the rim of the canvas bucket in which he crouched sixty feet above the deck as the ship went about. The mast canted over sharply as she thrust her head through the wind. The ship was a caravel named the *Lady Edwina*, after the mother whom the boy could barely remember.

Far below in the pre-dawn darkness he heard the great bronze culverins slat against their blocks and come up with a thump against their straining tackle. The hull throbbed and resonated to a different impulse as she swung round and went plunging away back into the west. With the south-east wind now astern she was transformed, lighter and more limber, even with sails reefed and with three feet of water in her bilges.

It was all so familiar to Hal Courteney. He had greeted the last five and sixty dawns from the masthead in this manner. His young eyes, the keenest in the ship, had been posted there to catch the first gleam of distant sail in the rose of the new day.

Even the cold was familiar. He pulled the thick woollen Monmouth cap down over his ears. The wind sliced through his leather jerkin but he was inured to such mild discomfort. He gave it no heed and strained his eyes out into the darkness. 'Today the Dutchmen will come,' he said aloud, and felt the excitement and dread throb beneath his ribs.

High above him the splendour of the stars began to pale and fade, and the firmament was filled with the pearly promise of new day. Now, far below him, he could make out the figures on the deck. He could recognize Ned Tyler, the helmsman, bowed over the whipstaff, holding the ship true; and his own father stooping over the binnacle to read the new course, the lantern lighting his lean dark features and his long locks tangling and whipping in the wind.

With a start of guilt Hal looked out into the darkness; he should not be mooning down at the deck in these vital minutes when, at any moment, the enemy might loom close at hand out of the night.

By now it was light enough to make out the surface of the sea rushing by the hull. It had the hard iridescent shine of new-cut coal. By now he knew this southern sea so well; this broad highway of the ocean that flowed eternally down the eastern coast of Africa, blue and warm and swarming with life. Under his father's tutelage he had studied it so that he knew the colour, the taste and run of it, each eddy and surge.

One day he also would glory in the title of Nautonnier Knight of the Temple of the Order of St George and the Holy Grail. He would be, as his father was, a Navigator of the Order. His father was as determined as Hal himself to bring that about, and, at seventeen years of age, his goal was no longer merely a dream.

This current was the highway upon which the Dutchmen must sail to make their westings and their landfall on the mysterious coast that still lay veiled out there in the night. This was the gateway through which all must pass who sought to round that wild cape that divided the Ocean of the Indies from the Southern Atlantic.

This was why Sir Francis Courteney, Hal's father, the Navigator, had chosen this position, at 34 degrees 25 minutes south latitude, in which to wait for them. Already they had waited sixty-five tedious days, beating monotonously back and forth, but today the Dutchmen might come, and Hal stared out into the gathering day with parted lips and straining green eyes.

A cable's length off the starboard bow he saw the flash of wings high enough in the sky to catch the first rays of the sun, a long flight of gannets coming out from the land, snowy chests and heads of black and yellow. He watched the leading bird dip and turn, breaking the pattern, and twist its head to peer down into the dark waters. He saw the disturbance below it, the shimmer of scales and the seething of the surface as a shoal came up to the light. He watched the bird fold its wings and plunge downwards, and each bird that followed began its dive at the same point in the air, to strike the dark water in a burst of lacy foam.

Soon the surface was thrashed white by the diving birds and the struggling silver anchovies on which they gorged. Hal turned away his gaze and swept the opening horizon.

His heart tripped as he caught the gleam of a sail, a tall ship square-rigged, only a league to the eastward. He had filled his lungs and opened his mouth to hail the quarterdeck before he recognized her. It was the *Gull of Moray*, a frigate, not a Dutch East Indiaman. She was far out of position, which had tricked Hal.

The *Gull of Moray* was the other principal vessel in the blockading squadron. The Buzzard, her captain, should be lying out of sight below the eastern horizon. Hal leaned out over the edge of the canvas crow's nest and looked down at the deck. His father, fists on his hips, was staring up at him.

Hal called down the sighting to the quarterdeck, 'The *Gull* hull up to windward!' and his father swung away to gaze out to the east. Sir Francis picked out the shape of the Buzzard's ship, black against the darkling sky, and raised the slender brass tube of the telescope to his eye. Hal could sense anger in the set of his shoulders and the way in which he slammed the instrument shut and tossed his mane of black hair. Before this day was out words would be exchanged between the two commanders. Hal grinned to himself. With his iron will and spiked tongue, his fists and blade, Sir Francis struck terror into those upon whom he turned them – even his brother Knights of the Order held him in awe. Hal was thankful that this day his father's temper would be directed elsewhere than at him.

He looked beyond the *Gull of Moray*, sweeping the horizon as it extended swiftly with the coming of day. Hal needed no telescope to aid his bright young eyes – besides, only one of these costly instruments was aboard. He made out the others' sails then exactly where they should be, tiny pale flecks against the dark sea. The two pinnaces maintaining their formation, beads in the necklace, were spread out fifteen leagues on each side of the *Lady Edwina*, part of the net his father had cast wide to ensnare the Dutchmen.

The pinnaces were open vessels, with a dozen heavily armed men crowded into each. When not needed they could be broken down and stowed in the *Lady Edwina*'s hold. Sir Francis changed their crews regularly, for neither the tough West Country men nor the Welsh nor the even hardier ex-slaves that made up most of his crew could endure the conditions aboard those little ships for long and still be fit for a fight at the end of it.

At last the full steely light of day struck as the sun rose from the eastern ocean. Hal gazed down the fiery path it threw across the waters. He felt his spirits slide as he found the ocean empty of a strange sail. Just as on the sixty-five preceding dawns, there was no Dutchman in sight.

Then he looked northwards to the land mass that crouched like a great rock sphinx, dark and inscrutable, upon the horizon. This was the Agulhas Cape, the southernmost tip of the African continent.

'Africa!' The sound of that mysterious name on his own lips raised goose pimples along his arms and made the thick dark hair prickle on the back of his neck.

'Africa!' The uncharted land of dragons and other dreadful creatures, who ate the flesh of men, and of dark-skinned savages who also ate men's flesh and wore their bones as decoration.

'Africa!' The land of gold and ivory and slaves and other treasures, all

3

waiting for a man bold enough to seek them out, and, perhaps, to perish in the endeavour. Hal felt daunted yet fascinated by the sound and promise of that name, its menace and challenge.

Long hours he had pored over the charts in his father's cabin when he should have been learning by rote the tables of celestial passages, or declining his Latin verbs. He had studied the great interior spaces, filled with drawings of elephants and lions and monsters, traced the outlines of the Mountains of the Moon, and of lakes and mighty rivers confidently emblazoned with names such as 'Khoikhoi', and 'Camdeboo', 'Sofala' and 'the Kingdom of Prester John'. But Hal knew from his father that no civilized man had ever travelled into that awesome interior and wondered, as he had so many times before, what it would be like to be the first to venture there. Prester John particularly intrigued him. This legendary ruler of a vast and powerful Christian empire in the depths of the African continent had existed in the European mythology for hundreds of years. Was he one man, or a line of emperors? Hal wondered.

Hal's reverie was interrupted by shouted orders from the quarterdeck, faint on the wind, and the feel of the ship as she changed course. Looking down, he saw that his father intended to intercept the *Gull of Moray*. Under top sails only, and with all else reefed, the two ships were now converging, both running westward towards the Cape of Good Hope and the Atlantic. They moved sluggishly – they had been too long in these warm southern waters, and their timbers were infested with the Toredo worm. No vessel could survive long out here. The dreaded shipworms grew as thick as a man's finger and as long as his arm, and they bored so close to each other through the planks as to honeycomb them. Even from his seat at the masthead Hal could hear the pumps labouring in both vessels to lower the bilges. The sound never ceased: it was like the beating of a heart that kept the ship afloat. It was yet another reason why they must seek out the Dutchmen: they needed to change ships. The *Lady Edwina* was being eaten away beneath their feet.

As the two ships came within hailing distance the crews swarmed into the rigging and lined the bulwarks to shout ribald banter across the water.

The numbers of men packed into each vessel never failed to amaze Hal when he saw them in a mass like this. The *Lady Edwina* was a ship of 170 tons burden, with an overall length of little more than 70 feet, but she carried a crew of a hundred and thirty men if you included those now manning the two pinnaces. The *Gull* was not much larger, but with half as many men again aboard.

4

Every one of those fighting men would be needed if they were to overwhelm one of the huge Dutch East India galleons. Sir Francis had gathered intelligence from all the corners of the southern ocean from other Knights of the Order, and knew that at least five of these great ships were still at sea. So far this season twenty-one of the Company's galleons had made the passage and had called at the tiny victualling station below the towering Tafelberg, as the Dutch called it, or Table Mountain at the foot of the southern continent before turning north-wards and voyaging up the Atlantic towards Amsterdam.

Those five tardy ships, still straggling across the Ocean of the Indies, must round the Cape before the south-easterly trades fell away and the wind turned foul into the north-west. That would be soon.

When the *Gull of Moray* was not cruising in the *guerre de course*, which was a euphemism for privateering, Angus Cochran, Earl of Cumbrae, rounded out his purse by trading for slaves in the markets of Zanzibar. Once they had been shackled to the ringbolts in the deck of the long narrow slave hold, they could not be released until the ship docked at the end of her voyage in the ports of the Orient. This meant that even those poor creatures who succumbed during the dreadful tropical passage of the Ocean of the Indies must lie rotting with the living in the confined spaces of the 'tween decks. The effluvium of decaying corpses, mingled with the waste odour of the living, gave the slave ships a distinctive stench that identified them for many leagues down wind. No amount of scouring with even the strongest lyes could ever rid a slaver of her characteristic smell.

As the *Gull* crossed upwind, there were howls of exaggerated disgust from the crew of the *Lady Edwina*. 'By God, she stinks like a dung-heap.'

'Did you not wipe your backsides, you poxy vermin? We can smell you from here!' one yelled across at the pretty little frigate. The language bawled back from the *Gull* made Hal grin. Of course, the human bowels held no mysteries for him, but he did not understand much of the rest of it, for he had never seen those parts of a woman to which the seamen in both ships referred in such graphic detail, nor knew of the uses to which they could be put, but it excited his imagination to hear them so described. His amusement was enhanced when he imagined his father's fury at hearing it.

Sir Francis was a devout man who believed that the fortunes of war could be influenced by the god-fearing behaviour of every man aboard.

He forbade gambling, blasphemy and the drinking of strong spirits. He led prayers twice a day and exhorted his seamen to gentle and dignified behaviour when they put into port – although Hal knew that

5

this advice was seldom followed. Now Sir Francis frowned darkly as he listened to his men exchange insults with those of the Buzzard but, as he could not have half the ship's company flogged to signal his disapproval, he held his tongue until he was in easy hail of the frigate.

In the meantime he sent his servant to his cabin to fetch his cloak. What he had to say to the Buzzard was official and he should be in regalia. When the man returned, Sir Francis slipped the magnificent velvet cloak over his shoulders before he lifted his speaking trumpet to his lips. 'Good morrow, my lord!'

The Buzzard came to his rail and lifted one hand in salute. Above his plaid he wore half-armour, which gleamed in the fresh morning light, but his head was bare, his red hair and beard bushed together like a haystack, the curls dancing on the wind as though his head was on fire. 'Jesus love you, Franky!' he bellowed back, his great voice easily transcending the wind.

'Your station is on the eastern flank!' The wind and his anger made Sir Francis short. 'Why have you deserted it?'

The Buzzard spread his hands in an expressive gesture of apology. 'I have little water and am completely out of patience. Sixty-five days are enough for me and my brave fellows. There are slaves and gold for the taking along the Sofala coast.' His accent was like a Scottish gale.

'Your commission does not allow you to attack Portuguese shipping.'

'Dutch, Portuguese or Spanish,' Cumbrae shouted back. 'Their gold shines as prettily. You know well that there is no peace beyond the Line.'

'You are well named the Buzzard,' Sir Francis roared in frustration, 'for you have the same appetite as that carrion bird!' Yet what Cumbrae had said was true. There was no peace beyond the Line.

A century and a half ago, by Papal Bull *Inter Caetera* of 25 September 1493, the Line had been drawn down the mid-Atlantic, north to south, by Pope Alexander VI to divide the world between Portugal and Spain. What hope was there that the excluded Christian nations, in their envy and resentment, would honour this declaration? Spontaneously, another doctrine was born: 'No peace beyond the Line!' It became the watchword of the privateer and the corsair. And its meaning extended in their minds to encompass all the unexplored regions of the oceans.

Within the waters of the northern continent, acts of piracy, rapine and murder – whose perpetrator previously would have been hunted down by the combined navies of Christian Europe and hanged from his own yard-arm – were condoned and even applauded when committed beyond the Line. Every embattled monarch signed Letters of Marque that, at a stroke, converted his merchantmen into privateers, ships of war, and sent them out marauding on the newly discovered oceans of the expanding globe.

Sir Francis Courteney's own letter had been signed by Edward Hyde, Earl of Clarendon, the Lord Chancellor of England, in the name of His Majesty King Charles II. It sanctioned him to hunt down the ships of the Dutch Republic, with which England was at war.

'Once you desert your station, you forfeit your rights to claim a share of any prize!' Sir Francis called across the narrow strip of water between the ships, but the Buzzard turned away to issue orders to his helmsman.

He shouted to his piper, who stood at the ready, 'Give Sir Francis a tune to remember us by!' The stirring strains of 'Farewell to the Isles' carried across the water to the *Lady Edwina*, as the Buzzard's topmast men clambered like monkeys high into the rigging, and loosed the reefs. The *Gull*'s top-hamper billowed out. The main sail filled with a boom like the discharge of cannon, she heeled eagerly to the south-easter and pressed her shoulder into the next blue swell, bursting it asunder.

As the Buzzard pulled away rapidly he came back to the stern rail, and his voice lifted above the skirling of the pipes and the whimper of the wind. 'May the peace of our Lord Jesus Christ shield you, my revered brother Knight.' But on the Buzzard's lips it sounded like blasphemy.

With his cloak, which was quartered by the crimson *croix patté* of the Order, billowing and flapping from his wide shoulders, Sir Francis watched him go.

Slowly the ironic cheering and heavy banter of the men died away. A sombre new mood began to infect the ship as the company realized that their forces, puny before, had been more than halved in a single stroke. They had been left alone to meet the Dutchmen in whatever force they might appear. The seamen that crowded the *Lady Edwina*'s deck and rigging were silent now, unable to meet each other's eyes.

Then Sir Francis threw back his head and laughed. 'All the more for us to share!' he cried, and they laughed with him and cheered as he made his way to his cabin below the poop deck.

For another hour Hal stayed at the masthead. He wondered how long the men's buoyant mood could last, for they were down to a mug of water twice a day. Although the land and its sweet rivers lay less than half a day's sailing away, Sir Francis had not dared detach even one of the pinnaces to fill the casks. The Dutchmen might come at any hour, and when they did he would need every man.

At last a man came aloft to relieve Hal at the lookout. 'What is there to see, lad?' he asked, as he slipped into the canvas crow's nest beside Hal.

7

'Precious little,' Hal admitted, and pointed out the tiny sails of the two pinnaces on the distant horizon. 'Neither carry any signals,' Hal told him. 'Watch for the red flag – it'll mean they have the chase in sight.'

The sailor grunted. 'You'll be teaching me to fart next.' But he smiled at Hal in avuncular fashion – the boy was the ship's favourite.

Hal grinned back at him. 'God's truth, but you need no teaching, Master Simon. I've heard you at the bucket in the heads. I'd rather face a Dutch broadside. You nigh crack every timber in the hull.'

Simon let out an explosive guffaw, and punched Hal's shoulder. 'Down with you, lad, before I teach you to fly like an albatross.'

Hal began to scramble down the shrouds. At first he moved stiffly, his muscles cramped and chilled after the long vigil, but he soon warmed up and swung down lithely.

Some of the men on the deck paused at their labours on the pumps, or with palm and needle as they repaired wind-ripped canvas, and watched him. He was as robust and broad-shouldered as a lad three years older, and long in limb – he already stood as tall as his father. Yet he still retained the fresh smooth skin, the unlined face and sunny expression of boyhood. His hair, tied with a thong behind his head, spilled from under his cap and glistened blue-black in the early sunlight. At this age his beauty was still almost feminine, and after more than four months at sea – six since they had laid eyes on a woman – some, whose fancy lay in that direction, watched him lasciviously.

Hal reached the main yard and left the security of the mast. He ran out along it, balancing with the ease of an acrobat forty feet above the curling rush of the bow wave and the planks of the main deck. Now every eye was on him: it was a feat that few aboard would care to emulate.

'For that you have to be young and stupid,' Ned Tyler growled, but shook his head fondly as he leaned against the whipstaff and stared up. 'Best the little fool does not let his father catch him playing that trick.'

Hal reached the end of the yard and without pause swung out onto the brace and slid down it until he was ten feet above the deck. From there he dropped to land lightly on his hard bare feet, flexing his knees to absorb the impact on the scrubbed white planks.

He bounced up, turned towards the stern – and froze at the sound of an inhuman cry. It was a primordial bellow, the menacing challenge of some great predatory animal.

Hal remained pinned to the spot for only an instant then instinctively spun away as a tall figure charged down upon him. He heard the fluting sound in the air before he saw the blade and ducked under it. The silver

8

steel flashed over his head and his attacker roared again, a screech of fury.

Hal had a glimpse of his adversary's face, black and glistening, a cave of a mouth lined with huge square white teeth, the tongue as pink and curled as a leopard's as he screamed.

Hal danced and swayed as the silver blade came arcing back. He felt a tug at the sleeve of his jerkin as the sword point split the leather, and fell back.

'Ned, a blade!' he yelled wildly at the helmsman behind him, never taking his eyes off those of his assailant. The pupils were black and bright as obsidian, the iris opaque with fury, the whites engorged with blood.

Hal leaped aside at the next wild charge, and felt on his cheek the draught of the blow. Behind him he heard the scrape of a cutlass drawn from the boatswain's scabbard, and the weapon slide across the deck towards him. He stooped smoothly and gathered it up, the hilt coming naturally to his hand, as he went into the guard stance and aimed the point at the eyes of his attacker.

In the face of Hal's menacing blade, the tall man checked his next rush and when, with his left hand, Hal drew from his belt his ten-inch dirk and offered that point also, the mad light in his eyes turned cold and appraising. They circled each other on the open deck below the mainmast, their blades weaving, touching and tapping lightly, as each sought an opening.

The seamen on the deck left their tasks – even those on the handles of the pumps – and came running to form a ring around the swordsmen as though they watched a cockfight, their faces alight with the prospect of seeing blood spurt. They growled and hooted at each thrust and parry, and urged on their favourites.

'Hack out his big black balls, young Hal!'

'Pluck the cockerel's saucy tail feathers for him, Aboli.'

Aboli stood five inches taller than Hal, and there was no fat on his lean, supple frame. He was from the eastern coast of Africa, of a warrior tribe highly prized by the slavers. Every hair had been carefully plucked from his pate, which gleamed like polished black marble, and his cheeks were adorned with ritual tattoos, whorls of raised cicatrices that gave him a terrifying appearance. He moved with a peculiar grace, on those long muscular legs, swaying from the waist like some huge black cobra. He wore only a petticoat of tattered canvas, and his chest was bare. Each muscle in his torso and upper arms seemed to have a life of its own, serpents slithering and coiling beneath the oiled skin.

He lunged suddenly, and with a desperate effort Hal turned the blade, but almost in the same instant Aboli reversed the blow, aiming once more at his head. There was such power in his stroke that Hal knew he could not block it with cutlass alone. He threw up both blades, crossing them, and trapped the Negro's high above his head. Steel rang and thrilled on steel, and the crowd howled at the skill and grace of the parry.

But at the fury of the attack Hal gave a pace, and another then another as Aboli pressed him again and again, giving him no respite, using his greater height and superior strength to counter the boy's natural ability.

Hal's face mirrored his desperation. He gave more readily now and his movements were uncoordinated: he was tired and fear dulled his responses. The cruel watchers turned against him, yelling for blood, urging on his implacable opponent.

'Mark his pretty face, Aboli!'

'Give us a look at his guts!'

Sweat greased Hal's cheeks and his expression crumpled as Aboli drove him back against the mast. He seemed much younger suddenly, and on the point of tears, his lips quivering with terror and exhaustion. He was no longer counter-attacking. Now it was all defence. He was fighting for his life.

Relentlessly Aboli launched a fresh attack, swinging at Hal's body, then changing the angle to cut at his legs. Hal was near the limit of his strength, only just managing to fend off each blow.

Then Aboli changed his attack once more: he forced Hal to overreach by feinting low to the left hip, then shifted his weight and lunged with a long right arm. The shining blade flew straight through Hal's guard and the watchers roared as at last they had the blood they craved.

Hal reeled sideways off the mast and stood panting in the sunlight, blinded by his own sweat. Blood dripped slowly onto his jerkin – but from a nick only, made with a surgeon's skill.

'Another scar for you each time you fight like a woman!' Aboli scolded him.

With an expression of exhausted disbelief, Hal raised his left hand, which still held the dirk, and with the back of his fist wiped the blood from his chin. The tip of his earlobe was neatly split and the quantity of blood exaggerated the severity of the wound.

The spectators bellowed with derision and mirth.

'By Satan's teeth!' one of the coxswains laughed. 'The pretty boy has more blood than he has guts!'

At the gibe, a swift transformation came over Hal. He lowered his

10

dirk and extended the point in the guard position, ignoring the blood that still dripped from his chin. His face was blank, like that of a statue, and his lips set and blanched frosty white. From his throat issued a low growl, and he launched himself at the Negro.

He exploded across the deck with such speed that Aboli was taken by surprise and driven back. When they locked blades he felt the new power in the boy's arm, and his eyes narrowed. Then Hal was upon him like a wounded wild-cat bursting from a trap.

Pain and rage put wings on his feet. His eyes were pitiless and his clenched jaws tightened the muscles of his face into a mask that retained no trace of boyishness. Yet his fury had not robbed him of reason and cunning. All the skill that the lad had accumulated, over hundreds of hours and days upon the practice deck, suddenly coalesced.

The watchers bayed as this miracle took place before their eyes. It seemed that, in that instant, the boy had become a man, had grown in stature so that he stood chin to chin and eye to eye with his dark adversary.

It cannot last, Aboli told himself, as he met the attack. His strength cannot hold out. But this was a new man he confronted, and he had not yet recognized him.

Suddenly he found himself giving ground – He will tire soon – but the twin blades that danced before his eyes seemed dazzling and ethereal, like the dread spirits of the dark forests that had once been his home.

He looked into the pale face and burning eyes and did not know them. He felt a superstitious awe assail him, which slowed his right arm. This was a demon, with a demon's unnatural strength. He knew that he was in danger of his life.

The next coup sped at his chest, glancing through his guard like a sunbeam. He twisted aside his upper body, but the thrust raked under his raised left arm. He felt no pain but heard the rasp of the razor edge against his ribs, and the warm flood of blood down his flank. And he had ignored the weapon in Hal's left fist and the boy used either hand with equal ease.

At the edge of his vision he saw the shorter, stiffer blade speed towards his heart and threw himself back to avoid it. His heel caught in the tail of the yard brace, coiled on the deck, and he went sprawling. The elbow of his sword arm slammed into the gunwale, numbing it to the fingertips, and the cutlass flew from his fingers.

On his back, Aboli looked up helplessly and saw death above him in those terrifying green eyes. This was not the face of the child who had been his ward and special charge for the last decade, the boy he had cherished and trained and loved over ten long years. This was a man

11

who would kill him. The bright point of the cutlass started down, aimed at his throat, with the full weight of the lithe young body behind it.

'Henry!' A stern, authoritative voice rang across the deck, cutting through the hubbub of the blood-crazed spectators.

Hal started, and stood still with the point against Aboli's throat. A bemused expression spread across his face, like that of an awakening dreamer, and he looked up at his father on the break of the poop.

'Avast that tomfoolery. Get you down to my cabin at once.'

Hal glanced around the deck, at the flushed, excited faces surrounding him. He shook his head in puzzlement, and looked down at the cutlass in his hand. He opened his fingers and let it drop to the planks. His legs turned to water under him and he sank down on top of Aboli and hugged him as a child hugs his father.

'Aboli!' he whispered, in the language of the forests that the black man had taught him and which was a secret no other white man on the ship shared with them. 'I have hurt you sorely. The blood! By my life, I could have killed you.'

Aboli chuckled softly and answered in the same language, 'It was past time. At last you have tapped the well of warrior blood. I thought you would never find it. I had to drive you hard to it.'

He sat up and pushed Hal away, but there was a new light in his eyes as he looked at the boy, who was a boy no longer. 'Go now and do your father's bidding!'

Hal stood up shakily and looked again round the circle of faces, seeing an expression in them that he did not recognize: it was respect mingled with more than a little fear.

'What are you gawking at?' bellowed Ned Tyler. 'The play is over. Do you have no work to do? Man those pumps. Those topgallants are luffing. I can find mastheads for all idle hands.' There was the thump of bare feet across the deck as the crew rushed guiltily to their duties.

Hal stooped, picked up the cutlass, and handed it back to the boatswain, hilt first.

'Thank you, Ned. I had need of it.'

'And you put it to good use. I have never seen that heathen bested, except by your father before you.'

Hal tore a handful of rag from the tattered hem of his canvas pantaloons, held it to his ear to staunch the bleeding, and went down to the stern cabin.

Sir Francis looked up from his log-book, his goose quill poised over the page. 'Do not look so smug, puppy,' he grunted at Hal. 'Aboli toyed with you, as he always does. He could have spitted you a dozen times before you turned it with that lucky coup at the end.'

When Sir Francis stood up there was hardly room for them both in the tiny cabin. The bulkheads were lined from deck to deck with books, more were stacked about their feet and leather-bound volumes were crammed into the cubby-hole that served his father as a bunk. Hal wondered where he found place to sleep.

His father addressed him in Latin. When they were alone he insisted on speaking the language of the educated and cultivated man. 'You will die before you ever make a swordsman, unless you find steel in your heart as well as in your hand. Some hulking Dutchman will cleave you to the teeth at your first encounter.' Sir Francis scowled at his son, 'Recite the law of the sword.'

'An eye for his eyes,' Hal mumbled in Latin.

'Speak up, boy!' Sir Francis's hearing had been dulled by the blast of culverins – over the years a thousand broadsides had burst around his head. At the end of an engagement, blood would be seen dripping from the ears of the seamen beside the guns and for days after even the officers on the poop heard heavenly bells ring in their heads.

'An eye for his eyes,' Hal repeated roundly, and his father nodded.

'His eyes are the window to his mind. Learn to read in them his intentions before the act. See there the stroke before it is delivered. What else?'

'The other eye for his feet,' Hal recited.

'Good.' Sir Francis nodded. 'His feet will move before his hand. What else?'

'Keep the point high.'

'The cardinal rule. Never lower the point. Keep it aimed at his eyes.'

Sir Francis led Hal through the catechism, as he had countless times before. At the end, he said, 'Here is one more rule for you. Fight from the first stroke, not just when you are hurt or angry, or you might not survive that first wound.'

He glanced up at the hourglass hanging from the deck above his head. 'There is yet time for your reading before ship's prayers.' He spoke in Latin still. 'Take up your Livy and translate from the top of page twenty-six.'

For an hour Hal read aloud the history of Rome in the original, translating each verse into English as he went. Then, at last, Sir Francis closed his Livy with a snap. 'There is improvement. Now, decline the verb *durare*.'

That his father should choose this one was a mark of his approval. Hal recited it in a breathless rush, slowing when he came to the future indicative. '*Durabo*. I shall endure.'

That word formed the motto of the Courteney coat-of-arms, and Sir Francis smiled frostily as Hal voiced it.

'May the Lord grant you that grace.' He stood up. 'You may go now but do not be late for prayers.'

Rejoicing to be free, Hal fled from the cabin and went bounding up the companionway.

Aboli was squatting in the lee of one of the hulking bronze culverins near the bows. Hal knelt beside him. 'I wounded you.'

Aboli made an eloquent dismissive gesture. 'A chicken scratching in the dust wounds the earth more gravely.'

Hal pulled the tarpaulin cloak off Aboli's shoulders, seized the elbow and lifted the thickly muscled arm high to peer at the deep slash across the ribs. 'None the less, this little chicken gave you a good pecking,' he observed drily, and grinned as Aboli opened his hand and showed him the needle already threaded with sailmaker's yarn. He reached for it, but Aboli checked him.

'Wash the cut, as I taught you.'

'With that long black python of yours you could reach it yourself,' Hal suggested, and Aboli emitted his long, rolling laugh, soft and low as distant thunder.

'We will have to make do with a small white worm.'

Hal stood and loosed the cord that held up his pantaloons. He let them drop to his knees, and with his right hand drew back his foreskin.

'I christen you Aboli, lord of the chickens!' He imitated his own father's preaching tone faithfully, and directed a stream of yellow urine into the open wound.

Although Hal knew how it stung, for Aboli had done the same many times for him, the black features remained impassive. Hal irrigated the wound with the very last drop and then hoisted his breeches. He knew how efficacious this tribal remedy of Aboli's was. The first time it had been used on him he had been repelled by it, but in all the years since then he had never seen a wound so treated mortify.

He took up the needle and twine, and while Aboli held the lips of the wound together with his left hand, Hal laid neat sailmaker's stitches across it, digging the needle point through the elastic skin and pulling his knots up tight. When he was done, he reached for the pot of hot tar that Aboli had ready. He smeared the sewn wound thickly and nodded with satisfaction at his handiwork.

Aboli stood up and lifted his canvas petticoats. 'Now we will see to your ear,' he told Hal, as his own fat penis overflowed his fist by half its length.

14

Hal recoiled swiftly. 'It is but a little scratch,' he protested, but Aboli seized his pigtail remorselessly and twisted his face upwards.

At the stroke of the bell the company crowded into the waist of the ship, and stood silent and bare-headed in the sunlight – even the black tribesmen, who did not worship exclusively the crucified Lord but other gods also whose abode was the deep dark forests of their homes.

When Sir Francis, great leather-bound Bible in hand, intoned sonorously, 'We pray you, Almighty God, deliver the enemy of Christ into our hands that he shall not triumph . . .' his eyes were the only ones still cast heavenward. Every other eye in the company turned towards the east from where that enemy would come, laden with silver and spices.

Half-way through the long service a line squall came boring up out of the east, wind driving the clouds in a tumbling dark mass over their heads and deluging the decks with silver sheets of rain. But the elements could not conspire to keep Sir Francis from his discourse with the Almighty, so while the crew huddled in their tar-daubed canvas jackets, with hats of the same material tied beneath their chins, and the water streamed off them as off the hides of a pack of beached walrus, Sir Francis missed not a beat of his sermon. 'Lord of the storm and the wind,' he prayed, 'succour us. Lord of the battle-line, be our shield and buckler . . .'

The squall passed over them swiftly and the sun burst forth again, sparkling on the blue swells and steaming on the decks.

Sir Francis clapped his wide-brimmed cavalier hat back on his head, and the sodden white feathers that surmounted it nodded in approval. 'Master Ned, run out the guns.'

It was the proper course to take, Hal realized. The rain squall would have soaked the priming and wet the loaded powder. Rather than the lengthy business of drawing the shot and reloading, his father would give the crews some practice.

'Beat to quarters, if you please.'

The drum-roll echoed through the hull, and the crew ran grinning and joking to their stations. Hal plunged the tip of a slow-match into the charcoal brazier at the foot of the mast. When it was smouldering evenly, he leapt into the shrouds and, carrying the burning match in his teeth, clambered up to his battle station at the masthead.

On the deck he saw four men sway an empty water cask up from the hold and stagger with it to the ship's side. At the order from the poop, they tossed it over and left it bobbing in the ship's wake. Meanwhile the guncrews knocked out the wedges and, heaving at the tackles, ran out the culverins. On either side of the lower deck there were eight, each loaded with a bucketful of powder and a ball. On the upper deck were ranged ten demi-culverins, five on each side, their long barrels crammed with grape.

The *Lady Edwina* was low on iron shot after her two-year-long cruise, and some of the guns were loaded with water-rounded flint marbles hand-picked from the banks of the river mouths where the watering parties had gone ashore. Ponderously she came about, and settled on the new tack, beating back into the wind. The floating cask was still two cables' length ahead but the range narrowed slowly. The gunners strode from cannon to cannon, pushing in the elevation wedges and ordering the training tackles adjusted. This was a specialized task: only five men aboard had the skill to load and lay a gun.

In the crow's nest, Hal swung the long-barrelled falconet on its swivel and aimed down at a length of floating kelp that drifted past on the current. Then with the point of his dirk he scraped the damp, caked powder out of the pan of the weapon, and carefully repacked it with fresh powder from his flask. After ten years of instruction by his father, he was as skilled as Ned Tyler, the ship's master gunner, in the esoteric art. His rightful battle station should have been on the gundeck, and he had pleaded with his father to place him there but had been answered only with the stern retort, 'You will go where I send you.' Now he must sit up here, out of the hurly-burly, while his fierce young heart ached to be a part of it.

Suddenly he was startled by the crash of gunfire from the deck below. A long dense plume of smoke billowed out and the ship heeled slightly at the discharge. A moment later a tall fountain of foam rose dramatically from the surface of the sea fifty yards to the right and twenty beyond the floating cask. At that range it was not bad shooting, but the deck erupted in a chorus of jeers and whistles.

Ned Tyler hurried to the second culverin, and swiftly checked its lay. He gestured for the men on the tackle to train it a point left then stepped forward and held the burning match to the touch hole. A fizzling puff of smoke blew back and then, from the gaping muzzle, came a shower of sparks, half-burned powder and clods of damp, caked muck. The ball rolled down the bronze barrel and fell into the sea less than half-way to the target cask. The crew howled with derision.

The next two weapons misfired. Cursing furiously, Ned ordered the crews to draw the charges with the long iron corkscrews as he hurried on down the line.

'Great expense of powder and bullet!' Hal recited to himself the words of the great Sir Francis Drake – for whom his own father had been christened – spoken after the first day of the epic battle against the Armada of Philip II, King of Spain, led by the Duke of Medina Sidonia. All that long day, under the dun fog of gunsmoke, the two great fleets had loosed their mighty broadsides at each other, but the barrage had sent not a single ship of either fleet to the bottom.

'Fright them with cannon,' Hal's father had instructed him, 'but sweep their decks with the cutlass,' and he voiced his scorn for the rowdy but ineffectual art of naval gunnery. It was impossible to aim a ball from the plunging deck of one ship to a precise point on the hull of another: accuracy was in the hands of the Almighty rather than those of the master gunner.

As if to illustrate the point, after Ned had fired every one of the heavy guns on board six had misfired and the nearest he had come to striking the floating cask was twenty yards. Hal shook his head sadly, reflecting that each of those shots had been carefully laid and aimed. In the heat of a battle, with the range obscured by billowing smoke, the powder and shot stuffed in haste into the muzzles, the barrels heating unevenly and the match applied to pan by excited and terrified gunners, the results could not be even that satisfactory.

At last his father looked up at Hal. 'Masthead!' he roared.

Hal had feared himself forgotten. Now, with a thrill of relief, he blew on the tip of the smouldering slow-match in his hand. It glowed bright and fierce.

From the deck Sir Francis watched him, his expression stern and forbidding. He must never let show the love he bore the boy. He must be hard and critical at all times, driving him on. For the boy's own sake – nay, for his very life – he must force him to learn, to strive, to endure, to run every step of the course ahead of him with all his strength and all his heart. Yet, without making it apparent, he must also help, encourage and assist him. He must shepherd him wisely, cunningly towards his destiny. He had delayed calling upon Hal until this moment, when the cask floated close alongside.

If the boy could shatter it with the small weapon where Ned had failed with the great cannon, then his reputation with the crew would be enhanced. The men were mostly boisterous ruffians, simple illiterates, but one day Hal would be called upon to lead them, or others like them. He had made a giant stride today by besting Aboli before them all. Here was a chance to consolidate that gain. 'Guide his hand, and the flight of the shot, oh God of the battle-line!' Sir Francis prayed silently, and the ship's company craned their necks to watch the lad high above them.

17

Hal hummed softly to himself as he concentrated on the task, conscious of the eyes upon him. Yet he did not sense the importance of this discharge and was oblivious of his father's prayers. It was a game to him, just another chance to excel. Hal liked to win, and each time he did so he liked it better. The young eagle was beginning to rejoice in the power of his wings.

Gripping the end of the long brass monkey tail, he swivelled the falconet downwards, peering over the yard-long barrel, lining up the notch above the pan with the pip on the muzzle end.

He had learned that it was futile to aim directly at the target. There would be a delay of seconds from when he applied the slow-match, to the crash of the shot, and in the meantime ship and cask would be moving in opposite directions. There was also the moment when the discharged balls were in flight before they struck. He must gauge where the cask would be when the shot reached it and not aim for the spot where it had been when he pressed the match to the pan.

He swung the pip of the foresight smoothly over the target, and touched the glowing end of the match to the pan. He forced himself not to flinch away from the flare of burning powder nor to recoil in anticipation of the explosion but to keep the barrels swinging gently in the line he had chosen.

With a roar that stung his ear-drums the falconet bucked heavily against its swivel, and everything disappeared in a cloud of grey smoke. Desperately he craned his head left and right, trying to see around the smoke, but it was the cheers from the decks below that made his heart leap, reaching him even through his singing ears. When the wind whisked away the smoke, he could see the ribs of the shattered cask swirling and tumbling astern in the ship's wake. He hooted with glee, and waved his cap at the faces on the deck far below.

Aboli was at his place in the bows, coxswain and gun captain of the first watch. He returned Hal's beatific grin and beat his chest with one fist, while with the other he brandished the cutlass over his bald head.

The drum rolled to end the drill and stand down the crew from their battle stations. Before he dropped down the shrouds Hal reloaded the falconet carefully and bound a strip of tar-soaked canvas around the pan to protect it from dew, rain and spray.

As his feet hit the deck he looked to the poop, trying to catch his father's eye and glean his approbation. But Sir Francis was deep in conversation with one of his petty officers. A moment passed before he glanced coldly over his shoulder at Hal. 'What are you gawking at, boy? There are guns to be reloaded.'

As he turned away Hal felt the bite of disappointment, but the rowdy congratulations of the crew, the rough slaps across his back and shoulders as he passed down the gundeck, restored his smile.

When Ned Tyler saw him coming he stepped back from the breech of the culverin he was loading and handed the ramrod to Hal. 'Any oaf can shoot it, but it takes a good man to load it,' he grunted, and stood back critically to watch Hal measure a charge from the leather powder bucket. 'What weight of powder?' he asked, and Hal gave the same reply he had a hundred times before.

'The same weight as that of the round shot.'

The blackpowder comprised coarse granules. There had been a time when, shaken and agitated by the ship's way or some other repetitive movement, the three essential elements, sulphur, charcoal and saltpetre, might separate out and render it useless. Since then the process of 'corning' had evolved, whereby the fine raw powder was treated with urine or alcohol to set it into a cake, which was then crushed in a ball mill to the required size of granules. Yet the process was not perfect and a gunner must always have an eye for the condition of his powder. Damp or age could degrade it. Hal tested the grains between his fingers and tasted a dab. Ned Tyler had taught him to differentiate between good and degenerate powder in this way. Then he poured the contents of the bucket into the muzzle, and followed it with the oakum wadding.

Then he tamped it down with the long wooden-handled ramrod. This was another crucial part of the process: tamped too firmly, the flame could not pass through the charge and a misfire was inevitable, but not tamped firmly enough, and the blackpowder would burn without the power to hurl the heavy projectile clear of the barrel. Correct tamping was an art that could only be learned from prolonged practice, but Ned nodded as he watched Hal at work.

It was much later when Hal scrambled up again into the sunlight. All the culverins were loaded and secured behind their ports and Hal's bare upper body was glistening with sweat from the heat of the cramped gundeck and his labours with the ramrod. As he paused to wipe his streaming face, draw a breath and stretch his back, after crouching so long under the cramped headspace of the lower deck, his father called to him with heavy irony, 'Is the ship's position of no interest to you, Master Henry?'

With a start Hal glanced up at the sun. It was high in the heavens above them: the morning had sped away. He raced to the companionway, dropped down the ladder, burst into his father's cabin, and snatched the heavy backstaff from its case on the bulkhead. Then he turned and ran back to the poop deck.

'Pray God, I'm not too late,' he whispered to himself, and glanced up at the position of the sun. It was over the starboard yard-arm. He positioned himself with his back to it and in such a way that the shadow cast by the main sail would not screen him, yet so that he had a clear view of the horizon to the south.

Now he concentrated all his attention on the quadrant of the backstaff. He had to keep the heavy instrument steady against the ship's motion. Then he must read the angle that the sun's rays over his shoulder subtended onto the quadrant, which gave him the sun's inclination to the horizon. It was a juggling act that required strength and dexterity.

At last he could observe noon passage, and read the sun's angle with the horizon at the precise moment it reached its zenith. He lowered the backstaff with aching arms and shoulders, and hastily scribbled the reading on the traverse slate.

Then he ran down the ladder to the stern cabin, but the table of celestial angles was not on its shelf. In distress he turned to see that his father had followed him down and was watching him intently. No word was exchanged, but Hal knew that he was being challenged to provide the value from memory. Hal sat at his father's sea-chest, which served as a desk, and closed his eyes as he reviewed the tables in his mind's eye. He must remember yesterday's figures and extrapolate from them. He massaged his swollen ear-lobe, and his lips moved soundlessly.

Suddenly his face lightened, he opened his eyes and scribbled another number on the slate. He worked for a minute longer, translating the angle of the noon sun into degrees of latitude. Then he looked up triumphantly. 'Thirty-four degrees forty-two minutes south latitude.'

His father took the slate from his hand, checked his figures, then handed it back to him. He inclined his head slightly in agreement. 'Close enough, if your sun sight was true. Now what of your longitude?'

The determination of exact longitude was a puzzle that no man had ever solved. There was no timepiece, hourglass or clock that could be carried aboard a ship and still be sufficiently accurate to keep track of the earth's majestic revolutions. Only the traverse board, which hung beside the compass binnacle, could guide Hal's calculation. Now he studied the pegs that the helmsman had placed in the holes about the rose of the compass each time he had altered his heading during the previous watch. Hal added and averaged these values, then plotted them on the chart in his father's cabin. It was only a crude approximation of longitude and, predictably, his father demurred. 'I would have given it a touch more of east, for with the weed on her bottom and the water in her bilges she pays off heavily to leeward – but mark her so in the log.'

Hal looked up in astonishment. This was a momentous day indeed.

No other hand but his father's had ever written in the leather-bound log that sat beside the Bible on the lid of the sea-chest.

While his father watched, he opened the log and, for a minute, stared at the pages filled with his father's elegant, flowing script, and the beautiful drawings of men, ships and landfalls that adorned the margins. His father was a gifted artist. With trepidation Hal dipped the quill in the gold inkwell that had once belonged to the captain of the *Heerlycke Nacht*, one of the Dutch East India Company's galleons that his father had seized. He wiped the superfluous drops from the nib, lest they splatter the sacred page. Then he trapped the tip of his tongue between his teeth and wrote with infinite care: 'One bell in the afternoon watch, this 3rd day of September in the year of our Lord Jesus Christ 1667. Position 34 degrees 42 minutes South, 20 degrees 5 minutes East. African mainland in sight from the masthead bearing due North.' Not daring to add more, and relieved that he had not marred the page with scratchings or splutterings, he set aside the quill and sanded his well-formed letters with pride. He knew his hand was fair – though perhaps not as fair as his father's, he conceded as he compared them.

Sir Francis took up the pen he had laid aside and leaning over his shoulder wrote: 'This forenoon Ensign Henry Courteney severely wounded in an unseemly brawl.' Then, beside the entry he swiftly sketched a telling caricature of Hal with his swollen ear sticking out lopsidedly and the knot of the stitch like a bow in a maiden's hair.

Hal gagged on his own suppressed laughter, but when he looked up he saw the twinkle in his father's green eyes. Sir Francis laid one hand on the boy's shoulder, which was as close as he would ever come to an embrace, and squeezed it as he said, 'Ned Tyler will be waiting to instruct you in the lore of rigging and sail trimming. Do not keep him waiting.'

Though it was late when Hal made his way forward along the upper deck, it was still light enough for him to pick his way with ease over the sleeping bodies of the off-duty watch. The night sky was filled with stars, such an array as must dazzle the eyes of any northerner. This night Hal had no eyes for them. He was exhausted to the point where he reeled on his feet.

Aboli had kept a place for him in the bows, under the lee of the forward cannon where they were out of the wind. He had spread a straw-filled pallet on the deck and Hal tumbled gratefully onto it. There were no quarters set aside for the crew, and the men slept wherever they could find a space on the open deck. In these warm southern nights they all preferred the topsides to the stuffy lower deck. They lay in rows, shoulder to shoulder, but the proximity of so much stinking humanity was natural to Hal, and even their snoring and mutterings could not keep him long from sleep. He moved a little closer to Aboli. This was how he had slept each night for the last ten years and there was comfort in the huge figure beside him.

'Your father is a great chief amongst lesser chieftains,' Aboli murmured. 'He is a warrior and he knows the secrets of the sea and the heavens. The stars are his children.'

'I know all this is true,' Hal answered, in the same language.

'It was he who bade me take the sword to you this day,' Aboli confessed.

Hal raised himself on one elbow, and stared at the dark figure beside him. 'My father wanted you to cut me?' he asked incredulously.

'You are not as other lads. If your life is hard now, it will be harder still. You are chosen. One day you must take from his shoulders the great cloak of the red cross. You must be worthy of it.'

Hal sank back on his pallet, and stared up at the stars. 'What if I do not want this thing?' he asked.

'It is yours. You do not have a choice. The one Nautonnier Knight chooses the Knight to follow him. It has been so for almost four hundred years. Your only escape from it is death.'

Hal was silent for so long that Aboli thought sleep had overcome him, but then he whispered, 'How do you know these things?'

'From your father.'

'Are you also a Knight of our Order?'

Aboli laughed softly. 'My skin is too dark and my gods are alien. I could never be chosen.'

'Aboli, I am afraid.'

'All men are afraid. It is for those of us of the warrior blood to subdue fear.'

'You will never leave me, will you, Aboli?'

'I will stay at your side as long as you need me.'

'Then I am not so afraid.'

Hours later Aboli woke him with a hand on his shoulder from a deep and dreamless sleep. 'Eight bells in the middle watch, Gundwane.' He used Hal's nickname: in his own language it meant 'Bush Rat'. It was not meant pejoratively, but was the affectionate name he had bestowed on the four-year-old who had been placed in his care over a decade before.

Four o'clock in the morning. It would be light in an hour. Hal scrambled up and, rubbing his eyes, staggered to the stinking bucket in the heads and eased himself. Then, fully awake, he hurried down the heaving deck, avoiding the sleeping figures that cluttered it.

The cook had his fire going in the brick-lined galley and passed Hal a pewter mug of soup and a hard biscuit. Hal was ravenous and gulped the liquid, though it scalded his tongue. When he crunched the biscuit he felt the weevils in it pop between his teeth.

As he hurried to the foot of the mainmast he saw the glow of his father's pipe in the shadows of the poop and smelled a whiff of his tobacco, rank on the sweet night air. Hal did not pause but went up the shrouds noting the change of tack and the new setting of the sails that had taken place while he slept.

When he reached the masthead and had relieved the lookout there, he settled into his nest and looked about him. There was no moon and, but for the stars, all was dark. He knew every named star, from the mighty Sirius to tiny Mintaka in Orion's glittering belt. They were the ciphers of the navigator, the signposts of the sky, and he had learned their names with his alphabet. His eye went, unbidden, to pick out Regulus in the sign of the Lion. It was not the brightest star in the zodiac, but it was his own particular star and he felt a quiet pleasure at the thought that it sparkled for him alone. This was the happiest hour of his long day, the only time he could ever be alone in the crowded vessel, the only time he could let his mind dance among the stars and his imagination have full rein.

His every sense seemed heightened. Even above the whimper of the wind and the creak of the rigging he could hear his father's voice and recognize its tone if not the words, as he spoke quietly to the helmsman on the deck far below. He could see his father's beaked nose and the set of his brow in the ruddy glow from the pipe bowl as he drew in the tobacco smoke. It seemed to him that his father never slept.

He could smell the iodine of the sea, the fresh odour of kelp and salt. His nose was so keen, purged by months of sweet sea air, that he could even whiff the faint odour of the land, the warm, baked smell of Africa like biscuit hot from the oven.

Then there was another scent, so faint he thought his nostrils had played a trick on him. A minute later he caught it again, just a trace, honey-sweet on the wind. He did not recognize it and turned his head back and forth, questing for the next faint perfume, sniffing eagerly.

Suddenly it came again, so fragrant and heady that he reeled like a drunkard smelling the brandy pot, and had to stop himself crying aloud in his excitement. With an effort he kept his mouth closed and, with the aroma filling his head, tumbled from the crow's nest, and fled down the shrouds to the deck below. He ran on bare feet so silently that his father started when Hal touched his arm.

'Why have you left your post?'

'I could not hail you from the masthead – they are too close. They might have heard me also.'

'What are you babbling about, boy?' His father came angrily to his feet. 'Speak plainly.'

'Father, do you not smell it?' He shook his father's arm urgently.

'What is it?' His father took the pipe stem from his mouth. 'What is it that you smell?'

'Spice!' said Hal. 'The air is full of the perfume of spice.'

They moved swiftly down the deck, Ned Tyler, Aboli and Hal, shaking the off-duty watch awake, cautioning each man to silence as they shoved him towards his battle stations. There was no drum to beat to quarters. Their excitement was infectious. The waiting was over. The Dutchman was out there some-where close, to windward in the darkness. They could all smell his fabulous cargo now.

Sir Francis extinguished the candle in the binnacle so that the ship showed no lights, then passed the keys of the arms chests to his boatswains. They were kept locked until the chase was in sight for the dread of mutiny was always in the back of every captain's mind. At other times only the petty officers carried cutlasses.

In haste the chests were opened and the weapons passed from hand to hand. The cutlasses were of good Sheffield steel, with plain wooden hilts and basket guards. The pikes had six-foot shafts of English oak and heavy hexagonal iron heads. Those of the crew who lacked skill with the sword chose either these robust spears or the boarding axes that could lop a man's head at a stroke from his shoulders.

The muskets were racked in the blackpowder magazine. They were brought up, and Hal helped the gunners load them with a handful of lead pellets on top of a handful of powder. They were clumsy, inaccurate weapons, with an effective range of only twenty or thirty yards. After the lock was triggered, and the burning match mechanically applied, the weapon fired in a cloud of smoke, but then had to be reloaded. This operation took two or three vital minutes, during which the musketeer was at the mercy of his foes.

Hal preferred the bow; the famous English longbow that had deci-

24

mated the French knights at Agincourt. He could loose a dozen shafts in the time it took to reload a musket. The longbow carried fifty paces with the accuracy to strike a foe in the centre of the chest and with the power to spit him to the backbone, even though he wore a breastplate. He already had two bundles of arrows lashed to the sides of the crow's nest, ready to hand.

Sir Francis and some of his petty officers strapped on their half armour, light cavalry cuirasses and steel pot helmets. Sea salt had rusted them and they were dented and battered from other actions.

In short order the ship was readied for battle, and the crew armed and armoured. However, the gunports were closed and the demi-culverins were not run out. Most of the men were hustled below by Ned and the other boatswains, while the rest were ordered to lie flat on the deck concealed below the bulwarks. No slow-match was lit – the glow and smoke might alert the chase to her danger. However, charcoal braziers smouldered at the foot of each mast, and the wedges were knocked out of the gunports with muffled wooden mallets so that the sound of the blows would not carry.

Aboli pushed his way through the scurrying figures to where Hal stood at the foot of the mast. Around his bald head he wore a scarlet cloth whose tail hung down his back, and thrust into his sash was a cutlass. Under one arm he carried a rolled bundle of coloured silk. 'From your father.' He thrust the bundle into Hal's arms. 'You know what to do with them!' He gave Hal's pigtail a tug. 'Your father says that you are to remain at the masthead no matter which way the fight goes. Do you hear now?'

He turned and hurried back towards the bows. Hal grimaced rebel-liously at his broad back, but climbed dutifully into the shrouds. When he reached the masthead he scanned the darkness swiftly, but as yet there was nothing to see. Even the aroma of spice had evaporated. He felt a stab of concern that he might only have imagined it. 'It is only that the chase has come out of our wind,' he reassured himself. 'She is probably abeam of us by now.'

He attached the banner Aboli had given him to the signal halyard, ready to fly it at his father's order. Then he removed the cover from the pan of the falconet. He checked the tension of the string before setting his longbow into the rack beside the bundles of yard-long arrows. Now there was nothing to do but wait. Below him the ship was unnaturally quiet, not even a bell to mark the passage of the hours, only the soft song of the sails and the muted accompaniment of the rigging.

The day came upon them with the suddenness that in these African seas he had come to know so well. Out of the dying night rose a tall bright tower, shining and translucent as an ice-covered alp – a great ship under a mass of gleaming canvas, her masts so tall they seemed to rake the last pale stars from the sky.

'Sail ho!' he pitched his voice so that it would carry to the deck below but not to the strange ship that lay, a full league away, across the dark waters. 'Fine on the larboard beam!'

His father's voice floated back to him. 'Masthead! Break out the colours!'

Hal heaved on the signal halyard, and the silken bundle soared to the masthead. There it burst open and the tricolour of the Dutch Republic streamed out on the south-easter, orange and snowy white and blue. Within moments the other banners and long pennants burst out from the head of the mizzen and the foremast, one emblazoned with the cipher of the VOC, die Verenigde Oostindische Compagnie, the United East India Company. The regalia was authentic, captured only four months previously from the *Heerlycke Nacht*. Even the standard of the Council of Seventeen was genuine. There would scarce have been time for the captain of the galleon to have learned of the capture of his sister ship and so to question the credentials of this strange caravel.

The two ships were on converging courses – even in darkness Sir Francis had judged well his interception. There was no call for him to alter course and alarm the Dutch captain. But within minutes it was clear that the *Lady Edwina*, despite her worm-riddled hull, was faster through the water than the galleon. She must soon begin to overtake the other ship, which he must avoid at all costs.

Sir Francis watched her through the lens of his telescope, and at once he saw why the galleon was so slow and ungainly: her mainmast was jury-rigged, and there was much other evidence of damage to her other masts and rigging. He realized that she must have been caught in some terrible storm in the eastern oceans – which would also account for her belated arrival off her landfall on the Agulhas Cape. He knew that he could not alter sail without alarming the Dutch captain, but he had to pass across her stern. He had prepared for this: he signed to the carpenter, at the rail, who with his mate lifted a huge canvas drogue and dropped it over the stern. Like the curb on a headstrong stallion it bit deep in the water and pulled up the *Lady Edwina* sharply. Again Sir Francis judged the disparate speeds of the two vessels, and nodded with satisfaction.

Then he looked down his own deck. The majority of the men were concealed below decks or lying under the bulwarks where they were invisible even to the lookouts at the galleon's masthead. There was no weapon in sight, all the guns hidden behind their ports. When Sir

Francis had captured this caravel she had been a Dutch trader, operating off the west African coast. In converting her to a privateer, he had been at pains to preserve her innocent air and prosaic lines. Only a dozen or so men were visible on the decks and in the rigging, which would be normal for a sluggish merchantman.

As he looked up again the banners of the Republic and the Company broke out at the Dutchman's mastheads. Only a trifle tardily she was acknowledging his salute.

'She accepts us,' Ned grunted, as he held the *Lady Edwina* stolidly on course. 'She likes our sheep's clothing.'

'Perhaps!' Sir Francis replied. 'And yet she cracks on more sail.' As they watched, the galleon's royals and top-gallants bloomed against the morning sky.

'There!' he exclaimed a moment later. 'She is altering course, sheering away from us. The Dutchman is a cautious fellow.'

'Satan's teeth! Just sniff her!' Ned whispered, almost to himself, as a trace of spices scented the air. 'Sweet as a virgin, and twice as beautiful.'

'It's the richest smell you'll ever have in your nostrils.' Sir Francis spoke loudly enough for the men on the deck below to hear him. 'There lies fifty pounds a head in prize money if you have the notion to fight for it.' Fifty pounds was ten years of an English workman's wages, and the men stirred and growled like hunting hounds on the leash.

Sir Francis went forward to the poop rail and lifted his chin to call softly up to the men in the rigging, 'Make believe that those cheese-heads over there are your brothers. Give them a cheer and a brave welcome.'

The men aloft howled with glee, and waved their bonnets at the tall ship as the *Lady Edwina* edged in under her stern.

K atinka van de Velde sat up and frowned at Zelda, her old nurse. 'Why have you woken me so early?' she demanded petulantly, and tossed the tumble of golden curls back from her face. Even so freshly aroused from sleep, it was rosy and angelic. Her eyes were of a startling violet colour, like the lustrous wings of a tropical butterfly.

'There is another ship near us. Another Company ship. The first we have seen in all these terrible stormy weeks. I had begun to think there was not another Christian soul left in all the world,' Zelda whined. 'You are always complaining of boredom. It might divert you for a while.'

27

Zelda was pale and wan. Her cheeks, once fat, smooth and greased with good living, were sunken. Her great belly was gone, and hung in folds of loose skin almost to her knees. Katinka could see it through the thin stuff of her nightgown.

She has puked away all her fat and half her flesh, Katinka thought, with a twinge of disgust. Zelda had been prostrated by the cyclones that had assailed the *Standvastigheid* and battered her mercilessly ever since they had left the Trincomalee coast.

Katinka threw back the satin bedclothes and swung her long legs over the edge of the gilded bunk. This cabin had been especially furnished and redecorated to accommodate her, a daughter of one of the omnipotent *Zeventien*, the seventeen directors of the Company. The décor was all gilt and velvet, silken cushions and silver vessels. A portrait of Katinka by the fashionable Amsterdam artist Pieter de Hoogh hung on the bulkhead opposite her bed, a wedding present from her doting father. The artist had captured her lascivious turn of head. He must have scoured his paint pots to reproduce so faithfully the wondrous colour of her eyes – and their expression, which was at once both innocent and corrupt.

'Do not wake my husband,' she cautioned the old woman as she flung a gold-brocade wrap over her shoulders and tied the jewelled belt around her hourglass waist. Zelda's eyelid drooped in conspiratorial agreement. At Katinka's insistence the Governor slept in the smaller, less grand cabin beyond the door that was locked from her side. Her excuse was that he snored abominably, and that she was indisposed by the *mal-de-mer*. In truth, caged in her quarters all these weeks, she was restless and bored, bursting with youthful energy and aflame with desires that the fat old man could never extinguish.

She took Zelda's hand and stepped out onto the narrow stern gallery. This was a private balcony, ornately carved with cherubs and angels, looking out over the ship's wake and hidden from the vulgar eyes of the crew.

It was a morning dazzling with sunlit magic, and as she filled her lungs with the salt tang of the sea she felt every nerve and muscle of her body quiver with the impetus of life. The wind kicked creamy feathers from the tops of the long blue swells, and played with her golden curls. It ruffled the silk over her breasts and belly with the caress of a lover's fingers. She stretched and arched her back sensuously like a sleek, golden cat.

Then she saw the other ship. It was much smaller than the galleon but with pleasing lines. The pretty flags and pennants that streamed from her masts contrasted with the pile of her white sails. She was close

28

enough for Katinka to make out the figures of the few men that manned her rigging. They were waving a greeting, and she could see that some were young and clad only in short petticoats.

She leaned over the rail and stared across. Her husband had commanded that the crew of the galleon observe a strict dress code while she was aboard, so the figures on this strange ship fascinated her. She folded her arms over her bosom and squeezed her breasts together, feeling her nipples harden and engorge. She wanted a man. She burned for a man, any man, just as long as he was young and hard and raging for her. A man like those she had known in Amsterdam before her father had discovered her taste for strong game and sent her out to the Indies, to a safe old husband who had a high position in the Company and even higher prospects. His choice had been Petrus Jacobus van de Velde who, now that he was married to Katinka, was assured of the next vacancy on the Company's board, where he would join the pantheon of the *Zeventien*.

'Come inside, *Lieveling*.' Zelda tugged at her sleeve. 'Those ruffians over there are staring at you.'

Katinka shrugged off Zelda's hand, but it was true. They had recognized her as a female. Even at this distance their excitement was almost palpable. Their antics had become frenzied and one strapping figure in the bows took a double handful of his own crotch and thrust his hips towards her in a rhythmic and obscene gesture.

'Revolting! Come inside!' Zelda insisted. 'The Governor will be furious if he sees what that animal is doing.'

'He should be furious that he cannot perform as nimbly,' Katinka replied angelically. She pressed her thighs tightly together the better to savour the sudden moist warmth at their juncture. The caravel was much closer now, and she could see that what the seaman was offering her was bulky enough to overflow his cupped hands. The tip of her pink tongue dabbed at her pouting lips.

'Please, mistress.'

'In a while,' Katinka demurred. 'You were right, Zelda. This does amuse me.' She raised one white hand and waved back at the other ship. Instantly the men redoubled their efforts to hold her attention.

'This is so undignified,' Zelda moaned.

'But it's fun. We'll never see those creatures again, and being always dignified is so dull.' She leaned further out over the rail and let the front of her gown bulge open.

At that moment there was a heavy pounding on the door to her husband's cabin. Without further urging Katinka fled from the gallery, rushed to her bunk and threw herself upon it. She pulled the satin

29

bedclothes up to her chin, before she nodded at Zelda, who lifted the cross bar and dropped into an ungainly curtsy as the Governor burst in. He ignored her and, belting his robe around his protruding belly, waddled to the bunk where Katinka lay. Without his wig his head was covered by sparse silver bristles.

'My dear, are you well enough to rise? The captain has sent a message. He wishes us to dress and stand to. There is a strange vessel in the offing, and it is behaving suspiciously.'

Katinka stifled a smile as she thought of the suspicious behaviour of the strange seamen. Instead she made a brave but pitiful face. 'My head is bursting, and my stomach—'

'My poor darling.' Petrus van de Velde, Governor-elect of the Cape of Good Hope, bent over her. Even on this cool morning his jowls were basted with sweat, and he reeked of last evening's dinner, Javanese curried fish, garlic and sour rum.

This time her stomach truly churned, but Katinka offered her cheek dutifully. 'I may have the strength to rise,' she whispered, 'if the captain orders it.'

Zelda rushed to the bedside and helped her sit up, and then lifted her to her feet, and with an arm around her waist, led her to the small Chinese screen in the corner of the cabin. Seated on the bench opposite, her husband was afforded only vague glimpses of shining white skin from behind the painted silk panels, even though he craned his head to see more.

'How much longer must this terrible journey last?' Katinka complained.

'The captain assures me that, with this wind holding fair, we should drop anchor in Table Bay within ten days.'

'The Lord give me strength to survive that long.'

'He has invited us to dine today with him and his officers,' replied the Governor. 'It is a pity, but I will send a message that you are indisposed.'

Katinka's head and shoulders popped up over the screen. 'You will do no such thing!' she snapped. Her breasts, round and white and smooth, quivered with agitation.

One of the officers interested her more than a little. He was Colonel Cornelius Schreuder, who, like her own husband, was *en route* to take up an appointment at the Cape of Good Hope. He had been appointed military commander of the settlement of which Petrus van de Velde would be Governor. He wore pointed moustaches and a fashionable van Dyck beard, and bowed to her most graciously each time she went on deck. His legs were well turned, and his dark eyes were eagle bright and gave her goose pimples when he looked at her. She read in them more than just respect for her position, and he had responded most gratifyingly to the sly appraisal she had given him from under her long eyelashes.

When they reached the Cape, he would be her husband's subordinate. Hers also to command – and she was sure that he could relieve the monotony of exile in the forsaken settlement at the end of the world that was to be her home for the next three years.

'I mean,' she changed her tone swiftly, 'it would be churlish of us to decline the captain's hospitality, would it not?'

'But your health is more important,' he protested.

'I will find the strength.' Zelda slipped petticoats over her head, one after another, five in all, each fluttering with ribbons.

Katinka came from behind the screen and raised her arms. Zelda lowered the blue silk dress over them and drew it down over the petticoats. Then she knelt and carefully tucked up the skirts on one side to reveal the petticoats beneath, and the slim ankles clad in white silk stockings. It was the very latest fashion. The Governor watched her, entranced. If only the other parts of your body were as big and busy as your eyeballs, Katinka thought derisively, as she turned to the long mirror and pirouetted before it.

Then she screamed wildly and clutched her bosom as, from the deck directly above them, there came the sudden deafening roar of gunfire. The Governor screamed as shrilly and flung himself from the bench onto the Oriental carpets that covered the deck.

'*De Standvastigheid*!' Through the lens of the telescope Sir Francis Courteney read the galleon's name off her high gilded transom. '*The Resolution*.' He lowered the glass and grunted, 'A name which we will soon put to the test!'

As he spoke a long bright plume of smoke spurted from the ship's upper deck, and a few seconds later the boom of the cannon carried across the wind. Half a cable's length ahead of their bows, the heavy ball plunged into the sea, making a tall white fountain. They could hear drums beating urgently in the other ship, and the gunports in her lower decks swung open. Long barrels prodded out.

'I marvel that he waited so long to give us a warning shot,' Sir Francis drawled. He closed the telescope, and looked up at the sails. 'Put up your helm, Master Ned, and lay us under his stern.' The display of false colours had won them enough time to duck in under the menace of the galleon's crushing broadside.

Sir Francis turned to the carpenter, who stood ready at the stern rail with a boarding axe in his hands. 'Cut her loose!' he ordered.

The man raised the axe above his head and swung it down. With a crunch the blade sliced into the timber of the stern rail, the drogue line parted with a whiplash crack and, free of her restraint, the *Lady Edwina* bounded forward, then heeled as Ned put up the helm.

Sir Francis's manservant, Oliver, came running with the red-quartered cloak and plumed cavalier hat. Sir Francis donned them swiftly and bellowed at the masthead, 'Down with the colours of the Republic and let's see those of England!' The crew cheered wildly as the Union flag streamed out on the wind.

They came boiling up from below decks, like ants from a broken nest, and lined the bulwarks, roaring defiance at the huge vessel that towered over them. The Dutchman's decks and rigging swarmed with frantic activity.

The cannons in the galleon's ports were training around, but few could cover the caravel as she came flying down on the wind, screened by the Dutchman's own high counter.

A ragged broadside thundered out across the narrowing gap but most of the shot fell wide by hundreds of yards or howled harmlessly overhead. Hal ducked as the blast of a passing shot lifted the cap from his head and sent it sailing away on the wind. A neat round hole had appeared miraculously in the sail six feet above him. He flicked his long hair out of his face, and peered down at the galleon.

The small company of Dutch officers on the quarterdeck were in disarray. Some were in shirtsleeves, and one was stuffing his night-shirt into his breeches as he came up the companion-ladder.

One officer caught his eye in the throng: a tall man in a steel helmet with a van Dyck beard was rallying a company of musketeers on the foredeck. He wore the gold-embroidered sash of a colonel over his shoulder, and from the way he gave his orders and the alacrity with which his men responded seemed a man to watch, one who might prove a dangerous foe.

Now at his bidding the men ran aft, each carrying a murderer, one of the small guns especially used for repelling boarders. There were slots in the galleon's stern rail into which the iron pin of the murderer would fit, allowing the deadly little weapon to be traversed and aimed at the decks of an enemy ship as it came alongside. When they had boarded the *Heerlycke Nacht* Hal had seen the execution the murderer could wreak at close range. It was more of a threat than the rest of the galleon's battery.

He swivelled the falconet, and blew on the slow-match in his hand.

32

To reach the stern the file of Dutch musketeers must climb the ladder from the quarterdeck to the poop. He aimed at the head of the ladder as the gap between the two ships closed swiftly. The Dutch colonel was first up the ladder, sword in hand, his gilded helmet sparkling bravely in the sunlight. Hal let him cross the deck at a run, and waited for his men to follow him up.

The first musketeer tripped at the head of the ladder and sprawled on the deck, dropping his murderer as he fell. Those following were bunched up behind him, unable to pass for the moment that it took him to recover and regain his feet. Hal peered over the crude sights of the falconet at the little knot of men. He pressed the burning tip of the match to the pan, and held his aim deliberately as the powder flared. The falconet jumped and bellowed and, as the smoke cleared he saw that five of the musketeers were down, three torn to shreds by the blast, the others screaming and splashing their blood on the white deck.

Hal felt breathless with shock as he looked down at the carnage. He had never before killed a man, and his stomach heaved with sudden nausea. This was not the same as shattering a water cask. For a moment he thought he might vomit.

The Dutch colonel at the stern rail looked up at him. He lifted his sword and pointed it at Hal's face. He shouted something up at Hal, but the wind and the continuous roll of gunfire obliterated his words. But Hal knew that he had made a mortal enemy.

This knowledge steadied him. There was no time to reload the falconet, it had done its work. He knew that that single shot had saved the lives of many of his own men. He had caught the Dutch musketeers before they could set up their murderers to scythe down the boarders. He knew he should be proud, but he was not. He was afraid of the Dutch colonel.

Hal reached for the longbow. He had to stand tall to draw it. He aimed his first arrow down at the colonel. He drew to full reach, but the Dutchman was no longer looking at him: he was commanding the survivors of his company to their positions at the galleon's stern rail. His back was turned to Hal.

Hal held off a fraction, allowing for the wind and the ship's movement. He loosed the arrow and watched it flash away, curling as the wind caught it. For a moment he thought it would find its mark in the colonel's broad back, but the wind thwarted it. It missed by a hand's breadth and thudded into the deck timbers where it stood quivering. The Dutchman glanced up at him, scorn curling his spiked moustaches. He made no attempt to seek cover, but turned back to his men.

Hal reached frantically for another arrow, but at that instant the two

33

ships came together, and he was almost catapulted over the rim of the crow's nest.

There was a grinding, crackling uproar, timbers burst, and the windows in the galleon's stern galleries shattered at the collision. Hal looked down and saw Aboli in the bows, a black colossus as he swung a boarding grapnel around his head in long swooping revolutions then hurled it upwards, the line snaking out behind.

The iron hook skidded across the poop deck, but when Aboli jerked it back it lodged firmly in the galleon's stern rail. One of the Dutch crew ran across and lifted an axe to cut it free. Hal drew the fletchings of another arrow to his lips and loosed. This time his judgement of the windage was perfect and the arrowhead buried itself in the man's throat. He dropped the axe and clutched at the shaft as he staggered backwards and collapsed.

Aboli had seized another grapnel and sent that up onto the galleon's stern. It was followed by a score of others, from the other boatswains. In moments the two vessels were bound to each other by a spider's web of manila lines, too numerous for the galleon's defenders to sever though they scampered along the gunwale with hatchets and cutlasses.

The *Lady Edwina* had not fired her culverins. Sir Francis had held his broadside for the time when it would be most needed. The shot could do little damage to the galleon's massive planking, and it was far from his plans to mortally injure the prize. But now, with the two ships locked together, the moment had come.

'Gunners!' Sir Francis brandished his sword over his head to attract their attention. They stood over their pieces, smoking slow-match in hand, watching him. 'Now!' he roared, and slashed his blade downwards.

The line of culverins thundered in a single hellish chorus. Their muzzles were pressed hard against the galleon's stern, and the carved, gilded woodwork disintegrated in a cloud of smoke, flying white splinters and shards of stained glass from the windows.

It was the signal. No command could be heard in the uproar, no gesture seen in the dense fog that billowed over the locked vessels, but a wild chorus of warlike yells rose from the smoke and the *Lady Edwina*'s crew poured up into the galleon.

They boarded in a pack through the stern gallery, like ferrets into a rabbit warren, climbing with the nimbleness of apes and swarming over the gunwale, screened from the Dutch gunners by the rolling cloud of smoke. Others ran out along the *Lady Edwina*'s yards and dropped onto the galleon's decks.

'Franky and St George!' Their war-cries came up to Hal at the

34

masthead. He saw only three or four shot down by the murderers at the stern before the Dutch musketeers themselves were hacked down and overwhelmed. The men who followed climbed unopposed to the galleon's poop. He saw his father go across, moving with the speed and agility of a much younger man.

Aboli stooped to boost him over the galleon's rail and the two fell in side by side, the tall Negro with the scarlet turban and the cavalier in his plumed hat, cloak swirling around the battered steel of his cuirass.

'Franky and St George!' the men howled, as they saw their captain in the thick of the fight, and followed him, sweeping the poop deck with ringing, slashing steel.

The Dutch colonel tried to rally his few remaining men, but they were beaten back remorselessly and sent tumbling down the ladders to the quarterdeck. Aboli and Sir Francis went down after them, their men clamouring behind them like a pack of hounds with the scent of fox in their nostrils.

Here they were faced with sterner opposition. The galleon's captain had formed up his men on the deck below the mainmast, and now their musketeers fired a close-range volley and charged the *Lady Edwina*'s men with bared steel. The galleon's decks were smothered with a struggling mass of fighting men.

Although Hal had reloaded the falconet, there was no target for him. Friend and foe were so intermingled that he could only watch helplessly as the fight surged back and forth across the open deck below him.

Within minutes it was apparent that the crew of the *Lady Edwina* were heavily outnumbered. There were no reserves – Sir Francis had left no one but Hal aboard the caravel. He had committed every last man, gambling all on surprise and this first wild charge. Twenty-four of his men were leagues away across the water, manning the two pinnaces, and could take no part. They were sorely needed now, but when Hal looked for the tiny scout vessels he saw that they were still miles out. Both had their gaff main sails set, but were making only snail's progress against the south-easter and the big curling swells. The fight would be decided before they could reach the two embattled ships and intervene.

He looked back at the deck of the galleon and to his consternation, realized that the fight had swung against them. His father and Aboli were being driven back towards the stern. The Dutch colonel was at the head of the counter-attack, roaring like a wounded bull and inspiring his men by his example.

From the back ranks of the boarding-party broke a small group of the *Lady Edwina*'s men, who had been hanging back from the fight. They were led by a weasel of a man, Sam Bowles, a forecastle lawyer, whose greatest talent lay in his ready tongue, his skill at arguing the division of spoils and in brewing dissension and discontent among his fellows.

Sam Bowles darted up into the galleon's stern and dropped over the rail to the *Lady Edwina*'s deck, followed by four others.

The interlocked ships had swung round ponderously before the wind, so that now the *Lady Edwina* was straining at the grappling lines that held them together. In panic and terror, the five deserters fell with axe and cutlass upon the lines. Each parted with a snap that carried clearly to Hal at the masthead.

'Avast that!' he screamed down, but not one man raised his head from his treacherous work.

'Father!' Hal shrieked towards the deck of the other ship. 'You'll be stranded! Come back! Come back!'

His voice could not carry against the wind or the noise of battle. His father was fighting three Dutch seamen, all his attention locked onto them. Hal saw him take a cut on his blade, and then riposte with a gleam of steel. One of his opponents staggered back, clutching at his arm, his sleeve suddenly sodden red.

At that moment the last grappling line parted with a crack, and the *Lady Edwina* was free. Her bows swung clear swiftly, her sails filled and she bore away, leaving the galleon wallowing, her flapping sails taken all aback, making ungainly sternway.

Hal launched himself down the shrouds, his palms scalded by the speed of the rope hissing through them. He hit the deck so hard that his teeth cracked together in his jaws and he rolled across the planks. In an instant he was on his feet, and looking desperately around him. The galleon was already a cable's length away across the blue swell, the sounds of the fighting growing faint on the wind. Then he looked to his own stern and saw Sam Bowles scurrying to take the helm.

A fallen seaman was lying in the scupper, shot down by a Dutch murderer. His musket lay beside him, still unfired, the match spluttering and smoking in the lock. Hal snatched it up and raced back along the deck to head off Sam Bowles.

He reached the whipstaff a dozen paces before the other man and rounded on him, thrusting the gun's gaping muzzle into his belly. 'Back, you craven swine! Or I'll blow your traitor's guts over the deck.'

Sam recoiled, and the other four seamen backed up behind him, staring at Hal with faces still pale and terrified from their flight.

'You can't leave your shipmates. We're going back!' Hal screamed, his eyes blazing green with wild rage and fear for his father and Aboli. He waved the musket at them, the smoke from the match swirling around his head. His forefinger was hooked around the trigger. Looking into those eyes, the deserters could not doubt his resolve and retreated down the deck.

Hal seized the whipstaff and held it over. The ship trembled under his feet as she came under his command. He looked back at the galleon, and his spirits quailed. He knew that he could never drive the *Lady Edwina* back against the wind with this set of sail: they were flying away from where his father and Aboli were fighting for their lives. At the same moment Bowles and his gang realized his predicament. 'Nobody ain't going back, and there's naught you can do about it, young Henry.' Sam cackled triumphantly. 'You'll have to get her on the other tack, to beat back to your daddy, and there's none of us will handle the sheets for you. Is there, lads? We have you strapped!'

Hal looked about him hopelessly. Then, suddenly, his jaw clenched with resolution. Sam saw the change in him and turned to follow his gaze. His own expression collapsed in consternation as he saw the pinnace only half a league ahead, crowded with armed sailors.

'Have at him, lads!' he exhorted his companions. 'He has but one shot in the musket, and then he's ours!'

'One shot and my sword!' Hal roared, and tapped the hilt of the cutlass on his hip. 'God's teeth, but I'll take half of you with me and glory in it.'

'All together!' Sam squealed. 'He'll never get the blade out of its sheath.'

'Yes! Yes!' Hal shouted. 'Come! Please, I beg you for the chance to have a look at your cowardly entrails.'

They had all watched this young wildcat at practice, had seen him fight Aboli, and none wanted to be at the front of the charge. They growled and shuffled, fingered their cutlasses and looked away.

'Come on, Sam Bowles!' Hal challenged. 'You were quick enough from the Dutchman's deck. Let's see how quick you are to come at me now.'

Sam steeled himself and then, grimly and purposefully, started forward, but when Hal poked the muzzle of the musket an inch forward, aiming at his belly, he pulled back hurriedly and tried to push one of his gang forward.

'Have at him, lad!' Sam croaked. Hal changed his aim to the second man's face, but he broke out of Sam's grip and ducked behind his neighbour.

The pinnace was close ahead now – they could hear the eager shouts of the seamen in her. Sam's expression was desperate. Suddenly he fled. Like a scared rabbit he shot down the ladder to the lower deck, and in an instant the others followed him in a panic-stricken mob.

Hal dropped the musket to the deck, and used both hands on the whipstaff. He gazed forward over the plunging bows, judging his moment carefully, then threw his weight against the lever and spun the ship's head up into the wind.

She lay there hove to. The pinnace was nearby and Hal could see Big Daniel Fisher in the bows, one of the *Lady Edwina*'s best boatswains. Big Daniel seized his opportunity, and shot the small boat alongside. His sailors latched onto the trailing grappling lines that Sam and his gang had cut, and came swarming up onto the caravel's deck.

'Daniel!' Hal shouted at him. 'I'm going to wear the ship around. Get ready to train her yards! We're going back into the fight!'

Big Daniel flashed him a grin, his teeth jagged and broken as a shark's, and led his men to the yard braces. Twelve men, fresh and eager, Hal exulted, as he prepared for the dangerous manoeuvre of bringing the wind across the ship's stern rather than over her bows. If he misjudged it, he would dismast her, but if he succeeded in bringing her round, stern first to the wind, he would save several crucial minutes in getting back to the embattled galleon.

Hal put the whipstaff hard alee, but as she struggled wildly to feel the wind come across her stern, and threatened to gybe with all standing, Daniel paid off the yard braces to take the strain. The sails filled like thunder, and suddenly she was on the other tack, clawing up into the wind, tearing back to join the fight.

Daniel hooted and lifted his cap, and they all cheered him, for it had been courageously and skilfully done. Hal hardly glanced at the others, but concentrated on holding the *Lady Edwina* close hauled, heading back for the drifting Dutchman. The fight must still be raging aboard her, for he could hear the faint shouts and the occasional pop of a musket. Then there was a flash of white off to leeward, and he saw the gaff sail of the second pinnace ahead, the crew waving wildly to gain his attention. Another dozen fighting men to join the muster, he thought. Was it worth the time to pick them up? Another twelve sharp cutlasses? He let the *Lady Edwina* drop off a point, to head straight for the tiny vessel.

Daniel had a line ready to heave across and, within seconds, the second pinnace had disgorged her men and was on tow behind the *Lady Edwina*.

'Daniel!' Hal called him. 'Keep those men quiet! No sense in warning the cheese-heads we're coming.'

'Right, Master Hal. We'll give 'em a little surprise.'

'Batten down the hatches on the lower decks! We have a cargo of cowards and traitors hiding in our holds. Keep 'em locked down there until Sir Francis can deal with them.'

Silently the *Lady Edwina* steered in under the galleon's tumblehome. Perhaps the Dutchmen were too busy to see her coming in under shortened sail for not a single head peered down from the rail above as the two hulls came together with a jarring grinding impact. Daniel and his crew hurled grappling irons over the galleon's rail, and immediately stormed up them, hand over hand.

Hal took only a moment to lash the whipstaff hard over, then raced across the deck and seized one of the straining lines. Close on Big Daniel's heels, he climbed swiftly and paused as he reached the galleon's rail. With one hand on the line and both feet planted firmly on the galleon's timbers, he drew his cutlass and clamped the blade between his teeth. Then he swung himself up and, only a second behind Daniel, dropped over the rail.

He found himself in the front rank of the fresh boarding party. With Daniel beside him, and the sword in his right fist he took a moment to glance around the deck. The fight was almost over. They had arrived with only seconds to spare for his father's men were scattered in tiny clusters across the deck, surrounded by its crew and fighting for their lives. Half their number were down, a few obviously dead. A head, hacked from its torso, leered up at Hal from the scupper where it rolled back and forth in a puddle of its own blood. With a shudder of horror, Hal recognized the *Lady Edwina*'s cook.

Others were wounded, and writhed, rolled and groaned on the deck. The planks were slick and slippery with their blood. Still others sat exhausted, disarmed and dispirited, their weapons thrown aside, their hands clasped over their heads, yielding to the enemy.

A few were still fighting. Sir Francis and Aboli stood at bay below the mainmast, surrounded by howling Dutchmen, hacking and stabbing. Apart from a gash on his left arm, his father seemed unhurt – perhaps the steel cuirass had saved him from serious injury – and he fought with all his usual fire. Beside him, Aboli was huge and indestructible, roaring a war-cry in his own tongue when he saw Hal's head pop over the rail.

Without a thought but to go to their aid, Hal started forward. 'For Franky and St George!' he screamed at the top of his lungs, and Big Daniel took up the cry, running at his left hand. The men from the pinnaces were after them, shrieking like a horde of raving madmen straight out of Bedlam.

The Dutch crew were themselves almost spent, a score were down, and of those still fighting many were wounded. They looked over their shoulders at this latest phalanx of bloodthirsty Englishmen rushing upon them. The surprise was complete. Shock and dismay was on every tired and sweat-lathered face. Most flung down their weapons and, like any defeated crew, rushed to hide below decks.

A few of the stouter souls swung about to face the charge, those around the mast led by the Dutch colonel. But the yells of Hal's boarding-party had rallied their exhausted and bleeding shipmates, who sprang forward with renewed resolve to join the attack. The Dutchmen were surrounded.

Even in the confusion and turmoil Colonel Schreuder recognized Hal, and whirled to confront him, aiming a cut, backhanded, at his head. His moustaches bristled like a lion's whiskers, and the blade hummed in his hand. He was miraculously unhurt and seemed as strong and fresh as any of the men that Hal led against him. Hal turned the blow with a twist of his wrist and went for the counter-stroke.

In order to meet Hal's charge the colonel had turned his back on Aboli, a foolhardy move. As he trapped Hal's thrust and shifted his feet to lunge, Aboli rushed at him from behind. For a moment Hal thought he would run him through the spine, but he should have guessed better. Aboli knew the value of ransom as well as any man aboard: a dead enemy officer was merely so much rotting meat to throw overboard to the sharks that followed in their wake but a captive was worth good gold guilders.

Aboli reversed his grip, and brought the steel basket of the cutlass hilt cracking into the back of the colonel's skull. The Dutchman's eyes flew wide open with shock, then his legs buckled under him and he toppled face down on the deck.

As the colonel went down, the last resistance of the galleon's crew collapsed with him. They threw down their weapons, and those of the *Lady Edwina*'s crew who had surrendered leapt to their feet, wounds and exhaustion forgotten. They snatched up the discarded weapons and turned them on the beaten Dutchmen, herding them forward, forcing them to squat in ranks with their hands clasped behind their heads, dishevelled and forlorn.

Aboli seized Hal in a bear-hug. 'When you and Sam Bowles set sail, I thought it was the last we would see of you,' he panted.

Sir Francis came striding towards his son, thrusting his way through the milling, cheering pack of his seamen. 'You deserted your post at the masthead!' He scowled at Hal as he bound a strip of cloth around the nick in his upper arm and knotted it with his teeth.

'Father,' Hal stammered, 'I thought—'

'And for once you thought wisely!' Sir Francis's dark expression cracked and his green eyes sparkled. 'We'll make a warrior of you yet, if you remember to keep your point up on the riposte. This great cheese-head,' he prodded the fallen colonel with his toe, 'was about to skewer you, until Aboli tapped his noggin.' Sir Francis slipped his sword back into its scabbard. 'The ship is not yet secure. The lower decks and holds are crawling with them. We'll have to drive them out. Stay close to Aboli and me!'

'Father, you're hurt,' Hal protested.

'And perhaps I would have been more sorely wounded had you come back to us even a minute later than you did.'

'Let me see to your wound.'

'I know the tricks Aboli has taught you – would you piss on your own father?' He laughed, and clapped Hal on the shoulder. 'Perhaps I'll give you that pleasure a little later.' He turned and bellowed across the deck, 'Big Daniel, take your men below and winkle out those cheese-heads who are hiding there. Master John, put a guard on the cargo hatches. See to it there is no looting. Fair shares for all! Master Ned, take the helm and get this ship on the wind before she flogs her canvas to rags.'

Then he roared at the others, 'I'm proud of you, you rascals! A good day's work. You'll each go home with fifty gold guineas in your pocket. But the Plymouth lassies will never love you as well I do!'

They cheered him, hysterical with the release from desperate action and the fear of defeat and death.

'Come on!' Sir Francis nodded to Aboli and started for the ladder that led down into the officers' and passengers' quarters in the stern.

Hal followed at a run as they crossed the deck, and Aboli grunted over his shoulder, 'Be on your mettle. There are those below who would be happy to stick a dirk between your ribs.'

Hal knew where his father was going, and what would be his first concern. He wanted the Dutch captain's charts, log and sailing directions. They were more valuable to him than all the fragrant spices and precious metals and bright jewels the galleon might be carrying. With those in his hands he would have the key to every Dutch harbour and fort in the Indies. He would read the sailing orders of the spice convoys and the manifest of their cargoes. To him they were worth ten thousand pounds in gold.

Sir Francis stormed down the ladder and tried the first door at the bottom. It was locked from within. He stepped back and charged. At his flying kick, the door flew open and crashed back on its hinges.

The galleon's captain was crouched over his desk, his cropped pate wigless and his clothing sweat-soaked. He looked up in dismay, blood

41

dripping from a cut on his cheek onto his silken shirt, its wide fashionable sleeves slashed with green.

At the sight of Sir Francis, he froze in the act of stuffing the ship's books into a weighted canvas bag, then snatched it up and rushed to the stern windows. The casements and glass had been shot away by the *Lady Edwina*'s culverins, and they gaped open, the sea breaking and swirling under her counter. The Dutch captain lifted the bag to hurl it through the opening but Sir Francis seized his raised arm and flung him backwards onto his bunk. Aboli grabbed the bag, and Sir Francis made a courteous little bow. 'You speak English?' he demanded.

'No English,' the captain snarled back, and Sir Francis changed smoothly into Dutch. As a Nautonnier Knight of the Order he spoke most of the languages of the great seafaring nations, French, Spanish and Portuguese, as well as Dutch. 'You are my prisoner, Mijnheer. What is your name?'

'Limberger, captain of the first class, in the service of the VOC. And you, Mijnheer, are a corsair,' the captain retorted.

'You are mistaken, sir! I sail under Letters of Marque from His Majesty King Charles the second. Your ship is now a prize of war.'

'You flew false colours,' the Dutchman accused.

Sir Francis smiled bleakly. 'A legitimate ruse of war.' He made a dismissive gesture and went on, 'You are a brave man, Mijnheer, but the fight is over now. As soon as you give me your word, you will be treated as my honoured guest. The day your ransom is paid, you will go free.'

The captain wiped the blood and sweat from his face with his silken sleeve, and an expression of resignation dulled his features. He stood and handed his sword hilt first to Sir Francis.

'You have my word. I will not attempt to escape.'

'Nor encourage your men to resistance?' Sir Francis prompted him. The captain nodded glumly. 'I agree.'

'I will need your cabin, Mijnheer, but I will find you comfortable quarters elsewhere.' Sir Francis turned his attention eagerly to the canvas bag and dumped its contents on the desk.

Hal knew that, from now on, his father would be absorbed in his reading, and he glanced at Aboli on guard in the doorway. The Negro nodded permission at him, and Hal slipped out of the cabin. His father did not see him go.

Cutlass in hand, he moved cautiously down the narrow corridor. He could hear the shouts and clatter from the other decks as the crew of the *Lady Edwina* cleared out the defeated Dutch seamen and herded them up onto the open deck. Down here it was quiet and deserted. The first door he tried was locked. He hesitated then followed his father's earlier example. The door resisted his first onslaught, but he backed off and charged again. This time it burst open and he went flying through into the cabin beyond, off balance and skidding on the magnificent Oriental rugs that covered the deck. He sprawled on the huge bed that seemed to fill half the cabin.

As he sat up and gazed at the splendour that surrounded him, he was aware of an aroma more heady than any spice he had ever smelt. The boudoir odour of a pampered woman, not merely the precious oils of flowers, procured by the perfumer's art, but blended with these the more subtle scents of skin and hair and a healthy young female body. It was so exquisite, so moving that when he stood his legs felt strangely weak under him, and he snuffed it up rapturously. It was the most delicious smell that had ever set his nostrils a-quiver.

Sword in hand he gazed around the cabin, only vaguely aware of the rich tapestries and silver vessels filled with sweetmeats, dried fruits and pot-pourri. The dressing table against the port bulkhead was covered with an array of cut-glass cosmetic and perfume bottles with stoppers of chased silver. He moved across to it. Laid out beside the bottles was a set of silver-backed brushes and a tortoiseshell comb. Trapped between the teeth of the comb was a single strand of hair, long as his arm, fine as a silk thread.

Hal lifted the comb to his face as though it were a holy relic. There was that entrancing odour again, that giddy woman's smell. He wound the hair about his finger and freed it from the teeth of the comb, then reverently tucked it into the pocket of his stained and sweat-stinking shirt.

At that moment there came a soft but heartbreaking sob from behind the gaudy Chinese screen across one end of the cabin.

'Who's there?' Hal challenged, cutlass poised. 'Come out or I'll thrust home.'

There was another sob, more poignant than the last. 'By all the saints, I mean it!' Hal stalked towards the screen.

He slashed at the screen, slicing through one of the painted panels. At the force of the blow it toppled and crashed to the deck. There was a terrified shriek, and Hal stood gaping at the wondrous creature who knelt, cowering, in the corner of the cabin.

Her face was buried in her hands, but the mass of shining hair that tumbled to the deck glowed like freshly minted gold escudos, and the skirts spread around were the blue of a swallow's wings.

'Please, madam!' Hal whispered. 'I mean you no ill. Please do not cry.'

43

His words had no effect. Clearly they were not understood and, inspired by the moment, Hal switched into Latin. 'You need not fear. You are safe. I will not harm you.'

The shining head lifted. She had understood. He looked into her face, and it was as though he had received a charge of grape shot in the centre of his chest. The pain was so intense that he gasped aloud. He had never dreamed that such beauty could exist.

'Mercy!' she whispered pitifully in Latin. 'Please do not harm me.' Her eyes were liquid and brimming, but her tears served only to enhance their magnitude and intensify their iridescent violet. Her cheeks were blanched to the translucent lustre of alabaster, and the tears upon them gleamed like tiny seed pearls.

'You are beautiful,' Hal said, still in Latin. His voice sounded like that of a victim on the rack, breathless and agonized. He was tortured by emotions that he had never dreamed existed. He wanted to protect and cherish this woman, to keep her for ever for himself, to love and worship her. All the words of chivalry, which, until he looked upon her, he had read and mouthed but never truly understood, rushed to his tongue demanding utterance, but he could only stand and stare.

Then he was distracted by another soft sound from behind him. He spun round, cutlass at the ready. From under the satin sheets that trailed over the edge of the huge bed crawled a porcine figure. The back and belly were so well larded as to wobble with every movement the man made. Rolls of fat swaddled the back of his neck and hung down his pendulous jowls. 'Yield yourself!' Hal bellowed, and prodded him with the point of the blade. The Governor screamed shrilly and collapsed on the deck. He wriggled like a puppy.

'Please do not kill me. I am a rich man,' he sobbed, also in Latin. 'I will pay any ransom.'

'Get up!' Hal prodded him again, but Petrus van de Velde had only enough strength and courage to reach his knees. He knelt there, blubbering.

'Who are you?'

'I am the Governor of the Cape of Good Hope, and this lady is my wife.'

These were the most terrible words Hal had ever heard spoken. He stared at the man aghast. The wondrous lady he already loved with his very life was married – and to this grotesque burlesque of a man who knelt before him.

'My father-in-law is a director of the Company, one of the richest and most powerful merchants in Amsterdam. He will pay – he will pay anything. Please do not kill us.'

44

The words made little sense to Hal. His heart was breaking. Within moments he had gone from wild elation to the depths of the human spirit, from soaring love to plunging despair.

But the Governor's words meant more to Sir Francis Courteney, who stood now in the entrance to the cabin with Aboli at his back.

'Please calm yourself, Governor. You and your wife are in safe hands. I will make the arrangements for your ransom with all despatch.' He swept off his plumed cavalier hat, and bent his knee towards Katinka. Even he was not entirely proof against her beauty. 'May I introduce myself, madam? Captain Francis Courteney, at your command. Please take a while to compose yourself. At four bells – that is in an hour's time – I would be obliged if you would join me on the quarterdeck. I intend to hold a muster of the ship's company.'

Both ships were under sail, the little caravel under studding-sails and top sails only, the great galleon with her mainsail set. They sailed in close company on a north-easterly heading, away from the Cape and on a closing course with the eastern reaches of the African mainland. Sir Francis looked down paternally upon his crew in the galleon's waist.

'I promised you fifty guineas the man as your prize,' he said, and they cheered him wildly. Some were stiff and crippled with their wounds. Five were laid on pallets against the rail, too weak from loss of blood to stand but determined not to miss a word of this ceremony. The dead were already stitched in their canvas shrouds, each with a Dutch cannonball at his feet, and laid out in the bows. Sixteen Englishmen and forty-two Dutch, comrades in the truce of death. None of the living now gave them a thought.

Sir Francis held up one hand. They fell silent and crowded forward so as not to miss his next words.

'I lied to you,' he told them. There was a moment of stunned disbelief and then they groaned and muttered darkly. 'There is not a man amongst you . . .' he paused for effect '. . . but is the richer by two hundred pounds for this day's work!'

The silence persisted as they stared incredulously at him, and then they went mad with joy. They capered and howled, and whirled each other around in a delirious jig. Even the wounded sat up and crowed.

Sir Francis smiled down on them benignly for a while as he let them give vent to their joy. Then he waved a sheaf of manuscript pages over his head and they fell silent again. 'This is the extract I have made of the ship's manifest!'

'Read it!' they pleaded.

The recital went on for almost half an hour, for they cheered each item of the bill of lading that he translated from the Dutch as he read aloud. Cochineal and pepper, vanilla and saffron, cloves and cardamom with a total weight of forty-two tons. The crew knew that, weight for weight and pound for pound, those spices were as precious as bars of silver. They were hoarse with shouting, and Sir Francis held up his hand again. 'Do I weary you with this endless list? Have you had enough?'

'No!' they roared. 'Read on!'

'Well, then, there are a few sticks of timber in her holds. Balu and teak and other strange wood that has never been seen north of the equator. Over three hundred tons.' They feasted on his words with shining eyes. 'There is still more, but I see that I weary you. You want no more?'

'Read it to us!' they pleaded.

'Finest Chinese blue and white ceramic ware, and silk in bolts. That will please the ladies!' They bellowed like a herd of bull elephants in musth at the mention of women. When they reached the next port, with two hundred pounds in each purse, they could have as many women, of whatever quality and comeliness their fancies ordered.

'There is also gold and silver, but that is boarded over in sealed steel chests in the bottom of the main hold, with three hundred tons of timber on top of it. We will not get our hands on it until we reach port and unload the main cargo.'

'How much gold?' they pleaded. 'Tell us how much silver.'

'Silver in coin to the value of fifty thousand guilders. That's over ten thousand good English pounds. Three hundred ingots of gold from the mines of Kollur on the Krishna river in Kandy, and the Good Lord alone knows what those will bring in when we sell them in London.'

Hal hung in the mainmast shrouds, a vantage point from which he could look down on his father on the quarterdeck. Hardly a word of what he was saying made sense to Hal, but he realized dimly that this must be one of the greatest prizes ever taken by English sailors during the course of this war with the Dutch. He felt dazed and light-headed, unable to concentrate on anything but the greater treasure he had captured with his own sword, and which now sat demurely behind his father, attended by her maid. Chivalrously Sir Francis had placed one of the carved, cushioned chairs from the captain's cabin on the quarterdeck for the Dutch governor's wife. Now Petrus van de Velde stood behind her, splendidly dressed, wearing high rhinegraves of soft Spanish leather

46

that reached to his thighs, bewigged and beribboned, his corpulence covered with the medallions and silken sashes of his office.

To his surprise Hal found that he hated the man bitterly, and lamented that he had not skewered him as he crawled from under the bed, and so made the angel who was his wife into a tragic widow.

He imagined devoting his life to playing Lancelot to her Guinevere. He saw himself humble and submissive to her every whim but inspired to deeds of outstanding valour by his pure love for her. At her behest, he might even undertake a knightly errand to search for the Holy Grail and place the sacred relic in her beautiful white hands. He shuddered with pleasure at the thought, and stared down longingly at her.

While Hal daydreamed in the rigging, the ceremony on the deck below him drew to its conclusion. Behind the Governor were ranked the Dutch captain and the other captured officers. Colonel Cornelius Schreuder was the only one without a hat, for a bandage swathed his head. Despite the blow Aboli had dealt him his eye was still keen and unclouded and his expression fierce as he listened to Sir Francis list the spoils.

'But that is not all, lads!' Sir Francis assured his crew. 'We are fortunate enough to have aboard, as our honoured guest, the new Governor of the Dutch settlement of the Cape of Good Hope.' With an ironic flourish he bowed to van de Velde, who glowered at him: now that his captors had realized his value and position, he felt more secure.

The Englishmen cheered, but their eyes were on Katinka, and Sir Francis obliged them by introducing her.

'We are also fortunate to have with us the Governor's lovely wife—' He broke off as the crew sounded their appreciation of her beauty.

'Coarse peasant cattle,' van de Velde growled and laid his hand protectively upon Katinka's shoulder. She gazed upon the men with wide violet eyes, and her beauty and innocence shamed them into an embarrassed silence.

'Mevrouw van de Velde is the only daughter of Burgher Hendrik Coetzee, the *stadhouder* of the City of Amsterdam, and the Chairman of the governing board of the Dutch East India Company.'

The crew stared at her in awe. Few understood the importance of such an exalted personage, but the manner in which Sir Francis had recited these titles had impressed them.

'The Governor and his wife will be held on board this ship until their ransom is paid. One of the captured Dutch officers will be despatched to the Cape of Good Hope with the ransom demand to be transmitted by the next Company ship to the Council in Amsterdam.'

The crew goggled at the couple as they considered this, then Big Daniel asked, 'How much, Sir Francis? What is the amount of the ransom you have set?'

'I have set the Governor's ransom at two hundred thousand guilders in gold coin.'

The ship's company was stunned, for such a sum surpassed their understanding.

Then Daniel bellowed again, 'Let's have a cheer for the captain, lads!' And they yelled until their voices cracked.

Sir Francis walked slowly down the ranks of captured Dutch seamen. There were forty-seven, eighteen of them wounded. He examined the face of each man as he passed: they were rough stock, coarse-featured and unintelligent of expression. It was obvious that none had any ransom value. They were, rather, a liability, for they had to be fed and guarded, and there was always the danger that they might recover their courage and attempt an insurrection.

'The sooner we are rid of them the better,' he murmured to himself, then addressed them aloud in their own language. 'You have done your duty well. You will be set free and sent back to the fort at the Cape. You may take your ditty bags with you, and I will see to it that you are paid the wages owing you before you go.' Their faces brightened. They had not expected that. That should keep them quiet and docile, he thought, as he turned away to the ladder down to his newly acquired cabin, where his more illustrious prisoners were waiting for him.

'Gentlemen!' he greeted them, as he entered and took his seat behind the mahogany desk. 'Would you care for a glass of Canary wine?'

Governor van de Velde nodded greedily. His throat was dry and although he had eaten only half an hour previously his stomach growled like a hungry dog. Oliver, Sir Francis's servant, poured the yellow wine into the long-stemmed glasses and served the sugared fruits he had found in the Dutch captain's larder. The captain made a sour face as he recognized his own fare, but took a large gulp of the Canary.

Sir Francis consulted the pile of manuscript on which he had made his notes, then glanced at one of the letters he had found in the captain's desk. It was from an eminent firm of bankers in Holland. He looked up at the captain and addressed him sternly. 'I wonder that an officer of your service and seniority with the VOC should indulge in trade for his own account. We both know it is strictly forbidden by the Seventeen.'

The captain looked as though he might protest, but when Sir Francis tapped the letter he subsided and glanced guiltily at the Governor, who sat beside him.

'It seems that you are a rich man, Mijnheer. You will hardly miss a ransom of two hundred thousand guilders.' The captain muttered and scowled darkly, but Sir Francis went on smoothly, 'If you will pen a letter to your bankers, the matter can be settled as between gentlemen, just as soon as I receive that amount in gold.' The captain inclined his head in acquiescence.

'Now, as to the ship's officers,' Sir Francis went on, 'I have examined your enlistment register.' He drew the book towards him and opened it. 'It seems that they are all men without high connections or financial substance.' He looked up at the captain. 'Is that the case?'

'That is true, Mijnheer.'

'I will send them to the Cape with the common seamen. Now it remains to decide to whom we shall entrust the ransom demand to the Council of the Company for Governor van de Velde and his good lady – and, of course, your letter to your bankers.'

Sir Francis looked up at the Governor. Van de Velde stuffed another candied fruit into his mouth and replied around it, 'Send Schreuder.'

'Schreuder?' Sir Francis riffled through the papers until he found the colonel's commission. 'Colonel Cornelius Schreuder, the newly appointed military commander of the fort at Good Hope?'

'Ja, that one.' Van de Velde reached for another sweetmeat. 'His rank will give him more standing when he presents your demand for my ransom to my father-in-law,' he pointed out.

Sir Francis studied the man's face as he chewed. He wondered why the Governor wanted to be rid of the colonel. He seemed a good man and resourceful; it would make more sense to keep him at hand. However, what van de Velde said of his status was true. And Sir Francis sensed that Colonel Schreuder might play the devil if he were kept captive aboard the galleon for any length of time. Much more trouble than he's worth, he thought, and said aloud, 'Very well, I will send him.'

The Governor's sugar-coated lips pouted with satisfaction. He was fully aware of his wife's interest in the dashing colonel. He had been married to her for only a few years, and yet he knew for a certainty that she had taken at least eighteen lovers in that time, some for only an hour or an evening.

Her maid, Zelda, was in the pay of van de Velde and reported to him each of her mistress's adventures, taking a deep vicarious pleasure in relating every salacious detail.

When van de Velde had first become aware of Katinka's carnal appetite, he had been outraged. However, his initial furious remonstrations had had no effect upon her and he learned swiftly that over her he had no control. He could neither protest too much nor send her away for on the one hand he was besotted by her, and on the other her father was too rich and powerful. The advancement of his own fortune and status depended almost entirely upon her. In the end his only course of action had been, as far as possible, to keep temptation and opportunity from her. During this voyage he had succeeded in keeping her a virtual prisoner in her quarters, and he was sure that, had he not done so, his wife would have already sampled the colonel's wares, which were ostentatiously on display. With him sent off the ship, her choice of diversion would be severely curtailed and, after a prolonged fast, she might even become amenable to his own sweaty advances.

'Very well,' Sir Francis agreed, 'I will send Colonel Schreuder as your emissary.' He turned the page of the almanac on the desk in front of him. 'With fair winds, and by the grace of Almighty God, the round trip from the Cape to Holland and back here to the rendezvous should not occupy more than eight months. We can hope that you might be free to take up your duties at the Cape by Christmas.'

'Where will you keep us until the ransom is received? My wife is a lady of quality and delicate disposition.'

'In a safe place, and in comfort. That I assure you, sir.'

'Where will you meet the ship returning with our ransom monies?'

'At thirty-three degrees south latitude and four degrees thirty minutes east.'

'Where, pray, might that be?'

'Why, Governor van de Velde, at the very spot upon the ocean where we are at this moment.' Sir Francis would not be tricked so readily into revealing the whereabouts of his base.

In a misty dawn the galleon dropped anchor in the gentler waters behind a rocky headland of the African coast. The wind had dropped and begun to veer. The end of the summer season was at hand; they were fast approaching the autumnal equinox. The *Lady Edwina*, her pumps pounding ceaselessly, came alongside and, with fenders of matted oakum between the hulls, she made fast to the larger vessel.

At once the work of clearing her out began. Blocks and tackle had already been rigged from the galleon's yards. They took out the guns first. The great bronze barrels on their trains were swayed aloft. Thirty seamen walked away with the tackle and then lowered each culverin to the galleon's deck. Once these guns were sited, the galleon would have the firepower of a ship of the line and would be able to attack any Company galleon on better than equal terms.

Watching the cannon come on board, Sir Francis realized that he now had the force to launch a raid on any of the Dutch trading harbours in the Indies. This capture of the *Standvastigheid* was only a beginning. From here he planned to become the terror of the Dutch in the Ocean of the Indies, just as Sir Francis Drake had scourged the Spanish on their own main in the previous century.

Now the powder kegs were lifted out of the caravel's magazine. Few remained filled after such a long cruise and the heavy actions she had fought. However, the galleon still carried almost two tons of excellent quality gunpowder, sufficient to fight a dozen battles, or to capture a rich Dutch entrepôt on the Trincomalee or Javanese coast.

When the furniture and stores had been brought across, water casks and weapons chests, brine barrels of pickled meats, bread bags and barrels of flour, the pinnaces were also hoisted aboard and broken down by the carpenters. They were stowed away in the galleon's main cargo hold on top of the stacks of rare oriental timbers. So bulky were they and so heavily laden with her own cargo was the galleon that to accommodate their bulk the hatch coamings had to be left off the main holds until the prize was taken into Sir Francis's secret base.

Stripped to her planks, the *Lady Edwina* rode high in the water when Colonel Schreuder and the released Dutch crew were ready to board her. Sir Francis summoned the colonel to the quarterdeck and handed him back his sword and the letter addressed to the Council of the Dutch East India Company in Amsterdam. It was stitched in a canvas cover, the seams sealed with red wax, and tied with ribbon. It made an impressive bundle, which Colonel Schreuder placed firmly under his arm.

'I hope we meet again, Mijnheer,' Schreuder said ominously to Sir Francis.

'In eight months from now I will be at the rendezvous,' Sir Francis assured. 'Then I shall be delighted to see you again, as long as you have the two hundred thousand gold guilders for me.'

'You miss my meaning,' said Cornelius Schreuder grimly.

'I assure you I do not,' responded Sir Francis quietly.

Then the colonel looked to the break in the poop where Katinka van de Velde stood at her husband's side. The deep bow that he made towards them and the look of longing in his eyes were not for the Governor alone. 'I shall return with all haste to end your suffering,' he told them.

'God be with you,' said the Governor. 'Our fate is in your hands.'

51

'You will be assured of my deepest gratitude on your return, my dear Colonel,' Katinka whispered, in a breathless little girl's voice, and the colonel shivered as though a bucket of icy water had been poured down his back. He drew himself to his full height, saluted her, then turned and strode to the galleon's rail.

Hal was waiting at the port with Aboli and Big Daniel. The colonel's eyes narrowed and he stopped in front of Hal and twirled his moustache. The ribbons on his coat fluttered in the breeze, and the sash of his rank shimmered as he touched the sword at his side.

'We were interrupted, boy,' he said softly, in good unaccented English. 'However, there will be a time and a place for me to finish the lesson.'

'Let us hope so, sir.' Hal was brave with Aboli at his side. 'I am always grateful for instruction.'

For a moment they held each other's eyes, and then Schreuder dropped over the galleon's side to the deck of the caravel. Immediately the lines were cast off and the Dutch crew set the sails. The *Lady Edwina* threw up her stern like a skittish colt and heeled to the press of her canvas. Lightly she turned away from the land to make her offing.

'We also will get under way, if you please, Master Ned!' Sir Francis said. 'Up with her anchor.'

The galleon bore away from the African coast, heading into the south. From the masthead where Hal crouched the *Lady Edwina* was still in plain view. The smaller vessel was standing out to clear the treacherous shoals of the Agulhas Cape, before coming around to run before the wind down to the Dutch fort below the great table-topped mountain that guarded the south-western extremity of the African continent.

As Hal watched, the silhouette of the caravel's sails altered drastically. He leaned out and shouted down, 'The *Lady Edwina* is altering course.'

'Where away?' his father yelled back.

'She's running free,' Hal told him. 'Her new course looks to be due west.'

She was doing precisely what they expected of her. With the sou'-easter well abaft her beam, she was now heading directly for Good Hope.

'Keep her under your eye.'

As Hal watched her, the caravel dwindled in size until her white sails merged with the tossing manes of the wind-driven white horses on the horizon.

'She's gone!' he shouted at the quarterdeck. 'Out of sight from here!'

Sir Francis had waited for this moment before he brought the galleon around onto her true heading. Now he gave the orders to the helm that brought her around towards the east, and she went back on a broad reach parallel with the African coast. 'This seems to be her best point of sailing,' he said to Hal, as his son came down to the deck after being relieved at the masthead. 'Even with her jury-rigging, she's showing a good turn of speed. We must get to know the whims and caprice of our new mistress. Make a cast of the log, please.'

With the glass in hand, Hal timed the wooden log on its reel, dropped from the bows on its journey back along the hull until it reached the stern. He made a quick calculation on the slate, and then looked up at his father. 'Six knots through the water.'

'With a new mainmast she will be good for ten. Ned Tyler has found a spar of good Norwegian pine stowed away in her hold. We will step it as soon as we get into port.' Sir Francis looked delighted: God was smiling upon them. 'Assemble the ship's company. We will ask God's blessing on her and rename her.'

They stood bare-headed in the wind, clutching their caps to their breasts, their expressions as pious as they could muster, anxious not to attract the disfavour of Sir Francis.

'We thank you, Almighty God, for the victory you have granted us over the heretic and the apostate, the benighted followers of the son of Satan, Martin Luther.'

'Amen!' they cried loudly. They were all good Anglicans, apart from the black tribesmen amongst them, but these Negroes cried, 'Amen!' with the rest. They had learned that word their first day aboard Sir Francis's ship.

'We thank you also for your timely and merciful intervention in the midst of the battle and your deliverance of us from certain defeat—'

Hal shuffled in disagreement, but without looking up. Some of the credit for the timely intervention was his, and his father had not acknowledged this as openly.

'We thank you and praise your name for placing in our hands this fine ship. We give you our solemn oath that we will use her to bring humiliation and punishment upon your enemies. We ask your blessing upon her. We beg you to look kindly upon her, and to sanction the new name which we now give her. From henceforth she will become the *Resolution*.'

His father had simply translated the galleon's Dutch name, and Hal was saddened that this ship would not bear his mother's name. He wondered if his father's memory of his mother was at last fading, or if he had some other reason for no longer perpetuating her memory. He knew, though, that he would never have the courage to ask, and he must simply accept this decision.

'We ask your continued help and intervention in our endless battle against the godless. We thank you humbly for the rewards you have so bountifully heaped upon us. And we trust that if we prove worthy you will reward our worship and sacrifice with further proof of the love you bear us.'

This was a perfectly reasonable sentiment, one with which every man on board, true Christian or pagan, could be in full accord. Every man devoted to God's work on earth was entitled to his rewards, and not only in the life to come. The treasures that filled the *Resolution*'s holds were proof and tangible evidence of his approval and consideration towards them.

'Now let's have a cheer for *Resolution* and all who sail in her.'

They cheered until they were hoarse, and Sir Francis silenced them at last. He replaced his broad-brimmed hat and gestured for them to cover their heads. His expression became stern and forbidding. 'There is one more task we have to perform now,' he told them, and looked at Big Daniel. 'Bring the prisoners on deck, Master Daniel.'

Sam Bowles was at the head of the forlorn file that came up from the hold, blinking in the sunlight. They were led aft and forced to kneel, facing the ship's company.

Sir Francis read their names from the sheet of parchment he held up. 'Samuel Bowles. Edward Broom. Peter Law. Peter Miller. John Tate. You kneel before your shipmates accused of cowardice and desertion in the face of the enemy, and dereliction of your duty.'

The other men growled and glared at them.

'How say you to these charges? Are you the cowards and traitors we accuse you of being?'

'Mercy, your grace. It was a madness of the moment. Truly we repent. Forgive us, we beg you for the sakes of our wives and the sweet babes we left at home,' Sam Bowles pleaded as their spokesman.

'The only wives you ever had were the trulls in the bawdy houses of Dock Street,' Big Daniel mocked him, and the crew roared.

'String them up at the yard-arm! Let's watch them dance a little jig to the devil.'

'Shame on you!' Sir Francis stopped them. 'What kind of English justice is this? Every man, no matter how base, is entitled to a fair trial.' They sobered and he went on. 'We will deal with this matter in proper order. Who brings these charges against them?'

'We do!' roared the crew in unison.

'Who are your witnesses?'

'We are!' they replied, with a single voice.

'Did you witness any act of treachery or cowardice? Did you see these foul creatures flee from the fight and leave their shipmates to their fate?'

'We did.'

'You have heard the testimony against you. Do you have aught to say in your defence?'

'Mercy!' whined Sam Bowles. The others were dumb.

Sir Francis turned back to the crew. 'And so what is your verdict?'

'Guilty!'

'Guilty as hell!' added Big Daniel, lest there be any lingering doubts.

'And your sentence?' Sir Francis asked, and immediately an uproar broke out.

'Hang 'em.'

'Hanging's too good for the swine. Keel haul 'em.'

'No! No! Draw and quarter 'em. Make them eat their own balls.'

'Let's fry some pork! Burn the bastards at the stake.'

Sir Francis silenced them again. 'I see we have some differences of opinion.' He gestured to Big Daniel. 'Take them down below and lock them up. Let them stew in their own stinking juices for a day or two. We will deal with them when we get into port. Until then there are more important matters to attend to.'

For the first time in his life aboard ship, Hal had a cabin of his own. He need no longer share every sleeping and waking moment of his life crammed in enforced intimacy with a horde of other humanity.

The galleon was spacious by comparison with the little caravel, and his father had found a place for him alongside his own magnificent quarters. It had been the cupboard of the Dutch captain's servant, and was a mere cubby-hole. 'You need a lighted place to continue your studies,' Sir Francis had justified this indulgence. 'You waste many hours each night sleeping when you could be working.' He ordered the ship's carpenter to knock together a bunk and a shelf on which Hal could lay out his books and papers.

An oil lamp swung above his head, blackening the deck overhead with its soot, but giving Hal just enough light to make out his lines and allow him to write the lessons his father set him. His eyes burned with fatigue and he had to stifle his yawns as he dipped his quill and peered at the sheet of parchment onto which he was copying the extract from the Dutch captain's sailing directions that his father had captured. Every navigator had his own personal manual of sailing directions, a priceless journal in which he kept details of oceans and seas, currents and coasts, landfalls and harbours; tables of the compass's changeable and mysterious deviations as a ship voyaged in foreign waters, and charts of the night sky, which altered with the latitudes. This was knowledge that each navigator painstakingly accumulated over his lifetime, from his own observations or gleaned from the experience and anecdotes of others. His father would expect him to complete this work before his watch at the masthead, which began at four in the morning.

A faint noise from behind the bulkhead distracted him, and he looked up with the quill still in his hand. It was a footfall so soft as to be almost inaudible and came from the luxurious quarters of the Governor's wife. He listened with every fibre of his being, trying to interpret each sound that reached him. His heart told him that it was the lovely Katinka, but he could not be certain of that. It might be her ugly old maid, or even the grotesque husband. He felt deprived and cheated at the thought.

However, he convinced himself that it was Katinka and her nearness thrilled him, even though the planking of the bulkhead separated them. He yearned so desperately for her that he could not concentrate on his task or even remain seated.

He stood, forced to stoop by the low deck above his head, and moved silently to the bulkhead. He leaned against it and listened. He heard a light scraping, the sound of a something being dragged across the deck, the rustle of cloth, some further sounds that he could not place, and then the purling sound of liquid flowing into a basin or bowl. With his ear against the panel, he visualized every movement beyond. He heard her dip water with her cupped hands and dash it into her face, heard her small gasps as the cold struck her cheeks, and then the drops splash back into the basin.

He looked down and saw that a faint ray of candlelight was shining through a crack in the panelling, a narrow sliver of yellow light that wavered in rhythm to the ship's motion. Without regard to the consequence of what he was doing, he sank to his knees and placed his eye to the crack. He could see little, for it was narrow, and the soft light of the candle was directly in his eye.

Then something passed between him and the candle, a swirl of silks and lace. He stared then gasped as he caught the pearly gleam of flawless white skin. It was merely a flash, so swift that he barely had time to make out the line of a naked back, luminous as mother-of-pearl in the yellow light.

He pressed his face closer to the panel, desperate for another glimpse of such beauty. He fancied that over the normal sound of the ship's timbers working in the seaway he could hear soft breathing, light as the whisper of a tropic zephyr. He held his own breath to listen until his lungs burned, and he felt light-headed with awe.

At that moment the candle in the other cabin was whisked away, the ray of light through the crack sped across his straining eye and was gone. He heard soft footfalls move away, and darkness and silence fell beyond the panelling.

He stayed kneeling for a long while, like a worshipper at a shrine, and then rose slowly and seated himself once more at his work shelf. He tried to force his tired brain to attend to the task his father had set him, but it kept breaking away like an unruly colt from the trainer's noose. The letters on the page before him dissolved in images of alabaster skin and golden hair. In his nostrils was a memory of that tantalizing odour he had smelt when first he burst into her cabin. He covered his eyes with one hand in an attempt to prevent the visions invading his aching brain.

It was to no avail: his mind was beyond his control. He reached for his Bible, which lay beside his journal, and opened the leather cover. Between the pages was a fine gold filigree, that single strand of hair that he had stolen from her comb.

He touched it to his lips, then gave a low moan: he fancied he could still detect a trace of her perfume on it, and he closed his eyes tightly.

It was some time before he became aware of the actions of his treacherous right hand. Like a thief it had crept under the skirts of the loose canvas petticoat that was his only garment in the hot, stuffy little cubby-hole. By the time he realized what he was doing it was too late to stop himself. He surrendered helplessly to the pumping and tugging of his own fingers. The sweat ran from his every pore and slicked down his hard young muscles. The rod he held between his fingers was hard as bone and endowed with a throbbing life of its own.

The scent of her filled his head. His hand beat fast but not as fast as his heart. He knew this was sin and folly. His father had warned him, but he could not stop. He writhed on his stool. He felt the ocean of his love for her pressing against the dyke of his restraint, like a high and irresistible tide. He gave a small cry and the tide burst from him. He felt the warm flood of it spray down his rigid straining thighs, heard it splatter the deck, and then its musky odour drove the sacred perfume of her hair from his nostrils.

He sat, sweating and panting softly, and let the waves of guilt and self-disgust overwhelm him. He had betrayed his father's trust, the promise he had made him, and with his profane lust, he had besmirched the pure and lovely image of a saint.

He could not remain in his cabin a moment longer. He flung on his canvas sea-jacket and fled up the ladder to the deck. He stood for a while at the rail breathing deeply. The raw salt air cleansed his guilt and self-disgust. He felt steadier, and looked about him to take stock of his surroundings.

The ship was still on the larboard tack, with the wind abeam. Her masts swung back and forth across the brilliant canopy of stars. He could just make out the lowering mass of the land down to leeward. The Great Bear stood a finger's breadth above the dark silhouette of the land. It was a nostalgic reminder of the land of his birth, and the childhood he had left behind.

To the south the sky was dazzling with the constellation of Centaurus standing above his right shoulder, and the mighty Southern Cross, burning in its heart. This was the symbol of this new world beyond the Line.

He looked to the helm and saw his father's pipe glow in a sheltered corner of the quarterdeck. He did not want to face him now, for he was certain that his guilt and depravity would still be so engraved on his features that his father would recognize it even in the gloom. Yet he knew that his father had seen him, and would count it as odd if he did not pay him respect. He went to him quickly. 'Your indulgence, please, Father. I came up for a breath of air to clear my head,' he mumbled, not able to meet Sir Francis's eyes.

'Don't idle up here too long,' his father cautioned him. 'I will want to see your task completed before you take your watch at the masthead.'

Hal hurried forward. This expansive deck was still unfamiliar. Much of the cargo and goods from the caravel could not fit into the galleon's already crammed holds and was lashed down on the deck. He picked his way among the casks and chests, and bronze culverins.

Hal was still so deep in remorse and guilt that he was aware of little around him, until he heard a soft, conspiratorial whispering near at hand. His wits returned to him with a rush, and he looked towards the bows.

A small group of figures was hiding in the shadows cast by the cargo stacked under the rise of the forecastle. Their furtive movements alerted him to something out of the ordinary.

After their trial by their peers, Sam Bowles and his men had been frogmarched down into the galleon's lower decks and thrown into a small compartment, which must have been the carpenter's store. There was no light and little air. The reek of pepper and bilges was stifling, and the space so confined that all five could not stretch out at the same time on the deck. They settled

58

themselves as best they could into this hellhole, and lapsed into a forlorn, despairing silence.

'Whereabouts are we? Below the waterline, do you think?' Ed Broom asked miserably.

'None of us knows his way about this Dutch hulk,' Sam Bowles muttered.

'Do you reckon they're going to murder us?' Peter Law asked.

'You can be sure they ain't about to give us a hug and a kiss,' Sam grunted.

'Keel-hauling,' Ed whispered. 'I seen it done once. When they'd dragged the poor bastard under the ship and got him out t'other side he was drowned dead as a rat in a beer barrel. There weren't much meat on his carcass – it were all scraped off by the barnacles under the hull. You could see his bones sticking out all white, like.'

They thought about that for a while. Then Peter Law said, 'I saw 'em hang and draw the regicides at Tyburn back in 'fifty-nine. Them as murdered King Charlie, the Black Boy's father. They opened they bellies like fish, then they stuck in an iron hook and twisted it until they had caught up all they guts, and they pulled their intestines out of them like ropes. After that they hacked off their cocks and their balls—'

'Shut your mouth!' Sam snarled, and they lapsed into abject silence in the darkness.

An hour later Ed Broom murmured, 'There's air coming in here some place. I can feel it on my neck.'

After a moment Peter Law said, 'He's right, you know. I can feel it too.'

'What's behind this bulkhead?'

'Ain't nobody knows. Maybe the main cargo hold.'

There was a scrabbling sound, and Sam demanded, 'What you doing?'

'There's a gap in the planking here. That's where the air's coming in.'

'Let me see.' Sam crawled across and, after a few moments, agreed. 'You're right. I can get my fingers through the hole.'

'If we could open her up.'

'If Big Daniel catches you at it, you're in bad trouble.'

'What's he going to do? Draw and quarter us? He aims to do that already.'

Sam worked in the darkness for a while and then growled, 'If I had something to prise this planking open.'

'I'm sitting on some loose timber.'

'Let's have a piece of it here.'

They were all working together now, and at last they forced the end of a sturdy wooden strut through the gap in the bulkhead. Using it as a lever they threw their weight on it together. The wood tore with a crack and Sam thrust his arm into the opening. 'There's open space beyond. Could be a way out.'

They all pushed forward for a chance to tear at the edges of the opening, ripping out their fingernails and driving splinters into the palms of their hands in their haste.

'Back! Get back!' Sam told them, and wriggled head-first into the opening. As soon as they heard him crawling away on the far side they scrambled through after him.

Groping his way forward Sam choked as the fiery reek of pepper burned his throat. They were in the hold that contained the spice casks. There was a little more light in here: it came in through the gaps where the hatch coaming had not been secured.

They could hardly make out the huge casks, each taller than a man, stacked in ranks, and there was no room to crawl over the top, for the deck was too low. However, they could just squeeze between them, but it was a hazardous passage.

The heavy casks shifted slightly with the action of the ship. They scraped and thumped on the timbers of the deck and fretted against the ropes that restrained them. A man would be crushed like a cockroach if he were caught between them.

Sam Bowles was the smallest. He crawled ahead and the others followed. Suddenly a piercing scream rang through the hold and froze them all.

'Quiet, you stupid bastard!' Sam turned back in fury. 'You'll have 'em down on us.'

'My arm!' screamed Peter Law. 'Get it off me.'

One of the huge casks had lifted with the roll of the hull and then come down again, its full weight trapping the man's arm against the deck. It was still sliding and pounding down on his limb, and they could hear the bones in his forearm and elbow crushing like dry wheat between millstones. He was screeching in hysteria and there was no quieting him: pain had driven him beyond all reasoning.

Sam crawled back and reached his side. 'Shut your mouth!' He grabbed Peter's shoulder and heaved, trying to drag him clear. But the arm was jammed, and Peter screamed all the louder.

'Ain't nothing for it,' Sam growled, and from around his waist he pulled the length of rope that served him as a belt. He dropped a loop over the other man's head and drew the noose tight round his throat. He leaned back on it, anchoring both feet between his victim's shoulder blades, and pulled with all his strength. Abruptly Peter's wild screams were cut off. Sam kept the noose tight for some time after the struggles had ceased, then freed it and retied it about his waist. 'I had to do it,' he muttered to the others. 'Better one man dead than all of us.'

No one spoke, but they followed Sam as he crawled forward, leaving the strangled corpse to be crushed to mincemeat by the shifting casks.

'Give me a hand here,' Sam said and the others boosted him up onto one of the casks below the hatch.

'There's naught but a piece of canvas 'tween us and the deck now,' he whispered triumphantly, and reached up to touch the tightly stretched cover.

'Come on, let's get out of here,' Ed Broom whispered.

'Still broad day out there.' Sam held him as he tried to loosen the ropes that held the canvas cover in place. 'Wait for dark. Won't be long now.'

Gradually the light filtering down through the chinks around the canvas cover dulled and faded. They could hear the ship's bell tolling the watches.

'End of the last dog watch,' said Ed. 'Let's go now.'

'Give it a while more,' Sam urged. After another hour, he nodded. 'Loose those sheets.'

'What we going to do out there?' Now that it was time to move they were fearful. 'You'll not be thinking of trying to take the ship?'

'Nay, you donkey. I've had enough of your bloody Captain Franky. Find anything that floats and then it's over the side for me. The land's not far off.'

'What of the sharks?'

'Captain Franky bites worse than any sodding shark you'll meet out there.'

No one argued with that.

They freed a corner of the canvas, and Sam lifted the flap and peered out. 'All clear. There's some of the empty water casks at the foot of the foremast. They'll do us just Jack-a-dandy.'

He wriggled out from under the canvas and darted across the deck. The others followed, one at a time, and helped him tear at the lashing that held the empty casks in place. Within seconds they had two clear.

'Together now, lads,' Sam whispered, and they trundled the first across the deck. They heaved up the cask between them and flung it over the rail, ran back and grabbed a second.

'Hey! You men! What are you doing?' The challenge from close at hand shocked them all and they turned pale faces to look back. They all recognized Hal.

61

'It's Franky's whelp!' one cried, and they dropped the cask and scampered for the ship's side. Ed Broom was first over. He dived headlong, with Peter Miller and John Tate close behind him.

Hal took a moment to realize what they were up to, and then bounded forward to intercept Sam Bowles. He was the ringleader, the most guilty of the gang, and Hal tackled him as he reached the ship's rail.

'Father!' he shouted, loud enough for his voice to carry to every quarter of the deck. 'Father, help me!'

Locked chest to chest they struggled. Hal fastened a head-lock on him, but Sam threw back his head then butted forward in the hope of breaking Hal's nose. But Big Daniel had taught Hal his wrestling, and he had been ready: he dropped his chin on his chest so that his skull clashed with Sam's. Both men were half stunned by the impact, and broke from each other's grip.

Instantly Sam lurched for the rail but, on his knees, Hal grabbed at his legs. 'Father!' he screamed again. Sam tried to kick him off but Hal held on grimly. Then Sam looked up and saw Sir Francis Courteney charging down from the quarterdeck. His sword was out and the blade flashed in the starlight.

'Hold hard, Hal! I'm coming!'

There was no time for Sam to free the rope belt from around his middle, and drop the loop over Hal's head. Instead he reached down and locked both hands around his throat. He was a small man, but his fingers were work-toughened, hard as iron marlinspikes. He found Hal's windpipe and blocked it off ruthlessly.

The pain choked Hal, and his grip loosened on Sam's legs. He seized the man's wrists, trying to break his stranglehold, but Sam placed one foot on his chest, kicked him over backwards, then darted to the side of the ship. Sir Francis aimed a sword cut at him as he ran up, but Sam ducked under it and dived over the rail.

'The treacherous vermin will get clear away!' Sir Francis howled. 'Boatswain, call all hands to tack ship. We will go back to pick them up.'

Sam Bowles was driven deep by the force with which he hit the water, and the shock of the cold drove the wind from his lungs. He felt himself drowning, but fought and clawed his way up. At last his head broke the surface, he sucked in a lungful of air and felt the dizziness, and the weakness in his limbs, pass.

He looked up at the hull of the ship, trundling majestically past him, and then he was left in her wake, which glistened slick and oily in the starlight. That was the highway that would guide him back to the cask. He must follow it before the swells wiped it away and left him with no signpost in the darkness. His feet were bare and he wore only a ragged cotton shirt and his canvas petticoats, which would not encumber his movements. He struck out overarm for, unlike most of his fellows, he was a strong swimmer.

Within a dozen strokes he heard a voice in the darkness nearby. 'Help me, Sam Bowles!' He recognized Ed Broom's wild cries. 'Give me a hand, shipmate, or I'm done for.'

Sam stopped to tread water and, in the starlight, saw the splashes of Ed's struggles. Beyond him he saw something else lift on the crest of a dark swell, something black and round.

The cask!

But Ed was between him and this promise of survival. Sam started swimming again, but he sheered away from Ed Broom. It was dangerous to come too close to a drowning man, for he would always seize you and hang on with a death grip, until he had taken you down with him.

'Please, Sam! Don't leave me.' Ed's voice was growing fainter.

Sam reached the floating cask and got a handhold on the protruding spigot. He rested a while then roused himself as another head bobbed up beside him. 'Who's that?' he gasped.

'It's me, John Tate,' the swimmer blurted out, coughing up sea water as he tried to find a hold on the barrel.

Sam reached down and loosened the rope belt from around his waist. He used it to take a turn around the spigot and thrust his arm through the loop. John Tate grabbed at the loop too.

Sam tried to push him away. 'Leave it! It's mine.' But John's grip was desperate with panic and after a minute Sam let him be. He could not afford to squander his own strength in wrestling with a bigger man.

They hung together on the rope in a hostile truce. 'What happened to Peter Miller?' John Tate demanded.

'Bugger Peter Miller!' snarled Sam.

The water was cold and dark, and both men imagined what might be lurking beneath their feet. A pack of the monstrous tiger sharks always followed the ship in these latitudes, to pick up the offal and contents of the latrine buckets as they were emptied overboard. Sam had seen one of these fearsome creatures as long as the *Lady Edwina*'s pinnace and he thought about it now. He felt his lower body cringe and tremble with cold and the dread of those serried ranks of fangs closing over it to shear him in two, as he might bite into a ripe apple.

'Look!' John Tate choked as a wave hit him in the face and flooded his open mouth. Sam raised his head and saw a dark, mountainous shape loom out of the night close by.

'Bloody Franky come back to find us,' he growled, through chattering teeth. They watched in horror as the galleon bore down on them, growing larger with each second until she seemed to blot out all the stars and they could hear the voices of the men on her deck.

'Do you see anything there, Master Daniel?' That was Sir Francis's hail.

'Nothing, Captain,' Big Daniel's voice boomed from the bows. Looking down onto the black, turbulent water it would be nigh on impossible to make out the dark wood of the cask or the two heads bobbing beside it.

They were hit by the bow wave the galleon threw up as she passed and were left twisting and bobbing in her wake as her stern lantern receded into the darkness.

Twice more during the night they saw its glimmer, but each time the ship passed further from them. Many hours later, as the dawn light strengthened, they looked with trepidation for *Resolution*, but she was nowhere in sight. She must have given them up for drowned and headed off on her original course. Stupefied with cold and fatigue, they hung on to their precarious handhold.

'There's the land,' Sam whispered, as a swell lifted them high, and they could make out the dark shoreline of Africa. 'It's so close you could swim to it easy.'

John Tate made no reply but stared at him sullenly through eyes scalded red and swollen.

'It's your best chance. Strong young fellow like you. Don't worry about me.' Sam's voice was rough with salt.

'You'll not get rid of me that easy, Sam Bowles,' John grated, and Sam fell silent again, husbanding his strength, for the cold had sapped him almost to his limit. The sun rose higher and they felt it on their heads, first as a gentle warmth that gave them new strength and then like the flames of an open furnace that seared their skin and dazzled and blinded them with its reflection off the sea around them.

The sun climbed higher, but the land came no closer: the current bore them inexorably parallel to the rocky headlands and white beaches. Idly Sam noticed a patch of cloud shadow that passed close by them, moving darkly across the surface of the water. Then the shadow turned and came back, moving against the wind, and Sam stirred and lifted his head. There was no cloud in the aching blue vault of the sky to cast such a shadow. Sam looked down again and concentrated his full attention on that dark presence on the sea. A swell lifted the cask so high that he could look down upon it.

'Sweet Jesus!' he croaked, through cracked salt-seared lips. The water was as clear as a glass of gin, and he had seen a great dappled shape move beneath, the dark zebra stripes upon its back. He screamed.

John Tate lifted his head. 'What is it? The sun's got you, Sam Bowles.' He stared into Sam's wild eyes, then turned his head slowly to follow their gaze. Both men saw the massive forked tail swing ponderously from side to side, driving the long body forward. It was coming up towards the surface and the tip of the tall dorsal fin broke through, only to the length of a man's finger, the rest still hidden deep beneath.

'Shark!' John Tate hissed. 'Tiger!' He kicked frantically, trying to turn the cask to interpose Sam between himself and the creature.

'Stay still,' Sam snarled. 'He's like a cat. If you move he'll come for you.'

They could see its eye, small for such girth and length of body. It stared at them implacably as it began the next circle. Round it went, and round again, each circle narrower, with the cask at its centre.

'Bastard's hunting us like a stoat after a partridge.'

'Shut your mouth. Don't move,' Sam moaned, but he could no longer control his terror. His sphincter loosened, and he felt the fetid warm rush under his petticoats as involuntarily his bowels emptied. Immediately the creature's movements became more excited and its tail beat to a faster rhythm as it tasted his excrement. The dorsal fin rose to its full height above the surface, as long and curved as the blade of a harvester's scythe.

The shark's tail beat the surface white and foamy as it drove forward until its snout crashed into the side of the cask. Sam watched in terror as a miraculous transformation came over the sleek head. The upper lip bulged outwards as the wide jaws gaped. The ranks of fangs were thrust forward, fanning open, and clashed against the side of the wooden cask.

Both men panicked and scrabbled at their damaged raft, trying to lift their lower bodies clear of the water. They were screaming incoherently, clawing wildly at the barrel staves and at each other.

The shark backed off and started another of those terrible circles. Beneath the staring eye the mouth was a grinning crescent. Now the thrashing legs of the struggling men gave it a new focus, and it surged in again, its broad back thrusting aside the waters.

John Tate's shriek was cut off abruptly, but his mouth was still wide open, so that Sam looked down his pink gulping throat. No sound came from it but a soft hiss of expelled breath. Then he was jerked beneath the surface. His left wrist was still twisted into the loop of line and, as he was pulled under, the cask bobbed and ducked like a cork.

'Leave go!' Sam howled as he was thrown around, the rope biting deep into his own wrist. Suddenly the cask flew to the surface, John Tate's wrist still twisted into the bight of line. A dark roseate cloud spread to discolour the surface around them.

Then John's head broke out. He made a harsh, cawing sound, and his bloodstained spittle sprayed into Sam's eyes. His face was icy white as his life's blood drained from him. The shark came surging back and, beneath the surface, latched onto John's lower body, worrying and shaking him so that the damaged cask was again pulled under. As it shot once more to the surface, Sam sucked in a breath, and tugged at John's wrist. 'Get away!' he screamed at both man and shark. 'Get away from me.' With the strength of a madman, he pulled the loop free and he kicked at the other man's chest, pushing him clear, screaming all the while, 'Get away!'

John Tate did not resist. His eyes were still wide open but although his lips writhed, no sound came from them. Below the surface his body had been bitten away below the waist, and his blood turned the waters dark red. The shark seized him once again, then swam off, gulping down lumps of John Tate's flesh.

The damaged cask had taken in water and now floated low, but this gave it a stability it had lacked when it rode high and lightly. At the third attempt Sam dragged himself up onto it. He draped both arms and legs over it, straddling it. The cask's balance was precarious and he dared not lift even his head for fear of upsetting it and being rolled back into the sea. After a while he saw the great dorsal fin pass before his eyes as the creature came back once more to the cask. He dared not lift his head to follow the narrowing circles, so he closed his eyes and tried to shut his mind to the beast's presence.

Suddenly the cask lurched under him and his resolve was forgotten. His eyes flew wide and he shrieked. But after having bitten into the wood the shark was backing away. Twice more it returned, each time nudging the cask with its grotesque snout. However, each attempt was less determined, perhaps because it had assuaged its appetite on John Tate's carcass and was now discouraged by the taste and smell of the splinters of wood. Eventually Sam saw it turn and move away, its tall fin wagging from side to side as it swam up-current.

He lay unmoving, draped over the cask, riding the salty belly of the ocean, rising and falling to her thrusts like an exhausted lover. The night fell over him, and now he could not have moved even if he had wished to. He fell into delirium and bouts of oblivion.

He dreamed that it was morning again, that he had survived the night. He dreamed that he heard human voices near at hand. He dreamed that when he opened his eyes he saw a tall ship, hove to close alongside. He knew it was fantasy for, in a twelve-month span, fewer than two dozen ships rounded this remote cape at the end of the world. Yet, as he watched, a boat was lowered from the ship's side and rowed towards him. Only when he felt rough hands seize his legs did he realize dully that this was no dream.

The *Resolution* edged in towards the land with only a feather of canvas set and the crew standing ready for the order to whip it off and furl it on her masts.

Sir Francis's eyes darted from the sails to the land close ahead. He listened intently to the chant of the leadsman as he swung the line and let the weight drop ahead of their bows. As the ship passed over it, and the line came straight up and down, he read the sounding. 'By the deep twenty!'

'Top of the tide in an hour.' Hal looked up from the slate. 'And full moon in three days. She'll be making springs.'

'Thank you, pilot,' Sir Francis said, with a touch of sarcasm. Hal was only performing his duty, but the lad was not the only one aboard who had pored for hours over the almanac and the tables. Then Sir Francis relented. 'Get up to the masthead, lad. Keep your eyes wide open.'

He watched Hal race up the shrouds, then glanced at the helm and said quietly, 'Larboard a point, Master Ned.'

'A point to larboard it is, Captain.' With his teeth Ned moved the stem of his empty clay pipe from one corner of his mouth to the other. He, too, had seen the white surge of reef at the entrance to the channel.

The land was so close now that they could make out the individual branches of the trees that grew tall on the rocky heads that guarded the entrance. 'Steady as she goes,' Sir Francis said, as the *Resolution* crept forward between these towering cliffs of rock. He had never seen this entrance marked on any chart that he had either captured or purchased. This coast was depicted always as forbidding and dangerous, with few safe anchorages for a thousand miles north from Table Bay at Good Hope. Yet as the *Resolution* thrust deeper into the green water channel, a lovely broad lagoon opened ahead of her, surrounded on all sides by high hills, densely forested.

'Elephant Lagoon!' Hal exulted at the masthead. It was over two months since last they had sailed from this secret sallyport. As if to justify the name that Sir Francis had given this harbour, there came a clarion blast from the beach below the forest.

Hal laughed with pleasure as he picked out on the beach four huge grey shapes. They stood shoulder to shoulder in a solid rank, facing the ship, their ears spread wide. Their trunks were raised straight and high, the nostrils at the tips questing the air for the scent of this strange apparition they saw coming towards them. The bull elephant lifted his long yellow tusks and shook his head until his ears clapped like the tattered grey canvas of an unfurling main sail. He trumpeted again.

In the ship's bows, Aboli returned the greeting, raising his hand above his head in salute and calling out in the language that only Hal could understand, 'I see you, wise old man. Go in peace, for I am of your totem and I mean you no harm.'

At the sound of his voice the elephants backed away from the water's edge, then turned as one and headed back into the forest at a shambling run. Hal laughed again, at Aboli's words and to watch the great beasts go, trampling and shaking the forest with their might.

Then he concentrated once more on picking out the sandbanks and shoals, and in calling down directions to his father on the quarterdeck. The *Resolution* followed the meandering channel down the length of the lagoon until she came out into a wide green pool. The last scrap of her canvas was stripped and furled on her yards, and her anchor splashed into its depths. She swung round gently and snubbed at her anchor chain.

She lay only fifty yards off the beach, hidden behind a small island in the lagoon, so that she was concealed from the casual scrutiny of a passing ship looking in through the entrance between the heads. The way was scarcely off her before Sir Francis was shouting his orders. 'Carpenter! Get the pinnaces assembled and launched.'

Before noon the first was lowered from the deck to the water, and ten men went down into her with their ditty bags. Big Daniel took charge of the oarsmen, who rowed them down the lagoon and put them ashore at the foot of the rocky heads. Through his telescope Sir Francis watched them climb the steep elephant path to the summit. From there they would keep a lookout and warn him of the approach of any strange sail.

'On the morrow we will move the culverins to the entrance and set them up in stone emplacements to cover the channel,' he told Hal. 'Now, we will celebrate our arrival with fresh fish for our dinner. Get out the hooks and lines. Take Aboli and four men with you in the other pinnace. Dig some crabs from the beach and bring me back a load of fish for the ship's mess.'

Standing in the bows as the pinnace was rowed out into the channel, Hal peered down into the water. It was so clear that he could see the sandy bottom. The lagoon teemed with fish and shoal after shoal sped away before the boat. Many were as long as his arm, some as long as the spread of both arms.

When they anchored in the deepest part of the channel, Hal dropped a handline over the side, the hooks baited with crabs they had taken from their holes on the sandy beach. Before it touched the bottom, the bait was seized with such rude power that before he could check it the line scorched his fingers. Leaning back against the line he brought it in hand over hand, and swung a flapping, glistening body of purest silver over the gunwale.

While it still thumped upon the deck and Hal struggled to twist the barbed hook from its rubbery lip, Aboli shouted with excitement and heaved back on his own line. Before he could swing his fish over the side, all the other sailors were laughing and straining to pull heavy darting fish aboard.

Within the hour the deck was knee-deep in dead fish and they were all smeared to the eyebrows with slime and scales. Even the hard, rope-calloused hands of the seamen were bleeding from line burn and the prick of sharp fins. It was no longer sport but hard work to keep the inverted waterfall of living silver streaming over the side.

Just before sunset Hal called a halt, and they rowed back towards the anchored galleon. They were still a hundred yards from her when, on an impulse, Hal stood up in the stern and stripped off his stinking slime-coated clothes. Stark mother naked he balanced on the thwart, and called to Aboli, 'Take her alongside and unload the catch. I will swim from here.' He had not bathed in over two months, since last they had anchored in the lagoon, and he longed for the feel of cool clear water on his skin. He gathered himself and dived overboard. The men at the galleon's rail shouted ribald encouragement and even Sir Francis paused and watched him indulgently.

'Let him be, Captain. He's still a carefree boy,' said Ned Tyler. 'It's just that he's so big and tall that we sometimes forget that.' Ned had been with Sir Francis for so many years that he could be forgiven such familiarity.

'There's no place for a thoughtless boy in the *guerre de course*. This is man's work and it needs a hard head on even the most youthful shoulders or there'll be a Dutch noose for that thoughtless head.' But he made no effort to reprimand Hal as he watched his naked white body slide through the water, supple and agile as a dolphin.

K atinka heard the commotion on the deck above, and raised her eyes from the book she was reading. It was a copy of François Rabelais' *Gargantua and Pantagruel* which had been printed privately in Paris with beautifully detailed erotic illustrations, hand-coloured and lifelike. A young man she had known in Amsterdam before her hasty marriage had sent it to her. From close and intimate experience, he knew her tastes well. She glanced idly through the window and her interest quickened. She dropped the book and stood up for a better view.

'*Lieveling*, your husband,' Zelda warned her.

'The devil with my husband,' said Katinka, as she stepped out onto the stern gallery and shaded her eyes against the slanting rays of the setting sun.

The young Englishman who had captured her stood in the stern of a small boat, not far across the quiet lagoon waters. As she watched he stripped off his soiled and tattered clothing, until he stood naked and unashamed, balancing with easy grace on the gunwale.

As a young girl she had accompanied her father to Italy. There she had bribed Zelda to take her to see the collection of sculptures by Michelangelo, while her father was meeting with his Italian trading partners. She had spent almost an hour of that sultry afternoon standing before the statue of David. Its beauty had aroused in her a turmoil of emotion. It was the first depiction of masculine nudity she had ever looked upon, and it had changed her life.

Now she was looking at another David sculpture, but this one was not of cold marble. Of course, since their first encounter in her cabin she had seen the boy often. He dogged her footsteps like an over-affectionate puppy. Whenever she left her cabin he appeared miraculously, to moon at her from afar. His transparent adoration afforded her only the mildest amusement, for she was accustomed to no less from every man between the ages of fourteen and eighty. He had barely warranted more than a glance, this pretty boy, in baggy, filthy rags. After their first violent meeting, the stink of him had lingered in her cabin, so pungent that she had ordered Zelda to sprinkle perfume to dispel it. But, then, she knew from bitter experience that all sailors stank for there was no water on the ship other than for drinking, and little enough of that.

Now that the lad had shed his noisome clothing, he had become a thing of striking beauty. Though his arms and face were bronzed by the sun, his torso and legs were carved in pure unsullied white. The low sun gilded the curves and angles of his body and his dark hair tumbled down his back. His teeth were very white in the tanned face, and his laughter so musical and filled with such zest that it brought a smile to her own lips.

Then she looked down his body and her mouth opened. The violet eyes narrowed and became calculating. The sweet lines of his face were deceiving. He was a lad no longer. His belly was flat, ridged with fine young muscle like the sands of a wind-sculpted dune. At its base flared a dark bush of crisp curls, and his rosy genitals hung full and weighty, with an authority that those of Michelangelo's David had lacked.

When he dived into the lagoon, she could follow his every movement beneath the clear water. He came to the surface and, laughing, flung the sodden hair from his face with a toss of his head. The flying droplets sparkled like the sacred nimbus of light around the head of an angel.

He struck out towards where she stood, high in the stern, gliding through the water with a peculiar grace that she had not noticed he possessed when clothed in his canvas tatters. He passed almost directly under where she was but did not look up at her, unaware of her scrutiny. She could make out the knuckles of his spine flanked by ridges of hard muscle that ran down to merge with the deep crease between his lean, round buttocks, which tightened erotically with every kick of his legs, as though he were making love to the water as he passed through it.

She leaned out to follow him with her eyes, but he swam out of her view around the stern. Katinka pouted with frustration and went to retrieve her book. But the illustrations in it had lost their appeal, paling against the contrast of real flesh and glossy young skin.

She sat with it open on her lap and imagined that hard young body all white and glistening above her and those tight young buttocks bunching and changing shape as she dug her sharp fingernails into them. She knew instinctively that he was a virgin – she could almost smell the honey-sweet odour of chastity upon him and felt herself drawn to it, like a wasp to an overripe fruit. It would be her first time with a sexual innocent. The thought of it added spice to his natural beauty.

Her erotic daydreams were aggravated by the long period of her enforced abstinence and she lay back and pressed her thighs tightly together, beginning to rock gently back and forth in her chair, smiling secretly to herself.

Hal spent the next three nights camped on the beach below the heads. His father had placed him in charge of ferrying the cannon ashore and building the stone emplacements to house them, overlooking the narrow entrance to the lagoon.

Naturally Sir Francis had rowed across to approve the sites his son had chosen, but even he could find no fault with Hal's eye for a field of fire that would rake an enemy ship seeking to pass through the heads.

On the fourth day, when the work was done and Hal was rowed back down the lagoon, he saw from afar that the work of repairing the galleon was well in hand. The carpenter and his mates had built scaffolds over her stern, from which platform they were fitting new timbers to replace those damaged by gunfire, to the great discomfort of the guests aboard. The ungainly jurymast, raised by the Dutch captain to replace his gale-shattered main, had been taken down and the galleon's lines were awkward and unharmonious with one mast missing.

However, when Hal climbed up to the deck through the entryport, he saw that Ned Tyler and his work gang were swaying up the massive baulks of exotic timber that made up the heaviest part of the ship's cargo and lowering them into the lagoon to float across to the beach.

The spare mast was stowed at the bottom of the hold, where the sealed compartment contained the coin and ingots. The cargo had to be removed to reach them.

'Your father has sent for you,' Aboli greeted Hal, and Hal hurried aft.

'You have missed three days of your studies while you were ashore,' Sir Francis told him, without preamble.

'Yes, Father.' Hal knew that it was vain to point out that he had not deliberately evaded them. But, at least, I will not apologize for it, he determined silently, and met his father's gaze unflinchingly.

'After your supper this evening, I will rehearse you in the catechism of the Order. Come to my cabin at eight bells in the second dog watch.'

The catechism of initiation to the Order of St George and the Holy Grail had never been written down and for nearly four centuries the two hundred esoteric questions and answers had been passed on by word of mouth; master instructing novice in the Strict Observance.

Sitting beside Aboli on the foredeck, Hal wolfed hot biscuit, fried in dripping, and baked fresh fish. Now with an unlimited supply of firewood and fresh food on hand, the ship's meals were substantial, but Hal was silent as he ate. In his mind he went over his catechism, for his father would be strict in his judgement. Too soon the ship's bell struck and, as the last note faded, Hal tapped on the door to his father's cabin.

While his father sat at his desk Hal knelt on the bare planks of the deck. Sir Francis wore the cloak of his office over his shoulders, and on his breast sparkled the magnificent seal fashioned of gold, the insignia of a Nautonnier Knight who had passed through all the degrees of the Order. It depicted the lion rampant of England holding aloft the croix patté and, above it, the stars and crescent moon of the mother goddess. The lion's eyes were rubies and the stars were diamonds. On the second finger of his right hand he wore a narrow gold ring, engraved with a compass and a backstaff, the tools of the navigator, and above these a crowned lion. The ring was small and discreet, not as ostentatious as the seal.

His father conducted the catechism in Latin. The use of this language ensured that only literate, educated men could ever become members of the Order.

'Who are you?' Sir Francis asked the first question.

'Henry Courteney, son of Francis and Edwina.'

'What is your business here?'

'I come to present myself as an acolyte of the Order of St George and the Holy Grail.'

'Whence come you?'

'From the ocean sea, for that is my beginning and at my ending will be my shroud.' With this response Hal acknowledged the maritime roots of the Order. The next fifty questions examined the novice's understanding of the history of the Order.

'Who went before you?'

'The Poor Knights of Christ and of the Temple of Solomon.' The Knights of the Temple of the Order of St George and the Holy Grail were the successors to the extinct Order of the Knights Templar.

After that Sir Francis made Hal outline the history of the Order; how in the year 1312 the Knights Templar had been attacked and destroyed by the King of France, Philippe Le Bel, in connivance with his puppet Pope Clement V of Bordeaux. Their vast fortune in bullion and land was confiscated by the Crown, and most of them were tortured and burned at the stake. However, warned by their allies, the Templar mariners slipped their moorings in the French channel harbours and stood out to sea. They steered for England, and sought the protection of King Edward II. Since then, they had opened their lodges in Scotland and England under new names, but with the basic tenets of the Order intact.

Next Sir Francis made his son repeat the arcane words of recognition, and the grip of hands that identified the Knights to each other.

'In Arcadia habito. I dwell in Arcadia,' Sir Francis intoned, as he stooped over Hal to take his right hand in the double grip.

'*Flumen sacrum bene cognosco!* I know well the sacred river!' Hal replied reverently, interlocking his forefinger with his father's in the response.

'Explain the meaning of these words,' his father insisted.

'It is our covenant with God and each other. The Temple is Arcadia, and we are the river.'

The ship's bell twice sounded the passage of the hours before the two hundred questions were asked and answered, and Hal was allowed to rise stiffly from his knees.

When he reached his tiny cabin he was too weary even to light the oil lamp and dropped to his bunk fully clothed to lie there in a stupor of mental exhaustion. The questions and responses of the catechism echoed, an endless refrain, through his tired brain, until meaning and reality seemed to recede.

Then he heard faint sounds of movement from beyond the bulkhead and, miraculously, his fatigue cleared. He sat up, his senses tuned to the other cabin. He would not light the lamp for the sound of steel striking flint would carry through the panel. He rolled off his bunk and, in the darkness, moved on silent bare feet to the bulkhead.

He knelt and ran his fingers lightly along the joint in the woodwork until he found the plug he had left there. Quietly he removed it and placed his eye to the spyhole.

Each day his father allowed Katinka van de Velde and her maid, with Aboli to guard them, to go ashore and walk on the beach for an hour. That afternoon while the women had been away from the ship, Hal had found a moment to steal down to his cabin. He had used the point of his dirk to enlarge the crack in the bulkhead. Then he had whittled a plug of matching wood to close and conceal the opening.

Now he was filled with guilt, but he could not restrain himself. He placed his eye to the enlarged aperture. His view into the small cabin beyond was unimpeded. A tall Venetian mirror was fixed to the bulkhead opposite him and, in its reflection, he could see clearly even those areas of the cabin that otherwise would have been hidden from him. It was apparent that this smaller cabin was an annexe to the larger and more splendid main cabin. It seemed to serve as a dressing and retiring place where the Governor's wife could take her bath and attend to her private and intimate toilet. The bath was set up in the centre of the deck, a heavy ceramic hip bath in the Oriental style, the sides decorated with scenes of mountain landscapes and bamboo forests.

Katinka sat on a low stool across the cabin and her maid was tending her hair with one of the silver-backed brushes. It flowed down to her waist, and each stroke made it shimmer in the lamp-light. She wore a gown of brocade, stiff with gold embroidery, but Hal marvelled that her hair was more brilliant than the precious metal thread.

He gazed at her, entranced, trying to memorize each gesture of her white hands, and each delicate movement of her lovely head. The sound of her voice and her soft laughter were balm to his exhausted mind and body. The maid finished her task, and moved away. Katinka stood up from her stool and Hal's spirits plunged, for he expected her to take up the lamp and leave the cabin. But instead she came towards him. Though she passed out of his direct line of sight he could still see her reflection in the mirror. There was only the thickness of the panel between them now, and Hal was afraid she might become aware of his hoarse breathing.

He gazed at her reflection as she stooped and lifted the lid of the night cabinet that was affixed to the opposite side of the bulkhead against which Hal pressed. Suddenly, before he realized what she intended, she swept the skirts of her gown above her waist and, in the same movement, perched like a bird on the seat of the cabinet.

She continued to laugh and chat to her maid as her water purred into the chamber-pot beneath her. When she rose again Hal was given one more glimpse of her long pale legs before the skirts dropped over them and she swept gracefully from the cabin.

Hal lay on his hard bunk in the dark, his hands clasped across his chest, and tried to sleep. But the images of her beauty tormented him. His body burned and he rolled restlessly from side to side. 'I will be strong!' he whispered aloud, and clenched his fists until the knuckles cracked. He tried to drive the vision from his mind, but it buzzed in his brain like a swarm of angry bees. Once again he heard, in his imagination, her laughter mingle with the merry tinkle she made in her chamber-pot, and he could resist no longer. With a groan of guilt he capitulated and reached down with both hands to his swollen, throbbing loins.

Once the cargo of timber had been lifted out of the main hold, the spare mast could be raised to the deck. It was a labour that required half the ship's company. The massive spar was almost as long as the galleon and had to be carefully manoeuvred from its resting place in the bowels of the hold. It was floated across the channel and then dragged up the beach. There, in a clearing beneath the spreading forest canopy, the carpenters set it on trestles and began to trim and shape it, so that it could be stepped into the hull to replace the gale-shattered mast.

Only once the hold was emptied could Sir Francis call the entire ship's company to witness the opening of the treasure compartment that the Dutch authorities had deliberately covered with the heaviest cargo. It was the usual practice of the VOC to secure the most valuable items in this manner. Several hundred tons of heavy timber baulks stacked over the entrance to the strong room would deter even the most determined thief from tampering with its contents.

While the crew crowded the opening of the hatch above them Sir Francis and the boatswains went down, each carrying a lighted lantern, and knelt in the bottom of the hold to examine the seals that the Dutch Governor of Trincomalee had placed on the entrance.

'The seals are intact!' Sir Francis shouted, to reassure the watchers, and they cheered raucously.

'Break the hinges!' he ordered Big Daniel, and the boatswain went to it with a will.

Wood splintered and brass screws squealed as they were ripped from their seats. The interior of the strong room was lined with sheets of copper, but Big Daniel's iron bar ripped through the metal and a hum of delight went up from the spectators as the contents of the compartment were revealed.

The coin was sewn into thick canvas bags of which there were fifteen. Daniel dragged them out and stacked them into a cargo net to be hoisted to the deck. Next, the ingots of gold bullion were raised. They were packed ten at a time into chests of raw, unplaned wood on which the number and weight of the bars had been branded with a red-hot iron.

When Sir Francis climbed up out of the hold he ordered all but two of the sacks of coin, and all the chests of gold bars, to be carried down to his own cabin.

'We will divide only these two sacks of coin now,' Sir Francis told them. 'The rest of your share you will receive when we get home to dear old England.' He stooped over the two remaining canvas sacks of coin with a dagger in his hand and he slit the stitching. The men howled like a pack of wolves as a stream of glinting silver ten-guilder coins poured onto the planking.

'No need to count it. The cheese-heads have done that job for us.' Sir Francis pointed out the numbers stencilled on the sacks. 'Each man will come forward as his name is called,' he told them. With excited laughter and ribald repartee, the men formed lines. As each was called, he shuffled forward with his cap held out, and his share of silver guilders was doled out to him.

Hal was the only man aboard who drew no part of the booty. Although he was entitled to a midshipman's share, one two-hundredth part of the crew's portion, almost two hundred guilders, his father would take care of it for him. 'No fool like a boy with silver or gold in his purse,' he had explained reasonably to Hal. 'One day you'll thank me for saving it for you.' Then he turned with mock fury on his crew. 'Just because you're rich now, doesn't mean I have no more work for you,' he roared. 'The rest of the heavy cargo must go ashore before we can beach and careen her and clean her foul bottom and step the new mast and put the culverins into her. There's enough work in that to keep you busy for a month or two.'

No man was ever allowed to remain idle for long in one of Sir Francis's ships. Boredom was the most dangerous enemy he would ever encounter. While one of the watches went ahead with the work of unloading, he kept the off-duty watches busy. They must never be allowed to forget that this was a fighting ship and that they must be ready at any moment to face a desperate enemy.

With the hatches open and the huge casks of spice being lifted out, there was no space on the deck for weapons practice so Big Daniel took the off-duty men to the beach. Shoulder to shoulder, they formed ranks and worked through the manual of arms. Swinging the cutlass – cut to the left, thrust and recover, cut to the right, thrust and recover – until the sweat streamed from them and they gasped for breath.

'Enough of that!' Big Daniel told them at last, but they were not to be released yet.

'A bout or two of wrestling now, just to warm your blood,' he shouted, and strode amongst them matching man against man, seizing a pair by the scruff of their necks and thrusting them at each other, as though they were fighting-birds in the cockpit.

Soon the beach was covered with struggling, shouting pairs of men naked to the waist, heaving and spinning each other off their feet and rolling in the white sand.

Standing back among the first line of forest trees, Katinka and her maid watched with interest. Aboli stood a few paces behind them, leaning against the trunk of one of the giant forest yellow-woods.

Hal was matched against a seaman twenty years his elder. They were

77

of the same height, but the other man was a stone heavier. Both struggled for a hold on each other's neck and shoulders as they danced in a circle, trying to force one another off balance or to hook a heel for a trip throw.

'Use your hip. Throw him over your hip!' Katinka whispered, as she watched Hal. She was so carried along by the spectacle that unconsciously she had clenched her fists and was beating them on her own thighs in excitement as she urged Hal on, her cheeks pinker than either the rouge pot or the heat had coloured them.

Katinka loved to watch men or animals pitted against each other. At every opportunity, her husband was made to accompany her to the bull-baiting and the cock-fights or the ratting contests with terriers.

'Whenever the red wine is poured, my lovely little darling is happy.' Van de Velde was proud of her unusual penchant for blood sport. She never missed a tournament of épée, and had even enjoyed the English sport of bare-fisted fighting. However, wrestling was one of her favourite diversions, and she knew all the holds and throws.

Now she was enchanted by the lad's graceful movements and impressed by his technique. She could tell that he had been well instructed, for although his opponent was heavier Hal was quicker and stronger. He used his opponent's weight against him, and the older man had to grunt and thrash around to recover himself as Hal tipped him to the edge of his balance. At his next lunge Hal offered no resistance but gave to his opponent's rush, and went over backwards, still maintaining his grip. As he struck the ground, he broke his own fall with an arch to his back, at the same time thrusting his heels into his opponent's belly to catapult him overhead. While the older man lay stunned, Hal whipped round to straddle his back and pin him face down. He grabbed the man's pigtail and forced his face into the fine white sand, until he slapped the earth with both hands to signal his surrender.

Hal released him and sprang to his feet with the agility of a cat. The seaman came to his knees gasping and spitting sand. Then, unexpectedly, he launched himself at Hal just as he was beginning to turn away. From the corner of his eye Hal spotted the swing of the bunched fist coming at his head and rolled away from the blow, but not quite quickly enough. It swiped across his face, bringing a flash of blood from one nostril. He seized the man's wrist as he reached the limit of his swing, twisting his arm and then lifting his wrist up between his shoulder-blades. The seaman squealed as he was forced him up on his toes.

'Mary's milk, Master John, but you must like the taste of sand.' Hal placed one bare foot on his backside and sent him sprawling head first on to the beach once more.

'You grow too clever and cocky, Master Hal!' Big Daniel strode up to him, frowning, and his voice was gruff as he tried to hide his delight at his pupil's performance. 'Next time I'll give you a harder match. And don't let the captain hear that milky blasphemy of yours or it's more than good clean beach sand you'll be tasting yourself.'

Still laughing, delighting in Daniel's ill-concealed approbation and in the hoots of encouragement from the other wrestlers, Hal swaggered to the lagoon's edge and scooped up a double handful of water to wash the blood from his upper lip.

'Joseph and Mary, but he loves to win.' Daniel grinned behind his back. 'Try as he will, Captain Franky will not break that one down. The old dog has sired a puppy of his own blood.'

'How old do you think he is?' Katinka asked her maid, in a reflective tone.

'I'm sure I don't know,' said Zelda primly. 'He's just a child.'

Katinka shook her head, smiling, remembering him standing naked in the stern of the pinnace. 'Ask our blackamoor watch-dog.'

Obediently Zelda looked back at Aboli, and asked in English, 'How old is the boy?'

'Old enough for what she wants from him,' Aboli grunted in his own language, a puzzled frown on his face as he pretended not to understand. These last few days, while he guarded her, he had studied this woman with sun-coloured hair. He had recognized the bright, predatory glimmer in the depths of those demure violet eyes. She watched a man the way a mongoose watches a plump chicken, and she carried her head in an affectation of innocence that was belied by the wanton swing of her hips beneath the layers of bright silks and gossamer lace. 'A whore is still a whore, whatever the colour of her hair and no matter if she lives in a beehive hut or a governor's palace.' The deep cadence of his voice was punctuated by the staccato clicks of his tribal speech.

Zelda turned away from him with a flounce. 'Stupid animal. He understands nothing.'

Hal left the water's edge and came up into the trees. He reached up to the branch on which hung his discarded shirt. His hair was still wet and his naked chest and shoulders were blotched red with the rough contact of the wrestling. A smear of blood was still streaked across his cheek.

His hand raised towards his shirt, he looked up. His eyes met Katinka's level violet regard. Until that moment he had been unaware of her presence. Instantly his arrogant swagger evaporated, and he stepped back as though she had slapped him unexpectedly. Now a dark blush spread over his face, obliterating the lighter blotches left by his opponent's blows.

Coolly Katinka looked down at his bare chest. He folded his arms across it, as if ashamed.

'You were right, Zelda,' she said, with a dismissive flick of her hand. 'Just a grubby child,' she added in Latin, to make certain that he understood. Hal stared after her miserably as she gathered her skirts and, followed by Aboli and her maid, sailed regally down the beach to the waiting pinnace.

That night, as he lay on the lumpy straw pallet on his narrow bunk, he heard movement, soft voices and laughter from the cabin next door. He propped himself up on one elbow. Then he recalled the insult she had thrown at him so disdainfully. 'I will not think of her ever again,' he promised himself, as he sank back onto the pallet and placed his hands over his ears to block out the lilting cadence of her voice. In an attempt to drive her from his mind, he repeated softly, '*In Arcadia habito.*' But it was long before weariness allowed him at last to fall into a deep black dreamless sleep.

At the head of the lagoon, almost two miles from where the *Resolution* lay at anchor, a stream of clear sweet water tumbled down through a narrow gorge to mingle with the brackish waters below.

As the two longboats moved slowly against the current into the mouth of the gorge, they startled the flocks of water birds from the shallows into the air. They rose in a cacophony of honks, quacks and cackles, twenty different varieties of ducks and geese unlike any they knew from the north. There were other species, too, with strangely shaped bills or disproportionately long legs trailing, and herons, curlews and egrets that were not quite the same as their English counterparts, bigger or brighter in plumage. The sky was darkened with their numbers, and the men rested for a minute upon their oars to gaze in astonishment at these multitudes.

'It's a land of marvels,' Sir Francis murmured, staring up at this wild display. 'Yet we have explored only a trivial part of it. What other wonders lie beyond this threshold, deep in the hinterland, that no man has ever laid eyes upon?'

His father's words excited Hal's imagination, and conjured up once more the images of dragons and monsters that decorated the charts he had studied.

'Heave away!' his father ordered, and they bent to the long sweeps again. The two were alone in the leading boat: Sir Francis pulled the starboard oar with a long powerful stroke that matched Hal's tirelessly. Between them stood the empty water casks, the refilling of which was the ostensible purpose of this expedition to the head of the lagoon. The real reason, however, lay on the floorboards at Sir Francis's feet. During the night Aboli and Big Daniel had carried the canvas sacks of coin and the chests of gold ingots down from the cabin and had hidden them under the tarpaulin in the bottom of the boat. In the bows they had stacked five kegs of powder and an array of weapons, captured along with the treasure from the galleon, cutlass, pistol and musket, and leather bags of lead shot.

Ned Tyler, Big Daniel and Aboli followed closely in the second boat, the three men in his crew whom Sir Francis trusted above all others. Their boat, too, was loaded with water casks.

Once they were well into the mouth of the stream, Sir Francis stopped rowing and leaned over the side to scoop a mugful of water and taste it. He nodded with satisfaction. 'Pure and sweet.' He called across to Ned Tyler, 'Do you begin to refill here. Hal and I will go on upstream.'

As Ned steered the boat in towards the riverbank, a wild, booming bark echoed down the gorge. They all looked up. 'What are those creatures? Are they men?' demanded Ned. 'Some kind of strange hairy dwarfs?' There was fear and awe in his voice, as he stared up at the ranks of human-like shapes that lined the edge of the precipice high above them.

'Apes.' Sir Francis called to him as he rested on his oar. 'Like those of the Barbary Coast.'

Aboli chuckled, then threw back his head and faithfully mimicked the challenge of the bull baboon that led the pack. Most of the younger animals leaped up and nervously skittered along the cliff at the sound.

The huge bull ape accepted the challenge. He stood on all fours at the edge of the precipice, and opened his mouth wide to display a set of terrible white fangs. Emboldened by this show, some of the younger animals returned and began to hurl small stones and debris down upon them. The men were forced to duck and dodge the missiles.

'Give them a shot to see them off,' Sir Francis ordered.

'It's a long one.' Daniel unslung his musket and blew on the burning tip of the slow-match as he raised the butt to his shoulder. The gorge echoed to the thunderous blast, and they all burst out laughing at the antics of the baboon pack, as it panicked at the shot. The ball knocked a chip off the lip of the ledge, and the youngsters of the troop somersaulted backwards with shock. The mothers seized their offspring,

81

slung them under their bellies and scrambled up the sheer face, and even the brave bull abandoned his dignity and joined the rush for safety. Within seconds, the cliff was deserted and the sounds of the terror-stricken retreat dwindled.

Aboli jumped over the side, waist deep into the river, and dragged the boat onto the bank while Daniel and Ned unstoppered the water casks to refill them. In the other boat Sir Francis and Hal bent to the oars and rowed on upstream. After half a mile the river narrowed sharply, and the cliffs on both sides became steeper. Sir Francis paused to get his bearings and then turned the longboat in under the cliff and moored the bows to the stump of a dead tree that sprang from a crack in the rock. Leaving Hal in the boat he jumped out onto the narrow ledge below the cliff and began to climb upwards. There was no obvious path to follow but Sir Francis moved confidently from one handhold to another. Hal watched him with pride: in his eyes, his father was an old man – he must have long passed the venerable age of forty years – yet he climbed with strength and agility. Suddenly, fifty feet above the river, he reached a ledge invisible from below and shuffled a few paces along it. Then he knelt to examine the narrow cleft in the cliff face; the opening was blocked with neatly packed rocks. He smiled with relief when he saw that they were exactly as he had left them many months previously. Carefully he pulled them out of the cleft and laid them aside, until the opening was wide enough for him to crawl through.

The cave beyond was in darkness but Sir Francis stood up and reached to a stone shelf above his head where he groped for the flint and steel he had left there. He lit the candle he had brought with him, and then looked around the cave.

Nothing had been touched since his last visit. Five chests stood against the back wall. That was the booty from the *Heerlycke Nacht*, mostly silver plate and a hundred thousand guilders in coin that had been intended for payment of the Dutch garrison in Batavia. A pile of gear was stacked beside the entrance, and Sir Francis began work on this immediately. It took him almost half an hour to rig the heavy wooden beam as a gantry from the ledge outside the cave entrance, and then to lower the tackle to the boat moored below.

'Make the first chest fast!' he called down to Hal.

Hal tied it on and his father hauled it upwards, the sheave squeaking at each heave. The chest disappeared and a few minutes later the rope end dropped back and dangled where Hal could reach it. He tied on the next chest.

It took them well over an hour to hoist all the ingots and the sacks of coin and stack them in the back of the cave. Then they started work on the powder kegs and the bundles of weapons. The last item to go up was the smallest: a box into which Sir Francis had packed a compass and backstaff, a roll of charts taken from the *Standvastigheid*, flint and steel, a set of surgeon's instruments in a canvas roll, and a selection of other equipment that could make the difference between survival and a lingering death to a party stranded on this savage, unexplored coast.

'Come up, Hal,' Sir Francis called down at last, and Hal went up the cliff with the speed and ease of one of the young baboons.

When Hal reached him, his father was sitting comfortably on the narrow ledge, his legs dangling and his clay-stemmed pipe and tobacco pouch in his hands.

'Give me a hand here, lad.' He pointed with his empty pipe at the vertical crack in the face of the cliff. 'Close that up again.'

Hal spent another half-hour packing the loose rock back into the entrance, to conceal it and to discourage intruders. There was little chance of men finding the cache in this deserted gorge, but he and his father knew that the baboons would return. They were as curious and mischievous as any human.

When Hal would have started back down the cliff, Sir Francis stopped him with a hand on his shoulder. 'There is no hurry. The others will not have finished refilling the water casks.'

They sat in silence on the ledge while Sir Francis got his long-stemmed pipe to draw sweetly. Then he asked, through a cloud of blue smoke, 'What have I done here?'

'Cached our share of the treasure.'

'Not only our share alone, but that of the Crown and of every man aboard,' Sir Francis corrected him. 'But why have I done that?'

'Gold and silver is temptation even to an honest man.' Hal repeated the lore his father had drummed into his head so many times before.

'Should I not trust my own crew?' Sir Francis asked.

'If you trust no man, then no man will ever disappoint you.' Hal repeated the lesson.

'Do you believe that?' Sir Francis turned to watch his face as he replied, and Hal hesitated. 'Do you trust Aboli?'

'Yes, I trust him,' Hal admitted, reluctantly, as though it were a sin.

'Aboli is a good man, none better. But you see that I do not bring even him to this place.' He paused, then asked, 'Do you trust me, lad?'

'Of course.'

'Why? Surely I am but a man and I have told you to trust no man?'

'Because you are my father and I love you.'

Sir Francis's eyes clouded and he made as if to caress Hal's cheek. Then he sighed, dropped his hand and looked down at the river below.

Hal expected his father to censure his reply, but he did not. After a while Sir Francis asked another question. 'What of the other goods I have cached here? The powder and weapons and charts and the like. Why have I placed those here?'

'Against an uncertain future,' Hal replied confidently – he had heard the answer often enough before. 'A wise fox has many exits to his earth.'

Sir Francis nodded. 'All of us who sail in the *guerre de course* are always at risk. One day, those few chests may be worth our very lives.'

His father was silent again as he smoked the last few shreds of tobacco in the bowl of his pipe. Then he said softly, 'If God is merciful, the time will come, perhaps not too far in the future, when this war with the Dutch will end. Then we will return here and gather up our prize and sail home to Plymouth. It has long been my dream to own the manor of Gainesbury that runs alongside High Weald—' He broke off, as if not daring to tempt fate with such imagining. 'If harm should befall me, it is necessary that you should know and remember where I have stored our winnings. It will be my legacy to you.'

'No harm can ever come your way!' Hal exclaimed in agitation. It was more a plea than a statement of conviction. He could not imagine an existence without this towering presence at the centre of it.

'No man is immortal,' said Sir Francis softly. 'We all owe God a death.' This time he allowed his right hand to settle briefly on Hal's shoulder. 'Come, lad. We must still fill the water casks in our own boat before dark.'

As the longboats crept back down the edge of the darkening lagoon, Aboli had taken Sir Francis's place on the rowing thwart, and now Hal's father sat in the stern, wrapped in a dark woollen cloak against the evening chill. His expression was remote and sombre. Facing aft as he worked one of the long oars, Hal could study him surreptitiously. Their conversation at the mouth of the cave had left him troubled with a presentiment of ill-fortune ahead.

He guessed that since they had anchored in the lagoon his father had cast his own horoscope. He had seen the zodiacal chart covered with arcane notations lying open on his desk in his cabin. That would account for his withdrawn and introspective mood. As Aboli had said, the stars were his children and he knew their secrets.

Suddenly his father lifted his head and sniffed the cool evening air. Then his face changed as he studied the forest edge. No dark thoughts could absorb him to the point where he was unaware of his surroundings.

'Aboli, take us in to the bank, if you please.'

They turned the boat towards the narrow beach, and the second followed. After they had all jumped out onto the beach and moored both boats, Sir Francis gave a quiet order. 'Bring your arms. Follow me, but quietly.'

He led them into the forest, pushing stealthily through the under-growth, until he stepped out suddenly onto a well-used path. He glanced back to make certain they were following him, then hurried along.

Hal was mystified by his father's actions until he smelt a trace of woodsmoke on the air and noticed for the first time the bluish haze along the tops of the dense forest trees. This must have been what had alerted his father.

Suddenly Sir Francis stepped out into a small clearing in the forest and stopped. The four men who were already there had not noticed him. Two lay like corpses on a battlefield, one still clutching a squat brown hand-blown bottle in his inert fingers, the other drooling strings of saliva from the corner of his mouth as he snored.

The second pair were wholly absorbed by the stacks of silver guilders and the ivory dice lying between them. One scooped up the dice and rattled them at his ear before rolling them across the patch of beaten bare earth. 'Mother of a pig!' he growled. 'This is not my lucky day.'

'You should not speak unkindly of the dam who gave birth to you,' said Sir Francis softly. 'But the rest of what you say is the truth. This is not your lucky day.'

They looked up at their captain in horrified disbelief, but made no attempt to resist or escape as Daniel and Aboli dragged them to their feet and roped them neck to neck in the manner used by the slavers.

Sir Francis walked over to inspect the still that stood at the far end of the clearing. They had used a black iron pot to boil the fermented mash of old biscuit and peelings, and copper tubing stolen from the ship's stores for the coil. He kicked it over and the colourless spirits flared in the flames of the charcoal brazier on which the pot stood. A row of filled bottles, stoppered with wads of leaves, was laid out beneath a yellow-wood tree. He picked them up one at a time and hurled them against the tree-trunk. As they shattered the evaporating fumes were pungent enough to make his eyes water. Then he walked back to Daniel and Ned, who had kicked the drunks out of their stupor and had dragged them across the clearing to rope them to the other captives.

'We'll give them a day to sleep it off, Master Ned. Then tomorrow, at the beginning of the afternoon watch, have the ship's company assemble to witness their punishment.' He glanced at Big Daniel. 'I trust you can still make your cat whistle, Master Daniel.'

'Please, Captain, we meant no harm. Just a little fun.' They tried to crawl to where he stood, but Aboli dragged them back like dogs on the leash.

'I will not grudge you your fun,' said Sir Francis, 'if you do not grudge me mine.'

The carpenter had knocked up a row of four tripods on the quarterdeck, and the drunkards and gamblers were lashed to them by wrist and ankle. Big Daniel walked down the line and ripped their shirts open from collar to waist, so that their naked backs were exposed. They hung helplessly in their bonds like trussed pigs on the back of a market cart.

'Every man aboard knows full well that I will tolerate no drunkenness and no gaming, both of which are an offence and abomination in the eyes of the Lord.' Sir Francis addressed the company, assembled in solemn ranks in the ship's waist. 'Every man aboard knows the penalty. Fifty licks of the cat.' He watched their faces. Fifty strokes of the knotted leather thongs could cripple a man for life. A hundred strokes was a sentence of certain and horrible death. 'They have earned themselves the full fifty. However, I remember that these four fools fought well on this very deck when we captured this vessel. We still have some hard fighting ahead of us, and cripples are of no use to me when the culverins are smoking and the cutlasses are out.'

He paused to watch their faces, and saw the terror of the cat in their eyes, mixed with relief that it was not them bound to the tripods. Unlike the captains of many privateers, even some Knights of the Order, Sir Francis took no pleasure in this punishment. Yet he did not flinch from necessity. He commanded a ship full of tough, unruly men, whom he had handpicked for their ferocity and who would take any show of kindness as weakness.

'I am a merciful man,' he told them, and somebody in the rear ranks chuckled derisively. Sir Francis paused and, with a bleak eye, singled out the offender. When the culprit hung his head and shuffled his feet, he went on smoothly, 'But these rascals would test my mercy to its limits.'

He turned to Big Daniel, who stood beside the first tripod. He was stripped to the waist and his great muscles bulged in arms and shoulders. He had tied back his long greying hair with a strip of cloth, and from his scarred fist the lashes of the cat hung to the planks of the deck like the serpents of Medusa's head.

86

'Make it fifteen for each, Master Daniel,' Sir Francis ordered, 'but comb your cat well between the strokes.'

Unless Daniel's fingers separated the lashes of the cat after each stroke, the blood would matt them together and clot them into a single heavy instrument that would cut human flesh like a sword blade. Even fifteen with an uncombed cat would strip the meat off a man's back down to the vertebrae of his spine.

'Fifteen it is, Captain,' Daniel acknowledged, and shaking out the whip to separate the knotted thongs, stepped up to his first victim. The man twisted his head to watch him over his shoulder, his expression blanched with fear.

Daniel raised his arm high and let the lash stream out over his shoulder then, with a peculiar grace for such a big man, he swung forward. The lash whistled like the wind in the leaves of a tall tree and clapped loudly on bare skin.

'One!' chanted the crew in unison, as the victim shrieked on a high note of shock and agony. The lash left a grotesque pattern over his back, each red line studded with a row of brighter crimson stars where the knots had broken the skin. It looked like the sting from the venomous tendrils of a Portuguese man-of-war.

Daniel combed out the lash, and the fingers of his left hand were smeared with bright fresh blood.

'Two!' The watchers counted, and the man shrieked again and writhed in his bonds, his toes dancing a tattoo of pain on the deck timbers.

'Avast punishment!' Sir Francis called, as he heard a mild commotion at the head of the companionway leading down to the cabins in the stern. Obediently Daniel lowered the whip, and waited as Sir Francis strode to the ladder.

Governor van de Velde's plumed hat appeared above the coaming, followed by his fat flushed face. He stood wheezing in the sunlight, mopping his jowls with a silk handkerchief, and looked about him. His face brightened with interest as he saw the men hanging on the row of tripods. 'Ja! Goed! I see we are not too late,' he said, with satisfaction.

Close behind him Katinka emerged from the hatch with a light, eager step, holding her skirts just high enough to reveal satin slippers embroidered with seed pearls.

'Good morrow, Mijnheer,' Sir Francis greeted the Governor with a perfunctory bow, 'there is punishment in progress. It is an unsuitable spectacle for a lady of your wife's delicate breeding to witness.'

'Truly, Captain,' Katinka laughed lightly as she intervened, 'I am not

87

a child. Heaven knows, there is a great paucity of diversion aboard this ship. Just think, you would collect no ransom if I were to die of boredom.' She tapped Sir Francis's arm with her fan, but he pulled away from this condescending touch, and spoke again to her husband.

'Mijnheer, I think you should escort your wife to her quarters.'

Katinka stepped between them as though he had not spoken, and beckoned Zelda who followed her. 'Place my stool there in the shade.' She spread out her skirts as she settled herself on the stool and pouted prettily at Sir Francis. 'I will be so quiet that you will not even know that I am here.'

Sir Francis glared at the Governor, but van de Velde spread his pudgy hands in a theatrical gesture of helplessness. 'You know how it is, Mijnheer, when a beautiful woman sets her heart on something.' He moved up behind Katinka and placed a proud and indulgent hand on her shoulder.

'I cannot be responsible for your wife's sensibilities, if they should be offended by the spectacle,' Sir Francis warned grimly, relieved at least that his men could not understand this exchange in Dutch and be aware that he had bowed to pressure from his captives.

'I think you need not trouble yourself too deeply. My wife has a strong stomach,' van de Velde murmured. During their tour of duty in Kandy and Trincomalee his wife had never missed the executions that were carried out regularly on the parade ground of the fort. Depending on the nature of the offence these punishments had ranged from burning at the stake to branding, garrotting and beheading. Even on those days when she had been suffering the break-bone pains of dengue fever and, in accordance with her doctor's orders, should have remained in bed, her carriage had always been parked in its accustomed place overlooking the scaffold.

'Then it shall be at your own responsibility, Mijnheer.' Sir Francis nodded curtly, and turned back to Daniel.

'Proceed with the punishment, Master Daniel,' he ordered. Daniel threw back the whip, high behind his shoulder, and the coloured tattoos that decorated his great biceps rippled with a life of their own.

'Three!' yelled the crew, as the lash sang and snapped.

Katinka stiffened, and leaned forward slightly on her stool.

'Four!' She started at the crack of the cat and the high scream of pain that followed it. Slowly her face turned pale as candle tallow.

'Five!' Thin snakes of scarlet crawled down the man's back and soaked into the waistband of his canvas petticoat. Katinka let her long golden eyelashes droop half closed to hide the gleam in her violet eyes.

'Six!' Katinka felt a tiny drop of liquid strike her, like a single spot of warm tropical rain. She tore her eyes from the wriggling, moaning body on the tripod, and looked down at her graceful hand.

A drop of blood, flung from the sodden lash, had landed on her forefinger. Like a ruby set in a precious ring it sparkled against her white skin. She cupped her other hand over it, hiding it in her lap while she glanced around at the faces that surrounded her. Every eye was fixed in total fascination upon the gruesome spectacle in front of them. No one had seen the blood splash her. No one was watching her now.

She lifted her hand to her full soft lips as though in an involuntary gesture of dismay. The pink tip of her tongue darted out and dabbed away the droplet from her finger. She savoured its metallic salt taste. It reminded her of a lover's sperm, and she felt the viscous wetness welling up between her legs, so that when she rubbed her thighs together they slid against each other, slippery as mating eels.

There would be a need for lodgings on shore while the *Resolution* was careened on the beach, her hull cleaned of weed and examined for any sign of shipworm.

Sir Francis put Hal in charge of building the compound that was to accommodate their hostages. Hal took particular care over the hut that would house the Governor's wife, making it spacious and comfortable and siting it for privacy and security from wild animals. Then he had his men build a stockade of thorn branches around the entire prison compound.

When darkness brought the first day's work to a halt, he went down to the beach of the lagoon and soaked himself in the warm, brackish waters. Then he scrubbed his body with handfuls of wet sand until his skin tingled. Yet he still felt sullied by the memory of the floggings he had been forced to watch that morning. Only when he smelt the tantalizing odour of hot biscuit floating across the water from the ship's galley did his mood change, and he thrust his legs into his breeches and ran down the beach to scramble into the pinnace as it pulled away from the shore.

While he had been ashore his father had written on the slate a series of navigational problems for him to solve. He tucked it under his arm, grabbed a pewter mug of small beer, a bowl of fish stew and, holding a hot biscuit between his teeth, darted down the ladder to his cabin, the only place on the ship where he could be alone to concentrate on his task.

Suddenly he looked up as he heard water being poured in the cabin next door. He had noticed the buckets of fresh river water standing over the charcoal fire in the galley and laughed when the cook had complained bitterly that his fire was being used to heat water to bathe in. Now Hal knew for whom those steaming pails had been prepared. Zelda's guttural tones carried to him through the panel as she harangued Oliver, his father's servant. Oliver's reply was truculent. 'I don't understand a word you say, you grisly old bitch. But if you don't like it you can fill the sodding bath yerself.'

Hal grinned to himself, half with amusement and half in anticipation, as he blew out his lamp and knelt to remove the wooden plug from his peephole. He saw that the cabin was filled with clouds of steam, which frosted the mirror on the far bulkhead so that his view was restricted. Zelda was shooing Oliver from the cabin as Hal adjusted his eye to the aperture.

'All right, you old trull!' Oliver baited her, as he lugged the empty buckets from the cabin. 'There's nothing you've got that would keep me here a minute longer.'

When Oliver was gone, Zelda went through into the main cabin and Hal heard her speaking to her mistress. A minute later she ushered Katinka through the doorway. Katinka paused beside the steaming bath and dabbled her fingers in the water. She exclaimed sharply and jerked away her hand. Zelda hurried forward, apologizing, and poured cold water from the bucket that stood beside the bath. Katinka tested the temperature again. This time she nodded with satisfaction, and went to sit on the stool. Zelda came up behind her, lifted the splendid shimmering bundle of her hair with both hands to pile it on top of her head and pinned it there, like a sheaf of ripe wheat.

Katinka leaned forward and, with her fingertips, wiped a small clear window in the clouded surface of the mirror. She examined the vignette of herself in this clear spot. She thrust out her tongue to examine it for any trace of white coating. It was pink as a rose petal. Then she opened her eyes wide and peered into their depths, touching the skin beneath them with her fingertips. 'Look at these horrid wrinkles!' she lamented.

Zelda denied it vehemently. 'Not a single one!'

'I never want to grow old and ugly.' Katinka's expression was tragic.

'Then you had best die now!' said Zelda. 'That's the only way you'll avoid it.'

'What a terrible thing to say. You are so cruel to me,' Katinka complained.

Hal could not understand what they said but the tone of her voice touched him to the depths of his being.

'Come now,' Zelda chided her. 'You know you're beautiful.'

'Am I, Zelda? Do you really think so?'

'Yes. And so do you.' Zelda lifted her to her feet. 'But if you don't bathe now, you will stink just as beautifully.'

She unfastened her mistress's gown, then moved behind her, lifted the gown from her shoulders and Katinka stood naked before the mirror. Hal's involuntary gasp was muffled by the panel and the small sounds of the ship's hull.

From that slender neck down to her tiny ankles Katinka's body formed a line of heartbreaking purity. Her buttocks swelled out into two perfectly symmetrical orbs, like a pair of the ostrich eggs Hal had seen offered for sale in the markets of Zanzibar. But there were childish, vulnerable dimples at the back of her knees.

Katinka's own image in the clouded mirror was ethereal and could not hold her attention for long. She turned away from it and stood facing him. Hal's gaze flew to her breasts. They were large for her narrow shoulders. Each would have filled his cupped hands, yet they were not perfectly round as he had expected them to be.

Hal stared at them until his eye watered and he was forced at last to blink. Then he let his gaze sink down, over the slight but enthralling bulge of her belly, and onto the misty cloud of fine curls that nestled between her thighs. The lamp-light struck them and they sparked purest gold.

She stood a long time thus, longer than he had dared hope she might, staring down into the bath while Zelda poured perfumed oil from a crystal bottle into the water, and then knelt to stir it with her hand. Katinka continued to stand, her weight on one leg so that her pelvis was tilted at an enchanting angle, and there was a small sly smile on her lips as she reached up slowly and took one of her nipples between thumb and forefinger. For a moment Hal thought she stared directly at him, and he began to pull away guiltily from his peep-hole. Then he knew that it was an illusion for she dropped her eyes and looked down at the fat little berry that poked out rosily between her fingers.

She rolled it softly back and forth, and while Hal stared in amazement it changed colour and shape. It swelled and hardened and darkened. He had never imagined anything quite like this – a little miracle that should have filled him with reverence but instead tore at his loins with the claws of lust.

Zelda looked up from the bath she was mixing and, when she saw what her mistress was doing, snapped a prim reprimand. Katinka laughed and stuck out her tongue, but dropped her hand and stepped into the

91

bath. With a luxurious sigh she sank into the hot, perfumed water, until only the thick coil of golden hair on top of her head showed above the rim of the bath.

Zelda fussed over her, lathering soap on a flannel, wiping and washing, murmuring endearments and cackling at her mistress's replies. Suddenly she rocked back on her heels and gave another instruction, in response to which Katinka stood up and the soapy water cascaded down her body. Her back was turned to Hal, and now the rounds of her bottom glowed pinkly from the hot water. At Zelda's instructions she moved compliantly to allow the old woman to soap down each leg in turn.

At last Zelda climbed stiffly to her feet and shuffled out of the cabin. As soon as she was gone Katinka, still standing in the bath, glanced over her shoulder. Again, Hal had the guilty illusion that she was looking directly into his own staring eye. It was only for a moment, then slowly and voluptuously she bent. Her buttocks changed shape at the movement. Katinka reached behind herself with both hands. She laid those small white hands on each of her glowing pink buttocks and drew them gently apart. This time Hal could not choke back the little abandoned cry that rose to his lips as the deep crease of her bottom opened to his feverish gaze.

Zelda bustled back into the cabin bearing an armful of towels. Katinka straightened and the enchanted crevice closed firmly, its secrets hidden once more from his eyes. She stepped from the bath and Zelda draped a towel over her shoulders that hung to her ankles. Zelda loosened the coil of her mistress's hair and brushed it out, and then braided it into a thick golden rope. She stood behind Katinka and held a gown for her to slip her arms into the sleeves, but Katinka shook her head and gave a peremptory order. Zelda protested but Katinka insisted and the maid threw the gown over the stool and left the cabin in an obvious pet.

When she was gone Katinka let the towel drop to the deck and, naked once more, crossed to the door and slid the locking bolt into place. Then she turned back and passed out of Hal's sight.

He saw a fuzzy pink blur of movement in the clouded mirror but could not be sure what she was doing until, abruptly and shockingly, her lips were an inch from the opposite side of his peep-hole and she hissed viciously at him, 'You filthy little pirate!' She spoke in Latin, and he recoiled as though she had flung a kettle of boiling water into his face.

Even in his confusion, though, the taunt had stung him to the quick, and he answered her, without thinking, 'I am not a pirate. My father carries Letters of Marque.'

'Don't you dare to contradict me.' Confusingly she was switching

92

between Latin, Dutch and English. But her tone was sharp and stinging as a scourge.

Again he was stung into a reply. 'I did not mean to offend you.'

'When my noble husband finds out that you have been spying on me, he will go to your pirate father, and they will have you flogged on the tripod like those other men this morning.'

'I was not spying on you—'

'Liar!' She would not let him finish. 'You dirty lying pirate.' For a moment she had run out of breath and insults.

'I only wanted to—'

Her fury was recharged. 'I know what you wanted. You wanted to look at my *katjie* – ' he knew that was the Dutch word for kitten ' – and then you wanted to take your cock in your hand and pull it—'

'No!' Hal almost shouted. How had she known his shameful secret? He felt sick and mortified.

'Quiet! Zelda will hear you,' she hissed again. 'If they catch you it will be the lash.'

'Please!' he whispered back. 'I meant no harm. Please forgive me. I did not mean it.'

'Then show me. Prove your innocence. Show me your cock.'

'I can't.' His voice quivered with shame.

'Stand up! Put it here next to the hole so I can see if you are lying.'

'No. Please don't make me do that.'

'Quickly or I will scream for my husband to come.'

Slowly he came to his feet. The peep-hole was at almost exactly the same level as his aching crotch.

'Now, show me. Open your breeches,' her voice goaded him.

Slowly, consumed by shame and embarrassment he lifted the canvas skirt, and before it was fully raised his penis jumped out like the springy branch of a sapling. He knew she must be nauseated and speechless with disgust to see such a thing. After a minute of thick, charged silence that seemed the longest in his life, he began to lower his skirt over himself.

Instantly she stopped him in a voice that seemed to him to tremble with revulsion, so that he could hardly understand her distorted English words.

'No! Do not seek to cover your shame. This thing of yours condemns you. Do you still pretend you are guiltless?'

'No,' he admitted miserably.

'Then you must be punished,' she told him. 'I must tell your father.'

'Please don't do that,' he pleaded. 'He would kill me with his own hands.'

'Very well. I shall have to punish you myself. Bring your cock closer.'

Obediently he pushed his hips forward.

'Closer, so I can reach it. Closer.'

He felt the tip of his distended penis touch the rough wood that surrounded the peep-hole, and then shockingly cool soft fingers closed over the tip. He tried to pull away, but her grip tightened and her voice was sharp. 'Stay still!'

Katinka knelt at the bulkhead and threaded his glans through the opening, then eased it out into the lamp-light. It was so swollen that it could barely fit through the hole.

'No, do not pull away,' she told him, making her voice stern and angry, as she took a firmer grip upon him. Obediently he relaxed and gave himself over to the insistent pressure of her fingers, allowing her to draw his full length through the opening.

She gazed at it, fascinated. At his age she had not expected him to be so large. The engorged head was the glossy purple of a ripe plum. She drew the loose prepuce over it, like a monk's cowl, and then pulled back the skin again as far it would go. The head seemed to swell harder as though on the point of bursting, and she felt the shaft jump in her hands.

She repeated the movement, slowly forward and then back again, and heard him groan beyond the panel. It was strange but she had almost forgotten the boy. This mannikin she held in her hands had a life and existence of its own.

'This is your punishment, you dirty, shameless boy.'

She could hear his fingernails scratching at the wood, as her hand began to fly back and forth along the full length of him as though she were working the shuttle of a weaver's loom.

It happened sooner than she had expected. The hot glutinous spurting against her sensitive breasts was so powerful that it startled her, but she did not pull away.

After a time, she said, 'Do not think that I have forgiven you yet for what you have done to me. Your penitence has only just begun. Do you understand?'

'Yes.' His voice was ragged and hoarse.

'You must make a secret opening in this wall.' She tapped the bulkhead softly with her knuckle. 'Loosen this panel so that you can come through to me, and I can punish you more severely. Do you understand?'

'Yes,' he panted.

'You must conceal the opening. No one else must know.'

'It is my observation,' Sir Francis told Hal, 'that filth and sickness have a peculiar affinity, one for the other. I know not why this should be, but it is so.'

He was responding to his son's cautious enquiry as to why it was necessary to go through the onerous and odious business of fumigating the ship. With all the cargo out of her and most of the crew billeted ashore Sir Francis was determined to try to rid the hull of vermin. It seemed that every crack in the woodwork swarmed with lice, and the holds were overrun with rats. The galley was littered with the black pellets of their droppings, and Ned Tyler had reported finding some of the stinking bloated carcasses rotting in the water casks.

Since the day of their arrival in the lagoon a shore party had been burning cordwood and leaching the ashes to obtain the lye, and Sir Francis had sent Aboli into the forest to search for those special herbs that his tribe used to keep their huts clear of the loathsome vermin. Now a party of seamen waited on the foredeck, armed with buckets of the caustic substance.

'I want every crack and joint of the hull scrubbed out, but be careful,' Sir Francis warned them. 'The corrosive fluid will burn the skin from your hands—' He broke off abruptly. Every head on board turned towards the distant rocky heads, and every man upon the beach paused in what he was doing and cocked his head to listen.

The flat boom of a cannon shot echoed from the cliffs at the entrance to the lagoon and reverberated across the still waters of the wide bay.

''Tis the alarm signal from the lookout on the heads, Captain,' shouted Ned Tyler, and pointed across the water to where a puff of white gunsmoke still hung over one of the emplacements that guarded the entrance. As they stared, a tiny black ball soared to the top of the makeshift flag-pole on the crest of the western headland then unfurled into a red swallow-tail. It was the general alarm signal, and could only mean that a strange sail was in sight.

'Beat to quarters, Master Daniel!' Sir Francis ordered crisply. 'Unlock the weapons chests and arm the crew. I am going across to the entrance. Four men to row the longboat and the rest take up their battle stations ashore.'

Although his face remained expressionless, inwardly he was furious that he should have allowed himself to be surprised like this, with the masts unstepped and all the cannon out of the hull. He turned to Ned Tyler. 'I want the prisoners taken ashore and placed under your strictest guard, well away from the beach. If they learn that there is a strange ship off the coast, it might give them the notion to try to attract attention.'

Oliver rushed up the companionway with Sir Francis's cloak over his arm. While he spread it over his master's shoulders, Sir Francis finished issuing his orders. Then he turned and strode to the entryport where the longboat lay alongside and Hal was waiting, where his father could not ignore him, fretting that he might not be ordered to join him.

'Very well, then,' Sir Francis snapped. 'Come with me. I might have need of those eyes of yours.' And Hal slid down the mooring line ahead, and cast off the moment his father stepped into the boat.

'Pull till you burst your guts!' Sir Francis told the men at the oars and the boat skittered across the lagoon. Sir Francis sprang over the side and waded ashore below the cliff with the water slopping over the tops of his high boots. Hal had to run to catch up with him on the elephant path.

They came out on the top, three hundred feet above the lagoon, looking out over the ocean. Although the wind that buffeted them on the heights had kicked the sea into a welter of breaking waves, Hal's sharp eyes picked out the brighter flecks that persisted among the ephemeral whitecaps even before the lookout could point them out to him.

Sir Francis stared through his telescope. 'What do you make of her?' he demanded of Hal.

'There are two ships,' Hal told him.

'I see but one – no, wait! You are right. There is another, a little further to the east. Is she a frigate, do you think?'

'Three masts,' Hal shaded his eyes, 'and full rigged. Yes, I'd say she's a frigate. The other vessel is too far off. I cannot tell her type.' It pained Hal to admit it, and he strained his eyes for some other detail. 'Both ships are standing in directly towards us.'

'If they are intending to head for Good Hope, then they must go about very soon,' Sir Francis murmured, never lowering the telescope. They watched anxiously.

'They could be a pair of Dutch East Indiamen still making their westings,' Hal hazarded hopefully.

'Then why are they pushing so close into a lee shore?' Sir Francis asked. 'No, it looks very much as though they are headed straight for the entrance.' He snapped the telescope closed. 'Come along!' At a trot he led the way back down the path to where the longboat waited on the beach. 'Master Daniel, row across to the batteries on the far side. Take command there. Do not open fire until I do.'

They watched the longboat move swiftly over the lagoon and Daniel's men drag it into a narrow cove where it was concealed from view. Then Sir Francis strode along the gun emplacements in the cliff and gave a curt set of orders to the men who crouched over the culverins with the burning slow-match.

'At my command, fire on the leading ship. One salvo of round shot,' he told them. 'Aim at the waterline. Then load with chain shot and bring down their rigging. They'll not want to try manoeuvring in these confined channels with half their sails shot away.' He jumped up onto the parapet of the emplacement and stared out at the sea through the narrow entrance, but the approaching vessels were still hidden from view by the rocky cliffs.

Suddenly, from around the western point of the heads, a ship with all sail set drew into view. She was less than two miles offshore, and even as they watched in consternation she altered course, and trimmed her yards around, heading directly for the entrance.

'Their guns are run out, so it's a fight they're looking for,' said Sir Francis grimly, as he sprang down from the wall. 'And we shall give it to them, lads.'

'No, Father,' Hal cried. 'I know that ship.'

'Who—' Before Sir Francis could ask the question, he was given the answer. From the vessel's maintop a long swallow-tailed banner unfurled. Scarlet and snowy white, it whipped and snapped on the wind.

'The *croix patté*!' Hal called. 'It's the *Gull of Moray*. It's Lord Cumbrae, Father!'

'By God, so it is. How did that red-bearded butcher know we were here?'

Astern of the *Gull of Moray* the strange ship hove into view. It also trained its yards around, and in succession altered its heading, following the Buzzard as he stood in towards the entrance.

'I know that ship also,' Hal shouted, on the wind. 'There, now! I can even recognize her figurehead. She's the *Goddess*. I know of no other ship on this ocean with a naked Venus at her bowsprit.'

'Captain Richard Lister, it is,' Sir Francis agreed. 'I feel easier for having him here. He's good man – though, God knows, I trust neither of them all the way.'

As the Buzzard came sailing in down the channel past the gun emplacements, he must have picked out the bright spot of Sir Francis's cloak against the lichen-covered rocks, for he dipped his standard in salute.

Sir Francis lifted his hat in acknowledgement, but grated between his teeth, 'I'd rather salute you with a bouquet of grape, you Scottish bastard. You've smelt the spoils, have you? You're come to beg or steal, is that it? But how did you know?'

97

'Father!' Hal shouted again. 'Look there, in the futtock-shrouds! I'd know that grinning rogue anywhere. That's how they knew. He led them here.'

Sir Francis swivelled his glass. 'Sam Bowles. It seems that even the sharks could not stomach that piece of carrion. I should have let his shipmates deal with him while we had the chance.'

The *Gull* moved slowly past them, reducing sail progressively, as she threaded her way deeper into the lagoon. The *Goddess* followed her, at a cautious distance. She also flew the *croix patté* at her masthead, along with the cross of St George and the Union flag. Richard Lister was also a Knight of the Order. They picked out his diminutive figure on his quarterdeck as he came to the rail and shouted something across the water that was jumbled by the wind.

'You are keeping strange company, Richard.' Even though the Welshman could not hear him, Sir Francis waved his hat in reply. Lister had been with him when they captured the *Heerlycke Nacht*, they had shared the spoils amicably, and he counted him a friend. Lister should have been with them, Sir Francis and the Buzzard while they spent those dreary months on blockade off Cape Agulhas. However, he had missed the rendezvous in Port Louis on the island of Mauritius. After waiting a month for him to appear, Sir Francis had been obliged to accede to the Buzzard's demands, and they had sailed without him.

'Well, we'd best put on a brave face, and go to greet our uninvited guests,' Sir Francis told Hal, and went down to the beach as Daniel brought the longboat across the channel between the heads.

As they rowed back up the lagoon the two newly arrived vessels lay at anchor in the main channel. The *Gull of Moray* was only half a cable's length astern of the *Resolution*. Sir Francis ordered Daniel to steer directly to the *Goddess*. Richard Lister was at the entryport to greet him as he and Hal came aboard.

'Flames of hell, Franky. I heard the word that you had taken a great prize from the Dutch. Now I see her lying there at anchor.' Richard seized his hand. He did not quite stand as tall as Sir Francis's shoulder but his grip was powerful. He sniffed the air with the great florid bell of his nose, and went on, in his singing Celtic lilt, 'And is that not spice I smell on the air? I curse meself for not having found you at Port Louis.'

'Where were you, Richard? I waited thirty-two days for you to arrive.'

'It grieves me to have to admit it but I ran full tilt into a hurricane just south of Mauritius. Dismasted me and blew me clear across to the coast of St Lawrence Island.'

'That would be the same storm that dismasted the Dutchman.' Sir

Francis pointed across the channel at the galleon. 'She was under jury-rig when we captured her. But how did you fall in with the Buzzard?'

'I thought that as soon as the *Goddess* was fit for sea again I would look for you off Cape Agulhas, on the off-chance that you were still on station there. That's when I came across him. He led me here.'

'Well, it's good to see you, my old friend. But, tell me, do you have any news from home?' Sir Francis leaned forward eagerly. This was always one of the foremost questions men asked each other when they met out here beyond the Line. They might voyage to the furthest ends of the uncharted seas, but always their hearts yearned for home. Almost a year had passed since Sir Francis had received news from England.

At the question, Richard Lister's expression turned sombre. 'Five days after I sailed from Port Louis I fell in with *Windsong*, one of His Majesty's frigates. She was fifty-six days out from Plymouth, bound for the Coromandel coast.'

'So what news did she have?' Sir Francis interrupted impatiently.

'None good, as the Lord is my witness. They say that all of England was struck by the plague, and that men, women and children died in their thousands and tens of thousands, so they could not bury them fast enough and the bodies lay rotting and stinking in the streets.'

'The plague!' Sir Francis crossed himself in horror. 'The wrath of God.'

'Then while the plague still raged through every town and village, London was destroyed by a mighty fire. They say that the flames left hardly a house standing.'

Sir Francis stared at him in dismay. 'London burned? It cannot be! The King — is he safe? Was it the Dutch that put the torch to London? Tell me more, man, tell me more.'

'Yes, the Black Boy is safe. But no, this time it was not the Dutch to blame. The fire was started by a baker's oven in Pudding Lane and it burned for three days without check. St Paul's Cathedral is burned to the ground and the Guildhall, the Royal Exchange, one hundred parish churches and God alone knows what else besides. They say that the damage will exceed ten million pounds.'

'Ten millions!' Sir Francis stared at him aghast. 'Not even the richest monarch in the world could rise to such an amount. Why, Richard, the total Crown revenues for a year are less than one million! It must beggar the King and the nation.'

Richard Lister shook his head with gloomy relish. 'There's more bad news besides. The Dutch have given us a mighty pounding. That devil, de Ruyter, sailed right into the Medway and the Thames. We lost sixteen ships of the line to him, and he captured the *Royal Charles* at her moorings in Greenwich docks and towed her away to Amsterdam.'

'The flagship, the flower and pride of our fleet. Can England survive such a defeat, coming as it does so close upon the heels of the plague and the fire?'

Lister shook his head again. 'They say the King is suing for peace with the Dutch. The war might be over at this very moment. It may have ended months ago, for all we know.'

'Let us pray most fervently that is not so.' Sir Francis looked across at the *Resolution*. 'I took that prize barely three weeks past. If the war was over then, my commission from the Crown would have expired. My capture might be construed as an act of piracy.'

'The fortunes of war, Franky. You had no knowledge of the peace. There is none but the Dutch will blame you for that.' Richard Lister pointed with his inflamed trumpet of a nose across the channel at the *Gull of Moray*. 'It seems that my lord Cumbrae feels slighted at being excluded from this reunion. See, he comes to join us.'

The Buzzard had just launched a boat. It was being rowed down the channel now towards them, Cumbrae himself standing in the stern. The boat bumped against the *Goddess*'s side and the Buzzard came scrambling up the rope ladder onto her deck.

'Franky!' he greeted Sir Francis. 'Since we parted, I have not let a single day go past without a prayer for you.' He came striding across the deck, his plaid swinging. 'And my prayers were heard. That's a bonny wee galleon we have there, and filled to the gunwales with spice and silver, so I hear.'

'You should have waited a day or two longer, before you deserted your station. You might have had a share of her.'

The Buzzard spread his hands in amazement. 'But, my dear Franky, what's this you're telling me? I never left my station. I took a short swing into the east, to make certain the Dutchies weren't trying to give us the slip by standing further out to sea. I hurried back to you just as soon as I could. By then you were gone.'

'Let me remind you of your own words, sir. "I am completely out of patience. Sixty-five days are enough for me and my brave fellows?"'

'My words, Franky?' The Buzzard shook his head, 'Your ears must have played you false. The wind tricked you, you did not hear me fairly.'

Sir Francis laughed lightly. 'You waste your talent as Scotland's greatest liar. There is no one here for you to amaze. Both Richard and I know you too well.'

'Franky, I hope this does not mean you would try to cheat me out of my fair share of the spoils?' He contrived to look both sorrowful and incredulous. 'I agree that I was not in sight of the capture, and I would not expect a full half share. Give me a third and I will not quibble.'

'Take a deep breath, sir.' Sir Francis laid his hand casually on the hilt of his sword. 'That whiff of spice is all the share you'll get from me.'

The Buzzard cheered up miraculously and gave a huge, booming laugh. 'Franky, my old and dear comrade in arms. Come and dine on board my ship this evening, and we can discuss your lad's initiation into the Order over a dram of good Highland whisky.'

'So it's Hal's initiation that brings you back to see me, is it? Not the silver and spice?'

'I know how much the lad means to you, Franky – to us all. He's a great credit to you. We all want him to become a Knight of the Order. You have spoken of it often. Isn't that the truth?'

Sir Francis glanced at his son, and nodded almost imperceptibly.

'Well, then, you'll not get a chance like this again in many a year. Here we are, three Nautonnier Knights together. That's the least number it takes to admit an acolyte to the first degree. When will you find another three Knights to make up a Lodge, out here beyond the Line?'

'How thoughtful of you, sir. And, of course, this has no bearing on a share of my booty that you were claiming but a minute ago?' Sir Francis's tone dripped with irony.

'We'll not speak about that again. You're an honest man, Franky. Hard but fair. You'd never cheat a brother Knight, would you?'

Sir Francis returned long before the midnight watch from dining with Lord Cumbrae aboard the *Gull of Moray*. As soon as he was in his cabin he sent Oliver to summon Hal.

'On the coming Sunday. Three days from now. In the forest,' he told his son. 'It is arranged. We will open the Lodge at moonrise, a little after two bells in the second dog watch.'

'But the Buzzard,' Hal protested. 'You do not like or trust him. He let us down—'

'And yet Cumbrae was right. We might never have three knights gathered together again until we return to England. I must take this opportunity to see you safely ensconced within the Order. The good Lord knows there might not be another chance.'

'We will leave ourselves at his mercy while we are ashore,' Hal warned. 'He might play us foul.'

Sir Francis shook his head. 'We will never leave ourselves at the

101

mercy of the Buzzard, have no fear of that.' He stood up and went to his sea-chest.

'I have prepared against the day of your initiation.' He lifted the lid. 'Here is your uniform.' He came across the cabin with a bundle in his hands and dropped it on his bunk. 'Put it on. We will make certain that it fits you.' He raised his voice and shouted, 'Oliver!'

His servant came at once with his housewife tucked under his arm. Hal stripped off his old worn canvas jacket and petticoats and, with Oliver's help, began to don the ceremonial uniform of the Order. He had never dreamed of owning such splendid clothing.

The stockings were of white silk and his breeches and doublet of midnight-blue satin, the sleeves slashed with gold. His shoes had buckles of heavy silver and the polished black leather matched that of his cross belt. Oliver combed out his thick tangled locks, then placed the Cavalier officer's hat on his head. He had picked the finest ostrich feathers in the market of Zanzibar to decorate the wide brim.

When he was dressed, Oliver circled Hal critically, his head on one side, 'Tight on the shoulders, Sir Francis. Master Hal grows wider each day. But it will take only a blink of your eye to fix that.'

Sir Francis nodded, and reached again into the chest. Hal's heart leaped as he saw the folded cloak in his father's hands. It was the symbol of the Knighthood he had studied so hard to attain. Sir Francis came to him and spread it over his shoulders, then fastened the clasp at his throat. The folds of white hung to his knees and the crimson cross bestrode his shoulders.

Sir Francis stood back and scrutinized Hal carefully. 'It lacks but one detail,' he grunted, and returned to the chest. From it he brought out a sword, but no ordinary sword. Hal knew it well. It was a Courteney family heirloom, but still its magnificence awed him. As his father brought it to where he stood, he recited to Hal its history and provenance one more time. 'This blade belonged to Charles Courteney, your great-grandfather. Eighty years ago, it was awarded to him by Sir Francis Drake himself for his part in the capture and sack of the port of Rancheria on the Spanish Main. This sword was surrendered to Drake by the Spanish governor, Don Francisco Manso.'

He held out the scabbard of chased gold and silver for Hal to examine. It was decorated with crowns and dolphins and sea sprites gathered around the heroic figure of Neptune enthroned. Sir Francis reversed the weapon and offered Hal the hilt. A large star sapphire was set in the pommel. Hal drew the blade and saw at once that this was not just the ornament of some Spanish fop. The blade was of the finest Toledo steel

102

inlaid with gold. He flexed it between his fingers, and rejoiced in its spring and temper.

'Have a care,' his father warned him. 'You can shave with that edge.'

Hal returned it to its scabbard and his father slipped the sword into the leather bucket of Hal's cross belt, then stood back again to examine him critically. 'What do you think of him?' he asked Oliver.

'Just the shoulders.' Oliver ran his hands over the satin of the doublet. 'It's all that wrestling and sword-play that changes his shape. I shall have to resew the seams.'

'Then take him to his cabin and see to it.' Sir Francis dismissed them both and turned back to his desk. He sat and opened his leather-bound log-book.

Hal paused in the doorway. 'Thank you, Father. This sword—' He touched the sapphire pommel at his side, but could not find words to continue. Sir Francis grunted without looking up, dipped his quill and began to write on the parchment page. Hal lingered a little longer in the entrance until his father looked up again in irritation. He backed out and shut the door softly. As he turned into the passage, the door opposite opened and the Dutch Governor's wife came through it so swiftly, in a swirl of silks, that they almost collided.

Hal jumped aside and swept the plumed hat from his head. 'Forgive me, madam.'

Katinka stopped and faced him. She examined him slowly, from the gleaming silver buckles of his new shoes upwards. When she reached his eyes she stared into them coolly and said softly, 'A pirate whelp dressed like a great nobleman.' Then, suddenly, she leaned towards him until her face almost touched his and whispered, 'I have checked the panel. There is no opening. You have not performed the task I set you.'

'My duties have kept me ashore. I have had no chance.' He stammered as he found the Latin words.

'See to it this very night,' she ordered, and swept by him. Her perfume lingered and the velvet doublet seemed too hot and constricting. He felt sweat break out on his chest.

Oliver fussed over the fit of his doublet for what seemed to Hal half the rest of the night. He unpicked and resewed the shoulder seams twice before he was satisfied and Hal fumed with impatience.

When at last he left, taking all Hal's newly acquired finery with him, Hal could barely wait to set the locking bar across his door, and kneel at the bulkhead. He discovered that the panel was fixed to the oak framework by wooden dowels, driven flush with the woodwork.

One at a time, with the point of his dirk, he prised and whittled the dowels from their drilled seats. It was slow work and he dared make no noise. Any blow or rasp would reverberate through the ship.

It was almost dawn before he was able to remove the last peg and then to slip the blade of his dagger into the joint and lever open the panel. It came away suddenly, with a squeal of protesting wood against the oak frame that seemed to carry through the hull, and must surely alarm both his father and the Governor.

With bated breath he waited for terrible retribution to fall around his head, but the minutes slid by, and at last he could breathe again.

Gingerly he stuck his head and shoulders through the rectangular opening. Katinka's toilet cabin beyond was in darkness, but the odour of her perfume made his breath come short. He listened intently, but could hear nothing from the main cabin beyond. Then, faintly, the sound of the ship's bell reached him from the deck above and he realized with dismay that it was almost dawn and in half an hour his watch would begin.

He pulled his head out of the opening, and replaced the panel, securing it with the wooden dowels, but so lightly that they could be removed in seconds.

'Should you allow the Buzzard's men ashore?' Hal asked his father respectfully. 'Forgive me, Father, but can you trust him that far?'

'Can I stop him without provoking a fight?' Sir Francis answered with another question. 'He says he needs water and firewood, and we do not own this land or even this lagoon. How can I forbid it to him?'

Hal might have protested further, but his father silenced him with a quick frown, and turned to greet Lord Cumbrae as the keel of his longboat kissed the sands of the beach and he sprang ashore his legs beneath the plaid furred with wiry ginger hair like a bear's.

'All God's blessings upon you this lovely morning, Franky,' he shouted, as he came towards them. His pale blue eyes darted restlessly as minnows in a pool under his beetling red brows.

'He sees everything,' Hal murmured. 'He has come to find out where we have stored the spice.'

'We cannot hide the spice. There's a mountain of it,' Sir Francis told him. 'But we can make the thieving of it difficult for him.' Then he smiled bleakly at Cumbrae as he came up. 'I hope I see you in good health, and that the whisky did not trouble your sleep last night, sir.'

'The elixir of life, Franky. The blood in my veins.' His eyes were bloodshot as they darted about the encampment at the edge of the forest. 'I need to fill my water casks. There must be good sweet water hereabouts.'

'A mile up the lagoon. There's a stream comes in from the hills.'

'Plenty of fish.' The Buzzard gestured at the racks of poles set up in the clearing upon which the split carcasses were laid out over the slow smoking fires of green wood. 'I'll have my lads catch some for us also. But what about meat? Are there any deer or wild cattle in the forest?'

'There are elephants, and herds of wild buffalo. But all are fierce, and even a musket ball in the ribs does not bring them down. However, as soon as the ship is careened I intend sending a band of hunters inland, beyond the hills to see if they cannot find easier prey.'

It was apparent that Cumbrae had asked the question to give himself space, and he hardly bothered to listen to the reply. When his roving eyes gleamed, Hal followed their gaze. The Buzzard had discovered the row of thatched lean-to shelters a hundred paces back among the trees, under which the huge casks of spice stood in serried ranks.

'So you plan to beach and careen the galleon.' Cumbrae turned away from the spice store, and nodded across the water at the hull of the *Resolution*. 'A wise plan. If you need help, I have three first-rate carpenters.'

'You are amiable,' Sir Francis told him. 'I may call upon you.'

'Anything to help a fellow Knight. I know you would do the same for me.' The Buzzard clapped him warmly on the shoulder. 'Now, while my shore party goes to refill the water casks, you and I can look for a suitable place to set up our Lodge. We must do young Hal here proud. It's an important day for him.'

Sir Francis glanced at Hal. 'Aboli is waiting for you.' He nodded to where the big black man stood patiently a little further down the beach.

Hal watched his father walk away with Cumbrae and disappear down a footpath into the forest. Then he ran down to join Aboli. 'I am ready at last. Let us go.'

Aboli set off immediately, trotting along the beach towards the head of the lagoon. Hal fell in beside him. 'You have no sticks?'

'We will cut them from the forest.' Aboli tapped the shaft of the hand axe, the steel head of which was hooked over his shoulder, and turned off the beach as he spoke. He led Hal a mile or so inland until they reached a dense thicket. 'I marked these trees earlier. My tribe call them the *kweti*. From them we make the finest throwing sticks.'

As they pushed into the dense thicket, there was a explosion of flying leaves and crashing branches as some huge beast charged away ahead of them. They caught a glimpse of scabby black hide and the flash of great bossed horns.

'Nyati!' Aboli told Hal. 'The wild buffalo.'

'We should hunt him.' Hal unslung the musket from his shoulder, and reached eagerly for the flint and steel in his pouch to light his slow-match. 'Such a monster would give us beef for all the ship's company.'

Aboli grinned and shook his head. 'He would hunt you first. There is no fiercer beast in all the forest, not even the lion. He will laugh at your little lead musket balls as he splits your belly open with those mighty spears he carries atop his head.' He swung the axe from his shoulder. 'Leave old Nyati be, and we will find other meat to feed the crew.'

Aboli hacked at the base of one of the kweti saplings and, with a dozen strokes, exposed the bulbous root. After a few more strokes he lifted it out from the earth, with the stem attached to it.

'My tribe call this club an iwisa,' he told Hal, as he worked, 'and today I will show you how to use it.' With skilful cuts, he sized the length of the shaft and peeled away the bark. Then he trimmed the root into an iron-hard ball, like the head of a mace. When he was finished he hefted the club, testing its weight and balance. Then he set it aside and searched for another. 'We need two each.'

Hal squatted on his heels and watched the wood chips fly under the steel. 'How old were you when the slavers caught you, Aboli?' he asked, and the dextrous black hands paused in their task.

A shadow passed behind the dark eyes, but Aboli started working again before he replied, 'I do not know, only that I was very young.'

'Do you remember it, Aboli?'

'I remember that it was night when they came, men in white robes with long muskets. It was so long ago, but I remember the flames in the darkness as they surrounded our village.'

'Where did your people live?'

'Far to the north. On the shores of a great river. My father was a chief yet they dragged him from his hut and killed him like an animal. They killed all our warriors, and spared only the very young children and the women. They chained us together in lines, neck to neck, and made us march, many days, towards the rising of the sun, down to the coast.' Aboli stood up abruptly, and picked up the bundle of clubs he had finished. 'We talk like old women while we should be hunting.'

He started back through the trees the way they had come. When they reached the lagoon again, he looked back at Hal. 'Leave your musket and powder flask here. They will be no use to you in the water.'

As Hal hid his weapon in the undergrowth, Aboli selected a pair of the lightest and straightest of the iwisa. When Hal returned he handed

106

him the clubs. 'Watch me. Do what I do,' he ordered, as he stripped off his clothing and waded out into the shallows of the lagoon. Hal followed him, naked, into the thickest stand of reeds.

Waist deep, Aboli stopped and pulled the stems of the tall reeds over his head plaiting them together to form a screen over himself. Then he sank down into the water, until only his head was exposed. Hal took up a position not far from him, and quickly built himself a similar roof of reeds. Faintly he could hear the voices of the watering party from the *Gull*, and the squeaking of their oars as they rowed back from the head of the lagoon where they had filled their casks from the sweet-water stream.

'Good!' Aboli called softly, 'Be ready now, Gundwane! They will put the birds into the air for us.'

Suddenly there was a roar of wings, and the sky was filled with the same vast cloud of birds they had watched before. A flight of ducks that looked like English mallard, except for their bright yellow bills, sped in a low V-formation towards where they were hidden.

'Here they come,' Aboli warned him, in a whisper, and Hal tensed, his face turned upwards to watch the old drake that led the flock. His wings were like knife blades as they stabbed the air with quick, sharp strokes.

'Now!' shouted Aboli, and sprang up to his full height, his right arm already cocked back with the *iwisa* in his fist. As he hurled it cartwheeling into the air, the line of wild duck flared in panic.

Aboli had anticipated this reaction and his spinning club caught the drake in the chest and stopped him dead. He fell in a tangle of wings and webbed feet, trailing feathers, but long before he struck the water Aboli had hurled his second club. It spun up to catch a younger bird, snapping her outstretched neck and dropping her close beside the floating carcass of the old drake.

Hal hurled his own sticks in quick succession, but both flew well wide of his mark and the splintered flock raced away low over the reed beds.

'You will soon learn, you were close with both your throws,' Aboli encouraged him, as he splashed through the reeds, first to pick up the dead birds, and then to recover his *iwisa*. He floated the two carcasses in a pool of open water in front of him, and within minutes they had decoyed in another whistling flock that dropped almost to the tops of the reeds before he threw at them.

'Good throw, Gundwane!' Aboli laughed at Hal as he waded out to pick up another two dead birds. 'You were closer then. Soon you may even hit one.'

Despite this prophecy, it was mid-morning before Hal brought down his first duck. Even then it was broken-winged, and he had to plunge and swim after it half-way down the lagoon before he could get a hand to it and wring its neck. In the middle of the day the birds stopped flighting and sat out in the deeper water where they could not be reached.

'It's enough!' Aboli put an end to the hunt, and gathered up his kill. From a tree at the water's edge he cut strips of bark and twisted these into strings to tie the dead ducks into bunches. They made up a load almost too heavy for even his broad shoulders to bear but Hal carried his own meagre bag without difficulty as they trudged back along the beach.

When they came round the point and could look into the bay where the three ships lay at anchor, Aboli dropped his burden of dead birds to the sand. 'We will rest here.' Hal sank down beside him, and for a while they sat in silence, until Aboli asked, 'Why has the Buzzard come here? What does your father say?'

'The Buzzard says he has come to make a Lodge for my initiation.'

Aboli nodded. 'In my own tribe the young warrior had to enter the circumcision lodge before he became a man.'

Hal shuddered and fingered his crotch as if to check that all was still in place. 'I am glad I will not have to give myself to the knife, as you did.'

'But that is not the true reason that the Buzzard has followed us here. He follows your father as the hyena follows the lion. The stink of treachery is strong upon him.'

'My father has smelt it also,' Hal assured him softly. 'But we are at his mercy, for the *Resolution* has no mainmast and the cannon are out of her.'

They both stared down the lagoon at the *Gull of Moray*, until Hal stirred uneasily. 'What is the Buzzard up to now?'

The longboat from the *Gull* was rowing out from her side to where her anchor cable dipped below the surface of the lagoon. They watched the crew of the small boat latch onto it and work there for several minutes.

'They are screened from the beach, so my father cannot see what they are up to.' Hal was thinking aloud. "Tis a furtive air they have about them, and I like it not at all.'

As he spoke the men finished their secretive task and began to row back to the *Gull*'s side. Now Hal could make out that they were laying a second cable over their stern as they went. At that he sprang to his feet in agitation. 'They are setting a spring to their anchor!' he exclaimed.

'A spring?' Aboli looked at him. 'Why would they do that?'

'So that with a few turns of the capstan the Buzzard can swing his ship in any direction he chooses.'

Aboli stood up beside him, his expression grave. 'That way he can train his broadside of cannon on our helpless ship or sweep our encampment on the beach with grape shot,' he said. 'We must hurry back to warn the captain.'

'No, Aboli, do not hurry. We must not alert the Buzzard to the fact that we have spotted his trick.'

Sir Francis listened intently to what Hal was saying, and when his son had finished he stroked his chin reflectively. Then he sauntered to the rail of the *Resolution* and casually raised his telescope to his eye. He made a slow sweep of the wide expanse of the lagoon, barely pausing as his gaze passed over the *Gull* so that no one could mark his sudden interest in the Buzzard's ship. Then he closed the telescope and came back to where Hal waited. There was respect in Sir Francis's eyes as he said, 'Well done, my boy. The Buzzard is up to his usual tricks. You were right. I was on the beach and could not see him setting the spring. I might never have noticed it.'

'Are you going to order him to remove it, Father?'

Sir Francis smiled and shook his head. 'Better not to let him know we have tumbled to him.'

'But what can we do?'

'I already have the culverins on the beach trained on the *Gull*. Daniel and Ned have warned every man—'

'But, Father, is there no ruse we can prepare for the Buzzard to match the surprise he clearly plans for us?' In his agitation Hal found the temerity to interrupt, but his father frowned quickly and his reply was sharp.

'No doubt you have a suggestion, Master Henry.'

At this formal address Hal was warned of his father's rising anger, and he was immediately contrite. 'Forgive my presumption, Father, I meant no impertinence.'

'I am pleased to hear that.' Sir Francis began to turn away, his back still stiff.

'Was not my great-grandfather, Charles Courteney, with Drake at the battle of Gravelines?'

'He was, indeed.' Sir Francis looked round. 'But as you already know the answer well enough, is this not a strange question to put to me now?'

'So it may well have been Great-grandfather himself who proposed to Drake the use of devil ships against the Spanish Armada as it lay anchored in Calais Roads, may it not?'

Slowly Sir Francis turned his head and stared at his son. He began to smile, then to chuckle, and at last burst out laughing. 'Dear Lord, but the Courteney blood runs true! Come down to my cabin this instant and show me what it is you have in mind.'

Sir Francis stood at Hal's shoulder as he sketched a design on the slate. 'They need not be sturdily constructed, for they will not have far to sail, and will have no heavy seas to endure,' Hal explained deferentially.

'Yes, but once they are launched they should be able to hold a true course, and yet carry a goodly weight of cargo,' his father murmured, and took the chalk from his son. He drew a few quick lines on the slate. 'We might lash two hulls together. It would not do to have them capsize or expend themselves before they reach their destination.'

'The wind has been steady from the sou'-east ever since we have been anchored here,' said Hal. 'There is no sign of it dropping. So we must hold them up-wind. If we place them on the small island across the channel, then the wind will work for us when we launch them.'

'Very well.' Sir Francis nodded. 'How many do we need?' He could see how much pleasure he gave the lad by consulting him in this fashion.

'Drake sent in eight against the Spaniards, but we do not have the time to build so many. Five, perhaps?' He looked up at his father, and Sir Francis nodded again.

'Yes, five should do it. How many men will you need? Daniel must remain in command of the culverins on the beach. The Buzzard may spring his trap before we are ready. But I will send Ned Tyler and the carpenter to help you build them – and Aboli, of course.'

Hal stared at his father in awe. 'You will trust me to take charge of the building?' he asked.

'It is your plan so if it fails I must be able to lay full blame upon you,' his father replied, with only the faintest smile upon his lips. 'Take your men and go ashore at once to begin work. But be circumspect. Don't make it easy for the Buzzard.'

al's axemen cleared a small opening on the far side of the heavily forested island across the channel where they were hidden from the *Gull of Moray*. After a circuitous detour through the forest on the mainland, he was also able to ferry his men and material across to the island out of sight of the lookouts on the Buzzard's vessel.

That first night they worked by the wavering light of pitch-soaked torches until after midnight. All of them were aware of the urgency of their task, and when they were exhausted they simply threw themselves on the soft bed of leaf mould under the trees and slept until the dawn gave enough light to begin work again.

By noon of the following day all five of the strange craft were ready to be carried to their hiding place in the grove at the edge of the lagoon. At low tide, Sir Francis waded across from the mainland and made his way down the footpath through the dense forest that covered the island to inspect the work.

He nodded dubiously. 'I hope sincerely that they will float,' he mused, as he walked slowly round one of the ungainly vessels.

'We will only know that when we send them out for the first time.' Hal was tired, and his temper was short. 'Even to please you, Father, I cannot arrange a prior demonstration for the benefit of Lord Cumbrae.'

His father glanced at him, concealing his surprise. The puppy grows into a young dog and learns how to growl, he thought, with a twinge of paternal pride. He demands respect, and, truth to tell, he has earned it.

Aloud he said, 'You have done well in the time at your disposal,' which deftly turned aside Hal's anger. 'I will send fresh men to help you transport them, and place them in the grove.'

al was so tired that he could barely drag himself up the rope ladder to the entryport of the *Resolution*. But even though his task was complete, his father would not let him escape to his cabin.

'We are anchored directly behind the *Gull*.' He pointed across the moonlit channel at the dark shape of the other ship. 'Have you thought what might happen if one of your fiendish vessels drifts past the mark and comes down upon us here? Dismasted as we are, we cannot manoeuvre the ship.'

'Aboli has already cut long bamboo poles in the forest.' Hal's tone could not conceal that he was weary to his bones. 'We will use them to deflect any drifters from us and send them harmlessly up onto the beach over there.' He turned and pointed back towards where the fires of the encampment flickered among the trees. 'The Buzzard will be taken by surprise, and will not be equipped with bamboo poles.'

At last his father was satisfied. 'Go to your rest now. Tomorrow night we will open the Lodge, and you must be able to make your responses to the catechism.'

Hal came back reluctantly from the abyss of sleep into which he had sunk. For some moments he was not certain what had woken him. Then the soft scratching came again from the bulkhead.

Instantly he was fully awake, every vestige of fatigue forgotten. He rolled off his pallet, and knelt at the panel. The scratching was now impatient and demanding. He tapped a swift reply on the woodwork, then fumbled in the darkness to find the stopper of his peep-hole. The moment he removed it, a yellow ray of lamp-light shone through but was cut off as Katinka placed her lips to the opening on the far side and whispered angrily, 'Where were you last night?'

'I had duties ashore,' he whispered back.

'I do not believe you,' she told him. 'You try to escape your punishment. You deliberately disobey me.'

'No, no, I would not—'

'Open this panel at once.'

He groped for his dirk, which hung on his belt on the hook at the foot of his bunk, and prised out the dowels. The panel came away in his hands with only the faintest scraping sound. He set it aside, and a square of soft light fell through the hatch.

'Come!' her voice ordered, and he wriggled into the gap. It was a tight squeeze, but after a short struggle he found himself on his hands and knees on the deck of her cabin. He started to rise to his feet, but she stopped him.

'Stay down there.' He looked up at her as she stood over him. She was dressed in a flowing night-robe of some gossamer material. Her hair was loose and hung in splendour to her waist. The lamp-light shone through the cloth of her robe and silhouetted her body, the lustre of her skin gleaming through the transparent folds of silk.

'You have no shame,' she told him, as he knelt before her as though she were the sacred image of a saint. 'You come to me naked. You show me no respect.'

112

'I am sorry!' he gasped. In his anxiety to obey her he had forgotten his own nudity, and now he cupped his hands over his privy parts. 'I meant no disrespect.'

'No! Do not cover your shame.' She reached down and pulled away his hands. Both stared down at his groin. They watched him slowly stretch out and thicken, thrusting out towards her, his prepuce peeling back of its own accord.

'Is there nothing I can do to stop such revolting behaviour? Are you too far gone in Satan's ways?'

She seized a handful of his hair and dragged him to his feet and after her into the splendid cabin where first he had laid eyes on her beauty.

She dropped onto the quilted bed, and sat facing him. The white silk skirts parted and fell back on each side of her long slim thighs. She twisted the handful of his curls, and said, in a voice that was suddenly breathless, 'You must obey me in all things, you child of the dark pit.'

Her thighs fell apart, and she pulled his face down and pressed it hard at their apex against the impossibly soft and silky mound of golden curls.

He smelt the sea in her, brine and kelp, and the scent of the sparkling living things of the oceans, the warm soft odour of the islands, of salt surf breaking on a sun-baked beach. He drank it in through flaring nostrils, and then tracked down the source of this fabulous aroma with his lips.

She wriggled forward on the satin covers to meet his mouth, her thighs spread wider, and she tilted her hips forward to open herself to him. With a handful of his curls, she moved his head, guiding him to that tiny bud of pink, taut flesh that nestled in its hidden crevice. As he found it with the tip of his tongue she gasped and she began to move herself against his face as though she rode bareback upon a galloping stallion. She gave small incoherent contradictory cries. 'Oh, stop! Please stop! No! Never stop! Go on for ever!'

Then suddenly she wrenched his head out from between her straining thighs, and fell backwards upon the covers lifting him over her. He felt her hard little heels dig into the small of his back as she wrapped her legs around him, and her fingernails, like knives, cutting into the tensed muscles of his shoulders. Then the pain was lost in the sensation of slippery engulfing heat as he slid deeply into her, and he smothered his cries in the golden tangle of her hair.

The three Knights had set up the Lodge on the slope of the hills above the lagoon, at the foot of a small waterfall that dropped into a basin of dark water surrounded by tall trees hung with lichens and lianas.

The altar stood within the circle of stones, the fire burning before it. Thus all the ancient elements were represented. The moon was in its first quarter, signifying rebirth and resurrection.

Hal waited alone in the forest while the three Knights of the Order opened the Lodge in the first degree. Then his father, his bared sword in his hand, came striding through the darkness to fetch him, and led him back along the path.

The other two Knights were waiting beside the fire in the sacred circle. Their swords were drawn, the blades gleaming in the reflection of the flames. Lying upon the stone altar under a velvet cloth, he saw the shape of his great-grandfather's Neptune sword. They paused outside the circle of stones and Sir Francis begged entrance to the Lodge.

'In the name of the Father, the Son and the Holy Ghost!'

'Who would enter the Lodge of the Temple of the Order of St George and the Holy Grail?' Lord Cumbrae thundered, in a voice that rang against the hills, his long two-edged claymore glinting in his hairy red fist.

'A novice who presents himself for initiation into the mysteries of the Temple,' Hal replied.

'Enter on peril of your eternal life,' Cumbrae warned him, and Hal stepped into the circle. Suddenly the air seemed colder and he shivered, even as he knelt in the radiance of the watchfire.

'Who sponsors this novice?' the Buzzard demanded again.

'I do.' Sir Francis stepped forward and Cumbrae turned back to Hal.

'Who are you?'

'Henry Courteney, son of Francis and Edwina.' The long catechism began as the starry wheel of the firmament turned slowly overhead and the flames of the watchfire sank lower.

It was after midnight when, at last, Sir Francis lifted the velvet covering from the Neptune sword. The sapphire on the hilt reflected a pale blue beam of moonlight into Hal's eyes as his father placed the hilt in his hands.

'Upon this blade you will confirm the tenets of your faith.'

'These things I believe,' Hal began, 'and I will defend them with my life. I believe there is but one God in Trinity, the Father eternal, the Son eternal and the Holy Ghost eternal.'

'Amen!' chorused the three Nautonnier Knights.

'I believe in the communion of the Church of England, and the divine right of its representative on earth, Charles, King of England, Scotland, France and Ireland, Defender of the Faith.'

'Amen!'

Once Hal had recited his beliefs, Cumbrae called upon him to make his knightly vows.

'I will uphold the Church of England. I will confront the enemies of my sovereign lord, Charles.' Hal's voice quivered with conviction and sincerity. 'I renounce Satan and all his works. I eschew all false doctrines and heresies and schisms. I turn my face away from all other gods and their false prophets.'

'I will protect the weak. I will defend the pilgrim. I will succour the needy and those in need of justice. I will take up the sword against the tyrant and the oppressor.'

'I will defend the holy places. I will search out and protect the precious relics of Christ Jesus and his Saints. I will never cease my quest for the Holy Grail that contained his sacred blood.'

The Nautonnier Knights crossed themselves as he made this vow, for the Grail quest stood at the centre of their belief. It was the granite column that held aloft the roof of their Temple.

'I pledge myself to the Strict Observance. I will obey the code of my Knighthood. I will abstain from debauchery and fornication,' Hal's tongue tripped on the word, but he recovered swiftly, 'and I will honour my fellow Knights. Above all else, I will keep secret all the proceedings of my Lodge.'

'And may the Lord have mercy on your soul!' the three Nautonnier Knights intoned in unison. Then they stepped forward and formed a ring around the kneeling novice. Each laid one hand on his bowed head and the other on the hilt of his sword, their hands overlapping each other.

'Henry Courteney, we welcome you into the Grail company, and we accept you as brother Knight of the Temple of the Order of St George and the Holy Grail.'

Richard Lister spoke first, in his sonorous Welsh voice, almost singing his blessing. 'I welcome you into the Temple. May you always follow the Strict Observance.'

Cumbrae spoke next. 'I welcome you into the Temple. May the waters of far oceans open wide before the bows of your ship, and may the force of the wind drive you on.'

Then Sir Francis Courteney spoke with his hand firmly set on Hal's brow. 'I welcome you into the Temple. May you always be true to your vows, to your God and to yourself.'

Then between them the Nautonnier Knights lifted him to his feet and, one after another, embraced him. Lord Cumbrae's whiskers were stiff and pricking as a garland of thorns from the traitor's bush.

'I have a hold filled with my share of the spices that you and I took from *Heerlycke Nacht*, enough to buy me a castle and five thousand acres of the finest land in Wales,' said Richard Lister, as he clasped Sir Francis's right hand in his, using the secret grip of the Nautonniers. 'And I have a young wife and two stout sons upon whom I have not laid eyes for three years. A little rest in green and pleasant places with those I love, and then, I know, the wind will summon. Perhaps we will meet again on far waters, Francis.'

'Take the tide of your heart, then, Richard. I thank you for your friendship, and for what you have done for my son.' Sir Francis returned his grip. 'I hope one day to welcome both your boys into the Temple.'

Richard turned away towards his waiting longboat, but hesitated and came back. He placed one arm around Sir Francis's shoulders and his brow was grave, his voice low, as he said, 'Cumbrae had a proposition for me concerning you, but I liked it not at all and told him so to his face. Watch your back, Franky, and sleep with one eye open when he is around you.'

'You are a good friend,' Sir Francis said, and watched Richard walk to his longboat and cross to the *Goddess*. As soon as he went up the ladder to the quarterdeck his crew weighed the anchor. All her sails filled and she moved down the channel, dipping her pennant in farewell as she disappeared out through the heads into the open sea.

'Now we have only the Buzzard to keep us company.' Hal looked across at the *Gull of Moray* where she lay in the centre of the channel, her boats clustered around her discharging water casks, bundles of firewood and dried fish into her holds.

'Make your preparations to beach the ship, please, Mr Courteney,' Sir Francis replied, and Hal straightened his spine. He was unaccustomed to his father addressing him thus. It was strange to be treated as a Knight and a full officer, instead of as a lowly ensign. Even his mode of dress had changed with his new status. His father had provided the shirt of fine white Madras cotton on his back, as well as his new moleskin breeches, which felt soft as silk against his skin after the rags of rough canvas he had worn before today.

He was even more surprised when his father deigned to explain his order. 'We must go about our business as if we suspect no treachery. Besides which the *Resolution* will be safer upon the beach if it comes to a fight.'

'I understand, sir.' Hal looked up at the sun to judge the time. 'The tide will be fair for us to take her aground at two bells in tomorrow's morning watch. We will be prepared.'

All the rest of that morning the crew of the *Gull* behaved like that of any other ship preparing for sea, and though Daniel and his guncrews, with cannon loaded and aimed, and with slow-match burning, watched the *Gull* from their hidden emplacements dug into the sandy soil along the edge of the forest, she gave them no hint of treachery.

A little before noon Lord Cumbrae had himself rowed ashore and came to find Sir Francis where he stood by the fire upon which the cauldron of pitch was bubbling, ready to begin caulking the *Resolution*'s hull when she was careened.

'It's farewell, then.' He embraced Sir Francis, throwing a thick red arm around his shoulders. 'Richard was right. There's no prize to be won if we sit here upon the beach and scratch our backsides.'

'So you're ready to sail?' Sir Francis kept his tone level, not betraying his astonishment.

'With tomorrow morning's tide, I'll be away. But how I hate to leave you, Franky. Will you not take a last dram aboard the *Gull* with me now? I would fain discuss with you my share of the prize money from the *Standvastigheid*.'

'My lord, your share is nothing. That ends our discussion, and I wish you a fair wind.'

Cumbrae let fly a great blast of laughter. 'I've always loved your sense of fun, Franky. I know you only wish to spare me the labour of carrying that heavy cargo of spice back to the Firth of Forth.' He turned and pointed with his curling beard at the spice store under the forest trees. 'So I shall let you do it for me. But, in the meantime, I trust you to keep a fair accounting of my share, and to deliver it to me when next we meet – plus the usual interest, of course.'

'I trust you as dearly, my lord.' Sir Francis lifted his hat and swept the sand with the plume as he bowed.

Cumbrae returned the bow and, still rumbling with laughter, went down to the longboat and had himself rowed to the *Gull*.

During the course of the morning the Dutch hostages had been brought ashore and installed in their new lodgings, which Hal and his gang had built for them. These were set well back from the lagoon and separated from the compound in which the *Resolution*'s crew were housed.

117

Now the ship was empty and ready for beaching. As the tide pushed in through the heads the crew, under the direction of Ned Tyler and Hal, began warping it in towards the beach. They had secured the strongest sheaves and blocks to the largest of the trees. Heavy hawsers were fastened to the *Resolution*'s bows and stern, and with fifty men straining on the lines, the ship came in parallel to the beach.

When her bottom touched the white sand they secured her there. As the tide receded they hove her down with tackle attached to her mizzen and foremasts, which were still stepped. The ship heeled over steeply until her mastheads touched the tree-tops. The whole of the starboard side of her hull, down as far as the keel, was exposed, and Sir Francis and Hal waded out to inspect it. They were delighted to find little sign of shipworm infestation.

A few sections of planking had to be replaced and the work began immediately. When darkness fell the torches were lit, for the work on the hull would continue until the return of the tide put a halt to it. When this happened Sir Francis went off to dine in his new quarters, while Hal gave orders to secure the hull for the night. The torches were doused and Ned led away the men to find their own belated dinner.

Hal was not hungry for food. His appetites were of a different order, but it would be at least another hour before he could satisfy them. Left alone on the beach, he studied the *Gull* across the narrow strip of water. It seemed that she was settled in quietly enough for the night. Her small boats still lay alongside, but it would not take long to lift them on board and batten down her hatches ready for sea.

He turned away and moved back into the trees. He went down the line of gun emplacements, speaking softly to the men on watch behind the culverins. He checked once more the laying of each, making sure that they were truly aimed at the dark shape of the *Gull*, as she lay in a spangle of star reflections on the surface of the still, dark lagoon.

For a while he sat next to Big Daniel, dangling his legs into the gunpit.

'Don't worry, Mr Henry.' Even Daniel used the new and more respectful form of address naturally enough. 'We're keeping a weather eye on that red-bearded bastard. You can go off and get your supper.'

'When did you last sleep, Daniel?' Hal asked.

'Don't worry about me. The watch changes pretty soon now. I'll be handing over to Timothy.'

Outside his hut Hal found Aboli sitting as quietly as a shadow by the fire, waiting for him with a bowl that contained roasted duck and hunks of bread, and a jug of small beer.

'I'm not hungry, Aboli,' Hal protested.

'Eat.' Aboli thrust the bowl into his hands. 'You will need your strength for the task that lies ahead of you this night.'

Hal accepted the bowl, but he tried to determine Aboli's expression and to read from it the deeper meaning of his admonition. The firelight danced on his dark enigmatic features, like those of a pagan idol, highlighting the tattoos on his cheeks, but his eyes were inscrutable.

Hal used his dirk to split the carcass of the duck in half and offered one portion to Aboli. 'What task is this that I have to perform?' he asked carefully.

Aboli tore a piece off the duck's breast and shrugged as he chewed. 'You must be careful not to scratch the tenderest parts of yourself on a thorn as you go through the hole in the stockade to do your duty.'

Hal's jaw stopped moving and the duck in his mouth lost its taste. Aboli must have discovered the narrow passage through the thorn fence behind Katinka's hut that Hal had so secretly left open.

'How long have you known?' he asked, through his mouthful.

'Was I supposed not to know?' Aboli asked. 'Your eyes are like the full moon when you look in a certain direction, and I have heard your roars like those of a wounded buffalo coming from the stern at midnight.'

Hal was stunned. He had been so careful and cunning.

'Do you think my father knows?' he asked with trepidation.

'You are still alive,' Aboli pointed out. 'If he knew, that would not be so.'

'You would tell no one?' he whispered. 'Especially not him?'

'Especially not him,' Aboli agreed. 'But take a care that you do not dig your own grave with that spade between your legs.'

'I love her, Aboli,' Hal whispered. 'I cannot sleep for the thought of her.'

'I have heard you not sleeping. I thought you might wake the entire ship's company with your sleeplessness.'

'Do not mock me, Aboli. I will die for lack of her.'

'Then I must save your life by taking you to her.'

'You would come with me?' Hal was shocked by the offer.

'I will wait at your hole in the stockade. To guard you. You might need my help if the husband finds you where he would like to be.'

'That fat animal!' Hal said furiously, hating the man with all his heart.

'Fat, perhaps. Sly, almost certainly. Powerful, without doubt. Do not underrate him, Gundwane.' Aboli stood up. 'I will go first to make sure the way is clear.'

The two slipped quietly through the darkness, and paused at the rear of the stockade.

119

'You don't have to wait for me, Aboli,' Hal whispered, 'I might be a little while.'

'If you were not, I would be disappointed in you,' Aboli told Hal in his own language. 'Remember this advice always, Gundwane, for it will stand you in good stead all the days of your life. A man's passion is like a fire in tall, dry grass, hot and furious but soon spent. A woman is like a magician's cauldron that must simmer long upon the coals before it can bring forth its spell. Be swift in all things but love.'

Hal sighed in the darkness. 'Why must women be so different from us, Aboli?'

'Thank all your Gods, and mine also, that they are.' Aboli's teeth gleamed in the darkness as he grinned. He pushed Hal gently towards the opening. 'If you call I will be here.'

The lamp still burned in her hut. The slivers of yellow light shone through the weak places in the thatch. Hal listened softly at the wall, but heard no voices. He crept to the door, which stood open a crack. He peered through it, at the huge four-poster bed that his men had carried from her cabin in the *Resolution*. The curtains were closed to keep out the insects, so he could not be certain that there was only one person behind them.

Soundlessly he slipped through the door and crept to the bed. As he touched the curtains, a small white hand reached through the folds, seized his outstretched hand and dragged him in. 'Do not speak!' she hissed at him. 'Say not a word!' Her fingers flew nimbly down the buttons of his shirt front, opening it to the waist, then her nails dug painfully into his breast.

At the same time her mouth covered his. She had never kissed him before and the heat and softness of her lips astonished him. He tried to grasp her breasts but she seized his wrists and held them at his sides as her tongue slipped into his mouth and twined with his, slithering and twisting like a live eel, goading and teasing him slowly, higher than he had ever been before.

Then still holding his hands at his side she forced him over backwards. Her swift fingers opened the fastening of his moleskin breeches, and then in a flurry of silks and laces she bestrode his hips and pinned him to the satin coverlet. Without using her hands she searched with her pelvis until she found him and sucked him into her secret heat.

Much later, Hal fell into a sleep so deep that it was like a little death.

An insistent hand on his bare arm woke him, and he started up in alarm. 'What—' he began, but the hand whipped over his mouth and gagged his next word.

120

'Gundwane! Make no noise. Find your clothes and come with me. Quickly!'

Hal rolled gently off the bed, careful not to disturb the woman beside him, and found his breeches where she had thrown them.

Neither spoke again until they had crept out through the gap in the stockade. There, they paused as Hal glanced up at the sky and saw, by the angle of the great Southern Cross to the horizon, that it lacked only an hour or so till dawn. This was the witching hour when all human resources were at their lowest ebb. Hal peered back at Aboli's dark shape. 'What is it, Aboli?' Hal demanded. 'Why did you call me?'

'Listen!' Aboli laid a hand on his shoulder and Hal cocked his head.

'I hear nothing.'

'Wait!' Aboli squeezed his shoulder for silence.

Then Hal heard it, far off and faint, blanketed by the trees, a shout of uncontrolled laughter.

'Where . . . ?' Hal was puzzled.

'At the beach.'

'God's wounds!' Hal blurted. 'What devilry is this now?' He began to run, Aboli at his side, heading for the lagoon, stumbling in the darkness on the uneven forest floor with low branches whipping into their faces.

As they reached the first huts of the encampment, they heard more noise ahead, a snatch of slurred song and a hoot of crazed laughter.

'The gunpits,' Hal panted, and at that moment saw, in the last glimmer from the dying watchfire, a pale human shape ahead.

Then his father's voice challenged him. 'Who is that?'

''Tis Hal, Father.'

'What is happening?' It was clear that Sir Francis had only just awakened for he was in his shirt sleeves and his voice was groggy with sleep, but his sword was in his hand.

'I don't know,' Hal said. There was another roar of stupid laughter. 'It comes from the beach. The gunpits.'

Without another word, all three ran on, and came together to the first culverin. Here, at the edge of the lagoon, the canopy of leaves overhead was thinner, allowing the last rays of the moon to shine through, giving them enough light to see one of the guncrew draped over the long bronze barrel. When Sir Francis aimed an angry kick at him he collapsed in the sand.

It was then that Hal spotted the small keg standing on the lip of the pit. Oblivious to their arrival, one of the other gunners was on his hands and knees in front of it, like a dog, lapping up the liquid that dribbled from the spigot. Hal smelt the sugary aroma, heavy on the night air like the emanation of some poisonous flower. He jumped down into the pit and seized the gunner by his hair.

'Where did you get the rum?' he snarled. The man peered back at him blearily. Hal drew back his fist and struck him a blow that made his teeth clash together in his jaw. 'Damn you for a sot! Where did you get it?' Hal pricked him with the point of his dirk. 'Answer me or I'll split your windpipe.'

The pain and the threat rallied his victim. 'A parting gift from his lordship,' he gasped. 'He sent a keg across from the *Gull* for us to drink his health and wish him God speed.'

Hal flung the drunken creature from him and leapt onto the parapet. 'The other guncrews? Has the Buzzard sent gifts to all of them?'

They ran down the line of emplacements, and in each found sweetly reeking oaken kegs and inert bodies. Few of the crews were still on their feet, but even those who were, were staggering and slobbering in intoxication. Few English seamen could resist the ardent essence of the sugar cane.

Even Timothy Reilly, one of Sir Francis's trusted coxswains, had succumbed, and although he tried to answer Sir Francis's accusation, he reeled on his feet. Sir Francis struck him a blow with the hilt of his sword across the side of his head and the fellow collapsed in the sand.

At that moment, Big Daniel came running from the encampment. 'I heard the uproar, Captain. What has happened?'

'The Buzzard has plied the guncrews with liquor. They are all of them witless.' His voice shook with fury. 'It can only mean one thing. There is not a moment to lose. Rouse the camp. Stand the men to arms – but softly, mind!'

As Daniel raced away, Hal heard a faint sound from the dark ship across the still lagoon waters, a distant clank of ratchet and pawl, that sent tingling shocks up his spine.

'The capstan!' he exclaimed. 'The *Gull* is tightening up on her anchor spring.'

They stared across the channel, and in the moonlight saw the silhouette of the *Gull* begin to alter, as the hawser running from the anchor to her capstan pulled her stern round, and her full broadside was presented to the beach.

'Her guns are run out!' Sir Francis exclaimed, as the moonlight glinted on the barrels. Behind each they could now make out the faint glow of the burning slow-match in the hands of the *Gull*'s gunners.

'Satan's breath, they're going to fire on us! Down!' shouted Sir Francis. 'Get down!' Hal leapt over the parapet of the gunpit and flung himself flat on the sandy floor.

Suddenly the night was lit brightly, as if by a flash of lightning. An instant later the thunder smote their ear-drums and the tornado of shot swept across the beach and thrashed into the forest around them. The *Gull* had fired all her cannon into the encampment in a single devastating broadside.

The grape shot tore through the foliage above and branches, clusters of leaves and slabs of wet bark rained down upon them. The air was filled with a lethal swarm of splinters blasted from the tree-trunks.

The frail huts gave no protection to the men within. The broadside slashed through, sending poles flying and flattening the flimsy structures as though they had been hit by a tidal wave. They heard the terrified yells of men awakening into a nightmare, and the sobs, screams and groans of those cut down by the hail of shot or skewered by the sharp, ragged splinters.

The *Gull* had disappeared behind the pall of her own gunsmoke, but Sir Francis leapt to his feet and snatched the smouldering match from the senseless hand of the drunken gunner. He glanced over the sights of the culverin and saw that it was still aimed into the swirling smoke behind which the *Gull* lay. He pressed the match to the touch hole. The culverin bellowed out a long silver gush of smoke and bounded back against its tackle. He could not see the strike of his shot, but he roared an order to those gunners down the line still sober enough to obey. 'Fire! Open fire! Keep firing as fast as you can!'

He heard a ragged salvo but then saw many of the guncrews heave themselves up and stagger away drunkenly among the trees.

Hal jumped onto the lip of the emplacement, shouting for Aboli and Daniel. 'Come on! Each of you bring a match and follow me. We must get across to the island!'

Daniel was already helping Sir Francis reload the culverin, swabbing out the smoking barrel to douse the burning sparks.

'Avast that, Daniel. Leave that work to others. I need your help.'

As they started off together along the shore, the fog bank that covered the *Gull* drifted aside and she fired her next broadside. It had been but two minutes since the first. Her gunners were fast and well trained and they had the advantage of surprise. Again the storm of shot swept the beach and ploughed into the forest with deadly effect.

Hal saw one of their culverin struck squarely by a lead ball. The tackle snapped and it was hurled backwards off its train, so that its muzzle pointed to the stars.

The cries of the wounded and dying swelled in the pandemonium of despair as men deserted their posts and fled among the trees. The desultory return fire from the gunpits shrivelled until there was only an occasional bang and flash of cannon. Once the battery was silenced, the Buzzard turned his guns on the remaining huts and the clumps of bush in which the *Resolution*'s crew had taken shelter.

Hal could hear the crew of the *Gull* cheering wildly as they reloaded and fired. 'The *Gull* and Cumbrae!' they shouted.

There were no more broadsides, but a continuous stuttering roll of thunder as each gun fired as soon as it was ready. Their muzzle flashes flickered and flared within the sulphurous white smoke bank like the flames of hell.

As he ran Hal heard his father's voice behind him, fading with distance as he tried to rally his shattered, demoralized crew. Aboli ran at his shoulder and Big Daniel was a few paces further back, losing ground to the two swifter runners.

'We will need more men to launch,' Daniel panted. 'They're heavy.'

'You will not find them to help you now. They're all hog drunk or running for their very lives,' Hal grunted, but even as he spoke he saw Ned Tyler speed out of the forest just ahead, leading five of his seamen. All seemed sober enough.

'Good man, Ned!' Hal shouted. 'But we must hurry. The Buzzard will be sending his men onto the beach as soon as he has silenced our batteries.'

They charged in a group across the shallow channel between them and the island. The tide was low so at first they staggered through the glutinous mud-flat that sucked at their feet, then plunged into the open water. They waded, swam and dragged themselves across, the thunder of the *Gull*'s barrage spurring them onwards.

'There is only a breath of wind from the sou'-west,' Big Daniel gasped, as they staggered out, streaming water, onto the beach of the island. 'It will not be enough to serve us.'

Hal did not reply but broke off a dead branch and lit it from his slow-match. He held it high to give himself light to see the path and ran on into the forest. In minutes they had crossed the island and reached the beach on the far side. Here Hal paused and looked across at the *Gull* in the main channel.

The dawn was coming on apace, and the night fled before it. The light was turning grey and silvery, the lagoon gleaming softly as a sheet of polished pewter.

The Buzzard was training his guns back and forth, with the use of his anchor spring, swinging the *Gull* on her moorings so that he could pick out any target on the shore.

There was only the odd flash of answering fire from the gunpits on the beach, and the Buzzard responded immediately to these, swinging his ship and bringing to bear the full power of his broadside, snuffing them out with a whirlwind of grape, flying sand and falling trees.

All of Hal's party were blown by the hard run across the mud-flats and the plunge through the channel. 'No time to rest.' Hal's breath whistled in his throat. The devil ships were covered with mounds of cut branches and they dragged them clear. Then they formed a ring round the first of these vessels, and each took a handhold.

'Together now!' Hal exhorted them, and between them they just lifted the keels of the double-hulled vessel clear of the sand. It was heavy with its cargo, faggots of dried wood drenched with pitch to make it more flammable.

They staggered down the beach with it, and dropped it into the shallows, where it wallowed and rolled in the wavelets, the square of dirty canvas on the stubby mast stirring idly in the light puffs of wind coming down from the heads. Hal took a turn of the painter around his wrist to prevent it drifting away.

'Not enough wind!' Big Daniel lamented, looking to the sky. 'For the sweet love of God, send us a breeze.'

'Keep your prayers for later.' Hal secured the vessel, and led them back at a run into the trees. They carried, shoved and dragged two more of the boats down to the water's edge.

'Still not enough wind.' Daniel looked across at the *Gull*. In the short time it had taken them to launch, the morning light had strengthened, and now, as they paused for a moment to regain their breath, they saw the Buzzard's men leave their guns, and, cheering wildly, brandishing cutlass and pike, swarm down into the boats.

'Will you look at those swine! They reckon the fight's over,' grunted Ned Tyler. 'They're going in for the looting.'

Hal hesitated. Two more devil ships still lay at the edge of the forest, but to launch them would take too long. 'Then we must give them aught to change their opinion,' he said grimly, and gripped the burning match between his teeth. He waded out as deep as his armpits to where the first devil ship bobbed, just off the beach, and lobbed the slow-match onto the high pile of cordwood. It spluttered and flared, blue smoke poured from it and drifted away on the sluggish breeze as the pitch-soaked logs caught fire.

Hal grabbed the painter attached to the bows, and dragged her out into the channel. Within a dozen yards he was into deeper water and had lost the bottom. He swam round to the stern, and found a purchase on it, kicked out strongly with both legs and the boat moved away.

Aboli saw what he was doing and plunged headlong into the lagoon. With a few powerful strokes he reached Hal's side. With both of them swimming it out, the boat moved faster.

With one hand on the stern Hal lifted his head clear of the water to orientate himself and saw the flotilla of small boats from the *Gull* heading in towards the beach. They were crowded with wildly yelling seamen, their weapons glinting in the morning light. So certain was the Buzzard of his victory that he could have left only a few men aboard to guard the ship.

Hal glanced over his shoulder and saw that both Ned and Daniel had followed his example. They had led the rest of the gang into the water and were clinging to the sterns of two more craft, kicking the water to a white froth behind them as they pushed out into the channel. From all three boats rose tendrils of smoke as the flames took hold in the loads of pitch-soaked firewood.

Hal dropped back beside Aboli and set himself to work doggedly with both legs, pushing the boat ahead of him, down the channel to where the *Gull* lay at anchor. Then the incoming tide caught them firmly in its flood and, like a trio of crippled ducks, bore them along more swiftly.

As Hal's boat swung its bows around he had a better view of the beach. He recognized the flaming red head and beard of the Buzzard in the leading longboat heading into the attack on the encampment, and fancied that, even in the uproar, he heard peals of his laughter carrying over the water.

Then he had something else to think about for the fire in the cargo above him gained a firm hold and roared into boisterous life. The flames crackled and leapt high in columns of dense black smoke. They danced and swayed as their heat created its own draught, and the single sail filled with more determination.

'Keep her moving!' Hal panted to Aboli beside him. 'Steer her two points more to larboard.'

A gust of heat swept over him so fiercely that it seemed to suck the air from his lungs. He ducked his head beneath the surface and came up snorting, water cascading down his face from his sodden hair, but still kicking with all his strength. The *Gull* lay less than a cable's length dead ahead. Daniel and Ned followed close behind him, both their vessels wreathed in tarry black smoke and dark orange flame. The air over them quivered and throbbed with the heat like a desert mirage.

'Keep her going,' Hal blurted. His legs were beginning to ache unbearably, and he spoke more to himself than to Aboli. The painter tied to the bows of the devil ship trailed back, threatening to wrap around his legs, but he kicked it away – there was no time to loosen it.

126

He saw the first of the *Gull*'s longboats reach the beach and Cumbrae leap ashore, swinging his claymore in flashing circles around his head. As he landed on the sand he threw back his head, uttered a blood-curdling Gaelic war-cry, then went bounding up the steep beach. As he reached the trees he looked back to make certain his men were following him. There he paused with his sword held high, and stared back across the channel at the tiny squadron of devil ships, blooming with smoke and flame and bearing down steadily upon his anchored *Gull*.

'Nearly there!' Hal gasped, and the waves of heat that broke over his head seemed to fry his eyeballs in their sockets. He plunged his head underwater again to cool it, and this time when he came up he saw that the *Gull* lay only fifty yards ahead.

Even above the crackling roar of the flames he heard the Buzzard's roar: 'Back! Back to the *Gull*. The bastards are sending fireships at her.' The frigate was stuffed with the booty of a long, hard privateering cruise, and her crew sent up a wild chorus of outrage as they saw the fruits of three years so endangered. They raced back to their boats even faster than they had charged up the beach.

The Buzzard stood in the bows of his, prancing and gesticulating so that he threatened to upset her balance. 'Let me get my hands on the pox-ridden swine. I'll rip out their windpipes, I'll split their stinking—' At that moment he recognized Hal's head at the stern of the leading fireship, lit by the full glare of the swirling flames, and his voice rose a full octave. 'It's Franky's brat, by God! I'll have him! I'll roast his liver in his own fire!' he shrieked, then lapsed into crimson-faced, inarticulate rage and hacked at the air with his claymore to spur his crew to greater speed.

Hal was only a dozen yards now from the *Gull*'s tall side, and found fresh strength in his exhausted legs. Tirelessly Aboli swam on, using a powerful frog-kick that pushed back the water in a swirling wake behind him.

With the Buzzard's longboat bearing down swiftly upon them, they covered the last few yards and Hal felt the fireship's bows thump heavily into the *Gull*'s stern timbers. The push of the tide pinned her there, swinging her broadside so that the flames were fanned by the rising morning breeze to lick up along the *Gull*'s side, scorching and blackening the timbers.

'Latch onto her!' bellowed the Buzzard. 'Get a line on her and tow her off!' His oarsmen shot straight in towards the fireship but, as they felt the full heat blooming out to meet them, they quailed. In the bows the Buzzard threw up his hands to cover his face, and his red beard crisped and singed. 'Back off!' he roared. 'Or we'll fry.' He looked at his coxswain. 'Give me the anchor! I'll grapple her, and we'll tow her off.'

127

Hal was on the point of diving and swimming under water out of the circle of heat but he heard Cumbrae's order. The painter still trailed around his legs, and he groped beneath the surface for the end, clenching it between his feet. Then he sank below the water and swam under the fireship's hull, coming up in the narrow gap between it and the *Gull*.

The *Gull*'s rudder stock broke the surface and, spitting lagoon water from his mouth, Hal threw a loop of the painter around the pintle. His face felt as though it were blistering as the heat beat down upon his head with hammer strokes, but he hitched the flaming craft securely to the *Gull*'s stern.

Then he dived again and came up next to Aboli. 'To the beach!' he gasped. 'Before the fire reaches the *Gull*'s powder store.'

Both struck out overarm, and Hal saw the longboat, close by, almost close enough to touch, but the Buzzard had lost all interest in them. He was whirling the small anchor around his head, and as Hal watched he hurled it out over the burning vessel, hooking onto her.

'Lie back on your oars!' he shouted at his crew. 'Tow her off.' The boatmen went to it with all their strength, but immediately the fireship came up short on the mooring line Hal had tied, and their blades beat the water vainly. She would not tow, and now the planking of the *Gull*'s side was smouldering ominously.

Fire was the terror of all seamen. The ship was built of combustibles and stuffed with explosives, wood and pitch, canvas and hemp, tallow, spice barrels and gunpowder. The faces of the longboat's crew were contorted with terror. Even the Buzzard was wild-eyed in the firelight as he looked up and saw the other two fireships drifting remorselessly upon him. 'Stop those others!' he pointed with his claymore. 'Turn them away!' Then he turned his attention back to the burning vessel moored to the *Gull*.

By now Hal and Aboli were fifty yards away, swimming for the beach, but Hal rolled onto his back to watch and trod water. He saw at once that the Buzzard's efforts to tow away the fireship had failed.

Now he rowed around to the *Gull*'s bows and scrambled up onto her deck. As his crew followed him he roared, 'Buckets! Get a bucket chain going. Pumps! Ten men on the pumps. Spray the flames!' They scurried to obey, but the fire was spreading swiftly, eating into the stern and dancing along the gunwale, reaching up hungrily towards the furled sails on their outstretched yards.

One of the *Gull*'s longboats had grappled Ned's fireship and, with frantically beating oars, was dragging it clear. Another was trying to get a line on Big Daniel's fireship, but the flames forced them to keep their distance. Each time they succeeded in hooking on, Daniel swam round

128

and cut the rope with a stroke of his knife. The men in the longboat who carried muskets and pistols were firing wildly at his bobbing head, but though the balls kicked up spray all around him, he seemed invulnerable.

Aboli had swum on ahead, and now Hal rolled onto his belly and followed him back to the beach. Together they raced up the white sand, and into the shot-shattered forest. Sir Francis was still in the gunpit where they had left him, but he had gathered around him a scratch crew of the *Resolution*'s survivors. They were reloading the big gun as Hal ran up to him and shouted, 'What do you want me to do?'

'Take Aboli with you to find some more of the men. Load another culverin. Bring the *Gull* under fire.' Sir Francis did not look up from the gun, and Hal ran back among the trees. He found half a dozen men, and he and Aboli kicked and dragged them out of the holes and bushes where they were cowering, and led them back to the silenced battery.

In the few short minutes it had taken him to gather the guncrew, the scene out on the lagoon had changed completely. Daniel had guided his fireship up to the *Gull*'s side and had secured her there. Her flames were adding to the confusion and panic on board the frigate. Now he was swimming back to the beach. He had seized two of his men, who could not swim, and was dragging them through the water.

The *Gull*'s crew had snared Ned's fireship – they had lines on it and were dragging it clear. Ned and his three fellows had abandoned it, and were also floundering back towards the shore. But, even as Hal watched, one gave up and slipped below the surface.

The sight of the drowning spurred Hal's anger: he poured a handful of powder into the culverin's touch hole as Aboli used an iron marlinspike to train the barrel around. It bellowed deafeningly, and Hal's men shouted with delight as the full charge of grape smashed into the longboat towing Ned's abandoned craft. It disintegrated at the blast, and the men packed into her were hurled into the lagoon. They splashed about, screaming for aid and trying to clamber into another longboat nearby, but it was already overcrowded and the men in her tried to beat off the frantic seamen with their oars. Some, though, managed to get a hold on the gunwale, and yelling and fighting among themselves, they caused the longboat to list heavily, until suddenly she capsized. The water around the burning hulks was filled with wreckage and the heads of struggling swimmers.

Hal was concentrating on reloading, and when he looked up again, he saw that some of the men in the water had reached the *Gull* and were climbing the rope ladders to the deck.

The Buzzard had at last got his pumps working. Twenty men were bobbing up and down like monks at prayer as they threw their weight on the handles, and white jets of water were spurting from the nozzles of the canvas hoses, aimed at the base of the flames, which were now spreading over the Gull's stern.

Hal's next shot shattered the wooden rail on the Gull's larboard side, and went on to sweep through the gang serving the bow pump. Four were snatched away, as though by an invisible set of claws, their blood splattering the others beside them on the handles. The jet of water from the hose shrivelled away.

'More men here!' Cumbrae's voice resounded across the lagoon, as he sent others to take the places of the dead. At once the jet of water was revived, but it made little impression on the leaping flames that now engulfed the Gull's stern.

Big Daniel reached the shore, and dropped the two men he had rescued on the sand. He ran up into the trees, and Hal shouted, 'Take command of one of the guns. Load with grape and aim at her decks. Keep them from fighting the fire.'

Big Daniel grinned at Hal with black teeth and knuckled his forehead. 'We'll play his lordship a pretty tune to dance to,' he promised.

The crew of the Resolution, who had been demoralized by the Gull's sneak attack, now began to take heart again at the swing in fortunes. One or two more emerged from where they had been skulking in the forest. Then, as the fire started to crash from the beach batteries and thump into the Gull's hull, the others grew bold and rushed back to serve the guns.

Soon a sheet of flame and smoke was tearing from out of the trees across the water. Flames had reached the Gull's mizzen-yards and were taking hold in the furled sails.

Hal saw the Buzzard striding through the smoke, lit by the flames of his burning ship, an axe in his hand. He stood over the anchor rope where it was drawn tightly through its fair lead and, with one gigantic swing he cut it free. Immediately the ship began to drift across the wind. He raised his head and bellowed an order to his seamen, who were clambering up the shrouds.

They shook out the main sail and the ship responded quickly. As she caught the rising breeze, the flames poured outwards, and the fire-fighters were able to run forward and direct the water from the hoses onto the base of the fire.

She towed the two fireships for a short distance, but when the lines that secured them burned through, the Gull left them as she headed slowly down the channel.

Along the beach the culverins continued to pour salvo after salvo

130

into her but, as she drew out of range, the battery fell silent. Still streaming smoke and orange flame behind her, the *Gull* headed for the open sea. Then, as she entered the channel between the heads and looked to have sailed clear away, the batteries hidden in the cliffs opened up on her. Gunsmoke billowed out from among the grey rocks and cannonballs kicked up spouts of foam along the *Gull*'s waterline or punched holes in her sails.

Painfully she ran this gauntlet, and at last left the smoking batteries out of range.

'Mr Courteney!' Sir Francis shouted at Hal – even in the heat of the battle he had used the formal address. 'Take a boat and cross to the heads. Keep the *Gull* under observation.'

Hal and Aboli reached the far side of the bay, and climbed up to the high ground on top of the heads. The *Gull* was already a mile offshore, reaching across the wind with sail set on her two forward masts. Wisps of dark grey smoke trailed from her stern, and Hal could see that her mizzen sails and her spanker were blackened and still smouldering. Her decks seethed with the tiny figures of her crew as they snuffed out the last of the fire and laboured to get the ship under full control and sailing handily again.

'We have given his lordship a lesson he'll long remember,' Hal exulted. 'I doubt we'll be having any more trouble from him for a while.'

'The wounded lion is the most dangerous,' Aboli grunted. 'We have blunted his teeth, but he still has his claws.'

When Hal stepped out of the boat onto the beach below the encampment he found that his father already had a gang of men at work, repairing the damage to the battery of culverins along the shore. They were building up the parapets and levelling the two guns that had been shot off their mountings by the *Gull*'s broadsides.

Where she lay careened on the beach, the *Resolution* had been hit by shot. The *Gull*'s fire had knocked great raw wounds in the timbers. Grape shot had peppered her sides but had not penetrated her stout planks. The carpenter and his mates were already at work cutting out the damaged sections and checking the frames beneath them, preparatory to replacing them with new oak planking from the ship's stores. The pitch cauldrons were bubbling and smoking over the coals, and the rasping of saws and soughing of planes resounded through the camp.

Hal found his father further back among the trees, where the wounded

131

had been laid out under a makeshift canvas shelter. He counted seventeen and, at a glance, could tell that at least three were unlikely to see tomorrow's dawn. Already the aura of death hung over them.

Ned Tyler doubled as the ship's surgeon – he had been trained for the role in the rough empirical school of the gundeck, and he wielded his instruments with the same rude abandon as the carpenters working on the *Resolution*'s punctured hull.

Hal saw that he was performing an amputation. One of the topmast-men had taken a blast of grape in his leg just below the knee and the limb hung by a tatter of flesh and exposed stringy white sinew from which protruded sharp white splinters of the shin bone. Two of Ned's mates were trying to hold down the patient on a sheet of blood-soaked canvas, as he bucked and writhed. They had thrust a doubled layer of leather belt between his teeth. The sailor bit down so hard upon it that the sinews in his neck stood out like hempen ropes. His eyes started out of his straining crimson face and his lips were drawn back in a terrifying rictus. Hal saw one of his rotten black teeth explode under the pressure of his bite.

He turned his eyes away and began his report to Sir Francis. 'The *Gull* was heading west the last I saw of her. The *Buzzard* seems to have the fire in hand, although she is still making a cloud of smoke—'

He was interrupted by screams as Ned laid aside his knife and took up the saw to trim off the shattered bone. Then, abruptly, the man lapsed into silence and slumped back in the grip of the men who held him. Ned stepped back and shook his head. 'Poor bastard's taken shore leave. Bring one of the others.' He wiped the sweat and smoke from his face with a blood-caked hand and left a red smear down his cheek.

Although Hal's stomach heaved, he kept his voice level as he went on with his report. 'Cumbrae was cracking on all the sail the *Gull* would carry.' He was determined not to show weakness in front of his men and his father, but his voice trailed off as near at hand Ned started to pluck a massive wood splinter from another seaman's back. Hal could not drag away his eyes.

Ned's two brawny assistants straddled the patient's body and held him down, while he got a grip on the protruding end of the splinter with a pair of blacksmith's tongs. He placed one foot on the man's back to give himself purchase and leaned back with all his weight. The raw splinter was as thick as his thumb, barbed like an arrowhead and relinquished its grip in the living flesh only with the greatest reluctance. The man's screams rang through the forest.

At that moment Governor van de Velde came waddling towards them through the trees. His wife was on his arm, weeping pitifully and barely able to support her own weight. Zelda followed her closely, attempting to thrust a green bottle of smelling-salts under her mistress's nose.

'Captain Courteney!' van de Velde said. 'I must protest in the strongest possible terms. You have placed us in the most dire danger. A ball passed through the roof of my abode. I might have been killed.' He mopped at his streaming jowls with his neckcloth.

At that moment the wretch who had been receiving Ned's ministrations let out a piercing shriek as one of the assistants poured hot pitch to staunch the bleeding into the deep wound in his back.

'You must keep these oafs of yours quiet.' Van de Velde waved disparagingly towards the severely wounded seaman. 'Their barnyard bleatings are frightening and offending my wife.'

With a last groan the patient sagged back limply into silence, killed by Ned's kindness. Sir Francis's expression was grim as he lifted his hat to Katinka. 'Mevrouw, you cannot doubt our consideration for your sensibilities. It seems that the rude fellow prefers to die rather than offend you further.' His expression was hard and unkind as he went on, 'Instead of caterwauling and indulging in the vapours, perhaps you might like to assist Master Ned with his work of tending the wounded?'

Van de Velde drew himself to his full height at the suggestion and glared at him. 'Mijnheer, you insult my wife. How dare you suggest that she might act as a servant to these coarse peasants?'

'I apologize to your lady, but I suggest that if she is to serve no other purpose here other than beautifying the landscape you take her back to her hut and keep her there. There will almost certainly be further unpleasant sights and sounds to test her forbearance.' Sir Francis nodded at Hal to follow him, and turned his back on the Governor. Side by side, he and his son strode towards the beach, past where the sailmakers were stitching the dead into their canvas shrouds and a gang was already digging their graves. In such heat they must be buried the same day. Hal counted the canvas-covered bundles.

'Only twelve are ours,' his father told him. 'The other seven are from the *Gull*, washed up on the beach. We have taken eight prisoners too. I'm going to deal with them now.'

The captives were under guard on the beach, sitting in a line with their hands clasped behind their heads. As they came up to them Sir Francis said, loudly enough for all to hear, 'Mr Courteney, have your men set eight nooses from that tree.' He pointed to the outspreading branches of a huge wild fig. 'We will hang some new fruit from them.' He gave a chuckle so macabre that Hal was startled.

The eight sent up a wail of protest. 'Don't hang us, sir. It were his lordship's orders. We only did as we was bade.'

Sir Francis ignored them. 'Get those ropes hung up,' Mr Courteney.

For a moment longer Hal hesitated. He was appalled at the prospect of having to carry out such a cold-blooded execution, but then he saw his father's expression and hurried to obey.

In short order ropes were thrown over the stout branches and the nooses were knotted at the hanging ends. A team of the *Resolution*'s sailors stood ready to heave their victims aloft.

One at a time the eight prisoners from the *Gull* were dragged to a rope's end, their hands bound behind their backs, their heads thrust through the waiting nooses. At his father's orders Hal went down the line and adjusted the knots under each victim's ears. Then he turned back to face his father, pale-faced and sick to the stomach. He touched his forehead. 'Ready to proceed with the execution, sir.'

Sir Francis's face was turned away from the condemned men and he spoke softly from the corner of his mouth. 'Plead for their lives.'

'Sir?' Hal looked bewildered.

'Damn you.' Sir Francis's voice cracked. 'Beg me to spare them.'

'Beg your pardon, sir, but will you not spare these men?' Hal said loudly.

'The blackguards deserve nothing but the rope's end,' Sir Francis snarled. 'I want to see them dance a jig to the devil.'

'They were only carrying out the orders of their captain.' Hal warmed to the role of advocate. 'Will you not give them a chance?'

The noosed heads of the eight men swung back and forth as they followed the argument. Their expressions were abject, but their eyes held a faint glimmer of hope.

Sir Francis fingered his chin. 'I don't know.' His face was still ferocious. 'What would we do with them? Turn them loose into the wilderness to serve as fodder for wild beasts and cannibals? It would be more merciful to string them up.'

'You could swear them in as crew to replace the men we have lost,' Hal pleaded.

Sir Francis looked still more dubious. 'They would not take an oath of allegiance, would they?' He glared at the condemned men who, had not the nooses restrained them, might have fallen to their knees.

'We will serve you truly, sir. The young gentleman is right. You'll not find better men nor more loyal than us.'

'Bring my Bible from my hut,' Sir Francis growled, and the eight seamen took their oath of service with the nooses round their necks.

Big Daniel freed them and led them away, and Sir Francis watched them go with satisfaction. 'Eight prime specimens to replace some of our losses,' he murmured. 'We'll need every hand we can find if we are

134

to have the *Resolution* ready for sea before the end of this month.' He glanced across the lagoon at the entrance between the headlands. 'Only the good Lord knows who our next visitors might be if we linger here.'

He turned back to Hal. 'That leaves only the drunken sots who lapped up the Buzzard's rum. Do you fancy another flogging, Hal?'

'Is this the time to render half our crew useless with the cat, Father? If the Buzzard returns before we are fit for sea, then they'll fight no better with half the meat stripped off their backs.'

'So you say let them go scot free?' Sir Francis asked coldly, his face close to Hal's.

'Why not fine them their share of the spoils from the *Standvastigheid* and divide it among the others who fought sober?'

Sir Francis stared at him a moment longer, then smiled grimly. 'The judgement of Solomon! Their purses will give them more pain than their backs, and it will add a guilder or three to our own share of the prize.'

Angus Cochran, Earl of Cumbrae, stepped out on the saddle of the mountain pass at least a thousand feet above the beach where he had come ashore from the *Gull*. His boatswain and two seamen followed him. They all carried muskets and cutlasses. One of the men balanced a small keg of drinking water on his shoulder, for the African sun speedily sucks the moisture from a man's body.

It had taken half the morning of hard hiking, following the game trails along the steep and narrow ledges, to reach this lookout point, which Cumbrae knew well. He had used it more than once before. A Hottentot they had captured on the beach had first led him to it. Now as he settled comfortably on a rock that formed a throne-like seat, the Hottentot's white bones lay at his feet in the undergrowth. The skull gleamed like a pearl, for it had lain here three years and the ants and other insects had picked it clean. It would have been foolhardy of Cumbrae to allow the savage to carry tales of his arrival to the Dutch colony at Good Hope.

From his stone throne Cumbrae had a breathtaking panoramic view of two oceans and of rugged mountain scenery spread out all around him. When he looked back the way he had come he could see the *Gull of Moray* anchored not far off a tiny rind of beach that clung precariously to the foot of the soaring rocky cliffs where the mountains fell into the sea. There were twelve distinct peaks in this maritime range, marked on the Dutch charts he had captured as the Twelve Apostles.

He stared at the *Gull* through his telescope but could see little evidence of the fire damage she had suffered to her stern. He had been able to replace the mizzen yards, and furled new sails upon them. From this great height and distance she looked lovely as ever, tucked away from inquisitive eyes in the green water cove below the Apostles.

The longboat that had brought Cumbrae through the surf was still drawn up on the beach, ready for a swift departure if he should run into trouble ashore. However, he expected none. He might encounter a few Hottentots among the bushes but they were a harmless, half-naked tribe, a pastoral people with high cheekbones and slanted Asiatic eyes, who could be scattered willy-nilly by a musket shot over their heads.

Much more dangerous were the wild animals that abounded in this harsh, untamed land. The previous night, from the deck of the anchored *Gull*, they had heard terrifying, blood-chilling roars, rising and falling, then ending in a diminishing series of grunts and groans that sounded like the chorus of all the devils of hell.

'Lions!' the older hands who knew the coast had whispered to each other, and the ship's company had listened in awed silence. In the dawn they had seen one of the terrible yellow cats, the size of a pony, with a dense dark mane of hair covering its head and reaching back behind its shoulder, sauntering along the white beach sands with a regal indolence. After that it had taken the threat of the lash to force the boat crew to row Cumbrae and his party to the shore.

He reached into the leather pouch that hung in front of his plaid and brought out a pewter flask. He tipped its base to the sky and swallowed twice, then sighed with pleasure and screwed the stopper back into the neck. His boatswain and the two seamen watched him intently, but he grinned at them and shook his head. 'It would do you no good. Mark my words, whisky is the devil's own hot piss. If you have no pact with him, as I have, you should never let it past your lips.'

He slipped the flask back into the pouch, and lifted the telescope to his eye. On his left hand rose the sphinx-shaped mountain top that the earliest mariners had named Lion's Head, when viewing it from the sea. At his right hand stood the sheer cliff that towered up to the flat top of the mighty Table Mountain that dominated the horizon and gave its name to the bay that opened out beneath it.

Far below where he sat, Table Bay was a lovely sweep of open water, nursing a small island in its arms. The Dutch called it Robben Island, for that was their name for the thousands of seals that infested it.

Beyond that was the endless wind-flecked expanse of the south

Atlantic. Cumbrae scrutinized it for any sign of a strange sail, but when he could pick out nothing he transferred his attention below to the Dutch settlement of Good Hope.

There was little to make it stand out from the wild and rocky wilderness that surrounded it. The roofs of the few buildings were of thatch and blended into their surroundings. The Company gardens, which had been laid out to grow provisions for the VOC ships on their passage to the east, were the most obvious sign of man's intrusion. The regular rectangular fields were either bright green with crops or chocolate brown with new-turned earth.

Just above the beach was the Dutch fort. Even from this distance Cumbrae could see that it was unfinished. He had heard from other captains that since the outbreak of war with England the Dutch had tried to speed up the construction, but there were still raw gaps in the defensive outer walls, like missing teeth.

The fort, and its half-completed state, were of interest to Cumbrae only in as much as it could afford protection to the ships that lay at anchor in the bay, under its guns. At this moment three large vessels were there, and he fastened his attention on them.

One looked like a naval frigate. She flew the ensign of the Republic, orange, white and blue, from her masthead. Her hull was painted black, but the gunports were picked out in white. He counted sixteen on the side she presented to him. He judged that she would outgun the *Gull* if it ever came to a set-piece engagement with her. But that was not his intention. He wanted easier pickings, and that meant one of the other two vessels in the bay. Both were merchantmen, and both flew the Company ensign.

'Which one is it to be?' he mused, as he glassed them with the closest attention.

One looked familiar. She rode high in the water, and he reckoned that she was probably in ballast and on the eastern leg of her voyage, heading out to the Dutch possessions to take on valuable cargo.

'No, by God, I recognize the cut of her jib now,' he exclaimed aloud. 'She's the *Lady Edwina*, Franky's old ship. He told me he'd sent her back to the Cape with his ransom demand.' He studied her a while longer. 'She's been stripped bare – even the guns are out of her.'

Losing interest in her as a possible prize, Cumbrae turned his telescope on the second merchantman. This ship was slightly smaller than the *Lady Edwina* but she was heavy with her cargo, riding so low that her lower ports were almost awash. Clearly she was on her return voyage, and stuffed with the treasures of the Orient. What made her even more attractive was that she was anchored further off the beach than the

137

other merchantman, at least two cables' length from the walls of the fort. Even under the best conditions that would be impossibly long cannon-shot for the Dutch gunners on the shore.

'A lovely sight.' The Buzzard grinned to himself. 'Fair makes one's mouth water to behold her.'

He spent another half-hour studying the bay, noting the lines of foam and spindrift that marked the flow of current along the beach and the set of the wind as it swirled down from the heights. He planned his entry into Table Bay. He knew that the Dutch had a small post on the slopes of Lion's Head whose lookouts would warn the settlement of the approach of a strange ship with a cannon-shot.

Even at midnight, with the present phase of the moon, they might be able to pick out the gleam of his sails while he was still well out at sea. He would have to make a wide circle, out below the horizon and then come in from the west, using the bulk of Robben Island as a stalking horse to creep in unobserved by even the sharpest lookout.

His crew were well versed in the art of cutting out a prize from under the shore batteries. It was a special English trick, one beloved of both Hawkins and Drake. Cumbrae had polished and refined it, and considered himself the master of either of those great Elizabethan pirates. The pleasure of plucking out a prize from under the enemy's nose rewarded him far beyond the spoils it yielded. 'Mounting the good wife while the husband snores in the bed beside her – so much sweeter than tipping up her skirts while he's off across the seas with no danger in it.' He chuckled, and swept the bay with his telescope, checking that nothing had changed since his last visit, that there were no lurking dangers such as newly emplaced cannon along the shore.

Even though the sun was past its noon and it was a long journey back to where the longboat waited on the beach, he spent a little longer studying the rigging of the prize through the glass. Once he had seized her, his men must be able to get her sails up speedily, and work her off the lee shore in the darkness.

It was after midnight when the Buzzard, using as his landmark the immense bulk of Table Mountain which blotted out half the southern sky, brought the *Gull* into the bay from the west. He was confident that, even on a clear starry night like this with half a moon shining, he was still well out of sight of the lookout on Lion's Head.

The dark whale shape of Robben Island rose with startling suddenness out of the gloom ahead. He knew there was no permanent settlement on this barren piece of rock so he was able to bring the *Gull* close into its lee, and drop his anchor in seven fathoms of protected water.

The longboat on deck was ready to launch. No sooner had the catted anchor splashed into the easy swells, than it was swung outboard and dropped to the surface. The Buzzard had already inspected the boarding-party. They were armed with pistol and cutlass and oak clubs, and their faces were darkened with lamp-black so that they looked like a party of wild savages with only their eyes and teeth gleaming. They were dressed in pitch-blackened sea-jackets, and two men had axes to cut the anchor cable of the prize.

The Buzzard was the last man down the ladder into the longboat, and as soon as he was aboard they pushed off. The oars were muffled, the rowlocks padded, and the only sound was the dip of the blades, but even this was lost in the breaking of the waves and the gentle sighing of the wind.

Almost immediately they crept out from behind the island they could see the lights on the mainland, two or three pinpricks from the watchfires on the walls of the fort, and lantern beams from the buildings outside the walls, spread out along the seafront.

The three vessels he had spotted from the saddle of the mountains were still anchored in the roads. Each showed a riding lantern at the masthead, and another at the stern. Cumbrae grinned in the darkness. 'Most obliging of the cheese-heads to put out a welcome for us. Don't they know there's a war a-raging?'

From this distance he was not yet able to distinguish one ship from the others, but his boat-crews pulled eagerly, the scent of the prize in their nostrils. Half an hour later, even though they were still well out in the bay, Cumbrae was able to pick out the *Lady Edwina*. He discarded her from his calculations and switched all his interest to the other vessel, which had not changed position and still lay furthest away from the batteries of the fort.

'Steer for the ship on the larboard side,' he ordered his boatswain in a whisper. The longboat altered a point, and the beat of the oars picked up. The second boat was close astern, like a hunting dog at heel, and Cumbrae peered back at its dark shape, grunting with approval. All the weapons were covered, there was no reflection of moonlight off a naked blade or pistol barrel to flash a warning to the watch on board the chase. Neither was there a lit match to send the reek of smoke down the wind, or a glow of light ahead of their arrival.

As they glided in towards the anchored vessel Cumbrae read her name from her transom, *De Swael*, the *Swallow*. He was alert for any sign of an anchor watch: this was a lee shore, with the sou'-easter swirling unpredictably around the mountain, but either the Dutch captain was remiss or the watch was asleep for there was no sign of life aboard the dark ship.

Two sailors stood ready to fend off from the side of the *Swallow* as they touched, and mats of knotted oakum hung over the longboat's side to soften the impact. A solid contact of timbers against hull would carry through the ship like the sounding body of a viol and wake every hand aboard.

They touched with the gentleness of a virgin's kiss, and one of the men, chosen for his simian climbing prowess, shot up the side and immediately made a line fast to the shackle of a gun train and dropped the coil back into the boat below.

Cumbrae paused long enough to lift the shutter of the storm lantern and light the slow-match from the flame, then seized the line and went up on bare feet hardened by hunting the stag without boots. In a silent rush the crews of both boats, also barefoot, followed him.

Cumbrae jerked the marlinspike from his belt and, his boatswain at his side, raced silently to the bows. The anchor watch was curled on the deck, out of the wind, sleeping like a hound in front of the hearth. The Buzzard stooped over him and clipped his skull with one sharp blow of the iron spike. The man sighed, uncurled his limbs and sagged into an even deeper state of unconsciousness.

His men were already at each of the *Swallow*'s hatches, leading to the lower decks, and as Cumbrae ran back towards the stern they were quietly closing the covers and battening them down, imprisoning the Dutch crew below decks.

'There'll no' be more than twenty of a crew on board her,' he muttered to himself. 'And, like as not, de Ruyter will have taken most of the prime seamen for the Navy. They'll be only boys and fat old fools on their last legs. I doubt they'll give us too much trouble.'

He looked up at the dark figures of his men silhouetted against the stars as they raced up the shrouds and danced out along the yards. As the sails unfurled, he heard from forward the soft clunk of an axe blow as the anchor cable was severed. Immediately the *Swallow* came alive and unfettered under his feet as she paid off before the wind. Already his boatswain was at the whipstaff.

'Take her straight out. Due west!' Cumbrae snapped, and the man put her head up into the wind as close as she would point.

Cumbrae saw at once that the heavily laden ship was surprisingly handy, and that they would be able to weather Robben Island on this tack. Ten armed men waited ready to follow him. Two carried shuttered storm lanterns, all had match burning for their pistols. Cumbrae seized one of the lanterns and led his men at a run down into the officers' quarters in the stern. He tried the door of the cabin that must open out onto the stern galleries and found it unlocked. He went through it swiftly and silently. When he flashed the lantern, a man in a tasselled night cap sat up in the bunk.

'Wie is dit?' he challenged sleepily. Cumbrae swept the bedclothes over his head to smother any further outcry, left his men to subdue and bind the captain, ran out into the passageway and burst into the next cabin. Here another Dutch officer was already awake. Plump and middle-aged, his greying hair tangled in his eyes, he was still staggering groggily with sleep as he groped for his sword where it hung in its scabbard at the foot of his bunk. Cumbrae shone the lantern in his eyes, and placed the sharp point of his claymore at the man's throat.

'Angus Cumbrae, at your service,' said the Buzzard. 'Yield, or I'll feed you to the gulls a wee bittie at a time.'

The Dutchman might not have understood the burred Scots accent, but Cumbrae's meaning was unmistakable. Gaping at him, he raised both hands above his head and the boarding-party swarmed over him and bore him to the deck, wrapping his bedclothes around his head.

Cumbrae ran on to the last cabin but, as he laid his hand on the door, it was flung open from inside with such force that he was thrown across the passage into the bulkhead. A huge figure charged out of the darkened doorway with a blood-curdling yell. He aimed a full overhead blow at the Buzzard, but in the narrow confines of the passageway the blade of his sword slashed into the door lintel, giving Cumbrae an instant to recover. Still bellowing with rage the stranger cut at him again. This time the Buzzard parried and the blade sped over his shoulder to shatter the panel behind him. The two big men raged down the passageway, fighting at close range, almost chest to chest. The Dutchman was shouting insults in a mixture of English and his own language, and Cumbrae answered him in full-blooded Scottish tones: 'You blethering cheese-headed nun-raper! I'll stuff your giblets down your ear-holes.' His men danced around them with clubs raised, waiting for an opportunity to cut down the Dutch officer, but Cumbrae shouted, 'Don't kill him! He's a dandy laddie, and he'll fetch a pretty price at ransom!'

Even in the uncertain lantern light, he had recognized his adversary's quality. Freshly roused from his bunk the Dutchman wore no wig on his shaven head but his fine pointed moustaches showed him to be a man of fashion. His embroidered linen nightshirt and the sword he wielded with the panache of a duelling master all proved that he was a gentleman, and no mistake.

The longer blade of the claymore was a disadvantage in the restricted space, and Cumbrae was forced to use the point rather than the double edges. The Dutchman thrust, then feinted low and slipped in under his guard. Cumbrae hissed with anger as the steel flew under his raised right arm, missing him by a finger's width and slashing a shower of splinters from the panel behind him.

Before his adversary could recover, the Buzzard whipped his left arm around the man's neck and enfolded him in a bear-hug. Locked together in the narrow passage, neither man could use his sword. They dropped them and wrestled from one end of the corridor to the other, snarling and snapping like a pair of fighting dogs, then grunting and howling with pain and outrage as first one then the other threw a telling fist to the head or smashed his elbow into the other's belly.

'Crack his skull,' Cumbrae gasped at his men. 'Knock the brute down.' He was unaccustomed to being bested in a straight trial of muscle, but the other was his match. His upthrust knee crashed into the Buzzard's crotch, and he howled again, 'Help me, damn your poxy yellow livers! Knock the rogue down!'

He managed to get one hand free and lock it round the man's waist then, bright crimson in the face with the effort, he lifted him and swung him round so that his back was presented to a seaman waiting with a raised oak club in his fist. It cracked down with a practised and controlled blow on the back of the shaven pate, not hard enough to shatter bone, but with just sufficient force to stun the Dutchman and turn his legs to jelly under him. He sagged in Cumbrae's arms.

Puffing, the Buzzard lowered him to the deck, and all four seamen bounced on him, pinning his limbs and straddling his back. 'Get a rope on this hellion,' he panted, 'afore he comes to and wrecks us and smashes up our prize.'

'Another filthy English pirate!' the Dutchman mouthed weakly, shaking his head to clear his wits and thrashing around on the deck as he tried to throw off his captors.

'I'll not put up with your foul insults,' Cumbrae told him genially, as he smoothed his ruffled red beard and retrieved his claymore. 'Call me a filthy pirate if you will, but I'm no Englishman and I'll thank you to remember it.'

'Pirates! All you scum are pirates.'

'And who are you to call me scum, you with your great hairy arse sticking in the air?' In the scuffle the Dutchman's night shirt had rucked up around his waist leaving him bare below. 'I'll not argue with a man in such indecent attire. Get your clothes on, sir, and then we will continue this discourse.'

Cumbrae ran up onto the deck, and found that they were already well out to sea. Muffled shouts and banging were coming from under the battened-down hatches, but his men had full control of the deck. 'Smartly done, you canty bunch of sea-rats. The easiest fifty guineas you'll ever put in your purses. Give yerselves a cheer, and cock a snook at the devil,' he roared so that even those up on the yards could hear him.

Robben Island was only a league dead ahead, and as the bay opened before them they could make out the *Gull* lying on the moonlit waters.

'Hoist a lantern to the masthead,' Cumbrae ordered, 'and we'll put a wee stretch of water between us before the cheese-heads in the fort rub the sleep out of their eyes.'

As the lantern went aloft, the *Gull* repeated the signal to acknowledge. Then she hoisted her anchor and followed the prize out to sea.

'There is bound to be a good breakfast in the galley,' Cumbrae told his men. 'The Dutchies know how to tend their bellies. Once you have them locked neatly in their own chains, you can try their fare. Boatswain, keep her steady as she goes. I'm going below to have a peep at the manifest, and to find what we've caught ourselves.'

The Dutch officers were trussed hand and foot, and laid out in a row on the deck of the main cabin. An armed seaman stood over each man. Cumbrae shone the lantern in their faces, and examined them in turn. The big warlike officer lifted his head and bellowed up at him, 'I pray God that I live to see you swinging on the rope's end, along with all the other devil-spawned English pirates who plague the oceans.' It was obvious that he had fully recovered from the blow to the back of his head.

'I must commend you on your command of the English language,' Cumbrae told him. 'Your choice of words is quite poetic. What is your name, sir?'

'I am Colonel Cornelius Schreuder in the service of the Dutch East India Company.'

'How do you do, sir? I am Angus Cochran, Earl of Cumbrae.'

'You, sir, are nothing but a vile pirate.'

'Colonel, your repetitions are becoming just a wee bit tiresome. I implore you not to spoil a most promising acquaintanceship in this manner. After all, you are to be my guest for some time until your ransom is paid. I am a privateer, sailing under the commission of His Majesty King Charles the Second. You, gentlemen, are prisoners of war.'

143

'There is no war!' Colonel Schreuder roared at him scornfully. 'We gave you Englishmen a good thrashing and the war is over. Peace was signed over two months ago.'

Cumbrae stared at him in horror, then found his voice again. 'I do not believe you, sir.' Suddenly he was subdued and shaken. He denied it more to give himself time to think than with any conviction. News of the English defeat at the Medway and the battle of the Thames had been some months old when Richard Lister had given it to him. He had also reported that the King was suing for peace with the Dutch Republic. Anything might have happened in the meantime.

'Order these villains of yours to release me, and I will prove it to you.' Colonel Schreuder was still in a towering rage, and Cumbrae hesitated before he nodded at his men.

'Let him up and untie him,' he ordered.

Colonel Schreuder sprang to his feet and smoothed his rumpled moustaches as he stormed off to his own cabin. There, he took down a silk robe from the head of his bunk. Tying the belt around his waist he went to his writing bureau and opened the drawer. With frosty dignity, he came back to Cumbrae and handed him a thick bundle of papers.

The Buzzard saw that most were official Dutch proclamations in both Dutch and English, but that one was an English news-sheet. He unfolded it with trepidation, and held it at arm's length. It was dated August 1667. The headline was in heavy black type two inches tall:

PEACE SIGNED WITH DUTCH REPUBLIC!

As his eye raced down the page, his mind tried to adjust to this disconcerting change in circumstances. He knew that with the signing of the peace treaty all Letters of Marque, issued by either side in the conflict, had become null and void. Even had there been any doubt about it, the third paragraph on the page confirmed it:

All privateers of both combatant nations, sailing under commission and Letters of Marque, have been ordered to cease warlike expeditions forthwith and to return to their home ports to submit themselves to examination by the Admiralty assizes.

The Buzzard stared at the news-sheet without reading further, and pondered the various courses of action open to him. The *Swallow* was a rich prize, the Good Lord alone knew just how rich. Scratching his beard he toyed with the idea of flouting the orders of the Admiralty assizes,

144

and hanging on to it at all costs. His great-grandfather had been a famous outlaw, astute enough to back the Earl of Moray and the other Scottish lords against Mary, Queen of Scots. After the battle of Carberry Hill they had forced Mary to abdicate and placed her infant son James upon the throne. For his part in the campaign his ancestor had received his earldom.

Before him all the Cochrans had been sheep thieves and border raiders, who had made their fortunes by murdering and robbing not only Englishmen but members of other Scottish clans as well. The Cochran blood ran true, so the consideration was not a matter of ethics. It was a calculation of his chances of getting away with this prize.

Cumbrae was proud of his lineage but also aware that his ancestors had come to prominence by adroitly avoiding the gibbet and the hangman's ministrations. During this last century, all the seafaring nations of the world had banded together to stamp out the scourge of the corsair and the pirate that, since the times of the pharaohs of ancient Egypt, had plagued the commerce of the oceans.

Ye'll not get away with it, laddie, he decided silently, and shook his head regretfully. He held up the news-sheet before the eyes of his sailors, none of whom was able to read. 'It seems the war is over, more's the pity of it. We will have to set these gentlemen free.'

'Captain, does this mean that we lose out on our prize money?' the coxswain asked plaintively.

'Unless you want to swing from the gallows at Greenwich dock for piracy, it surely does.'

Then he turned and bowed to Colonel Schreuder. 'Sir, it seems that I owe you an apology.' He smiled ingratiatingly. 'It was an honest mistake on my part, which I hope you will forgive. I have been without news of the outside world these past months.'

The Colonel returned his bow stiffly, and Cumbrae went on, 'It gives me pleasure to return your sword to you. You fought like a warrior and a true gentleman.' The Colonel bowed a little more graciously. 'I will give orders to have the crew of this ship released at once. You are, of course, free to return to Table Bay and to continue your voyage from there. Whither were you bound, sir?' he asked politely.

'We were on the point of sailing for Amsterdam before your intervention, sir. I was carrying letters of ransom to the council of the VOC on behalf of the Governor designate of the Cape of Good Hope who, together with his saintly wife, was captured by another English pirate, or rather,' he corrected himself, 'by another English privateer.'

Cumbrae stared at him. 'Was your Governor designate named Petrus van de Velde, and was he captured on board the company ship the *Standvastigheid?*' he asked. 'And was his captor an Englishman, Sir Francis Courteney?'

Colonel Schreuder looked startled. 'He was indeed, sir. But how do you know these details?'

'I will answer your question in due course, Colonel, but first I must know. Are you aware that the *Standvastigheid* was captured *after* the peace treaty was signed by our two countries?'

'My lord, I was a passenger on board the *Standvastigheid* when she was captured. Certainly I am aware that she was an illegal prize.'

'One last question, Colonel. Would not your reputation and professional standing be greatly enhanced if you were able to capture this pirate Courteney, to secure by force of arms the release of Governor van de Velde and his wife, and to return to the treasury of the Dutch East India Company the valuable cargo of the *Standvastigheid?*'

The Colonel was struck speechless by such a magnificent prospect. That image of violet-coloured eyes and hair like sunshine, which since he had last looked upon it had never been far from his mind, now returned to him in every vivid detail. The promise that those sweet red lips had made him outweighed even the treasure of spice and bullion that was at stake. How grateful the lady Katinka would be for her release, and her father also, who was president of the governing board of the VOC. This might be the most significant stroke of fortune that would ever come his way.

He was so moved that he could barely manage a stiff nod of agreement to the Buzzard's proposition.

'Then, sir, I do believe that you and I have matters to discuss that might redound to our mutual advantage,' said the Buzzard, with an expansive smile.

The following morning the *Gull* and the *Swallow* sailed in company back into Table Bay, and as soon as they had anchored under the guns of the fort the Colonel and Cumbrae went ashore. They landed through the surf, where a party of slaves and convicts waded out shoulder deep to drag their boat up the beach before the next wave could capsize it, and stepped out onto dry land without wetting their boots. As they strode together towards the gates of the fort they made a striking and unusual pair: Schreuder was in full uniform, his sashes, ribbons and the plumes in his hat fluttering in the sou'-easter. Cumbrae was resplendent in his plaid of red, russet, yellow and black. The population of this remote way-station had never seen a man dressed in such garb and crowded to the verge of the unpaved parade ground to gape at him.

Some of the doll-like Javanese slave girls caught Cumbrae's attention, for he had been at sea for months without the solace of feminine company. Their skin shone like polished ivory, and their dark eyes were languid. Many had been dolled up in European style by their owners, and their small, neat bosoms were jaunty under their lacy bodices.

Cumbrae acknowledged their admiration like royalty on a progress, lifting his beribboned bonnet to the youngest and prettiest of the girls, reducing them to titters and blushes with the bold stare of his blue eyes over the fiery bush of his whiskers.

The sentries at the gates of the fort saluted Schreuder, who was well known to them, and they went through into the interior courtyard. Cumbrae glanced around him with a penetrating eye, assessing the strength of the defences. It might be peace now, but who could tell what might transpire a few years from now? One day he might be leading a siege against these walls.

He saw that the fortifications were laid out in the shape of a five-pointed star. Clearly they had as their model the new fortress of Antwerp, which had been the first to adopt this innovative ground-plan. Each of the five points was crowned by a redoubt, the salient angles of which made it possible for the defenders to lay down a covering fire on the curtain walls of the fort, which before would have been dead ground, and indefensible. Once the massive outer walls of masonry were completed, the fort would be wellnigh impregnable to anything other than an elaborate siege. It might take many months to sap and mine the walls before they could be breached.

However, the work was far from finished. Gangs of hundreds of slaves and convicts were labouring in the moat and on top of the half-raised walls. Many of the cannon were stored in the courtyard and had not yet been sited in their redoubts atop the walls overlooking the bay.

'An opportunity lost!' the Buzzard wailed. This intelligence had come to him too late to be of profit. 'With another few Knights of the Order to help me – Richard Lister, and even Franky Courteney, before we fell out – I could have taken this fort and sacked the town. If we had combined our forces, the three of us could have sat here in comfort, commanding the entire southern Atlantic and snapping up every Dutch galleon that tried to round the Cape.'

As he looked around the courtyard, he saw that part of the fort was also used as a prison. A file of convicts and slaves in leg-irons was being led up from the dungeons under the northern wall. Barracks for the military garrison had been built above these foundations.

Although piles of masonry and scaffolding littered the courtyard, a company of musketeers in the green and gold doublets of the VOC was drilling in the only open space in front of the armoury.

Ox-drawn wagons, heavily laden with lumber and stone, rumbled in and out of the gates or cluttered the yard, and a coach, standing in splendid isolation, waited outside the entrance to the south wing of the building. The horses were a matching team of greys, groomed so that their hides gleamed in the sunlight. The coachman and footmen were in the green and gold Company livery.

'His excellency is in his office early this morning. Usually we don't see him before noon,' Schreuder grunted. 'News of your arrival must have reached the residence.'

They went up the staircase of the south wing and entered through teak doors with the Company crest carved into them. In the entrance lobby, with its polished yellow-wood floors, an aide-de-camp took their hats and swords, and led them through to the antechamber. 'I will tell his excellency that you are here,' he excused himself, as he backed out of the room. He returned in minutes. 'His excellency will see you now.'

The Governor's audience room overlooked the bay through narrow slit windows. It was furnished in a strange mixture of heavy Dutch furniture and Oriental artifacts. Flamboyant Chinese rugs covered the polished floors, and the glass-fronted cabinets displayed a collection of delicate ceramic ware in the distinctive and colourful glazes of the Ming dynasty.

Governor Kleinhans was a tall, dyspeptic man in late middle age, his skin yellowed by a life in the tropics and his features creased and wrinkled by the cares of his office. His frame was skeletal, his Adam's apple so prominent as to seem deformed, and his full wig too young in style for the withered features beneath it.

'Colonel Schreuder.' He greeted the officer stiffly, without taking his faded eyes, in their pouches of jaundiced skin, off the Buzzard. 'When I woke this morning and saw your ship was gone I thought you had sailed for home without my leave.'

'I beg your pardon, sir. I will give you a full explanation, but may I first introduce the Earl of Cumbrae, an English nobleman.'

'Scots, not English,' the Buzzard growled.

However, Governor Kleinhans was impressed by the title, and switched into good grammatical English, marred only slightly by his guttural accent. 'Ah, I bid you welcome to the Cape of Good Hope, my lord. Please be seated. May I offer you a light refreshment – a glass of Madeira, perhaps?'

With long-stemmed glasses of the amber wine in their hands, their high-backed chairs drawn up in a circle, the colonel leaned towards Kleinhans and murmured, 'Sir, what I have to tell you is a matter of the utmost delicacy,' and he glanced at the hovering servants and aide-de-camp. The Governor clapped his hands and they disappeared like smoke on the wind. Intrigued, he inclined his head towards Schreuder. 'Now, Colonel, what is this secret you have for me?'

Slowly, as Schreuder talked, the Governor's gloomy features lit with greed and anticipation, but, when Schreuder had finished his proposition he made a show of reluctance and scepticism. 'How do we know that this pirate, Courteney, will still be anchored where last you saw him?' he asked Cumbrae.

'As recently as twelve days ago the stolen galleon, the *Standvastigheid*, was careened upon the beach with all her cargo unloaded and her mainmast unstepped. I am a mariner, and I can assure you that Courteney could not have had her ready for sea again within thirty days. That means that we still have over two weeks in which to make our preparations and to launch our attack upon him,' the Buzzard explained.

Kleinhans nodded. 'So whereabouts is the anchorage in which this rascal is hiding?' The Governor tried to make the question casual, but his fever-yellowed eyes glinted.

'I can only assure you that he is well concealed.' The Buzzard side-stepped the question with a dry smile. 'Without my help your men will not be able to hunt him down.'

'I see.' With his bony forefinger the Governor picked at his nostril, then inspected the flake of dried snot he had retrieved. Without looking up, he went on, still casually, 'Naturally you would not require a reward for thus performing what is, after all, merely your bounden and moral duty, to root out this pirates' nest.'

'I would not ask for a reward, other than a modest amount to compensate me for my time and expenses,' Cumbrae agreed.

'One hundredth part of what we are able to recover of the galleon's cargo,' Kleinhans suggested.

'Not quite so modest,' Cumbrae demurred. 'I had in mind a half.'

'Half!' Governor Kleinhans sat bolt upright and his complexion turned the colour of old parchment. 'You are jesting, surely, sir.'

'I assure you, sir, that when it comes to money I seldom jest,' said the Buzzard. 'Have you considered how grateful the director-general of your company will be when you return his daughter to him unharmed, and without having to make the ransom payment? That alone would be a

149

compelling factor in augmenting your pension, without even taking into account the value of the cargo of spice and bullion.'

While Governor Kleinhans considered this he began to excavate his other nostril, and remained silent.

Cumbrae went on persuasively, 'Of course, once van de Velde is released from the clutches of this villain and arrives here, you will be able to hand over your duties to him, and then you will be free to return home to Holland where the rewards of your long and loyal service await you.' Colonel Schreuder had remarked on how avidly the Governor was looking forward to his imminent retirement, after thirty years in the Company's service.

Kleinhans stirred at such an inviting prospect, but his voice was harsh. 'A tenth of the value of the recovered cargo, but not to include the value of any pirates captured and sold on the slave block. A tenth, and that is my final offer.'

Cumbrae looked tragic. 'I shall have to divide the reward with my crew. I could not consider a lesser figure than a quarter.'

'A fifth,' grated Kleinhans.

'I agree,' said Cumbrae, well content.

'And, of course, I will need the services of that fine naval frigate anchored in the bay, and three companies of your musketeers with Colonel Schreuder here to command them. And my own vessel needs to be replenished with powder and cartridge, not to mention water and other provisions.'

It had taken a prodigious effort by Colonel Schreuder, but by late afternoon the following day the three companies of infantry, each comprising ninety men, were drawn up on the parade ground outside the walls of the fort, ready to embark. The officers and non-commissioned officers were all Dutch, but the musketeers were a mixture of native troops, Malaccans from Malaysia, Hottentots recruited from the tribes of the Cape, and Sinhalese and Tamils from the Company's possessions in Ceylon. They were bowed like hunchbacks under their weapons and heavy back-packs but, incongruously, they were barefoot.

As Cumbrae watched them march out through the gates, in their flat black caps, green doublets and white cross belts, their muskets carried at the trail, he remarked sourly, 'I hope they fight as prettily as they march, but I think they may be in for a wee surprise when they meet Franky's sea-rats.'

He could carry only a single company with all its baggage on board the *Gull*. Even then her decks would be crowded and uncomfortable, especially if they ran into heavy weather on the way.

The other two companies of infantry went on board the naval frigate. They would have the easier passage, for *De Sonnevogel*, the *Sun Bird*, was a fast and commodious vessel. She had been captured from Oliver Cromwell's fleet by the Dutch Admiral de Ruyter during the battle of the Kentish Knock, and had been in de Ruyter's squadron during his raid up the Thames only months previously to her arrival off the Cape. She was sleek and lovely in her glossy black paint, and snowy-white trim. It was easy to see that her sails had been renewed before she sailed from Holland, and all her sheets and rigging were spanking new. Her crew were mostly veterans of the two recent wars with England, prime battle-hardened warriors.

Her commander, Captain Ryker, was also a tough, rugged deep-water mariner, wide in the shoulder and big in the gut. He made no attempt to hide his displeasure at finding himself under the direction of a man who, until recently, had been his enemy, an irregular whom he considered little short of a greedy pirate. His bearing towards Cumbrae was cold and hostile, his scorn barely concealed.

They had held a council of war aboard *De Sonnevogel* which had not gone smoothly, Cumbrae refusing to divulge their destination and Ryker making objection to every suggestion and arguing every proposal that he put to him. Only the arbitration of Colonel Schreuder had kept the expedition from breaking down irretrievably before they had even left the shelter of Table Bay.

It was with a profound feeling of relief that the Buzzard at last watched the frigate weigh anchor and, with almost two hundred musketeers lining her rail waving fond farewells to the throng of gaudily dressed or half-naked Hottentot women on the beach, follow the little *Gull* out towards the entrance to the bay.

The *Gull*'s own deck was crowded with infantrymen, who waved and jabbered and pointed out the landmarks on the mountain and on the beach to each other, and hampered the seamen as they worked the *Gull* off the lee shore.

As the ship rounded the point below Lion's Head and felt the first majestic thrust of the south Atlantic, a strange quiet fell over the noisy passengers, and as they tacked and went onto a broad easterly reach, the first of the musketeers rushed to the ship's side, and shot a long yellow spurt of vomit directly into the eye of the wind. A hoot of laughter went up from the crew as the wind sent it all back into the wretch's pallid face and splattered his green doublet with the bilious evidence of his last meal.

151

Within the hour most of the other soldiers had followed his example, and the decks were so slippery and treacherous with their offerings to Neptune that the Buzzard ordered the pumps to be manned and both decks and passengers to be sluiced down.

'It's going to be an interesting few days,' he told Colonel Schreuder. 'I hope these beauties will have the strength to carry themselves ashore when we reach our destination.'

Before they had half completed their journey, it became apparent that what he had said in jest was in fact dire reality. Most of the troops seemed moribund, laid out like corpses on the deck with nothing left in their bellies to bring up. A signal from Captain Ryker indicated that those aboard the *Sonnevogel* were in no better case.

'If we put these men straight from the deck into a fight, Franky's lads will eat them up without spitting out the bones. We'll have to change our plans,' the Buzzard told Schreuder, who sent a signal across to the *Sonnevogel*. While he hove to, Captain Ryker came across in his skiff with obvious bad grace to discuss the new plan of assault.

Cumbrae had drawn up a sketch map of the lagoon and the shoreline that lay on each side of the heads. The three officers pored over this in the tiny cabin of the *Gull*. Ryker's mood had been alleviated by the disclosure of their final destination, by the prospect of action and prize money, and by a dram of whisky that Cumbrae poured for him. For once he was disposed to agree with the plan with which Cumbrae presented him.

'There is a another headland here, about eight or nine leagues west of the entrance to the lagoon.' The Buzzard laid his hand on the map. 'With this wind there will be enough calm water in the lee to send the boats ashore and land Colonel Schreuder and his musketeers on the beach. Then he will begin his approach march.' He stabbed at the map with a forefinger bristling with ginger hair. 'The interlude on dry land and the exercise will give his men an opportunity to recover from their malaise. By the time they reach Courteney's lair they should have some fire in them again.'

'Have the pirates set up any defences at the entrance to the lagoon?' Ryker wanted to know.

'They have batteries here and here, covering the channel.' Cumbrae drew a series of crosses down each side of the entrance. 'They are so well protected as to be invulnerable to return fire delivered by a ship entering or leaving the anchorage.' He paused as he remembered the rousing send-off those culverins had given the *Gull* as she fled from the lagoon after his abortive attack on the encampment.

152

Ryker looked sober at the prospect of subjecting his ship to close-range salvoes from entrenched shore batteries.

'I will be able to deal with the batteries on the western approaches,' Schreuder promised them. 'I will send a small detachment to climb down the cliffs. They will not be expecting an attack from their rear. However, I will not be able to cross the channel and reach the guns on the eastern headland.'

'I will send in another raiding party to put those guns out of the game,' Ryker cut in. 'As long as we can devise a system of signals to co-ordinate our attacks.' They spent another hour working out a code with flag and smoke between the ships and the shore. By this time the blood of both Ryker and Schreuder was a-boil, and they were vying for the opportunity to win battle honours.

Why should I risk my own sailors when these heroes are eager to do the work for me? the Buzzard thought happily. Aloud he said, 'I commend you, gentlemen. That is excellent planning. I take it you will delay the attacks on the batteries at the entrance until Colonel Schreuder has brought up his main force of infantry through the forest and is in a position to launch the main assault on the rear of the pirate encampment.'

'Yes, quite so,' Schreuder agreed eagerly. 'But as soon as the batteries on the heads have been put out of action, your ships will provide the diversion by sailing in through them and bombarding the pirates' encampment. That will be the signal for me to launch my land attack into their rear.'

'We will give you our full support.' Cumbrae nodded, thinking comfortably to himself, How hungry he is for glory, and restrained an avuncular urge to pat him on the shoulder. The idiot is welcome to my share of the cannonballs, just as long as I can get my hands on the prize.

Then he looked speculatively at Captain Ryker. It only remained to arrange that the *Sonnevogel* lead the squadron through the heads into the lagoon, and in the process draw the main attentions of Franky's culverins along the edge of the forest. It might be to his advantage if she were to sustain heavy damage before Franky was overwhelmed. If the Buzzard were in command of the only seaworthy ship at the end of the battle, he would be able to dictate his own terms when it came to disposing of the spoils of war.

'Captain Ryker,' he said with an arrogant flourish, 'I claim the honour of leading the squadron into the lagoon in my gallant little *Gull*. My ruffians would not forgive me if I let you go ahead of us.'

Ryker's lips set stubbornly. 'Sir!' he said stiffly. 'The *Sonnevogel* is more heavily armed, and better able to resist the balls of the enemy. I must insist that you allow me to lead the entry into the lagoon.'

And that takes care of that, thought the Buzzard, as he bowed his head in reluctant acquiescence.

Three days later they put Colonel Schreuder and his three companies of seasick musketeers ashore on a deserted beach and watched them march away into the African wilderness in a long untidy column.

The African night was hushed but never silent. When Hal paused on the narrow path, his father's light footfalls dwindled ahead of him, and Hal could hear the soft sounds of myriad life that teemed in the forest around him: the warbling call of a night bird, more hauntingly beautiful than ever musician coaxed from stringed instrument; the scrabbling of rodents and other tiny mammals among the dead leaves and the sudden murderous cry of the small feline predators that hunted them; the singing and hum of the insects and the eternal soughing of the wind. All were part of the hidden choir in this temple of Pan.

The beam of the storm lantern disappeared ahead of him, and now he stepped out to catch up. When they had left the encampment, his father had ignored his question, but when at last they emerged from the forest at the foot of the hills, he knew where they were going. The stones that still marked the Lodge within which he had taken his vows formed a ghostly circle in the glow of the waning moon. At the entry to it Sir Francis went down on one knee and bowed his head in prayer. Hal knelt beside him.

'Lord God, make me worthy,' Hal prayed. 'Give me the strength to keep the vows I made here in your name.'

His father lifted his head at last. He stood up, took Hal's hand and raised him to his feet. Then, side by side, they stepped into the circle and approached the altar stone. '*In Arcadia habito!*' Sir Francis said, in his deep, lilting voice, and Hal gave the response.

'*Flumen sacrum bene cognosco!*'

Sir Francis set the lantern upon the tall stone and, in its yellow light, they knelt again. For a long while they prayed in silence, until Sir Francis looked up at the sky. 'The stars are the ciphers of the Lord. They light our comings and our goings. They guide us across uncharted oceans. They hold our destiny in their coils. They measure the number of our days.'

154

Hal's eyes went immediately to his own particular star, Regulus. Timeless and unchanging it sparkled in the sign of the Lion.

'Last night I cast your horoscope,' Sir Francis told him. 'There is much that I cannot reveal, but this I can tell you. The stars hold a singular destiny in store for you. I was not able to fathom its nature.'

There was a poignancy in his father's tone, and Hal looked at him. His features were haggard, the shadows beneath his eyes deep and dark. 'If the stars are so favourably inclined, what is it that troubles you, Father?'

'I have been harsh to you. I have driven you hard.'

Hal shook his head. 'Father—'

But Sir Francis quieted him with a hand on his arm. 'You must remember always why I did this to you. If I had loved you less, I would have been kinder to you.' His grip on Hal's arm tightened as he felt Hal draw breath to speak. 'I have tried to prepare you and give you the knowledge and strength to meet that particular destiny that the stars have in store for you. Do you understand that?'

'Yes. I have known this all along. Aboli explained it to me.'

'Aboli is wise. He will be with you when I have gone.'

'No, Father. Do not speak of that.'

'My son, look to the stars,' Sir Francis replied, and Hal hesitated, uncertain of his meaning. 'You know which is my own star. I have shown it to you a hundred times before. Look for it now in the sign of the Virgin.'

Hal raised his face to the heavens, and turned it to the east where Regulus still showed, bright and clear. His eyes ran on past it into the sign of the Virgin, which lay close beside the Lion, and he gasped, his breath hissing through his lips with superstitious dread.

His father's sign was slashed from one end to the other by a scimitar of flame. A fiery red feather, red as blood.

'A shooting star,' he whispered.

'A comet,' his father corrected him. 'God sends me a warning. My time here draws to its close. Even the Greeks and the Romans knew that the heavenly fire is the portent of disaster, of war and famine and plague, and the death of kings.'

'When?' Hal asked, his voice heavy with dread.

'Soon,' replied Sir Francis. 'It must be soon. Most certainly before the comet has completed its transit of my sign. This may be the last time that you and I will be alone like this.'

'Is there nothing that we can do to avert this misfortune? Can we not fly from it?'

'We do not know whence it comes,' Sir Francis said gravely. 'We cannot escape what has been decreed. If we run, then we will certainly run straight into its jaws.'

'We will stay to meet and fight it, then,' said Hal, with determination.

'Yes, we will fight,' his father agreed, 'even if the outcome has been ordained. But that was not why I brought you here. I want to hand over to you, this night, your inheritance, those legacies both corporal and spiritual which belong to you as my only son.' He took Hal's face between his hands and turned it to him so that he looked into his eyes.

'After my death, the rank and style of baronet, accorded to your great-grandfather, Charles Courteney, by good Queen Bess after the destruction of the Spanish Armada, falls upon you. You will become Sir Henry Courteney. You understand that?'

'Yes, Father.'

'Your pedigree has been registered at the College of Arms in England.' He paused as a savage cry echoed down the valley, the sawing of a leopard hunting along the cliffs in the moonlight. As the dreadful rasping roars died away Sir Francis went on quietly, 'It is my wish that you progress through the Order until you attain the rank of Nautonnier Knight.'

'I will strive towards that goal, Father.'

Sir Francis raised his right hand. The band of gold upon his second finger glinted in the lantern light. He twisted it off, and held it to catch the moonlight. 'This ring is part of the regalia of the office of Nautonnier.' He took Hal's right hand, and tried the ring on his second finger. It was too large, so he placed it on his son's forefinger. Then he opened the high collar of his cloak, and exposed the great seal of his office that lay against his breast. The tiny rubies in the eyes of the lion rampant of England, and the diamond stars above it, sparkled softly in the uncertain light. He lifted the chain of the seal from around his own neck, held it high over Hal's head and then lowered it onto his shoulders. 'This seal is the other part of the regalia. It is your key to the Temple.'

'I am honoured but humbled by the trust you place in me.'

'There is one other part to the spiritual legacy I leave for you,' Sir Francis said, as he reached into the folds of his cloak. 'It is the memory of your mother.' He opened his hand and in his palm lay a locket bearing a miniature of Edwina Courteney.

The light was not strong enough for Hal to make out the detail of the portrait, but her face was graven in his mind and in his heart. Wordlessly he placed it in the breast pocket of his doublet.

'We should pray together for the peace of her soul,' said Sir Francis quietly, and both bowed their heads. After many minutes Sir Francis again raised his head. 'Now, it remains only to discuss the earthly

156

inheritance that I leave to you. There is firstly High Weald, our family manor in Devon. You know that your uncle Thomas administers the house and lands in my absence. The deeds of title are with my lawyer in Plymouth . . .' Sir Francis went on speaking for a long while, listing and detailing his possessions and estates in England. 'I have written all this in my journal for you, but that book may be lost or plundered before you can study it. Remember all that I have told you.'

'I will not forget any of it,' Hal assured him.

'Then there are the prizes we have taken on this cruise. You were with me when we cached the spoils from both the *Heerlycke Nacht* and from the *Standvastigheid*. When you return with that booty to England, be sure to pay over to each man of the crew the share he has earned.'

'I will do so without fail.'

'Pay also every penny of the Crown's share to the King's customs officers. Only a rogue would seek to cheat his sovereign.'

'I will not fail to render to my king.'

'I should never rest easy if I were to know that all the riches that I have won for you and my king were to be lost. I require you to make an oath on your honour as a Knight of the Order,' Sir Francis said. 'You must swear that you will never reveal the whereabouts of the spoils to any other person. In the difficult days that lie ahead of us, while the red comet rules my sign and dictates our affairs, there may be enemies who will try to force you to break this oath. You must bear always in the forefront of your mind the motto of our family. *Durabo!* I shall endure.'

'On my honour, and in God's name, I shall endure,' Hal promised. The words slipped lightly over his tongue. He could not know then that when they returned to him their weight would be grievous and heavy enough to crush his heart.

For his entire military career Colonel Cornelius Schreuder had campaigned with native troops rather than with men of his own race and country. He much preferred them, for they were inured to hardship and less likely to be affected by heat and sun, or by cold and wet. They were hardened against the fevers and plagues that struck down the white men who ventured into these tropical climes, and they survived on less food. They were able to live and fight on what frugal fare this savage and terrible land provided, whereas European troops would sicken and die if forced to undergo similar privations.

There was another reason for his preference. Whereas the lives of

Christian troops must be reckoned dear, these heathen could be expended without such consideration, just as cattle do not have the same value as men and can be sent to the slaughter without qualm. Of course, they were famous thieves and could not be trusted near women or liquor, and when forced to rely upon their own initiative they were as little children, but with good Dutch officers over them, their courage and fighting spirit outweighed these weaknesses.

Schreuder stood on a rise of ground and watched the long column of infantry file past him. It was remarkable how swiftly they had recovered from the terrible affliction of seasickness that only the previous day had prostrated most of them. A night's rest on the hard earth and a few handfuls of dried fish and cakes of sorghum meal baked over the coals, and this morning they were cheerful and strong as when they had embarked. They strode past him on bare feet, following their white petty-officers, moving easily under their burdens, chattering to each other in their own tongues.

Schreuder felt more confidence in them now than at any time since they had embarked in Table Bay. He lifted his hat and mopped at his brow. The sun was only just showing above the tree-tops but already it was hot as the blast from a baker's oven. He looked ahead at the hills and forest that awaited them. The map that the red-haired Scotsman had drawn for him was a rudimentary sketch that merely adumbrated the shoreline and gave no warning of this rugged terrain that they had encountered.

At first he had marched along the shore, but this proved heavy-going – under their packs the men sank ankle deep into sand at each pace. Also, the open beaches were interspersed with cliffs and rocky capes, which could cause further delay. So Schreuder had turned inland and sent his scouts ahead to find a way through the hills and forest.

At that moment there was a shout from up ahead. A runner was coming back down the line. Panting, the Hottentot drew himself up and saluted with a flourish. 'Colonel, there is a wide river ahead.' Like most of these troops he spoke good Dutch.

'Name of a dog!' Schreuder cursed. 'We will fall further behind and our rendezvous is only two days from now. Show me the way.' The scout led him towards the crest of the hill.

At the top of the slope a steep river valley opened beneath his feet. The sides were almost two hundred feet deep and densely covered with forest. At the bottom the estuary was broad and brown, racing out into the sea with the tide. He drew his telescope from its leather case and carefully scanned the valley where it cut deeply into the hills of the hinterland. 'There does not seem to be an easier way to cross and I cannot afford the time to search further.' He looked down at the drop. 'Fix ropes to those trees at the top to give the men purchase on the slope.'

It took them half the morning to get two hundred men down into the valley. At one stage a rope snapped under the weight of fifty men leaning on it to keep their footing as they descended. However, although most sustained grazes, cuts and sprains as they rolled down to the riverbank, there was one serious casualty. A young Sinhalese infantryman's right leg caught in a tree root as he fell, and was fractured in a dozen places below the knee, the sharp splinters of bone sticking out of his shin.

'Well, we're down with only one man lost,' Schreuder told his lieutenant, with satisfaction. 'It could have been more costly. We might have spent days searching for another crossing.'

'I will have a litter made for the injured man,' Lieutenant Maatzuyker suggested.

'Are you soft in the head?' Schreuder snapped. 'He would hold up the march. Leave the clumsy fool here with a loaded pistol. When the hyena come for him he can make his own decision who to shoot, one of them or himself. Enough talk! Let's get on with the crossing.'

From the bank Schreuder looked across a hundred-yard sweep of river, the surface dimpled with small whirlpools as the outgoing tide spurred the muddy waters on their race for the sea.

'We will have to build rafts—' Lieutenant Maatzuyker ventured, but Schreuder snarled, 'Nor can I afford the time for that. Get a rope across to the other bank. I must see if this river is fordable.'

'The current is strong,' Maatzuyker pointed out tactfully.

'Even a simpleton can see that, Maatzuyker. Perhaps that is why you had no difficulty in making the observation,' said Schreuder ominously. 'Pick your strongest swimmer!'

Maatzuyker saluted and hurried down the ranks of troops. They guessed what was in store and every one found something of interest to study in sky or forest, rather than meeting Maatzuyker's eye.

'Ahmed!' he shouted at one of his corporals, grabbed his shoulder and pulled him out of the huddle of men where he was trying to make himself inconspicuous.

Resignedly Ahmed handed his musket to a man in his troop and began to strip. His naked body was hairless and yellow, sheathed in lithe, hard muscle.

Maatzuyker knotted the rope under his armpits and sent him into the

159

water. As Ahmed edged out into the current it rose gradually to his waist. Schreuder's hopes for a swift, easy crossing rose with it. Ahmed's mates on the bank shouted encouragement as they paid out the line.

Then, when he was almost half-way across, Ahmed stumbled abruptly into the main channel of the river, and his head disappeared below the surface.

'Pull him back!' Schreuder ordered, and they hauled Ahmed back into the shallower water, where he struggled to regain his footing, snorting and coughing up the water he had swallowed.

Suddenly Schreuder shouted, with more urgency, 'Pull! Get him out of the water!'

Fifty yards upstream he had seen a mighty swirl on the surface of the opaque waters. Then a swift V-shaped wake sped down the channel to where the corporal was splashing about in the shallows. The team on the rope saw it then and, with yells of consternation, they hauled Ahmed in so vigorously that he was plucked over backwards and dragged thrashing and kicking towards the bank. However, the thing below the surface moved more swiftly still and arrowed in on the helpless man.

When it was only yards from him its deformed black snout, gnarled and scaled as a black log, thrust through the surface, and twenty feet behind the head a crested saurian tail exploded out. The hideous monster raced across the gap, and rose high out of the water, its jaws open to display the ragged files of yellow teeth.

Then Ahmed saw it, and shrieked wildly. With a crash like a falling portcullis the jaws closed over his lower body. Man and beast plunged below the surface in a whirlpool of creaming foam. The men on the line were jerked off their feet and dragged in a struggling heap down the bank.

Schreuder leapt after them and seized the rope's end. He took two turns around his wrist and flung his weight back on the line. Out in the brown tide-race there was another boiling explosion of foam as the huge crocodile, its fangs locked in Ahmed's belly, rolled over and over at dizzying speed. The other men on the line recovered their footing and hung on grimly. There was a sudden stain of red on the brown water as Ahmed was torn in half, the way a glutton might twist the leg off the carcass of a turkey.

The bloodstain was whipped away and dissipated downstream by the swift current, and the straining men fell back as the resistance at the other end of the rope gave way. Ahmed's upper torso was dragged ashore, arms jerking and mouth opening and shutting convulsively, like that of a dying fish.

160

Far out in the river the crocodile rose again, holding Ahmed's legs and lower torso crosswise in its jaws. It lifted its head to the sky and gulped and strained to swallow. As the dismembered carcass slid down into its maw, they saw it bulge the soft, pale scaly throat.

Schreuder was roaring with rage. 'This foul beast will delay us for days, if we allow it.' He rounded on the shaken musketeers who were dragging away Ahmed's sundered corpse. 'Bring that piece of meat back here!'

They dropped the corpse at his feet and watched in awe as he stripped off his own clothing, and stood naked before them, flat, hard muscle rippling his belly and his thick penis jutting out of the mat of dark hair at its base. At his impatient order they tied a rope under his armpits, then handed him a loaded musket with the match burning in the lock, which Schreuder shouldered. With his other hand he grabbed Ahmed's limp dead arm. An incredulous hum of amazement went up from the bank as Schreuder stepped into the river dragging the bleeding remnants with him. 'Come, then, filthy beast!' he bellowed angrily, as the water reached his knees and he kept going. 'You want to eat? Well, I have something for you to chew on.'

A moan of horror burst from every throat as, upstream from where Schreuder stood, with the water at his hips, there was another tremendous swirl and the crocodile rushed down-river towards him, leaving a long slick wake across the brown surface.

Schreuder braced himself and then, with a round-arm swing, hurled the upper half of Ahmed's dripping, dismembered corpse ahead of him into the path of the crocodile's flailing charge. 'Eat that!' he shouted, as he lifted the musket from his shoulder and levelled it at the human bait that bobbed only two arms' span ahead of him.

The monstrous head burst through the surface and the mouth opened wide enough to engulf Ahmed's pitifully shredded remains. Over the sights of the gun Schreuder looked down into its gaping jaws. He saw the ragged spikes of teeth, still festooned with shreds of human flesh, and beyond them the lining of the throat, which was a lovely buttercup yellow. As the jaws opened, a tough membrane automatically closed off the throat to prevent water rushing down it into the beast's lungs.

Schreuder aimed into the depths of the open throat and snapped the lock. The burning match dropped and there was an instant of delay as the powder flared in the pan. Then, as Schreuder held his aim unwaveringly, came a deafening roar and a long silver-blue spurt of smoke flew from the muzzle straight down the throat of the crocodile. Three ounces of antimony-hardened lead pellets drove through the membrane, tearing through windpipe, artery and flesh, lancing deep into the chest cavity, ripping through the cold reptilian heart and lungs.

Such a mighty convulsion racked the great lizard that fifteen feet of its length arched clear of the water and the grotesque head almost touched the crested tail before it fell back in a tall spout of foam. Then it rolled, dived and burst out again, swirling in leviathan contortions.

Schreuder did not pause to watch these hideous death throes, but dropped the smoking musket and dived head-first into the deepest part of the channel. Relying on the beast's frenzy to confuse and distract any other of the deadly reptiles, he lashed out towards the far bank with a full overarm stroke.

'Pay out the rope to him!' Maatzuyker yelled at the men who stood paralysed with shock, and they recovered their wits. Holding it high to keep it clear of the current they let it out as Schreuder clawed himself across the channel.

'Look out!' Maatzuyker shouted, as first one then another crocodile pushed through the surface. Their eyes were set on protuberant horny knuckles so they were able to watch the convulsions of their dying fellow without exposing the whole of their heads.

The softer splashes thrown up by Schreuder did not attract their attention until he was only a dozen strokes from the far bank, when one of the monsters sensed his presence. It turned and sped towards him, ripples spreading like a fan on each side of the twin lumps on its forehead.

'Faster!' Maatzuyker bellowed. 'He's after you!' Schreuder redoubled his stroke as the crocodile closed in swiftly upon him. Every man on the bank roared encouragement at him, but the crocodile was only a body length behind as Schreuder's feet touched the bottom. It raced in the last yard as Schreuder flung himself forward and the mighty jaws snapped closed only inches behind his feet.

Dragging the rope like a tail he staggered towards the tree-line – but still he was not clear of danger for the dragonlike creature raised itself on its stubby bowed legs as it came ashore, and waddled after him at a speed that the watchers could hardly credit. Schreuder reached the first tree of the forest only feet ahead of it and sprang for an overhanging branch. As the snaggle-toothed jaws clashed shut he was just able to lift his legs beyond their bite and, with the last of his strength, draw himself higher into the branches.

The frustrated reptile lurked below, circling the bole of the tree. Then, uttering a hissing roar, it retreated slowly down the bank. It carried high its long tail, crested like a gigantic cockscomb, but as it reached the river it lowered itself and slid back beneath the surface.

Even before it had disappeared, Schreuder shouted across the river, 'Make your end fast!'

He looped his own rope end around the thick trunk beside which he was perched, and knotted it. Then he yelled, 'Maatzuyker! Get those men busy building a raft. They can pull themselves over on the rope against the current.'

T he hull of the *Resolution* had been cleaned of weed and barnacles, and as the crew paid off her hoving lines she righted herself slowly against the press of the incoming tide.

While she had been careened on the beach, the carpenters had finished shaping and dressing the new mainmast, and it was at last ready to step. It took every hand to carry the long, heavy spar down to the beach and lift the thick end over the gunwale. The tackle was made fast to her other two standing masts, and the slings were adjusted to raise the new spar.

With gangs heaving cautiously on the lines, and Big Daniel and Ned directing them, they raised the massive length of gleaming pine towards the vertical. Sir Francis trusted no one else to supervise the crucial business of fitting the heel of the mast through the hole in the main deck and then sliding its length down through the hull to the step on the keelson of the ship. It was a delicate operation that needed the strength of fifty men, and took most of that day.

'Well done, lads!' Sir Francis told them, when at last the massive spar slid home the last few inches and the heel clunked heavily into its prepared step. 'Slack off!' No longer supported by the ropes, the fifty-foot mast stood of its own accord.

Big Daniel shouted up to the deck from where he stood waist deep in the lagoon, 'Now woe betide those cheese-heads. Ten days from today, we'll sail her out through the heads, you mark my words.'

Sir Francis smiled down at him from the rail. 'Not before we get the shrouds on that mainmast. And that will not happen while you stand there with your mouth open and your tongue wagging.'

He was about to turn away when suddenly he frowned at the shore. The Governor's wife had come out of the trees, followed by her maid, and now she stood at the top of the beach, spinning the handle of her parasol between her long white fingers so it revolved over her head, a brightly coloured wheel that drew the eye of every man of his crew. Even Hal, who was overseeing the gang on the foredeck, had turned from his work to gawk at her like a ninny. Today she was dressed in a fetching new costume, cut so low in front that her bosom bulged out almost to her nipples.

'Mr Courteney,' Sir Francis called, loud enough to shame his son in front of his men, 'give a mind to your work. Where are the wedges to steady that spar?'

Hal started, and flushed darkly under his tan as he turned from the rail and seized the heavy mallet. 'You heard the captain,' he snapped at his gang.

'That strumpet is the Eve in this paradise,' Sir Francis dropped his voice, and spoke from the side of his mouth to Aboli at his shoulder. 'I have seen Hal mooning at her before and, sweet heavens, she looks back at him bold as a harlot with her dugs sticking out. He is only a boy.'

'You see him through a father's eyes.' Aboli smiled and shook his head. 'He is a boy no longer. He is a man. You told me once that your holy book speaks of an eagle in the sky and a serpent on a rock, and a man with a maid.'

Although Hal could steal little time from his duties, he responded to Katinka's summons like a salmon returning to its native river in the spawning season. When she called him, nothing could stop him answering. He ran up the path with his heart keeping time to his flying feet. It was almost a full day since last he had been alone with Katinka, which was much too long for his liking. Sometimes he was able to sneak away from the camp to meet her twice or even thrice in a single day. Often they could be together only for a few minutes, but that was time enough to get the business done. The two wasted little of their precious time together in ceremony or debate.

They had been forced to find a meeting place other than her hut. Hal's midnight visits to the hostage stockade had almost ended in disaster. Governor van de Velde could not have been sleeping as soundly as his snores suggested and they had grown careless and rowdy in their love play.

Roused by his wife's unrestrained cries and Hal's loud responses, Governor van de Velde seized the lantern and crept up on her hut. Aboli, on guard without, saw the glimmer of it in time to hiss a warning, giving Hal a space to snatch up his clothing and duck out of the hole in the stockade wall, just as van de Velde burst into the hut with the lantern in one hand and a naked sword in the other.

164

He had complained bitterly to Sir Francis the following morning. 'One of your thieving sailors,' he accused.

'Is there any item of value missing from your wife's hut?' Sir Francis wanted to know and, when van de Velde shook his head, he was heavy with innuendo. 'Perhaps your wife should not make such a show of her jewels for they excite avaricious thoughts. In future, sir, it might be prudent to take better care of *all* your possessions.'

Sir Francis questioned the off-duty watch, but as the Governor's wife could supply no description of the intruder – she had been fast asleep at the time – the matter was soon dropped. That had been the last nocturnal visit Hal dared risk to the stockade.

Instead they had found this secret place to meet. It was well hidden but situated close enough to the camp for Hal to be able respond to her summons and to reach it in just a few minutes. He paused briefly on the narrow terrace in front of the cave, breathing deeply in his haste and excitement. He and Aboli had discovered it as they returned from one of their hunting forays in the hills. It was not really a cave, but an overhang where the soft red sandstone had been eroded from the harder rock strata to form a deep veranda.

They were not the first men to have passed this way. There were old ashes in the stone hearth against the back wall of the shelter, and the low roof was soot-stained. Littering the floor were the bones of fish and small mammals, remnants of meals that had been prepared at the hearth. The bones were dry and picked clean, and the ashes were cold and scattered. The hearth was long disused.

However, these were not the only signs of human occupation. The rear wall was covered from floor to roof with a wild and exuberant cavalcade of paintings. Horned antelope and gazelle that Hal did not recognize streamed in great herds across the smooth rock face, hunted by stick-like human archers with swollen buttocks and incongruously erect sexual members. The paintings were childlike and colourful, the perspective and the relative size of men and beasts fantastical. Some human figures dwarfed the elephant they pursued, and eagles were twice the size of the herds of black buffalo beneath their outstretched wings. Yet Hal was enchanted by them. Often in the intervals of quiet between wild bouts of lovemaking, he would lie staring up at these strange little men as they hunted the game and fought battles with each other. At those times he felt a strange longing to know more about the artists, and these heroic little hunters and warriors they had depicted.

When he asked Aboli about them, the big black man shrugged disdainfuly. 'They are the San. Not really men, but little yellow apes. If you are ever unfortunate enough to meet one of them, a fate from which

165

your three gods should protect you, you will find out more about their poison arrows than their paint pots.'

Today the paintings could hold his interest for only a moment, for the bed of grass that he had laid on the floor against the wall was empty. This was no surprise, for he was early to the tryst. Still, he wondered if she would come or if her summons had been capricious. Then, behind him, he heard the snap of a breaking twig from further down the slope.

He glanced around quickly for a place to hide. Down one side of the entrance trailed a curtain of vines, their dark green foliage starred with startlingly yellow blossoms, their light, sweet perfume wafting through the cave. Hal slipped behind it and shrank back against the rock wall.

A moment later Katinka sprang lightly onto the terrace outside the entrance and peered expectantly into the interior. When she realized it was empty, her frame stiffened with anger. She said one word in Dutch that, from her regular use of it, he had come to know well. It was obscene, and he felt his skin crawl with excitement at the delights presaged by that word.

Silently he slipped out from his hiding place and crept up behind her. He whipped one hand over her eyes and, with the other arm around her waist, lifted her off her feet and ran with her towards the bed of grass.

Much later Hal lay back on the grass mattress, his naked chest still heaving and running with sweat. She nibbled lightly at one of his nipples as though it were a raisin. Then she played with the golden medallion that hung from his neck.

'This is pretty,' she murmured. 'I like the red ruby eyes of the lion. What is it?' He did not understand this complex question in her language, and shrugged. She repeated it slowly and clearly.

'It is something given me by my father. It has great value to me,' he replied evasively.

'I want it,' she said. 'Will you give it to me?'

He smiled lazily. 'I could never do that.'

'Do you love me?' she pouted. 'Are you mad for me?'

'Yes, I love you madly,' he admitted, as with the back of his forearm he wiped the sweat out of his eyes.

'Then give me the medallion.'

He shook his head wordlessly and then, to avoid the looming argument, he asked, 'Do you love me as I love you?'

She gave a merry laugh. 'Don't be a silly goat! Of course I do not love you. Lord Cyclops is the only one I love.' She had nicknamed his sex after the one-eyed giant of the legend, and to affirm it she reached down to his groin. 'But even him I do not love when he is so soft and small.'

Her fingers were busy for a moment, and then she laughed again, this time throatily. 'There now, I love him better already. Ah, yes! Better still. The bigger he grows, the more I love him. I am going kiss him now to show him how much I love him.'

She slid the tip of her tongue down over his belly, but as she pushed her face into the dark bush of his pubic hair, a sound arrested her. It came rolling in across the lagoon below, and broke in a hundred booming echoes from the hills.

'Thunder!' Katinka cried, and sat up. 'I hate thunder. Ever since I was a little girl.'

'Not thunder!' Hal said, and pushed her away so roughly that she cried out again.

'Oh! You son of a pig, you have hurt me.'

But Hal took no heed of her complaint, and sprang to his feet. Naked, he rushed to the entrance of the cave and stared out. The entrance was situated high enough to enable him to see over the tops of the forest trees surrounding the lagoon. The bare masts of the *Resolution* towered into the blue noon sky. The air was filled with seabirds – the thunderous sound had startled them from the surface of the water and the sunlight sparkled on their wings so that circling high overhead they seemed to be creatures of ice and crystal.

A softly rolling bank of mist obscured half the lagoon. It blanketed the rocky cliffs of the heads in silvery-blue billows that were suddenly shot through with strange flickering lights. But this was not mist.

The thunder broke again, reaching Hal long after the flare of lights, the distant sound taking time to reach his ears. The swirling clouds thickened, spilling densely and heavily as oil across the lagoon waters. Above this cloud bank, the tall masts and sails of two great ships floated as though suspended above the waters. He stared at them, stupefied, as they sailed in serenely between the heads. Another broadside broke from the leading ship. He saw at once that she was a frigate, her black hull trimmed with white, her gunports gaping and the fire and smoke boiling out of her. High above the smoke banks the tricolour of the Dutch Republic rippled in the light noon breeze. In line behind her the *Gull of Moray* followed daintily, the colours of St George and St Andrew and the great red cross of the Temple bedecking her masts and rigging, her culverins bellowing out their warlike chorus.

'Merciful God!' Hal cried. 'Why do not the batteries at the entrance return their fire?'

Then with his naked eye he saw strange soldiers in green uniform overrunning the gun emplacements at the foot of the cliffs, their swords and the steel heads of their pikes flashing in the sunlight as they

167

slaughtered the gunners, and flung their bodies over the parapets into the sea below.

'They have surprised our men in the forts. The Buzzard has led the Dutch to us, and shown them where our guns are placed.' His voice trembled with outrage. 'He will pay with his blood for this day, I swear it.'

Katinka sprang up from the grass mattress and ran to the entrance beside him. 'Look! It is a Dutch ship, come to rescue me from the den of your foul pirate father. I give thanks to God! Soon I will be away from this forsaken place and safe at Good Hope.' She danced with excitement. 'When they hang you and your father from the gibbet on the parade outside the fort, I shall be there to blow you one last kiss and to wave you farewell.' She laughed mockingly.

Hal ignored her. He ran back into the cave, pulled on his clothing hastily and belted on the Neptune sword.

'There will be fighting and great danger, but you will be safe if you stay here until it is over,' he told her, and started down.

'You cannot leave me alone here!' she screamed after him. 'Come back here, I command you!'

But he took no notice of her pleas and raced down the footpath through the trees. *I should never have allowed her to tempt me from my father's side,* he lamented silently as he ran. *He warned me of the danger of the red comet. I deserve whatever cruel fate awaits me now.*

He was in such distress that he was oblivious to all but the need to take up his neglected duties and almost ran full tilt into the lines of skirmishing soldiers moving through the trees ahead of him. Just in time, he smelt the smoke of their burning match and then picked out their green doublets and the white cross belts as they wove their way through the trees of the forest. He flung himself to the ground and rolled behind the trunk of a tall wild fig tree. He peered out from behind it, and saw that the strange green-clad ranks were moving away from him, advancing on the encampment, pikes and muskets at the ready, keeping good order under the direction of a white officer.

Hal heard the officer call softly in Dutch, 'Keep your spacing. Do not bunch up!' There could be no doubt now whose troops these were. The Dutchman's back was still turned, and Hal had a moment's respite to think. *I must reach the camp to warn my father, but there is not enough time to find a way round. I will have to fight my way through the enemy ranks.* He drew the sword from its scabbard and rose on one knee, then paused as a thought struck him with force. *We are outnumbered on land and on the water. This time there are no fireships to drive off the Buzzard and the Dutch frigate. The battle may go hard for us.*

Using the point of his sword, he scratched a hole in the soft, loamy soil at the base of the wild fig. Then he slipped the ring from his finger and the locket with the miniature of his mother from his pocket and dropped them into the hole. After that he lifted the seal of the Nautonnier from his neck and laid it on top of his other treasures. He swept the loose soil back over them, and tamped it down with the flat of his hand.

It had taken him only a minute but when he started to his feet the Dutch officer had disappeared into the forest ahead. Hal crept forward, guided to his quarry by the rustle and crackle of the undergrowth. Without their officers these men will not fight so well, he thought. If I can take this one I will quench some of the fire in their bellies. He slowed as he drew closer to the man he was stalking, and came up behind the Dutchman as he pushed his way through the undergrowth, the noise of his progress masking the fainter sounds of Hal's approach.

The Dutchman was sweating in dark wet patches down the back of his serge coat. By his epaulettes Hal realized that he was a lieutenant in the Company's army. He was thin and lanky, with angry red pustules studding the back of his scrawny neck. He carried his bared sword in his right hand. He had not bathed for many days and smelt like a wild boar.

'On guard, Mijnheer!' Hal challenged him in Dutch, for he could not run him through the back. The lieutenant spun round to face him, lifting his blade into the guard.

His eyes were pale blue, and they flew wide with shock and fright as he found Hal so close behind him. He was not much older than Hal, and his face blanched with terror, emphasizing the rash of purple acne that covered his chin.

Hal thrust and their blades rasped as they crossed. He recovered swiftly, but with that first light touch he had assessed his adversary. The Dutchman was slow and his wrist lacked the snap and power of a practised swordsman. His father's words rang in his ears. 'Fight from the first stroke. Do not wait until you are angry.' And he gave his heart over to a cold, murderous rage to kill. 'Ha!' he grunted, and feinted high, aiming the point at the Dutchman's eyes but balanced for his parry. The lieutenant was slow to counter, and Hal knew he could risk the flying attack that Daniel had taught him against such a foe. He could go for the quick kill.

His wrist tempered to steel by hours with Aboli on the practice deck, he caught up the Dutchman's blade, and whirled it with a stirring motion that threw the point off the line of defence. He had created an opening, but to exploit it with the flying attack he must open his own

169

guard and place himself in full jeopardy of the Dutchman's natural riposte – suicide in the face of a skilled opponent.

He committed himself, throwing his weight forward over his left foot, and sped his point in through the other man's guard. The riposte came too late, and Hal's steel spiked through the sweat-stained serge cloth. It glanced off a rib and then found the gap between them. Despite the days he had spent with a sword in his hand this was Hal's first kill with the cold steel, and he was unprepared for the sensation of his blade running through human flesh.

It was a soggy, dead feeling, which smothered the speed of his thrust. Lieutenant Maatzuyker gasped and dropped his own sword as Hal's point stopped at last against his spine. He clutched at Hal's razor-sharp blade with bare hands. It slashed his palms to the bone, severing the sinews in a quick flush of bright blood. His fingers opened nervelessly, and he sank to his knees staring up into Hal's face with watery blue eyes, as though he were about to burst into tears.

Hal stood over him, and tugged at the sapphire pommel of the Neptune sword, but the Toledo blade clung fast in the wet flesh. Maatzuyker gasped in agony and held up his mutilated hands in appeal.

'I am sorry,' Hal whispered in horror, and heaved again on his sword hilt. This time Maatzuyker opened his mouth wide and whimpered. The blade had passed through his right lung, and a sudden gout of blood burst through his pale lips, poured down his coat front and splashed Hal's boots.

'Oh God!' Hal muttered, as Maatzuyker toppled backwards with the blade between his ribs. For a moment, he stood helplessly, watching the other man choke on and drown in his own blood. Then, close behind him, came a wild shout from the bushes.

A green-jacketed soldier had spotted him. A musket boomed, the pellets rattled into the foliage above Hal's head and sang off the tree trunk beside him. He was galvanized. All along he had known what he must do but, until that moment, he had not been able to bring himself to do it. Now he placed his booted heel firmly on Maatzuyker's heaving chest and leaned back against the resistance of the trapped blade. He tugged once and then again with all his weight behind it. Reluctantly the blade slid out until suddenly it came free and Hal reeled backwards.

Instantly he recovered his balance and leapt over Maatzuyker's body just as another musket shot crashed out and the pellets hissed past his head. The soldier who had fired was fumbling with his powder flask as he tried to reload and Hal ran straight at him. The musketeer looked up in fright, then dropped his empty weapon and turned his back to run.

Hal would not use the point again but slashed at the man's neck, just below his ear. The razor edge cut to the bone, and the side of his neck opened like a grinning red mouth. The man dropped without a sound. But all around him the bushes were alive with green-jacketed figures. Hal realized there must be hundreds of them. This was not a raiding party but a small army attacking the encampment.

He heard shouts of alarm and anger, and now a constant barrage of musket fire, much of it wild and undirected, but some slashing into the undergrowth close on either side of him as he ran with all his speed and strength. In the midst of the uproar Hal recognized, by its power and authority, one stentorian voice.

'Get that man!' it bellowed in Dutch. 'Don't let him get away! I want that one.' Hal glanced in the direction from which it was coming, and almost tripped with the shock of seeing Cornelius Schreuder racing through the trees to head him off. His hat and wig flew from his head, but the ribbons and sash of his rank were gold. His shaven head gleamed like an eggshell. His moustaches were scored heavily across his face. For such a big man, he was fast on his feet, but fear made Hal faster.

'I want you!' Schreuder yelled. 'This time you will not get away.'

Hal put on a burst of speed and, within thirty flying paces, had forged ahead to see the stockade of the encampment through the trees. It was deserted and he realized that his father and every other man would have been decoyed away to the lagoon's edge by the heavy fire of the two warships, and that they must be manning the culverins in the emplacements.

'To arms!' he screamed as he ran, with Schreuder pounding along only ten paces behind him. 'Rally to me, the *Resolution*. In your rear!'

As he burst into camp he saw, with huge relief, Big Daniel and a dozen seamen responding to his call, rushing back from the beach to support him. Immediately Hal rounded on the Dutchman.

'Come, then,' he said, and went on guard. But Schreuder came up short as he saw the *Resolution*'s men bearing down on him and realized that he had outrun his own troops, had left them without a leader, and was now outnumbered twelve to one.

'Again you are lucky, puppy,' he snarled at Hal. 'But before this day ends, you and I will speak again.'

Thirty paces behind Hal, Big Daniel pulled up short and lifted the musket he carried. He aimed at Schreuder but, as the lock snapped, the Colonel ducked and spun on his heels, the shot went wide and he bounded back into the forest, shouting to rally his attacking musketeers as they came swarming forward through the trees.

'Master Daniel,' Hal panted, 'the Dutchman leads a strong force. The forest is full of men.'

'How many?'

'A hundred or more. There!' He pointed as the first of the attackers came running and dodging towards them, stopping to fire and reload their muskets, then running forward again.

'What's worse, there are two warships in the bay,' Daniel told him. 'One is the *Gull* but the other is a Dutch frigate.'

'I saw them from the hill.' Hal had recovered his breath. 'We are outgunned in front and outnumbered in the rear. We cannot stand here. They will be on us in a minute. Back to the beach.'

The coloured troops behind them clamoured like a pack of hounds as Hal turned and led his men back at a run. Ball and shot thrummed and whistled around them, kicking up spurts of damp earth at their heels, speeding them on their way.

Through the trees he could see the piled earth of the gun emplacements and the drifting bank of gunsmoke. He could make out the heads of his own gunners as they reloaded the culverins. Out in the lagoon the stately Dutch frigate bore down on the shore, wreathed in her own powder smoke. As Hal watched, she put her helm over, bringing her broadside to bear, and again her gunports bloomed with great flashes of flame. Seconds later the thunder of the cannonade and the blast of howling grape shot swept over them.

Hal flinched in the turmoil of disrupted air, his eardrums singing. Whole trees crashed down, and branches and leaves rained upon them. Directly in front of him he saw one of the culverins hit squarely, and hurled off its train. The bodies of two of the *Resolution*'s sailors were sent spinning high into the air.

'Father, where are you?' Hal tried to make himself heard in the pandemonium but then, through it all, he heard Sir Francis's voice.

'Stand to your guns, lads. Aim at the Dutchmen's ports. Give those cheese-heads out there some of our good English cheer.'

Hal leapt down into the gunpit beside his father, seized his arm and shook it urgently.

'Where have you been, boy?' Sir Francis glanced at him, but when he saw the blood on his clothing he did not wait for an answer. Instead he grunted, 'Take command of the guns on the left flank. Direct your fire—'

Hal interrupted, in a breathless rush, 'The enemy ships are only creating a diversion, Father. The real danger is in our rear. The forest is full of Dutch soldiers, hundreds of them.' He pointed back with his blood-stained blade. 'They'll be on us in a minute.'

Sir Francis did not hesitate. 'Go down the line of guns. Order every second culverin to be swung round and loaded with grape. The front guns continue to engage the ships, but hold your fire with the back guns until the attack in our rear is point-blank. I will give the order to fire. Now, go!' As Hal scrambled out of the pit, Sir Francis turned to Big Daniel. 'Take these men of yours, and any other loafers you can find, go back and slow the enemy advance in our rear.'

Hal raced down the line, pausing beside each gunpit to shout his orders and then running on. The sound of the barrage and the answering fire from the beach was deafening and confusing. He reeled and almost went sprawling to the ground as another broadside from the black frigate swept over him like the devil-winds of a typhoon, smashing through the forest and ploughing the earth around him. He shook his head to clear it and ran on, hurdling a fallen tree-trunk.

As he passed each emplacement and alerted the gunners, they began to train the culverins around, aiming them back into the forest. Back there they could already hear musket fire and angry shouts as Big Daniel and his small band of seamen charged into the advancing hordes that poured from the forest.

Hal reached the gunpit at the end of the line and jumped down beside Aboli, who was captaining the team of gunners there. Aboli thrust his burning match into the touch hole. The culverin leapt and thundered. As the stinking smoke swirled back over them, Aboli grinned at Hal, his dark face stained even darker with soot and his eyes bloodshot with smoke. 'Ah! I thought you might never pull your root out of the sugar field in time to join the fight. I feared I might have to come up to the cave, and prise you loose with an iron bar.'

'You will grin less happily with a musket ball in your tail feathers,' Hal told him grimly. 'We are surrounded. The woods behind us are full of Dutchmen. Daniel is holding them, but not for much longer. There are hundreds of them. Train this piece around and load with grape.' While they reloaded, Hal went on giving his orders. 'We'll have time for only one shot, then we'll charge them in the smoke,' he said as he tamped down the charge with the long ramrod. As he pulled it out, a sailor lifted the heavy canvas bag filled with lead shot, and forced it down the muzzle. Hal drove it down to sit upon the powder charge. Then they ducked behind the parapet on both sides of the gun, keeping clear of the area where the train would recoil, and stared past the stockade into the forest beyond. They could hear the ring of steel on steel and the wild shouts as Daniel's men charged then fell back before the counter-charge of the green-jackets. Musket fire hammered steadily as Schreuder's men reloaded and ran forward to fire again.

Now they caught glimpses through the trees of their own seamen coming back. Daniel towered above the others: he was carrying a wounded man over one shoulder and swinging a cutlass in his other hand. The green-jackets were pressing him and his party hard.

'Ready now!' Hal grated at the seamen around him, and they crouched below the parapet and fingered their pikes and cutlasses. 'Aboli, don't fire until Daniel is out of the line.'

Suddenly Daniel threw down his burden, and turned back. He raced into the thick of the enemy, and scattered them with a great swipes of his cutlass. Then he ran to the wounded seaman, slung him over his shoulder and came on again towards where Hal crouched.

Hal glanced down the line of gunpits. Although the forward-pointing cannon were still banging away at the ships in the lagoon, every second culverin was directed into the forest, waiting for the moment to loose a storm of shot into the lines of attacking infantry.

'At such short range the shot will not spread, and they are keeping their spaces,' Aboli muttered.

'Schreuder has them well under control,' Hal agreed grimly. 'We can't hope to bring too many down with a single volley.'

'Schreuder!' Aboli's eyes narrowed. 'You did not tell me it was him.'

'There he is!' Hal pointed at the tall wigless figure striding towards them through the trees. His sash glittered and his moustache bristled as he urged his musketeers forward.

Aboli grunted, 'That one is the devil. We'll have trouble from him.' He thrust an iron bar under the culverin and turned it round a few degrees, trying to bring the sights to bear on the colonel.

'Stand still,' he urged, 'for just long enough to give me a shot.' But Schreuder was moving up and down the ranks of his men, waving them on. He was so close now that his voice carried to Hal as he snapped at his men, 'Keep your line! Keep the advance going. Steady now, hold your fire!'

His control over them was apparent in the determined but measured advance. They must have been aware of the line of waiting guns, but they came forward without wavering, holding their fire, not wasting the one fair shot they carried in their muskets.

They were close enough for Hal to make out their individual features. He knew that the Company recruited most of its troops in its eastern colonies, and this was apparent in the Asiatic faces of many of the advancing soldiers. Their eyes were dark and almond-shaped and their skins a deep amber.

Suddenly Hal realized that the broadsides from the two warships had ceased and snatched a glance over his shoulder. He saw that both the

174

black frigate and the *Gull* had anchored a cable's length or so off the beach. Their guns were silent, and Hal realized that Cumbrae and the frigate captain must have arranged with Schreuder a code of signals. They had ceased firing for fear of hitting their own men.

That gives us a breathing space, he thought, and looked ahead again.

He saw that Daniel's band was much depleted: they had lost half their number, and the survivors were clearly exhausted by their foray and the fierce skirmishing. Their gait was erratic – many could barely drag themselves along. Their shirts were sodden with sweat and the blood from their wounds. One at a time they stumbled up and flopped over the parapet to lie panting in the bottom of the pit.

Daniel alone was indefatigable. He passed the wounded man over the parapet to the gunners and, so murderous was his mood, would have turned back and rushed at the enemy once more had not Hal stopped him. 'Get back here, you great ox! Let us soften them up with a little grape shot. Then you can have at them again.'

Aboli was still trying to line up the barrel on Schreuder's elusive shape. 'He is worth fifty of the others,' he muttered to himself, in his own language. Hal, though, was no longer paying him any heed, but trying anxiously to catch a glimpse of his father in the furthest emplacement, and take a lead from him.

'By God, he's letting them get too close!' he fretted. 'A longer shot would give the grape a chance to spread, but I'll not open fire before he gives the order.'

Then he heard Schreuder's voice again: 'Front rank! Prepare to fire!' Fifty men dropped obediently to their knees, right in front of the parapet, and grounded the butts of their muskets.

'Ready now, men!' Hal called softly to the sailors crowded around him. He had realized why his father had delayed the salvo of culverin until this moment: he had been waiting for the attackers to discharge their muskets, and then he would have them at a fleeting disadvantage as they tried to reload.

'Steady now!' Hal repeated. 'Wait for their volley!'

'Present your arms!' Schreuder's command rang out in the sudden silence. 'Take your aim!' The file of kneeling men lifted their muskets and aimed at the parapet. The blue smoke from the slow-match in the locks swirled about their heads, and they slitted their eyes to aim through it.

'Heads down!' Hal yelled.

The seamen in the gunpits ducked below the parapet, just as Schreuder roared, 'Fire!'

The long, ragged volley of musketry rattled down the file of kneeling men, and lead balls hissed over the heads of the gunners and thumped into the earth ramp. Hal leapt to his feet and looked down to the far end of the line of gunpits. He saw his father jump onto the parapet, brandishing his sword, and, although it was too far for his order to carry clearly, his gestures were unmistakable.

'Fire!' yelled Hal at the top of his lungs, and the line of guns erupted in a solid blast of smoke, flame and buzzing grape shot. It swept through the thin green line of Dutch infantry at point-blank range.

Directly in front of him Hal saw one of them hit by the full fury of the volley. He disintegrated in a burst of torn green serge and pink shredded flesh. His head spun high in the air, then fell back to earth and rolled like a child's ball. After that, all was obscured by the dense cloud of smoke, but though his ears still sang from the thunderous discharge, Hal could hear the screams and moans of the wounded resounding in the reeking blue fog.

'All together!' Hal shouted, as the smoke began to clear. 'Take the steel to them now, lads!'

After the mind-stopping blast of the guns their voices were thin and puny as they rose together from the gunpits. 'For Franky and King Charley!' they shouted, and the steel of cutlass and pike winked and twinkled as they jumped from the parapet and charged at the shattered rank of green uniforms.

Aboli was at Hal's left side and Daniel at his right as he led them into the mêlée. By unspoken agreement the two big men, one white the other black, placed protective wings over Hal but they had to run at their best speed to keep up with him.

Hal saw that his misgivings had been fully borne out. The volley of grape had not wrought the devastation among the Dutch infantry that they might have hoped for. The range had been too short: five hundred lead balls from each culverin had cut through them like a single charge of round shot. Men caught by the discharge had been obliterated, but for every one blown to nothingness, five others were unscathed.

These survivors were stunned and bewildered, their eyes dazed and their expressions blank. Most knelt blinking and shaking their heads, making no attempt to reload their empty muskets.

'Have at them, before they pull themselves together!' Hal screamed, and the seamen following him cheered again more lustily. In the face of the charge the musketeers started to recover. Some leapt to their feet, flung down their empty guns and drew their swords. One or two petty-officers had pistols tucked in their belts, which they drew and fired wildly at the seamen who rushed down on them. A few turned their backs and tried to flee back among the trees, but Schreuder was there to head them off. 'Back, you dogs and sons of dogs. Stand your ground like men!' They turned again, and formed up around him.

Every man of the *Resolution*'s crew who could still stand on his feet was in that charge – even the wounded hobbled along behind the rest, cheering as loudly as their comrades.

The two lines came together and immediately all was confusion. The solid rank of attackers split up into little groups of struggling men, mingled with the green serge coats of the Dutch. All around Hal fighting men were cursing, shouting and hacking at each other. His existence closed in, became a circle of angry, terrified faces and the clatter of steel weapons, most already dulled with new gore.

A green-jacket stabbed a long pike at Hal's face. He ducked under it and, with his left hand, seized the shaft just behind the spearhead. When the musketeer heaved back, Hal did not resist but used the impetus to launch his counter-attack, leading with the Neptune sword in his right hand. He aimed at the straining yellow throat above the high green collar, and his point slid in cleanly. As the man dropped the pike and fell back, Hal allowed the weight of his dropping body to pull him free of the blade.

Hal went smoothly back on guard, and glanced quickly around for his next opponent, but the charge of seamen had almost wiped out the file of musketeers. Few were left standing, and they were surrounded by clusters of attackers.

He felt his spirits soar. For the first time since he had seen those two ships sail into the lagoon, he felt that there was a chance that they might win this fight. In these last few minutes, they had broken up the main attack. Now they had only to deal with the sailors from the Dutch frigate and the *Gull* as they tried to come ashore.

'Well done, lads. We can do it! We can thrash them,' he shouted, and the seamen who heard him cheered again. Looking about him, he could see triumph on the face of every one of his men as they cut down the last of the green-jackets. Aboli was laughing and singing one of his pagan war-chants in a voice that carried over the din of the battle and inspired every man who heard it. They cheered him and themselves, rejoicing deliriously, in the ease of their victory.

Daniel's tall figure loomed at Hal's right side. His face and thick muscular arms were speckled with blood thrown from the wounds he had inflicted on his victims, and his mouth was wide open as he laughed ferociously, showing his carious teeth.

'Where is Schreuder?' Hal yelled, and Daniel sobered instantly. The laughter died as his mouth snapped shut and he glared around the quietening battlefield.

Then Hal's question was answered unequivocally by Schreuder himself. 'Second wave! Forward!' he bellowed lustily. He was standing on the edge of the forest, only a hundred paces from them. Hal, Aboli and Daniel started towards him, then came up short as another massed column of green-jackets poured out of the forest from behind where Schreuder stood.

'By God!' Hal breathed in despair. 'We haven't seen the half of them yet. The bastard has kept his main force in reserve.'

'There must be two hundred of the swine!' Daniel shook his head in disbelief.

'Quarter columns!' Schreuder shouted, and the advancing infantry changed their formation: they spread out behind him three deep in precisely spaced ranks. Schreuder led them forward at a trot, their ranks neatly dressed and their weapons advanced. Suddenly he held his sword high to halt them. 'First rank! Prepare to fire!' His men sank to their knees, while behind them the other two ranks stood steady.

'Present your arms!' A line of muskets was raised and levelled at the knots of dumbstruck seamen.

'Fire!' roared Schreuder.

The volley crashed out. From a distance of only fifty paces it swept through Hal's men, and almost every shot told. Men dropped and staggered as the heavy lead pellets struck. The line of Englishmen reeled and wavered. There was a chorus of yells – of pain and anger and fear.

'Charge!' Hal cried. 'Don't stand and let them shoot you down!' He lifted the Neptune sword high. 'Come on, lads. Have at them!'

On each side of him Aboli and Daniel started forward, but most of the others hung back. It was dawning on them that the fight was lost, and many looked back towards the safety of the gun emplacements. That was a dangerous signal. Once they glanced over their shoulders it was all up.

'Second rank,' shouted Schreuder, 'prepare to fire!' Fifty more musketeers stepped forward, their weapons loaded and the matches burning. They walked through the gaps in the kneeling rank that had just fired, advanced another two paces in a brisk businesslike manner, then knelt.

'Present your arms!' Even Hal and the dauntless pair flanking him wavered as they gazed into the muzzles of fifty levelled muskets, while a moan of fear and horror went up from their men. They had never before faced such disciplined troops.

'Fire!' Schreuder dropped his sword, and the next volley slashed into the wavering seamen. Hal flinched as a ball passed his ear so closely that the wind of it flipped a curl of his hair into his eyes.

At his side Daniel gasped, 'I am struck!' jerked around like a marionette and sat down heavily. The volley had knocked over another dozen of the *Resolution*'s men and wounded as many more. Hal stooped to aid Daniel, but the big boatswain growled, 'Don't dither about here, you fool. Run! We're beaten, and there's another volley coming.'

As if to prove his words, Schreuder's next orders rang out close at hand. 'Third rank, present your arms!'

All around them the *Resolution*'s men who were still on their feet, broke and scattered in the face of the levelled muskets, running and staggering towards the gunpits.

'Help me, Aboli,' Hal shouted, and Aboli grabbed Daniel's other arm. Between them they hauled him to his feet and started back towards the beach.

'Fire!' Schreuder shouted, and at that instant, not waiting for a word from each other, Hal and Aboli flung themselves flat to earth, pulling Daniel down with them. The gunsmoke and the shot of the third volley crashed over their heads. Immediately they sprang up again and, dragging Daniel, ran for the shelter of the pits.

'Are you hit?' Aboli grunted at Hal, who shook his head, saving his breath. Few of his seamen were still on their feet. Only a handful had reached the line of gunpits and jumped into their shelter.

Half carrying Daniel, they staggered on, while behind them there were jubilant cheers, and the green-clad musketeers surged forward, brandishing their weapons. The three reached the gunpit and pulled Daniel down into it.

There was no need to ask of his wound for the whole of his left side ran red with blood. Aboli jerked the cloth from around his head, wadded it into a ball and stuffed it hurriedly into the front of Daniel's shirt.

'Hold that on the wound,' he told Daniel. 'Press as hard as you can.' He left him lying on the floor of the pit, and stood up beside Hal.

'Oh, sweet Mary!' Hal whispered. His sweat-streaked face was pale with horror and fury at what he beheld over the parapet. 'Look at those bloody butchers!'

As the green-jackets came clamouring forward, they paused only to stab the wounded seamen who lay in their path. Some of their victims rolled on their backs and lifted their bare hands to try to ward off the thrust, others screamed for mercy and tried to crawl away but, laughing and hooting, the musketeers ran after them, thrusting and hacking. This bloody work was quickly done, with Schreuder bellowing at them to close up and keep advancing.

In this moment of respite Sir Francis came dodging down the line and jumped into the pit beside his son.

179

'We are beaten, Father!' Hal said, dispiritedly, and they looked around at their dead and wounded. 'We have lost over half our men already.'

'Hal is right,' Aboli agreed. 'It is over. We must try to get away.'

'Where to?' Sir Francis asked, with a grim smile. 'That way?' He pointed through the trees towards the lagoon, where they saw boats speeding in towards the beach, driven by the oars of enemy sailors eager to join the fight.

Both the frigate and the *Gull* had lowered their boats which were crowded with men. Their cutlasses were drawn and the smoke of their matchlocks blued the air, trailing out across the surface of the water. They were shouting and cheering as wildly as the green-jackets in front.

As the first boats touched the beach the armed men spilled out of them and raced across the narrow strip of white sand. Howling with savage zeal, they stormed at the line of gunpits in which the empty culverins gaped silently, and the *Resolution*'s remaining crew cowered bewildered.

'We cannot hope for quarter, lads,' Sir Francis shouted. 'Look at what those bloodthirsty heathen do to those who try to yield to them.' With his sword he indicated the corpses of the murdered men that littered the ground in front of the guns. 'One more cheer for King Charley, and we'll go down fighting!'

The voices of his tiny band were small and hoarse with exhaustion as they dragged themselves over the parapet once more and sallied out to meet the charge of two hundred fresh and eager musketeers. Aboli was a dozen paces ahead, and hacked at the first green-jacket in his path. His victim went down under the blow but Aboli's blade snapped off at the hilt. He tossed it aside, stooped and picked up a pike from the dead hands of one of the fallen English seamen.

As Hal and Sir Francis ran up beside him, he hefted the long oak shaft and thrust at the belly of another musketeer who rushed at him with his sword held high. The pike-head caught him just under the ribs and transfixed him, standing out half an arm's length between his shoulder blades. The man struggled like a fish on a gaff, and the heavy shaft snapped off in Aboli's hands. He used the stub like a cudgel to strike down the third musketeer who rushed at him. Aboli looked around, grinning like a crazed gargoyle, his great eyes rolling in their sockets.

Sir Francis was engaged with a white Dutch sergeant, trading cut for thrust, their blades clanking and rasping against each other.

Hal killed a corporal with a single neat thrust into his throat, then glanced at Aboli. 'The men from the boats will be on us in an instant.'

They could hear wild cries in their rear as the enemy seamen swept over the gunpits, dealing out short shrift to the few men hiding there. Hal and Aboli did not need to look back – they both knew it was over.

'Farewell, old friend,' Aboli panted. 'They were good times. Would that they had lasted longer.'

Hal had no chance to reply, for at that moment a hoarse voice said in English, 'Hal Courteney, you bold puppy, your luck has just this moment ended.' Cornelius Schreuder pushed aside two of his own men and strode forward to face Hal.

'You and me!' he shouted and came in fast, leading with his right foot, taking the quick double paces of the master swordsman, recovering instantly from each of the swift series of thrusts with which he drove Hal backwards.

Hal was shocked anew at the power in those thrusts, and it taxed all his skill and strength to meet and parry them. The Toledo steel of his blade rang shrilly under the mighty blows and he felt despair as he realized that he could not hope to hold out against such magisterial force.

Schreuder's eyes were blue, cold and merciless. He anticipated each of Hal's moves, offering him a wall of glittering steel when once he attempted the riposte, beating his blade aside then coming on again remorselessly.

Close by, Sir Francis was absorbed in his own duel and had not seen Hal's deadly predicament. Aboli had only the stump of the pike-shaft in his hand – no weapon with which to take on a man like Cornelius Schreuder. He saw Hal, his immature strength already spent by his earlier exertions, wilting visibly before the overwhelming force of these attacks.

Aboli knew by Schreuder's expression when he judged his moment and gathered himself to make the kill. It was certain, inevitable, for Hal could never withstand the thunderbolt which was ready to loose itself upon him.

Aboli moved with the speed of a striking black cobra, faster even than Schreuder could send home his final thrust. He darted up behind Hal, and lifted the oak club. He struck Hal down with a crack over his ear, rapping him sharply across the temple.

Schreuder was amazed to have his victim drop to the ground, senseless, just as he was about to launch the death thrust. While he hesitated Aboli dropped the shattered pike-shaft and stood protectively over Hal's inert body.

'You cannot kill a fallen man, Colonel. Not on the honour of a Dutch officer.'

181

'You black Satan!' Schreuder roared with frustration. 'If I can't kill the puppy, at least I can kill you.'

Aboli showed him his empty hands, holding up his pale palms before Schreuder's eyes. 'I am unarmed,' he said softly.

'I would spare an unarmed Christian.' Schreuder glared. 'But you are a godless animal.' He drew back his blade and aimed the point at the centre of Aboli's chest, where the muscles glistened with sweat in the sunlight. Sir Francis Courteney stepped lightly in front of him, ignoring the colonel's blade.

'On the other hand, Colonel Schreuder, I am a Christian gentleman,' he said smoothly, 'and I yield myself and my men to your grace.' He reversed his own sword and proffered the hilt to Schreuder.

Schreuder glared at him, speechless with fury and frustration. He made no move to accept Sir Francis's sword, but placed the point of his weapon on the other man's throat and pricked him lightly. 'Stand aside, or by God I'll cut you down, Christian or heathen.' The knuckles of his right hand turned white on the hilt of his weapon as he prepared himself to make good the threat.

Another hail made him hesitate. 'Come now, Colonel, I am loath to interfere in a matter of honour. If you murder the brother of my bosom, Franky Courteney, then who will lead us to the treasure from your fine galleon the *Standvastigheid?*'

Schreuder's gaze flicked to the face of Cumbrae as he came striding up to them, the great blood-streaked claymore in his hand.

'The cargo?' Schreuder demanded. 'We have captured this pirate's nest. We will find the treasure is here.'

'Now don't you be so certain of that.' The Buzzard waggled his bushy red beard sadly. 'If I know my dear brother in Christ, Franky, he'll have squirrelled the best part of it away somewhere.' His eye glinted greedily from under his bonnet. 'No, Colonel, you are going to have to keep him alive, at least until we have been able to recompense ourselves with a handful of silver rix-dollars for doing God's work this day.'

When Hal recovered consciousness, he found his father kneeling over him. He whispered, 'What happened, Father? Did we win?' His father shook his head, without looking into his eyes, and made a fuss of wiping the sweat and soot from his son's face with a strip of grubby cloth torn from the hem of his own shirt.

'No, Hal. We did not win.' Hal looked beyond him, and it all came

182

back. He saw that a pitiful few of the *Resolution*'s crew had survived. They were huddled together around where Hal lay, guarded by green-jackets with loaded muskets. The rest were scattered where they had fallen in front of the gunpits, or were draped in death upon the parapets.

He saw that Aboli was tending Daniel, binding up the wound in his chest with the red bandanna. Daniel was sitting up and seemed to have recovered somewhat, although clearly he had lost a great deal of blood. His face beneath the grime of battle was as white as the ashes of last night's camp-fire.

Hal turned his head and saw Lord Cumbrae and Colonel Schreuder standing nearby, in deep and earnest conversation. The Buzzard broke off at last and shouted an order to one of his men. 'Geordie, bring the slave chains from the *Gull*! We don't want Captain Courteney to leave us again.' The sailor hurried back to the beach, and the Buzzard and the colonel came to where the prisoners squatted under the muskets of their guards.

'Captain Courteney.' Schreuder addressed Sir Francis ominously. 'I am arresting you and your crew for piracy on the high seas. You will be taken to Good Hope to stand trial on those charges.'

'I protest, sir.' Sir Francis stood up with dignity. 'I demand that you treat my men with the consideration due to prisoners of war.'

'There is no war, Captain,' Schreuder told him icily. 'Hostilities between the Republic of Holland and England ceased under treaty some months ago.'

Sir Francis stared at him, aghast, while he recovered from the shock of this news. 'I was unaware that a peace had been concluded. I acted in good faith,' he said at last, 'but in any event I was sailing under a commission from His Majesty.'

'You spoke of this Letter of Marque during our previous meeting. Will you consider me presumptuous if I insist on having sight of the document?' Schreuder asked.

'My commission from His Majesty is in my sea-chest in my hut.' Sir Francis pointed into the stockade, where many of the huts had been destroyed by cannon fire. 'If you will allow me I will bring it to you.'

'Please don't discommode yourself, Franky my old friend.' The Buzzard clapped him on the shoulder. 'I'll fetch it for you.' He strode away and ducked into the low doorway of the hut that Sir Francis had indicated.

Schreuder rounded on him again. 'Where are you holding your hostages, sir? Governor van de Velde and his poor wife, where are they?'

'The Governor must still be in his stockade with the other hostages, his wife and the captain of the galleon. I have not seen them since the beginning of the fight.'

Hal stood up shakily, holding the cloth to his head. 'The Governor's wife has taken refuge from the fighting in a cave in the hillside, up there.'

'How do you know that?' Schreuder asked sharply.

'For her own safety, I led her there myself.' Hal spoke up boldly, avoiding his father's stern eye. 'I was returning from the cave when I ran into you in the forest, Colonel.'

Schreuder looked up the hill, torn by duty and the desire to rush to the aid of the woman whose rescue was, for him at least, the main object of this expedition. But at that moment the Buzzard swaggered out of the hut. He carried a roll of parchment tied with a scarlet ribbon. The royal seals of red wax dangled from it.

Sir Francis smiled with satisfaction and relief. 'There you have it, Colonel. I demand that you treat me and my crew as honourable prisoners, captured in a fair fight.'

Before he reached them, the Buzzard paused and unrolled the parchment. He held up the document at arm's length, and turned it so that all could see the curlicue script penned by some clerk of the Admiralty in black indian ink. At last, with a jerk of his head, he summoned one of his own seamen. He took the loaded pistol from the man's hand, and blew upon the burning match in the lock. Then he grinned at Sir Francis and applied the flame to the foot of the document in his hand.

Sir Francis stood appalled as the flame caught and the parchment began to curl and blacken as the pale yellow flame ran up it. 'By God, Cumbrae, you treacherous bastard!' He started forward, but the tip of Schreuder's blade lay on his chest.

'It would give me the greatest pleasure to thrust home,' he murmured. 'For your own sake, do not try my patience any further, sir.'

'That swine is burning my commission.'

'I can see nothing,' Schreuder told him, his back deliberately turned to the Buzzard. 'Nothing, except a notorious pirate standing before me with the blood of innocent men still warm and wet on his hands.'

Cumbrae watched the parchment burn, a great wide grin splitting his ginger whiskers. He passed the crackling sheet from hand to hand as the heat reached his fingertips, turning it to allow the flames to consume every scrap.

'I have heard you prate of your honour, sir,' Sir Francis flared at Schreuder. 'It seems that that is an illusory commodity.'

'Honour?' Schreuder smiled coldly. 'Do I hear a pirate speak to me of honour? It cannot be. Surely my ears play me false.'

184

Cumbrae allowed the flames to lick the tips of his fingers before he dropped the last blackened shred of the document to the earth and stamped on the ashes, crushing them to powder. Then he came up to Schreuder. 'I am afraid Franky's up to his tricks again. I can find no Letter of Marque signed by the royal hand.'

'I suspected as much.' Schreuder sheathed his sword. 'I place the prisoners in your charge, my lord Cumbrae. I must see to the welfare of the hostages.' He glanced at Hal. 'You will take me immediately to the place where you left the Governor's wife.' He looked round at his Dutch sergeant who stood attentively at his shoulder. 'Bind his hands behind his back and put a rope round his neck. Lead him on a leash like the mangy puppy he is.'

Colonel Schreuder delayed the rescue expedition while a search was conducted for his lost wig. His vanity would not allow him go to Katinka in a state of disarray. They found it lying in the forest through which he had chased Hal. It was covered with damp earth and dead leaves, but Schreuder beat it against his thigh then rearranged the curls carefully before placing it on his head. His beauty and dignity restored, he nodded at Hal. 'Show us the way!'

By the time they came out on the terrace in front of the cave Hal was a sorry object. Both hands were trussed behind his back and the sergeant had another rope round his neck. His face was blackened with dirt and gunsmoke and his clothing torn and smeared with blood diluted with his own sweat. Despite his exhaustion and distress, his concern was still for Katinka, and he felt a tremor of alarm as he went into the cave.

There was no sign of her. I cannot live if anything has happened to her, he thought, but aloud he told Schreuder, 'I left Mevrouw van de Velde here. No ill can have befallen her.'

'For your sake, you had better be correct in that.' The threat was more terrifying for having been uttered so softly. Then Schreuder raised his voice. 'Mevrouw van de Velde!' he called. 'Madam, you are safe. It is Colonel Schreuder, come to rescue you!'

The vines veiling the entrance to the cave rustled softly, and Katinka stepped out timidly from behind them. Her huge violet eyes were brimming with tears, and her face was pale and tragic, adding to her appeal. 'Oh!' she choked with emotion. Then, dramatically, she held out both hands towards Cornelius Schreuder. 'You came! You kept your promise!' She flew to him and stood on tiptoe to fling both her slim arms round his neck. 'I knew you would come! I knew you would never leave me to be humiliated and molested by these dreadful criminals.'

For one moment Schreuder was taken aback by her embrace, then he folded her in his arms, shielding and comforting her as she sobbed against the ribbons and sashes that covered his chest. 'If you have suffered the slightest affront, I swear I will avenge it a hundredfold.'

'My ordeal has been too terrible to relate,' she whimpered.

'This one?' Schreuder looked at Hal and demanded, 'Was he one of those who mistreated you?'

Katinka looked sideways at Hal, her cheek still pressed against Schreuder's chest. Her eyes narrowed viciously and a small sadistic smile twisted her luscious lips. 'He was the worst of all.' She sobbed. 'I cannot bring myself to tell you what disgusting things he said to me, or how he has harassed and humiliated me.' Her voice broke. 'I only thank God for the strength that he gave me to hold out against that man's importunity.'

Schreuder seemed to swell with the strength of his fury. Gently he set Katinka aside, then turned on Hal. He bunched his right fist and punched him hard in the side of his head. Hal was taken by surprise, and staggered back. Schreuder followed him swiftly, and his next punch caught Hal in the pit of his stomach, driving the wind from his lungs and doubling him over.

'How dare you insult and mistreat a high-born lady?' Schreuder was shaking with fury. He had lost all control of his temper.

Hal's forehead was almost touching his knees, as he gasped and wheezed to recover his breath. Schreuder aimed a kick at his face, but Hal saw it coming and jerked his head aside. The boot glanced off his shoulder, and sent him reeling backwards.

Schreuder's rage boiled over. 'You are not fit to lick the soles of this lady's slippers.' He braced himself to punch again, but Hal was too quick. Although his hands were tied behind his back he stepped forward to meet Schreuder and aimed a kick at his groin, but because he was hampered by his bonds the kick lacked power.

Schreuder was more startled than hurt. 'By God, puppy, you go too far!' Hal was still off-balance, and Schreuder's next blow knocked his legs out from under him. He collapsed and Schreuder set on him, using both feet, his boots thumping into Hal's curled-up body. Hal grunted and rolled over, trying desperately to avoid the barrage of kicks that slogged into him.

'Yes! Oh, yes!' Katinka trilled with excitement. 'Punish him for what he has done to me.' She goaded Schreuder, driving his violent temper to its limit. 'Make him suffer, as I was made to do.'

Hal knew in his heart that she was forced to reject him now in front of this man and even in his hurt he forgave her. He doubled over to protect his more vulnerable parts, taking most of the kicks on his shoulders and thighs, but he could not ride them all. One caught him in the side of the mouth and blood trickled down his chin.

Katinka squeaked and clapped her hands to see it flow. 'I hate him. Yes! Hurt him! Smash his pretty, insolent face!' But the blood seemed to bring Schreuder to his senses again. With an obvious effort, he curbed his wild temper and stepped back, breathing heavily and still trembling with rage. 'That is just a small taste of what is in store for him. Believe me, Mevrouw, he will be paid out in full when we reach Good Hope.' He turned back to Katinka and bowed. 'Please let me take you back to the safety of the ship that waits in the bay.'

Katinka gave a pathetic little cry, her fingers on her soft pink lips. 'Oh, Colonel, I fear I shall swoon.' She swayed on her feet, and Schreuder leapt forward to steady her. She leant against him. 'I do not think my legs can carry me.'

He swept her into his arms, and set off down the hill carrying her lightly. She clung to him as though she were a child being taken to her bed.

'Come along, gallows-bait!' The sergeant yanked Hal to his feet by the loop around his neck, and led him, still bleeding, down towards the camp. 'Better for you had the Colonel finished you off here and now. The executioner at Good Hope is famous. He's an artist, he is.' He tugged hard on the rope. 'He'll have some sport with you, I'll warrant.'

A pinnace brought the chains to the beach where the survivors of the *Resolution*'s crew, both wounded and unharmed, were squatting under guard in the blazing sun.

They carried the first set to Sir Francis. 'It's good to see you again, Captain.' The sailor with the irons in his hands stood over him. 'I have thought of you every day since last we met.'

'I, on the other hand, have never given you another thought, Sam Bowles.' Sir Francis barely glanced at him, but scorn was in his voice.

'It's Boatswain Sam Bowles, now. His lordship has promoted me,' said Sam, with an insolent grin.

'Then I wish the Buzzard joy of his new boatswain. 'Tis a marriage made in heaven.'

'Hold out your hands, Captain. Let's see how high and mighty you are with bracelets of iron on you,' Sam Bowles gloated. 'By Christ, you'll never know how much pleasure this gives me.' He snapped the shackles onto Sir Francis's wrists and ankles, and with the key screwed them so tight that they bit into his flesh. 'I hope that fits you as well as your

187

fancy cloak ever did.' He stepped back and spat suddenly into Sir Francis's face, then burst out laughing. 'I give you my solemn promise that, the day they reef your top sails for you, I will be at the Parade at Good Hope to wish you Godspeed. I wonder what way they will send you. Do you think it will be the fire, or will they hang and draw you?' Sam chuckled again and went on to Hal. 'Good day to you, young Master Henry. It's your humble servant Boatswain Sam Bowles come to tend to your needs.'

'I did not get a glimpse of your yellow hide during the fighting,' Hal said quietly. 'Where were you hiding this time?' Sam flushed and swung the handful of heavy chains against Hal's head. Hal recovered and stared coldly into his eyes. Sam would have struck again, but a huge black hand reached up and seized his wrist. He looked down into the smoky eyes of Aboli, who crouched beside Hal. Aboli said not a word but Sam Bowles stayed the blow. He could not hold that murderous stare, and dropped his eyes, keeping them averted as he knelt hurriedly to clamp the chains on Hal's limbs.

He stood up and came to Aboli, who watched him with the same expressionless gaze as he hurriedly screwed the shackles onto him, then passed on to where Big Daniel lay. Daniel winced but uttered no sound as Sam Bowles tugged brutally at his arms. The bullet wound had stopped bleeding, but with this rough treatment it opened again and began to weep watery blood from under the red headcloth that Aboli had used to bandage it. The blood trickled over his chest and dripped into the sand.

When they were all shackled together they were ordered to their feet. Supporting him between them, Hal and Aboli half carried Daniel as they were led in a file to one of the larger trees. Again they were forced to sit while the end of the chain was passed around the trunk and made fast with two heavy iron padlocks.

There were only twenty-six survivors from the *Resolution*'s complement. Amongst these were four ex-slaves, of which Aboli was one. Nearly all were at least lightly wounded, but four, including Daniel, were gravely injured and must be in danger of their lives.

Ned Tyler had received a deep cutlass slash in his thigh. Hampered by their manacles, Hal and Aboli bound it up with another strip of cloth salvaged from the shirt of one of the dead men who littered the battlefield like flotsam on the windswept beach.

Parties of green-jacketed musketeers were working under their Dutch sergeants to gather up the corpses. Dragging them by the heels to a clearing among the trees, they stripped the bodies and searched them for the silver coins and other items of value that had been their share of the booty from the *Standvastigheid*.

A pair of petty-officers painstakingly searched through the discarded clothing, ripping out seams and tearing the soles off boots. Another team of three men, their sleeves rolled high and their fingers dipped in a pot of grease, probed the body orifices of the corpses, searching for any valuables that might be tucked away in these traditional hiding places.

The recovered booty was thrown into an empty water cask, over which a white sergeant stood with a loaded pistol as the keg filled slowly with a rich booty. When the ghoulish trio had finished with the naked corpses another gang dragged them away and threw them onto tall funeral pyres. Fuelled by dry logs the flames reached so high that they shrivelled the green leaves on the tall trees that surrounded the clearing. The smoke of charring flesh was sweet and nauseating, like burnt pork fat.

In the meantime, Schreuder and Cumbrae, assisted by Limberger, the captain of the galleon, were taking stock of the spice barrels. They were as officious as tax collectors, with their lists and books, checking the contents and weights of the recovered goods against the original ship's manifest, and marking the staves of the kegs with white chalk.

When they had made their tallies other gangs of seamen rolled the great barrels down to the beach and loaded them into the largest pinnace to be taken out to the galleon, which lay anchored out in the channel, under her new mainmast and rigging. The work went on all that night by the light of lantern and bonfire and the yellow flames of the cremation pyres.

As the hours passed Big Daniel became feverish. His skin was hot, and at times he raved. The bandage had at last staunched his wound, and under it a soft crusty scab had begun to form over the ugly puncture. But the skin around it was swollen and turning livid.

'The ball is still in there,' Hal whispered to Aboli. 'There is no wound in his back for it to have left his body.'

Aboli grunted, 'If we try to cut it out, we will kill him. From the angle which it entered, it must lie close to his heart and lungs.'

'I fear it will mortify.' Hal shook his head.

'He is strong as a bull.' Aboli shrugged. 'Perhaps strong enough to defeat the demons.' Aboli believed that all sickness was caused by demons that had invaded the blood. It was a groundless superstition, but Hal humoured him in his belief.

'We should cauterize the wounds of all the men with hot tar.' This was the sailor's cure-all and Hal pleaded in Dutch with the Hottentot guards to bring one of the pitch pots from the carpenter's shop in the stockade, but they ignored him.

It was after midnight before they saw Schreuder again. He strode out of the darkness and went directly to where Sir Francis lay chained to the others at the foot of the tree. Like the rest of his men, he was exhausted but able to snatch only brief moments of broken sleep, disturbed by the restless din and movements of the work gangs and the weak cries and groans of the wounded.

'Sir Francis.' Schreuder stooped and shook him fully awake. 'May I trouble you for a few minutes of your time?' From the tone of his voice, it seemed that his temper was on an even keel.

Sir Francis sat up. 'First, Colonel, may I trouble you for a little compassion? None of my men has had a drop of water since yesterday afternoon. As you can see, four are grievously wounded.'

Schreuder frowned, and Sir Francis guessed that he had not given orders for the prisoners to be deliberately mistreated. He himself had never thought that Schreuder was a brutal or sadistic man. His savage behaviour earlier had almost certainly been caused by his excitable nature, and by the strain and exigencies of battle. Now Schreuder turned to the guards and gave orders for water and food to be brought to the prisoners, and sent a sergeant to find the chest of medical supplies in Sir Francis's shattered hut.

While they waited for his orders to be carried out, Schreuder paced back and forth in the sand, his chin on his breast and his hands clasped behind his back. Hal suddenly sat up straighter.

'Aboli,' he whispered. 'The sword.'

Aboli grunted as he realized that on Schreuder's sword belt hung the inlaid and embossed Neptune sword of Hal's knighthood, that had once belonged to his grandfather. Aboli laid a calming hand on the young man's shoulder to prevent him accosting Schreuder, and said softly, 'The spoils of war, Gundwane. It is lost to you, but at least a real warrior still wears it.' Hal subsided, realizing the cruel logic of the other man's advice.

At last Schreuder turned back to Sir Francis. 'Captain Limberger and I have tallied the spice and timber cargo that you have stored in the godowns, and we find that most of it is accounted for and still intact. The shortfall would probably be due to seawater damage sustained during the taking of the galleon. I have been told that one of your culverin balls pierced the main hold, and part of the cargo was flooded.'

'I am pleased,' Sir Francis nodded with weary irony, 'that you have been able to recover all of your Company's property.'

'Alas, that is not the case, Sir Francis, as you are well aware. There is still a large part of the galleon's cargo missing.' He paused as the sergeant returned, and gave him an order. 'Take the chains off the black and the boy. Let them water the others.' Some men were following with a water cask, which they placed at the foot of the tree. Hal and Aboli immediately began to pour fresh water for their wounded, and all of them drank, gulping down the precious stuff with closed eyes and bobbing throats.

The sergeant reported to Colonel Schreuder, 'I have found the surgeon's instruments.' He displayed the canvas roll. 'But, Mijnheer, it contains sharp knives, which could be used as weapons, and the contents of the pitch pots could be used against my men.'

Schreuder looked down at Sir Francis where he squatted, haggard and dishevelled, beside the tree-trunk. 'Do I have your word as a gentleman not to use these medical supplies to harm my men?'

'You have my solemn word,' Sir Francis agreed.

Schreuder nodded at the sergeant. 'Give all of it into Sir Francis's charge,' he ordered, and the sergeant handed over the small chest of medical supplies, the tar pot and a bolt of clean cloth that could be used as bandages.

'Now, Captain,' Schreuder picked up the conversation where he had left off, 'we have retrieved the plundered spice and timber, but more than half the coin and all of the gold bullion that was in the hold of the *Standvastigheid* is still missing.'

'The spoils were distributed to my crew.' Sir Francis smiled humourlessly. 'I do not know what they have done with their share, and most are too dead to be able to enlighten us.'

'We have recovered what I calculate must be the greater part of your crew's share.' Schreuder gestured at the barrel containing the valuables collected in such macabre fashion from the battlefield casualties. It was being carried by a party of seamen down to a waiting pinnace and guarded by Dutch officers with drawn swords. 'My officers have searched the huts of your men in the stockade, but there is still no sign of the other half.'

'Much as I would like to be of service to you, I am unable to account to you for the missing portion,' Sir Francis told him quietly. At this denial, Hal looked up from ministering to the wounded men, but his father never glanced in his direction.

'Lord Cumbrae believes that you have cached the missing treasure,' Schreuder remarked. 'And I agree with him.'

'Lord Cumbrae is a famous liar and cheat,' Sir Francis said. 'And you, sir, are mistaken in your belief.'

'Lord Cumbrae is of the opinion that were he given the opportunity to question you in person he would be able to extract from you the

191

whereabouts of the missing treasure. He is anxious to try to persuade you to reveal what you know. It is only with the greatest difficulty that I have been able to prevent him doing so.'

Sir Francis shrugged. 'You must do as you feel fit, Colonel, but unless I am a poor judge, the torture of captives is not something that a soldier like you would condone. I am grateful for the compassion that you have shown my wounded.'

Schreuder's reply was interrupted by an agonized scream from Ned Tyler as Aboli poured a ladleful of steaming tar into the sword gash in his thigh. As the scream subsided into sobbing, Schreuder went on smoothly. 'The tribunal that tries you for piracy at the fort at Good Hope will be headed by our new governor. I have serious doubts that Governor Petrus Jacobus van de Velde will feel himself so constrained to mercy as I am.' Schreuder paused and then went on, 'By the way, Sir Francis, I am reliably informed that the executioner employed by the Company at Good Hope prides himself on his skills.'

'I will have to give the Governor and his executioner the same answer I gave you, Colonel.'

Schreuder squatted on his heels and lowered his voice to a conspiratorial, almost friendly, tone. 'Sir Francis, in our short acquaintance I have formed a high regard for you as a warrior, a sailor and a gentleman. If I were to give evidence before the tribunal that your Letter of Marque existed, and that you were a legitimate privateer, the outcome of your trial might go differently.'

'You must have faith in Governor van de Velde that I lack,' Sir Francis replied. 'I wish I could further your career for you by producing the missing bullion, but I cannot help you, sir. I know nothing of its whereabouts.'

Schreuder's face stiffened as he stood up. 'I have tried to help you. I regret that you reject my offer. However, you are correct, sir. I do not have the stomach to have you put to the question under torture. What is more, I will prevent Lord Cumbrae from taking that task upon himself. I will simply do my duty and deliver you to the mercy of the tribunal at Good Hope. I beg you, sir, will you not reconsider?'

Sir Francis shook his head. 'I regret I cannot help you, sir.'

Schreuder sighed. 'Very well. You and your men will be taken aboard the *Gull of Moray* as soon as she is ready to sail tomorrow morning. The frigate *Sonnevogel* has other duties in the Indies and she will sail at the same time to go her separate way. The *Standvastigheid* will remain here under her true commander, Captain Limberger, to take on her cargo of spice and timber before she resumes her interrupted voyage to Amsterdam.'

He turned on his heel and disappeared back into the shadows, in the direction of the spice godown.

When they were aroused by their captors the following morning, four of the wounded, including Daniel and Ned Tyler, were unable to walk and their comrades were forced to carry them. The slave chains allowed little freedom of movement, and it was a clumsy line of men that shambled down to the beach. Each step was hampered by the clanking shackles, so that they could not lift their feet high enough to step over the gunwale of the pinnace, and had to be shoved in by their guards.

When the pinnace tied onto the foot of the rope ladder down the side of the *Gull*, the climb that faced the chained men to the deck was daunting and dangerous. Sam Bowles stood at the entryport above them. One of the guards in the pinnace shouted up to him, 'Can we loose the prisoners' chains, Boatswain?'

'Why do you want to do that?' Sam called down.

'The wounded can't help themselves. The others will not be able to hoist them. They'll not be able to make it up the ladder otherwise.'

'If they don't make it they're the ones that will be the poorer for it,' Sam answered. 'His lordship's orders. The manacles must stay on.'

Sir Francis led the climb, his every movement hampered by the string of men linked behind him. The four wounded men, moaning in their delirium, were dead weights that had to be dragged up by force. Big Daniel, in particular, tested all their strength. If they had allowed him to slip from their grasp, he would have plummeted into the pinnace and pulled the whole string of twenty-six men with him, almost certainly capsizing the small boat. Once in the lagoon, the weight of their heavy iron chains would have plucked them all to the bottom, four fathoms down.

If it had not been for the bull strength of Aboli, they would never have reached the deck of the *Gull*. Yet even he was completely played out when, at last, he heaved Daniel's inert form over the gunwale and collapsed beside him on the scrubbed white deck. They all lay there gasping and panting, to be roused at last by a tingling peal of laughter.

With an effort Hal raised his head. On the *Gull*'s quarterdeck, under a canvas awning, a breakfast table was laid. The glass was crystal and the silverware sparkled in the early sunlight. He smelt the heady aroma of bacon, fresh eggs and hot biscuit rising from the silver chafing dish.

At the head of the table sat the Buzzard. He raised his glass towards that sprawling heap of human bodies in the waist of his ship.

'Welcome aboard, gentlemen, and your astounding good health!' He drank the toast in whisky, then wiped his ginger whiskers with a damask napkin. 'The finest quarters on board have been prepared for you. I wish you a pleasant voyage.'

Katinka van de Velde laughed again, a musical sound. She sat at the Buzzard's left hand. Her head was bare, her golden curls piled high, her violet eyes wide and innocent in the flawless oval of her powdered face, and a beauty spot drawn carefully at the corner of her pretty, painted mouth.

The Governor sat opposite his wife. He stopped in the act of lifting a silver fork loaded with crisped bacon and cheese to his mouth, but continued to chew. A yellow drop of egg yolk escaped from between his pendulous lips and ran down his chin as he guffawed. 'Do not despair, Sir Francis. Remember your family motto. I am sure you will endure.' He stuffed the forkful into his mouth, and spoke through it. 'This is really excellent fare, fresh from Good Hope. What a pity you cannot join us.'

'How thoughtful of your lordship to provide us with entertainment. Will these troubadours sing for us, or will they amuse us with more acrobatics?' Katinka asked in Dutch, then made a pretty little *moue* and tapped Cumbrae's arm with her painted Chinese fan.

At that moment Big Daniel rolled his head from side to side, thumping it on the planks, and cried out in delirium. The Buzzard howled with laughter. 'As you see, they try their best, madam, but their repertoire does not suit every taste.' He nodded at Sam Bowles. 'Pray show them to their quarters, Master Samuel, and make sure they are well cared for.'

With a knotted rope end, Sam Bowles whipped the prisoners to their feet. They lifted their wounded and shambled down the companion ladder. In the depths of the hull, below the main hold, stretched the low slave deck. When Sam Bowles lifted the hatch that opened into it, the stench that rose to greet them made even him recoil. It was the essence of the suffering of hundreds of doomed souls who had languished here.

The headspace in this deck was no higher than a man's waist so they were forced to crawl down it and drag the wounded men with them. Iron rings were set into the bulkhead, bolted into the heavy oak beam that ran the length of the hold. Sam and his four mates crawled down after them and shackled their chains into the ringbolts. When they had finished, the captives were laid out like herrings in a barrel, side by side, secured at wrist and ankle, only just able to sit up, but unable to turn over or to move their limbs more than the few inches that their chains allowed.

Hal lay with his father on one side and the inert hulk of Big Daniel on the other. Aboli was on the far side of Daniel and Ned Tyler beyond him.

When the last man had been secured, Sam crawled back to the hatch and smirked down at them. 'Ten days to Good Hope with this wind. One pint of water a day for each man, and three ounces of biscuit, when I remember to bring it to you. You're free to shit and piss where you lie. See you at Good Hope, my lovelies.'

He slammed the hatch closed, and they heard him on the far side hammering the locking pins into their seats. When the mallet blows ceased, the sudden quiet was frightening. At first the darkness was complete, but then as their eyes adjusted they could just make out the dark forms of their mates packed around them.

Hal looked for the source of light and found a small iron grating set into the deck directly above his head. Even without the bars, it would not have been large enough to admit the head of a grown man, and he discounted it immediately as a possible escape route. At least it provided a whiff of fresh air.

The stench was hard to bear and they all gasped in the suffocating atmosphere. It smelt like a bear-pit. Big Daniel moaned, and the sound loosened their tongues. They started to talk all at once.

'Love of God, it smells like a shit-house in apricot season down here.'

'Do you think there's a chance of escaping from here, Captain?'

'Of course there is, my bully,' one of the men answered for Sir Francis. 'When we reach Good Hope.'

'I would give half my share of the richest prize that ever sailed the seven seas for five minutes alone with Sam Bowles.'

'All my share for the another five with that bloody Cumbrae.'

'Or that cheese-headed bastard, Schreuder.'

Suddenly Daniel gabbled, 'Oh, Mother, I see your lovely face. Come, kiss your little Danny.' The plaintive cry disheartened them, and the silence of despair fell over the dark, noisome slave deck. Gradually they sank into a torpor of despondency, broken occasionally by the groans of delirium and the clank of the links as they tried to find a more comfortable position.

Slowly, the passage of time lost all significance, and none were sure whether it was night or day when the sound of the anchor capstan from the upper deck reverberated through the hull and they heard the faint shouts of the petty-officers relaying the orders to get the *Gull* under way.

195

Hal tried to judge the ship's course and direction by the momentum and heel of the hull, but soon lost track. It was only when the *Gull* plunged suddenly and began to work with a light, frolicsome motion to the scend of the open sea that he knew they had left the lagoon and passed out through the heads.

For hour after hour the *Gull* battled with the sou'-easter to make good her offing. The motion threw them back and forth on the bare planks, sliding on their backs the few inches that their chains allowed before coming up hard on their manacles, and then sliding back the other way. It was a great relief when, at last, she settled into an easier reach.

'There now. That's a sight better.' Sir Francis spoke for them all. 'The Buzzard has made his offing. He has come about and we are running free with the sou'-easter abaft our beam, heading west for the Cape.'

As time passed, Hal made some estimate of the passage of the days by the intensity of light from the grating above his head. During the long nights there was a crushing blackness in the slave deck, like that at the bottom of a coal shaft. Then the softest light filtered down on him as the dawn broke, which grew in strength until he could make out the shape of Aboli's dark round head beyond the lighter face of Big Daniel.

However, even at noon the further reaches of the slave deck were hidden in darkness, from which the sighs and moans, and the occasional whispers of the other men echoed eerily between the oaken bulkheads. Then again the light faded away into that utter darkness to mark the passing of another day.

On the third morning a whispered message was passed from man to man. 'Timothy O'Reilly is dead.' He was one of the wounded: he had taken a sword thrust in his chest from one of the green-jackets.

'He was a good man.' Sir Francis voiced his epitaph. 'May God rest his soul. I would that we were able to afford him a Christian burial.' By the fifth morning, Timothy's corpse added to the miasma of decay and rot that permeated the slave deck and filled their lungs with each breath.

Often, as Hal lay in a stupor of despair, the scampering grey rats, big as rabbits, clambered over his body. Their sharp claws raised painful scratches across his bare skin. In the end he gave up the hopeless task of trying to drive them away by kicking and hitting out at them, and set himself to endure the discomfort. It was only when one sank its sharp, curved teeth into the back of his hand that he shouted and managed to seize it, squeaking shrilly, by the throat and throttle it with his bare hands.

When Daniel cried out in pain beside him, he realized then that the rats had found him also, and that he was unable to defend himself from

196

their attacks. After that he and Aboli took turns at sitting up and trying to keep the voracious rodents away from the unconscious man.

Their fetters prevented them from squatting over the narrow gutter that ran along the foot of the bulkhead, designed to carry away their sewage. Every once in a while Hal heard the spluttering release as one of the men voided where he lay, and immediately afterwards came the fetid stench of fresh faeces in the confined and already musty spaces.

When Daniel emptied his bladder, the warm liquid spread to flood the planks under Hal and soaked into his shirt and breeches. There was nothing he could do to avoid it, except lift his head from the deck.

Most days, around what Hal judged to be noon, the locking pins on the hatch were suddenly driven out with thunderous mallet blows. When it was lifted the feeble light that flooded the hold almost blinded them, and they lifted their hands, heavy with chains, to shield their eyes.

'I have a special posset for you merry gentlemen today,' Sam Bowles's voice sang out. 'A mug of water from our oldest barrels, with a few little beasties swimming in it and just a drop of my spittle to give it flavour.' They heard him spit heartily, and then bray with laughter before he handed down the first pewter mug. Each mugful had to be passed along the deck, from hand to clumsy manacled hand, and when one was spilled there was none to replace it.

'One for each of our gentlemen. That's twenty-six mugs, and no more,' Sam Bowles told them cheerily.

Big Daniel was now too far gone to drink unaided, and Aboli had to lift his head while Hal dribbled water between his lips. The other sick men had to be treated in the same way. Much of the water was lost when it ran out of their slack mouths, and it was a long-drawn-out business. Sam Bowles lost patience before they were half through. 'None of you want any more? Well, I'll be off, then.' And he slammed the hatch closed and drove home the pins, leaving most of the captives pleading vainly, through parched throats and flaking lips for their share. But he was unrelenting, and they were forced to wait another day for their next ration.

After that Aboli filled his own mouth with water from the mug, placed his lips over Daniel's and forced it into the unconscious man's mouth. They did the same for the other wounded. This method was quick enough to satisfy even Sam Bowles, and less of the precious fluid was lost.

Sam Bowles chuckled when one of the men shouted up at him, 'For God's sweet sake, Boatswain, there's a dead man down here. Timothy O'Reilly is stinking to the high heavens. Can you not smell him?'

197

He answered, 'I'm glad you told me. That means he will not be using his water ration. It will be only twenty-five mugs I'll be serving from tomorrow.'

Daniel was dying. He no longer groaned or thrashed about in delirium. He lay like a corpse. Even his bladder had dried up and no longer emptied itself spontaneously on the reeking planks on which they lay. Hal held his head and whispered to him, trying to cajole him into staying alive. 'You can't give up now. Hold on just a while longer and we will be at the Cape before you know it. All the sweet fresh water you can drink, pretty slave girls to nurse you. Just think on that, Danny.'

At noon, on what he thought must be their sixth day at sea, Hal called across to Aboli, 'I have something to show you here. Give me your hand.' He took Aboli's fingers and guided them over Daniel's ribs. The skin was so hot that it was almost painful to the touch, and the flesh so wasted that the ribs stood out like barrel staves.

Hal rolled Daniel over as far as his chains would allow, and directed Aboli's fingers onto his shoulder blade. 'There. Can you feel that lump?'

Aboli grunted, 'I can feel it, but I cannot see.' He was so restricted by his chains that he could not look over the bulk of Daniel's inert body.

'I'm not sure, but I think I know what it is.' Hal put his face closer and strained his eyes in the dim light. 'There is a swelling the size of a walnut. It's black like a bruise.' He touched it gently, and even this light pressure made Daniel groan and fret against his bonds.

'It must be very tender.' Sir Francis had roused himself and leaned as close as he was able. 'I cannot see well. Where is it?'

'In the middle of his shoulder blade,' Hal answered. 'I believe that it is the musket ball. It has passed clean through his chest and is lying here under the skin.'

'Then that is what is killing him,' Sir Francis said. 'It is the seat and source of the mortification that is eating him up.'

'If we had a knife,' Hal murmured, 'we could try to cut it out. But Sam Bowles took the medical chest.'

Aboli said, 'Not before I hid one of the knives.' He searched in the waistband of his breeches and held up the thin blade. It glinted softly in the faint light from the grating above Hal's head. 'I was waiting for a chance to cut Sam's throat with it.'

'We must risk cutting,' Sir Francis told him. 'If it stays in his body the ball will kill him more certainly than the scalpel.'

'I cannot see to make the cut from where I lie,' Aboli said. 'You will have to do it.'

There was a scuffling and clinking of the chain links, then Sir Francis grunted, 'My chains are too short. I cannot lay a finger on him.'

They were all silent for a short while, then Sir Francis said, 'Hal.'

'Father,' Hal protested, 'I do not have the knowledge or the skill.'

'Then Daniel will die,' Aboli said flatly. 'You owe him a life, Gundwane. Here, take the knife.'

In Hal's hand the knife seemed heavy as a bar of lead. His mouth dry with dread, he tested the edge of the blade against the ball of his thumb and found it dulled by much use.

'It is blunt,' he protested.

'Aboli is right, my son.' Sir Francis laid a hand on Hal's shoulder and squeezed. 'You are Daniel's only chance.'

Slowly Hal reached out with his left hand, and felt the hard lump in Daniel's hot flesh. It moved under his fingers, and he felt it grate softly against the bone of the shoulder blade.

The pain roused Daniel, and he struggled against his chains. He shouted, 'Help me, Jesus. I have sinned against God and man. The devil comes for me. He is dark. Everything grows dark.'

'Hold him, Aboli,' Hal whispered. 'Hold him still.'

Aboli wrapped his arms around Daniel, like the coils of a great black python. 'Do it,' he said. 'Do it swiftly.'

Hal leaned in close to Daniel, as close as his chains would let him, his face a hand's breadth from the other man's back. Now he could see the swelling more clearly. The skin was stretched so tightly over it that it was glossy and purple as an overripe plum. He placed the fingers of his left hand on each side of it and spread the skin even tighter.

He took a deep breath, and placed the tip of the scalpel against the swelling. He steeled himself, counting silently to three, then pressed down with the strength of a trained sword arm. He felt the blade slide deep into Daniel's back, and then strike something hard and unyielding, metal on metal.

Daniel shrieked and then went slack in Aboli's enfolding arms. A spurt of purple and yellow pus erupted from the deep scalpel cut. Hot and thick as carpenter's glue, it struck Hal in the mouth and splattered across his chin. The smell was worse than all the other odours of the slave deck, and Hal's gorge rose to scald the back of his throat. He swallowed back his own vomit, and wiped the pus from his face with the back of his arm, before he could bring himself to peer gingerly once more at the wound.

Black pus still bubbled from it, but he saw extraneous matter caught

199

in the mouth of the fresh cut. He dug at it with the tip of the scalpel, and freed a plug of dark and fibrous material, in which bone chips from the shattered scapula were mingled with jellied blood and pus.

'It's a piece of Danny's jacket,' he gasped. 'The ball must have pulled it into the wound.'

'Have you found the ball?' Sir Francis demanded.

'No, it must still be in there.'

He probed deeper into the wound. 'Yes. There it is.'

'Can you get it out?'

For a few minutes Hal worked in silence, thankful that Daniel was unconscious and did not have to suffer during this crude exploration. The flow of pus dwindled and now fresh clean blood oozed from the dark wound.

'I can't get it with the knife. It keeps slipping away,' he whispered. He put the aside the blade and pushed his finger into Daniel's hot, living flesh. Breath rasping with horror, he worked in deeper and still deeper, until he could get his fingertip behind the lump of lead.

'There!' he exclaimed suddenly, as the musket ball popped out of the wound and dropped onto the planks with a thump. It was deformed by its violent contact with bone, and there was a mirror-bright smear in the soft lead. He stared at it in vast relief, then snatched his finger from the wound.

It was followed by another soft rush of pus and lumpy foreign matter. 'There is the musket wad.' He gagged. 'I think everything is out now.' He looked down at his besmeared hands. The stench from them struck him like a blow in the face.

For a while they were all silent. Then Sir Francis whispered, 'Well done, Hal!'

'I think he is dead,' Hal answered, in a small voice. 'He is so still.'

Aboli released Daniel from his grip, then groped down his naked chest. 'No, he is alive. I can feel his heart. Now, Gundwane, you must wash out the wound for him.'

Between them they dragged Daniel's inert body to the limit of his fetters and Hal half knelt above him. He opened his filthy breeches and dehydrated by the limited ration of water, strained to squirt a weak stream of urine into the wound. It was enough to wash out the last rotting shreds of wadding and corruption. Hal used the last few drops of his own water to cleanse some of the filth from his hands and then fell back, spent by the effort.

'Done like a man, Gundwane,' Aboli told him, and offered Hal the red headcloth, black and crackling with dried blood and pus. 'Use this to staunch the wound. It is all we have.'

While Hal bandaged the wound, Daniel lay like a corpse. He no longer groaned or fought against his chains.

Three days later, as Hal leaned over to give him water, Daniel suddenly reached up, pushed away his head and took the mug from Hal's hands. He drained it in three long swallows. Then he belched thunderously and said, in a weak but lucid voice, 'By God, that was good. I'll have a drop more of that.'

Hal was so delighted and relieved that he handed him his own ration and watched him drink it. By the following day, Daniel was able to sit up as much as his chains would allow.

'Your surgery would have killed a dozen ordinary mortals,' Sir Francis murmured, as he watched Big Daniel's recovery with amazement, 'but Daniel Fisher thrives upon it.'

On the ninth day of their voyage Sam Bowles opened the hatch and sang out cheerily, 'Good news for you, gentlemen. Wind has played us false these last fifty leagues. His lordship reckons it will be another five days before we round the Cape. So your pleasure cruise will last a little longer.'

Few had the strength or interest to rail at this dread news, but they reached up for the pewter water mug with frantic hands. When the daily ceremony of watering was done, this time Sam Bowles altered the routine. Instead of slamming the hatch closed for another day, he stuck his head down and called, 'Captain Courteney, sir, his lordship's compliments, and if you have no previous engagement, he would be obliged if you would take dinner with him.' He scrambled down into the slave deck and, with two of his mates to help him, unscrewed Sir Francis's shackles from his wrists and ankles, and withdrew them from the ringbolts in the bulkhead.

Even once Sir Francis was free, it took all three men to lift him to his feet. He was so weak and cramped that he swayed and staggered like a drunkard as they helped him climb painfully through the hatch. 'Begging your pardon, Captain,' Sam laughed in his face, 'you ain't exactly no bed of roses, you ain't. I've smelt pig-sties and cesspools a sight sweeter than you, that I have, Franky me lad.'

They dragged him up on deck, and stripped the stinking rags from his shrunken body. Then four seamen worked the handles of the deck pump while Sam turned the stream from the canvas hose full on him. The *Gull* had entered the tail end of the cold green Benguela current that sweeps down the west coast of the continent. The jet of icy seawater from the hose almost knocked Sir Francis from his feet, and he had to cling to the shrouds to keep his balance. Shivering and choking when Sam directed the hose full into his face, he was able yet to scrub most of the crusted filth from his hair and body. It was of no concern to him that Katinka van de Velde leaned on the rail of the poop deck and scrutinized his nudity without the least indication of modesty.

Only when the hose was turned off and he was left to stand in the wind to dry off did Sir Francis have a chance to look about him and form some estimate of the *Gull's* position and condition. Although his emaciated body was blue with cold, he felt refreshed and strengthened by the dousing. His teeth chattered and his whole frame shuddered with involuntary spasms of cold as he looked overside, and he folded his arms over his chest to try to warm himself. The African mainland lay ten leagues or so to the north, and he recognized the cliffs and crags of the point that guarded the entrance to False Bay. They would have to weather that savage point before they could enter Table Bay on the far side of the peninsula.

The wind was almost dead calm, and the surface of the sea as slick as oil, with long, low swells rising and falling like the breathing of a sleeping monster. Sam Bowles was telling the truth: unless the wind picked up it would be many more days before they rounded the Cape and dropped anchor in Table Bay. He wondered how many more of his men would follow Timothy before they were released from the confines of the slave deck.

Sam Bowles threw a few pieces of threadbare but clean clothing on the deck at his feet. 'His lordship is expecting you. Don't keep him waiting now.'

'Franky!' Cumbrae rose to greet him as he stooped through the doorway into the *Gull's* stern cabin. 'I am so pleased to see that you look none the worse for your little sojourn below decks.' Before Sir Francis could avoid it, Cumbrae seized him in a bear-hug. 'I must apologize deeply for your treatment but it was at the insistence of the Dutch Governor and his wife. I would never have treated a brother Knight in such a scurvy fashion.'

While he spoke the Buzzard ran his great hands quickly down Sir Francis's body, checking for a concealed knife or other weapon, then pushed him into the largest and most comfortable chair in the cabin.

'A glass of wine, my dear old friend?' He poured it with his own hand, then gestured for his steward to place a bowl of stew in front of Sir Francis. Though saliva flooded into his mouth at the aroma of the first hot food he had been offered in almost two weeks, Sir Francis made no move to touch the glass or the spoon beside the bowl of stew.

202

Cumbrae noticed his refusal and, although he raised one bushy ginger eyebrow, he did not urge him but seized his own spoon and slurped up a mouthful from his own bowl. He chewed with all the sounds of appetite and approval, then washed it down with a hearty swallow from his wine glass, and wiped his red whiskers with the back of his hand. 'No, Franky, left to my own choice I would never have treated you so shabbily. You and I have had our differences in the past, but it has always been in the spirit of gentlemanly sport and competition, has it not?'

'Such sport as firing your broadside into my camp without warning?' Sir Francis asked.

'Now, let us not waste time in idle recrimination.' The Buzzard waved away the remark. 'That would never have been necessary if only you had agreed to share the booty from the galleon with me. What I really mean was that you and I understand each other. At heart we are brothers.'

'I think that I understand you.' Sir Francis nodded.

'Then you will know that what gives you pain, pains me even more. I have suffered every minute of your incarceration with you.'

'I hate to see you suffer, my lord, so why not release me and my men?'

'That is my fervent wish and intention, I assure you. However, there remains one small impediment that prevents me doing so. I need from you a sign that my warm feelings towards you are reciprocated. I am still deeply hurt that you would not share with me, your old friend, what was rightly mine in the terms of our agreement.'

'I am certain that the Dutch have given you the share you lacked before. In fact I saw you loading what seemed to me a generous portion of the spice aboard this very ship. I wonder what the Lord High Admiral of England will make of such traffic with the enemy.'

'A few barrels of spice – barely worth the breath to mention it.' Cumbrae smiled. 'But there ain't nothing like silver and gold to rouse my fraternal instincts. Come, now, Franky, we have wasted enough time in the pleasantries. You and I know that you have the bullion from the galleon cached somewhere close by your encampment on Elephant Lagoon. I know I will find it if I search long enough, but by then you will be dead, sent messily on your way by the executioner at Good Hope.'

Sir Francis smiled and shook his head. 'I have cached no treasure. Search if you will, but there is nothing for you to find.'

'Think on it, Franky. You know what the Dutch did to the English merchants they captured on the isle of Bali? They crucified them and burnt off their hands and feet with sulphur flares. I want to save you from that.'

203

'If you have nothing further to discuss, I will return to my crew.' Sir Francis stood up. His legs were stronger now.

'Sit down!' the Buzzard snapped. 'Tell me where you hid it, man, and I will put you and your men ashore with no further harm done, I swear it on my honour.' Cumbrae wheedled and blustered for another hour. Then at last he sighed. 'You drive a hard bargain, Franky. I tell you what I'll do for you. I would do it for no one else, but I love you like a brother. If you take me back and lead me to the booty, I'll share it with you. Fifty-fifty, right down the middle. Now I can't be more fair than that, can I?'

Sir Francis met even this offer with a calm, detached smile, and Cumbrae could hide his fury no longer. He slapped the table so viciously with the palm of his hand, that the glasses overturned and the wine sprayed across the cabin. He bellowed furiously for Sam Bowles. 'Take this arrogant bastard away, and chain him up again.' As Sir Francis left the cabin he shouted after him, 'I will find where you hid it, Franky, I swear it to you. I know more than you think. Just as soon as I have seen you topped on the Parade at Good Hope, I will be going back to the lagoon, and I won't leave until I find it.'

One more of Sir Francis's seamen died in his chains before they anchored off the foreshore in Table Bay. The others were so stiff and weak that they were forced to crawl like animals up the ladder to the upper deck. They huddled there, their ragged clothing crusted with their own filth, gazing around them, blinking and trying to shield their eyes from the brilliant morning sunshine.

Hal had never been this close inshore of Good Hope. On the outward leg of their cruise, at the beginning of the war, they had stood well off and looked into the bay from a great distance. However, that brief glimpse had not prepared him for the splendour of this seascape, where the royal blue of the Atlantic, flecked with wind spume, washed up on beaches so dazzling they hurt his weakened eyes.

The fabled flat-topped mountain seemed to fill most of the blue African sky, a great cliff of yellow rock slashed by deep ravines choked with dense green forest. The top of the mountain was so geometrically level, and its proportions so pleasing, that it seemed to have been designed by a celestial architect. Over the top of this immense table-land spilled a standing wave of shimmering cloud, frothy as milk boiling over the rim of a pot. This silver cascade never reached the lower slopes of the mountain, but as it fell it evaporated in mid-flight with a magical suddenness, leaving the lower slopes resplendent in their cloaking of verdant natural forest.

The grandeur dwarfed and rendered inconsequential the buildings that spread like an irritating rash along the shore above the snowy beach, from which a fleet of small boats put out to meet the *Gull* as soon as she dropped her anchor.

Governor van de Velde refused to climb down the ladder, and was hoisted from the deck, swung outboard in a boatswain's chair, all the while shouting nervous instructions at the men on the ropes. 'Careful now, you clumsy oafs! Drop me and I will have the skin thrashed off your backs.'

He was lowered into the longboat at the *Gull*'s side, in which his wife already waited. Assisted by Colonel Cornelius Schreuder, her descent had been considerably more graceful than her husband's.

They were rowed to the foreshore, where five strong slaves lifted the new Governor from the boat that danced in the shore break of white foam at the edge of the beach. They waded ashore with him and deposited him on the sand.

As the Governor's feet touched African soil the first cannon shot of a salute of fourteen rang out. A long plume of silver gunsmoke shot from the embrasure on the top of the southern redoubt, and the thunderous report so startled the new representative of the Company that he leapt a foot in the air and almost lost his plumed hat to the sou'-easter.

Governor Kleinhans, overjoyed that his successor in office had at last arrived, was at the foreshore to meet him. The garrison commander, equally anxious to hand over to Colonel Schreuder and shake from his feet the rank African dust, was on the ramparts of the fortress, his telescope focused on the arriving dignitaries.

The state carriage was waiting above the beach, six beautiful greys in the traces. Governor Kleinhans dismounted from it to greet the new arrivals, clutching his hat in the wind. An honour guard from the garrison was drawn up around the carriage. Gathered along the water-front were several hundred men, women and children. Every resident of the settlement who could walk or crawl had turned out to welcome Governor van de Velde as he struggled through the loose sand.

When at last he reached firm footing and had gathered his breath and dignity he accepted Governor Kleinhans' welcome. They shook hands to cheering and applause from the Company officials, free burghers and slaves gathered to watch. The military escort presented their arms, and the band launched into a spirited patriotic air. The music ended with a clash of cymbals and a roll of kettle drums. The two Governors spontaneously embraced each other, Kleinhans delighted to be free to return to Amsterdam, and van de Velde overjoyed at having escaped death by storm and piracy and to have Dutch soil under his feet once more.

While Sam Bowles and his mates were removing the corpses from the slave chains and tossing them overboard, Hal squatted in the rank of captives and watched from afar as Katinka was ushered into the carriage by Governor Kleinhans on one arm and Colonel Schreuder on the other.

He felt his heart tear with love for her, and he whispered to Daniel and Aboli, 'Is she not the most beautiful lady in the world? She will use her influence for us. Now that her husband has full powers, she will persuade him to treat us justly.' Neither of the two big men replied, but they exchanged a glance. Daniel grinned with broken teeth and Aboli rolled his eyes.

Once Katinka was settled on the leather seats, they boosted her husband aboard. The carriage swayed and rocked under his weight. As soon as he was safely installed beside his wife, the band struck up a lively march and the escort shouldered their muskets and stepped out, a stirring sight in their white cross belts and green jackets. The procession streamed across the open parade ground towards the fort, with the crowds running ahead of the carriage and lining both sides of the route.

'Farewell, gentlemen. It has been a pleasure and a privilege to have you aboard.' The Buzzard touched the brim of his hat in an ironic salute as Sir Francis shambled across the deck dragging his chains, and led the file of his crew down the ladder into the boat moored alongside. So many men in chains made a heavy load for it in this condition of swell. They were left with only a few inches of freeboard as they pushed off from the *Gull*'s side.

The oarsmen struggled to hold the longboat's stern into the breaking white waves as they approached the beach, but a taller swell got under her and threw her off line. She broached heavily, dug in her shoulder and rolled over in four feet of water. Crew and passengers were thrown into the white water, and the capsized boat was caught up in the wash.

Choking and coughing up seawater, the prisoners managed to drag each other from the surf by their chains. Miraculously none was drowned, but the effort taxed most to their limit. When the guards from the fortress hectored them to their feet and drove them with musket butt and curses up the beach, they were streaming water and coated with a sugaring of white sand.

Having seen the state carriage safely through the gates of the fort, the crowds poured back to the water-front to have a little sport with these wretched creatures. They studied them as though they were livestock at a market, and their laughter was unrestrained, their comments ribald.

'Look more like gypsies and beggars than English pirates to me.'

'I'm saving my guilders. I'll not be bidding when that lot go up on the slave block.'

'They don't sell pirates, they burn them.'

'They don't look much, but at least they'll give us all some sport. We haven't had a really good execution since the slave revolt.'

'There's Stadige Jan over there, come to look them over. I'll warrant he'll have a few lessons to teach these corsairs.'

Hal turned his head in the direction the speaker pointed to where a tall burgher in dark, drab clothing and a puritan hat stood a head above the crowd. He looked at Hal with pale expressionless yellow eyes.

'What do you think of these beauties, Stadige Jan? Will you be able to get them to sing a pretty tune for us?'

Hal sensed the repulsion and fascination this man held for those around him. None stood too close to him, and they looked at him in such a way that Hal instinctively knew that this was the executioner of whom they had been warned. He felt his flesh crawl as he looked into those faded eyes.

'Why do you think that they call him Slow John?' he asked Aboli, from the side of his mouth.

'Let us hope we never have to find out,' Aboli replied, as they passed where the tall, cadaverous figure stood.

Small boys, both brown and white, danced beside the column of chained men, jeering and pelting them with pebbles and filth from the open gutters that carried the sewage from the town down to the sea front. Encouraged by this example a pack of mongrel dogs snapped at their heels. The adults in the crowd were turned out in their best clothes for such an unusual occasion and laughed at the antics of the children. Some of the women held sachets of herbs to their noses when they smelt the bedraggled file of prisoners, shuddering in horrified fascination.

'Oh! What dreadful creatures!'

'Look at those cruel and savage faces.'

'I have heard that they feed those Negroes on human flesh.'

Aboli contorted his face and rolled his eyes at them. The tattoos on his cheeks stood proud, and his great white teeth were bared in a fearsome grin. The women squealed with delicious terror, and their little daughters hid their faces in their mothers' skirts as he passed.

At the rear of the crowd, hanging back from the company of their betters, taking no part in the sport of baiting the captives, were those men and women who, Hal guessed, must be the domestic slaves of the burghers. The slaves in the crowd ranged in colour from the anthracite black of Africa to the amber and gold skins of the Orient. Most were simply dressed in the cast-off clothing of their owners, although some of the prettier women wore the flamboyant finery that marked them as the favourite playthings of their masters.

They looked on quietly as the seamen trudged past in their clanking chains, and there was no sound of laughter among them. Rather, Hal sensed a certain empathy behind their closed impassive expressions for they were captives also. Just before they entered the gate to the fort, Hal noticed one girl in particular at the back of the crowd. She had climbed up on a pile of masonry blocks for a better view and stood higher than the intervening ranks of spectators. This was not the only reason why Hal had singled her out.

She was more beautiful than he had ever expected any woman to be. She was a flower of a girl, with thick glossy black hair and dark eyes that seemed too large for her delicate oval face. For one moment their eyes met over the heads of the crowd, and it seemed to Hal that she tried to pass him some message that he was unable to grasp. He knew only that she felt compassion for him, and that she shared in his suffering. Then he lost sight of her as they were marched through the gateway into the courtyard of the fort.

The image of her stayed with him over the dreadful days that followed. Gradually it began to supersede the memory of Katinka, and in the nights sometimes returned to give him the strength he needed to endure. He felt that if there were but one person of such loveliness and tenderness out there, beyond the gaunt stone walls, who cared for his abject condition, then it was worth fighting on.

In the courtyard of the fort, a military armourer struck off their shackles. A shore party under the command of Sam Bowles stood by to collect the discarded chains to take back aboard the *Gull*. 'I will miss you all, my shipmates.' Sam grinned. 'The lower decks of the old *Gull* will be empty and lonely without your smiling faces and your good cheer.' He gave them a salute from the gateway as he led his shore party away. 'I hope they look after you as well as your good friend Sam Bowles did. But, never fear, I'll be at the Parade when you give your last performance there.'

When Sam was gone, Hal looked around the courtyard. He saw that the fortress had been designed on a substantial scale. As part of his training his father had made him study the science of land fortifications, so he recognized the classical defensive layout of the stone walls and redoubts. He realized that once these works were completed, it would take an army equipped with a full siege train to reduce them.

However, the work was less than half finished, and on the landward side of the fort or, as their new gaolers referred to it, *het kasteel*, the castle, there were merely open foundations from which the massive stone walls would one day rise. Yet it was clear that the work was being hastened along. Almost certainly the two recent Anglo-Dutch wars had imparted this impetus. Both Oliver Cromwell, the Lord Protector of the Commonwealth of England, Scotland and Ireland, during the interregnum, and King Charles, son of the man he had beheaded, could claim some credit for the frenzy of construction that was going on around them. They had forcibly reminded the Dutch of the vulnerability of their far-flung colonies. The half-finished walls swarmed with hundreds of workmen, and the courtyard in which they stood was piled with building timber and blocks of dressed masonry hewn from the mountain that loomed over it all.

As dangerous captives they were kept apart from the other prisoners. They were marched from the courtyard down the short spiral staircase below the south wall of the fort. The stone blocks that lined floor, vaulted roof and walls glistened with moisture that had seeped in from the surrounding waterlogged soil. Even on such a sunny day in autumn the temperature in these dank forbidding surroundings made them shiver.

At the foot of the first flight of stairs Sir Francis Courteney was dragged out of the file by his gaolers and thrust into a small cell just large enough to hold one man. It was one in a row of half a dozen or so identical cells, whose doors were of solid timber studded with iron bolts and the tiny barred peep-hole in each was shuttered and closed. They had no sight of the other inmates. 'Special quarters for you, Sir Pirate,' the burly Dutch gaoler told him as he slammed the door on Sir Francis and turned the lock with a huge iron key from the bunch on his belt. 'We are putting you in the Skellum's Den, with all the really bad ones, the murderers and rebels and robbers. You will feel at home here, of that I'm sure.'

The rest of the prisoners were herded down to the next level of the dungeon. The sergeant gaoler unlocked the grille door at the end of the tunnel and they were shoved into a long narrow cell. Once the grille was locked behind them there was barely room for them all to stretch out on the thin layer of damp straw that covered the cobblestoned floor. A single latrine bucket stood in one corner, but murmurs of pleasure from all the men greeted the sight of the large water cistern beside the grille gate. At least this meant they were no longer on shipboard water rations.

There were four small windows set in the top of one wall and, once they had inspected their surroundings, Hal looked up at them. Aboli hoisted him onto his shoulders and he was able to reach one of these narrow openings. It was heavily barred, like the others, but Hal tried the gratings with his bare hands. They were set rock-firm, and he was forced to put out of his mind any notion of escaping this way.

Hanging on the grating, he drew himself up and peered through it. He found that his eyes were a foot or so above ground level, and from there he had a view of part of the interior courtyard of the castle. He could see the entrance gateway and the grand portals of what he guessed must be the Company offices and the Governor's suite. To one side, through the gap where the walls had not yet been raised, he could see a portion of the cliffs of the table-topped mountain, and above them the sky. Against the cloudless blue sailed a flock of white gulls.

Hal lowered himself and pushed his way through the throng of seamen, stepping over the bodies of the sick and wounded. When he reached the grille he looked up the staircase but could not see the door to his father's cell.

'Father!' he called tentatively, expecting a rebuke from one of the gaolers, but when there was no response he raised his voice and shouted again.

'I hear you, Hal,' his father called back.

'Do you have any orders for us, Father?'

'I expect they'll leave us in peace for a day or two, at least until they have convened a tribunal. We will have to wait it out. Tell the men to be of good heart.'

At that a strange voice intervened, speaking in English but with an unfamiliar accent. 'Are you the English pirates we have heard so much about?'

'We are honest sailors, falsely accused,' Sir Francis shouted back. 'Who and what are you?'

'I am your neighbour in the Skellum's Den, two cells down from you. I am condemned to die, as you are.'

'We are not yet condemned,' Sir Francis protested.

'It is only a matter of time. I hear from the gaolers that you soon will be.'

'What is your name?' Hal joined in the exchange. He was not interested in the stranger, but this conversation served to pass the time and divert them from their own predicament. 'What is your crime?'

'I am Althuda, and my crime is that I strive to be free and to set other men free.'

'Then we are brothers, Althuda, you and I and every man here. We all strive for freedom.'

There was a ragged chorus of assent, and when it subsided Althuda spoke again. 'I led a revolt of the Company slaves. Some were recaptured. Those Stadige Jan burned alive, but most of us escaped into the mountains. Many times they sent soldiers after us, but we fought and drove them off and they could not enslave us again.' His was a vital young voice, proud and strong, and even before Hal had seen his face he found himself drawn to this Althuda.

'Then if you escaped, how is it that you are back here in the Skellum's Den?' one of the English seamen wanted to know. They were all listening now. Althuda's story had moved even the most hardened of them.

'I came back to rescue somebody, another slave who was left behind,' Althuda told them. 'When I entered the colony again I was recognized and betrayed.'

They were all silent for a space.

'A woman?' a voice asked. 'You came back for a woman?'

'Yes,' said Althuda. 'A woman.'

'There is always an Eve in the midst of Eden to tempt us into folly,' one sang out and they all laughed.

Then somebody else asked, 'Was she your sweetheart?'

'No,' Althuda answered. 'I came back for my little sister.'

Thirty guests sat down to the banquet that Governor Kleinhans gave to welcome his successor. All the most important men in the administration of the colony, together with their wives, were seated around the long board.

From the place of honour Petrus van de Velde gazed with delighted anticipation down the length of the rosewood table above which hung massive chandeliers, each burning fifty perfumed candles. They lit the great hall as if it was day, and sparkled on the silverware and crystal glasses.

For months now, ever since sailing from the coast of Trincomalee, van de Velde had been forced to subsist on the swill and offal cooked on the galleon and then on the coarse fare that the English pirates had provided for him. Now his eyes shone and saliva flooded his mouth as he contemplated the culinary extravaganza spread before him. He reached for the tall glass in front of him, and took a mouthful of the rare

211

wine from Champagne. The tiny seething bubbles tickled his palate and spurred his already unbridled appetite.

Van de Velde considered this a most fortunate posting, for which his wife's connection in the Council of Seventeen was to be thanked. Positioned here, at the tip of Africa, a constant procession of ships passed in both directions bringing the luxuries of Europe and the Orient into Table Bay. They would want for nothing.

Silently he cursed Kleinhans for his long-winded speech of welcome, of which he heard barely a word. All his attention was on the array of silver dishes and chargers that were laid before him, one after another.

There were little sucking pigs in crisp suits of golden crackling; barons of beef running with their own rich juices set around with steaming ramparts of roasted potatoes; heaps of tender young pullets and pigeons and ducks and fat geese; five different types of fresh fish from the Atlantic, cooked five different ways, fragrant with the curries and spices of Java and Kandy and Further India; tall pyramids of the huge clawless crimson lobsters that abounded in this southern ocean; a vast array of fruits and succulent vegetables from the Company gardens; and sherbets and custards and sugar dumplings and cakes and trifles and confitures and every sweet delight that the slave chefs in the kitchens could conceive. All this was backed by stalwart ranks of cheese brought by Company ships from Holland, and jars of pickled North-Sea herring, and smoked sides of wild boar and salmon.

In contrast to this superabundance, the service was all of delicate blue and white pattern. Behind each chair stood a house slave in the green uniform of the Company, ready to recharge glass and plate with nimble white-gloved hands. Would the man never stop talking and let them at the food, van de Velde wondered, and smiled and nodded at Kleinhans' inanities.

At last, with a bow to the new Governor and a much deeper one to his wife, Kleinhans sank back into his chair, and everyone looked expectantly at van de Velde. He gazed around at their asinine faces, and then with a sigh rose to his feet to reply. Two minutes will do it, he told himself, and gave them what they expected to hear, ending jovially, 'In conclusion, I want only to wish Governor Kleinhans a safe return to the old country, and a long and happy retirement.'

He sat down with alacrity and reached for his spoon. This was the first time the burghers had been privileged to witness the new Governor at table, and an amazed and respectful silence fell upon the company as they watched the level in his soup bowl fall like the outgoing tide across the mud-flats of the Zuider Zee. Then, suddenly realizing that when the guest of honour finished one course, the plates would be changed and

212

the next course served, they fell to in a frenzied effort to catch up. There were many stout trenchermen amongst them, but none to match the Governor, especially when he had had a head start.

As his soup bowl emptied, every bowl was whisked away and replaced with a plate piled high with thick cuts of sucking pig. The first two courses were completed in virtual silence, broken only by slurping and gulping.

During the third course Kleinhans rallied and, as host, made a valiant attempt to revive the conversation. He leaned forward to distract van de Velde's attention from his plate. 'I expect that you will wish to deal with the matter of the English pirates before any other business,' he asked, and van de Velde nodded vigorously, although his mouth was too full of succulent lobster to permit a verbal reply.

'Have you decided yet how you will go about their trial and sentencing?' Kleinhans enquired lugubriously. Van de Velde swallowed noisily, before he replied, 'They will be executed, of course, but not before their captain, this notorious corsair Francis Courteney, reveals the hiding place of the missing Company cargo. I would like to convene a tribunal immediately for this purpose.'

Colonel Schreuder coughed politely, and van de Velde glanced at him impatiently. 'Yes? You wanted to say something? Out with it, then!'

'Today I had opportunity to inspect the work proceeding on the kasteel fortifications, sir. The good Lord alone knows when we will be at war with England again, but it may be soon. The English are thieves by nature, and pirates by vocation. It is for these reasons, sir, that the Seventeen in Amsterdam have placed the highest priority on the completion of our fortifications. That fact is spelt out very clearly in my orders and my letter of appointment to the command of the kasteel.'

Every man at the table looked grave and attentive at the mention of the sacred Seventeen, as though the name of a deity had been invoked. Schreuder let the silence run on for a while to make good his point, then said, 'The work is very much behind what their excellencies have decreed.'

Major Loten, the outgoing garrison commander, interjected, 'It is true that the work is somewhat behindhand, but there are good reasons for this.' The construction was his prime responsibility, and Governor van de Velde's eyes switched to his face. He placed another forkful of lobster in his mouth. The sauce was truly delicious, and he sighed with pleasure as he contemplated another five years of meals of this order. He must certainly buy the chef from Kleinhans before he sailed. He formed his features into a more solemn pattern as he listened to Loten making his excuses. 'I have been hampered by a shortage of labour. This most 'regrettable revolt among the slaves has left us severely undermanned,' he said lamely, and van de Velde frowned.

'Precisely the point I was about to make,' Schreuder picked up smoothly. 'If we are so short of men to meet the expectations of the Seventeen, would we be wise to execute twenty-four strong and able-bodied English pirates, instead of employing them in the workings?'

Every eye at the table turned to van de Velde to judge his reaction, waiting for him to give them a lead. The new Governor swallowed, then used his forefinger to free a shred of lobster leg caught in his back teeth before he spoke. 'Courteney cannot be spared,' he said at last. 'Not even to work on the fortifications. According to Lord Cumbrae, whose opinion I respect,' he gave the Buzzard a seated bow, 'the Englishman knows where the missing cargo is hidden, besides which my wife and I,' he nodded towards Katinka, who sat between Kleinhans and Schreuder, 'have been forced to suffer many indignities at his hands.'

'I quite agree,' said Schreuder. 'He must be made to tell all he knows of the missing bullion. But the others? Such a waste to execute them when they are needed on the walls, don't you think, sir. They are, after all, dull-witted cattle, with little understanding of the gravity of their offence but with strong backs to pay for it.'

Van de Velde grunted noncommittally. 'I would like to hear the opinion of Governor Kleinhans on this matter,' he said, and filled his mouth again, his head lowered on his shoulders and his small eyes focused on his predecessor. Sagely, he passed on the responsibility of making the decision. Later, if there were repercussions, he could always unload a share of the blame.

'Of course,' said Governor Kleinhans, with an airy wave of the hand, 'prime slaves are selling for almost a thousand guilders a head at the moment. Such a large addition to the Company purse would commend itself highly to their excellencies. The Seventeen are determined that the colony must pay for itself and not become a drain on the Company exchequer.'

All present gave this their solemn consideration. In the silence Katinka said, in ringing crystal tones, 'I, for one, will need slaves for my household. I would welcome the opportunity to acquire good workers even at those exorbitant prices.'

'By international accord and protocol it is forbidden to sell Christians into slavery,' Schreuder pointed out, as he saw the prospects of procuring labour for his fortifications beginning to recede. 'Even Englishmen.'

'Not all the captured pirates are Christians,' Kleinhans persisted. 'I saw a number of black faces amongst them. Negro slaves are much in demand in the colony. They are good workers and breeders. Would it

214

not be a most desirable compromise to sell them for guilders to please the Seventeen? We could then condemn the English pirates to lifelong hard labour. They could be used to hasten the completion of the works, also to please the Seventeen.'

Van de Velde grunted again, and scraped his plate noisily to draw attention to the fact that he was ready to sample the beef. He pondered these conflicting arguments while a freshly loaded plate was placed in front of him. There was another consideration to take into account of which no one else was aware: his bitter hatred of Colonel Schreuder. He did not want to ease his lot in life and, truth to tell, he would be delighted if the Colonel failed dismally in his new command and was ordered home in disgrace – just as long as that failure did not redound to his own discredit.

He stared hard at Schreuder as he toyed with the idea of refusing him. He knew, all too well, what that one had in mind, and he turned his attention from the Colonel to his wife. Katinka looked radiant this evening. Within a few days of arriving at the Cape and moving into their temporary quarters in the castle, she was fully recovered from the long voyage and from the captivity forced upon them by Sir Francis Courteney. She was, of course, young and resilient, not yet twenty-four years of age, but that alone did not account for her gaiety and vivacity this evening. Whenever the bumptious Schreuder spoke, which was too often, she turned those huge, innocent eyes upon him, with full attention. When she spoke directly to him, which was also too often, she touched him, laying one of her delicate white hands on his sleeve, and once, to van de Velde's intense mortification, actually placing her fingers on Schreuder's bony paw, letting them linger there for all the company to see and smirk at.

It almost, but not quite, spoiled his appetite to have this blatant courtship ritual take place not only under his nose but under the collective noses of the entire colony. It would have been bad enough if, in private, he had been forced to face the fact that the valiant Colonel would soon be rummaging around under those rustling petticoats. It was insufferable that he must share this knowledge with all his underlings. How could he demand respect and sycophantic obedience from them while his wife was set on publicly placing horns upon his head? When I packed him off to Amsterdam to negotiate my ransom, I thought we had seen the last of Colonel Schreuder, he thought sullenly. It seems I will have to take sterner measures in the future. And as he ploughed his way through all sixteen courses, he turned over in his mind the various alternatives.

Van de Velde was so stuffed with good food that the short walk from

215

the great hall of the castle to the council chamber was only accomplished with much heavy breathing and the occasional pause, ostensibly to admire the paintings and other works of art that decorated the walls, but in reality to recover his resources.

In the chamber he settled with a vast sigh into the cushions of one of the high-backed chairs, and accepted a glass of brandy and a pipe of tobacco.

'I will convene the court to try the pirates this coming week, that is immediately after I formally take over the governorship from Mijnheer Kleinhans,' he announced. 'No point in wasting any more time on this riff-raff. I appoint Colonel Schreuder to act as attorney-general and to prosecute the case. I will take on the duties of judge.' He looked across the table at his host. 'Will you have your officers make the necessary arrangements please, Mijnheer Kleinhans.'

'Certainly, Mijnheer van de Velde. Have you given any thought to appointing an advocate to defend the accused pirates?'

It was clear from van de Velde's expression that he had not, but now he waved a pudgy paw and said airily, 'See to that, will you? I am sure one of your clerks has sufficient knowledge of the law to perform the duty adequately. After all, what is there to defend?' he asked, and chuckled throatily.

'A name comes to mind.' Kleinhans nodded. 'I will appoint him and arrange for him to have access to the prisoners to receive their statements.'

'Dear God!' Van de Velde looked scandalized. 'Why would you do that? I don't want that English rogue Courteney putting all sorts of ideas into the man's head. I will set out the facts for him. He need only recite them to the court.'

'I understand,' Kleinhans agreed. 'It will all be ready to hand over to you before I step down next week.' He looked across at Katinka. 'My dear lady, you, of course, will wish to move out of your temporary quarters here in the castle, and into the much more commodious and comfortable Governor's residence as soon as possible. I thought that we could arrange an inspection of your new home after the church service on Sunday. I would be honoured to personally conduct you on a tour of the establishment.'

'That is kind, sir.' Katinka smiled at him, glad to be the focus of attention once more. For a moment Kleinhans basked in the warmth of her approval, then went on diffidently, 'As you can well imagine, I have acquired a considerable household during my term of office in the colony. Coincidentally, the cooks who prepared the humble little meal of which we partook this evening are part of my own span of slaves.' He

216

glanced at van de Velde. 'I hope that their efforts met with your approval?' When the Governor nodded comfortably, he turned back to Katinka. ' As you know, very soon I shall return to the old country, and into retirement on my small country estate. Twenty slaves will be far in excess of my future requirements. You, Mevrouw, voiced your interest in purchasing quality slaves. I would like to take the opportunity of your visit to the residence to show you those creatures that I have for sale. They have all been hand-picked, and I think you will find it more convenient and cheaper to make a private acquisition than to bid at public auction. The trouble with buying slaves is that those who look good value on the auction block can have serious hidden defects. It is always comforting to know that the seller has sound and sufficient reasons for selling, is it not?'

Hal set a constant lookout at the high window of the cell. There was always one man standing on another's shoulders, clinging to the bars, to keep a watch on the castle courtyard. The lookout called down all sightings to Hal, who in turn relayed these up the stairwell to his father.

Within the first few days they were able to work out the timetable of the garrison, and to note the routine comings and goings of the Company officials, and of the free burghers who visited the castle regularly.

Hal called a description of each of these persons to the unseen leader of the slave rebellion in the Skellum's Den. Althuda knew the personal details of every person in the settlement and passed on all this accumulated knowledge, so that within the first few days Hal came to know not only the appearance but also the personality and character of each one.

He started a calendar, marking the passage of each day with a scratch on a slab of sandstone in one corner of the cell and registering the more important events beside it. He was not certain that anything was to be gained from these records, but at least it gave the men something to talk about, and fostered the illusion that he had a plan of action for their release or, failing that, for their escape.

'Governor's carriage at the staircase!' the lookout warned, and Hal jumped up from where he was sitting between Aboli and Daniel against the far wall.

'Come down,' he ordered. 'Let me up.'

Through the bars he saw the state carriage parked at the foot of the broad staircase that led up to the Company offices and the Governor's suite. The coachman's name was Fredricus, an elderly Javanese slave

217

who belonged to Governor Kleinhans. According to Althuda, he was no friend. For thirty years he had been Kleinhans' dog, and he could not be trusted. Althuda suspected that he was the one who had betrayed him, and had reported his return from the mountains to Major Loten. 'We will probably be rid of him when Kleinhans leaves the colony. He is sure to take Fredricus back with him to Holland,' Althuda told them.

There was a sudden stir as a detachment of soldiers hurried across the courtyard from the armoury and formed up at the foot of the staircase.

'Kleinhans going out,' Hal called, recognizing these preparations, and as he spoke the double doors swung open and a small party emerged into the sunlight and descended towards the waiting carriage.

The tall, stooped figure of Kleinhans, with his sour dyspeptic face, contrasted sharply with the lovely young woman on his arm. Hal's heart tripped as he recognized Katinka but his feelings were no longer as intense as once they had been. Instead, his eyes narrowed as he saw that the Neptune sword hung in its chased and gold-encrusted scabbard at Schreuder's side as the colonel followed Katinka down the stairs. Each time he saw Schreuder wearing it his anger was rekindled.

Fredricus climbed stiffly from his high seat, folded down the steps, opened the carriage door, then stood aside to allow the two gentlemen to hand Katinka up and settle her comfortably.

'What is happening down there?' his father called and, with a guilty start, Hal realized that he had not spoken since he had laid eyes on the woman he loved. By now, though, she had been carried out of his sight. The carriage rolled out smoothly through the castle gates, and the sentries saluted as Fredricus shook the horses into a trot across the parade.

It was a sparkling autumn day, and the constant sou'-easter of summer had dropped. Katinka sat beside Governor Kleinhans, facing forward. Cornelius Schreuder sat opposite her. She had left her husband in his office in the castle, labouring over his reports for the Seventeen, and now she felt the devil in her. She flounced out her skirts and the rustling crinolines covered the Colonel's soft leather boots.

While still chatting animatedly to Kleinhans, she reached out one slippered foot under cover of her skirts and found Schreuder's toe. She pressed it coquettishly, and felt him start. She pressed again, and felt him respond sheepishly. Then she turned from Kleinhans and addressed Schreuder directly. 'Don't you agree, Colonel, that an avenue of oaks leading up to the residence would look splendid? I can imagine their thick hard trunks standing up vigorously. How beautiful that would be.' She opened her violet eyes wide to give the remark significance, and pressed his foot again.

'Indeed, Mevrouw.' Schreuder's voice was husky with double meaning. 'I agree with you entirely. In fact the image you paint is so vivid that you should be able to see the stem growing before your very eyes.'

At this invitation she glanced down at his lap and, to her amusement, saw the effect that she was having upon him. He is putting up a tent in his breeches for my sake!

Almost a mile beyond the forbidding pile of the castle, the Governor's residence stood at the mountain end of the Company gardens. It was a graceful building, with dark thatched roof and whitewashed walls, surrounded by wide shady verandas. Laid out in the shape of a cross, the gables at each of the four ends of the house were decorated with plaster friezes depicting the seasons. The gardens were well established; a succession of Company gardeners had lavished love and care upon them.

Even from a distance Katinka was delighted with her new home. She had dreaded being lodged in some ugly, bucolic hovel, but this far surpassed her most optimistic expectations. The entire domestic staff of the residence was drawn up on the wide front terrace to greet her.

The carriage rolled to a standstill and her two escorts hastened to help Katinka to earth. At a prearranged signal all the waiting man-servants lifted their hats, and bowed so low as to sweep the ground before her with their headgear, while the females dropped into deep curtsies. Katinka acknowledged their greeting with a cool nod, and Kleinhans introduced each of them in turn to her. Most were merely brown or yellow faces that made no impression whatsoever on her, and she glanced vaguely in their direction then passed on, hurrying through this tedious little ritual as swiftly as she could.

However, one or two caught and held her attention for more than a few moments.

'This is the head gardener.' Kleinhans summoned the man with a snap of his fingers, and he stood bareheaded before her, holding over his chest the high-crowned Puritan hat with its silver buckled band and wide brim. 'He is a man of some importance in our community,' Kleinhans said. 'Not only is he responsible for these beautiful surroundings,' he indicated the wide green lawns and splendid flower beds, 'and for providing each Company ship that calls into Table Bay with fresh fruit and vegetables, but he is also the official executioner.'

Katinka had been on the point of passing on, but now, with a small thrill of excitement, she turned back to study this creature. He towered above her, and she looked up into his strange pale eyes, imagining what dread sights they had seen. Then she glanced down at his hands. They were farmer's hands, broad and strong and calloused, the backs covered with stiff bristles. She imagined them holding a spade or a branding iron, a pitchfork or the knotted coil of the strangling cord.

'They call you Stadige Jan?' She had heard the name spoken with fascination and revulsion, the way one speaks of a deadly, venomous snake.

'Ja, Mevrouw.' He nodded. 'That is what they call me.'

'A strange name. Why?' She found his level yellow stare disquieting, as though he was looking at something far behind her.

'Because I speak slowly. Because I never rush. Because I am thorough. Because plants grow slowly and fruitfully under my hands. Because men die slowly and painfully under these same hands.' He held up one for her to examine. His voice was sonorous yet melodious. She found herself swallowing hard with a strange, perverse arousal.

'We are soon to have a chance to watch you work, Stadige Jan.' She smiled slightly breathlessly. 'I believe that the dungeon of the castle is full of rogues awaiting your ministrations.' She had a sudden image of those broad strong hands working on Hal Courteney's slim straight body, the body she knew so well, changing it, gradually breaking it down. The muscles in her thighs and lower belly tightened at the thought. It would be the ultimate thrill to see the beautiful toy of which she had tired being maimed and disfigured, but slowly and slowly.

'We must talk again, Stadige Jan,' she said huskily. 'I am sure you have many amusing stories to tell me, about cabbages and other things.' He bowed again, replaced the hat on his shaven head and stepped back into the line of servants. Katinka passed on.

'This is my housekeeper,' Kleinhans said, but Katinka was so engrossed in her thoughts that, for several seconds, she gave no indication that she had heard him. Then she threw an idle glance at the female Kleinhans was presenting, and suddenly her eyes widened. She turned her full attention on the woman. 'Her name is Sukeena.' There was something in Kleinhans' tone that she could not immediately fathom.

'She is very young for such an important position,' Katinka said, to gain time in which to allow her instincts to have play. In an entirely different manner, she found this woman as enthralling as the executioner. She was so exquisitely small and dainty as to seem an artist's creation and not flesh and blood.

'It is a characteristic of her race to appear much younger than their years,' Kleinhans told her. 'They have such small childlike bodies – you will observe her tiny waist and her hands and feet, like those of a doll.'

He broke off abruptly, as he realized that he might have committed a solecism in discussing another woman's bodily parts.

Katinka's expression did not change to reveal the amusement she felt. The old goat lusts for her, she thought, and she studied the jewel-like qualities to which he had drawn her attention. The girl wore a high collar, but the stuff of her blouse was sheer and light as gossamer. Like the rest of her, her breasts were tiny but perfect. Katinka could see the shape and colour of her nipples through the silk: they were like a pair of imperial rubies wrapped in gossamer. That dress, although simple and of classical Eastern design, must have cost fifty guilders at the very least. Her sandals were gold-embroidered, rich raiment for a house slave. At her throat she wore an ornament of carved jade, a jewel fit for a mandarin's favourite. The girl must certainly be Kleinhans' pretty bauble, she decided.

Katinka's first carnal fulfilment had been at the age of thirteen, on the threshold of puberty. In the seclusion of the nursery, her nurse had introduced her to those forbidden delights. Occasionally, when her fancy dictated and opportunity presented, she still voyaged to the enchanted isles of Lesbos. Often she had found there enchantments that no man had been able to afford her. Now as she looked up from the childlike body to the dark eyes, she felt a tremor of desire run down her own belly and melt into her loins.

Sukeena's gaze smouldered like the lavas of the volcanoes of her native Bali. These were not the eyes of a subservient child slave but those of a proud, defiant woman. Katinka felt herself challenged and aroused. To subdue her, and have her, and then to break her. She felt her pulse quicken and her breath come short as she pictured it happening.

'Follow me, Sukeena,' she commanded. 'I want you to show me the house.'

'My lady.' Sukeena placed the palms of her hands together and touched her fingertips to her lips as she bowed, but her eyes held Katinka's with the same dark, furious expression. Was it hatred, Katinka wondered, and the idea increased her excitement.

Sukeena has intrigued her, as I knew she must. She will buy her from me, Kleinhans thought. I will be rid of the witch at last. He had been aware of that interplay of passions and emotions between the two women. Although he did not flatter himself that he could fathom the slave girl's oriental mind, she had been his chattel for almost five years and he had learned to recognize many of the nuances of her moods. The thought of parting with her filled him with dismay but for his own peace and sanity he knew he must do it. She was destroying him. He could not remember what it was to have a quiet mind, not to be plagued and tormented by passions and unfulfilled desires, not to be in the witch's thrall. Because of her he had lost his health. His stomach was being eaten away by the hot acids of dyspepsia, and he could not remember a night of unbroken sleep in all those long five years.

At least he was rid of her brother, who had been almost as great a torment to him. Now she, too, must go. He could no longer endure this blight on his existence.

Sukeena stepped out of the line of servants and fell in dutifully behind the three, her loathsome master, the boorish giant of a soldier and this beautiful cruel golden lady, who, she sensed somehow, already held her destiny in those slim white hands.

I will wrest it from her, Sukeena vowed. This vile old man could not own me, although for the last five years he has dreamed of nothing else. Neither will this golden tiger woman ever own me. I swear it on my father's sacred memory.

They passed in a group through the high airy rooms of the residence. Through the green-painted shutters spilled the mellow Cape sunshine, casting stark zebra shadows on the tiled floors. Katinka felt a lightness of the spirit in these sunny colonies. She felt a recklessness in herself, an eagerness for strange adventures and for unfathomed excitements.

In every room she encountered a subtle, delicate feminine influence. It was not only the lingering perfume of flowers and incense, but some other living presence that she knew could never have emanated from the sad and sick old man at her side. She did not have to glance behind her to be aware of the girl who had created this aura, her silk clothing whispering and the susurration of the golden sandals on her tiny feet, the scent of the jasmine blossom in her coal-dark hair and the sweet musk of her skin.

In counterpoint, there was the crisp staccato click of the Colonel's heels on the tiles, the creak of his leather and the clink of his scabbard as it swung at his side. His scent was more powerful than that of the girl. It was masculine and rank, sweat and leather and animal, like a stallion pushed hard, bounding between her thighs. In this emotional hothouse in which she found herself, every one of her senses was fully engaged.

At last Governor Kleinhans led them out of the house and across the lawns to where a small gazebo stood, secluded beneath the oaks. An alfresco repast had been laid for them, and Sukeena stood in close attendance, directing the service of the meal with a glance or a subtle, graceful gesture.

Katinka noticed that as each dish or bottle was presented Sukeena tasted a morsel or took a delicate sip, like a butterfly at an open orchid. Her silence was not self-effacing, for all three seated at the table were intensely aware of her presence.

Cornelius Schreuder sat so close to Katinka that his leg pressed against hers whenever he leaned close to speak to her. They looked down towards the bay, where the *Standvastigheid* lay at anchor, not far from the *Gull of Moray*. The galleon had come in during the night, fully laden with her cargo of recovered spices and timber. She would carry Kleinhans northwards on the next leg of her voyage, so he was in haste to settle his affairs here in the Cape. Katinka smiled sweetly at the old man over the rim of her wine glass, knowing that she had him at a disadvantage in the bargaining.

'I wish to sell fifteen of my slaves,' he told her, 'and I have prepared a list of them, setting out their personal details, their skills and training, their ages and the state of their health. Five of the females are pregnant, so already the buyer will be assured of an increase on his, or her, investment.'

Katinka glanced at the document he handed her, then dropped it on the table top. 'Tell me about Sukeena,' she commanded. 'Am I mistaken, or have I detected in her a drop of northern blood? Was her father Dutch?'

Although Sukeena stood close by, Katinka spoke about the girl as though she were an inanimate object, without hearing or human sensitivity, a pretty piece of jewellery or a miniature painting, perhaps.

'You are observant, Mevrouw.' Kleinhans inclined his head. 'But no, her father was not Dutch. He was an English trader and her mother was a Balinese but, nonetheless, a woman of high breeding. When I saw her she was in her middle age. However, I understand that in her youth she was a great beauty. Although she was merely his concubine, the English trader treated her like a wife.'

All three studied Sukeena's features openly. 'Yes, you can see the European blood. It is the tone of her skin, and the set and shape of her eyes,' said Katinka.

Sukeena kept her eyes lowered, and her expression did not change. Smoothly she continued with her duties.

'What do you think of her appearance, Colonel?' Katinka turned to Schreuder, and pressed her leg against his. 'I am always interested in what a man finds attractive. Do you not think her a delicious little creature?'

Schreuder flushed slightly, and moved his chair so that he was no longer looking directly at Sukeena.

'Mevrouw, I have never had a penchant for native girls, even if they

223

are half-castes.' Sukeena's face remained impassive even though, at six feet from him, she had heard the derogatory description clearly. 'My tastes incline very much towards our lovely Dutch girls. I would not trade the dross for the pure gold.'

'Oh, Colonel, you are so gallant. I envy the pure golden Dutch girl who catches your fancy.' She laughed, and he gave her a look more eloquent than the words that rose to his lips, but perforce remained unspoken.

Katinka turned back to Kleinhans. 'So if her father was English, does she speak that language? That would be a useful accomplishment, would it not?'

'Indeed, she speaks it with great fluency, but that is not all. She has a way with guilders and runs the household with great economy and efficiency. The other slaves respect and obey her. She has intimate knowledge of Oriental medicines and remedies for all illness—'

'A paragon!' Katinka interrupted his recital. 'But what of her nature? Is she tractable, docile?'

'She is as she appears,' said Kleinhans, concealing the evasion with a ready reply and open face. 'I assure you, Mevrouw, that I have owned her for five years and have always found her completely compliant.'

Sukeena's face remained as if carved in jade, lovely and remote, but her soul seethed with outrage at the lie. For five years she had withstood him, and only on the few occasions when he had beaten her unconscious had he been able to invade her body. But that had been no victory for him, she knew, and took comfort from that knowledge. Twice she had recovered her senses while he was still grunting and straining over her like an animal, forcing himself into her dry, reluctant flesh. She did not count this as defeat, she did not even admit to herself that he had conquered her, for the moment that she regained consciousness she had begun to fight him again, with all the strength and determination of before.

'You are not a woman,' he had cried in despair, as she thrashed and kicked and wormed out from under him, 'you are a devil,' and, bleeding where she had bitten him and covered with deep gouges and scratches, he had slunk away, leaving her battered but triumphant. In the end he had given up any attempt at forcing her into submission, and instead had tried every other blandishment.

Once, weeping like an old woman, he had even offered her freedom and marriage, her deed of emancipation on the day that she married him. She spat like a cat at the thought.

Twice she had tried to kill him. Once with a dagger and once with poison. Now he made her taste every dish or bowl she served him, but the thought sustained her that one day she might succeed and watch his death throes.

'She does seem to have an angelic presence,' Katinka agreed, knowing instinctively that the description would enrage its subject. 'Come here, Sukeena,' she ordered, and the girl came to her moving like a reed in the wind.

'Kneel down!' said Katinka, and Sukeena knelt before her, her eyes modestly downcast. 'Look at me!' She raised her head.

Katinka studied her face, and spoke to Kleinhans without looking at him. 'You say she is healthy?'

'Young and healthy, never a day's illness in her life.'

'Is she pregnant?' Katinka asked, and ran her hand lightly over the girl's stomach. It was flat and hard.

'No! No!' Kleinhans exclaimed. 'She is a virgin.'

'There is never any guarantee of that state. The devil enters even the most heavily barred fortress.' Katinka smiled. 'But I will accept your word on it. I want to see her teeth. Open your mouth.' For a moment she thought Sukeena would refuse, but then her lips parted, and her small teeth sparkled in the sunlight, whiter than freshly carved ivory.

Katinka laid the tip of her finger on the girl's lower lip. It felt soft as a rose petal, and Katinka let the moment hang, drawing out the pleasure, prolonging Sukeena's humiliation. Then, slowly and voluptuously, she ran her finger between the girl's lips. The gesture was sexually fraught, a parody of the masculine penetration of the woman. As he watched, Kleinhans' hand began to tremble so violently that the sweet Constantia wine spilled over the rim of the glass he held. Cornelius Schreuder scowled and moved uneasily in his seat, crossing one leg over the other.

The inside of Sukeena's mouth was soft and moist. The two women stared at each other. Then Katinka began to move her finger slowly back and forth, exploring and probing while she asked Kleinhans, 'Her father, this Englishman, what happened to him? If he loved his concubine, as you say he did, why did he allow her children to be sold on the slave block?'

'He was one of the English bandits that were executed while I was Governor of Batavia. I am sure you are acquainted with the incident, are you not, Mevrouw?'

'Yes, I recall it well. The accused men were tortured by the Company executioner to ascertain the extent of their villainy,' Katinka said softly, still gazing into Sukeena's eyes. The extremity of the suffering she saw in them amazed and intrigued her. 'I did not know that you were the Governor at that time. The girl's father was executed at your orders, then?' Katinka asked, and Sukeena's lips quivered and closed softly around Katinka's long white finger.

'I have heard that they were crucified,' Katinka breathed huskily, and Sukeena's eyes filled with tears although her features remained serene. 'I have heard that burning sulphur flares were applied to their feet,' Katinka said, and felt the girl's tongue slide over her finger as she swallowed her grief. 'And then the flares were held under their hands.' Sukeena's sharp little teeth closed on her finger, not hard enough to be painful and certainly not hard enough to break or mark the white skin, but the threat was in her eyes, which were filled with hatred.

'I regret that it was necessary. The man's obstinacy was extraordinary. It must be a national trait of the English.' Kleinhans nodded. 'To endorse the punishment I ordered that the condemned man's concubine, her name was Ashreth, be made to watch the execution, she and the two children. Of course, at the time I knew nothing of Sukeena and her brother. It was not idle cruelty on my part but Company policy. These people do not respond to kindness, which they mistake for weakness.' Kleinhans gave a sigh of regret at such intransigence.

The tears were sliding silently down Sukeena's cheeks as Kleinhans went on, 'Once they had fully confessed their guilt, the criminals were burned. The flares were thrown onto the faggots of wood at their feet and the whole lot went up in the flames, which was a merciful release for all of us.'

With a small shudder Katinka withdrew her finger from between the girl's trembling lips. With the tenderness of a satisfied lover she stroked the satiny cheek, her finger still wet with the girl's saliva leaving damp streaks on the amber skin.

'What happened to the woman, the concubine? Was she also sold into slavery with the children?' Katinka asked, not taking her gaze from those grief-wet eyes in front of her.

'No,' Kleinhans said. 'That is the strange part of the story. Ashreth threw herself into the flames and perished on the same pyre as her English lover. There is no understanding the native mind, is there?'

There was a long silence, and when a cloud passed over the sun the day seemed suddenly dark and chill.

'I will take her,' Katinka said, so softly that Kleinhans cupped a hand to his ear.

'Please excuse me, Mevrouw, but I did not catch what you said.'

'I will take her,' Katinka repeated. 'This girl, Sukeena, I will buy her from you.'

'We have not yet agreed a price.' Kleinhans looked startled: he had not expected it to be so easy.

226

'I am certain your price will be reasonable – that is, if you also wish to sell me the other slaves in your span.'

'You are a lady of great compassion.' Kleinhans shook his head in admiration. 'I see that Sukeena's story has touched your heart and that you want to take her into your care. Thank you. I know you will treat her kindly.'

H al hung on the grating of the cell window and called his sighting to Aboli, who held him on his shoulders.

'They have returned in the Governor's carriage. The three of them, Kleinhans, Schreuder and Governor van de Velde's wife. They are going back up the staircase—' He broke off and exclaimed, 'Wait! There is someone else alighting from the carriage. Someone I do not know. A woman.'

Daniel, who was standing at the grille gate, relayed this message up the staircase to the solitary cells at the top.

'Describe this strange woman,' Sir Francis called.

At that moment the woman turned to say something to Fredricus the driver and, with a start, Hal recognized her as the slave girl who had stood in the crowd while they were being marched across the parade.

'She is small and young, almost a child. Balinese, perhaps, or Malaccan, something about the look of her.' He hesitated. 'She is probably of mixed blood, and almost certainly a servant or a slave. Kleinhans and Schreuder walk ahead of her.'

Daniel passed this on, and suddenly Althuda's voice came back to them down the stairwell. 'Is she very pretty? Long dark hair twisted up on top of her head, with flowers in it. Does she wear a green jade ornament at her throat?'

'All those things,' Hal shouted back. 'Except that she is not pretty, she is lovely beyond the telling of it. Do you know her? Who is she?'

'Her name is Sukeena. She is the one for whom I came back from the mountains. She is my little sister.'

Hal watched Sukeena mount the stairs, moving with the lightness and alacrity of an autumn leaf in a gust of wind. Somehow, while he watched this girl, his thoughts of Katinka were not so all-consuming. When she disappeared from his sight, the light filtering into the dungeon seemed dimmer and the stone walls more damp and cold.

At first they had all been amazed by the treatment meted out to them in the castle dungeons. They were allowed to slop out the latrine bucket every morning, drawing lots for the privilege. At the end of the first week, a load of fresh straw was delivered by one of the Company field slaves, driving an oxcart, and they were allowed to throw out the verminous old straw that covered the floors. Through a copper pipe the water cistern was fed continuously from one of the streams that rushed down from the mountain, so they suffered no hardship from thirst. Each evening a loaf of coarse-grained bread, the size of a wagon wheel, and a great iron pot were sent down from the kitchens. The pot was filled with the peelings and offcuts of vegetables, boiled up with the meat of seals captured on Robben Island. This stew was more plentiful and tastier than much of the food they had eaten aboard ship.

Althuda laughed when he heard them discussing it. 'They also feed their oxen well. Dumb animals work better when they are strong.'

'We ain't doing much work here and now,' Daniel remarked comfortably, and patted his belly.

Althuda laughed again. 'Look out of the window,' he advised them. 'There is a fort to build. You will not be sitting down here much longer. Believe me when I say it.'

'Ahoy there, Althuda,' Daniel shouted, 'your sister isn't English, so it makes sense that you aren't an Englishman either. How is it that you speak like one?'

'My father was from Plymouth. I have never been there. Do you know the place?'

There was a roar of laughter and comment and clapping, and Hal spoke for them all. 'By God, except for Aboli and these other African knaves, we are all Devon men and true. You are one of us, then, Althuda!'

'You have never seen me. I must warn you that I don't look like you,' Althuda warned them.

'If you look half as good as your little sister, then you'll do well enough,' Hal replied, and the men hooted with laughter.

For the first week of their captivity, they saw the sergeant gaoler, named Manseer, only when the stew pot was brought in or when the bedding straw was changed. Then, suddenly, on the eighth morning, the iron door at the head of the stairs was thrown open with a crash and Manseer bellowed down the well, 'Two at a time, form up. We are taking you out to wash some of the stink off you, or the judge will suffocate before he has a chance to send you to Stadige Jan. Come on now, shake yourselves.'

With a dozen guards keeping watch over them they were taken out in pairs, made to strip naked and wash themselves and their clothing under the hand pump behind the stables.

The following morning they were turned out again with the dawn, and this time the castle armourer was waiting with his forge and anvil to shackle them together, not this time in one long ungainly file but into pairs.

When the iron-studded door to Sir Francis's cell was opened, and his father emerged with his hair hanging lankly to his shoulders and a grizzled beard covering his chin, Hal pushed himself forward so that they were shackled together.

'How are you, Father?' Hal asked with concern, for he had never seen his father looking so seedy.

Before Sir Francis could reply a bout of coughing overtook him. When it passed, he answered hoarsely, 'I prefer a good Channel gale to the air down here, but I am well enough for what has to be done.'

'I could not shout it to you, but Aboli and I have been working out a plan to escape,' Hal whispered to him. 'We have managed to lift one of the floor slabs in the back of the cell and we are going to dig a tunnel under the walls.'

'With your bare hands?' Sir Francis smiled at him.

'We need to find a tool,' Hal admitted, 'but when we do . . .'

He nodded with grim determination, and Sir Francis felt his heart might burst with love and pride. I have taught him to be a fighter, and to keep on fighting even when the battle is lost. Sweet God, I hope the Dutchies spare him the fate that they have in store for me.

In the middle of the morning they were marched from the court-yard up the staircase into the main hall of the castle, which had been converted into a courtroom. Shackled two by two, they were led to the four rows of low wooden benches in the centre of the floor and seated upon them, Sir Francis and Hal in the middle of the front row. Their guards, with drawn swords, lined up along the wall behind them.

A platform had been built against the wall before them and on it, facing the benches of the prisoners, was set a heavy table and a tall chair of dark teak. This was the judge's throne. At one end of the table was a stool, on which the court writer was already seated, scribbling busily in his journal. Below the platform was another pair of tables and chairs. At one of these sat someone Hal had seen many times before through the cell window. According to Althuda, he was a junior clerk in the Company administration. His name was Jacobus Hop and, after one nervous glance at the prisoners, he did not look at them again. He was rustling and scratching through a sheaf of documents, pausing from time to time to wipe his sweating face with a large white neckcloth.

At the second table sat Colonel Cornelius Schreuder. He was the romantic poet's image of the gallant and debonair soldier, all a-glitter with his medallions and stars and the wide sash across one shoulder. His wig was freshly washed, the curls hanging down to his shoulders. His legs were thrust out in front of him, his soft thigh-high boots crossed at the ankles. On the table top in front of him books and papers were scattered and laid carelessly upon them were his plumed hat and the Neptune sword. As he rocked backwards and forwards on his chair he stared relentlessly at Hal, and though Hal tried to match his gaze he was forced at last to drop his eyes.

There was a sudden uproar at the main doors, and when they swung open the crowds from the town burst in and scrambled to find seats on the benches down each side of the hall. As soon as the last seat was taken, the doors were forced closed again in the faces of those unfortunates at the rear. Now the hall was clamorous with excited comment and anticipation, as the lucky spectators studied the prisoners and loudly gave their opinions to each other.

To one side an area had been railed off, and two green-jackets with drawn swords stood guard over it. Behind the railing a row of comfortable cushioned chairs had been arranged. Now there was further hubbub, and the crowd's attention turned from the accused men to the dignitaries who filed out through the doors of the audience chamber. Governor Kleinhans led them, with Katinka van de Velde on his arm, followed by Lord Cumbrae and Captain Limberger, chatting casually together, ignoring the stir that their entrance was causing among the common folk.

Katinka took the chair in the centre of the row. Hal stared at her, willing her to look in his direction, to give him a sign of recognition and reassurance. He tried to sustain in himself the faith that she would never abandon him, and that she had already used her influence and had interceded with her husband for mercy, but she was deep in conversation with Governor Kleinhans and never as much as glanced at the ranks of English seamen. She does not want others to see her preference and concern for us, Hal consoled himself, but when the time comes for her to give her evidence she will surely speak out for us.

Colonel Schreuder clumped down his booted feet heavily and came to his feet. He stared around the crowded hall with huge disdain, and the female spectators gave little sighs and squeals of admiration.

'This tribunal is convened by virtue of the power conferred upon the honourable Dutch East India Company in the terms of the charter issued to the aforesaid Company by the government of the Republic of Holland and the Lowlands. Pray silence and stand for the president of the tribunal, His Excellency Governor Petrus van de Velde.'

The spectators came to their feet with a subdued murmur and stared in anticipation at the door behind the platform. Some of the prisoners struggled up, rattling their chains, but when they saw Sir Francis Courteney and Hal sit unmoving they subsided back onto the benches.

Through the far door appeared the president of the court. He mounted ponderously to the platform and glared down upon the seated rows of prisoners. 'Get those rogues on their feet!' he bellowed suddenly and the crowds quailed before his murderous expression.

In the stunned silence that followed this outburst, Sir Francis spoke out clearly in Dutch. 'Neither I nor any of my men recognize the authority of this assembly, nor do we accept the right of the self-appointed president to examine and sentence free-born Englishmen, subjects only of His Majesty King Charles the Second.'

Van de Velde seemed to swell like a great toad. His face turned a dark and furious shade of crimson, and he roared, 'You are a pirate and a murderer. By the sovereignty of the Republic and the charter of the Company, by the right of moral and international law, the authority is vested in me to conduct this trial.' He broke off to gasp for breath, then went on even louder than before. 'I find you guilty of gross and flagrant contempt of this court, and I sentence you to ten strokes of the cane to be administered forthwith.' He looked to the commander of the guard. 'Master of arms, take the prisoner into the courtyard and carry out the sentence at once.'

Four soldiers hurried forward from the back of the hall, and hauled Sir Francis to his feet. Hal, shackled to his father, was dragged with him to the main doors. Behind them, men and women leaped onto the benches and craned for a view, then rushed in a body to the doorway and the windows as Sir Francis and Hal were urged down the staircase into the yard.

Sir Francis kept silent, his head high and his back straight, as he was pushed to the hitching rail for officer's horses at the entrance of the armoury. At the shouted orders of the sergeant, he and Hal were placed on either side of the high rail, facing each other, their manacled wrists hooked into the iron rings.

Hal was powerless to intervene. The sergeant placed his forefinger in the back of the collar of Sir Francis's shirt and yanked down, splitting the cotton to the waist. Then he stepped back and swished his light malacca cane.

231

'You have made an oath on your Knighthood. Do you stand by it on your honour?' Sir Francis whispered to his son.

'I do, Father.'

The cane fluted and snapped on his bare flesh, and Sir Francis winced. 'This beating is but a little thing, the play of children compared to what must follow. Do you understand that?'

'I understand full well.'

The sergeant struck again. He was laying the stripes one on top of the other, the pain multiplying with each blow.

'No matter what you do or say, nothing and no one can change the flight of the red comet. The stars have laid out my destiny and you cannot intervene.'

The cane hummed and cracked, and Sir Francis's body stiffened, then relaxed.

'If you are strong and constant, you will endure. That will be my reward.'

This time he gave a small, hoarse gasp as the cane bit into the tautly stretched muscles of his back.

'You are my body and my blood. Through you I also will endure.'

The cane hummed and clapped, again and again.

'Swear it to me one last time. Reinforce your oath, that you will never reveal anything to these people in a futile attempt to save me.'

'Father, I swear it to you,' Hal whispered back, his face white as bleached bone, as the cane sang, a succession of cruel blows.

'I put all my faith and my trust in you,' said Sir Francis, and the soldiers lifted him down from the railing. As they marched back up the staircase, he leaned lightly on Hal's arm. When he stumbled Hal braced him, so that his head was still high and his bloody back straight as they entered the hall and marched together to their seats on the front bench.

Governor van de Velde was now seated on the dais. A silver tray was set at his elbow, loaded with small china bowls of appetizers and spiced savouries. He was munching contentedly on one of these and drinking from a pewter mug of small beer as he chatted to Colonel Schreuder at the table below him. As soon as Sir Francis and Hal were shoved by their guards onto the bench again his amiable expression changed dramatically. He raised his voice and an immediate, dense silence fell over the assembly. 'I trust that I have made it clear that I will brook no further hindrance to these proceedings.' He glowered at Sir Francis and then raised his eyes to sweep the hall. 'That goes for all persons gathered here. Anyone else who in any way attempts to make a mockery of this tribunal will receive the same treatment as the prisoner.' He looked down at Schreuder. 'Who appears for the prosecution?'

232

Schreuder stood up. 'Colonel Cornelius Schreuder, at your service, your excellency.'

'Who appears for the defence?' Van de Velde glowered at Jacobus Hop, and the clerk sprang to his feet, sending half the documents in front of him showering to the tiles.

'I do, your excellency.'

'State your name, man!' van de Velde roared at him, and Hop wriggled like a puppy.

He stammered, 'Jacobus Hop, clerk and writer to the Honourable Dutch East India Company.' This declaration took a long time to enunciate.

'In future speak out and speak clear,' van de Velde warned him, then turned back to Schreuder. 'You may proceed to present your case, Colonel.'

'This is a matter of piracy on the high seas, together with murder and abduction. The accused are twenty-four in number. With your indulgence, I will now read a list of their names. Each prisoner will stand when his name is read so that the court may recognize him.' From the sleeve of his tunic he drew a roll of parchment and held it at arm's length. 'The foremost accused person is Francis Courteney, captain of the pirate bark the *Lady Edwina*. Your excellency, he is the leader and instigator of all the criminal acts perpetrated by this pack of seawolves and corsairs.' Van de Velde nodded his understanding and Schreuder went on. 'Henry Courteney, officer and mate. Ned Tyler, boatswain. Daniel Fisher, boatswain . . .' He recited the name and rank of each man on the benches, and each stood briefly, some of them bobbing their heads and grinning ingratiatingly at van de Velde. The last four names on Schreuder's list were those of the black seamen.

'Matesi, a Negro slave.

'Jiri, a Negro slave.

'Kimatti, a Negro slave.

'Aboli, a Negro slave.

'The prosecution will prove that on the fourth day of September in the year of Our Lord sixteen sixty-seven, Francis Courteney, while commanding the caravel the *Lady Edwina*, of which the other prisoners were all crew members, did fall upon the galleon *De Standvastigheid*, Captain Limberger commanding . . .' Schreuder spoke without reference to notes or papers, and Hal felt a reluctant admiration for the thoroughness and lucidity of his accusations.

'And now, your excellency, if you please, I should like to call my first witness.' Van de Velde nodded, and Schreuder turned and looked across the floor. 'Call Captain Limberger.'

The captain of the galleon left his comfortable chair in the railed-off enclosure, crossed to the platform and stepped up onto it. The witness's chair stood beside the judge's table and Limberger seated himself.

'Do you understand the gravity of this matter and swear in the name of Almighty God to tell the truth before this court?' van de Velde asked him.

'I do, your excellency.'

'Very well, Colonel, you may question your witness.'

Swiftly Schreuder led Limberger through a recital of his name, rank and his duties for the Company. He then asked for a description of the *Standvastigheid*, her passengers and her cargo. Limberger read his replies from the list he had prepared. When he had finished Schreuder asked, 'Who was the owner of this ship and of the cargo she was carrying?'

'The honourable Dutch East India Company.'

'Now, Captain Limberger, on the fourth of September of this year was your ship voyaging in about latitude thirty-four degrees south and longitude four degrees east – that is approximately fifty leagues south of the Agulhas Cape?'

'It was.'

'That is some time after the cessation of hostilities between Holland and England?'

'Yes, it was.'

Schreuder picked up a leather-bound log-book from the table in front of him and passed it up to Limberger. 'Is this the log-book that you were keeping on board your ship during that voyage?'

Limberger examined it briefly, 'Yes, Colonel, this is my log.'

Schreuder looked at van de Velde. 'Your excellency, I think I should inform you that the log-book was found in the possession of the pirate Courteney after his capture by Company troops.' Van de Velde nodded, and Schreuder looked at Limberger. 'Will you please read to us the last entry in your log?'

Limberger turned the pages and then read aloud, '"Fourth September sixteen sixty-seven. Two bells in the morning watch. Position by dead reckoning four degrees twenty-three minutes south latitude thirty-four degrees, forty-five minutes east longitude. Strange sail in sight bearing south-south-east. Flying friendly colours."' Limberger closed the log and looked up. 'The entry ends there,' he said.

'Was that strange sail noted in your log the caravel the *Lady Edwina*, and was she flying the colours of the Republic and the Company?'

'Yes, to both questions.'

'Will you recount the events that took place after you sighted the *Lady Edwina*, please.'

Limberger gave a clear description of the capture of his ship, with Schreuder making him emphasize Sir Francis's use of false colours to get within striking distance. After Limberger had told of the boarding and fighting on board the galleon, Schreuder asked for a detailed account of the numbers of Dutch sailors wounded and killed. Limberger had a written list prepared and handed this to the court.

'Thank you, Captain. Can you tell us what happened to you, your crew and your passengers once the pirates had taken control of your ship?'

Limberger went on to describe how they had sailed east in company with the *Lady Edwina*, the transfer of cargo and gear from the caravel into the galleon, and the dispatch of the *Lady Edwina* in command of Schreuder to the Cape with letters of demand for ransom, the onward voyage aboard the captured galleon to Elephant Lagoon and the captivity of himself and his eminent passengers there until their salvation by the expeditionary force from the Cape, led by Schreuder and Lord Cumbrae.

When Schreuder had finished questioning him, van de Velde looked at Hop. 'Do you have any questions, Mijnheer?'

With both hands full of papers Hop stood up, blushed furiously, then took a deep, gulping breath and let out a long, unbroken stammer. Everybody in the hall watched his agony with interest, and at last van de Velde spoke. 'Captain Limberger intends sailing for Holland in two weeks' time. Do you think you will have asked your question by then, Hop?'

Hop shook his head. 'No questions,' he said at last, and sat down heavily.

'Who is your next witness, Colonel?' van de Velde asked, as soon as Limberger had left the witness chair and was seated back in the enclosure.

'I would like to call the Governor's wife, Mevrouw Katinka van de Velde. That is, if it does not inconvenience her.'

There was a masculine hum of approval as Katinka rustled her silk and her laces to the witness's chair. Sir Francis felt Hal stiffen beside him, but did not turn to look at his face. Only days before their capture, when Hal had been absent from the camp for long periods and had begun to neglect his duties, he had realized that his son had fallen into the golden whore's snare. By then it had been far too late to intervene, and in any case, he remembered what it was like to be young and in love, even with an utterly unsuitable woman, and had understood the futility of trying to prevent what had already happened. He had been waiting for the correct moment and the right means to end the liaison when Schreuder and the Buzzard had attacked the camp.

With great deference, Schreuder led Katinka gently through the recital of her name and position and then asked her to describe her voyage aboard the *Standvastigheid*, and how she had been taken prisoner. She answered in a sweet, clear voice that throbbed with emotion, and Schreuder went on, 'Please tell us, madam, how you were treated by your captors.'

Katinka began to sob softly. 'I have tried to put the memory from my mind, for it was too painful to bear thinking upon. But I will never be able to forget. I was treated like a caged animal, cursed and spat upon, kept locked up in a grass hut.' Even van de Velde looked amazed by the testimony, but realized that it would look impressive in the report that went to Amsterdam. After reading it Katinka's father and the other members of the Seventeen would have no other option but to approve even the harshest retribution visited on the prisoners.

Sir Francis was aware of the turmoil of emotion that Hal was suffering as he listened to the woman in whom he had placed so much trust pouring out her lies. He felt his son sag physically as she destroyed his faith in her.

'Be of good heart, my boy,' he said softly, from the corner of his mouth, and felt Hal sit up straighter on the hard bench.

'My dear lady, we know that you have suffered a terrible ordeal at the hands of these inhuman monsters.' By this time Schreuder was trembling with anger to hear of her ordeal. Katinka nodded and dabbed daintily at her eyes with a lace handkerchief. 'Do you believe that animals such as these should be shown mercy, or should they be subjected to the full force and majesty of the law?'

'Sweet Jesus knows that I am only a poor female, with a soft and loving heart for all God's creation.' Katinka's voice broke pitifully. 'But I know that everybody in this assembly will agree with me that a simple hanging is too good for these unspeakable wretches.' A murmur of agreement spread slowly along the benches of spectators, then turned into a deep growl. Like a pit full of bears at feeding time, they wanted blood.

'Burn them!' a woman screamed. 'They are not fit to be called men.'

Katinka lifted her head and, for the first time since entering the hall, she looked directly at Hal, staring through her tears straight into his eyes.

Hal lifted his chin and stared back. He felt the love and awe he had cherished for her withering, like a tender vine struck with the black mould. Sir Francis felt it too, and turned to look at him. He saw the ice in his son's eyes and could almost feel the heat of the flames in his heart.

'She was never worthy of you,' Sir Francis said softly. 'Now that you have renounced her, you have taken another mighty leap into manhood.'

Did his father really understand, Hal wondered. Did he know what had taken place? Did he know of Hal's feelings? If that were so, surely he would long ago have rejected him. He turned and looked into Sir Francis's eyes, fearing to see them filled with scorn and revulsion. But his father's gaze was mellow with understanding. Hal realized that he knew everything, and had probably known all along. Far from rejecting him, his father was offering him strength and redemption.

'I have committed adultery, and I have disgraced my Knighthood,' Hal whispered. 'I am no longer worthy to be called your son.'

The manacle on his wrist clinked as Sir Francis laid his hand on the boy's knee. ''Twas this harlot that led you astray. The blame is not yours. You will always be my son and I shall always be proud of you,' he whispered.

Van de Velde frowned down upon Sir Francis. 'Silence! No more of your muttering! Is it another touch of the cane you are seeking?' He turned back to his wife. 'Mevrouw, you have been very brave. I am sure Mijnheer Hop will not wish to trouble you further.' He transferred his gaze to the unfortunate clerk, who scrambled to his feet.

'Mevrouw!' The single word came out sharp and clear as a pistol shot, surprising Hop as much as everyone else in court. 'We thank you for your testimony, and we have no questions.' There was only one catch, on the word 'testimony', and Hop sat down again triumphantly.

'Well said, Hop.' Van de Velde beamed at him in avuncular fashion, and then turned a doting smile on his wife. 'You may return to your seat, Mevrouw.' There was a lust-laden hush and every man in the hall let his gaze drop as Katinka lifted her skirts just high enough to expose her perfect little ankles clad in white silk and stepped down from the platform.

As soon as she was seated, Schreuder said, 'Now, Lord Cumbrae, may we trouble you?'

In his full regalia the Buzzard mounted the platform, and as he took the oath placed one hand on the flashing yellow cairngorm in the hilt of his dagger. Once Schreuder had established who and what he was, he asked the Buzzard, 'Do you know the pirate captain, Courteney?'

'Like a brother.' Cumbrae smiled down on Sir Francis. 'Once we were close.'

'Not any more?' Schreuder asked sharply.

'Alas, it pains me but when my old friend began to change there was a parting of our ways, although I still feel great affection for him.'

'How did he change?'

'Well, he was always a braw laddie, was Franky. We sailed in company on many a day, through storm and the balmy days. There was no man I loved better, fair he was and honest, brave and generous to his friends—' Cumbrae broke off and an expression of deep sorrow knitted his brow.

'You speak in the past tense, my lord, what changed?'

''Twas Francis who changed. At first it was in little things – he was cruel to his captives and hard on his crew, flogging and hanging when it weren't called for. Then he changed towards his old friends, lying and cheating them out of their share of the prize. He became a hard man and bitter.'

'Thank you for this honesty,' Schreuder said, 'I can see it gives you no pleasure to reveal these truths.'

'No pleasure at all,' Cumbrae confirmed with sadness. 'I hate to see my old friend in chains, though God Almighty knows well he deserves no mercy for his murderous behaviour towards honest Dutch seamen, and innocent women.'

'When did you last sail in company with Courteney?'

'It was not too long ago, in April of this year. Our two ships were on patrol together off Agulhas, waiting to waylay the Company galleons as they rounded the Cape to call in here at Table Bay.' There was a murmur of patriotic anger from the spectators, which van de Velde ignored.

'Were you, then, also a corsair?' Schreuder glared at him. 'Were you also preying on Dutch shipping?'

'No, Colonel Schreuder, I was not a pirate or a corsair. During the recent war between our two countries, I was a commissioned privateer.'

'Pray, my lord, tell us the difference between a pirate and a privateer?'

''Tis simply that a privateer sails under Letters of Marque issued by his sovereign in times of war, and so is a legitimate man-of-war. A pirate is a robber and an outlaw, carrying out his depredations without any sanction, but that of the Lord of Darkness, Satan himself.'

'I see. So you had a Letter of Marque when you were raiding Dutch shipping?'

'Yes, Colonel. I did.'

'Are you able to show this document to us?'

'Naturally!' Cumbrae reached into his sleeve and drew out a roll of parchment. He leaned down and handed it to Schreuder.

'Thank you.' Schreuder unrolled it and held it up for all to see, heavy with scarlet ribbons and wax seals. He read aloud, 'Know you by these presents that our dearly beloved Angus Cochran, Earl of Cumbrae—'

238

'Very well, Colonel,' van de Velde interrupted testily. 'No need to read us the whole thing. Let me have it here, if you please.'

Schreuder bowed. 'As your excellency pleases.' He handed up the document. Van de Velde glanced at it then set it aside. 'Please go on with your questions.'

'My lord, did Courteney, the prisoner, also have one of these Letters of Marque?'

'Well, now, if he did I was not aware of it.' The Buzzard grinned openly at Sir Francis.

'Would you have expected to be aware of it, if the letter had, in fact, existed?'

'Sir Francis and I were very close. No secrets between us. Yes, he would have told me.'

'He never discussed the letter with you?' Schreuder looked annoyed, like a pedagogue whose pupil has forgotten his lines. 'Never?'

'Oh, yes. Now I do recall one occasion. I asked him if he had a royal commission.'

'And what was his reply?'

'He said, "It ain't nothing but a bit of paper anyway. I don't trouble meself with rubbish like that!"'

'So you knew he had no letter and yet you sailed in his company?'

Cumbrae shrugged. 'It was war-time, and it was none of my business.'

'So you were off Cape Agulhas with the prisoner after the peace had been signed, and you were still raiding Dutch shipping. Can you explain that to us?'

'It was simple, Colonel. We did not know about peace, that is until I fell in with a Portuguese caravel outward bound from Lisbon for Goa. I hailed her and her captain told me that peace had been signed.'

'What was the name of this Portuguese ship?'

'She was the *El Dragão*.'

'Was the prisoner Courteney present at this meeting with her?'

'No, his patrol station was north of mine. He was over the horizon and out of sight at the time.'

Schreuder nodded. 'Where is this ship now?'

'I have here a copy of a news-sheet from London, only three months old. It arrived three days ago on the Company ship lying in the bay at this moment.' The Buzzard produced the sheet from his sleeve with a magician's flourish. '*El Dragão* was lost with all hands in a storm in the Bay of Biscay while on her homeward voyage.'

'So, it would seem, then, that we will never have any way of disproving your meeting with her off Agulhas?'

239

'You'll just have to take my word for it, Colonel.' Cumbrae stroked his great red beard.

'What did you do when you heard of the peace between England and Holland?'

'As an honest man, there was only one thing I could do. I broke off my patrol, and went in search of the *Lady Edwina*.'

'To warn her that the war was over?' Schreuder suggested.

'Of course, and to tell Franky that my Letter of Marque was no longer valid and that I was going home.'

'Did you find Courteney? Did you give him that message?'

'I found him within a few hours' sailing. He was due north of my position, about twenty leagues distant.'

'What did he say when you told him the war was over?'

'He said, "It may be over for you, but it ain't over for me. Rain or shine, wind or calm, war or peace, I am going to catch myself a fat cheese-head."'

There was a ferocious clanking of chains and Big Daniel sprang to his feet, dragging the diminutive figure of Ned Tyler off the bench with him. 'There ain't a word of truth in it, you lying Scots bastard!' he thundered.

Van de Velde jumped up and wagged his finger at Daniel. 'Sit down, you English animal, or I'll have you thrashed, and not just with the light cane.'

Sir Francis turned and reached back to grab Daniel's arm. 'Calm yourself, Master Daniel,' he said quietly. 'Don't give the Buzzard the pleasure of watching us ache.' Big Daniel sank down, muttering furiously to himself, but he would not disobey his captain.

'I am sure Governor van de Velde will take notice of the unruly and desperate nature of these villains,' Schreuder said, then turned his attention back to the Buzzard. 'Did you ever see Courteney again before today?'

'Yes, I did. When I heard that, despite my warning, he had seized a Company galleon, I went to find him and remonstrate with him. To ask him to free the ship and its cargo, and to release the hostages he was holding to ransom.'

'How did he respond to your pleas?'

'He turned his guns upon my ship, killing twelve of my seamen, and he attacked me with fireships.' The Buzzard shook his head at the memory of this perfidious treatment by an old friend and shipmate. 'That was when I came here to Table Bay to inform Governor Kleinhans of the galleon's whereabouts and to offer to lead an expedition to recapture the ship and her cargo from the pirates.'

240

'As a soldier myself, I can only commend you, my lord, on your exemplary conduct. I have no further questions, your excellency.' Schreuder bowed at van de Velde.

'Hop, do you have any questions?' van de Velde demanded.

Hop looked confused, and glanced in appeal at Sir Francis.

'Your excellency,' he stuttered, 'might I speak to Sir Francis alone, if only for a minute?'

For a while it seemed that van de Velde might refuse the request, but he clasped his brow wearily. 'If you insist on holding up these proceedings all the time, Hop, we will be here all week. Very well, man, you may talk to the prisoner, but do try to be quick.'

Hop hurried across to Sir Francis and leaned close. He asked a question, and listened to the reply with an expression of dawning horror on his pale face. He nodded and kept nodding as Sir Francis whispered in his ear, then went back to his table.

He stared down at his papers, breathing like a pearl diver about to plunge out of his canoe into twenty fathoms of water. Finally he looked up and shouted at Cumbrae, 'The first you knew of the end of the war was when you tried to cut out the *Swallow* from under the fortress here in Table Bay and were told about it by Colonel Schreuder.'

It came out in a single rush, without check or pause, but it was a long speech and Hop reeled back, gasping from the exertion.

'Have you lost your wits, Hop?' van de Velde bellowed. 'Are you accusing a nobleman of lying, you little turd?'

Hop drew another full breath, took his fragile courage in both hands, and shouted again, 'You held Captain Courteney's Letter of Marque in your own two hands, then brandished it in his face while you burned it to ashes.' Again it came out fluently, but Hop was spent. He stood there gulping for air.

Van de Velde was on his feet now. 'If you are looking for advancement in the Company, Hop, you are going about it in a very strange way. You stand there hurling crazy accusations at a man of high rank. Don't you know your place, you worthless guttersnipe? How dare you behave like this? Sit down before I have you taken out and flogged.' Hop dropped into his seat as though he had received a musket ball in the head. Breathing heavily, van de Velde bowed towards the Buzzard. 'I must apologize, my lord. Every person here knows that you were instrumental in rescuing the hostages and saving the *Standvastigheid* from the clutches of these villains. Please ignore those insulting statements and return to your seat. We are grateful for your help in this matter.'

As Cumbrae crossed the floor, van de Velde suddenly became aware of the writer scribbling away busily beside him. 'Don't write that down, you fool. It was not part of the court proceedings. Here, let me see your journal.' He snatched it from the clerk, and as he read his face darkened. He leaned across and took the quill from the writer's hand. With a series of broad strokes he expurgated those parts of the text that offended him. Then he pushed the book back towards the writer. 'Use your intelligence. Paper is an expensive commodity. Don't waste it by writing down unimportant rubbish.' Then he transferred his attention to the two advocates. 'Gentlemen, I should like this matter settled today. I do not want to put the Company to unnecessary expense by wasting any more time. Colonel Schreuder, I think you have made a thoroughly convincing presentation of the case against the pirates. I hope that you do not intend to gild the lily by calling any more witnesses, do you?'

'As your excellency pleases. I had intended calling ten more—'

'Sweet heavens!' Van de Velde looked appalled. 'That will not be necessary at all.'

Schreuder bowed deeply and sat down. Van de Velde lowered his head like a bull about to charge and looked at the defence advocate. 'Hop!' he growled. 'You have just seen how reasonable Colonel Schreuder has been, and what an excellent example in the economy of words and time he has set for this court. What are your intentions?'

'May I call Sir Francis Courteney to give evidence?' Hop stuttered.

'I strongly advise against it,' van de Velde told him ominously. 'Certainly it will do your case little good.'

'I want to show that he did not know the war had ended and that he was sailing under a commission from the English King,' Hop ploughed on obstinately, and van de Velde flushed crimson.

'Damn you, Hop. Haven't you listened to a word I said? We know all about that line of defence, and I will take it into consideration when I ponder my verdict. You don't have to regurgitate those lies again.'

'I would like to have the prisoner say it, just for the court records.' Hop was close to tears, and his words limped painfully over his crippled tongue.

'You are trying my patience, Hop. Continue in this fashion, and you will be on the next ship back to Amsterdam. I cannot have a disloyal Company servant spreading dissension and sedition throughout the colony.'

Hop looked alarmed to hear himself described in such terms, and he capitulated with alacrity. 'I apologize for delaying the business of this honourable court. I rest the case for the defence.'

'Good man! You have done a fine job of work, Hop. I will make a notation to that effect in my next despatch to the Seventeen.' Van de

Velde's face resumed its natural colour and he beamed jovially about the hall. 'We will adjourn for the midday meal and for the court to consider its verdict. We will reconvene at four o'clock this afternoon. Take the prisoners back to the dungeons.'

To avoid having to remove their shackles Manseer, the gaoler, bundled Hal who was still chained to his father into the solitary cell near the top of the spiral staircase, while the rest went below.

Hal and Sir Francis sat side by side on the stone shelf that served as a bed. As soon as they were alone Hal blurted out, 'Father, I want to explain to you about Katinka – I mean about the Governor's wife.'

Sir Francis embraced him awkwardly, hampered by the chains. 'Unlikely as it now seems, I was young once. You do not have to speak about that harlot again. She is not worthy of your consideration.'

'I will never love another woman, not as long as I live,' Hal said bitterly.

'What you felt for that woman was not love, my son.' Sir Francis shook his head. 'Your love is a precious currency. Spend it only in the market where you will not be cheated again.'

At that there was a tapping on the iron bars of the next cell, and Althuda called, 'How goes the trial, Captain Courteney? Have they given you a good taste of Company justice?'

Sir Francis raised his voice to answer. 'It goes as you said it would, Althuda. It is obvious that you also have experienced it.'

'The Governor is the only god in this little heaven called Good Hope. Here, justice is that which pays a profit to the Dutch East India Company or a bribe to its servants. Has the judge pronounced your guilt yet?'

'Not yet. Van de Velde has gone to guzzle at his trough.'

'You must pray that he values labour for his walls more than revenge. That way you might still slip through Slow John's fingers. Is there anything you are hiding from them? Anything they want from you – to betray a comrade, perhaps?' Althuda asked. 'If there is not, then you might still escape the little room under the armoury where Slow John does his work.'

'We are hiding nothing,' Sir Francis said. 'Are we, Hal?'

'Nothing,' Hal agreed loyally.

'But,' Sir Francis went on, 'van de Velde believes that we are.'

'Then all I can say, my friend, is may Almighty Allah have pity on you.'

Those last hours together went too swiftly for Hal. He and his father spent the time talking softly together. Every so often Sir Francis broke off in a fit of coughing. His eyes glittered feverishly in the dim light, and

243

when Hal touched his skin it was hot and clammy. Sir Francis spoke of High Weald like a man who knows he will never see his home again. When he described the river and the hill, Hal dimly remembered them and the salmon coming upstream in the spring and the stags roaring in the rut. When he spoke of his wife, Hal tried to recall his mother's face, but saw only the woman in the miniature painting he had left buried at Elephant Lagoon, and not the real live person.

'These last years she has faded in my own memory,' Sir Francis admitted. 'But now her face comes back to me vividly, as young and fresh and sweet as she ever was. I wonder, is it because soon we will be together again? Is she waiting for me?'

'I know she is, Father.' Hal gave him the reassurance he needed. 'But I need you most and I know that we will be together many more years before you go to my mother.'

Sir Francis smiled regretfully, and looked up at the tiny window set high in the stone wall. 'Last night I climbed up and looked through the bars, and the red comet was still in the sign of Virgo. It seemed closer and fiercer, for its fiery tail had altogether obliterated my star.'

They heard the tramp of the guards approaching and the clash of keys in the iron door. Sir Francis turned to Hal. 'For the last time let me kiss you, my son.'

His father's lips were dry and hot with the fever in his blood. The contact was brief, then the door to the cell was thrown open.

'Don't keep the Governor and Slow John waiting now,' said Sergeant Manseer jovially. 'Out with the pair of you.'

The atmosphere among the spectators in the court room was like that at the cockpit just before the spurred birds are released to tear into each other in a cloud of flying feathers.

Sir Francis and Hal led in the long file of prisoners and, before he could prevent himself, Hal looked quickly towards the railed-off area at the far end of the hall. Katinka sat in her place in the centre of the front row with Zelda directly behind her. The maid leered viciously at Hal, but there was a soft contented smile on Katinka's face, and her eyes sparkled with violet lights that seemed to light the dim recesses of the room.

Hal looked away quickly, startled by the sudden hot hatred that had replaced the adoration he had so recently felt for her. How could it have happened so quickly, he wondered, and knew that if he had a sword in his hand he would not hesitate to drive the point between the peaks of her soft white breasts.

As he sank into his seat he felt compelled to look up again into the pack of spectators. This time he went cold as he saw another pair of eyes, pale and watchful as those of a leopard, fastened on his father's face.

Slow John sat in the front row of the gallery. He looked like a preacher in his puritanical black suit, the wide-brimmed hat set squarely upon his head.

'Do not look at him,' Sir Francis said softly, and Hal realized that his father, too, was intensely aware of the scrutiny of those strange, faded eyes.

As soon as the hall had settled into an expectant silence, van de Velde appeared through the door of the audience chamber beyond. When he lowered himself into his seat his smile was expansive and his wig was just the slightest bit awry. He belched softly, for clearly he had eaten well. Then he looked down on the prisoners with such a benign expression that Hal felt an unwarranted surge of hope for the outcome.

'I have considered the evidence that has been laid before this court,' the Governor began, without preamble, 'and I want to say right at the outset that I was impressed with the manner in which both the advocates presented their cases. Colonel Schreuder was a paradigm of succinct- ness—' He stumbled over both of the longer words, then belched again. Hal fancied that he detected a whiff of cumin and garlic on the warm air that reached him a few seconds later.

Next van de Velde turned a paternal eye on Jacobus Hop. 'The advocate for the defence behaved admirably and made a good job of a hopeless case, and I shall make a note to that effect in his Company file.' Hop bobbed his head and coloured with gratification.

'However!' He now looked squarely at the benches of the prisoners. 'While considering the evidence, I have given much thought to the defence raised by Mijnheer Hop, namely that the pirates were operating under a Letter of Marque issued by the King of England, and that when they attacked the Company galleon, the *Standvastigheid*, they were unaware of the cessation of hostilities between the belligerents in the recent war. I have been forced by irrefutable evidence to the contrary to reject this line of defence in its entirety. Accordingly, I find all twenty- four of the accused persons guilty of piracy on the high seas, of robbery and abduction and murder.'

The seamen on the benches stared at him in pale silence.

'Is there anything you wish to say before I pass sentence upon you?' van de Velde asked, and opened his silver snuff box.

Sir Francis spoke out, in a voice that rang the length and breadth of the hall. 'We are prisoners of war. You do not have the right to chain us like slaves. Neither do you have the right to try us nor to pass sentence upon us.'

Van de Velde took a pinch of snuff up each nostril and then sneezed deliciously, spraying the court writer who sat beside him. The clerk closed the one eye nearest to the Governor but kept his quill flying across the page in an effort to keep up with the proceedings.

'I believe that you and I have discussed this opinion before.' Van de Velde nodded mockingly towards Sir Francis. 'I will now proceed to sentence these pirates. I will deal firstly with the four Negroes. Let the following persons stand forth. Aboli! Matesi! Jiri! Kimatti!'

The four were shackled in pairs, and now the guards prodded them to their feet. They shuffled forward and stood below the dais. Van de Velde regarded them sternly. 'I have taken into account that you are ignorant savages, and therefore cannot be expected to behave like decent Christians. Although your crimes reek to heaven and cry for retribution, I am inclined to mercy. I condemn you to lifelong slavery. You will be sold by the auctioneer of the Dutch East India Company to the highest bidder at auction, and the monies received from this sale will be paid into the Company treasury. Take them away, Sergeant!'

As they were led from the hall Aboli looked across at Sir Francis and Hal. His dark face was impassive behind the mask of tattoos, but his eyes sent them the message of his heart.

'Next I will deal with the white pirates,' van de Velde announced. 'Let the following prisoners stand forth.' He read from the list in his hand. 'Henry Courteney, officer and mate. Ned Tyler, boatswain. Daniel Fisher, boatswain. William Rogers, seaman . . .' He read out every name except that of Sir Francis Courteney. When Sir Francis rose beside his son, van de Velde stopped him. 'Not you! You are the captain and the instigator of this gang of rogues. I have other plans for you. Have the armourer separate him from the other prisoner.' The man hurried forward from the back of the court with the leather satchel containing his tools, and worked swiftly to knock the shackle out of the links that bound Hal to his father.

Sir Francis sat alone on the long bench as Hal left him and went forward to take his place at the head of the row of prisoners below the dais. Van de Velde studied their faces, beginning at one end of the line and moving his brooding gaze slowly along until he arrived at Hal. 'A more murderous bunch of cutthroats I have never laid eyes upon. No honest man or woman is safe when creatures like you are at large. You are fit only for the gibbet.'

As he stared at Hal, a sudden thought occurred to him, and he glanced away towards the Buzzard, who sat beside the lovely Katinka at the side of the hall. 'My lord!' he called. 'May I trouble you for a word in private?' Leaving the prisoners standing, van de Velde heaved his bulk onto his feet and waddled back through the doors in the audience chamber behind him. The Buzzard made an elaborate bow to Katinka and followed the Governor.

As he entered the chamber he found van de Velde selecting a morsel from the silver tray on the polished yellow-wood table. He turned to the Buzzard, his mouth already filled. 'A sudden thought occurred to me. If I am to send Francis Courteney to the executioner for questioning as to the whereabouts of the missing cargo, should not his son go also? Surely Courteney would have told his son or had him with him when he secreted the treasure. What do you think, my Lord?'

The Buzzard looked grave and tugged at his beard as he pretended to consider the question. He had wondered how long it would take this great hog to come round to this way of thinking, and he had long ago prepared his answer. He knew he could rely on the fact that Sir Francis Courteney would never reveal the whereabouts of his wealth, not even to the most cunning and persistent tormentor. He was just too stubborn and pigheaded unless – and here was the one possible case in which he might capitulate – if it were to save his only son. 'Your excellency, I think you need have no fear that any living person knows where the treasure is, apart from the pirate himself. He is much too avaricious and suspicious to trust another human being.'

Van de Velde looked dubious and helped himself to another curried samosa from the tray. While he munched, the Buzzard mulled over his best line of argument, should van de Velde choose to debate it further. There was no question in the Buzzard's mind but that Hal Courteney knew where the treasure from the *Standvastigheid* lay. What was more, he almost certainly knew where the other hoard from the *Heerlycke Nacht* was hidden. Unlike his father, the youngster would be unable to withstand the questioning by Slow John and, even if he proved tougher than the Buzzard believed, his father would certainly break down when he saw his son on the rack. One way or the other the two would lead the Dutch to the hoard, and that was the last thing on this earth that the Buzzard wanted to happen.

His grave expression almost cracked into a grin as he realized the irony of his being forced to save Henry Courteney from the attentions of Slow John. But if he wanted the treasure for himself, he must make sure that neither father nor son led the cheese-heads to it first. The best place for Sir Francis was the gallows, and the best place for his brat was the dungeon under the castle walls.

This time he could not prevent the grin reaching his lips as he thought that while Slow John was still cooling his branding irons in Sir Francis's blood, the *Gull* would be flying back to Elephant Lagoon to winkle out those sacks of guilders and those bars of gold from whatever nook or cranny Sir Francis had tucked them into.

He turned the grin now on van de Velde. 'No, your excellency, I give you my assurance that Francis Courteney is the only man alive who knows where it is. He may look hard and talk bravely, but Franky will roll over and spread his thighs like a whore offered a gold guinea just as soon as Slow John gets to work on him. My advice is that you send Henry Courteney to work on the castle, and rely on his father to lead you to the booty.'

'Ja!' Van de Velde nodded. 'That's what I thought myself. I just wanted you to confirm what I already knew.' He popped one last samosa into his mouth and spoke around it. 'Let's go back and get the business finished, then.'

The prisoners were still waiting in their chains below the dais, like oxen in the traces, as van de Velde settled himself into his chair again.

'The gibbet and the gallows, these are your natural homes, but they are too good for you. I sentence every last man of you to a lifetime of labour in the service of the Dutch East India Company, which you conspired to cheat and rob, and whose servants you abducted and maltreated. Do not think this is kindness on my part, or weakness. There will come a time when you will weep to the Almighty and beg him for the easy death that I denied you this day. Take them away and put them to work immediately. The sight of them offends my eyes, and those of all honest men.'

As they were herded from the hall, Katinka hissed with frustration and made a gesture of annoyance. Cumbrae leaned closer to her and asked, 'What is it that troubles you, madam?'

'I fear my husband has made a mistake. He should have sent them to the pyre on the parade.' Now she would be denied the thrill of watching Slow John work on the beautiful brat, and listening to his screams. It would have been a deeply satisfying conclusion to the affair. Her husband had promised it to her, and he had cheated her of the pleasure. She would make him suffer for that, she decided.

'Ah, madam, revenge is best savoured like a pipe of good Virginia tobacco. Not gobbled up in a rush. Any time in the future that the fancy takes you, you need only look up at the castle walls and there they will be, being worked slowly to death.'

Hal passed close by where Sir Francis sat on the long bench. His father looked forlorn and sick, with his hair and beard in lank ropes and black shadows beneath his eyes, in dreadful contrast with his pale skin. Hal could not bear it and suddenly he cried, 'Father!' and would have run to him, but Sergeant Manseer had anticipated him and stepped in front of him with the long cane in his right hand. Hal backed away.

His father did not look up, and Hal realized that he had taken his farewell and had moved on into the far territory where only Slow John would be able now to reach him.

When the file of convicts had left the hall and the doors had closed behind them, a hush fell and every eye rested on the lonely figure on the bench.

'Francis Courteney,' van de Velde said loudly. 'Stand forth!'

Sir Francis threw back his head, flicking the greying hair out of his eyes. He shrugged off the guards' hands and rose unaided to his feet. He held his head high as he marched to the dais, and his torn shirt flapped around his naked back. The cane stripes had begun to dry into crusted black scabs.

'Francis Courteney, it is not by chance, I am certain, that you bear the same Christian name as that most notorious of all pirates, the rogue Francis Drake.'

'I have the honour to be named for the famous seafarer,' said Sir Francis softly.

'Then I have the even greater honour of passing sentence upon you. I sentence you to death.' Van de Velde waited for Sir Francis to show some emotion, but he stared back without expression. At last the Governor was forced to continue. 'I repeat, your sentence is death, but the manner of your death will be of your own choosing.' Abruptly and unexpectedly, he let out a mellow guffaw. 'There are not many rogues of your calibre that are treated with such beneficence and condescension.'

'With your permission, I shall withhold any expression of gratitude until I hear the rest of your proposal,' Sir Francis murmured, and van de Velde stopped laughing.

'Not all the cargo from the *Standvastigheid* has been recovered. By far the most valuable portion is still missing, and there is no doubt in my mind that you were able to secrete this before you were captured by the troops of the honourable Company. Are you prepared to reveal the hiding place of the missing cargo to the officers of the Company? In that case, your execution will be by a swift and clean beheading.'

'I have nothing to tell you,' said Sir Francis, in a disinterested tone.

'Then, I fear, you will be asked the same question under extreme compulsion by the state executioner.' Van de Velde smacked his lips softly, as though the words tasted good on his tongue. 'Should you answer fully and without reservation the headsman's axe will put an end to your suffering. Should you remain obstinate, the questioning will continue. At all times the choice will remain yours.'

249

'Your excellency is a paragon of mercy,' Sir Francis bowed, 'but I cannot answer the question, for I know nothing of the cargo of which you speak.'

'Then Almighty God have mercy on your soul,' said van de Velde, and turned to Sergeant Manseer. 'Take the prisoner away and place him in the charge of the state executioner.'

Hal balanced high on the scaffolding on the unfinished wall of the eastern bastion of the castle. This was only the second day of the labours that were to last the rest of his natural life, and already the palms of his hands and both his shoulders were rubbed raw by the ropes and the rough, undressed stone blocks. One of his fingertips was crushed and the nail was the colour of a purple grape. Each masonry block weighed a ton or more and had to be manhandled up the rickety scaffolding of bamboo poles and planks.

In the gang of convicts working with him were Big Daniel and Ned Tyler, neither of whom was fully recovered from his wounds. Their injuries were plain to see for all were dressed only in petticoats of ragged canvas.

The musket ball had left a deep, dark purple crater in Daniel's chest and a lion's claw across his back, where Hal had cut him. The scabs over these wounds had burst open with his exertions and were weeping watery blood-tinged lymph.

The sword wound crawled like a raw red vine around Ned's thigh, and he limped heavily as he moved along the scaffold. After their privations in the slave deck of the *Gull* they were all honed clean of the last ounce of fat. They were lean as hunting dogs, and stringy muscle and bone stood out clearly beneath their sun-reddened skins.

Though the sun still shone brightly, the winter wind whistled in from the nor-'west and seemed to abrade their bodies like ground glass. In unison they hauled at the tail of the heavy manila rope and the sheaves screeched in their blocks as the great yellow lump of stone lifted from the truck of the wagon far below and began its perilous ascent up the high structure.

The previous day a scaffolding on the south bastion had collapsed under the weight of the stones and had hurled three of the convicts working upon it to their death on the cobbles far below. Hugo Barnard, the overseer, had muttered as he stood over their crushed corpses, 'Three birds with one stone. I'll have the next careless bastard that kills himself thrashed within an inch of his life,' and burst out laughing at his own gallows' humour.

Daniel took a turn of the rope end around his good shoulder and anchored it as the rest of the team reached out, seized the swinging block and hauled it onto the trestle. Between them they manhandled it into the gap at the top of the wall, with the Dutch stonemason in his leather apron shouting instructions at them.

They stood back panting after it had dropped into place, every muscle in their bodies aching and trembling from the effort, but there was no time to rest. From the courtyard below Hugo Barnard was already yelling, 'Get that cradle down here. Swiftly now or I'll come up and give you a touch of the persuader,' and he flicked out the knotted leather thongs of his whip.

Daniel peered over the edge of the scaffold. Suddenly he stiffened and glanced over his shoulder at Hal. 'There go Aboli and the other lads.'

Hal stepped up beside him and looked down. From the doorway to the dungeon a small procession emerged. The four black seamen were led out into the wintry sunshine. Once again, they were wearing light chains. 'Look at those lucky bastards,' Ned Tyler muttered. They had not been included in the labour teams, but had stayed in the dungeon, resting and being fed an extra meal each day to fatten them up while they waited to go on the auction block. This morning Manseer had ordered the four men to strip naked. Then Dr Saar, the Company surgeon, had come down to the cell and examined them, probing and peering into their ears and mouths to satisfy himself as to the state of their health. When the surgeon had left, Manseer ordered them to anoint themselves all over from a stone jar of oil. Now their skins shone in the sunlight like polished ebony. Though they were still lean and finely drawn from their stay aboard the *Gull*, the coating of oil made them appear sleek prime specimens of humanity. Now they were being led out through the gates of the castle onto the open Parade where already a crowd had gathered.

Before he passed through the gates Aboli raised his great round head and looked up at Hal on the scaffold, high above. For one moment their eyes met. There was no need for either to shout a message, chancing a cut of the cane from their keepers, and Aboli strode on without looking back.

The auction block was a temporary structure that at other times was used as a gibbet on which the corpses of executed criminals were placed on public view. The four men were lined up on the platform and Dr Saar mounted the platform with them and addressed the crowd. 'I have examined all of the four slaves being offered for sale today,' he stated, lowering his head to peer over the tops of his wire-framed eye-glasses. 'I can give the assurance that all of them are in good health. Their eyes and teeth are sound and they are hale in limb and body.'

The crowd was in a festive mood. They clapped at the doctor's announcement, and gave him an ironical cheer as he climbed down from the block and hurried back towards the castle gates. Jacobus Hop stepped forward and held up a hand for silence. Then he read from the proclamation of the sale, the crowd jeering and imitating him every time he stuttered. 'By order of His Excellency the Governor of this colony of the honourable Dutch East India Company, I am authorized to offer for sale, to the highest bidder, four Negro slaves—' He broke off and removed his hat respectfully as the Governor's open carriage came down the avenue from the residence, passing through the gardens and wheeling out onto the open Parade behind the six glossy greys. Lord Cumbrae and the Governor's wife sat side by side on the open leather seats facing forward, and Colonel Schreuder sat opposite them.

The crowd opened to let the carriage come to the foot of the block, where Fredricus, the coloured coachman, called the team to a halt and wound down the hand brake. None of the passengers dismounted. Katinka lolled elegantly on the leather seat, twirling her parasol, and chatting gaily to the two men.

On the platform Hop was thrown into confusion by the arrival of these exalted visitors, and stood flushing, stammering and blinking in the sunlight until Schreuder called out impatiently, 'Get on with it, fellow! We didn't come here to watch you goggle and gape.'

Hop replaced his hat and bowed first at Schreuder then at Katinka. He raised his voice. 'The first lot is the slave Aboli. He is about thirty years of age and is believed to be a member of the Qwanda tribe from the east coast of Africa. As you are aware, the Qwanda Negroes are much appreciated as field slaves and herdsmen. He could also be trained into an excellent wagon driver or coachman.' He paused to mop his sweaty face and gather his tripping tongue, then he went on, 'Aboli is said to be a skilled hunter and fisherman. He would bring in a good income to his owner from any of these occupations.'

'Mijnheer Hop, are you hiding anything from us?' Katinka called out, and Hop was once more thrown into disarray by the question. His stammer became so agonized that he could hardly get the words out.

'Revered lady, greatly esteemed lady,' he spread his hands helplessly, 'I assure you—'

'Would you offer for sale a bull wearing clothes?' Katinka demanded. 'Do you expect us to bid for something that we cannot see?'

As he caught her meaning, Hop's face cleared and he turned to Aboli.

'Disrobe!' he ordered loudly, to bolster his courage while facing this huge wild savage. For a moment Aboli stared at him unmoving then contemptuously slipped the knot of his loincloth and let it fall to the planks under his feet.

Naked and magnificent, he stared over their heads at the table-topped mountain. There was a hissing intake of breath from the crowd below. One of the women squealed and another giggled nervously, but none turned away their eyes.

'Hoots!' Cumbrae broke the pregnant pause with a chuckle. 'The buyer will be getting full measure. There is no makeweight in that load of blood-sausage. I'll start the bidding at five hundred guilders!'

'And a hundred more!' Katinka called out.

The Buzzard glanced at her and spoke softly from the corner of his mouth. 'I did not know you were intending to bid, madam.'

'I will have this one at any price, my lord,' she warned him sweetly, 'for he amuses me.'

'I would never stand in the way of a beautiful lady.' The Buzzard bowed. 'But you will not bid against me for the other three, will you?'

''Tis a bargain, my lord.' Katinka smiled. 'This one is mine, and you may have the others.'

Cumbrae folded his arms across his chest and shook his head when Hop looked to him to increase the bid. 'Too rich a price for my digestion,' he said, and Hop looked in vain for a buyer in the rest of the crowd. None was foolhardy enough to go up against the Governor's wife. Recently they had been given a glimpse of his excellency's temper in open court.

'The slave Aboli is sold to Mevrouw van de Velde for the sum of six hundred guilders!' Hop sang out, and bowed towards the carriage. 'Do you wish the chains struck off, Mevrouw?'

Katinka laughed. 'And have him bolt for the mountains? No, Mijnheer, these soldiers will escort him up to the slave quarters at the residence.' She glanced across at Schreuder who gave an order to a detachment of green-jackets waiting under their corporal at the edge of the crowd. They elbowed their way forward, dragged Aboli down from the block and led him away up the avenue towards the residence.

Katinka watched him go. Then she tapped the Buzzard on the shoulder with one finger. 'Thank you, my lord.'

'The next lot is the slave Jiri,' Hop told them, reading from his notes. 'He is, as you see, another fine strong specimen—'

'Five hundred guilders!' growled the Buzzard, and glared at the other buyers, as if daring them to bid at their peril. But without the Governor's wife to compete against, the burghers of the colony were bolder.

'And one hundred,' sang out a merchant of the town.

'And a hundred more!' called a wagoner in a jacket of leopardskins. The bidding went quickly to fifteen hundred guilders with only the wagoner and the Buzzard in the race.

'Damn and blast the clod!' Cumbrae muttered, and turned his head to catch the eye of his boatswain who, with three of his seamen, hovered beside the rear wheel of the carriage. Sam Bowles nodded and his eyes gleamed. With his men backing him he sidled through the press until he stood close behind the wagoner.

'Sixteen hundred guilders,' roared the Buzzard, 'and be damned to ye!'

The wagoner opered his mouth to push upwards and felt something prick him under the ribs. He glanced down at the knife in Sam Bowles's gnarled fist, closed his mouth and blanched white as baleen.

'The bid is against you, Mijnheer Tromp!' Hop called to him, but the wagoner scurried away across the Parade back towards the town.

Kimatti and Matesi were both knocked down to the Buzzard for well under a thousand guilders each. The other prospective buyers in the crowd had seen the little drama between Sam and the wagoner and none showed any further interest in bidding against Cumbrae.

All three slaves were dragged away by Sam Bowles's shore party towards the beach. When Matesi struggled to escape a shrewd crack over his scalp with a marlinspike quieted him and, with his mates, he was shoved into the longboat and rowed out to where the *Gull* lay anchored at the edge of the shoals.

'A successful expedition for both of us, my lord.' Katinka smiled at the Buzzard. 'To celebrate our acquisitions, I hope you will be able to dine with us at the residence this evening.'

'Nothing would have given me greater pleasure, but alas, madam, I was lingering only for the sale and the chance of picking up a few prime seamen. Now my ship lies ready in the bay, and the wind and the tide bid me away.'

'We shall miss you, my lord. Your company has been most diverting. I hope you will call on us and remain a while longer when next you round the Cape of Good Hope.'

'There is no power on this earth, no storm, ill wind or enemy which could prevent me doing so,' said Cumbrae and kissed her hand. Cornelius Schreuder glowered: he could not stand to see another man lay a finger on this woman who had come to rule his existence.

As the Buzzard's feet touched the deck of the *Gull* he shouted to the helm, 'Geordie, my lad, prepare to weigh anchor and get under way.'

Then he singled out Sam Bowles. 'I want the three Negroes on the quarterdeck, and swiftly.' As they were ranged before him, he looked them over carefully. 'Does any one of you three heathen beauties speak God's own language?' he asked, and they stared at him blankly. 'So it's only your benighted lingo, is it?' He shook his head sadly. 'That makes my life much harder.'

'Begging your pardon,' Sam Bowles tugged obsequiously at his Monmouth cap, 'I know them well, all three of them. We was shipmates together, we was. They're playing you for a patsy. They all three speak good English.'

Cumbrae grinned at them, with murder in his eyes. 'You belong to me now, my lovelies, from the tops of your woolly heads to the pink soles of your great flat feet. If you want to keep your black hides in one piece, you'll not play games with me again, do you hear me?' And with a swipe of his huge hairy fist he sent Jiri crashing to the deck. 'When I talk to you you'll answer clear and loud in sweet English words. We're going back to Elephant Lagoon and, for the sake of your health, you're going to show me where Captain Franky hid his treasure. Do you hear me?'

Jiri scrambled back onto his feet. 'Yes, Captain Lordy, sir! We hear you. You are our father.'

'I'd rather have lopped off my own spigot with a blunt spade than fathered the likes of one of you with it!' The Buzzard grinned at them. 'Now get ye up to the main yard to clap some canvas on her.' And he sent Jiri on his way with a flying kick in the backside.

Katinka sat in sunlight, in a protected corner of the terrace out of the wind, with Cornelius Schreuder beside her. At the serving table Sukeena poured the wine with her own hands, and carried the two glasses to the luncheon table with its decorations of fruit and flowers from Slow John's gardens. She placed a tall glass with a spiral stem in front of Katinka, who reached out and caressed her arm lightly.

'Have you sent for the new slave?' she asked with a purr in her voice.

'Aboli is being bathed and fitted with a uniform, as you ordered, mistress,' Sukeena answered softly, as if unaware of the other woman's touch. However, Schreuder had seen it, and it amused Katinka to watch him frown with jealousy.

She raised her glass to him and smiled over the rim. 'Shall we drink to a swift voyage for Lord Cumbrae?'

'Indeed.' He lifted his glass. 'A short swift voyage to the bottom of the ocean for him and all his countrymen.'

'My dear Colonel,' she smiled, 'how droll. But softly now, here comes my latest plaything.'

Two green-jackets from the castle escorted Aboli onto the terrace. He was dressed in a pair of tight-fitting black trousers and a white cotton shirt cut full to encompass his broad chest and massive arms. He stood silently before her.

Katinka switched into English. 'In future you will bow when you enter my presence and you will address me as mistress, and if you forget I will ask Slow John to remind you. Do you know who Slow John is?'

'Yes, mistress,' Aboli rumbled, without looking at her.

'Oh, good! I thought you might be tiresome, and that I would have to have you broken and tamed. This makes things easier for both of us.' She took a sip of the wine, then looked him over slowly with her head on one side. 'I bought you on a whim, and I have not decided what I shall do with you. However, Governor Kleinhans is taking his coachman home with him when he sails. I will need a new coachman.' She turned to Colonel Schreuder. 'I have heard these Negroes are good with animals. Is that your experience also, Colonel?'

'Indeed, Mevrouw. Being animals themselves they seem to have a rapport with all wild and domestic beasts.' Schreuder nodded, and studied Aboli unhurriedly. 'He is a fine physical specimen but, of course, one does not look for intelligence in them. I congratulate you on your purchase.'

'Later, I may breed him with Sukeena,' Katinka mused. The slave girl went still, but her back was turned so that they could not see her face. 'It might be diverting to see how the black blood mingles with the gold.'

'A most interesting mixture.' Schreuder nodded. 'But are you not worried that he may escape? I saw him fight on the deck of the *Standvastigheid* and he is a truculent savage. A leg iron might be suitable costume for him, at least until he has been broken in.'

'I do not think I need go to such pains,' Katinka said. 'I was able to observe him at length during my captivity. Like a faithful dog, he is devoted to the pirate Courteney and even more so to his brat. I believe he would never try to escape while either of them is alive in the castle dungeons. Of course, he will be locked in the slave quarters at night with the others, but during working hours he will be allowed to move around freely to attend to his duties.'

'I am sure you know best, Mevrouw. But I for one would never trust such a creature,' Schreuder warned her.

Katinka turned back to Sukeena. 'I have arranged with Governor Kleinhans that Fredricus is to teach Aboli his duties as coachman and driver. The *Standvastigheid* will not sail for another ten days. That should be ample time. See to it immediately.'

Sukeena made the gracious oriental obeisance. 'As Mistress commands,' she said, and beckoned for Aboli to follow her.

She walked ahead of him down the pathway to the stables where Fredricus had drawn up the coach and Aboli was reminded of the posture and carriage of the young virgins of his own tribe. As little girls they were trained by their mothers, carrying the water gourds balanced on their heads. Their backs grew straight and they seemed to glide over the ground, as this girl did.

'Your brother, Althuda, sends you his heart. He says that you are his tiger orchid still.'

Sukeena stopped so abruptly that, walking behind her, Aboli almost collided with her. She seemed like a startled sugarbird perched on a protea bloom on the point of flight. When she moved on again he saw that she was trembling.

'You have seen my brother?' she asked, without turning her head to look at him.

'I never saw his face, but we spoke through the door of his cell. He said that your mother's name was Ashreth and that the jade brooch you wear was given to your mother by your father on the day of your birth. He said that if I told you these things, you would know that I was his friend.'

'If he trusted you, then I also trust you. I, too, shall be your friend, Aboli,' she agreed.

'And I shall be yours,' Aboli said softly.

'Oh, do tell me, how is Althuda? Is he well?' she pleaded. 'Have they hurt him badly? Have they given him to Slow John?'

'Althuda is puzzled. They have not yet condemned him. He has been in the dungeon four long months and they have not hurt him.'

'I give all thanks to Allah!' Sukeena turned and smiled at him, her face lovely as the tiger orchid to which Althuda had likened her. 'I had some influence with Governor Kleinhans. I was able to persuade him to delay judgement on my brother. But now that he is going I do not know what will happen with the new one. My poor Althuda, so young and brave. If they give him to Slow John my heart will die with him, as slowly and as painfully.'

257

'There is one I love as you love your brother,' Aboli rumbled softly. 'The two share the same dungeon.'

'I think I know the one of whom you speak. Did I not see him on the day they brought all of you ashore in chains and marched you across the Parade? Is he straight and proud as a young prince?'

'That is the one. Like your brother, he deserves to be free.'

Again Sukeena's feet checked, but then she glided onwards. 'What are you saying, Aboli, my friend?'

'You and I together. We can work to set them free.'

'Is it possible?' she whispered.

'Althuda was free once. He broke his jesses and soared away like a falcon.' Aboli looked up at the aching blue African sky. 'With our help he could be free again, and Gundwane with him.'

They had come to the stableyard and Fredricus roused himself on the seat of the carriage. He looked down at Aboli and his lips curled back to show teeth discoloured brown by chewing tobacco. 'How can a black ape learn to drive my coach and my six darlings?' he asked the empty air.

'Fredricus is an enemy. Trust him not.' Sukeena's lips barely moved as she gave Aboli the warning. 'Trust nobody in this household until we can speak again.'

As well as the house slaves, and most of the furniture in the residence, Katinka had purchased from Kleinhans all the horses in his string and the contents of the tack room. She had written him an order on her bankers in Amsterdam. It was for a large sum, but she knew that her father would make good any shortfall.

The most beautiful of all the horses was a bay mare, a superb animal with strong graceful legs and a beautifully shaped head. Katinka was an expert horsewoman, but she had no feeling or love for the creature beneath her and her slim, pale hands were strong and cruel. She rode with a Spanish curb that bruised the mare's mouth savagely, and her use of the whip was wanton. When she had ruined a mount she could always sell it and buy another.

Despite these faults, she was fearless and had a dashing seat. When the mare danced under her and threw her head against the agony of the whip and the curb, Katinka sat easily and looked marvellously elegant. Now she was pushing the mare to the full extent of her pace and endurance, flying at the steep path, using the whip when she faltered or when it seemed as though she would refuse to jump a fallen tree that blocked the pathway.

The horse was lathered, soaked with sweat as though she had plunged through a river. The froth that streamed from her gaping mouth was tinged pink with blood from the edged steel of the curb. It splattered back onto Katinka's boots and skirt, and she laughed wildly with excitement as they galloped out onto the saddle of the mountain. She looked back over her shoulder. Schreuder was fifty lengths or more behind her: he had come by another route to meet her in secret. His black gelding was labouring heavily under his weight, and though Schreuder used the whip freely his mount could not hold the mare.

Katinka did not stop at the saddle but, with the whip and the tiny needle-sharp spur under her riding habit, goaded the mare onward and sent her plunging straight down the far slope. Here a fall would be disastrous, for the footing was treacherous and the mare was blown. The danger excited Katinka. She revelled in the feel of the powerful body beneath her, and of the saddle leather pounding against her sweating thighs and buttocks.

They came slithering off the scree slope and burst out into the open meadow beside the stream. She raced parallel with the stream for half a league, but when she reached a hidden grove of silverleaf trees she reined in the mare in a dozen lunges from full gallop to a wrenching halt.

She unhooked her leg from over the horn of the sidesaddle and in a swirl of skirts and laced underlinen dropped lightly to earth. She landed like a cat, and while the mare blew like the bellows of a smithy and reeled on her feet with exhaustion, Katinka stood, both fists clenched on her hips, and watched Schreuder come down the slope after her.

He reached the meadow and galloped to where she stood. There, he jumped from the gelding's back. His face was dark with rage. 'That was madness, Mevrouw,' he shouted. 'If you had fallen!'

'But I never fall, Colonel.' She laughed in his face. 'Not unless you can make me.' She reached up suddenly and threw both arms around his neck. Like a lamprey she fastened on his lips, sucking so powerfully that she drew his tongue into her own mouth. As his arms tightened around her she bit his lower lip hard enough to start his blood, and tasted the metallic salt on her own tongue. When he roared with pain, she broke from his embrace and, lifting the skirts of her habit, ran lightly along the bank of the stream.

'Sweet Mary, you'll pay dearly for that, you little devil!' He wiped his mouth, and when he saw the smear of blood on his palm, he raced after her.

These last days, Katinka had toyed with him, driving him to the frontiers of sanity, promising and then revoking, teasing and then dismissing, cold as the north wind one moment then hot as the tropical sun at noonday. He was dizzy and confused with lust and longing, but his desire had infected her. Tormenting him, she had driven herself as far and as hard. She wanted him now almost as much as he wanted her. She wanted to feel him deep inside her body, she had to have him quench the fires she had ignited in her womb. The time had come when she could delay no longer.

He caught up with her and she turned at bay. With her back against one of the silverleaf trees, she faced him like a hind cornered by the hounds. She saw the blind rage turn his eyes opaque as marble. His face was swollen and encarnadined, his lips drawn back to expose his clenched teeth.

With a thrill of real terror she realized that this rage into which she had driven him was a kind of madness over which he had no control. She knew that she was in danger of her life and, knowing that, her own lust broke its banks like a mighty river in full spate.

She threw herself at him and with both hands ripped at the fastenings of his breeches. 'You want to kill me, don't you?'

'You bitch,' he choked, and reached for her throat. 'You slut. I can stand no more. I will make you—'

She pulled him out through the opening in his clothes, hard and thick, swollen furious red and so hot he seemed to sear her fingers. 'Kill me with this, then. Thrust it into me so deeply that you pierce my heart.' She leaned back against the rough bark of the silverleaf and planted her feet wide apart. He swept her skirts up high, and with both hands she guided him into herself. As he lunged and bucked furiously against her, the tree against which she leaned shook as though a gale of wind had struck it. The silver leaves rained down over them glinting like newly minted coins as they spun and swirled in the sunlight. As she reached her climax Katinka screamed so that the echoes rang along the yellow cliffs high above them.

Katinka came down from the mountain like a fury, riding on the wings of the north-west gale that had sprung so suddenly out of the sunny winter sky. Her hair had broken free of her bonnet and streamed out like a brilliant banner, snapping and tangling in the wind. The mare ran as though pursued by lions. When she reached the upper vineyards, Katinka put her to the high stone wall, over which she soared like a falcon.

She galloped through the gardens down to the stableyard. Slow John turned to watch her go by. The green things he had nurtured were uprooted, torn and scattered beneath the mare's flying hoofs. When she had passed, Slow John stooped and picked up a shredded stem. He lifted it to his mouth and bit into it softly, tasting the sweet sap. He felt no resentment. The plants he grew were meant to be cut and destroyed, just as man is born to die. To Slow John, only the manner of the dying was significant.

He stared after the mare and her rider and felt the same reverence and awe that always overcame him at the moment when he released one of his little sparrows from this mortal existence. He thought of all the condemned souls who died under his hands as his little sparrows. The first time he had set his eyes on Katinka van de Velde he had fallen completely under her spell. He felt that he had waited all his life for this woman. He had recognized in her those mystical qualities that dictated his own existence but, compared to her, he knew that he was a thing crawling in primeval slime.

She was a cruel and untouchable goddess, and he worshipped her. It was as though these torn plants he held in his hands were a sacrifice to that goddess. As though he had laid them on her altar and she had accepted them. He was moved almost to the point of tears by her condescension. He blinked those strange yellow eyes and for once they mirrored his emotion. 'Command me,' he breathed. 'There is nothing that I would not do for you.'

Katinka spurred the mare at full gallop up the driveway to the front doors of the residence, and flung herself from its back before it had come fully to rest. She did not even glance at Aboli as he sprang down from the terrace, gathered up the reins and led the mare away to the stableyard.

He spoke gently to the horse in the language of the forests. 'She has made you bleed, little one, but Aboli will heal your hurt.' In the yard he unbuckled the girth and dried the mare's steaming sweat with the cloth, walking her in slow circles, then watering her before he led her to her stall.

'See where her whip and spurs have cut you. She is a witch,' he whispered, as he anointed the torn and bruised corners of the horse's mouth with salve. 'But Aboli is here now to protect and cherish you.'

Katinka strode through the rooms of the residence, singing softly to herself, her face lit with the afterglow of her loving. In her bedchamber she shouted for Zelda then, without waiting for the old woman to arrive, she stripped off her clothing and dropped it in a heap in the middle of the floor. The winter air through the shutters was cold on her body, which was damp with sweat and the juices of her passion. Her pale pink nipples rose in haloes of gooseflesh and she shouted again, 'Zelda, where are you?' When the maid came scurrying into the chamber she rounded on her, 'Sweet Jesus, where have you been, you lazy old baggage? Close those shutters! Is my bath ready, or have you been dozing off again in front of the fire?' But her words lacked their usual venom and when she lay back in the steaming, perfumed waters of her ceramic bathtub, which had been carted up from the cabin in the stern of the galleon, she was smiling warmly and secretly to herself.

Zelda hovered around the tub, lifting the thick strands of her mistress's hair out of the scented foam and pinning them atop her head, soaping her shoulders with a cloth.

'Don't fuss so! Leave me be for a while!' Katinka ordered imperiously. Zelda dropped the cloth and backed out of the bathroom.

Katinka lay for a while, humming softly to herself and lifting her feet one at a time above the foam to inspect her delicate ankles and pink toes. Then a movement in the steam-clouded mirror caught her attention and she sat up straight and stared incredulously. Quickly she stood up and stepped out of the tub, slipped a towel around her shoulders to soak up the drops of water that ran down her body and crept to the door of her bedroom.

What she had seen in the mirror was Zelda gathering up her soiled clothing from where she had dropped it on the tiles. The old woman stood now with Katinka's underlinen in her hands examining the stains upon it. As Katinka watched, she lifted the cloth to her face and sniffed at it like an old bitch scenting the entrance to a rabbit warren.

'You like the smell of a man's ripe cream, do you?' Katinka asked coldly.

At the sound of her voice Zelda spun about to face her. She hid the clothing behind her back and her cheeks went pale as ash as she stammered incoherently.

'You dried-up old cow, when did you last have a sniff of it?' Katinka asked.

She dropped the towel and glided across the floor, slim and sinuous as an erect female cobra and her gaze as icy and venomous. Her riding whip lay where she had dropped it and she scooped it up as she passed.

Zelda backed away in front of her. 'Mistress,' Zelda whined, 'I was worried only that your pretty things might be spoiled.'

'You were snuffling it up like a fat old sow with a truffle,' Katinka told her, and her whip arm flashed out. The lash caught Zelda in the mouth. She squealed and fell back on the bed.

Katinka stood over her, naked, and plied the whip across her back and arms and legs, swinging with all her strength, so that the layers of fat wobbled and shook on the maid's limbs as the lash bit into them. 'This is a pleasure too long denied,' Katinka screamed, her own fury increasing as the old woman howled and wriggled on the bed. 'I have grown weary of your thieving ways and your gluttony. Now you revolt me with this prurient trespass into intimate areas of my life, you sneaking, spying, whining old baggage.'

'Mistress, you are killing me.'

'Good so! But if you live you will be on board the *Standvastigheid* when she sails for Holland next week. I can abide you around me no longer. I will send you back in the meanest cabin without a penny of pension. You can eke out the rest of your days in the poorhouse.' Katinka was panting wildly now, raining her blows on Zelda's head and shoulders.

'Please, mistress, you would not be so cruel to your old Zelda, who wet-nursed you as a baby.'

'The thought of having sucked on those great fat tits makes me want to puke.' Katinka lashed out at them, and Zelda whimpered and covered her chest with both arms. 'When you leave I will have your baggage searched so that you take with you nothing that you have stolen from me. There will be not a single guilder in your purse, I shall see to that. You thieving, lying crone.'

The threat transformed Zelda from a pathetic wriggling fawning creature into a woman possessed. Her arm shot out and her plump fist seized Katinka's wrist as she was about to strike again. Zelda held onto her with a strength that shocked her mistress and she glared into Katinka's face with a terrible hatred.

'No!' she said. 'You will not take everything I have from me. You will not beggar me. I have served you twenty-four years and you will not cast me off now. I will sail on the galleon, yes, and nothing will give me greater joy than to see the last of your poisonous beauty. But when I go I will take with me all I own and on top of that I will have in my purse the thousand gold guilders you will give to me as my pension.'

Katinka was stunned out of her rage, and stared in disbelief at her.

'You rave like a lunatic. A thousand guilders? More likely a thousand cuts with the whip.'

She tried to pull her arm free, but Zelda hung on with a mad strength. 'A lunatic you say! But what will his excellency do when I bring him proof of how you have been rutting with the Colonel?'

Katinka froze at the threat then slowly lowered her whip arm. Her mind was racing, and a hundred mysteries unravelled as she stared into Zelda's eyes. She had trusted this old bitch without question, never doubting her complete loyalty, never even thinking about it. Now she knew how her husband always seemed to have intimate knowledge of her lovers and her behaviour that should have been secret.

She thought quickly now, her impassive expression masking the outrage she felt at this betrayal. It mattered little if her husband learned of this new adventure with Cornelius Schreuder. It would simply be an annoyance, for Katinka had not yet tired of the colonel. The consequences would, of course, be more serious for her new lover.

Looking back, she realized just how vindictive Petrus van de Velde had been: all her lovers had suffered some grievous harm once her husband knew about them. How he knew had always been a mystery to Katinka until this moment. She must have been naïve, but it had never occurred to her that Zelda had been the serpent in her bosom.

'Zelda, I have wronged you,' Katinka said softly. 'I should not have treated you so harshly.' She reached down and stroked the angry weal on the maid's chubby cheek. 'You have been kind and faithful to me all these years and it is time you went to a happy retirement. I spoke in anger. I would never dream of denying you that which you deserve. When you sail on the galleon you will have not a thousand but two thousand guilders in your purse, and my love and gratitude will go with you.'

Zelda licked her bruised lips and grinned with malicious triumph. 'You are so kind and good to me, my sweet mistress.'

'Of course, you will say nothing to my husband about my little indiscretions with Colonel Schreuder, will you?'

'I love you much too much ever to do you harm, and my heart will break on the day that I have to leave you.'

Slow John knelt in the flower bed at the end of the terrace, his pruning knife in his powerful hands. As a shadow fell over him, he looked up and rose to his feet. He lifted his hat and held it across his chest respectfully. 'Good morrow, mistress,' he said, in his deep melodious voice.

'Pray continue with your task. I love to watch you work.'

He sank to his knees again and the blade of the sharp little knife flickered in his hands. Katinka sat on a bench close at hand and watched him in silence for a while.

'I admire your skills,' she said at last, and though he did not raise his head he knew that she referred not only to his dexterity with the pruning knife. 'I have dire need of those skills, Slow John. There would be a purse of a hundred guilders as your reward. Will you do something for me?'

'Mevrouw, there is nothing I would not do for you.' He lifted his head at last and stared at her with those pale yellow eyes. 'I would not flinch from laying down my life if you asked it of me. I do not ask for payment. The knowledge that I do your bidding is all the reward I could ever want.'

The winter nights had turned cold and squalls of rain roared down off the mountain to batter the panes of the windows and howl like jackals around the eaves of the thatched roof. Zelda pulled her nightdress over her ample frame. All the weight she had lost on the voyage from the east had come back to settle on her paunch and thighs. Since moving into the residence she had fed well at her corner in the kitchen, wolfing down the luscious scraps as they were carried through from the high table in the main dining hall, washing them down from her tankard filled with the dregs from the wine glasses of the gentry, Rhine and red wine mixed with gin and schnapps.

Her belly filled with good food and drink, she made ready for bed. First, she checked that the window casements in her small room were sealed against the draught. She stuffed wads of rags into the cracks and drew the curtains across them. She slid the copper warming pan under the covers of her bed and held it there until she smelt the linen begin to singe. Then she blew out the candle and crept under the thick woollen blankets.

Snuffling and sighing, she settled into the softness and warmth, and her last thoughts were of the purse of golden coins tucked under her mattress. She fell asleep, smiling.

An hour after midnight, when all the house was silent and sleeping, Slow John listened at the door of Zelda's room. When he heard her snores rattling louder than the wind at the casement, he eased open the door noiselessly and slipped through it the brazier of glowing charcoal. He listened for a minute, but the rhythm of the old woman's breathing was regular and unbroken. He closed the door softly and moved silently down the passage to the door at the end.

In the dawn Sukeena came to wake Katinka an hour before her appointed time. When she had helped her dress in a warm robe, she led her to the servants' quarters where a silent, frightened knot of slaves was gathered outside Zelda's door. They stood aside for Katinka to enter and Sukeena whispered, 'I know how much she meant to you, mistress. My heart breaks for you.'

'Thank you, Sukeena,' Katinka answered sadly, and glanced quickly around the tiny room. The brazier had been removed. Slow John had been thorough and reliable.

'She looks so peaceful and what a lovely colour she has.' Sukeena stood beside the bed. 'Almost as if she were alive still.'

Katinka came to stand beside her. The noxious fumes from the brazier had rouged the old woman's cheeks. In death she was more handsome than she had ever been in life. 'Leave me alone with her for a while, please, Sukeena,' she said quietly. 'I wish to say a prayer for her. She was so dear to me.'

As she knelt beside the bed Sukeena closed the door softly behind her. Katinka slid her hand under the mattress and drew out the purse. She could tell by its weight that none of the coins was missing. She slipped the purse into the pocket of her gown, clasped her hands in front of her and closed her eyes so tightly that the long golden lashes intermeshed.

'Go to hell, you old bitch,' she murmured.

Slow John came at last. Many long days and tormented nights they had waited for him, so long that Sir Francis Courteney had begun to imagine that he would never come.

Each evening, when darkness brought an end to the work on the castle walls, the prisoner teams came shuffling in, out of the night. Winter was tightening its grip on the Cape and they were often soaked by the driving rain and chilled to the bone.

Every evening, as he passed the iron-studded door of his father's cell, Hal called, 'What cheer, Father?'

The reply, in a voice hoarse and choked with the phlegm of his illness, was always the same. 'Better today, Hal. And with you?'

'The work was easy. We are all in good heart.'

Then Althuda would call from the next-door cell, 'The surgeon came this morning. He says that Sir Francis is well enough to be questioned by Slow John.' Or on another occasion, 'The fever is worse, Sir Francis has been coughing all day.'

As soon as the prisoners were locked into the lower dungeon they would gulp down their one meal of the day, scraping out the bowls with their fingers, and then drop like dead men on the damp straw.

In the darkness before dawn Manseer would rattle on the bars of the cell. 'Up! Up, you lazy bastards, before Barnard sends in his dogs to rouse you.'

They would struggle to their feet, and file out again into the rain and the wind. There, Barnard waited to greet them, with his two huge black boarhounds, growling and lunging against the leashes. Some of the seamen had found pieces of sacking or canvas with which to wrap their bare feet or cover their heads, but even these rags were still wet from the previous day. Most, though, were bare foot and half-naked in the winter gales.

Then Slow John came. He came at midday. The men on the high scaffolding fell silent and all work stopped. Even Hugo Barnard stood aside as he passed through the gates of the castle. In his sombre clothing, and with the wide-brimmed hat pulled low over his eyes, he looked like a preacher on his way to the pulpit.

Slow John stopped at the entrance to the dungeons, and Sergeant Manseer came running across the yard, jangling his keys. He opened the low door, stood aside for Slow John, then followed him through. The door closed behind the pair and the watchers roused themselves, as though they had awakened from a nightmare and resumed their tasks. But while Slow John was within a deep, brooding silence hung over the walls. No man cursed or spoke, even Hugo Barnard was subdued, and at every chance their heads turned to look down at the closed iron door.

Slow John went down the staircase, Manseer lighting the treads with a lantern, and stopped outside the door of Sir Francis's cell. The sergeant drew back the latch on the peep-hole and Slow John stepped up to it. There was a beam of light from the high window of the cell. Sir Francis sat on the stone shelf that served as his bunk, lifted his head and stared back into Slow John's yellow eyes.

Sir Francis's face was that of a sun-bleached skull, so pale as to seem luminous in the poor light, the long tresses of his hair dead black and his eyes dark cavities. 'I have been expecting you,' he said, and coughed until his mouth filled with phlegm. He spat it into the straw that covered the floor.

Slow John made no reply. His eyes, gleaming through the peep-hole, were fastened on Sir Francis's face. The minutes dragged by. Sir Francis was overwhelmed with a wild desire to scream at him, 'Do what you have to do. Say what you have to say. I am ready for you.' But he forced himself to remain silent and stared back at Slow John.

At last Slow John stepped away from the peep-hole and nodded at Manseer. He slammed the shutter closed and scurried back up the staircase to open the iron door for the executioner. Slow John crossed the courtyard with every eye upon him. When he went out through the gate men breathed again and there was once more the shouting of orders and the answering murmur of curse and complaint from the walls.

'Was that Slow John?' Althuda called softly from the cell alongside that of Sir Francis.

'He said nothing. He did nothing,' Sir Francis whispered hoarsely.

'It is the way he has,' Althuda said. 'I have been here long enough to see him play the same game many times. He will wear you down so that in the end you will want to tell him all he wants to know before he even touches you. That is why they named him Slow John.'

'Sweet Jesus, it half unmans me. Has he ever come to stare at you, Althuda?'

'Not yet.'

'How have you been so fortunate?'

'I know not. I know only that one day he will come for me also. Like you, I know how it feels to wait.'

Three days before the *Standvastigheid* was due to sail for Holland, Sukeena left the kitchens of the residence with her conical sunhat of woven grass on her dainty little head and her bag on her arm. Her departure caused no surprise among the other members of the household for it was her custom to go out several times a week along the slopes of the mountain to collect herbs and roots. Her skills and knowledge of the healing plants were famous throughout the colony.

From the veranda of the residence Kleinhans watched her go, and the knife blade of agony twisted in his guts. It felt as if an open wound were bleeding deep within him and often his stools were black with clotted blood. However, it was not only the dyspepsia that was devouring him. He knew that once the galleon sailed, with him aboard her, he would never again look upon Sukeena's beauty. Now that the time for this parting drew near he could not sleep at night, and even milk and bland boiled rice turned to acid in his stomach.

Mevrouw van de Velde, his hostess since she had taken over the residence, had been kind to him. She had even sent Sukeena out this morning to gather the special herbs that, when seeped and distilled with the slave girl's skills, were the only medicine that could alleviate his agony for even a short while – long enough at least to allow him to catch a few hours of fitful sleep. At Katinka's orders Sukeena would prepare enough of this brew to tide him over the long voyage northwards. He prayed that, once he reached Holland, the physicians there would be able to cure this dreadful affliction.

Sukeena moved quietly through the scrub that covered the slopes of the mountain. Once or twice she looked back but nobody had followed her. She went on, stopping only to cut a green twig from one of the flowering bushes. As she walked she stripped the leaves from it and, with her knife, trimmed the end into a fork.

All around her the wild blossom grew in splendid profusion; even now that winter was upon them, a hundred different species were on show. Some were as large as ripe artichoke heads, some as tiny as her little fingernail, all of them lovely beyond an artist's imagination or the powers of his palette to depict. She knew them all.

Meandering seemingly without direction, in reality she was moving gradually and circuitously towards a deep ravine that split the face of the table-topped mountain. With one more careful look around she darted suddenly down the steep, heavily bushed slope. There was a stream at the bottom, tumbling through a series of merry waterfalls and dreaming pools. As she approached one, she moved more slowly and softly. Tucked into a rocky crevice beside the dark waters was a small clay bowl. She had placed it there on her last visit. From the ledge above she looked down and saw that the milky white fluid, with which she had filled it, had been drunk. Only a few opalescent drops remained in the bottom.

Daintily she climbed cautiously into a position from which she could look deeper into the crack in the rock. Her breath caught as she saw in the shadows the soft gleam of ophidian scales. She opened the lid of the basket, took the forked stick in her right hand and moved closer. The serpent was coiled beside the bowl. It was not large, as slender as her forefinger. Its colour was a deep glowing bronze, each scale a tiny marvel. As she drew closer it raised its head an inch and watched her with black beady eyes. But it made no attempt to escape, sliding back into the depths of the crevice, as it had the first time she had discovered it.

It was lazy and somnolent, lulled by the milky concoction she had fed it. After a moment it lowered its head again and seemed to sleep. Sukeena was not tempted into any sudden or rash move. Well she knew that, from the bony needles in its upper jaw, the little reptile could dispense death in one of its most horrible and agonizing manifestations. She reached out gently with the twig and again the snake raised its head. She froze, the fork held only inches above its slim neck. Slowly the little reptile drooped back to earth and, as its head stretched out, Sukeena pinned it to the rock. It hissed softly and its body coiled and recoiled around the stick that held it.

Sukeena reached down and gripped it behind the head, with two fingers locked against the hard bones of the skull. It wrapped its long sinuous body around her wrist. She took hold of the tail and unwound it, then dropped the serpent into her basket. In the same movement she closed the lid upon it.

Retiring Governor Kleinhans went aboard the galleon on the evening before she sailed. Before the carriage took him down to the foreshore, all the household assembled on the front terrace of the residence to bid farewell to their former master. He moved slowly along the line with a word for each. When he reached Sukeena she made that graceful gesture, her fingertips together touching her lips, which made his heart ache with love and longing for her.

'Aboli has taken your luggage aboard the ship and placed all of it in your cabin,' she said softly. 'Your medicine chest is packed at the bottom of the largest trunk, but there is a full bottle in your small travelling case, which should last you several days.'

'I shall never forget you, Sukeena,' he said.

270

'And I shall never forget you, master,' she answered. For one mad moment he almost lost control of his emotions. He was on the point of embracing the slave girl, but then she looked up and he recoiled as he saw the undying hatred in her eyes.

When the galleon sailed in the morning with the dawn tide, Fredricus came to wake him and help him from his bunk. He wrapped the thick fur coat around his master's shoulders and Kleinhans went up on deck and stood at the stern rail as the ship caught the north-west wind and stood out into the Atlantic. He waited there until the great flat mountain sank away below the horizon and his vision was dimmed with tears.

Over the next four days the pain in his stomach was worse than he had ever known it. On the fifth night he woke after midnight, the acid scalding his intestines. He lit the lantern and reached for the brown bottle that would give him relief. When he shook it, it was already empty.

Doubled over with pain, he carried the lantern across the cabin and knelt before the largest of his trunks. He lifted the lid, and found the teak medicine chest where Sukeena had told him it was. He lifted it out and carried it to the table top against the further bulkhead, placing the lantern to light it so that he could fit the brass key into the lock.

He lifted the wooden lid and started. Laid carefully over the contents of the chest was a sheet of paper. He read the black print and, with amazement, realized that it was an ancient copy of the Company gazette. He read down the page and, as he recognized it, his stomach heaved with nausea. The proclamation was signed by himself. It was a death warrant. The warrant for the questioning and execution of one Robert David Renshaw. The Englishman who had been Sukeena's father.

'What devilry is this?' he blurted aloud. 'The little witch has placed it here to remind me of a deed committed long ago. Will she never relent? I thought she was out of my life for ever, but she makes me suffer still.'

He reached down to seize the paper and rip it to shreds but before his fingers touched it there was a soft, rustling sound beneath the sheet, and then a blur of movement.

Something struck him a light blow upon the wrist and a gleaming, sinuous body slid over the edge of the chest and dropped to the deck. He leapt back in alarm but the thing disappeared into the shadows and he stared after it in bewilderment. Slowly he became aware of a slight burning on his wrist and lifted it into the lamplight.

The veins on the inside of his wrist stood out like blue ropes under the pale skin blotched with old man's freckles. He looked closer at the seat of the burning sensation, and saw two tiny drops of blood gleaming in the lantern light like gemstones as they welled up from twin punctures.

271

He tottered backwards and sat on the edge of his bunk, gripping his wrist and staring at the ruby droplets.

Slowly, an image from long ago formed before his eyes. He saw two solemn little orphans standing hand in hand before the smoking ashes of a funeral pyre. Then the pain swelled within him until it filled his mind and his whole body.

There was only the pain now. It flowed through his veins like liquid fire and burrowed deep into his bones. It tore apart every ligament, sinew and nerve in his body. He began to scream and went on screaming until the end.

Sometimes twice a day Slow John came to the castle dungeon and stood at the peep-hole in the door of Sir Francis's cell. He never spoke. He stood there silently, with a reptilian stillness, sometimes for a few minutes and at others for an hour. In the end Sir Francis could not look at him. He turned his face to the stone wall, but still he could feel the yellow eyes boring into his back.

It was a Sunday, the Lord's day, when Manseer and four green-jacketed soldiers came for Sir Francis. They said nothing, but he could tell by their faces where they were taking him. They could not look into his eyes, and they wore the doleful expressions of a party of pall-bearers.

It was a cold, gusty day as Sir Francis stepped out into the courtyard. Although it was no longer raining, the clouds that hung low across the face of the mountain were an ominous blue grey, the colour of an old bruise. The cobbles beneath his feet were shining wetly with the rain squall that had just passed. He tried to stop himself shivering in the raw wind, lest his guards think it was for fear.

'God keep you safe!' A young clear voice carried to him above the wild wind, and he stopped and looked up. Hal stood high on the scaffold, his dark hair ruffled by the wind and his bare chest wet and shining with raindrops.

Sir Francis lifted his bound hands before him, and shouted back, '*In Arcadia habito!* Remember the oath!' Even from so far off, he could see his son's stricken face. Then his guards urged him on towards the low door that led down into the basement below the castle armoury. Manseer led him through the door and down the staircase. At the bottom he paused and knocked diffidently on the iron-bound door. Without waiting for a reply he pushed it open and led Sir Francis through.

The room beyond was well lit, a dozen wax candles flickering in their holders in the draught from the open door. To one side Jacobus Hop sat

272

at a writing table. There was parchment and an inkpot in front of him, and a quill in his right hand. He looked up at Sir Francis with a pale terrified expression. An angry red carbuncle glowed on his cheek. Quickly he dropped his eyes, unable to look at the prisoner.

Along the far wall stood the rack. Its frame was of massive teak, the bed long enough to accommodate the tallest man with his limbs stretched out to their full extent. There were sturdy wheels at each end, with iron ratchets and slots into which the levers could be fitted. On the side wall opposite the recording clerk's desk, a brazier smouldered. On hooks set into the wall above it hung an array of strange and terrible tools. The fire radiated a soothing, welcoming warmth.

Slow John stood beside the rack. His coat and his hat hung from a peg behind him. He wore a leather blacksmith's apron.

A pulley wheel was bolted into the ceiling and a rope dangled from it with an iron hook at its end. Slow John said nothing while his guards led Sir Francis to the centre of the stone floor and passed the hook through the bonds that secured his wrists. Manseer tightened the rope through the sheave until Sir Francis's arms were drawn at full stretch above his head. Although both his feet were firmly on the floor he was helpless. Manseer saluted Slow John, then he and his men backed out of the room and closed the door behind them. The panels were of solid teak, thick enough to prevent any sound passing through.

In the silence, Hop cleared his throat noisily and read from the transcript of the judgement passed upon Sir Francis by the Company court. His stutter was painful, but at the end he laid down the document and burst out clearly, 'As God is my witness, Captain Courteney, I wish I were a hundred leagues from this place. This is not a duty I enjoy. I beg of you to co-operate with this inquiry.'

Sir Francis did not reply but looked back steadily into Slow John's yellow eyes. Hop took up the parchment once more, and his voice quavered and broke as he read from it. 'Question the first: is the prisoner, Francis Courteney, aware of the whereabouts of the cargo missing from the manifest of the Company ship, the *Standvastigheid*?'

'No,' replied Sir Francis, still looking into the yellow eyes before him. 'The prisoner has no knowledge of the cargo of which you speak.'

'I beg you to reconsider, sir,' Hop whispered hoarsely. 'I have a delicate disposition. I suffer with my stomach.'

For the men on the windswept scaffolding the hours passed with agonizing slowness. Their eyes kept turning back towards the small, insignificant door below the armoury steps. There was no sound or movement from there, until suddenly, in the middle of the cold rainswept morning, the door burst open and Jacobus Hop scuttled out into the courtyard. He tottered to the officers' hitching rail and hung onto one of the iron rings as though his legs could no longer support him. He seemed oblivious to everything around him as he stood gasping for breath like a man freshly rescued from drowning.

All work on the walls came to a halt. Even Hugo Barnard and his overseers stood silent and subdued, gazing down at the miserable little clerk. With every eye upon him, Hop suddenly doubled over and vomited over the cobbles. He wiped his mouth with the back of his hand, and looked around him wildly as though seeking an avenue of escape.

He lurched away from the hitching rail and set off at a run, across the yard and up the staircase into the Governor's quarters. One of the sentries at the top of the stairs tried to restrain him but Hop shouted, 'I have to speak to his excellency,' and brushed past him.

He burst unannounced into the Governor's audience chamber. Van de Velde sat at the head of the long, polished table. Four burghers from the town were seated below him, and he was laughing at something that had just been said.

The laughter died on his fat lips as Hop stood trembling at the threshold, his face deathly pale, his eyes filled with tears. His boots were flecked with vomit.

'How dare you, Hop?' van de Velde thundered, as he dragged his bulk out of the chair. 'How dare you burst in here like this?'

'Your excellency,' Hop stammered, 'I cannot do it. I cannot go back into that room. Please don't insist that I do it. Send somebody else.'

'Get back there immediately,' van de Velde ordered. 'This is your last chance, Hop. I warn you, you will do your duty like a man or suffer for it.'

'You don't understand.' Hop was blubbering openly now. 'I can't do it. You have no idea what is happening in there. I can't—'

'Go! Go immediately, or you will receive the same treatment.'

Hop backed out slowly and van de Velde shouted after him, 'Shut those doors behind you, worm.'

Hop staggered back across the silent courtyard like a blind man, his eyes filled again with tears. At the little door he stood and visibly braced himself. Then he flung himself through it and disappeared from the view of the silent watchers.

In the middle of the afternoon the door opened again and Slow John came out into the courtyard. As always he was dressed in the dark suit and tall hat. His face was serene and his gait slow and stately as he passed out through the castle gates and took the avenue up through his gardens towards the residence.

Minutes after he had gone, Hop rushed out of the armoury and across to the main block. He came back leading the Company surgeon, who carried his leather bag, and disappeared down the armoury stairs. A long time afterwards the surgeon emerged and spoke briefly to Manseer and his men, who were hovering at the door.

The sergeant saluted and he and his men went down the stairs. When they came out again Sir Francis was with them. He could not walk unaided, and his hands and feet were swaddled in bandages. Red stains had already soaked through the cloth.

'Oh, sweet Jesus, they have killed him,' Hal whispered as they dragged his father, legs dangling and head hanging, across the yard.

Almost as if he had heard the words, Sir Francis lifted his head and looked up at him. Then he called in a clear, high voice, 'Hal, remember your oath!'

'I love you, Father!' Hal shouted back, choking on the words with sorrow, and Barnard slashed his whip across his back.

'Get back to work, you bastard.'

That evening as the file of convicts shuffled down the staircase past the door of his father's cell, Hal paused and called softly, 'I pray God and all his saints to protect you, Father.'

He heard his father move on the rustling mattress of straw, and then, after a long moment, his voice. 'Thank you, my son. God grant us both the strength to endure the days ahead.'

From behind the shutters of her bedroom Katinka watched the tall figure of Slow John coming up the avenue from the Parade. He passed out of her sight behind the stone wall at the bottom of the lawns and she knew he was going directly to his cottage. She had been waiting half the day for his return, and she was impatient. She placed the bonnet on her head, inspected her image in the mirror and was not satisfied. She looped a coil of her hair, arranged it carefully over her shoulder, then smiled at her reflection and left the room through the small door out to the back veranda. She followed the paved path under the naked black vines that covered the pergola, stripped of their last russet leaves by the onset of the winter gales.

Slow John's cottage stood alone at the edge of the forest. There was no person in the colony, no matter how lowly his station, who would live with him as a neighbour. When she reached it Katinka found the front door open and she went in without a knock or hesitation. The single room was bare as a hermit's cell. The floors were coated with cow dung, and the air smelled of stale smoke and the cold ashes on the open hearth. A simple bed, a single table and chair were the only furniture.

As she paused in the centre of the room she heard water splashing in the back yard and she followed the sound. Slow John stood beside the water trough. He was naked to the waist, and he was scooping water from the trough with a leather bucket and pouring it over his head.

He looked up at her, with the water trickling from his sodden hair down his chest and arms. His limbs were covered with the hard flat muscle of a professional wrestler or, she thought whimsically, of a Roman gladiator.

'You are not surprised to see me here,' Katinka stated. It was not a question for she could see the answer in his flat gaze.

'I was expecting you. I was expecting the Goddess Kali. Nobody else would dare come here,' he said, and Katinka blinked at this unusual form of address.

She sat down on the low stone wall beside the pump, and was silent for a while. Then she asked, 'Why do you call me that?' The death of Zelda had forged a strange, mystic bond between them.

'In Trincomalee, on the beautiful island of Ceylon beside the sacred Elephant Pool, stands the temple of Kali. I went there every day that I was in the colony. Kali is the Hindu Goddess of death and destruction. I worship her.' She knew then that he was mad. The knowledge intrigued her, and made the fine, colourless hairs on her forearms stand erect.

She sat for a long time in silence and watched him complete his toilet. He squeezed the water from his hair with both hands, and then wiped down those lean, hard limbs with a square of cloth. He pulled on his undershirt, then picked up the dark coat from where it hung over the wall, shrugged into it and buttoned it to his chin.

At last he looked at her. 'You have come to hear about my little sparrow.' With that fine melodious voice he should have been a preacher or an operatic tenor, she thought.

'Yes,' she said. 'That is why I have come.'

It was as though he had read her thoughts. He knew exactly what she wanted and he began to speak without hesitation. He told her what had taken place that day in the room below the armoury. He omitted no detail. He almost sang the words, making the terrible acts he was

276

describing sound as noble and inevitable as the lyrics from some Greek tragedy. He transported her, so that she hugged her own arms and began to rock slowly back and forth on the wall as she listened.

When he had finished speaking she sat for a long while with a rapturous expression on her lovely face. At last she shuddered softly and said, 'You may continue to call me Kali. But only when we are alone. No one else must ever hear you speak the name.'

'Thank you, Goddess.' His pale eyes glowed with an almost religious fervour as he watched her go to the gate in the wall.

There she paused and, without looking round at him, she asked, 'Why do you call him your little sparrow?'

Slow John shrugged. 'Because from this day onwards he belongs to me. They all belong to me and to the Goddess Kali, for ever.' Katinka gave a small ecstatic shiver at those words, then walked on down the path through the gardens towards the residence. Every step of the way she could feel his gaze upon her.

ukeena was waiting for her when she returned to the residence. 'You sent for me, mistress.'

'Come with me, Sukeena.'

She led the girl to her closet, and seated herself on the chaise-longue in front of the shuttered window. She gestured for Sukeena to stand before her. 'Governor Kleinhans often discussed your skills as a physician,' Katinka said. 'Who taught you?'

'My mother was an adept. At a very young age I would go out with her to gather the plants and herbs. After her death I studied with my uncle.'

'Do you know the plants here? Are they not different from those of the land where you were born?'

'There are some that are the same, and the others I have taught myself.'

Katinka already knew all this from Kleinhans, but she enjoyed the music of the slave girl's voice. 'Sukeena, yesterday my mare stumbled and almost threw me. My leg was caught on the saddle horn, and I have an ugly mark. My skin bruises easily. Do you have in your chest of medicines one that will heal it for me?'

'Yes, mistress.'

'Here!' Katinka leaned back on the sofa, and drew her skirts high above her knees. Slowly and sensually she rolled down one of the white stockings. 'Look!' she ordered, and Sukeena sank gracefully to the silk carpet in front of her. Her touch was as soft upon the skin as a butterfly alighting on a flower, and Katinka sighed. 'I can feel that you have healing hands.'

Sukeena did not reply and a wave of her dark hair hid her eyes.

'How old are you?' Katinka asked.

Sukeena's fingers stopped for an instant and then moved on to explore the bruise that spread around the back of her mistress's knee. 'I was born in the year of the Tiger,' she said, 'so on my next birthday I will be eighteen years of age.'

'You are very beautiful, Sukeena. But, then, you know that, don't you?'

'I do not feel beautiful, mistress. I do not think a slave can ever feel beautiful.'

'What a droll notion.' Katinka did not hide her annoyance at this turn in the conversation. 'Tell me, is your brother as beautiful as you are?'

Again Sukeena's fingers trembled on her skin. Ah! That shaft went home. Katinka smiled softly in the silence, and then asked, 'Did you hear my question, Sukeena?'

'To me Althuda is the most beautiful man who has ever lived upon this earth,' Sukeena replied softly, and then regretted having said it. She knew instinctively that it was dangerous to allow this woman to discover those areas where she was most vulnerable, but she could not recall the words.

'How old is Althuda?'

'He is three years older than I am.' Sukeena kept her eyes downcast. 'I need to fetch my medicines, mistress.'

'I shall wait for you to return,' Katinka replied. 'Be quick.'

Katinka lay back against the cushions and smiled or frowned at the vivid procession of images and words that ran through her mind. She felt expectant and elated, and at the same time restless and dissatisfied. Slow John's words sounded in her head like cathedral bells. They disturbed her. She could not remain still a moment longer. She sprang to her feet and prowled around the closet like a hunting leopard. 'Where is that girl?' she demanded, and then she glimpsed her own reflection in the long mirror and turned back to consider it.

'Kali!' she whispered, and smiled. 'What a marvellous name. What a secret and splendid name.'

She saw Sukeena's image appear in the mirror behind her but she did not turn immediately. The girl's dark beauty was a perfect foil for her own. She considered their two faces together, and felt the excitement charge her nerves and sing through her veins.

278

'I have the salve for your injury, mistress.' Sukeena stood close behind her, but her eyes were fathomless.

'Thank you, my little sparrow,' Katinka whispered. I want you to belong to me for ever, she thought. I want you to belong to Kali.

She turned back to the sofa and Sukeena knelt before her again. At first the salve was cool on the skin of her leg, and then a warm glow spread from it. Sukeena's fingers were cunning and skilful.

'I hate to see something beautiful destroyed needlessly,' Katinka whispered. 'You say your brother is beautiful. Do you love him very much, Sukeena?'

When there was no reply Katinka reached down and cupped her hand under Sukeena's chin. She lifted her face so that she could look into her eyes. The agony she saw there made her pulse race.

'My poor little sparrow,' she said. I have touched the deepest place in her soul, she exulted. As she removed her hand she let her fingers trail across the girl's cheek.

'This hour I have come from Slow John,' she said, 'but you saw me on the path. You were watching me, were you not?'

'Yes, mistress.'

'Shall I repeat to you what Slow John told me? Shall I tell you about his special room at the castle, and what happens there?' Katinka did not wait for the girl to reply but went on speaking quietly. When Sukeena's fingers stilled she broke off her narrative to order, 'Do not stop what you are doing, Sukeena. You have a magical touch.'

When at last she finished speaking, Sukeena was weeping without a sound. Her tears were slow and viscous as drops of oil squeezed from the olive press. They glistened against the red gold of her cheeks. After a while Katinka asked, 'How long has your brother been in the castle? I have heard that it is four months since he came back from the mountains to fetch you. Such a long time, and he has not been tried, no sentence passed upon him.'

Katinka waited, letting the moments fall, a slow drop at a time, slow as the girl's tears. 'Governor Kleinhans was remiss, or was he persuaded by somebody, I wonder. But my husband is an energetic and dedicated man. He will not let justice be denied. No renegade can escape him long.'

Now Sukeena was no longer making any pretence; she stared at Katinka with stricken eyes as she went on, 'He will send Althuda to the secret room with Slow John. Althuda will be beautiful no longer. What a dreadful pity. What can we do to prevent that happening?'

'Mistress,' Sukeena whispered, 'your husband, he has the power. It is in his hands.'

'My husband is a servant of the Company, a loyal and unbending servant. He will not flinch from his duty.'

'Mistress, you are so beautiful. No man can deny you. You can persuade him.' Sukeena slowly lowered her head and placed it on Katinka's bare knee. 'With all my heart, with all my soul, I beg you, mistress.'

'What would you do to save your brother's life?' Katinka asked. 'What price would you pay, my little sparrow?'

'There is no price too high, no sacrifice from which I would turn aside. Everything and anything you ask of me, mistress.'

'We could never hope to set him free, Sukeena. You understand that, don't you?' Katinka asked gently. Nor would I ever wish that, she thought, for while the brother is in the castle the little sparrow is safely in my cage.

'I will not even let myself hope for that.'

Sukeena lifted her head and again Katinka cupped her chin, this time with both her hands, and she leaned forward slowly. 'Althuda shall not die. We will save him from Slow John, you and I,' she promised, and kissed Sukeena full on the mouth. The girl's lips were wet with her tears. They tasted hot and salty, almost like blood. Slowly Sukeena opened her lips, like the petals of an orchid opening to the sunbird's beak as it quests for nectar.

Althuda. Sukeena steeled herself with the thought of her brother, as without breaking the kiss Katinka took her hand and moved it slowly up under her skirts until it lay on her smooth white belly. Althuda, this is for you, and for you alone, Sukeena told herself silently, as she closed her eyes and her fingers crept timorously over the satiny belly, down into the nest of fine dense golden curls at the base.

The next day dawned in a cloudless sky. Although the air was chill the sun was brilliant and the wind had dropped. From the scaffold Hal watched the closed door to the dungeons. Daniel stayed close by his side; in taking Hal's share of the work on his broad shoulders he was shielding him from Barnard's lash.

When Slow John came through the gates and crossed the courtyard to the armoury, with his measured undertaker's tread, Hal stared down at him with stricken eyes. Suddenly, as he passed below the scaffold, Hal snatched up the heavy mason's hammer that lay on the planking at his feet and lifted it to hurl it down and crush the executioner's skull. But

Daniel's great fist closed around his wrist. He eased the hammer from Hal's grip, as though he were taking a toy from a child, and placed it on top of the wall beyond his reach.

'Why did you do that?' Hal protested. 'I could have killed the swine.'

'To no purpose,' Daniel told him, with compassion. 'You cannot save Sir Francis by killing an underling. You would sacrifice your own life and achieve nothing by it. They would simply send another to your father.'

Manseer brought Sir Francis up from the dungeons. He could not walk unaided on his broken bandaged feet, but his head was high as they dragged him across the courtyard.

'Father!' Hal screamed, in torment. 'I cannot let this happen.'

Sir Francis looked up at him, and called in a voice just loud enough to reach him on the high wall, 'Be strong, my son. For my sake, be strong.' Manseer forced him down the steps below the armoury.

The day was long, longer than any that Hal had ever lived through, and the north side of the courtyard was in deep shadow when at last Slow John re-emerged from below the armoury.

'This time I will kill the poisonous swine,' Hal blurted, but again Daniel held him in a grip that he could not shake off as the executioner walked slowly beneath the scaffold and out through the castle gates.

Hop came scampering into the courtyard, his face ghastly. He summoned the Company surgeon and the two men disappeared once more down the stairs. This time the soldiers brought out Sir Francis on a litter.

'Father!' Hal shouted down to him, but there was neither reply nor sign of life in response.

'I have warned you often enough,' Hugo Barnard bellowed at him. He strode out onto the boards and laid half a dozen whip strokes across his back. Hal made no attempt to avoid the blows, and Barnard stepped back astonished that he showed no pain. 'Any more of your imbecile chattering, and I will put the dogs onto you,' he promised, as he turned away. Meanwhile, in the courtyard, the Company surgeon watched gravely as the soldiers carried Sir Francis's unconscious form down to his cell. Then, accompanied by Hop, he set off for the Governor's suite on the south side of the courtyard.

Van de Velde looked up in irritation from the papers that littered his desk. 'Yes? What is it, Dr Saar? I am a busy man. I hope you have not come here to waste my time.'

'It is the prisoner, your excellency.' The surgeon looked flustered and apologetic at the same time. Van de Velde did not allow him to continue but turned on Hop, who stood nervously behind the doctor, twisting his hat in his fingers.

'Well, Hop, has the pirate succumbed yet? Has he told us what we want to know?' he shouted, and Hop retreated a pace.

'He is so stubborn. I would never have believed it possible, that any human being—' He broke off in a long, tormented stammer.

'I hold you responsible, Hop.' Van de Velde came menacingly from behind his desk. He was warming to this sport of baiting the miserable little clerk, but the surgeon intervened.

'Your excellency, I fear for the prisoner's life. Another day of questioning – he may not survive it.'

Van de Velde rounded on him now. 'That, doctor, is the main object of this whole business. Courteney is a man condemned to death. He will die, and you have my solemn word on that.' He went back to his desk and lowered himself into the soft chair. 'Don't come here to give me news of his imminent decease. All I want to know from you is whether or not he is still capable of feeling pain, and if he is capable of speaking or at least giving some sign of understanding the question. Well, is he, doctor?' Van de Velde glared.

'Your excellency,' the doctor removed his eye-glasses and polished the lenses vigorously as he composed a reply. He knew what van de Velde wanted to hear, and he knew also that it was not politic to deny him. 'At the moment the prisoner is not *compos mentis*.'

Van de Velde scowled and cut in, 'What of the executioner's vaunted skills? I thought he never lost a prisoner, not unintentionally anyway.'

'Sir, I am not disparaging the skills of the state executioner. I am sure that by tomorrow the prisoner will have recovered consciousness.'

'You mean that tomorrow he will be healthy enough to continue questioning?'

'Yes, your excellency. That is my opinion.'

'Well, Mijnheer, I will hold you to that. If the pirate dies before he can be formally executed in accordance with the judgement of the court, you will answer to me. The populace must see justice performed. It is no good the man passing peacefully away in a closed room below the walls. We want him out there on the Parade for all to see. I want an example made of him, do you understand?'

'Yes, your excellency.' The doctor backed towards the door.

'You too, Hop. Do you understand, dolt? I want to know where he has hidden the galleon's cargo, and then I want a good rousing execution. For your own good, you had better deliver both those things.'

'Yes, your excellency.'

'I want to speak to Slow John. Send him to me before he starts work tomorrow morning. I want to make certain that he fully understands his responsibilities.'

'I will bring the executioner to you myself,' Hop promised.

Once more it was dark when Hugo Barnard stopped work on the walls and ordered the lines of exhausted prisoners down into the courtyard. As Hal passed his father's cell on the way down the staircase, he called desperately to him, 'Father, can you hear me?'

When there was no reply, he hammered on the door with both his fists. 'Father, speak to me. In the name of God, speak to me!' For once Manseer was indulgent. He made no attempt to force Hal to move on down the staircase and Hal pleaded again, 'Please, Father. It's Hal, your son. Do you not know me?'

'Hal,' croaked a voice he did not recognize. 'Is that you, my boy?'

'Oh, God!' Hal sank to his knees and pressed his forehead to the panel. 'Yes, Father. It is me.'

'Be strong, my son. It will not be for much longer, but I charge you, if you love me, then keep the oath.'

'I cannot let you suffer. I cannot let this go on.'

'Hal!' His father's voice was suddenly powerful again. 'There is no more suffering. I have passed that point. They cannot hurt me now, except through you.'

'What can I do to ease you? Tell me, what can I do?' Hal pleaded.

'There is only one thing you can do now. Let me take with me the knowledge of your strength and your fortitude. If you fail me now, it will all have been in vain.'

Hal bit into the knuckles of his own clenched fist, drawing blood in the vain attempt to stifle his sobs. His father's voice came again. 'Daniel, are you there?'

'Yes, Captain.'

'Help him. Help my son to be a man.'

'I give you my promise, Captain.'

Hal raised his head, and his voice was stronger. 'I do not need anybody to help me. I will keep my faith with you, Father. I will not betray your trust.'

'Farewell, Hal.' Sir Francis's voice began to fade, as though he were falling into an infinite pit. 'You are my blood and my promise of eternal life. Goodbye, my life.'

The following morning when they carried Sir Francis up from the dungeon Hop and Dr Saar walked on either side of the litter. They were both worried men, for there was no sign of life in the broken figure that lay between them. Even when Hal defied Barnard's whip, and called down to him from the walls, Sir Francis did not raise his head. They took him down the stairs to where Slow John already waited, but within a few minutes all three came out into the sunlight, Saar, Hop and Slow John, and stood talking quietly for a short while. Then they walked together across to the Governor's suite and mounted the stairs.

Van de Velde was standing by the stained-glass window, peering out at the shipping that lay anchored off the foreshore. Late the previous evening, another Company galleon had come into Table Bay and he was expecting the ship's captain to call upon him to pay his respects and to present an order for provisions and stores. Van de Velde turned impatiently from the window to face the three men as they filed into his chamber.

'Ja, Hop?' He looked at his favourite victim. 'You have remembered my orders, for once, hey? You have brought the state executioner to speak to me.' He turned to Slow John. 'So, has the pirate told you where he has hidden the treasure? Come on, fellow, speak up.'

Slow John's expression did not change as he said softly, 'I have worked carefully not to damage the respondent beyond usefulness. But I am nearing the end. Soon he will no longer hear my voice, nor be sensible to any further persuasion.'

'You have failed?' van de Velde's voice trembled with anger.

'No, not yet,' said Slow John. 'He is strong. I would never have believed how strong. But there is still the rack. I do not believe that he will be able to withstand the rack. No man can weather the rack.'

'You have not used it yet?' van de Velde demanded. 'Why not?'

'To me it is the last resort. Once they have been racked, there is nothing left. It is the end.'

'Will it work with this one?' van de Velde wanted to know. 'What happens if he still resists?'

'Then there is only the scaffold and the gibbet,' said Slow John.

Slowly van de Velde turned to Dr Saar. 'What is your opinion, doctor?'

'Your excellency, if you require an execution then it should be carried out very soon after the man is racked.'

'How soon?' van de Velde demanded.

'Today. Before nightfall. After racking, he will not last the night.'

Van de Velde turned back to Slow John. 'You have disappointed me.

I am displeased.' Slow John did not seem to hear the rebuke. His eyes did not even flicker as he stared back at van de Velde. 'However, we must do what we can to make the best of this whole sorry business. I will order the execution for three o'clock this afternoon. In the meantime you are to go back and place the pirate on the rack.'

'I understand, your excellency,' said Slow John.

'You have failed me once. Do not do so again. He must be alive when he goes to the scaffold.' Van de Velde turned to the clerk. 'Hop, send messengers through the town. I am declaring the rest of today to be a holiday throughout the colony, except for the work on the castle walls, of course. Francis Courteney will be executed at three o'clock this afternoon. Every burgher in the colony must be there. I want all to see how we deal with a pirate. Oh, and by the way, make certain that Mevrouw van de Velde is informed. She will be very angry if she misses the sport.'

At two o'clock they brought Sir Francis Courteney on a litter from the cell below the armoury. They had not bothered to cover his naked body. Even from high up on the south wall of the castle, and with his vision blurred by his tears, Hal could see that his father's body had been grotesquely deformed by the rack. Every one of the great joints in his limbs and at his shoulders and pelvis were dislocated, swollen and bruised purple black.

An execution detail of green-jackets was drawn up in the courtyard. Led by an officer with a drawn sword, they fell in around the litter. Twenty men marched in front, and twenty followed behind, their muskets at the slope. The tap-tap tap-tap of the death drum set the pace. The procession snaked through the castle gates, out onto the Parade.

Daniel placed his arm around Hal's shoulder, as the boy watched, white-faced and shivering, in the icy wind. Hal made no move to pull away from him. Those seamen who had coverings for their heads removed them, unwinding the filthy rags and standing grim and silent as the bier passed beneath them.

'God bless you, Captain,' Ned Tyler called out. 'You were as good a man as ever hoisted sail!' There was a hoarse and ragged cheer from the others, and one of Hugo Barnard's huge black hounds bayed mournfully, a strangely harrowing sound.

Out on the parade the crowd waited around the gibbet in tense and expectant silence. Every living soul in the colony seemed to have answered the summons. Above their heads Slow John waited high on

285

the platform. He wore his leather apron, and his head was covered with the mask of his office, the mask of death. His eyes and his mouth were all that showed through the slits in the black cloth.

Led by the drummer the procession marched with slow and measured tread towards him, and Slow John waited with his arms folded over his chest. Even he turned his head as the Governor's carriage came down the avenue through the gardens, and crossed the parade. Slow John bowed to the Governor and his wife as Aboli guided the six grey horses to the foot of the scaffold and bought the vehicle to a halt.

Slow John's yellow eyes met those of Katinka through the slits in his black headcloth. He bowed again, this time to her directly. She knew, without words being spoken, that he was dedicating the sacrifice to her, to his Goddess Kali.

'He has no reason to act so grand. The oaf has made a botch of the job so far,' van de Velde said grumpily. 'He has killed the man without getting a word out of him. I don't know what your father and the other members of the Seventeen are going to say when they hear that the cargo is lost. They are going to blame me, of course. They always do.'

'As always you will have me to protect you, my darling husband,' she said, and stood up in the carriage to have a better view. The escort stopped at the foot of the gallows and the litter with the still figure upon it was lifted high and placed at Slow John's feet. A low growl went up from the watchers as the executioner knelt beside it to begin his grisly task.

A little later when the crowd gave forth a lusty roar, made up of excitement and horror and obscene glee, the grey horses shied and fidgeted nervously in the traces at the sound and smell of fresh human blood. With an impassive face and gentle hands on the reins Aboli checked them and brought them back under control. Slowly he turned away his head from the dreadful spectacle taking place before his eyes and looked towards the unfinished walls of the castle.

He recognized the figure of Hal among the other convicts. He stood almost as tall as Big Daniel now, and he had the shape and set of a fully mature man. But he has a boy's heart still. He should not look upon this thing. No man or boy should ever have to watch his father die. Aboli's own great heart felt that it might burst in the barrel of his chest, but his face was still impassive beneath the cicatrice of tattoos. He looked back at the scaffold as Sir Francis Courteney's body rose slowly in the air and the crowd bellowed again. Slow John's pressure on the rope was gentle and sure as he lifted Sir Francis from the litter by his neck. It required a delicate touch not to snap the vertebrae, and end it all too soon. It was a matter of pride to him that the last spark of life

286

must not be snuffed out of that broken husk until after the drawing out of the viscera.

Firmly Aboli turned away his eyes and looked again to the bereft and tragic figure of Hal Courteney on the castle walls. We should not mourn for him, Gundwane. He was a man and he lived the life of a man. He sailed every ocean, and fought as a warrior must fight. He knew the stars and the ways of men. He called no man master, and turned aside from no enemy. No, Gundwane, we should not mourn him, you and I. He will never die while he lives on in our hearts.

For four days Sir Francis Courteney's dismembered body remained on public display. Every morning as the light strengthened, Hal looked down from the walls and saw it still hanging there. The gulls came from the beach in a shrieking cloud of black and white wings and squabbled raucously over the feast. When they had gorged, they perched on the railing of the gibbet and whitewashed the planks with their liquid dung.

For once Hal hated the clarity of his own eyesight, that spared him no detail of the terrible transformation that was taking place as he watched. By the third day the birds had picked the flesh from his father's skull so that it grinned at the sky with empty eye-sockets. The burghers crossing the open parade on their way to the castle walked well down-wind of the scaffold on which he hung, and the ladies held sachets of dried herbs to their faces as they passed.

However, on the dawning of the fifth day when Hal looked down upon it, the gibbet was empty. His father's pathetic remains no longer hung there, and the seagulls had gone back to the beach.

'Thank the merciful Lord,' Ned Tyler whispered to Daniel. 'Now young Hal can begin to heal.'

'Yet it is passing strange that they have taken the corpse away so soon.' Daniel was puzzled. 'I would not have thought that van de Velde could be so compassionate.'

Sukeena had shown him how to slip the grating on one of the small back windows of the slave quarters and squeeze his great body through. The night guard at the residence had become lax over the years, and Aboli had little difficulty in evading the watch. For three consecutive nights he escaped from the slave

287

quarters. Sukeena had warned him that he must return at least two hours before dawn for at that hour the watch would rouse themselves and put on a show of vigilance to impress the awakening household.

Once he had escaped over the walls it took Aboli less than an hour to run through the darkness to the boundary of the colony, marked by a hedge of bitter almond bushes planted at the order of the Governor. Although the hedge was still scraggy and there were more gaps than barriers in its length, it was the line over which no burgher might pass without the Governor's permission. On the other hand, none of the scattered Hottentot tribes that inhabited the limitless wilderness of plain, mountain and forest beyond were allowed to cross the hedge and enter the colony. On the orders of the Company, they were to be shot or hanged if they transgressed the boundary. The VOC was no longer prepared to tolerate the savages' treachery, their sly thieving ways or their drunkenness when they were able to get their hands on spirits. The wanton whoring of their women, who would lift their short leather skirts for a handful of beads or a trifling trinket, was a threat to the morals of the God-fearing burghers of the colony. Selected tribesmen, who might be useful as soldiers and servants, were allowed to remain in the colony but the rest had been driven out into the wilderness where they belonged.

Each night Aboli crossed this makeshift boundary and ranged like a silent black ghost across the flat plain whose wide expanses cut off Table Mountain and its bastion of lesser hills from the main ranges of the African hinterland. The wild animals had not been driven off these plains, for few white hunters had been allowed to leave the confines of the colony to pursue them. Here, Aboli heard again the wild, heart-stopping chorus of a pride of hunting lions that he remembered from his childhood. The leopards sawed and coughed in the thickets, and often he startled unseen herds of antelope, whose hoofs drummed through the night.

Aboli needed a black bull. Twice he had been so close as to smell the buffalo herd in the thickets. The scent reminded him of his father's herds of cattle, which he had tended in his childhood, before his circumcision. He had heard the grunting of the great beasts and the lowing of the weaning calves, he had followed their deeply ploughed hoofmarks and seen splashes of their wet dung still steaming in the moonlight. But each time as he closed with the herd, the wind had tricked him. They had sensed him and gone crashing away through the brush, galloping on until the sound of their flight dwindled into silence. Aboli could not pursue them further, for it was past midnight and he was still hours away from the bitter almond hedge and from his cell in the slave quarters.

On the third night he took the chance of creeping out of the window of the slave quarters an hour earlier than Sukeena had warned him was wise. One of the hounds rushed at him, but before it could alarm the watch, Aboli calmed it with a soft whistle. The hound recognized him and snuffled his hand. He stroked its head and whispered softly to it in the language of the forests and left it whining softly and wagging its tail as he slipped over the wall like a dark moon shadow.

During his previous hunts, he had discovered that each night the buffalo herd left the fastness of the dense forest to drink at a waterhole a mile or so beyond the boundary hedge. He knew that if he crossed it before midnight he might be able to catch them while they were still at the water. It was his best chance of being able to pick out a bull and make his stalk.

From the hollow tree at the edge of the forest he retrieved the bow that he had cut and carved from a branch of wild olive. Sukeena had stolen the single iron arrowhead from the collection of weapons that Governor Kleinhans had assembled during his service in the Indies, which now hung on the walls of the residence. It was unlikely that it would be missed from among the dozens of swords, shields and knives that made up the display.

'I will return it to you,' he promised Sukeena. 'I would not have you suffer if it should be missed.'

'Your need of it is great than my risk,' she told him as she slipped the arrowhead, wrapped in a scrap of cloth, beneath the seat of the carriage. 'I also had a father who was denied a decent burial.'

Aboli had fitted the arrowhead to a reed shaft and bound it in place with twine and pitch. He had fletched it with the moulted feathers from the hunting falcons housed in the mews behind the stables. However, he did not have time to search for the insect grubs from which to brew poison for the barbs, and so he must rely on this single shaft flying true to the mark.

Now as Aboli hunted in the shadows, himself another silent gliding shadow, he found old forgotten skills returning to him, and recalled the instruction that he had undergone as a young boy from the elders of his tribe. He felt the night wind softly caress his bare chest and flanks and was aware of its direction at all times as he circled the waterhole until it blew straight into his face. It brought down to him the rich bovine stench of the prey he sought.

The wind was strong enough to shake the tall reeds and cover any sound he might make so he could move in swiftly over the last hundred paces. Above the soughing of the north wind and the rustle of the reeds he heard a coughing grunt. He froze and nocked his single arrow. Had the lions come to the water ahead of the herd, he wondered, for that had been a leonine sound. He stared ahead, and heard the sound of great hoofs plodding and sucking in the mud of the waterhole. Above the rippling heads of the reeds a dark shape moved, mountainous in the moonlight.

'A bull,' he breathed. 'A bull of a bull!'

The bull had finished drinking. The crafty old beast had come ahead of the cows and calves of the breeding herd. His back was coated with glistening wet mud from the wallow, and he plodded towards where Aboli crouched, his hoofs squelching in the mud.

Aboli lost sight of the prey as he sank down among the swaying stems and let him come on. But he could mark him by the sound of his heavy breathing, and by the rasping of the reeds dragging down his flanks. The bull was very close, but still out of Aboli's sight, when suddenly he shook his head as the reed stems tangled in his horns, and his ears flapped against his cheeks. If I reach out now I could touch his snout, Aboli thought. Every nerve in his body was drawn as tight as the bowstring in his fingers.

The reed bank parted in front of Aboli, and the massive head came through, the moonlight gleaming on the curved bosses of the horns. Abruptly the bull became aware of something amiss, of danger lurking close at hand, and he stopped and raised his huge black head. As he lifted his muzzle to test the air, his nose was wet and shining and water drooled from his mouth. He flared his nostrils into dark pits and snuffled the air. Aboli could feel his breath hot upon his naked chest and his face.

The bull turned his head, questing for the scent of man or cat, for the hidden hunter. Aboli stayed still as a tree-stump. He was holding the heavy bow at full draw. The power of the olive branch and the gut bowstring were so fierce that even the granite muscles in his arms and shoulder bulged and trembled with the effort. As the bull turned his head he revealed the notch behind his ear where the neck fused with the bone of his skull and the massive boss of his horns. Aboli held his aim for one heartbeat longer, then loosed the arrow. It flashed and whirred in the moonlight, leaping from his hand and burying half its length in the massive black neck.

The bull reeled back. If the arrowhead had found the gap between the vertebrae of the spine, as Aboli had hoped, he would have dropped where he stood but the iron point struck the spine and was deflected by bone. It glanced aside but sliced through the great artery behind the jawbone. As the bull bucked and kicked to the stinging impact of the steel, the severed artery erupted and a spout of blood flew high in the air, black as an ostrich feather in the light of the moon.

The bull dashed past Aboli, hooking wildly with those wide curved horns. If Aboli had not dropped his bow and hurled himself aside, the burnished point that hissed by, a finger's width from his navel, would have skewered him and ripped open his bowels.

The bull charged on and reached the hard dry ground. On his knees Aboli strained his ears to follow his quarry's crashing rush through the scrub. Abruptly it came up short. There was a long, fraught pause, in which he could hear the animal's laboured breathing and the patter of streaming blood falling on the leaves of the low bushes around it. Then he heard the bull stagger and stumble backwards, trying to remain on his feet while the strength flowed out of his huge body on that tide of dark blood. The beast fell heavily so that the earth trembled under Aboli's bare feet. A moment later came the rasping death bellow, and thereafter an aching quietness. Even the night birds and the bullfrogs of the swamp had been silenced by that dreadful sound. It was as though all the forest held its breath at the passing of such a mighty creature. Then, slowly, the night came alive once again, the frogs piped and croaked from the reedbeds, a nightjar screeched and from afar an eagle owl hooted mournfully.

Aboli skinned the bull with the knife that Sukeena had stolen for him from the residence kitchens. He folded the green skin and tied it with bark rope. It was heavy enough to tax even his strength. He staggered with the bundle until he could get under it and balance it on his head. He left the naked carcass for the packs of night-prowling hyena and the flocks of vultures, carnivorous storks, kites and crows that would find it with the first light of morning, and set off back towards the colony and the table-topped mountain, silhouetted against the stars. Even under his burden he moved at the ground-eating trot of the warriors of his tribe that was becoming so natural to him again after his confinement for two decades in a small ship upon the seas. He was remembering so much long-forgotten tribal lore and wisdom, relearning old skills, becoming once more a true son of this baked African earth.

He climbed to the lower slopes of the mountain and left the bundled skin in a narrow crevice in the rock cliff. He covered it with large boulders, for the hyenas roamed here also, attracted by the rubbish and wastes and sewage generated by the human settlement of the colony.

When he had placed the last boulder he looked up at the sky and saw that the curling scorpion was falling fast towards the dark horizon. Only then he realized how swiftly the night had sped, and went bounding back down the slope. He reached the edge of the Company gardens just as the first rooster crowed in the darkness.

Later that morning, as he waited on the bench with the other slaves outside the kitchens for his breakfast bowl of gruel and thick, curdled sour milk, Sukeena passed on her way to tend the affairs of the household. 'I heard you return last night. You were out too late,' she whispered, without turning her head on the orchid stem of her neck. 'If you are discovered, you will bring great hardship on all of us, and our plans will come to naught.'

'My task is almost finished,' he rumbled softly. 'Tonight will be the last time I need to go out.'

'Have a care, Aboli. There is much at risk,' she said and glided away. Despite her warning she had given him any help he had asked for, and without watching her go Aboli whispered to himself, 'That little one has the heart of a lioness.'

That night, when the house had settled down for the night, he slipped through the grating. Again the dogs were stilled by his quiet whistle, and he had lumps of dried sausage for each of them. When he reached the wall below the lawns, he looked to the stars and saw in the eastern sky the first soft luminescence of the moonrise. He vaulted over it and, keeping well clear of the road, guided himself by touch along the outside of the wall, towards the settlement.

No more than three or four dim lights were showing from the cottages and buildings of the village. The four ships at anchor in the bay were all burning lanterns at their mastheads. The castle was a dark brooding shape against the starlight.

He waited at the edge of the Parade and tuned his ears to the sounds of the night. Once, as he was about to set out across the open ground, he heard drunken laughter and snatches of singing as a party of soldiers from the castle returned from an evening of debauchery among the rude hovels on the waterfront, which passed as taverns in this remote station, selling the rough raw spirit the Hottentots called *dop*. One of the revellers carried a tar-dipped torch. The flames wove uncertainly as the man stopped before the gibbet in the middle of the Parade, and shouted an insult at the corpse that still hung upon it. His companions bellowed with drunken laughter at his humour, and then reeled on, supporting each other, towards the castle.

When they had disappeared through the gates, and when silence and darkness fell, Aboli moved out swiftly across the Parade. Though he could not see more than a few paces ahead, the smell of corruption guided him; only a dead lion smells as strongly as a rotting human corpse.

292

Sir Francis Courteney's body had been beheaded and neatly quartered. Slow John had used a butcher's cleaver to hack through the larger bones. Aboli brought down the head from the spike on which it had been impaled. He wrapped it in a clean white cloth and placed it in the saddle-bag he carried. Then he retrieved the other parts of the corpse. The dogs from the village had carried off some of the smaller bones, but even working in darkness Aboli was able to recover what remained. He closed and buckled the leather flap of the bag, slung it over his shoulder and set off again at a run towards the mountain.

Sukeena knew the mountain intimately, every ravine, cliff and crag. She had explained to him how to find the narrow concealed entrance to the cavern where, the previous night, he had left the raw buffalo skin. In the light of the rising moon, he returned unerringly to it. When he reached the entrance he stooped and swiftly removed the boulders that covered the buffalo skin. Then he crawled further into the crevice and drew aside the bushes that hung down from the cliff above to conceal the dark throat of the cavern.

He worked deftly, with flint and steel, to light one of the candles Sukeena had provided. Shielding the flame with cupped hands from any watcher below the mountain he went forward and crawled into the low natural tunnel on hands and knees, dragging the saddle-bag behind him. As Sukeena had told him, the tunnel opened suddenly into a cavern high enough for him to stand. He held the candle above his head and saw that the cavern would make a fitting burial place for a great chief. There was even a natural rock shelf at the far end. He left the saddle bag upon it and crawled back to retrieve the buffalo skin. Before he entered the tunnel again he looked back over his shoulder and reoriented himself in the direction of the moonrise.

'I shall turn his face to greet ten thousand moons and all the sunrises of eternity!' he said softly, and dragged the heavy skin into the cavern and spread it on the rock floor.

He placed the candle on the rock shelf and began to unpack the bag. First he set aside those small offerings and ceremonial items he had brought with him. Then he lifted out Sir Francis's covered head and laid it in the centre of the buffalo hide. He unwrapped it reverently, and showed no repugnance for the thick cloying odour of decay that slowly filled the cavern. He assembled all the other dismembered parts of the body and arranged them in their natural order, binding them in place with slim strands of bark rope, until Sir Francis lay on his side, his knees drawn up beneath his chin and his arms hugging his legs, the foetal position of the womb and of sleep. Then he folded the wet buffalo hide tightly around him so that only his ravaged face was still exposed. He stitched the folds of the hide around him so they would dry into an iron-hard sarcophagus. It was a long and meticulous task, and when the candle burnt down and guttered in a pool of its own liquid wax he lit another from the stump and worked on.

When he had finished, he took up the turtleshell comb, another of Sukeena's gifts, and combed out the tangled tresses that still adhered to Sir Francis's skull, and braided them neatly. At last he lifted the seated body and placed it on the stone shelf. He turned it carefully to face the east; to gaze for ever towards the moonrise and the dawn.

For a long while he squatted below the ledge and looked upon the ravaged head, seeing it in his mind's eye as it once was. The face of the vigorous young mariner who had rescued him from the slavers' hold two decades before.

At last he rose and began to gather up the grave-goods he had brought with him. He laid them one at a time on the ledge before the body of Sir Francis. The tiny model of a ship he had carved with his own hands. There had not been time to lavish care upon its construction, and it was crude and childlike. However, the three masts had sails set upon them, and the name carved into the stern was *Lady Edwina*.

'May this ship carry you over the dark oceans to the landfall where the woman whose name she bears awaits you,' Aboli whispered.

Next he placed the knife and the bow of olive wood beside the ship. 'I have no sword with which to arm you, but may these weapons be your defence in the dark places.'

Then he offered the food bowl and the water bottle. 'May you never again hunger or thirst.'

Lastly, the cross of wood that Aboli had fashioned and decorated with green abalone shell, white-carved bone and small bright stones from the river-bed. 'May the cross of your God which guided you in life, guide you still in death,' he said as he placed the cross before Sir Francis's empty eyes.

Kneeling on the cavern floor he built a small fire and lit it from the candle. 'May this fire warm you in the darkness of your long night.' Then, in his own language, he sang the funeral chant and the song of the traveller on a long journey, clapping his hands softly to keep the time, and to show respect. When the flames of the fire burned low he stood and moved to the entrance of the cavern.

'Farewell, my friend,' he said. 'Goodbye, my father.'

Governor van de Velde was a cautious man. At first, he had not allowed Aboli to drive him in the carriage. 'This is a whim of yours that I will not deny, my dear,' he told his wife, 'but the fellow is a black savage. What does he know of horses?'

'He is really very good, better by far than old Fredricus.' Katinka laughed. 'And he looks so splendid in the new livery I have designed for him.'

'His fancy maroon coat and breeches will be of little interest to me when he breaks my neck,' van de Velde said, but despite his misgivings he watched the way Aboli handled the team of greys.

The first morning that Aboli drove the Governor down from the residence to his suite in the castle, there was a stir and a murmur among the convicts working on the walls as the carriage crossed the Parade and approached the castle gates. They had recognized Aboli sitting high on the coachman's seat with the long whip in his white-gloved hands.

Hal was on the point of shouting a greeting to him, but checked himself in time. It was not the sting of Barnard's whip that dissuaded him, but he realized that it would be unwise to remind his captors that Aboli had been his shipmate. The Dutch would expect him to regard a black man as a slave and not as a companion.

'Nobody to greet Aboli,' he whispered urgently to Daniel, sweating beside him. 'Ignore him. Pass it on.' The order went swiftly down the ranks of men on the scaffold and then to those labouring in the courtyard. When the carriage came in through the gates to a turnout of the honour guard and the salutes of the garrison's officers, none of the convicts paid any attention. They devoted themselves to the heavy work with block and tackle and iron bar.

Aboli sat like a carved figurehead on the coachman's seat, staring directly ahead. His dark eyes did not even flicker in Hal's direction. He drew the team of greys to a halt at the foot of the staircase and sprang down to lower the folding steps and hand out the Governor. Once van de Velde had waddled up the stairs and disappeared into his suite, Aboli returned to his seat and sat upon it, unmoving, facing straight ahead. In a short time the gaolers and guards forgot his silent presence, turned their attention to their duties and the castle fell into its routine.

An hour passed and one of the horses threw its head and fidgeted. From the corner of his eye Hal had noticed Aboli touch the reins to agitate the animal slightly. Now he climbed unhurriedly down and went to its head. He held its leather cheek-strap and stroked its head and murmured endearments to it. The grey quietened immediately under his touch, and Aboli went down on one knee and lifted first one front foot and then the other, examining the hoofs for any injury.

Still on one knee and screened by the horse's body from the view of any of the guards or overseers, he looked up for the first time at Hal. Their gaze touched for an instant. Aboli nodded almost imperceptibly and opened his right fist to give Hal a glimpse of the tiny curl of white paper he had in his palm, then closed his fist and stood up. He walked down the team of horses examining each animal and making minute adjustments to the harness. At last he turned aside and leaned against the stone wall beside him, stooping to wipe the fine flouring of dust from his boots.

Hal watched him take the quill of paper and surreptitiously stuff it into a joint in the stonework of the wall. He straightened and returned to the coachman's seat to await the Governor's pleasure. Van de Velde never showed consideration for servant, slave or animal. All that morning the team of greys stood patiently in the traces with Aboli soothing them at intervals. A little before noon the Governor re-emerged from the Company offices and had himself driven back to the residence for the midday meal.

In the dusk, as the convicts wearily climbed down into the courtyard, Hal stumbled as he reached the ground and put out his hand to steady himself. Neatly he picked the scrap of folded paper from the joint in the stonework where Aboli had left it.

Once in the dungeon there was just sufficient light filtering down from the torch in its bracket at the top of the staircase for Hal to read the message. It was written in a fine neat hand that he did not recognize. Despite all his father's and Hal's own instruction, Aboli's handwriting had never been better than large, sprawling and malformed. It seemed that another scribe had framed these words. A tiny nub of charcoal was wrapped in the paper, placed there for Hal to write his reply on the reverse of the scrap.

'The Captain buried with honour.' Hal's heart leapt as he read that. So it was Aboli who had taken down his father's mutilated corpse from the gibbet. I should have known he would give my father that respect.

There was only one more word. 'Althuda?' Hal puzzled over this until he understood that Aboli, or the writer, must be asking after the welfare of the other prisoner.

'Althuda!' he called softly. 'Are you awake?'

'Greetings, Hal. What cheer?'

'Somebody outside asks after you.'

There was a long silence as Althuda considered this. 'Who asks?'

'I know not.' Hal could not explain for he was certain that the gaolers eavesdropped on these exchanges.

Another long silence. 'I can guess,' Althuda called. 'And so can you.

296

We have discussed her before. Can you send a reply? Tell her I am alive.'

Hal rubbed the charcoal on the wall to sharpen a point on it and wrote, 'Althuda well.' Even though his letters were small and cramped, there was space for no more on the paper.

The following morning, as they were led out to begin the day's work on the scaffold, Daniel screened Hal for the moment he needed to push the scrap of paper into the same crack from which he had retrieved it.

In the middle of the morning Aboli drove the Governor down from the residence and parked once more beneath the staircase. Long after van de Velde had disappeared into his sanctum, Aboli remained on the coachman's seat. At last he looked up casually at a flock of red-winged starlings that had come down from the cliffs to perch on the walls of the eastern bastion and give vent to their low, mournful whistles. From the birds his eye passed over Hal, who nodded. Once again Aboli dismounted and tended his horses, pausing beside the wall to adjust the straps on his boots and, with a magician's sleight-of-hand, to recover the message from the crack in the wall. Hal breathed easier when he saw it, for they had established their letterbox.

They did not make the mistake of trying to exchange messages every day. Sometimes a week or more might pass before Aboli nodded at Hal, and placed a note in the wall. If Hal had a message, he would give the same signal and Aboli would leave paper and charcoal for him.

The second message Hal received was in that artistic and delicate script: 'A. is safe. Orchid sends her heart.'

'Is the orchid the one we spoke of?' Hal called to Althuda that night. 'She sends you her heart, and says you are safe.'

'I do not know how she has achieved that, but I must believe it and be thankful to her in this as in so many things.' There was a lift of relief in Althuda's tone. Hal held the scrap of paper to his nose, and fancied that he detected the faintest perfume upon it. He huddled on his damp straw in a corner of the cell. He thought about Sukeena until sleep overcame him. The memory of her beauty was like a candle flame in the winter darkness of the dungeon.

Governor van de Velde was passing drunk. He had swilled the Rhenish with the soup and Madeira with the fish and the lobster. The red wines of Burgundy had accompanied the mutton stew and the pigeon pie. He had quaffed the claret with the beef, and interspersed each with draughts of good Dutch gin. When at last he rose from the board, he steadied himself as he wove to his seat by the fire with a hand on his wife's arm. She was not usually so attentive, but all this evening she had been in an affectionate and merry mood, laughing at his sallies which on other occasions she would have ignored, and refilling his glass with her own gracious hand before it was half emptied. Come to think of it, he could not remember when last they had dined alone, just the two of them, like a pair of lovers.

For once, he had not been forced to put up with the company of the rustic yokels from the settlement, or with the obsequious flattery of ambitious Company servants or, greatest blessing of all, without the posturing and boasting of that amorous prig Schreuder.

He fell back in the deep leather chair beside the fire and Sukeena brought him a box of good Dutch cigars to choose from. As she held the burning taper for him, he peered with a lascivious eye down the front of her costume. The soft swell of girlish breasts, between which nestled the exotic jade brooch, moved him so that he felt his groin swell and engorge pleasantly.

Katinka was kneeling at the open hearth, but she regarded him so slyly that he worried for a moment that she had seen him ogle the slave girl's bosom. But then she smiled and took up the poker that was heating in the fire and plunged its glowing tip into the stone jug of scented wine. It boiled and fumed, and she filled a bowl with it and brought it to him before it had time to cool.

'My beautiful wife!' He slurred a little. 'My little darling.' He toasted her with the steaming bowl. He was not yet so intoxicated or gullible that he did not realize there would be some price to pay for this unusual kindness. There always was.

Kneeling in front of him, Katinka looked up at Sukeena, who hovered close at hand. 'That is all for tonight, Sukeena. You may go.' She gave the slave girl a knowing smile.

'I wish you sweet sleep and dreams of paradise, master and mistress.' Sukeena gave that graceful genuflection, and glided from the room. She slid the carved oriental screen door closed behind her, and knelt there quietly with her face close to the panel. These were her mistress's orders. Katinka wanted Sukeena to witness what transpired between her and her husband. She knew that it would tighten the knot that bound the slave girl to her.

Now Katinka moved behind her husband's chair. 'You have had such a difficult week,' she said softly, 'what with the affair of the pirate's body being stolen from the scaffold, and now the new census and taxation ordinances from the Seventeen. My poor darling husband, let me massage your shoulders for you.'

298

She removed his wig and kissed the top of his head. The stubble prickled her lips, and she stood back and dug her thumbs into his heavy shoulders. Van de Velde sighed with pleasure, not only with the sensation of the knots being eased from his muscles but because he recognized this as the prelude to the infrequent dispensation of her sexual favours.

'How much do you love me?' she asked, and leaned over him to nibble at his ear.

'I adore you,' he blurted out. 'I worship you.'

'You are always so kind to me.' Her voice took on that husky quality that made his skin tingle. 'I want to be kind to you. I have written to my father. I have explained to him the circumstances of the pirate's demise and how it was not your fault that it happened. I shall give the letter to the captain of the homeward-bound galleon, which is anchored in the bay at the moment, to hand to Papa in person.'

'May I see the letter before you dispatch it?' he asked warily. 'It would carry much weight if it could accompany my own report to the Seventeen, which I shall send on the same ship.'

'Of course you may. I shall bring it to you before you leave for the castle in the morning.' She brushed the top of his head with her lips again, and slid her fingers from his shoulders down over his chest. She unhooked the buttons of his doublet and slipped both hands into the opening. She took a handful of each of his pendulous dugs and kneaded them as though they were lumps of soft bread dough.

'You are such a good little wife,' he said. 'I would like to give you a sign of my love. What do you lack? A jewel? A pet? A new slave? Tell your old Petrus.'

'I do have a little whimsy,' she admitted coyly. 'There is a man in the dungeons.'

'One of the pirates?' he hazarded.

'No, a slave named Althuda.'

'Ah, yes! I know about him. The rebel and runaway! I shall deal with him this coming week. His death warrant is already on my desk waiting for my signature. Shall I give him to Slow John? Would you like to watch? Is that it? You want to enjoy the sport? How can I deny you?'

She reached down and began to unlace the fastening of his breeches. He spread his legs and lay back comfortably in the chair to make the task easier for her.

'I want you to grant Althuda a reprieve,' she whispered in his ear.

He sat bolt upright. 'You are mad,' he gasped.

'You are so cruel to call me mad.' She pouted.

'But – but he is a runaway. He and his gang of thugs murdered

299

twenty of the soldiers who were sent to recapture him. I could never free him.'

'I know you cannot release him. But I want you to keep him alive. You could set him to work on the walls of your castle.'

'I cannot do it.' He shook his shaven head. 'Not even for you.'

She came round from behind his chair and knelt in front of him. Her fingers began work again on the lacing of his breeches. He tried to sit up but she pushed him back and reached inside.

All the saints bear witness, the old sodomite makes it difficult for me. He is as soft and white as unrisen dough, she thought as she grasped him. 'Not even for your own loving wife?' she whispered, and looked up with swimming violet eyes, as she thought, That's a little better, I felt the drooping lily twitch.

'I mean, rather, that it would be difficult.' He was in a quandary.

'I understand,' she murmured. 'It was just as difficult for me to compose my letter to my father. I would hate to be forced to burn it.' She stood up and lifted her skirts as though she were about to climb over a stile. She was naked from the waist down and his eyes bulged like those of a cod hauled up abruptly from deep water. He struggled to sit up and at the same time tried to reach for her.

I'll not have you on top of me again, you great tub of pork lard, she thought as she smiled lovingly at him and held him down with both hands on his shoulders. Last time you nearly squashed the life out of me.

She straddled him as though she were mounting the mare. 'Oh, sweet Jesus, what a mighty man you are!' she cried, as she took him in. The only pleasure she received from it was the thought of Sukeena listening at the screen door. She closed her eyes and summoned up the image of the slave girl's slim thighs and the treasure that lay between them. The thought inflamed her, and she knew that her husband would feel her flowing response and think it was for him alone.

'Katinka,' he gurgled and snorted as though he was drowning, 'I love you.'

'The reprieve?' she asked.

'I cannot do it.'

'Then neither can I,' she said, and lifted herself onto her knees. She had to fight to keep herself from laughing aloud as she watched his face swell and his eyes bulge further out. He wriggled and heaved under her, thrusting vainly at the air.

'Please!' he whimpered. 'Please!'

'The reprieve?' she asked, keeping herself suspended tantalizingly above him.

300

'Yes,' he whinnied. 'Anything. I will give you anything you want.'

'I love you, my husband,' she whispered in his ear, and sank down like a bird settling on its nest.

Last time he lasted to a count of one hundred, she remembered. This time I shall try to bring him to the finishing line in under fifty. With rocking hips she set herself to better her own record.

M anseer opened the door of Althuda's cell and roared, 'Come out, you murderous dog. Governor's orders, you go to work on the wall.' Althuda stepped out through the iron door and Manseer glared at him. 'Seems you'll not be dancing a quadrille on the scaffold with Slow John, more's the pity. But don't crow too loud, you'll give us as much sport on the castle walls. Barnard and his hounds will see to that. You'll not last the winter out, I'll wager a hundred guilders on it.'

Hal led the file of convicts up from the lower cells, and paused on the stone step below Althuda. For a long moment they studied each other keenly. Both looked pleased at what they saw.

'If you give me a choice, then I think I prefer the cut of your sister's jib to yours.' Hal smiled. Althuda was smaller in stature than his voice had suggested and all the marks of his long captivity were plain to see: his skin was sallow and his hair matted and tangled. But the body that showed through the holes in his miserable rags was neat and strong and supple. His gaze was frank and his countenance comely and open. Although his eyes were almond-shaped and his hair straight and black, his English blood mingled well with that of his mother's people. There was a proud and stubborn set to his jaw.

'What cradle did you fall out of?' he asked Hal, with a grin. It was obvious that he was overjoyed to come out from the shadow of the gallows. 'I called for a man and they sent a boy.'

'Come on, you murdering renegade,' Barnard bellowed, as the gaoler handed over the convicts to his charge. 'You may have escaped the noose for the moment, but I have a few pleasures in store for you. You slit the throats of some of my comrades on the mountainside.' It was clear that all the garrison bitterly resented Althuda's reprieve. Then Barnard turned on Hal. 'As for you, you stinking pirate, your tongue is too loose by far. One word out of you today and I'll kick you off the wall, and feed the scraps to my dogs.'

Barnard separated the two of them: he sent Hal back onto the scaffold and set Althuda to work in the gangs of convicts down in the courtyard, unloading the masonry blocks from the ox-drawn wagons as they came down from the quarries.

However, that evening Althuda was herded into the general cell. Daniel and the rest crowded around him in the darkness to hear his story told in detail, and to ply him with all the questions that they had not been able to shout up the staircase. He was something new in the dreary, monotonous round of captivity and heart-breaking labour. Only when the kettle of stew was brought down from the kitchens and the men hurried to their frugal dinner did Hal have a chance to speak to him alone.

'If you escaped once before, Althuda, then there must be a chance we can do it again.'

'I was in a better state then. I had my own fishing boat. My master trusted me and I had the run of the colony. How can we escape from the walls that surround us? I fear it would be impossible.'

'You use the words fear and impossible. That is not a language that I understand. I thought perhaps I had met a man, not some faintheart.'

'Keep the harsh words for our enemies, my friend.' Althuda returned his hard stare. 'Instead of telling me what a hero you are, tell me instead now how you receive word from the outside.' Hal's stern expression cracked and he grinned at him. He liked the man's spirit, the way he could meet broadside with broadside. He moved closer and lowered his voice as he explained to Althuda how it was done. Then he handed him the latest message he had received. Althuda took it to the grille gate, and studied it in the torchlight that filtered down the staircase.

'Yes,' he said. 'That is my sister's hand. I know of no other who can pen her letters so prettily.'

That evening the two composed a message for Aboli to collect, to let him and Sukeena know that Althuda had been released from Skellum's Den.

However, it seemed that Sukeena already knew this, for the following day she accompanied her mistress on a visit to the castle. She rode beside Aboli on the driver's seat of the carriage. At the staircase she helped her mistress dismount. It was strange but Hal was by now so accustomed to Katinka's visits that he no longer felt angry and bitter when he looked upon her angelic face. She held his attention barely at all, and instead he watched the slave girl. Sukeena stood at the bottom of the staircase and darted quick birdlike glances in every direction as she searched for her brother's face among the gangs of convicts.

Althuda was working in the courtyard, chipping and chiselling the rough stone blocks into shape before they were swung up on the gantry to the top of the unfinished walls. His face and hair were powdered white as a miller's with the stone dust, and his hands were bleeding from the abrasion of tools and rough stone. At last Sukeena picked him out, and brother and sister stared at each other for one long ecstatic moment.

Sukeena's radiant expression was one of the most beautiful Hal had ever looked upon. But it was only for a fleeting instant, then Sukeena hurried up the stairs after her mistress.

A short time later they reappeared at the head of the staircase, but Governor van de Velde was with them. He had his wife on his arm and Sukeena followed then demurely. The slave girl seemed to be searching for someone other than her brother. When she mounted the driver's seat of the carriage, she murmured something to Aboli. In response, Aboli moved only his eyes, but she followed his gaze, up to the top of the scaffold where Hal was belaying a rope end.

Hal felt his pulse sprint as he realized that it was him she was seeking. They stared at each other solemnly and it seemed they were very close, for afterwards Hal could remember every angle and plane of her face and the graceful curve of her neck. At last she smiled, it was a brief, honeyed interlude, then dropped her eyes. That night in his cell he lay on the clammy straw and relived the moment.

Perhaps she will come again tomorrow, he thought, as sleep swept over him like a black wave. But she did not come again for many weeks.

 They made a place on the straw for Althuda to sleep near Hal and Daniel so that they could talk quietly in the darkness.

'How many of your men are in the mountains?' Hal wanted to know.

'There were nineteen of us to begin with, but three were killed by the Dutch and five others died after we escaped. The mountains are cruel and there are many wild beasts.'

'What weapons do they have?' Hal asked.

'They have the muskets and the swords that we captured from the Dutch, but there is little powder, and by now it might all be used up. My companions have to hunt to live.'

'Surely they have made other weapons?' Hal enquired.

'They have fashioned bows and pikes, but they lack iron points for these weapons.'

'How secure are your hiding places in the wilderness?' Hal persisted.

'The mountains are endless. The gorges are a tangled labyrinth. The cliffs are harsh and there are no paths except those made by the baboons.'

'Do the Dutch soldiers venture into these mountains?'

'Never! They dare not scale even the first ravine.'

These discussions filled all their evenings, as the winter gales came ravening down from the mountain like a pride of lions roaring at the castle walls. The men in the dungeons lay shivering on the straw pallets. Sometimes it was only the talking and the hoping that kept them from succumbing to the cold. Even so, some of the older, weaker convicts sickened: their throats and chests filled with thick yellow phlegm, their bodies burned up with fever and they died, choking and coughing.

The flesh was burned off those who survived. Although they became thin, they were hardened by the cold and the labour. Hal reached his full growth and strength in those terrible months, until he could match Daniel at belaying a rope or hefting the heavy hods. His beard grew out dense and black and the thick pigtail of his hair hung down between his shoulder blades. The whip marks latticed his back and flanks, and his gaze was hard and relentless when he looked up at the mountain tops, blue in the distance.

'How far is it to the mountains?' he asked Althuda in the darkness of the cell.

'Ten leagues,' Althuda told him.

'So far!' Hal whispered. 'How did you ever reach them over such a distance, with the Dutch in pursuit?'

'I told you I was a fisherman,' Althuda said. 'I went out each day to kill seals to feed the other slaves. My boat was small and we were many. It barely served to carry us across False Bay to the foot of the mountains. My sister Sukeena does not swim. That is why I would not let her chance the crossing.'

'Where is that boat now?'

'The Dutch who pursued us found where we had hidden it. They burned it.' Each night these councils were shortlived, for they were all being driven to the limit of their strength and endurance. But, gradually, Hal was able to milk from Althuda every detail that might be of use.

'What is the spirit of the men you took with you to the mountains?'

'They are brave men – and women too, for there are three girls with the band. Had they been less brave they would never have left the safety of their captivity. But they are not warriors, except one.'

'Who is he, this one amongst them?'

'His name is Sabah. He was a soldier until the Dutch captured him. Now he is a soldier again.'

'Could we send word to him?'

Althuda laughed bitterly. 'We could shout from the top of the castle walls or rattle our chains. He might hear us on his mountain top.'

'If I had wanted a jester, I would have called on Daniel here to amuse me. His jokes would make a dog retch, but they are funnier than yours. Answer me now, Althuda. Is there no way to reach Sabah?'

Though his tone was light, it had an edge of steel to it, and Althuda thought a while before he replied. 'When I escaped I arranged with Sukeena a hiding place beyond the bitter-almond hedge of the colony, where we could leave messages for each other. Sabah knew of this post, for I showed it to him on the night I returned to fetch my sister. It is a long throw of the dice, but Sabah may still visit it to find a message from me.'

'I will think on these things you have told me,' Hal said, and Daniel, lying near him in the dark cell, heard the power and authority in his voice and shook his head.

'Tis the voice and the manner of Captain Franky he has now, Daniel marvelled. What the Dutchies are doing to him here might have put a lesser man up on the reef but, by God, all they have done to him is filled his main sail with a strong wind. Hal had taken over his father's role, and the crew who had survived recognized it. More and more they looked to him for leadership, to give them courage to go on and to counsel them, to settle the petty disputes that rose almost daily between men in such bitter straits, and to keep a spark of hope and courage burning in all their hearts.

The next evening Hal took up the council of war that exhaustion had interrupted the night before. 'So Sukeena knows where to leave a message for Sabah?'

'Naturally, she knows it well – the hollow tree on the banks of the Eerste River, the first river beyond the boundary hedge,' Althuda replied.

'Aboli must try to make contact with Sabah. Is there something that is known only to you and Sabah that will prove to him the message comes from you and is not a Dutch trap?'

Althuda thought about it. 'Just say 'tis the father of little Bobby,' he suggested at last. Hal waited in silence for Althuda to explain, and after a pause he went on, 'Robert is my son, born in the wilderness after we had escaped from the colony. This August he will be a year old. His mother is one of the girls I spoke of. In all but name she is my wife. Nobody inside the bitter-almond hedge but I could know the child's name.'

'So, you have as good a reason as any of us for wanting to fly over these walls,' Hal murmured.

The content of the messages that they were able to pass to Aboli was severely restricted by the size of the paper they could safely employ without alerting the gaolers or the sharp, hungry scrutiny of Hugo

Barnard. Hal and Althuda spent hours straining their eyes in the dim light and flogging their wits to compose the most succinct messages that would still be intelligible. The replies that returned to them were the voice of Sukeena speaking, little jewels of brevity that delighted them with occasional flashes of wit and humour.

Hal found himself thinking more and more of Sukeena, and when she came again to the castle, following behind her mistress, her eyes went first to the scaffold where he worked before going on to seek out her brother. Occasionally, when there was space in the letters that Aboli placed in the crack of the wall, she made little personal comments; a reference to his bushing black beard or the passing of his birthday. This startled Hal, and touched him deeply. He wondered for a while how she had known this intimate detail, until he guessed that Aboli had told her. He encouraged Althuda to talk about her in the darkness. He learned little things about her childhood, her fancies and her dislikes. As he lay and listened to Althuda, he began to fall in love with her.

Now when Hal looked to the mountains in the north they were covered by a mantle of snow that shone in the wintry sunlight. The wind came down from it like a lance and seemed to pierce his soul. 'Aboli has still not heard from Sabah.' After four months of waiting, Hal at last accepted that failure. 'We will have to cut him out of our plans.'

'He is my friend, but he must have given me up,' Althuda agreed. 'I grieve for my wife for she also must be mourning my death.'

'Let us move on, then, for it boots us not to wish for what is denied us,' Hal said firmly. 'It would be easier to escape from the quarry on the mountain than from the castle itself. It seems that Sukeena must have arranged for your reprieve. Perhaps in the same fashion she can have us sent to the quarry.'

They dispatched the message, and a week later the reply came back. Sukeena was unable to influence the choice of their workplace, and she cautioned that any attempt to do so would arouse immediate suspicion. 'Be patient, Gundwane,' she told him in a longer message than she had ever sent before. 'Those who love you are working for your salvation.' Hal read that message a hundred times then repeated it to himself as often. He was touched that she should use his nickname; Gundwane. Of course, Aboli had told her that also.

'Those who love you'? Does she mean Aboli alone, or does she use the plural intentionally? Is there another who loves me too? Does she mean me alone or does she include Althuda, her brother? He alternated between hope and dismay. How can she trouble my mind so, when I have never even heard her voice? How can she feel anything for me, when she sees nothing but a bearded scarecrow in a beggar's rags? But, then, perhaps Aboli has been my champion and told her I was not always thus.

Plan as they would, the days passed and hope grew threadbare. Six more of Hal's seamen died during the months of August and September: two fell from the scaffold, one was struck down by a falling block of masonry and two more succumbed to the cold and the damp. The sixth was Oliver, who had been Sir Francis's manservant. Early in their imprisonment his right foot had been crushed beneath the iron-shod wheel of one of the ox-wagons that brought the stone down from the quarry. Even though Dr Saar had placed a splint upon the shattered bone, the foot would not mend. It swelled up and burst out in suppurating ulcers that smelt like the flesh of a corpse. Hugo Barnard drove him back to work, even though he limped around the courtyard on a crude crutch.

Hal and Daniel tried to shield Oliver, but if they intervened too obviously Barnard became even more vindictive. All they could do was take as much of the work as they could on themselves and keep Oliver out of range of the overseer's whip. When the day came that Oliver was too weak to climb the ladder to the top of the south wall, Barnard sent him to work as a mason's boy, trimming and shaping the slabs of stone. In the courtyard he was right under Barnard's eye, and twice in the same morning Barnard laid into him with the whip.

The last was a casual blow, not nearly as vicious as many that had preceded it. Oliver was a tailor by trade, and by nature a timid and gentle creature, but, like a cur driven into an alley from which there was no escape, he turned and snapped. He swung the heavy wooden mallet in his right hand, and though Barnard sprang back he was not swift enough and it caught him across one shin. It was a glancing blow that did not break bone but it smeared the skin, and a flush of blood darkened Barnard's hose and seeped down into his shoe. Even from his perch on the scaffold Hal could see by his expression that Oliver was appalled and terrified by what he had done.

'Sir!' he cried, and fell to his knees. 'I did not mean it. Please, sir, forgive me.' He dropped the mallet and held up both hands to his face in the attitude of prayer.

Hugo Barnard staggered back, then stooped to examine his injury. He ignored Oliver's frantic pleas, and peeled back his hose to expose the long graze down his shin. Then still without looking at Oliver, he limped to the hitching rail on the far side of the courtyard where his pair of black boarhounds were tethered. He held them on the leashes and pointed them at where Oliver still knelt.

'Get him!' They hurled themselves against the leashes, baying and gaping with wide red mouths and long white fangs.

'Get him!' Barnard urged, and at the same time restrained them. The fury in his voice enraged the animals, and they leapt against the leashes so that Barnard was almost pulled off his feet.

'Please!' screamed Oliver, struggling to rise, toppling back, then crawling towards where his crutch was propped against the stone wall.

Barnard slipped the hounds. They bounded across the yard and Oliver had time only to lift his hands to cover his face before they were on him.

They bowled him over and sent him rolling over the cobbles, then slashed at him with snapping jaws. One went for his face, but he lifted his arm and it buried its fangs in his elbow. Oliver was shirtless and the other hound caught him in the belly. Both held on.

From high on the scaffold Hal was powerless to intervene. Gradually Oliver's screams grew weaker and his struggles ceased. Barnard and his hounds never let up: they went on worrying the body long after the last flutter of life had been extinguished. Then Barnard gave the mutilated body one last kick and stepped back. He was panting wildly and sweat slimed his face and dripped onto his shirtfront, but he lifted his head and grinned up at Hal. He left Oliver's body lying on the cobbles until the end of the work shift when he singled out Hal and Daniel. 'Throw that piece of offal on the dungheap behind the castle. He will be more use to the seagulls and crows than he ever was to me.' And he chuckled with glee when he saw the murder in Hal's eyes.

When spring came round again only eight were left. Yet the eight were tempered by these hardships. Every muscle and sinew stood proud beneath the tanned and weathered skin of Hal's chest and arms. The palms of his hands were tough as leather, and his fingers powerful as a blacksmith's tongs. When he broke up a fight a single blow from one of his scarred fists could drop a big man to the paving.

The first promise of spring dispersed the gale-driven clouds, and the sun had new fire in its rays. A restlessness took over from the resigned gloom that had possessed them all during winter. Tempers were short, fighting amongst them more frequent, and their eyes looked often to the far mountains, from which the snows had thawed or turned out across the blue Atlantic.

Then there came a message from Aboli in Sukeena's hand: 'Sabah sends greetings to A. Bobby and his mother pine for him.' It filled them all with a wild and joyous hope that, in truth, had no firm foundation for Sabah and his band could only help them once they had passed the bitter-almond hedge.

Another month passed, and the wild flame of hope that had lit their hearts sank to an ember. Spring came in its full glory, and turned the mountain into a prodigy of wild flowers whose colours stunned the eye, and whose perfume reached them even on the high scaffold. The wind came singing out of the south-east, and the sunbirds returned from they knew not where, setting the air afire with their sparkling plumage.

Then there was a laconic message from Sukeena and Aboli. 'It is time to go. How many are you?'

That night they discussed the message in whispers that shook with excitement. 'Aboli has a plan. But how can he get all of us away?'

'For me he is the only horse in the race,' Big Daniel growled. 'I'm laying every penny I have on him.'

'If only you had a penny to lay.' Ned chuckled. It was the first time Hal had heard him laugh since Oliver had been ripped to pieces by Barnard's dogs.

'How many are going?' Hal asked. 'Think on it a while, lads, before you give answer.' In the bad light he looked around the circle of heads, whose expressions turned grim. 'If you stay here you will go on living for a while at least, and no man will think the worse of you. If we go and we do not reach the mountains, then you all saw the way my father and Oliver died. 'Twas not a fitting death for an animal, let alone a man.'

Althuda spoke first. 'Even if it were not for Bobby and my woman, I would go.'

'Aye!' said Daniel, and 'Aye!' said Ned.

'That's three,' Hal murmured, 'What about you, William Rogers?'

'I'm with you, Sir Henry.'

'Don't test me, Billy. I have told you not to call me that.' Hal frowned. When they used his title he felt himself a fraud, for he was not worthy of the honour that his grandfather had won at the right hand of Drake. The title that his father had carried with such distinction. 'Your last chance, Master Billy. If your tongue trips again I'll kick some sense into the other end of you. Do you hear?'

'Aye, I hear you sweet and clear, Sir Henry.' Billy grinned at him, and the others roared with laughter as Hal caught him by the scruff of his neck and boxed his ears. They were all bubbling over with excitement – all, that was, but Dick Moss and Paul Hale.

'I've grown too old for a lark such as this, Sir Hal. My bones are so stiff I could not climb a pretty lad if you tied him over a barrel for me, let alone climb a mountain.' Dick Moss the old pederast grinned. 'Forgive me, Captain, but Paul and me have talked it over, and we'll stay on here where we'll get a bellyful of stew and a bundle of straw each night.'

'Perhaps you are wiser than the rest of us.' Hal nodded, and he was not saddened by the decision. Dicky was long past his glory days when he had been the man to beat to the masthead when they reefed sail in a full gale. This last winter had stiffened his limbs and greyed his hair. He would be non-paying cargo to carry on this voyage. Paul was Dicky's shipwife. They had been together for twenty years, and though Paul was still a fury with a cutlass in his hand he would stay with his ageing lover.

'Good luck to both of you. You're as good a pair as I ever sailed with,' Hal said, and looked at Wally Finch and Stan Sparrow. 'What about you two birds? Will you fly with us, lads?'

'As high and as far as you're going.' Wally spoke for both of them, and Hal clapped his shoulder.

'That makes six of us, eight with Aboli and Althuda, and it'll be high and far enough to suit all our tastes, I warrant you.'

There was a final exchange of messages as Aboli and Sukeena explained the plan they had worked out. Hal suggested refinements and drew up a list of items that Aboli and Sukeena must try to steal to make their existence in the wilderness more certain. Chief amongst these were a chart and compass, and a backstaff if they could find one.

Aboli and Sukeena made their final preparation without letting their trepidation or excitement become apparent to the rest of the household. Dark eyes were always watching everything that happened in the slave quarters, and they trusted nobody now that they were so close to the chosen day. Sukeena gradually assembled those items for which Hal had asked, and added a few of her own that she knew they would need.

The day before the planned escape, Sukeena summoned Aboli into the main living area of the residence where before he had never been allowed to enter. 'I need your strength to move the carved armoire in the banquet hall,' she told him, in front of the cook and two others of the kitchen staff. Aboli followed her submissively as a trained hound on a leash. Once they were alone, Aboli dropped the demeanour of the meek slave.

'Be quick!' Sukeena warned him. 'The mistress will return very soon. She is with Slow John at the bottom of the garden.' She moved swiftly to the shutter of the window that overlooked the lawns, and saw that the ill-assorted couple were still in earnest conversation under the oak trees.

'There is no limit to her depravity,' she whispered to herself, as she watched Katinka laugh at something the executioner had said. 'She would make love to a pig or a poisonous snake if the fancy came upon her.' Sukeena shuddered at the memory of that ophidian tongue exploring the secret recesses of her own body. It will never happen again, she promised herself, only four more days to endure before Althuda will be safe. If she calls me to her nest before then I will plead that my courses are flowing.

She heard something whirl in the air like a great bird in flight and glanced back over her shoulder to see that Aboli had taken one of the swords from the display of weapons in the hallway. He was testing its balance and temper, swinging it in singing circles around his head, so that the reflections of light off the blade danced on the white walls.

He set it aside and chose another, but liked it not at all and placed it back with a frown. 'Hurry!' she called softly to him. Within minutes he had picked out three blades, not for the jewels that decorated the hilts but for the litheness and temper of their blades. All three were curved scimitars made by the armourers of Shah Jahan at Agra on the Indian continent. 'They were made for a Mogul prince and sit ill in the hand of a rough sailor, but they will do until I can find a cutlass of good Sheffield steel to replace them.' Then he picked out a shorter blade, a *kukri* knife used by the hill people of Further India, and he shaved a patch of hair off his forearm. 'This will do for the close work I have in mind.' He grunted with satisfaction.

'I have marked well those you have chosen,' Sukeena told him. 'Now leave them on the rack or their empty slots will be noticed by the other house slaves. I will pass them to you on the evening before the day.'

That afternoon she took her basket and, the conical straw hat on her head, went up into the mountain. Although any watcher would not have understood her intent, she made certain that she was out of sight, hidden in the forest that filled the great ravine below the summit. There was a dead tree that she had noted on many previous outings. From the rotting pith sprouted a thicket of tiny purple toadstools. She pulled on a pair of gloves before she began to pick them. The gills beneath the parasol-shaped tops were of a pretty yellow colour. These fungi were toxic, but only if eaten in quantity would they be fatal. She had chosen them for this quality – she did not want the lives of innocent men and their families on her conscience. She placed them in the bottom of the basket and covered them with other roots and herbs before she descended the steep mountainside and walked sedately back through the vineyards to the residence.

That evening Governor van de Velde held a gala dinner in the great hall, and invited the notables from the settlement and all the Company

311

dignitaries. These festivities continued late, and after the guests had left the household staff and slaves were exhausted. They left Sukeena to make her rounds and lock up the kitchens for the night.

Once she was alone she boiled the purple toadstools and reduced the essence to the consistency of new honey. She poured the liquid into one of the empty wine bottles from the feast. It had no odour and she did not have to sample it to know that it had only the faintest taste of the fungi. One of the women who worked in the kitchens at the castle barracks was in her debt: Sukeena's potions had saved her eldest son when he had been stricken by the smallpox. The next morning she left the bottle in a basket with remedies and potions in the carriage for Aboli to deliver to the woman.

When Aboli drove the Governor down to the castle, van de Velde was ashen-faced and grumpy with the effects of the previous night's debauchery. Aboli left a message in the slot in the wall that read, 'Eat nothing from the garrison kitchen on the last evening.'

That night Hal poured the contents of the stew kettle into the latrine bucket before any of the men were tempted to sample it. The steaming aroma filled the cell and to the starving seamen it smelled like the promise of eternal life. They groaned and gritted their teeth, and cursed Hal, their fates and themselves to see it wasted.

The next morning at the accustomed hour the dungeon began to stir with life. Long before dawn outlined the four small, barred windows, men groaned and coughed and then crept, one at a time to ease themselves, grunting and farting as they voided in the latrine bucket. Then, as the significance of the day dawned upon them, a steely, charged silence gripped them.

Slowly the light of day filtered down upon them from the windows and they looked at each other askance. They had never been left this late before. On every other morning they had been at work on the walls an hour earlier than this.

When at last Manseer's keys rattled in the lock, he looked pale and sickly. The two men with him were in no better case.

'What ails you, Manseer?' Hal asked. 'We thought you had changed your affections and that we would never see you again.' The gaoler was an honest simpleton, with little malice in him, and over the months Hal had cultivated a superficially amicable relationship with him.

'I spent the night sitting in the shithouse,' Manseer moaned. 'And I had company, for every man in the garrison was trying to get in there with me. Even at this hour half of them are still in their bunks—' He broke off as his belly rumbled like distant thunder, and a desperate expression came over his face. 'Here I go again! I swear I'll kill that poxy cook.' He started back up the stairs and left them waiting another half-hour before he returned to open the grille gate and lead them out into the courtyard.

Hugo Barnard was waiting to take over from him. He was in a foul mood. 'We have lost half a day's work,' he snarled at Manseer. 'Colonel Schreuder will blame me for this, and when he does I'll come back to you, Manseer!' He turned on the line of convicts. 'Don't you bastards stand there smirking! By God, you're going to give me a full day's work even if I have to keep you on the scaffold until midnight. Now leap to it, and quickly too!' Barnard was in fine fettle, his face ruddy and his temper already on the boil. It was clear that the colic and diarrhoea that afflicted the rest of the garrison had not touched him. Hal remembered Manseer remarking that Barnard lived with a Hottentot girl in the settlement down by the shore, and did not eat in the garrison mess.

He looked around quickly as he walked across the courtyard to the foot of the ladder. The sun was already well up and its rays lit the western redoubt of the castle. There were less than half the usual number of gaolers and guards: one sentry instead of four at the gates, none at the entrance to the armoury and only one more at the head of the staircase that led to the Company offices and the Governor's suite on the south side of the courtyard.

When he climbed the ladder and reached the top of the wall he looked across the parade to the avenue, and could just make out the roof of the Governor's residence among the trees.

'God speed, Aboli,' he whispered. 'We are ready for you.'

Aboli brought the carriage round to the front of the residence a few minutes earlier than the Governor's wife had ordered it, and pulled up the horses below the portico. Almost immediately Sukeena appeared in the doorway and called to him. 'Aboli! The mistress has some packages to take with us in the carriage.' Her tone was light and easy, with no hint of strain. 'Please come and carry them down.' This was for the benefit of the others whom she knew would be listening.

Obediently Aboli locked the brake on the carriage wheels and, with a quiet word to the horses, jumped down from the coachman's seat. He moved without haste and his expression was calm as he followed Sukeena into the house. He came out again a minute later carrying a rolled-up silk rug and a set of leather saddle-bags. He went to the back of the carriage and placed this luggage in the panniers, then closed the lid. There was no air of secrecy about his movements and no furtiveness to alert any of the other slaves. The two maids who were busy sweeping the front terrace did not even look up at him. He went back to his seat and picked up the reins, waiting with a slave's infinite patience.

Katinka was late, but that was not unusual. She came at last in a cloud of French perfume and rustling silks, sweeping down the stairs and scolding Sukeena for some fancied misdemeanour. Sukeena glided beside her on small, silent, slippered feet, contrite and smiling.

Katinka climbed up into the carriage like a queen on her way to her coronation, and imperiously ordered Sukeena, 'Come and sit here beside me!' Sukeena gave her a curtsy with her hands to her lips. She had hoped that Katinka would give her that command. When she was in the mood for physical intimacy, Katinka wanted her close enough to be able to stretch out her hand and touch her. At other times she was cold and aloof, but at all times unpredictable.

'Tis an omen for good that she does what I intended, Sukeena encouraged herself, as she took the seat opposite her mistress and smiled at her lovingly.

'Drive on, Aboli!' Katinka called and then, as the carriage pulled away, gave her attention to Sukeena. 'How does this colour suit me in the sunlight? Does it not make me seem pale and insipid?'

'It goes beautifully with your skin, mistress.' Sukeena told her what she wanted to hear. 'Even better than it does indoors. Also it brings out the violet lights in your eyes.'

'Should there not be a touch more lace in the collar, do you think?' Katinka tilted her head prettily.

Sukeena considered her reply. 'Your beauty does not rely on even the finest lace from Brussels,' she told her. 'It stands alone.'

'Do you think so, Sukeena? You are such a flatterer, but I must say you yourself are looking particularly fetching this morning.' She considered the girl thoughtfully. The carriage was now bowling down the avenue at a trot, the greys arching their necks and stepping out handsomely. 'There is colour in your cheeks and a twinkle in your eye. One might be forgiven for thinking that you were in love.'

Sukeena looked at her in a way that made Katinka's skin tingle. 'Oh, but I am in love with a special person,' she whispered.

'My naughty little darling,' Katinka purred.

The carriage came out into the parade and turned towards the castle. Katinka was so engrossed that for some while she did not realize where they were heading. Then a shadow of annoyance crossed her face and she called sharply, 'Aboli! What are you doing, idiot? Not the castle. We are going to Mevrouw de Waal.'

Aboli seemed not to have heard her. The greys trotted straight on towards the castle gates.

'Sukeena, tell the fool to turn round.'

Sukeena stood up quickly in the swaying carriage then sat down close beside Katinka and slipped her arm through that of her mistress, holding her firmly.

'What on earth are you doing, child? Not here. Have you lost your mind? Not in front of the whole colony.' She tried to pull away her arm, but Sukeena held it with a strength that shocked her.

'We are going into the castle,' Sukeena said quietly. 'And you are to do exactly what I tell you to do.'

'Aboli! Stop the carriage this instant!' Katinka raised her voice and made to stand up. But Sukeena jerked her down in her seat.

'Don't struggle,' Sukeena ordered, 'or I will cut you. I will cut your face first, so that you are no longer beautiful. Then if you still do not obey I will send this blade through your slimy, evil heart.'

Katinka looked down and, for the first time, saw the blade that Sukeena held to her side. That dagger had been a gift from one of Katinka's lovers and she knew just how sharp was its slender blade. Sukeena had stolen it from Katinka's closet.

'Are you mad?' Katinka blanched with terror, and tried to squirm away from the needle point.

'Yes. Mad enough to kill you and to enjoy doing it.' Sukeena pressed the dagger to her side and Katinka screamed. The horses pricked their ears. 'If you scream again I will draw your blood,' Sukeena warned. 'Now hold your tongue and listen while I tell you what you are to do.'

'I will give you to Slow John and laugh as he draws out your entrails,' Katinka blustered, but her voice shook and terror was in her eyes.

'You will never laugh again, not unless you obey me. This dagger will see to that,' and she pricked Katinka again, hard enough to pierce cloth and skin, so that a spot of blood the size of a silver guilder appeared on her bodice.

'Please!' Katinka whimpered. 'Please, Sukeena, I will do as you say. Please don't hurt me again. You said you loved me.'

'And I lied,' Sukeena hissed at her. 'I lied for my brother's sake. I hate you. You will never know the strength of my hatred. I loath the touch of your hands. I am revolted by every filthy, evil thing you forced me to do. So do not trade on any love from me. I will crush you with as little

315

pity as I would rid my hair of lice.' Katinka saw death in her eyes, and she was afraid as she had seldom been in her life before.

'I will do as you tell me,' she whispered, and Sukeena instructed her in a flat, hard tone that was more threatening than any shouting or raging.

As Aboli drove the carriage through the castle gates, the usual stir of activity heralded its arrival. The single sentry came to attention and presented his musket. Aboli wheeled the team of greys and brought the carriage to a halt in front of the Company offices. The captain of the guard hurried from the armoury, hastily strapping on his sword-belt. He was a young subaltern, freshly out from Holland, and he had been taken by surprise by the unexpected arrival of the Governor's wife.

'The devil's horns!' he muttered to himself. 'Why does the bitch pick today to arrive when half my men are sick as dogs?' He looked anxiously at the single guard at the door to the Company offices, and saw that the man's face still had a pale greenish tinge. Then he realized that the Governor's wife was beckoning to him from her seat in the carriage. He broke into a run across the courtyard, straightening his cap and tightening the strap under his chin as he went. He reached the carriage and saluted Katinka. 'Good morning, Mevrouw. May I assist you to dismount?'

The Governor's wife had a strained, nervous look and her voice was high and breathless. The subaltern was instantly alarmed. 'Is something amiss, Mevrouw?'

'Yes, something is very much amiss. Call my husband!'

'Will you go to his office?'

'No. I will remain here in the carriage. Go to him this instant and tell him that I say he must come immediately. It is a matter of the utmost importance. Life and death! Go! Hurry!'

The subaltern looked startled and saluted quickly, then bounded up the steps two at a time and shot through the double doors into the offices. While he was gone Aboli dismounted, went to the panniers at the back of the carriage and opened the lid. Then he glanced around the courtyard.

There was one guard at the gates and another at the head of the stairs but, as usual, the slow-match in their muskets was unlit. There was no sentry posted at the doors to the armoury, but from where he stood he could see through the window that three men were in the guard room.

316

Each of the five overseers in the courtyard carried swords as well as their whips and canes. Hugo Barnard was at the far end of the yard and had both his hounds on the leash. He was haranguing the gang of common convicts laying the paving stones along the foot of the east wall. These other convicts, not part of the crew of the *Resolution*, might be a hazard when they made their attempt to escape. Nearly two hundred were working on the walls, the multi-hued dregs of humanity. They could easily hamper the rescue attempt by blocking the escape route or even by trying to join in with the *Resolution*'s crew and mobbing the carriage when they realized what was happening.

We will deal with that when it happens, he thought grimly, and turned his full attention to the armed guards and overseers who were the primary threat. With Barnard and his gang, there were ten armed men in sight but any outcry could bring another twenty or thirty soldiers hurrying out of the barracks and across the yard. The whole business could get out of hand quickly.

He looked up to find Hal and Big Daniel watching him from the scaffold. Hal already had the rope of the gantry in his hand, the tail looped around his wrist. Ned Tyler and Billy Rogers were on the lower tier, and the two birds, Finch and Sparrow, were working near Althuda in the courtyard. They were all pretending to carry on with their tasks, but were eyeing Aboli surreptitiously.

Aboli reached into the pannier and loosened the twine that secured the rolled silk carpet. He opened a flap of it and, without lifting them clear, revealed the three Mogul scimitars and the single *kukri* knife that he had chosen for himself. He knew that, from their vantage point, Hal and Big Daniel could see into the pannier. Then he stood immobile and expressionless at the back wheel of the carriage.

Suddenly the Governor burst hatless and in his shirt sleeves through the double doors at the head of the staircase and came down at an ungainly lurching run.

'What is it, Mevrouw?' he called urgently to his wife, when he was half-way down. 'They say you sent for me, and it's a matter of life and death.'

'Hurry!' Katinka cried plaintively. 'I am in the most terrible predicament.'

He arrived at the door of the carriage, panting wildly. 'Tell me what ails you, Mevrouw!' he gasped.

Aboli stepped up behind him and hooked one great arm around his neck, pinning him helplessly. Van de Velde began to struggle. For all his obesity he was a powerful man and even Aboli had difficulty in holding him.

'What in the devil's name are you doing?' he roared in outrage. Aboli

317

placed the blade of the *kukri* at his throat. When van de Velde felt the cold touch of steel and the sting of the razor edge, his struggles ceased.

'I will slit your throat like the great hog you are,' Aboli whispered in his ear, 'and Sukeena has a dagger at your wife's heart. Tell your soldiers to stay where they are and throw down their arms.'

The subaltern had started forward at van de Velde's cry, and his sword was half-way out of its scabbard as he rushed down the stairs.

'Stop!' van de Velde shouted at him in terror. 'Don't move, you fool. You will have me killed.' The subaltern halted and dithered uncertainly.

Aboli tightened his lock around the Governor's throat. 'Tell him to throw down his sword.'

'Throw down your sword!' van de Velde whinnied. 'Do as he says. Can't you see he has a knife at my throat?' The subaltern dropped his sword, which clattered down the steps.

Fifty feet above the courtyard, Hal sprang out from the scaffold, hanging on the rope from the gantry, and Big Daniel belayed the other end, braking the speed of his fall. The sheave squealed as he plummeted down and landed in balance on the cobbles. He leaped to the rear of the carriage and seized one of the jewelled scimitars. With the next leap he was half-way up the steps where he stooped and swept up the subaltern's sword in his left hand. He placed the point under the officer's chin and said, 'Order your men to throw down their weapons!'

'Lay down your arms, all of you!' the subaltern yelled. 'If any man amongst you brings harm to the Governor or his lady, he will pay for it with his own life.' The sentries obeyed with alacrity, dropping their muskets and sidearms to the paving stones.

'You too!' van de Velde howled at the overseers, and with reluctance they obeyed. However, at that moment Hugo Barnard was screened by a pile of masonry blocks. He stepped quietly into the doorway to the kitchens, dragging his two hounds with him, and crouched there, waiting his opportunity.

Down from the scaffold scrambled the other seamen. Sparrow and Finch from the lower tier were first to reach the courtyard but Ned, Big Daniel and Billy Rogers were seconds behind them.

'Come on, Althuda!' Hal called, and Althuda dropped his mallet and chisel and ran to join him. 'Catch!' Hal lobbed the jewelled scimitar in a high, glinting parabola, and Althuda reached up and caught it by the hilt, plucking it neatly out of the air. Hal wondered what class of swordsman he was. As a fisherman it was unlikely that he would have had much practice.

I shall have to shield him if it comes to a fight, he thought, and looked around quickly. He saw Daniel pulling the other weapons out of the pannier at the back of the carriage. The twin scimitars looked like toys in his huge fist. He tossed one to Ned Tyler and kept the other for himself as he ran to join Hal.

Hal picked up a sword that a sentry had dropped and threw it to Big Daniel. 'This one is more your style, Master Danny,' he yelled, and Daniel grinned, showing his broken black teeth, as he caught the heavy infantry weapon and made it hiss in the air as he cut left and right.

'Sweet Jesus, it's good to have a real blade in my hand again!' he exulted, and tossed the light scimitar to Wally Finch. 'A tool for a man, but a toy for a boy.'

'Aboli, keep a firm hold on that great hog. Cut his ears off if he tries to be crafty,' Hal shouted. 'The rest of you follow me!' He dropped down the staircase and raced towards the doors of the armoury with Big Daniel and the others on his heels. Althuda began to follow him also, but Hal stopped him. 'Not you. You look after Sukeena!'

As Althuda turned back and they ran on across the courtyard, Hal snapped at Daniel, 'Where's Barnard?'

'The murdering bastard was here not a moment past, but I don't see him now.'

'Keep a good lookout for his top sails. We'll have trouble with that swine yet.'

Hal burst into the armoury. The three men in the guard room were slumped on the bench: two were asleep and the third scrambled to his feet in bewilderment. Before he could recover his wits, Hal's point was pressed to his chest. 'Stay where you are, or I'll look at the colour of your liver.' The man dropped back into his seat. 'Here, Ned!' Hal called to him as Ned rushed in. 'Play wet-nurse to these infants,' and left them in his charge as he ran after Daniel and the other seamen.

Daniel charged the heavy teak door at the end of the passage and it burst open before his rush. They had never before had a chance to look into the armoury, but now at a glance Hal saw that it was all laid out in a neat and orderly fashion. The weapons were in racks along the walls, and the powder kegs stacked to the ceiling at the far end.

'Pick your weapons and bring a keg of powder each,' he ordered, and they ran to the long racks of infantry swords, polished, gleaming and sharpened to a bright edge. Further back were the racks of muskets and pistols. Hal thrust a pair of pistols into the rope that served him as a belt. 'Remember, you'll have to carry everything you take with you up the mountains, so don't be greedy,' he warned them, and picked up a fifty-pound keg of gunpowder from the pyramid at the far end of the armoury, which he hoisted to his shoulder. Then he turned for the door. 'That's enough, lads. Get out! Daniel, lay a powder trail as you go!'

319

Daniel used the butt of a musket to stove in the bungs of two of the powder kegs. At the foot of the pyramid of barrels he poured a mound of black gunpowder. 'That lot will go off with an almighty bang!' He grinned, as he backed towards the door, the other keg under his arm spilling a long dark trail behind him.

Under their burdens they staggered out into the sunlight. Hal was the last to leave. 'Get out of here, Ned!' he ordered, and handed him the weapons he carried as Ned ran for the door. Then Hal turned on the three Dutch soldiers, who were cowering on the bench. Ned had disarmed them – their weapons were thrown in the corner of the guard room.

'I'm going to blow this place to hell,' he told them in Dutch. 'Run for the gates, and if you're wise you'll keep running without looking back. Go!' They sprang up and, in their haste to get clear, jammed in the doorway. They struggled and fought each other until they burst out into the courtyard and raced across it.

'Look out!' they yelled, as they sprinted for the gates. 'They're going to blow up the powder store!' The gaolers and the other common convicts who, until this point, had stood gaping at the carriage and the hostage Governor in Aboli's grip, now turned their heads towards the armoury and stared at it in stupid surprise.

Hal appeared in the armoury doorway with a sword in one hand and a burning torch that he had seized from its bracket in the other.

'I am counting to ten,' Hal shouted, 'and then I am lighting the powder train!' In his rags, and with his great bushy black beard and wild eyes, he looked like a maniac. A moan of horror and fear went up from every man in the yard. One of the convicts threw down his spade and followed the fleeing soldiers in a rush for the gate. Immediately pandemonium overwhelmed them all. Two hundred convicts and soldiers stormed the gates in a rush for safety.

Van de Velde struggled in Aboli's grip and screamed, 'Let me go! The idiot is going to blow us all to perdition. Let me go! Run! Run!' His shrieks added to the panic, and within the time it takes to draw and hold a long breath the courtyard was deserted except for the group of seamen around the carriage and Hal. Katinka was screaming and sobbing hysterically, but Sukeena slapped her hard across the face. 'Keep quiet, you simpering ninny, or I'll give you good reason to blubber,' and Katinka gulped back her distress.

'Aboli, get van de Velde into the carriage! He and his wife are coming with us,' Hal called, and Aboli lifted the Governor bodily and hurled him over the top of the door. He landed in an ungainly heap on the floorboards and struggled there, like an insect on a pin. 'Althuda, put your sword point to his heart and be ready to kill him when I give the word.'

'I look forward to it!' Althuda shouted, dragged van de Velde upright and thrust him into the seat facing his wife. 'Where should I give it to you?' he asked him. 'In your fat gut, perhaps?'

Van de Velde had lost his wig in the scuffle and his expression was abject, every inch of his huge frame seeming to quiver with despair. 'Don't kill me. I can protect you,' he pleaded, and Katinka started weeping and keening again. This time, Sukeena merely held her a little tighter, lifted the point of the dagger to her throat and whispered, 'We don't need you now we have the Governor. It won't matter at all if I kill you.' Katinka choked back the next sob.

'Daniel, load the powder and the spare weapons,' Hal ordered, and they piled them into the carriage. The elegant vehicle was no wagon, and the coachwork sagged under the load on its delicately sprung suspension.

'That's enough! It will take no more.' Aboli stopped them throwing the last few powder kegs on board.

'One man to each horse!' Hal commanded. 'Don't try to board them, lads. You're none of you riders. You'll fall off and break your necks, which won't matter much, but your weight will kill the poor beasts before we have gone a mile, and that will matter. Lay hold of their rigging and let them tow you along.' They ran to their places around the team of horses, and latched onto their harness. 'Leave space for me on the larboard bow, lads,' he called, and even in her excitement and agitation Sukeena laughed aloud at his use of the nautical terms. His men understood, though, and left the offside lead horse for him.

Aboli leaped to his place on the coachman's seat, while in the body of the carriage Althuda menaced van de Velde and Sukeena held her dagger to Katinka's white throat.

Aboli wheeled the team and shouted, 'Come on, Gundwane. It's time to go. The garrison will wake up at any moment now.' As he said it they heard the flat report of a pistol shot, and a garrison officer ran from the doorway of the barracks across the square waving his smoking pistol, shouting to his men to form up on him. 'Stand to arms! On me the First Company!'

Hal paused only a moment to light the slow-match of one of his pistols from the burning torch, then tossed the torch onto the powder train and waited to see it flare and catch. The smoking flame started snaking back through the doors of the armoury into the passageway that led to the main powder magazine. Then he sprang down the steps into the courtyard and raced to meet the overloaded carriage as Aboli drove the horses in a circle and lined up for the gates.

He was almost there, raising his hand to seize the bridle of the leading grey gelding, when suddenly Aboli shouted in agitation, 'Gundwane, behind you! Have a care!'

Hugo Barnard had appeared in the doorway where he and his hounds had taken shelter at the first sign of trouble. Now he slipped both dogs from the leash and with wild yells of encouragement sent them in pursuit of Hal. 'Vat hom! Catch him!' he yelled and the animals raced towards him in a silent rush, running side by side, striding out and covering the length of the courtyard like a pair of whippets coursing a hare.

Aboli's warning had given Hal just time enough to turn to face them. The dogs worked as a team, and one leaped for his face while the other rushed for his legs. Hal lunged at the first while it was in the air and sent his point into the base of the black throat where it joined the shoulders. The flying weight of the hound's body drove the blade in full length, transfixing it cleanly through heart and lung and on into its guts. Even though it was dead, the momentum of its flight drove it on to crash into Hal's chest, and he staggered backwards.

The second hound snaked in low to the ground and, while Hal was still off balance, sank its fangs into his left shin just below the knee, jerking him over backwards. His shoulder crashed into the stone paving, but when he tried to rise the animal still had him in its grip and pulled back on all four braced legs, sending him sprawling again. Hal felt its teeth grate on the bone of his leg.

'My hounds!' Barnard yelled. 'You are hurting my darlings.' With his drawn sword in his hand he rushed to intervene. Again Hal tried to rise, and again the hound pulled him down. Barnard reached them and raised his sword to his full height above Hal's unprotected head. Hal saw the blow coming and rolled aside. The blade struck the flint cobbles beside his ear in a sheet of sparks.

'You bastard!' Barnard roared, and lifted the sword again. Aboli swerved the team of horses and drove them deliberately at Barnard. The overseer's back was turned to the approaching carriage, and he was so engrossed with Hal that he did not see it coming. As he was about to strike again at Hal's head, the rear wheel caught him a glancing blow on the hip and sent him staggering aside.

With a violent effort Hal hauled himself into a sitting position, and before the hound could drag him flat again, he stabbed it in the base of the neck, driving his blade at an angle back between its shoulder blades like the bull-fighter's coup, finding the heart. The beast let out an agonized howl and released its grip on his leg, staggered around in a circle then collapsed on the cobbles, kicking feebly.

Hal heaved himself to his feet just as Barnard rushed at him. 'You have killed my beauties!' He was maddened with grief, and hacked again at Hal, a wild uncontrolled blow. Hal turned it effortlessly aside and let it fly an inch past his head.

'You filthy pirate, I'll cut you down!' Barnard gathered himself and rushed in again. With the same apparent ease Hal deflected the next thrust, and said softly, 'Do you remember what you and your dogs did to Oliver?' He feinted high left, forcing Barnard to open his guard in the mid-line, and then, like a bolt of lightning, thrust home. The blade took Barnard just under the sternum, and sprang half its length out of his back. He dropped his sword and fell to his knees.

'The debt to Oliver is paid!' Hal said, placed his bare foot on Barnard's chest and, against its resistance, pulled his blade clear. Barnard toppled and lay beside the carcass of his dying hound.

'Come on, Gundwane!' Aboli was struggling to hold the team of greys, for the shouting and the smell of blood had panicked them. 'The magazine!' It was only seconds since Hal had lighted the powder train, but when he glanced in that direction he saw clouds of acrid blue smoke billowing from the doorway of the armoury.

'Hurry, Gundwane!' Sukeena called softly. 'Oh, please, hurry!' Her voice was so filled with concern for his safety that it spurred him. Even in these dire straits, Hal realized that it was the first time he had ever heard her speak his nickname. He started forward. The dog had bitten deeply into his leg, but its fangs could not have severed nerves or sinews for Hal found that, if he ignored the pain, he could still run on it. He leaped across the yard and grabbed hold of the leading horse's bridle. It tossed its head and rolled its eyes until the pink lining showed, but Hal hung on and Aboli gave the team its head.

The carriage went rocking and clattering under the archway of the gates, across the bridge, over the moat and out onto the open Parade. Suddenly from behind them came a shattering explosion, and a shock-wave of disrupted air swept over them like a tropical line squall. The horses reared and plunged in terror, and Hal was lifted off his feet. He clung desperately to the traces and looked back. A tower of dun-coloured smoke rose swiftly from the interior courtyard of the castle, spinning and revolving upon itself, shot through with dark flames and scraps of debris and wreckage. In the midst of this plume of destruction a single human body cartwheeled a hundred feet into the sky.

323

'For Sir Hal and King Charley!' Big Daniel roared, and the other seamen took up the cheering, beside themselves with excitement at their escape.

However, when Hal looked back again he could see that the massive outer walls of the castle were untouched by the detonation. The barracks had been built of the same heavy stonework, and almost certainly had withstood the blast. Two hundred men were housed in there, three companies of green-jackets, and even now they were probably recovering their wits after the explosion. Soon they would come pouring out through the castle gates in full pursuit – and where, he wondered, was Colonel Cornelius Schreuder?

The carriage was pounding across the parade at a gallop. Ahead ran a mob of escaped convicts. They were scattering in every direction, some leaping over the stone wall of the Company gardens and heading for the mountain, others running for the beach to find a boat in which to make good their flight. Out on the Parade were the few stunned burghers and house slaves who were abroad at this time of the forenoon. They gawked in amazement at the tide of fugitives, then at the rolling cloud of smoke that enveloped the castle and then at the even more extraordinary sight of the advancing Governor's carriage, festooned with a motley array of desperate tatterdemalion outlaws and pirates, screaming like madmen and brandishing their weapons. As the vehicle bore down on them they scattered frantically.

'The pirates have escaped from the castle. Run! Run!' At last they recovered and spread the alarm. The cry was taken up and shouted ahead of them through the huts and hovels of the settlement. Hal could see the burghers and their slaves hurrying to escape the bloodthirsty pirate crew. One or two of the braver souls had armed themselves, and there was a desultory popping of musket fire from some of the cottage windows, but the range was long, the aim hurried and poor. Hal did not even hear the flight of the balls and none of the men or horses were hit. The carriage swept on past the first buildings, following the only road that skirted the curving beach of Table Bay, and headed out into the unknown.

Hal looked back at Aboli. 'Slow down, damn you! You'll blow the horses before we've got past the town.' Aboli stood upright and pulled the horses back. 'Whoa, Royal! Slow down, Cloud!' But the team were bolting and had almost reached the outskirts of the settlement before Aboli was able to wrestle them to a trot. They were all sweating and snorting from the gallop, but were far from spent.

As soon as they were under control, Hal loosed his grip on the harness and turned back to jog beside the carriage. 'Althuda,' he called, 'instead of sitting up there like a gentleman on a Sunday picnic, make sure all the muskets are primed and loaded. Here!' He passed up the pistol with the burning match. 'Use this to light the match on all the weapons. They'll be after us soon enough.' Then he looked from Althuda to his sister.

'We have not been introduced. Your servant, Henry Courteney.' He grinned at her, and she laughed delightedly at his formal manner.

'Good morrow, Gundwane. I know you well. Aboli has warned me of what a fierce young pirate you are.' Then she turned serious. 'You are hurt. I should see to your leg.'

'"Tis nothing that cannot wait until later,' he assured her.

'The bite of a dog will mortify swiftly if it is left untreated,' she told him.

'Later!' he repeated, and turned to Aboli.

'Aboli, are you acquainted with the road to the boundary of the colony?'

'There is only one road, Gundwane. We have to go straight through the village, skirt the marshland then head out across the sandy flatlands towards the mountains.' He pointed. 'The bitter-almond fence is five miles beyond the marsh.'

Looking beyond the settlement, Hal could already see marshland and the lagoon ahead, stands of reeds and open water, over which hovered flocks of water birds. He had heard that crocodiles and hippopotami lurked in the depths of the lagoon.

'Althuda, will there be any soldiers in our way?' Hal asked him.

'There are usually guards at the first bridge and there is always a patrol at the bitter-almond hedge to shoot any Hottentots who try to enter,' Althuda replied, without looking up from the musket he was loading.

Then Sukeena sang out, 'There will be no pickets or patrols today. From dawn I kept a watch on the crossroad. No soldiers went out to take up their posts. They are all too busy nursing their aching bellies.' She laughed gaily, as excited and wrought up as the rest of them. Suddenly she leaped up in the body of the carriage and called out in a ringing voice, 'Free! For the first time in my life I am free!' Her plait had tumbled down and come loose. Her hair streamed out behind her head. Her eyes sparkled, and she was so beautiful that she epitomized the dreams of every one of the ragged seamen.

Although they cheered her, 'You, and us also, darling!' it was Hal at whom she was looking with those laughing eyes.

As they passed the buildings of the settlement, the warning cries had been shouted ahead of them. 'Beware! The pirates have escaped. The pirates are on the rampage!' The good citizens of Good Hope scattered

325

before them. Mothers rushed into the street to seize their offspring and drag them indoors, to throw the door-bolts and slam down the shutters.

'You are safe now. You have escaped clean away. Please will you not let me free, Sir Henry?' Katinka had recovered from her shock sufficiently to plead for her life. 'I swear I have never meant you harm. I saved you from the gallows. I saved Althuda also. I'll do anything you say, Sir Henry. Just please set me free,' she whimpered, clinging to the side of the carriage.

'You may call me sir now and make me those declarations of goodwill but they would have stood my father in better stead while he was on his way to the gallows.' Hal's expression was so cold and remorseless that Katinka recoiled and fell back in the seat beside Sukeena, sobbing as though her heart were breaking.

The seamen running with Hal shouted their scorn and hatred at her. 'You wanted to see us hanged, you painted doxy, and we're going to feed you to the lions out there in the wilderness,' gloated Billy Rogers.

Katinka sobbed afresh and covered her face with her hands. 'I never meant any of you harm. Please let me go.'

The carriage rolled steadily down the empty street, and the last few huts and hovels of the settlement were all that lay ahead when Althuda rose from his seat and pointed back down the gravel-surfaced road towards the distant parade. 'Horseman coming at a gallop!' he cried.

'So soon?' Big Daniel muttered, shading his eyes. 'I had not expected the pursuit yet. Do they have cavalry to send after us?'

'Have no fear of that, lads,' Aboli reassured them. 'There are no more than twenty horses in the whole colony, and we have six of those.'

'Aboli is right. 'Tis only one horseman!' shouted Wally Finch.

The rider was leaving a pale ribbon of dust in the air behind him, leaning forward over his mount's neck as he drove the animal to its top speed, using the whip in his right hand to flog it onwards mercilessly. He was still far off, but Hal recognized him from the sash that flowed out behind him with the speed of his gallop.

'Sweet Mary, it's Schreuder! I knew he would join us before too long.' His jaw clenched in anticipation. 'The hot-headed idiot comes alone to fight us. Brains he lacks, but he has a full cargo of guts.' Even from his seat Aboli could see what Hal intended by the narrowing of his eyes and the way he changed his grip on his sword.

'Don't think of going back to give him satisfaction, Gundwane!' Aboli called sternly. 'You will place every soul here at risk for any delay.'

'I know you think I'm no match for Schreuder but things have changed, Aboli. I can beat him now. I'm sure of it in my heart.' Aboli thought that he might well do so, for Hal was no longer a boy. The months on the walls had toughened him, and Aboli had seen him match strength with Big Daniel. 'Leave me here to see to this business, man to man, and I will follow you later,' Hal cried.

'No, Sir Hal!' shouted Big Daniel. 'Maybe you *could* best him but not with that leg bitten to the bone. Leave your feud with the Dutchman for another time. We need you with us. There will be a hundred green-jackets following close behind him.'

'No!' agreed Wally and Stan. 'Stay with us, Captain.'

'We've put our trust in you,' said Ned Tyler. 'We can never find our way through the wilderness without a navigator. You can't desert us now.'

Hal hesitated, still glaring back at the swiftly approaching rider. Then his eyes flicked to the face of the girl in the carriage. Sukeena stared at him, her huge dark eyes full of entreaty. 'You are sorely wounded. Look at your leg.' She leaned over the door of the carriage, so that she was very close, and spoke so softly that he could only just make out the words above the din of men and wheels and horses. 'Stay with us, Gundwane.'

He glanced down at the blood and pale lymph oozing from the deep puncture wounds. While he wavered Big Daniel ran back and jumped up onto the step of the carriage.

'I'll take care of this one,' he said, and lifted the loaded musket from Althuda's hands. Holding it, he dropped from the step into the dirt of the road and stood there checking the burning matchlock and the priming in the pan. He took his time as the carriage trotted away from him and Colonel Schreuder galloped down on him.

Despite all their pleas and warnings Hal started back to intervene. 'Daniel, don't kill the fool.' He wanted to explain that he and Schreuder had a destiny to work out together. It was a matter of chivalric honour in which no other should come between them, but there was no time to give voice to such a romantic notion.

Schreuder galloped to within earshot and stood in his stirrups. 'Katinka!' he shouted. 'Have no fear, I am come to save you, my darling. I will never let these villains take you.'

He plucked the bell-muzzled pistol from his sash and held the matchlock in the wind so that the smouldering match flared. Then he lay flat along his horse's neck with his pistol arm outstretched. 'Out of my way, oaf!' he roared at Daniel, and fired. His right arm was thrown high by the discharge and a wreath of blue smoke swirled around his head, but the ball flew wide, hitting the earth a foot from Daniel's bare right leg, showering him with gravel.

Schreuder threw aside the pistol and drew the Neptune sword from its scabbard at his side. The gold inlay on the blade glinted as he wielded it. 'I'll cleave your skull to the teeth!' Schreuder roared, and raised the blade high. Daniel dropped on one knee and let the Colonel's horse come on the last few strides.

Too close, Hal thought. Much too close. If the musket misfires Danny is a dead man. But Daniel held his aim steadily and snapped the lock. For an instant Hal thought his worst fear had been realized but then, with a sharp report, a spurt of flame and silver smoke, the musket discharged.

Perhaps Daniel had heeded Hal's shout, or perhaps the horse was a bigger and surer target than the rider upon its back, but he had aimed into the animal's wide, sweat-drenched chest and the heavy lead ball for once flew true. At full charge Schreuder's steed collapsed under him. He was thrown over its head, slamming face and shoulder into the ground.

The horse struggled and kicked, lying on its back, thrashing its head from side to side while its heart-blood pumped from the wound in its chest. Then its head fell back to earth with a thump and, with one last snorting breath, it lay still.

Schreuder lay motionless on the sun-baked road, and Hal felt a moment's fear that his neck was broken. He almost ran back to aid him, but Schreuder made a few disjointed movements, and Hal paused. The carriage was drawing away swiftly, and the others were shouting to him, 'Come back, Gundwane!'

'Leave the bastard, Sir Henry.'

Daniel sprang up, grabbed Hal's arm. 'He ain't dead, but we soon will be if we lie becalmed here much longer,' and dragged him away.

For the first few steps Hal resisted and tried to shake off Daniel's hand. 'It can't end like this. Don't you understand, Danny?'

'I understand well enough,' Big Daniel grunted, and at that Schreuder sat up groggily in the middle of the road. The gravel had torn the skin off one side of his face, but he was trying to get to his feet, lurching and falling, then trying again.

'He's all right,' said Hal, with a relief that almost surprised him, and allowed Daniel to pull him away.

'Aye!' said Daniel, as they caught up with the carriage. 'He's right enough to crop your acorns for you when next you meet. We'll not be rid of that one so easily.'

Aboli braked the carriage to allow them to catch up, and Hal grabbed the bridle of the leading horse and allowed it to lift him off his feet. He looked back to see Schreuder on his feet in the middle of the road, dusty, and bleeding. He staggered after the carriage like a man with a bottle of cheap gin in his belly, still brandishing the sword.

They pulled away from him at a brisk trot and Schreuder gave up the attempt to overhaul the departing carriage, instead screamed abuse after it: 'By God, Henry Courteney, I'm coming after you, even if I have to follow you to the very gates of hell. I have you in my eye, sir, I have you in my heart.'

'When you come, bring with you that sword you stole from me,' Hal shouted back. 'I'll spit you with it like a sucking pig for the devil to roast.' His seamen hooted with laughter and gave the colonel an assortment of obscene farewell gestures.

'Katinka! My darling!' Schreuder changed his tone. 'Do not despair. I will rescue you. I swear it on my father's grave. I love you with my very life.'

Throughout all the shouting and the musket fire, van de Velde had been crouching on the floor of the carriage but now he heaved himself back onto the seat and glared at the battered figure in the road. 'Is he raving mad? How dare he address my wife in such odious terms?' He rounded on Katinka with a red face and wobbling jowls. 'Mevrouw, I trust you have given the dolt of a soldier no cause for such licence.'

'I assure you, Mijnheer, his language and address come as more of a shock to me than they do to you. I take great offence, and I implore you to take him seriously to task at the first opportunity,' replied Katinka, clinging to the door of the carriage with one hand and to her bonnet with the other.

'I will do better than that, Mevrouw. He will be on the next ship back to Amsterdam. I cannot abide with such impertinence. Moreover, he is responsible for the predicament we are now in. As commander of the castle, the prisoners are his responsibility. Their escape is due to his incompetence and the dereliction of his duty. The dastard has no right to speak to you in such a fashion.'

'Oh, yes, he does,' said Sukeena sweetly. 'Colonel Schreuder has the right of conquest in his favour. Your wife has been lying under him often enough with her legs in the air for him to call her darling, or even to call her whore and slut if he chose to be more honest.'

'Quiet, Sukeena!' shrilled Katinka. 'Are you out of your mind? Remember your place. You are a slave.'

'No, Mevrouw. A slave no longer. A free woman now, and your captor,' Sukeena told her, 'so I can say to you anything I please, especially if it is the truth.' She turned to van de Velde. 'Your wife and the gallant colonel have been playing the beast with two backs so blatantly as to delight every tattle-tale in the colony. They have set a pair of horns on your head that are too large for even your grossly bloated body.'

'I will have you thrashed!' van de Velde gurgled apoplectically. 'You slave bitch!'

'No, you won't,' said Althuda, and placed the point of the jewelled scimitar against the Governor's pendulous belly. 'Rather, you will apologize for that insult to my sister.'

'Apologize to a slave? Never!' van de Velde began in a bellow, but this time Althuda pricked him with more intent and the bellow turned into a squeal, like air escaping from a pig's bladder.

'Apologize not to a slave, but to a freeborn Balinese princess,' Althuda corrected him. 'And swiftly.'

'I beg your pardon, madam,' van de Velde gritted through clenched teeth.

'You are gallant, sir.' Sukeena smiled at him. Van de Velde sank back in his seat and said no more, but he fixed his wife with a venomous stare.

Once they had left the settlement behind them, the surface of the road deteriorated. There were deep wheel ruts left by the Company wagons going out to fetch firewood, and the carriage rocked and lurched dangerously through them. Along the edge of the lagoon the water had seeped in to turn the tracks to mud and slush and, in many places, the seamen were forced to put their shoulders to the tall rear wheels to help the horses drag the vehicle through. It was late morning before they saw ahead the framework of the wooden bridge over the first river.

'Soldiers!' Aboli called. From his high seat he had picked out the glint of a bayonet and the shape of the tall helmets.

'Only four,' said Hal. His eyes were still the sharpest of all. 'They'll not be expecting trouble from this direction.' He was right. The corporal of the bridge guard came forward to meet them, puzzled but unalarmed, his sword sheathed and the match on his pistols unlit. Hal and his crew disarmed him and his men, stripped them to their breeches and sent them running back towards the colony with a discharge of muskets over their heads.

While Aboli walked the carriage over the bridge and took it on along the rudimentary track, Hal and Ned Tyler climbed beneath the wooden structure and roped a barrel of gunpowder under the heavy timber kingpost. When it was secure Hal used the butt of his pistol to drive in the bung of the barrel, thrust a short length of slow-match into it and lit it. He and Ned scrambled back onto the roadway and ran after the carriage.

Hal's leg was painful now. It was swelling and stiffening, but he was looking back over his shoulder as he hobbled along through the ankle-

330

deep sand. The centre of the bridge suddenly erupted in a spout of mud, water, shattered planks and piers. The wreckage fell back into the river.

'That will not hold the good colonel long, but at least he will get his breeches wet,' Hal muttered, as they caught up with the carriage. Althuda jumped down and called to him, 'Take my place. You must favour that leg.'

'There is little wrong with my leg,' Hal protested.

'Other than that it can barely carry your weight,' said Sukeena sternly, leaning over the door. 'Come up here at once, Gundwane, or else you will do lasting damage to it.'

Meekly Hal climbed up into the coach and took the seat opposite Sukeena. Without looking at the pair, Aboli grinned to himself. Already she gives the orders and he obeys. It seems they have the tide and a fair wind behind them.

'Let me look at that leg,' Sukeena ordered, and Hal placed it on the seat between her and Katinka.

'Take care, clod!' Katinka snapped, and pulled away her skirts. 'You will bloody my dress.'

'If you do not have a care to your tongue, it will not be the only thing I will bloody,' Hal assured her, and scowled. She withdrew into the farthest corner of the seat.

Sukeena worked over the leg with swift, competent hands. 'I should lay a hot poultice on these bites, for they are deep and will certainly fester. But I need boiling water.' She looked up at Hal.

'You will have to wait for that until we reach the mountains,' he told her. Then, for a while, their conversation broke down and they gazed into each other's eyes bemusedly. This was as close as they had ever been and each found something in the other to amaze and delight them.

Then Sukeena roused herself. 'I have my medicines in the saddle-bags,' she said briskly, and climbed over the seat to reach the panniers on the back of the carriage. She hung there as she rummaged in the leather bags. The carriage jolted on over the rough track, and Hal looked with awe on her small rounded bottom, pointed skywards. Despite the ruffles and petticoats that shrouded it, he thought it almost as enchanting as her face.

She climbed back with cloths and a black bottle in her hand. 'I will swab out the wounds with this tincture and then bind them up,' she explained, without looking again into the distraction of his green eyes.

'Avast!' Hal gasped at the first touch of the tincture. 'That burns like the devil's breath.'

Sukeena scolded, 'You have endured whip and shot and sword and savaging by an animal. But the first touch of medicine and you cry like a baby. Now be still.'

Aboli's face creased into a bouquet of tattoos and merry laughter lines but, though his shoulders shook, he held his peace.

Hal sensed his amusement, and rounded on him. 'How far ahead is the bitter-almond hedge?'

'Another league.'

'Will Sabah meet us there?'

'That is what I believe, if the green-jackets don't catch up with us first.'

'Methinks we will have some respite. Schreuder made an error by rushing alone in pursuit of us. He should have mustered his troops and come after us in an orderly fashion. My guess is that most of the green-jackets will be chasing the other prisoners we turned free. They will concentrate on us only once Schreuder takes command.'

'And he has no horse,' Sukeena added. 'I think we will get clear away, and once we reach the mountains—' She broke off and lifted her eyes from Hal's leg. Both she and Hal looked ahead to the high blue rampart that filled the sky ahead.

Van de Velde had been avidly following this conversation, and now he broke in. 'The slave wench is right. You have succeeded in this underhand scheme of yours, more's the pity. However, I am a reasonable man, Henry Courteney. Set my wife and me free now. Give the carriage over to us and let us return to the colony. In exchange I will give you my solemn undertaking to call off the chase. I will order Colonel Schreuder to send his men back to their barracks.' He turned on Hal what he hoped was an open and guileless countenance. 'I offer you my word as a gentleman on it.'

Hal saw the cunning and malice in the Governor's eyes. 'Your excellency, I am uncertain of the validity of your claim to the title of gentleman, besides which I should hate to be deprived so soon of your charming company.'

At that moment one of the front wheels of the carriage crashed into a hole in the tracks. 'The aardvarks dig these burrows,' Althuda explained, as Hal clambered down from the lopsided vehicle.

'Pray, what manner of man or beast is that?'

'The earth pig, a beast with a long snout and a thick tail that digs up the burrows of ants with its powerful claws and devours them with its long sticky tongue,' Althuda told him.

Hal threw back his head and laughed. 'Of course, I believe that. I also believe that your earth pig flies, dances the hornpipe and tells fortunes by cards.'

'You have a few things yet to learn about the land that lies out there, my friend,' Althuda promised him.

Still chuckling, Hal turned from him. 'Come on, lads!' he called to his seamen. 'Let's get this ship off the reef and running before the wind again.'

He made van de Velde and Katinka get out and the rest of them strained with the horses to pull the carriage free. From here onwards, though, the track became barely passable, and the bush on either hand grew taller and more dense as they went on. Within the next mile they were stuck in holes twice more.

'It is almost time to get rid of the carriage. We can get on faster on our own shanks,' Hal told Aboli quietly. 'How much further to the hedge?'

'I thought we should have reached it by now,' Aboli replied, 'but it cannot be far.' They came to the boundary around the next kink in the narrow track. The famous bitter-almond hedge was a straggly and blighted excrescence, hardly shoulder high, but the road ended dramatically against it. There was also a rough hut, which served as a guard post to the border picket, and a notice in Dutch.

'WARNING!' the notice began, in vivid scarlet letters, and went on to forbid movement by any person beyond that point, with the penalty for infringement being imprisonment or the payment of a fine of a thousand guilders or both. The board had been erected in the name of the Governor of the Dutch East India Company.

Hal kicked open the door of the single room of the guard hut and found it deserted. The fire on the open hearth was cold and dead. A few articles of Company uniform hung on the wooden pegs in the wall, and a black kettle stood over the dead coals, with odd bowls, bottles and utensils lying on the rough wooden table or on shelves along the walls.

Big Daniel was about to put the slow-match to the thatch, but Hal stopped him. 'No point in giving Schreuder a smoke beacon to follow,' he said, 'and there's naught of value here. Leave it be,' and limped back to where the seamen were unloading the carriage.

Aboli was turning the horses out of the traces and Ned Tyler was helping him to improvise pack saddles for them, using the harness, leatherwork and canvas canopy from the carriage.

Katinka stood forlornly at her husband's side. 'What is to become of me, Sir Henry?' she whispered as he came up.

'Some of the men want to take you up into the mountains and feed you to the wild animals,' he replied. Her hand flew to her lips and she paled. 'Others want to cut your throat here and now for what you and your fat toad of a husband did to us.'

333

'You would never allow such a thing to happen,' van de Velde blustered. 'I only did what was my duty.'

'You're right,' Hal agreed. 'I think throat-cutting too good for you. I favour hanging and drawing, as you did to my father.' He glared at him coldly, and van de Velde quailed. 'However, I find myself sickened by you both. I want no further truck with either of you, and so I leave you and your lovely wife to the mercy of God, the devil and the amorous Colonel Schreuder.' He turned and strode away to where Aboli and Ned were checking and tightening the loads on the horses.

Three of the greys had kegs of gunpowder slung on each side of their backs, two carried bundles of weapons and the sixth horse was loaded with Sukeena's bulky saddle-bags.

'All shipshape, Captain.' Ned knuckled his forehead. 'We can up anchor and get under way at your command.'

'There's nothing to keep us here. The Princess Sukeena will ride on the lead horse.' He looked around for her. 'Where is she?'

'I am here, Gundwane.' Sukeena stepped out from behind the guard hut. 'And I need no mollycoddling. I will walk like the rest of you.'

Hal saw that she had shed her long skirts and that she now wore a pair of baggy Balinese breeches and a loose cotton shift that reached to her knees. She had tied a cotton headcloth over her hair, and on her feet were sturdy leather sandals that would be comfortable for walking. The men ogled the shape of her calves in the breeches, but she ignored their rude stares, took the lead rein of the nearest horse and led it towards the gap in the bitter-almond hedge.

'Sukeena!' Hal would have stopped her, but she recognized his censorious tone and ignored it. He realized the folly of persisting, and wisely tempered his next command. 'Althuda, you are the only one who knows the path from here. Go ahead with your sister.' Althuda ran to catch up with her, and brother and sister led them into the uncharted wilderness beyond the hedge.

Hal and Aboli brought up the rear of the column as it wound through the dense scrub and bush. No men had trodden this path recently. It had been made by wild animals: the marks of their hoofs and paws were plain to see in the soft sandy soil, and their dung littered the track.

Aboli could recognize each animal by these signs, and as they moved along at a forced pace, he pointed them out to Hal. 'That is leopard and there is the spoor of the antelope with the twisted horns we call kudu. At least we shall not starve,' he promised. 'There is a great plenty of game in this land.'

This was the first opportunity since the escape that they had had to

334

talk, and Hal asked quietly, 'This Sabah, the friend of Althuda, what do you know of him?'

'Only the messages he sent.'

'Should he not have met us at the hedge?'

'He said only that he would lead us into the mountains. I expected him to be waiting at the hedge,' Aboli shrugged, 'but with Althuda to guide us we do not need him.'

They made good progress, the grey mare trotting easily with them hanging onto her traces and running beside her. Whenever they passed a tree that would bear Aboli's weight he shinned up it and looked back for signs of pursuit. Each time he came down and shook his head.

'Schreuder will come,' Hal told him. 'I have heard men say that those green-jackets of his can run down a mounted man. They will come.'

They moved on steadily across the plain, stopping only at the swampy waterholes they passed. Hal hung onto the horse to ease his injured leg and, as he limped along, Aboli recounted all that had happened in the months since they had last been together. Hal was silent as he described, in his own language, how he had retrieved Sir Francis's body from the gibbet and the funeral he had given him. 'It was the burial of a great chief. I dressed him in the hide of a black bull and placed his ship and his weapons within his reach. I left food and water for his journey, and before his eyes I set the cross of his God.' Hal's throat was too choked for him to thank Aboli for what he had done.

The day wore on, and their progress slowed as men and horses tired in the soft sandy footing. At the next marshy swamp where they stopped for a few minutes' rest, Hal took Sukeena aside.

'You have been strong and brave but your legs are not as long as ours, and I have watched you stumble with fatigue. From now on you must ride.' When she started to protest he stopped her firmly. 'I obeyed you in the matters of my wounds, but in all else I am captain and you must do as I say. From here on you will ride.'

Her eyes twinkled. She made a pretty little gesture of submission, placing her fingertips together and touching them to her lips, 'As you command, master,' and allowed him to boost her up on top of the saddle-bags on the leading grey.

They skirted the swamp and went on a little faster now. Twice more Aboli climbed a tree to look back and saw no sign of pursuit. Against his natural instincts Hal began to hope that they might have eluded their pursuers, that they might reach the mountains that loomed ever closer and taller without being further molested.

In the middle of the afternoon they crossed a broad open *vlei*, a meadow of short green grass where herds of wild antelope with scimitar-curved horns were grazing. They looked up at the approach of the caravan of horses and men, standing frozen in wide-eyed astonishment, their coats a metallic blue-grey hue in the afternoon sunlight.

'Even I have never seen beasts of that ilk,' Aboli admitted.

As the herds fled before them, wreathed in their own dust, Althuda called back, 'Those are the animals the Dutch call *blaauwbok*, the blue buck. I have seen great herds of them on the plains beyond the mountains.'

Beyond the *vlei* the ground began to rise in a series of undulating ridges towards the foothills of the range. They climbed towards the first ridge, with Hal toiling along at the rear of the column. By now he was moving heavily, in obvious pain. Aboli saw that his face was flushed with fever, and that blood and watery fluid had seeped through the bandage that Sukeena had placed on his leg.

At the top of the ridge Aboli forced a halt. They looked back at the great Table Mountain, which dominated the western horizon. To their left, the wide blue curve of False Bay opened. However, they were all too exhausted to spend long admiring their surroundings. The horses stood, heads hanging, and the men threw themselves down in any shade they could find. Sukeena slid off her mount and hurried to where Hal had slumped with his back to a small tree-trunk. She knelt in front of him, unwrapped the bandage from his leg and drew a sharp breath when she saw how swollen and inflamed it was. She leaned closer and sniffed the oozing punctures. When she spoke her voice was stern.

'You cannot walk further on this. You must ride as you force me to do.' Then she looked up at Aboli. 'Make a fire to boil water,' she ordered him.

'We have no time for such tomfoolery,' Hal murmured half-heartedly, but they ignored him. Aboli lit a small fire with a slow-match and placed over it a tin mug of water. As soon as it boiled, Sukeena prepared a paste with the herbs she had in her saddle-bag, and spread it on a folded cloth. While it still steamed with heat she clapped the cloth over Hal's wounds. He moaned and said, 'I swear I would rather Aboli pissed on my leg, than you burned it off with your devilish concoctions.'

Sukeena ignored his immodest language and went on with her task. She bound the poultice in place with a fresh cloth, then from her saddle-bags she fetched a loaf of bread and a dried sausage. She cut these into slices, folded bread and sausage together, and handed one to each of the men.

'Bless you, Princess.' Big Daniel knuckled his forehead, before taking his ration from her.

'God love you, Princess,' said Ned, and all the others adopted the name. From then on she was their princess, and the rough seamen looked upon her with increasing respect and burgeoning affection.

'You can eat on the march, lads.' Hal hauled himself to his feet. 'We have been lucky too long. Soon the devil will want his turn.' They groaned and muttered but followed his lead.

As Hal was helping Sukeena to mount, there was a warning shout from Daniel. 'There the bastards come at last.' He pointed back down at the open *vlei* at the bottom of the slope. Hal pushed Sukeena up between the saddle-bags and limped back to the rear of the column. He looked down the hillside and saw the long file of running men who had emerged from the edge of the scrub and were crossing the open ground. They were led by a single horseman who came on at a trot.

'It's Schreuder again. He has found another mount.' Even at that range there was no mistaking the Colonel. He sat tall and arrogant in the saddle, and there was a sense of deadly purpose about the set of his shoulders and the way he lifted his head to look up the slope towards them. It was obvious that he had not yet spotted them, hidden in the thick scrub.

'How many men with him?' Ned Tyler asked, and they all looked at Hal to count them. He slitted his eyes and watched them come out of the thick scrub. With their swinging trot they kept up easily with Schreuder's horse.

'Twenty,' Hal counted.

'Why so few?' Big Daniel demanded.

'Almost certainly Schreuder has chosen his fastest runners to press us hard. The rest will be following at their best speed.' Hal shaded his eyes. 'Yes, by God, there they are, a league behind the first platoon, but coming fast. I can see their dust and the shape of their helmets above the scrub. There must be a hundred or more in that second detachment.'

'Twenty we can deal with,' Big Daniel muttered, 'but a hundred of those murdering green-backs is more than I can eat for breakfast without belching. What orders, Captain?' Every man looked at Hal.

He paused before replying, carefully studying the lie and the grain of the land below before he said, 'Master Daniel, take the rest of the party on with Althuda to guide you. Aboli and I will stay here with one horse to slow down their advance.'

'We cannot outrun them. They've proved that to us, Captain,' Daniel protested. 'Would it not be better to fight them here?'

'You have your orders.' Hal turned a cold, steely eye upon him.

Daniel again knuckled his brow. 'Aye, Captain,' and he turned to the others. 'You heard the orders, lads.'

Hal limped back to where Sukeena sat on her horse, with Althuda holding the lead rein. 'You must go on, whatever happens. Do not turn back for any reason,' he told Althuda, and then he smiled up at Sukeena. 'Not even if her royal highness commands it.'

She did not return his smile but leaned down closer and whispered, 'I will wait for you on the mountain. Do not make me wait too long.'

Althuda led the column of horses forward again, and as they crossed the skyline there was a distant shout from the *vlei* below.

'So they have discovered us,' Aboli muttered.

Hal went to the single remaining horse, and loosened one of the fifty-pound kegs of gunpowder. He lowered it to the ground, and told Aboli, 'Take the horse on. Follow the others. Let Schreuder see you go. Tether it out of sight beyond the ridge and then come back to me.'

He rolled the keg to the nearest outcrop of rock and crouched beside it. With only the top of his head showing, he again studied the slope below him, then turned his full attention to Schreuder and his band of green-jackets. Already they were much closer, and he could see that two of the Hottentots ran ahead of Schreuder's horse. They watched the ground as they came on, following exactly the route that Hal's party had blazed.

They read our sign from the earth, like hounds after the stag, he thought. They will come up the same path we followed.

At that moment Aboli dropped back over the ridge and squatted beside him. 'The horse is tethered and the others go on apace. Now what is your plan, Gundwane?'

''Tis so simple, there is no need to explain it to you,' said Hal, as he prised the bung from the keg with the point of his sword. Then he unwound the length of the slow-match he had tied around his waist. 'This match is the devil. It either burns too fast or too slow. But I will take a chance on three fingers' length,' he muttered as he measured, then lopped off a length. He rolled it gently between the palms of his hands in an attempt to induce it to burn evenly, then threaded one end into the bunghole of the keg and secured it by driving back the wooden plug.

'You had best hurry, Gundwane. Your old fencing partner, Schreuder, is in great haste to meet you again.'

Hal glanced up from his task and saw that the pursuers had crossed the meadow and were already starting up the slope towards them. 'Keep out of sight,' Hal told him. 'I want to let them get very close.' The two lay flat on their bellies and peered down the hillside. Sitting high in the saddle, Schreuder was in full view, but the two trackers who led him were obscured by the scrub and flowering bushes from the waist down. As they came on Hal could make out the ugly gravel graze down Schreuder's face, the rents and dirt smears on his uniform. He wore neither hat nor wig, had probably lost them along the way, perhaps in his fall. Vain though he was, he had wasted no time in trying to regain them, so urgent was his haste.

The sun had already reddened his shaven pate and his horse was lathered. Perhaps he had not bothered to water it during the long chase. Closer still he came. His eyes were fastened on the ridge where he had seen the fugitives cross. His face was a stony mask, and Hal could see that he was a man driven by his volcanic temper, ready to take any risk or brave any danger.

On the steep slope even his indefatigable trackers began to flag. Hal could see the sweat streaming down their flat yellow Asiatic faces and hear their gasping breath.

'Come on, you rogues!' Schreuder goaded them. 'You will let them get clear away. Faster! Run faster.' They came scrambling and straining up the slope.

'Good!' Hal muttered. 'They are sticking in our tracks, as I hoped.' He whispered his final instructions to Aboli. 'But wait until I give you the word,' he cautioned him.

Closer they came until Hal could hear the Hottentots' bare feet slapping the ground, the squeak of Schreuder's tack and the jingle of his spurs. On he came, until Hal saw the individual beads of sweat that decorated the points of his moustache, and the little veins in his bulging blue eyes as he fixed his obsessed and furious stare on the skyline of the ridge, overlooking the enemy who lay hidden much closer at hand.

'Ready!' whispered Hal, and held the burning slow-match to the fuse of the powder keg. It flared, spluttered, caught, then burned up fiercely. The flame raced down the short length of fuse towards the bung hole.

'Now, Aboli!' he snapped. Aboli seized the keg and leapt to his feet, almost under the hoofs of Schreuder's horse. The two Hottentots yelled with shock and ducked off the path, while the horse shied and reared, throwing Schreuder forward onto its neck.

For a moment Aboli stood poised, holding the keg high above his head with both hands. The fuse sizzled and hissed like an angry puff-adder, and the powder smoke blew around his great tattooed head like a blue nimbus. Then he hurled the keg out over the hillside. It turned lazily in the air before striking the rocky ground and bounding away, bouncing and leaping as it gathered speed. It jumped up into the face of

Schreuder's horse, which reared away just as its rider had recovered his balance. Schreuder was thrown forward again onto its neck, lost one of his stirrups and hung awkwardly out of the saddle.

The horse spun and leaped back down the slope, almost into the platoon of infantry that was following close upon its heels. As both maddened horse and bouncing powder keg came hurtling back amongst them, the column of green-jackets sent up a howl of consternation. Every one recognized that the smoking fuse was the harbinger of a fearsome detonation only seconds away, and they broke ranks and scattered. Most turned instinctively downhill, rather than breaking out to the sides, and the keg overhauled them, bouncing along in their midst.

Schreuder's horse went down on its bunched hindquarters as it slipped and slid down the hillside. The reins snapped in one of its rider's hands while the other lost its precarious hold on the pommel of the saddle. Schreuder fell clear of his mount's driving hoofs, and as he hit the earth the keg exploded. The fall saved his life for he had tumbled into the lee of a low rock outcrop and the main force of the blast swept over him.

However, it ripped through the horde of routed soldiers. Those closest to it were hurled about and thrown upwards like burning leaves from a garden fire. Their clothing was stripped from their mangled bodies, and a disembodied arm was thrown high to fall back at Hal's feet. Both Aboli and Hal were knocked down by the force of the blast. Ears buzzing, Hal scrambled upright again and stared down in awe at the devastation they had created.

Not one of the enemy was still on his feet. 'By God, you killed them all!' Hal marvelled, but at once there were confused cries and shouts among the flattened bushes. First one and then more of the enemy soldiers staggered dazedly upright.

'Come away!' Aboli seized Hal's arm and dragged him to the top of the ridge. Before they dropped over the crest Hal glanced back and saw that Schreuder had hoisted himself upright. Swaying drunkenly he was standing over the mutilated carcass of his mount. He was still so dazed that, even as Hal watched, his legs folded under him and he sat down heavily among the broken branches and torn leaves, covering his face with his hands.

Aboli released Hal's arm, and changed his sword into his right hand. 'I can run back and finish him off,' he growled, but the suggestion stirred Hal from his own daze.

'Leave him be! It would not be honourable to kill him while he is unable to defend himself.'

'Then let us go, and fast.' Aboli growled. 'We may have put this band of Schreuder's men up on the reef but, look! The rest of his green-jackets are not far behind.'

Hal wiped the sweat and dust from his face and blinked to stop his eyes blurring. He saw that Aboli was right. The dustcloud from the second detachment of the enemy rose from the scrub of the flatlands on the far side of the *vlei*, but it was coming on swiftly.

'If we run hard now, we might be able to hold them off until nightfall and by then we should be into the mountains,' Aboli estimated.

Within a few paces, Hal stumbled and hopped as his injured leg gave way under him. Without a word Aboli gave him his arm to help him over the rough ground to where he had tethered the horse. This time Hal did not protest when Aboli boosted him up onto its back and took the lead rein.

'Which direction?' Hal demanded. As he looked ahead the mountain barrier was riven into a labyrinth of ravines and soaring rock buttresses, of cliffs and deep gorges in which grew dense strips of forest and tangled scrub. He could pick out no path nor pass through this confusion.

'Althuda knows the way, and he has left signs for us to follow.' The spoor of five horses and the band of fugitives was deeply trodden ahead of them, but to enhance it Althuda had blazed the bark from the trees along his route. They followed at the best of their speed, and from the next ridge saw the tiny shapes of the five grey horses crossing a stretch of open ground two or three miles ahead. Hal could even make out Sukeena's small figure perched on the back of the leading horse. The silver colour of the horses made them stand out like mirrors in the dark, surrounding bush, and he murmured, 'They are beautiful animals, but they draw the eye of an enemy.'

'In the traces of a gentleman's carriage there could be no finer,' Aboli agreed, 'but in the mountains they would flounder. We must abandon them when we reach the rough ground, or else they will break their lovely legs in the rocks and crevices.'

'Leave them for the Dutch?' Hal asked. 'Why not a musket ball to end their suffering?'

'Because they are beautiful, and because I love them like my children,' said Aboli softly, reaching up and patting the animal's neck. The grey mare rolled an eye at him and whickered softly, returning his affection.

Hal laughed, 'She loves you also, Aboli. For your sake we will spare them.'

They plunged down the next slope and struggled up the far side. The ground grew steeper at each pace and the mountain crests seemed to hang suspended above their heads. At the top they paused again to let the mare blow, and looked ahead.

'It seems Althuda is aiming for that dark gorge dead ahead.' Hal shaded his eyes. 'Can you see them?'

'No,' Aboli grunted. 'They are hidden by the folds of the foothills and the trees.' Then he looked back again. 'But look behind you, Gundwane!'

Hal turned and stared where he pointed, and exclaimed as though he were in pain. 'How can they have come so quickly? They are gaining on us as though we were standing still.'

The column of running green-jackets was swarming over the ridge behind them like soldier ants from a disturbed nest. Hal could count their numbers easily and pick out the white officers. The mid-afternoon sunlight flashed from their bayonets and Hal could hear their faint but jubilant cries as they viewed their quarry so close ahead.

'There is Schreuder!' Hal exclaimed bitterly. 'By God, that man is a monster. Is there no means of stopping him?' The dismounted colonel was trotting along near the rear of the long, spread-out column but, as Hal watched him, he passed the man ahead of him on the path. 'He runs faster than his own Hottentots. If we linger here another minute, he will be up to us before we reach the mouth of the dark gorge.'

The ground ahead rose up so steeply that the horse could not take it straight up, and the path began to zigzag across the slope. There was another joyous cry from below, like the halloo of the fox hunter, and they saw their pursuers strung out over a mile or more of the track. The leaders were much closer now.

'Long musket shot,' Hal hazarded, and as he said it one of the leading soldiers dropped to his knee behind a rock and took deliberate aim before he fired. They saw the puff of muzzle smoke long before they heard the dull pop of the shot. The ball struck a blue chip off a rock fifty feet below where they stood. 'Still too far. Let them waste their powder.'

The grey mare leaped upwards over the rocky steps in the path, much surer on her feet than Hal could have hoped. Then they reached the outer bend in the wide dog-leg and started back across the slope. Now they were approaching their pursuers at an oblique angle, and the gap between them narrowed even faster.

The men on the path below welcomed them with joyous shouts. They flung themselves down to rest, to steady their pounding hearts and shaking hands. Hal could see them checking the priming in the pans of their muskets and lighting their slow-match, preparing themselves to make the shot as the grey mare and her rider came within fair musket range.

'Satan's breath!' Hal muttered. 'This is like sailing into an enemy broadside!' But there was nowhere to run or hide, and they laboured on up the path.

Hal could see Schreuder now: he had worked his way steadily towards the head of the column and was staring up at them. Even at this range Hal could see that he had driven himself far beyond his natural strength: his face was drawn and haggard, his uniform torn, filthy, soaked with sweat, and blood from a dozen scratches and abrasions. He heaved and strained for breath, but his sunken eyes burned with malevolence. He did not have the strength to shout or to shake a weapon but he watched Hal implacably.

One of the green-jackets fired and they heard the ball hum close over their heads. Aboli was urging on the mare at her best pace over the steep, broken path, but they would be within musket range for many more minutes. Now a ripple of fire ran along the line of soldiers along the path below. Musket balls thudded among the rocks around them, some flattening into shiny discs where they struck. Others sprayed chips of stone down upon them, or whined away in ricochet across the valley.

Unscathed, the grey mare reached the outward leg of the path and started back. Now the range was longer and most of the Hottentot infantrymen jumped to their feet and took up the pursuit. One or two started directly up the slope, attempting to cut the corner, but the hillside proved too sheer for even their nimble feet. They gave up, slid back to the angled pathway and hurried after their companions along the gentler but longer route.

A few soldiers remained kneeling in the path, and reloaded, stabbing the ramrods frantically down the muzzles of their muskets, then pouring blackpowder into the pan. Schreuder had watched the fusillade, leaning heavily against a rock while his pounding heart and laboured breathing slowed. Now he pushed himself upright and seized a reloaded musket from one of his Hottentots, elbowing the other man aside.

'We are beyond musket shot!' Hal protested. 'Why does he persist?'

'Because he is mad with hatred for you,' Aboli replied. 'The devil gives him strength to carry on.'

Swiftly Schreuder stripped off his coat and bundled it over the rock, making a cushion on which to rest the forestock of the musket. He looked down the barrel and picked up the pip of the foresight in the notch of the backsight. He settled it for an instant on Hal's bobbing head, then lifted it until he had a slice of blue sky showing beneath it, compensating for the drop of the heavy lead ball when it reached the limit of its carry. In the same motion he swept the sight ahead of the grey's straining head.

'He can never hope for a hit from there!' Hal breathed, but at that instant he saw the silver smoke bloom like a noxious flower on the stem of the musket barrel. Then he felt a mallet blow as the ball ploughed into the ribs of the grey mare an inch from his knee. Hal heard the air driven from the horse's punctured lungs. The brave animal reeled backwards and went down on its haunches. It tried to recover its footing by rearing wildly, but instead threw itself off the edge of the narrow path. Just in time, Aboli grabbed Hal's injured leg and pulled him from its back.

Hal and Aboli sprawled together on the rocks and looked down. The horse rolled until it struck the bend in the pathway, where it came to rest in a slide of small stones, loose earth and dust. It lay with all four legs kicking weakly in the air. A resounding shout of triumph went up from the pursuing soldiers, whose cries rang along the cliffs and echoed through the gloomy depths of the dark gorge.

Hal crawled shakily to his feet, and quickly assessed their circumstances. Both he and Aboli still had their muskets slung over their shoulders and their swords in their scabbards. In addition they each had a pair of pistols, a small powder horn and a bag containing musket balls strapped around their waists. But they had lost all else.

Below them their pursuers had been given new heart by this reverse in their fortunes and were clamouring like a pack of hounds with the smell of the chase hot in their nostrils. They came scrambling upwards.

'Leave your pistols and musket,' Aboli ordered. 'Leave the powder horn and sword also, or their weight will wear you down.'

Hal shook his head. 'We will need them soon enough. Lead the way on.' Aboli did not argue and went away at full stride. Hal stayed close behind him, forcing his injured leg to serve his purpose through the pain and the quivering weakness that spread slowly up his thigh.

Aboli reached back to hand him up over the more formidable steps in the pathway, but the incline became sharper as they laboured upwards and began to work round the sheer buttress of rock that formed one of the portals of the dark gorge. Now, at every pace forward, they were forced to step up onto the next level, as though they were on a staircase, and were skirting the sheer wall that dropped into the valley far below. The pursuers, though still close, were out of sight around the buttress.

'Are we sure this is the right path?' Hal gasped, as they stopped for a few seconds' rest on a broader step.

'Althuda is leaving sign for us still,' Aboli assured him, and kicked over the cairn of three small pebbles balanced upon each other which had been erected prominently in the centre of the path. 'And so are my grey horses.' He smiled as he pointed out a pile of shining wet balls of dung a little further ahead. Then he cocked his head. 'Listen!'

Now Hal could hear the voices of Schreuder's men. They were closer than they had been when last they had stopped. They sounded as though they were just round the corner of the buttress behind them. Hal looked at Aboli with dismay, and tried to balance on his good leg to conceal the weakness of the other. They could hear the clink of sword on rock and the clatter of loose stones underfoot. The soldiers' voices were so clear and loud that Hal could distinguish their words, and Schreuder's voice relentlessly urging his troops onwards.

'Now you will obey me, Gundwane!' said Aboli, and he leaned across and snatched Hal's musket. 'You will go on at your best speed while I hold them here for a while.' Hal was about to argue but Aboli looked hard into his eyes. 'The longer you argue the more danger you place me in,' he said.

Hal nodded. 'See you at the top of the gorge.' He clasped Aboli's arm in a firm grip, then hobbled on alone. As the path turned into the main gorge, Hal looked back and saw that Aboli had taken shelter crouching in the bend of the path, and that he had laid the two muskets on the rock in front of him, close to his hand.

Hal turned the corner, looked up and saw the gorge open up above him like a great gloomy funnel. The sides were sheer rock walls and it was roofed over by trees with tall thin stems that reached up for the sunlight. They were draped and festooned with lichens. A small stream came leaping down, in a series of pools and waterfalls, and the path took to this stream bed and climbed up over water-worn boulders. Hal dropped to his knees, plunged his face into the first pool and sucked up water, choking and coughing in his greed. As the water distended his belly he felt strength flow back into his swollen, throbbing leg.

From the other side of the buttress behind him there came the thud of a musket shot, then the thump of a ball striking flesh, followed immediately by the scream of a man thrown into the abyss, a scream that dwindled and faded as he fell away. It was cut off abruptly as he struck the rocks far below. Aboli had made certain of his first shot, and the pursuers would be thrown back in disarray. It would take them time to regroup and come on more cautiously, so he had won precious minutes for Hal.

Hal scrambled to his feet, and launched himself up the stream bed. Each of the huge, smooth boulders tested his injured leg to its limit. He grunted, groaned and dragged himself upward, listening at the same time for the sounds of fighting behind him, but he heard nothing more until he reached the next pool where he stopped in surprise.

Althuda had left the five grey horses tethered to a dead tree at the water's edge. When he looked beyond them to the next giant step in the stream bed, Hal knew why they had been abandoned here. They could no longer follow this dizzy path. The gorge was constricted into a narrow throat high above his head – and his own courage faltered as he surveyed the perilous route that he had to follow. But there was no other way, for the gorge had turned into a trap from which there was no escape. While he wavered, he heard from far below another musket shot and a clamour of angry shouts.

'Aboli has taken another,' he said aloud, and his own voice echoed weirdly from the high walls of the gorge. 'Now both his muskets are empty and he will have to run.' But Aboli had won this reprieve for him, and he dared not squander it. He drove himself at the steep path, dragging his wounded leg over glassy, water-polished rock, which was slippery and treacherous with slimy green algae.

His heart pounding with exhaustion, and his fingernails ripped to the quick, he crawled the last few feet upwards and reached the ledge in the throat of the gorge. Here he dropped flat on his belly and looked back over the edge. He saw Aboli coming up, leaping from rock to rock without hesitation, a musket clutched in each hand, not even glancing down to judge his footing on the treacherous boulders.

Hal looked up at the sky through the narrow opening of the gorge high above his head, and saw that day was fading. It would be dark soon, and the tops of the trees were turning to gold in the last rays of sunlight.

'This way!' he shouted down to Aboli.

'Go on, Gundwane!' Aboli shouted back. 'Do not wait for me. They are close behind!'

Hal turned and looked up the steep stream bed behind him. For the next two hundred paces it was in full view: if he and Aboli tried to continue the climb, then Schreuder and his men would reach this vantage point while their backs were still exposed. Before they could reach the next shelter they would be shot down by short-range musket fire.

We will have to make our stand here, he decided. We must hold them until nightfall, then try to slip away in the dark. Quickly he gathered loose rocks from the choked watercourse in which he hid and stacked them along the lip of the ledge. When he looked down he saw that Aboli had reached the foot of the rock wall and was climbing rapidly up towards him.

When Aboli was half-way up, and fully exposed, there was a shout from further down the darkening gorge. Through the gloom Hal made out the shape of the first of their pursuers. There came the flash and bang of a musket shot, and Hal peered down anxiously but Aboli was uninjured and still climbing fast.

Now the bottom of the gorge was swarming with men, and a fusillade of shots set the echoes booming and crashing. Hal picked out Schreuder down there in the gloom: his white face stood out among the darker ones that surrounded him.

Aboli reached the top of the rock-wall, and Hal gave him a hand on to the ledge. 'Why have you not gone on, Gundwane?' he panted.

'No time for talking.' Hal snatched one of the muskets from him and began to reload it. 'We have to hold them here until dark. Reload!'

'Powder almost finished,' Aboli replied. 'Only enough for a few more shots.' As he spoke he was plying the ramrod.

'Then we must make every shot tell. After that we will beat them back with rocks.' Hal primed the pan of his musket. 'And when we have run out of rocks to throw, we will take the steel to them.'

Musket balls began to buzz and crack around their heads as the men below opened up a sustained rolling volley. Hal and Aboli were forced to lie below the lip, every few seconds popping up their heads to take a quick glance down the wall.

Schreuder was using most of his men to keep up the fusillade, controlling them so that weapons were always loaded and ready to fire at his command while others reloaded. It seemed that he had chosen a team of his strongest men to scale the wall, while his marksmen tried to keep Hal and Aboli from defending themselves.

This first wave of a dozen or more climbers carrying only their swords rushed forward and hurled themselves at the rock wall, scrambling upwards. Then, as soon as Hal and Aboli's heads appeared over the lip, there came a thunderous volley of musket fire and the muzzle flashes lit the gloom.

Hal ignored the balls that flew around and splashed against the rock below him. He thrust out the barrel of his musket and aimed down at the nearest climber. This was one of the white Dutch corporals, and the range was point-blank. Hal's ball struck him in the mouth, smashed in his teeth and shattered his jawbone. He lost his grip on the slippery face, and fell backwards. He crashed into the three men below him, knocking them loose, and all four plummeted down to shatter on the rocks below.

Aboli fired and sent another two green-jackets slithering downwards. Then both he and Hal snatched up their pistols and fired again, then again, clearing the wall of climbers, except for two men who clung helplessly to a crevice half-way up the polished rock face.

Hal dropped the empty pistols and seized one of the boulders he had placed at hand. It filled his fist, and he hurled it down at the man below him. The green-jacket saw it coming, but could not avoid it. He tried to tuck his head into his shoulders but the rock caught him on the temple, his fingers opened and he fell.

'Good throw, Gundwane!' Aboli applauded him. 'Your aim is improving.' He threw at the last man on the wall and hit him under the chin. He teetered for a moment, then lost his grip and plunged down.

'Reload!' Hal snapped, and as he poured in powder he glanced at the strip of sky above them. 'Will the night never come?' he lamented, and saw Schreuder send the next wave of climbers to rush the wall. Darkness would not save them for, before they had reloaded the muskets, the enemy soldiers were already half-way up.

They knelt on the lip and fired again, but this time their two shots brought down only one of the attackers and the rest came on steadily. Schreuder sent another wave of climbers to join them and the entire wall seethed with dark figures.

'We cannot beat them all back,' Hal said, with black despair in his heart. 'We must retreat back up the gorge.' But when he looked up at the steep, boulder-strewn climb, his spirits quailed.

He flung down his musket and, with Aboli at his side, went at the treacherous slope. The first climbers came over the lip of the wall and rushed, shouting, after them.

In the gathering darkness Hal and Aboli struggled upwards, turning when the pursuers pressed them too closely to take them on with their blades and drive them back just far enough to give them respite to go on upwards. But now more and still more green-jackets had reached the top of the wall, and it was only a matter of minutes before they would be overtaken and overwhelmed.

Just ahead, Hal noticed a deep crevice in the side wall of the gorge and thought that he and Aboli might take shelter in its darkness. He abandoned the idea, however, as he came level with it and saw how shallow it was. Schreuder would hunt them out of there like a ferret driving out a couple of rabbits from a warren.

'Hal Courteney!' a voice called from the dark crack in the rock. He peered into it and, in its depths, saw two men. One was Althuda, who had called him, and the other was a stranger, a bearded, older man dressed in animal skins. It was too dark to see his face clearly, but when both he and Althuda beckoned urgently neither Hal nor Aboli hesitated. They threw themselves at the narrow opening and squeezed in, between the two men already there.

'Get down!' the stranger shouted in Hal's ear, and stood up with a short-handled axe in his hand. A soldier appeared in the opening of the crevice and raised his sword to thrust at the four men crowded into it, but Althuda threw up the pistol in his hand and shot him at close range in the centre of his chest.

At the same time the bearded stranger raised the axe high then

348

slashed down with a powerful stroke. Hal did not understand what he was doing, until he saw that the man had severed a rope of plaited bark, thick as a man's wrist and hairy. The axe bit cleanly through the taut rope, and as it parted the severed tail whipped away, as though impelled by some immense force. The end had been looped and knotted around a sturdy wooden peg, driven into a crack in the stone. The length of the rope ran round the corner of the crevice, then stretched upwards to some point lost in the gathering gloom higher up the steep gorge.

For a long minute nothing else happened, and Hal and Aboli stared at the other two in bewilderment. Then there was a creaking and a rustling from higher up the funnel of the gorge, a rumbling and a crackling as though a sleeping giant had stirred.

'Sabah has triggered the rockfall!' Althuda explained, and instantly Hal understood. He stared out into the gorge through the narrow entrance to the crevice. The rumbling became a gathering roar, and above it he could hear the wild, terrified screams of green-jackets caught full in the path of this avalanche. For them there was neither shelter nor escape. The gorge was a death trap into which Althuda and Sabah had lured them.

The roaring and grinding of rock rose to a deafening crescendo. The mountain seemed to tremble beneath them. The screams of the soldiers in its path were drowned, and suddenly a mighty river of racing boulders came sweeping past the entrance to the crevice. The light was blotted out, and the air was filled with dust and powdered rock so that the four men choked and gasped for breath. Blinded and suffocating, Hal lifted the tail of his ragged shirt and held it over his nose and mouth, trying to filter the air so that he could breathe in the tumultuous choking dust-storm thrown out by the tidal wave of rock and flying stone that poured past.

The avalanche went on for a long time but gradually the stream of moving rock dwindled to become a slow, intermittent slither and tumble of the last few fragments. At last silence, complete and oppressive, weighed down upon them, and the dust settled to reveal the outline of the opening to their shelter.

Aboli crawled out and balanced gingerly on the loose, unstable footing. Hal crept out beside him and both peered down the gloomy gorge. From wall to wall, it had been scoured clean by the avalanche. There was no sound or trace of their pursuers, not a last despairing cry or dying moan, not a shred of cloth or discarded weapon. It was as though they had never been.

Hal's injured leg could no longer bear his weight. He staggered and collapsed in the opening of the crevice. The fever in his blood from the festering wounds boiled up and filled his head with darkness and heat. He was aware of strong hands supporting him and then he lapsed into unconsciousness.

Colonel Cornelius Schreuder waited for an hour in the antechamber of the castle before Governor van de Velde condescended to see him. When, eventually, he was summoned by an aide-de-camp, he strode into the Governor's audience chamber, but still van de Velde declined to acknowledge his presence. He went on signing the documents and proclamations that Jacobus Hop laid before him, one at a time.

Schreuder was in full uniform, wearing all his decorations and stars. His wig was freshly curled and powdered, and his moustaches were dressed with beeswax into sharp spikes. Down one side of his face there were pink raw scars and scabs.

Van de Velde signed the last document and dismissed Hop with a wave of his hand. When the clerk had left and closed the doors behind him, van de Velde picked up Schreuder's written report from the desk in front of him as though it was a particularly revolting piece of excrement.

'So you lost almost forty men, Schreuder?' he asked heavily. 'Not to mention eight of the Company's finest horses.'

'Thirty-four men,' Schreuder corrected him, still standing stiffly to attention.

'Almost forty!' van de Velde repeated, with an expression of repugnance. 'And eight horses. The convicts and slaves you were pursuing got clean away from you. Hardly a famous victory, do you agree, Colonel?' Schreuder scowled furiously at the sculpted cornices on the ceiling above the Governor's head. 'The security of the castle is your responsibility, Schreuder. The minding of the prisoners is your responsibility. The safety of my person and that of my wife is also your responsibility. Do you agree, Schreuder?'

'Yes, your excellency.' A nerve beneath Schreuder's eye began to twitch.

'You allowed the prisoners to escape. You allowed them to plunder the Company's property. You allowed them to do grievous damage to this building with explosives. Look at my windows!' Van de Velde pointed at the empty casements from which the stained-glass panels had been blown. 'I have estimates from the Company surveyor that place the damage at over one hundred thousand guilders!' He was working himself steadily into a rage. 'A hundred thousand guilders! Then, on top of that,

350

you allowed the prisoners to abduct my wife and myself and to place us in mortal danger—' He had to break off to get his temper under control. 'Then you allowed almost forty of the Company's servants to be murdered, including five white men! What do you imagine will be the reaction of the Council of Seventeen in Amsterdam when they receive my full report detailing the depths of the dereliction of your duties, hey? What do you think they will say? Answer me, you jumped-up popinjay! What do you think they will say?'

'They may be somewhat displeased,' Schreuder replied stiffly.

'Displeased? Somewhat displeased?' shrieked van de Velde, and fell back in his chair, gasping for breath like a stranded fish. When he had recovered, he went on, 'You will be the first to know whether or not they are somewhat displeased, Schreuder. I am sending you back to Amsterdam in the deepest disgrace. You will sail in three days' time aboard the *Weltevreden*, which is anchored in the bay at this moment.'

He pointed out through the empty windows at the cluster of ships lying at anchor beyond the surf line. 'My report on the affair will go to Amsterdam on the same ship, together with my condemnation of you in the strongest possible terms. You will stand before the Seventeen and make your excuses to them in person.' He leered at the colonel gloatingly. 'Your military career is destroyed, Schreuder. I suggest you consider taking up the calling of whoremaster, a vocation for which you have demonstrated considerable aptitude. Goodbye, Colonel Schreuder. I doubt I shall have the pleasure of your company ever again.'

Aching with the Governor's insults as though he had taken twenty lashes of the cat, Schreuder strode out to the head of the staircase. To give himself time in which to regain his composure and his temper, he paused to survey the damage that the explosion had inflicted on the buildings surrounding the courtyard. The armoury had been destroyed, blown into a rubble heap. The roof timbers of the north wing were shattered and blackened by the fire that had followed the blast, but the outer walls were intact and the other buildings only superficially damaged.

The sentries who once would have leapt to attention at his appearance now delayed rendering him his honours, and when finally they tossed him a lackadaisical salute, one accompanied it with an impudent grin. In the tiny community of the colony news spread swiftly, and clearly his dishonourable discharge from the Company's service was already known to the entire garrison. Jacobus Hop must have taken pleasure in spreading the news, Schreuder decided, and he rounded on the grinning sentry. 'Wipe that smirk off your ugly face or, by God, I will shave it off with my sword.' The man sobered instantly and stared rigidly ahead. However, as Schreuder crossed the courtyard, Manseer and the overseers whispered together and smiled behind their fists. Even some of the recaptured prisoners, now wearing chains, who were repairing the damage to the armoury stopped work to grin slyly at him.

Such humiliation was painfully hard for a man of his pride and temperament to bear, and he tried to imagine how much worse it would become when he returned to Holland and faced the Council of Seventeen. His shame would be shouted in every tavern and port, in every garrison and regiment, in the salons of all the great houses and mansions of Amsterdam. Van de Velde was correct: he would become a pariah.

He strode out through the gates and across the bridge of the moat. He did not know where he was going, but he turned down towards the foreshore and stood above the beach staring out to sea. Slowly he brought his turbulent emotions under some control, and began to look for some escape from the scorn and the ridicule that he could not bear.

I shall swallow the ball, he decided. It's the only way open to me. Then, almost instantly, his whole nature revolted against such a craven course of action. He remembered how he had despised one of his brother officers in Batavia who, over the matter of a woman, had placed the muzzle of a loaded pistol in his mouth and blown away the back of his skull. 'It is the coward's way!' Schreuder said aloud. 'And not for me.'

Yet he knew he could never obey van de Velde's orders to return home to Holland. But neither could he remain here at Good Hope, nor travel to any Dutch possession anywhere upon this globe. He was an outcast, and he must find some other land where his shame was unknown.

Now his gaze focused on the cluster of shipping anchored out in Table Bay. There was the *Weltevreden*, upon which van de Velde wished to send him back to face the Seventeen. His eye moved on over the three other Dutch vessels lying near it. He would not sail on a Dutch ship but there were only two foreign vessels. One was a Portuguese slaver, outward-bound for the markets of Zanzibar. Even the thought of sailing on a slaver was distasteful – he could smell her from where he stood above the beach. The other ship was an English frigate and, by the looks of her, newly launched and well found. Her rigging was fresh and her paintwork only lightly marred by the Atlantic gales. She had the look of a warship, but he had heard that she was privately owned and an armed trader. He could read her name on her transom: the *Golden Bough*. She had fifteen gunports down the side, which she presented to him as she rode lightly at anchor, but he did not know whence she had come nor whither she was bound. However, he knew exactly where to find this

352

information so he settled his hat firmly over his wig and struck out along the shore, heading for the nearest of the insalubrious cluster of hovels that served as brothels and gin halls to the seafarers of the oceans.

Even at this hour of the morning the tavern was crowded, and the windowless interior was dark and rank with tobacco smoke and the fumes of cheap spirits and unwashed humanity. The whores were mostly Hottentots but there were one or two white women who had grown too old and pox-ridden to work in even the ports of Rotterdam or St Pauli. Somehow they had found ships to carry them southwards and had come ashore, like rats, to eke out their last days in these squalid surroundings before the French disease burned them out entirely.

His hand on the hilt of his sword, Schreuder cleared a small table for himself with a sharp word and haughty stare. Once he was seated he summoned one of the haggard serving wenches to bring him a tankard of small beer. 'Which are the sailors from the *Golden Bough*?' he asked, and tossed a silver rix-dollar onto the filthy table top. The trull snatched up this largesse and dropped it down the front of her grubby dress between her pendulous dugs before she jerked her head in the direction of three seamen at a table in the far corner of the room.

'Take each of those gentlemen another chamberpot filled with whatever foul piss you're serving them and tell them that I'm paying for it.'

When he left the tavern half an hour later Schreuder knew where the *Golden Bough* was heading, and the name and disposition of her captain. He sauntered down to the beach and hired a skiff to row him out to the frigate.

The anchor watch on board the *Golden Bough* spotted him as soon as he left the beach, and could tell by his dress and deportment that he was a man of consequence. When Schreuder hailed the deck of the frigate and asked for permission to come aboard, a stout, florid-faced Welsh petty-officer gave him a cautious greeting at the entryport, then led him down to the stern cabin where Captain Christopher Llewellyn rose to welcome him. Once he was seated, he offered Schreuder a pewter pot of porter. He was obviously relieved to find that Schreuder spoke good English. Llewellyn soon accepted him as a gentleman and an equal, relaxed and spoke easily and openly.

First they discussed the recent hostilities between their two countries, and expressed themselves pleased that a satisfactory peace had been concluded, then went on to speak about maritime trade in the eastern oceans and the temporal powers and politics that governed the regions of the East Indies and Further India. These were highly involved, and complicated by the rivalry between the European powers whose traders

353

and naval vessels were entering the Oriental seas in ever greater numbers.

'There are also the religious conflicts that embroil the eastern lands,' Llewellyn remarked. 'My present voyage is in response to an appeal by the Christian King of Ethiopia, the Prester John, for military assistance in his war against the forces of Islam.'

At the mention of war in the East Schreuder sat up a little straighter in his chair. He was a warrior, at the moment an unemployed warrior, and war was his trade. 'I had not heard of this conflict. Please tell me more about it.'

'The great Mogul has sent his fleet and an army under the command of his younger brother, Sadiq Khan Jahan, to seize the countries that make up the seaboard of the Great Horn of Africa from the Christian king.' Llewellyn broke off his explanation to ask, 'Tell me, Colonel, do you know much about the Islamic religion?'

Schreuder nodded. 'Yes, of course. Many of the men I have commanded over the last thirty years have been Muslims. I speak Arabic and I have made a study of Islam.'

'You will know, then, that one of the precepts of this militant belief is the *hadj*, the pilgrimage to the birthplace of the prophet at Mecca, which is situated on the eastern shores of the Red Sea.'

'Ah!' Schreuder said. 'I can see where you are heading. Any pilgrim from the Great Mogul's realm in India would be forced to enter the Red Sea by passing around the Great Horn of Africa. This would bring the two religions into confrontation in the region, am I correct in my surmise?'

'Indeed, Colonel, I commend you on your grasp of the religious and political implications. That is precisely the excuse being used by the Great Mogul to attack the Prester John. Of course, the Arabs have been trading with Africa since before the birth of either our Saviour, Jesus Christ, or the prophet Muhammad. From a foothold on Zanzibar island they have been gradually extending their domination onto the mainland. Now they are intent on the conquest and subjugation of the heartland of Christian Ethiopia.'

'And where, may I be so bold to ask, is your place in this conflict?' Schreuder asked thoughtfully

'I belong to a naval chivalric order, the Knights of the Temple of the Order of St George and the Holy Grail, committed to defend the Christian faith and the holy places of Christendom. We are the successors to the Knights Templar.'

'I know of your order,' Schreuder said, 'and I am acquainted with several of your brother knights. The Earl of Cumbrae, for one.'

'Ah!' Llewellyn sniffed. 'He is not a prime example of our membership.'

'I have also met Sir Francis Courteney,' Schreuder went on.

Llewellyn's enthusiasm was unfeigned. 'I know him well,' he exclaimed. 'What a fine seaman and gentleman. Do you know, by any chance, where I might find Franky? This religious war in the Great Horn would draw him like a bee to honey. His ship joined with mine would make a formidable force.'

'I am afraid that Sir Francis was a casualty of the recent war between our two countries.' Schreuder phrased it diplomatically, and Llewellyn looked distraught.

'I am saddened by that news.' He was silent for a while then roused himself. 'To give you the answer to your question, Colonel Schreuder, I am on my way to the Great Horn in response to the Prester's call for assistance to repel the onslaught of Islam. I intend sailing with the tide this very evening.'

'No doubt the Prester will be in need of military as well as naval assistance?' Schreuder asked abruptly. He was trying to disguise the excitement he felt. This was a direct answer to his prayers, 'Would you look kindly upon my request for passage aboard your fine ship to the theatre of war? I, also, am determined to offer my services.'

Llewellyn looked startled. 'A sudden decision, sir. Do you not have duties and obligations ashore? Would it be possible for you to sail with me at such short notice?'

'Indeed, Captain, your presence here in Table Bay seems like a stroke of destiny. I have this very day freed myself from the obligations of which you speak. It is almost as though I had divine premonition of this call to duty. I stand ready to answer the call. I would be pleased to pay for my passage, and that of the lady who is to be my wife, in gold coin.'

Llewellyn looked doubtful, scratched his beard and studied Schreuder shrewdly. 'I have only one small cabin unoccupied, hardly fit accommodation for persons of quality.'

'I would pay ten English guineas for the privilege of sailing with you,' Schreuder said, and the captain's expression cleared.

'I should be honoured by your company, and that of your lady. However, I cannot delay my departure by a single hour. I must sail with the tide. I will have a boat take you ashore and wait for you on the beach.'

As Schreuder was rowed away he was seething with excitement. The service of an oriental potentate in a religious war would surely offer opportunities for martial glory and enrichment far beyond what he could ever have expected in the service of the Dutch East India Company. He had been offered an escape from the threat of disgrace and ignominy. After this war, he might still return to Holland laden with gold and glory. This was the tide of fortune he had waited for all his life and, with the woman he loved beyond everything else at his side, he would take that tide at the full.

As soon as the boat beached he sprang out and tossed a small silver coin to the boatswain, 'Wait for me!' and strode off towards the castle. His servant was waiting in his quarters, and Schreuder gave him instructions to pack all his possessions, have them carried down to the foreshore and placed upon the *Golden Bough*'s longboat. It seemed that the entire garrison must know already of his dismissal. Even his servant was not surprised by his orders, so none would think it odd that he was moving out.

He shouted for his groom and ordered him to saddle his single remaining horse. While he waited for the horse to be brought round from the stables, he stood before the small mirror in his dressing room and rearranged his uniform, brushed out his wig and reshaped his moustaches. He felt a glow of excitement and a sense of release. By the time that the Governor realized that he and Katinka were gone, the *Golden Bough* would be well out to sea and on course for the Orient.

He hurried down the stairs, out into the yard where the groom now held his horse, and sprang into the saddle. He was in great haste, anxious to be away, and he pushed his mount to a gallop along the avenues towards the Governor's residence. His haste was not so great, however, as to deprive him of all caution. He did not ride up the front drive through the lawns in front of the mansion, but took the side road through the oak grove which was used by slaves and the suppliers of firewood and provisions from the village. He reined his horse in as soon as he was close enough for its hoofbeats to be heard in the residence, and walked the animal sedately into the stableyard behind the kitchens. As he dismounted a startled groom hurried out to take the horse, and Schreuder skirted the kitchen wall, entering the gardens through the small gate in the corner.

He looked about carefully for the gardeners were often working in this part of the estate, but he saw no sign of them. He walked across the lawns, neither dawdling nor hurrying, and entered the residence through the double doors that led into the library. The long, book-lined room was deserted.

Schreuder was well acquainted with the layout of the residence. He had visited Katinka often enough while her husband was about his duties in the castle. He went first to her reading room, which overlooked the lawns and a distant vista of the bay and the blue Atlantic. It was

Katinka's favourite retreat, but this noon she was not there. A female slave was on her knees in front of the bookshelves, taking down each volume one at a time and polishing the leather bindings with a soft cloth. She looked up, startled, as Schreuder burst in upon her.

'Where is your mistress?' he demanded, and when she gawked dumbly at him he repeated, 'Where is Mevrouw van de Velde?'

The slave girl scrambled to her feet in confusion. 'The mistress is in her bedroom. But she is not to be disturbed. She is unwell. She left strict instructions.'

Schreuder spun on his heel and went down the corridor. Gently he tried the handle of the door at the end of the passage, but it was locked from within. He exclaimed with impatience. Time was wasting away, and he knew Llewellyn would not hesitate to make good his threat to sail without him when the tide turned. He hurried back along the corridor and stepped through the glazed doors out onto the long veranda. He went down to the windows that opened into the principal bedroom suite. The windows to Katinka's closet were shuttered, and he raised his fist to knock upon them but restrained himself. He did not want to alert the house slaves. Instead he drew his sword, slipped the blade through the gap in the shutters and lifted the latch on the inside. He eased open the shutter and stepped inside over the sill.

Katinka's perfume assailed his senses and, for an instant, he felt giddy with his love and longing for her. Then with a surge of joy, he remembered that she would soon be his alone, the two of them voyaging out, hand in hand, to make a new life and fortune together. He crossed the wooden floor, stepping lightly so as not to frighten her, and gently drew aside the curtains from the door into the main bedroom. Here, also, the shutters were closed and latched and the room was in semi-darkness. He paused to allow his eyes to adjust to the dim light and saw that the bed was in disarray.

Then, in the gloom, he made out the pearly sheen of her flawless white skin amongst the tumbled bedlinen. She was nude, her back turned to him, her silver-gold hair cascading down to the cleft of her perfect buttocks. He felt a surge of lust, his loins engorged, and he was so overcome with wanting her that for a moment he could not move, could not even breathe.

Then she turned her head and looked straight at him. Her eyes flew wide and all the colour drained from her face.

'You despicable swine!' she said softly. 'How dare you spy upon me?' Her voice was low but filled with scorn and fury. He recoiled in astonishment. She was his lover, and he could not understand that she would speak to him thus, nor that she should look upon him with such contempt and fury. Then he saw that her naked breasts shone with the soft dew of her own sweat, and that she was seated astride a supine masculine form. The man beneath her lay upon his back, and she was impaled upon him, in the act of passion, riding him like a steed.

The man's body was muscular, white and hard, the body of a gladiator. With one explosive movement Katinka sprang off him and spun to face Schreuder. As she stood beside the bed trembling with outrage her inner thighs glistened with the overflow of her venery.

'What are you doing in my bedroom?' she hissed at Schreuder.

Stupidly he answered, 'I came to take you away with me.' But his eyes went down to the man's body. His pubic hair was wet and matted and his sex thrust up towards the ceiling, thick and swollen and glistening, with a shiny, viscous coating. The man sat upright and looked straight at Schreuder, with a flat yellow gaze.

A wave of unspeakable horror and revulsion swept over Schreuder. Katinka, his love, had been rutting with Slow John, the executioner.

Katinka was speaking, but her words barely made sense to him. 'You came to take me away? What gave you the notion that I would go with you, the Company clown, the laughing stock of the colony? Get out of here, you fool. Go into obscurity and shame where you belong.'

Slow John stood up from the bed. 'You heard her. Get out or I shall throw you out.' It was not the words but the fact that Slow John's penis was still fully tumescent that turned Schreuder into a maniac. His temper which, until now, he had been able to keep under restraint boiled over and took control of him. To the humiliation, insults and rejection that had been heaped upon him all that day was added the black rage of his jealousy.

Slow John stooped to the pile of his discarded clothing, which lay upon the tiles beside the bed, and straightened up again with a pruning knife in his right hand. 'I warn you,' he said in that deep, melodious voice, 'leave now, at once.'

With one fluid movement the Neptune sword sprang from its scabbard as though it were a living thing. Slow John was no warrior. His victims were always delivered to him trussed and chained. He had never been matched against a man like Schreuder. He jumped forward, the knife held low in front of him, but Schreuder flicked his own blade across the inner side of Slow John's wrist, severing the sinews so that the man's fingers opened involuntarily and the knife dropped to the tiles.

Then Schreuder thrust for the heart. Slow John had neither time nor chance to evade the stroke. The point took him in the centre of his broad, hairless chest and the blade buried itself right up to the jewelled pommel. The two men stood, locked together by the weapon. Gradually

358

Slow John's sex wilted and hung white and flaccid. His eyes glazed over and turned opaque and sightless as yellow pebbles. As he sank to his knees, Katinka began to scream.

Schreuder plucked the blade from the executioner's chest. Its burnished length was dulled by his blood. Katinka screamed again as a feather of bright heart-blood stood out of the wound in Slow John's chest, and he toppled headlong to the tiles.

'Don't scream,' Schreuder snarled, with the black rage still upon him, and advanced upon her with the sword in his hand. 'You have played me false with this creature. You knew I loved you. I came to fetch you. I wanted you to come away with me.' She backed away before him, both fists clenched upon her cheeks, and screamed in high, ringing hysteria.

'Don't scream,' he shouted. 'Be quiet. I cannot bear it when you do that.' The dreadful sound echoed in his head and made it ache, but she retreated from him, her cries louder now, a terrible sound, and he had to make her stop.

'Don't do that!' He tried to catch hold of her wrist, but she was too swift for him. She twisted out of his grip. Her screams grew even louder, and his rage broke its bounds as though it were some terrible black animal over which he had no control. The sword in his hand flew without his brain or his hand commanding it, and he stabbed her satiny white belly, just above the golden nest of her *mons veneris*.

Her scream turned to a higher, agonized shriek and she clutched at the blade as he jerked it from her flesh. It cut her palms to the bone, and he thrust again to quieten her, twice more in the belly.

'Quiet!' he roared at her and she turned away and tried to run for the doors of her closet, but he stabbed her in the back just above her kidneys, pulled out the blade and thrust between her shoulders. She fell and rolled on her back, and he stood over her and stabbed and hacked and thrust at her. Each time the blade passed clean through her body and struck the tiles on which she squirmed.

'Keep quiet!' he yelled, and kept on stabbing until her screams and sobs died away. Even then he continued to thrust at her, standing in the spreading pool of her blood, his uniform drenched with gouts of scarlet, his face and arms splashed and speckled so that he looked like a plague victim covered with the rash of the disease.

Then, slowly, the black rage drained from his brain, and he staggered back against the wall, leaving daubs of her blood across the whitewash.

'Katinka!' he whispered. 'I did not mean to hurt you. I love you so.'

She lay in the wide deep pool of her own blood. The wounds were like a choir of red mouths on her white skin. The blood still trickled from each of them. He had not dreamed there could be so much blood in that slim white body. Her head lay in a scarlet puddle, and her hair was soaked red. Her face was daubed thickly with it. Her features were twisted into a rictus of terror and agony that was no longer lovely to look upon.

'Katinka, my darling. Please forgive me.' He started across the floor towards her, stepping through the river of her blood that spread across the tiles. Then he stopped with the sword in his hand as, in the mirror across the room, he glimpsed a wild blood-smeared apparition staring back at him.

'Oh, sweet Mary, what have I done?' He tore his eyes from the creature in the mirror, and knelt beside the body of the woman he loved. He tried to lift her, but she was limp and boneless. She slid out of his embrace, and flopped into the puddle of her own blood.

He stood again and backed away from her. 'I did not mean you to die. You made me angry. I loved you, but you were unfaithful.'

Again he saw his own reflection in the mirror, 'Oh sweet God, the blood. There is so much.' He wiped, with sticky hands, at the mess of crimson that covered his jacket, then at his face, spreading the blood into a scarlet carnival mask.

For the first time he thought of flight, of the boat waiting for him on the beach and the frigate lying out in the bay. 'I cannot ride through the colony like this! I cannot go aboard like this!'

He staggered across the room to the door of the Governor's dressing room. He stripped off his sodden jacket and threw it from him. A pitcher of water was standing in a basin on the cabinet and he plunged his gory hands into it and sloshed it over his face. He seized the washcloth from its hook and soaked it in the pink water, then scrubbed at his arms and the front of his breeches.

'So much blood!' he kept repeating, as he wiped then rinsed the cloth and wiped again. He found a pile of clean white shirts on one of the shelves, and pulled one on over his damp chest. Van de Velde was a big man, and it fitted him well enough. He looked down and saw that the bloodstains were not so obvious on the dark serge of his breeches. His wig was stained so he pulled it off and flung it against the far wall. He chose another from the row set on blocks along the back wall. He found a woollen cloak that covered him from shoulders to calves. He spent a minute cleaning the blade and the sapphire of the Neptune sword, then thrust it back into its scabbard. When he looked again in the mirror he saw that his appearance would no longer shock or alarm. Then a thought struck him. He picked up his soiled jacket and ripped the stars and decorations from the lapels. He wrapped them in a clean neckcloth he

360

found on one of the shelves and stuffed them into the inner pocket of the woollen cloak.

He paused on the threshold of the Governor's dressing room and looked for the last time at the body of the woman he loved. Her blood was still moving softly across the tiles, like a fat, lazy adder. As he watched, it reached the edge of the smaller puddle in which Slow John lay. Their blood ran together, and Schreuder felt a deep sense of sacrilege that the pure should mingle thus with the base.

'I did not want this to happen,' he said hopelessly. 'I am so sorry, my darling. I wanted you to come with me.' He trod carefully over the rill of blood, went to the shuttered window and stepped out onto the veranda. He gathered the cloak around his shoulders and strode through the gardens to the small door in the stableyard where he shouted for the groom, who hurried up with his horse.

Schreuder rode down the avenue and crossed the Parade, looking straight ahead. The longboat was still on the beach and as he rode up the boatswain called to him, 'We was just about to give you up, Colonel. The *Golden Bough* is shortening her anchor cable and manning her yards.'

As he climbed to the deck of the frigate, Captain Llewellyn and his crew were so absorbed by the business of weighing anchor and getting the ship under sail that they paid him little heed. A midshipman showed him down to his small cabin, then hurried away leaving him alone. His travel chests had been brought aboard and were stowed under the narrow bunk. Schreuder stripped off all his soiled dress and found a clean uniform in one of his chests. Before donning it, he placed the stars and orders upon its lapels. His blood-smeared clothing he tied in a bundle, then looked around for something to weight it. Obviously the thin wooden bulkheads would be struck when the frigate was cleared for action, and his cabin would form part of the ship's gundeck. A culverin filled most of the available deck space. Beside the weapon was heaped a pyramid of iron cannonballs. He stuffed one into the bundle of blood-soaked clothing and waited until he felt the ship come on the wind and thrust out into the bay.

Then he opened the gunport a crack, and dropped the bundle through it into fifty fathoms of green water. When he went up on deck they were already a league offshore and running out strongly on the sou'easter to make their offing before coming about to round the cape.

Schreuder stared back at the land and made out the roof of the Governor's mansion among the trees at the base of the great mountain. He wondered if they had yet discovered Katinka's body, or whether she still lay joined in death to her base lover. He stood there at the stern rail until the great massif of Table Mountain was only a distant blue silhouette against the evening sky.

'Farewell, my darling,' he whispered.

It was only when he lay sleepless in his hard bunk at midnight that the enormity of his situation began to dawn upon him. His guilt was manifest. Every ship that left Table Bay would carry the tidings across the oceans and to every port in the civilized world. From this day forward he was a fugitive and an outlaw.

Hal woke to a sense of peace such as he had seldom known before. He lay with his eyes shut, too lazy and weak to open them. He realized that he was warm and dry and lying on a comfortable mattress. He expected the dungeon stench to assail him, the mouldy odour of damp, rotting straw, the latrine bucket and the smell of men who had not bathed for a twelve-month crowded together in a fetid hole in the earth. Instead he smelled fresh woodsmoke, perfumed and sweet, the scent of burning cedar faggots.

Suddenly the memories came flooding back, and, with a great lift of the spirits, he remembered their escape, that he was no longer a prisoner. He lay and savoured that knowledge. There were other smells and sounds. It amused him to try to recognize them without opening his eyes. There was the smell of the newly cut grass mattress on which he lay and the fur blanket that covered him, the aroma of meat grilling on the coals and another tantalizing fragrance that he could not place. It was a mingling of wild flowers and a warm kittenish musk that roused him strangely and added to his sense of well-being.

He opened his eyes slowly and cautiously, and was dazzled by the strong mountain light through the opening of the shelter in which he lay. He looked around and saw that it must have been built into the side of the mountain, for half the walls were of smooth rock and the sides nearest the opening were built of interwoven saplings daubed with red clay. The roof was thatch. Clay pots and crudely fashioned tools and implements were stacked against the inner wall. A bow and quiver hung from a peg near the door. Beside them hung his sword and pistols.

He lay and listened to the burble of a mountain stream, and then he heard a woman's laughter, merrier and more lovely than the tinkle of water. He raised himself slowly on one elbow, shocked by the effort it required, and tried to look through the doorway. The sound of an infant's laughter mingled with that of the woman. Through all his long

362

captivity he had heard nothing to equal it, and he could not help but chuckle with delight.

The sound of feminine laughter ceased and there was a quick movement outside the hut. A lissom gamine figure appeared in the opening, backlit by the sunshine so that she was only a lovely silhouette. Though he could not see her face, he knew straight away who it was.

'Good morrow, Gundwane, you have slept long, but did you sleep well?' Sukeena asked shyly. She had the infant on her hip and her hair was loose, hanging in a dark veil to her waist. 'This is my nephew, Bobby.' She joggled the baby on her hip and he gurgled with delight.

'How long did I sleep?' Hal asked, beginning to rise, but she passed the baby to someone outside, and came quickly to kneel beside the mattress. She restrained him with a small warm hand on his naked chest.

'Gently, Gundwane. You have been in fever sleep for many days.'

'I am well again now,' he said, and then recognized the mysterious perfume he had noticed earlier. It was her woman smell, the flowers in her hair and the soft warmth of her skin.

'Not yet,' she contradicted him, and he let her ease his head back onto the mattress. He was staring at her and she smiled without embarrassment.

'I have never seen anything so beautiful as you,' he said, then reached up and touched his own cheek. 'My beard?'

'It is gone.' She laughed, sitting back with her legs curled under her. 'I stole a razor from the fat Governor especially for the task.' She cocked her head on one side and studied him. 'With the beard gone, you also are beautiful, Gundwane.'

She blushed slightly as she realized the import of her words, and Hal watched in delight as the red-gold suffused her cheeks. She turned her full attention to his injured leg, drew back the fur blanket to expose it and unwound the bandage.

'Ah!' she murmured, as she touched it lightly. 'It heals marvellously well with a little help from my medicines. You have been fortunate. The bite from the fangs of a hound is always poisonous, and then the abuse to which you put the limb during our flight might have killed you or crippled you for the rest of your life.'

Hal smiled at her strictures as he lay back comfortably and surrendered himself to her hands.

'Are you hungry?' she asked, as she retied the dressing over his wound. At that question Hal realized that he was ravenous. She brought him the carcass of a wild partridge, grilled on the coals, and sat opposite him, watching with a proprietary air as he ate and then sucked the bones clean.

363

'You will soon be strong again.' She smiled. 'You eat like a lion.' She gathered up the scraps of his meal, then stood up. 'Aboli and your other seamen have been pleading with me for a chance to come to you. I will call them now.'

'Wait!' He stopped her. He wished that this intimate time alone with her would not end so soon. She sank down beside him once more and watched his face expectantly.

'I have not thanked you,' he said lamely. 'Without your care, I would probably have died of the fever.'

She smiled softly and said, 'I have not thanked you either. Without you, I would still be a slave.' For a time they looked at each other without speaking, openly examining each other's face in detail.

Then Hal asked, 'Where are we, Sukeena?' He made a gesture that took in their surroundings. 'This hut?'

'It is Sabah's. He has lent it to us. To you and me, and he has gone to live with the others of his band.'

'So we are in the mountains at last?'

'Deep in the mountains.' She nodded. 'At a place that has no name. In a place where the Dutch can never find us.'

'I want to see,' he said. For a moment she looked dubious, then nodded. She helped him to stand and offered her shoulder to support him as he hopped to the opening in the thatched shelter.

He sank down and leaned against the doorpost of rough cedar wood. Sukeena sat close beside him as he gazed about. For a long time neither spoke. Hal breathed deeply of the crisp, high air that smelled and tasted of the wild flowers that grew in such profusion about them.

''Tis a vision of paradise,' he said at last. The peaks that surrounded them were wild and splendid. The cliffs and gorges were painted with lichens that were all the colours of the artist's palette. The late sunlight fell full upon the mountain tops across the deep valley and crowned them with a golden radiance. The long shadow thrown by the peak behind them was royal purple. The water of the stream below was clear as the air they breathed, and Hal could see the fish lying like long shadows on the yellow sandbanks, fanning their dark tails to keep their heads into the current.

'It is strange, I have never seen this place nor any like it, and yet I feel as though I know it well. I feel a sense of homecoming, as though I was waiting to return here.'

''Tis not strange, Henry Courteney. I also was waiting.' She turned her head and looked deep into his eyes. 'I was waiting for you. I knew you would come. The stars told me. That day I first saw you on the Parade outside the castle, I recognized you as the one.'

364

There was so much to ponder in that simple declaration that he was silent again for a long while, watching her face.

'My father was also an adept. He was able to read the stars,' he said.

'Aboli told me.'

'So you, too, can divine the future from the stars, Sukeena.'

She did not deny it. 'My mother taught me many skills. I was able to see you from afar.'

He accepted her statement without question. 'So you must know what is to become of us, you and me?'

She smiled, and there was a mischievous gleam in her eye. She slipped a slim arm through his. 'I would not have to be a great sage to know that, Gundwane. But there is much else that I am able to tell of what lies ahead.'

'Tell me, then,' he ordered, but she smiled again and shook her head. 'There will be time later. We will have much time to talk while your leg heals and you grow strong again.' She stood up. 'But now I will fetch the others, I cannot deny them any longer.'

They came immediately, but Aboli was the first to arrive. He greeted Hal in the language of the forests. 'I see you well, Gundwane. I thought you would sleep for ever.'

'Without your help, I might indeed have done so.'

Then Big Daniel and Ned and the others came to touch their foreheads and mumble their self-conscious greetings and squat in a semi-circle in front of him. They were not much given to expressing their emotions in words, but what he saw in their eyes when they looked at him warmed and fortified him.

'This is Sabah, whom you already know.' Althuda led him forward.

'Well met, Sabah!' Hal seized his hand. 'I have never been happier to see another man than I was that night in the Gorge.'

'I would have liked to come to your aid much sooner,' Sabah replied in Dutch, 'but we are few and the enemy were as numerous as ticks on an antelope's belly in spring.' Sabah sat down in the ring of men and, with an apologetic air, began to explain. 'The fates have not been kind to us here in the mountains. We did not have the services of a physician such as Sukeena. We who were once nineteen are now only eight and two of those a woman and an infant. I knew we could not help you fight out in the open, for in hunting for food we have used up all our gunpowder. However, we knew Althuda would bring you up Dark Gorge. We built the rockfall knowing that the Dutch would follow you.'

'You did the brave and wise thing,' Hal said.

Althuda brought his woman out of the gathering darkness. She was a

365

pretty girl, small and darker-skinned than he was, but Hal could not doubt that Althuda was the father of the boy on her hip.

'This is Zwaantie, my wife, and this is my son, Bobby.' Hal held out his hands and Zwaantie handed him the child. He held Bobby in his lap, and the little boy regarded him with huge solemn black eyes.

'He is a likely lad, and strong,' Hal said, and father and mother smiled proudly.

Zwaantie lifted the infant and strapped him on her back. Then she and Sukeena built up the fire and began to cook the evening meal of wild game and the fruits of the mountain forests, while the men talked quietly and seriously.

First Sabah explained their circumstances, addressing himself directly to Hal, enlarging on the brief report he had already given. Hal soon understood that, despite the beauty of their surroundings now in the summertime and the seeming abundance of the meal that the women were preparing, the mountains were not always as hospitable. During winter the snows lay thick even in the valleys and game was scarce. However, they dared not move down to lower altitudes where they would be seen by the Hottentot tribes and their whereabouts reported to the Dutch at Good Hope.

'The winters here are fierce,' Sabah summed up. 'If we stay here for another, then few of us will be left alive this time next year.' During their captivity Hal's seamen had garnered enough knowledge of the Dutch language to enable them to follow what Sabah had to say, and when he had finished speaking they were all silent and stared glumly into the fire, munching disconsolately on the food the women brought to them.

Then, one at a time, their heads turned towards Hal. Big Daniel spoke for them all when he asked, 'What are we going to do now, Sir Henry?'

'Are you seamen or mountaineers?' Hal answered his question with a question, and some of the men chuckled.

'We were born in Davey Jones's locker and we were all of us given salt water for blood,' Ned Tyler answered.

'Then I will have to take you down to the sea and find you a ship, won't I?' said Hal. They looked confused but some chuckled again, though half-heartedly.

'Master Daniel, I want a manifest of all the weapons, powder and other stores that we were able to bring with us,' Hal said briskly.

'There weren't much of anything, Captain. Once we left the horses we had just about enough strength left to get ourselves up the mountains.'

'Powder?' Hal demanded.

'Only what we had in our flasks.'

'When you went on ahead, you had two full kegs on the horses.'

'Those kegs weighed fifty pounds apiece.' Daniel looked ashamed. 'Too much cargo for us to haul.'

'I have seen you carry twice that weight.' Hal was angry and disappointed. Without a store of powder they were at the mercy of this wild terrain, and the beasts and tribes that infested it.

'Daniel carried my saddle-bags up Dark Gorge.' Sukeena intervened softly. 'No one else could do it.'

'I'm sorry, Captain,' Daniel muttered.

But Sukeena supported him fiercely. 'There is not a thing in my bags that we could do without. That includes the medicines that saved your leg and will save every one of us from the hurts and pestilences that we will meet here in the wilderness.'

'Thank you, Princess,' Daniel murmured, and looked at her like an affectionate hound. If he had possessed a tail Hal knew he would have wagged it.

Hal smiled and clapped Daniel's shoulder. 'I find no fault with what you did, Big Danny. There is no man alive who could have done better.'

They all relaxed and smiled. Then Ned asked, 'Were you serious when you promised us a ship, Captain?'

Sukeena stood up from the fire. 'That's enough for tonight. He must regain his strength before you plague him further. You must go now. You may come again tomorrow.'

One at a time they came to Hal, shook his hand and mumbled something incoherent, then wandered off through the darkness towards the other huts spread out along the valley floor. When the last had gone Sukeena threw another cedar log on the fire then came and sat close beside him. In a natural, possessive manner, Hal placed his arm around her shoulders. She leaned her slim body against him and fitted her head into the notch of his shoulder. She sighed, a sweet, contented sound, and neither spoke for a while.

'I want to stay here at your side like this for ever, but the stars may not allow it,' she whispered. 'The season of our love may be short as a winter day.'

'Don't say that,' Hal commanded. 'Never say that.'

They both looked up at the stars, and here, in the high thin air, they were so brilliant that they lit the heavens with the luminescence of the mother-of-pearl that lines the inside of an abalone shell taken fresh from the sea. Hal looked upon them with awe and considered what she had said. He felt a sense of hopelessness and sadness come upon him. He shivered.

Immediately she sat up straight and said softly, 'You grow cold. Come, Gundwane!'

She helped him to his feet and led him into the hut, to the mattress against the far wall. She laid him upon it and then lit the wick of the small clay oil lamp and placed it on a shelf in the rock wall. She went to the fire and lifted off the clay pot of water that stood on the edge of the coals. She poured steaming water into an empty dish and mixed in cold water from the pot beside the door until the temperature suited her.

Her movements were unhurried and calm. Propped on one elbow, Hal watched her. She placed the dish of warm water in the centre of the floor then poured a few drops from a glass vial into it and stirred it again with her hand. He smelt its light, subtle perfume on the waft of steam.

She rose, went to the doorway and closed the animal-skin curtain over the opening, then came back and stood beside the dish of scented water. She removed the wild flowers from her hair and tossed them onto the fur blanket at Hal's feet. Without looking at him, she let down the coils of her hair and combed them out until they shimmered like a wave of obsidian. She began to sing in her own language as she combed, a lullaby or a love song, Hal could not be certain. Her voice was mellifluous; it soothed and delighted him.

She laid aside her comb, and let the shift slip from her shoulders. Her skin gleamed in the yellow lamplight and her breasts were pert as small golden pears. When she turned her back to him Hal felt deprived that they were hidden from his sight. Her song changed now – it had a lilt of joy and excitement in it.

'What is it you sing?' Hal asked.

Sukeena smiled at him over her bare shoulder. 'It is the wedding song of my mother's people,' she answered. 'The bride is saying that she is happy and that she loves her husband with the eternal strength of the ocean, and the patience of the shining stars.'

'I have never heard anything so pleasing,' Hal whispered.

With slow voluptuous movements, she unwrapped the sarong from around her waist and threw it aside. Her buttocks were small and neat, the deep cleft dividing them into perfect ovals. She squatted down beside the dish to soak a small cloth in the scented water and began to bathe herself. She started at her shoulders and washed each arm down to her long tapered fingertips. There were silky clusters of black curls in her armpits.

Hal realized that it was a ritual bath she was performing, part of some ceremony she was enacting before him. He watched avidly each move she made, and every now and then she looked up and smiled at him shyly. The soft hairs behind her ears were damp from the cloth, and water droplets gleamed on her cheeks and upper lip.

She stood at last and turned slowly to face him. Once he had thought her body boyish, but now he saw that it was so feminine that his heart swelled hard with desire for her. Her belly was flat but smooth as butter, and at its base was a triangle of dark fur, soft as a sleeping kitten.

She stepped away from the dish and dried herself on the cotton shift she had discarded. Then she went to the oil lamp, cupped one hand around the wick and leaned towards it as if to snuff out the flame.

'No!' said Hal. 'Leave the light. I want to look at you.'

At last she came to him, gliding across the stone floor on small bare feet, crept onto the bed beside him, into his arms, and folded her body against his. She held her lips to his mouth. Hers were soft and wet and warm, and her breath mingled with his, and smelled of the wild flowers she had worn in her hair.

'I have waited all my life for you,' she whispered into his mouth.

He whispered back, 'It was too long to wait, but I am here at last.'

In the morning she proudly displayed the treasures she had brought for him in her saddle-bags. She had somehow procured everything he had asked for in the notes he had left for Aboli in the wall of the castle.

He snatched up the charts. 'Where did you get these from, Sukeena?' he demanded, and she was delighted to see how much value he placed upon them.

'I have many friends in the colony,' she explained. 'Even some of the whores from the taverns came to me to treat their ailments. Dr Saar kills more of his patients than he saves. Some of the tavern ladies go aboard the ships in the bay to do their business, and come back with divers things, not all of them gifts from the seamen.' She laughed merrily. 'If something is not bolted to the deck of the galleon they think it belongs to them. When I asked for charts these are what they brought me. Are they what you wanted, Gundwane?'

'These are more than I ever hoped for, Sukeena. This one is valuable and so is this.' The charts were obviously some navigator's treasures, highly detailed and covered with notations and observations in a well-formed, educated hand. They showed the coasts of southern Africa in wondrous detail, and from his own knowledge he could see how accurate they were. To his amazement the location of Elephant Lagoon was marked on one, the first time he had ever seen it shown on any chart other than his father's. The position was accurate to within a few minutes of angle, and in the margin there was a sketch of the landfall and seaward elevation of the heads, which he recognized instantly as having been drawn from observation.

Although the coast and the immediate littoral were accurately recorded, the interior, as usual, had been left blank or filled with conjecture, apocryphal lakes and mountains that no eye had ever beheld. The outline of the mountains in which they were now sequestered was sketched in, as though the cartographer had observed them from the colony of Good Hope or from sailing into False Bay and had guessed their shape and extent. Somewhere, somehow, Sukeena had found him a Dutch mariners' almanac to go with the charts. It had been published in Amsterdam and listed the movements of the heavenly bodies until the end of the decade.

Hal laid aside these precious documents and took up the backstaff Sukeena had found. It was a collapsible model whose separate parts fitted into a small leather case, the interior of which was lined with blue velvet. The instrument itself was of extraordinarily fine workmanship: the bronze quadrant, decorated with embodiments of the four winds, needles and screws were all engraved and worked in pleasing artistic shapes and classical figures. A tiny bronze plaque inside the lid of the case was engraved 'Cellini. Venezia'.

The compass she had brought was contained in a sturdy leather case; the body was brass and the magnetic needle was tipped with gold and ivory, so finely balanced that it swung unerringly into the north as he rotated the case slowly in his hand.

'These are worth twenty pounds at least!' Hal marvelled. 'You're a magician to have conjured them up.' He took her hand and led her outside, not limping as awkwardly as he had on the previous day. Seated side by side on the mountain slope he showed her how to observe the noon passage of the sun and to mark their position on one of the charts. She delighted in the pleasure she had given him, and impressed him with her immediate grasp of the esoteric arts of navigation. Then he remembered that she was an astrologer, and that she understood the heavens.

With these instruments in his hands, he could move with authority through this savage wilderness, and his dream of finding a ship began to seem less forlorn than it had only a day before. He drew her to his chest, kissed her, and she merged herself tenderly to him. 'That kiss is better reward than the twenty pounds of which you spoke, my captain.'

'If one kiss is worth twenty pounds, then I have aught for you that must be worth five hundred,' he said, laid her back in the grass and made love to her. A long time later she smiled up at him and whispered, 'That was worth all the gold in this world.'

When they returned to the encampment they found that Daniel had assembled all the weapons, and that Aboli was polishing the sword blades and sharpening the edges with a fine-grained stone he had picked from the stream bed.

Hal went carefully over the collection. There were cutlasses enough to arm every man, and pistols too. However, there were only five muskets, all standard Dutch military models, heavy and robust. Their lack was in powder, slow-match and lead ball. They could always use pebbles as missiles, but there was no substitute for blackpowder. They had less than five pounds weight of this precious substance in the flasks, not enough for twenty discharges.

'Without powder, we can no longer kill the larger game,' Sabah told Hal. 'We eat partridges and dassies.' He used the diminutive of the Dutch name for badger, *dasc*, to describe the fluffy, rabbity creatures that swarmed in the caves and crevices of every cliff. Hal thought he recognized them as the coneys of the Bible.

The urine from the dassie colonies poured down the cliff face so copiously that as it dried it covered the rock with a thick coating that shone in the sunlight like toffee but smelt less sweet. With care and skill, these rock-rabbits could be killed and trapped in such numbers as to provide the little band with a staple of survival. Their flesh was succulent and delicious as suckling pig.

Now that Sukeena was with them their diet was much expanded by her knowledge of edible roots and plants. Each day Hal went out with her to carry her basket as she foraged along the slopes. As his leg grew stronger they ventured further and stayed out in the wilderness a little longer each day.

The mountains seemed to enfold them in their grandeur and to provide the perfect setting for the bright jewel of their love. When Sukeena's foraging basket was filled to overflowing, they found hidden pools in the numerous streams in which to bathe naked together. Afterwards they lay side by side on the smooth, water-polished rocks and dried themselves in the sun. With tantalizing slowness they toyed with each other's bodies and at last made love. Then they talked and explored each other's minds as intimately as they had explored their bodies, and afterwards made love yet again. Their appetites for each other seemed insatiable.

'Oh! Where did you learn to please a girl so?' Sukeena asked breathlessly. 'Who taught you all these special things that you do to me?'

It was not a question he cared to answer, and he said, "Tis simply that we fit together so perfectly. My special places were made to touch your special places. I seek pleasure in your pleasure. My pleasure is increased a hundredfold by yours.'

In the evenings when all the fugitives gathered around the cooking fire, they pressed Hal with questions about his plans for them, but he avoided these with an easy laugh or a shake of his head. A plan of action was indeed germinating in his mind but it was not yet ready to be disclosed, for there were still many obstacles he had to circumvent. Instead he questioned Sabah and the five escaped slaves, who with him had survived the mountain winter.

'How far to the east have you travelled across the range, Sabah?'

'In midwinter we travelled six days in that direction. We were trying to find food and a place where the cold was not so fierce.'

'What land lies to the east?'

'It is mountains such as these for many leagues, and then suddenly they fall away into plains of forest and rolling grassland, with glimpses of the sea on the right hand.' Sabah took up a twig and began to draw in the dust beside the fire. Hal memorized his descriptions, questioning him assiduously, urging him to recall every detail of what he had seen.

'Did you descend into these plains?'

'We went down a little way. We found strange creatures never before seen by the eyes of man – grey and enormous with long horns set upon their noses. One rushed upon us with terrible snorts and whistles. Though we fired our muskets at it, it came on and impaled the wife of Johannes upon its nose horn and killed her.'

They all looked at little one-eyed Johannes, one of Sabah's band of escaped slaves, who wept at the memory of his dead woman. It was strange to see tears squeezing out of his empty eye socket. They were all silent for a while, then Zwaantie took up the story. 'My little Bobby was only a month old, and I could not place him in such danger. Without powder for the muskets we could not go on. I prevailed on Sabah to turn back, and we returned to this place.'

'Why do you ask these questions? What is your plan, Captain?' Big Daniel wanted to know, but Hal shook his head.

'I'm not ready to explain it to you, but don't lose heart, lads. I have promised to find you a ship, have I not?' he said, with more confidence than he felt. In the morning, on the pretence of fishing, he led Aboli and Big Daniel up the stream to the next pool. When they were out of sight of the camp, they sat close together on the rocky bank.

'It is clear that unless we can better arm ourselves, we are trapped in these mountains. We will perish as slowly and despondently as most of Sabah's men already have. We must have powder for the muskets.'

'Where will we get that?' Daniel asked. 'What do you propose?'

'I have been thinking about the colony,' Hal told them.

Both men stared at him in disbelief. Aboli broke the silence. 'You plan to go back to Good Hope? Even there you will not be able to lay your hands on powder. Oh, perhaps you might steal a pound or two from the green-jackets at the bridge, or from a Company hunter, but that is not enough to see us on our journey.'

'I planned to break into the castle again,' Hal said.

Both men laughed bitterly. 'You lack not in enterprise or in heart, Captain,' Big Daniel said, 'but that is madness.'

Aboli agreed with him, and said, in his deep, thoughtful voice, 'If I thought there were even the poorest chance of success, I would gladly go alone. But think on it, Gundwane, I do not mean merely the impossibility of winning our way into the castle armoury. Say, even, that we succeeded in that, and that the store of powder we destroyed has since been replenished by shipments from Holland. Say that we were able to escape with some of it. How would we carry even a single keg back across the plains with Schreuder and his men pursuing us? This time we would not have the horses.'

In his heart Hal had known that it was madness, but he had hoped that even such a desperate and forlorn proposal might fire them to think of another plan.

At last, Aboli broke the silence. 'You spoke of a plan to find a ship. If you tell us that plan, Gundwane, then perhaps we can help you to bring it to pass.' Both men looked at him expectantly.

'Where do you suppose the Buzzard is at this very moment?' Hal asked.

Aboli and Big Daniel looked startled. 'If my prayers have prevailed he is roasting in hell,' Daniel replied bitterly.

Hal looked at Aboli. 'What do you think, Aboli? Where would you look for the Buzzard?'

'Somewhere out on the seven seas. Wherever he smells gold or the promise of easy pickings, like the carrion bird for which he is named.'

'Yes!' Hal clapped him on the shoulder. 'But where might the smell of gold be strongest? Why did the Buzzard buy Jiri and our other black shipmates at auction?'

Aboli stared blankly at him. Then a slow smile spread over his wide, dark face. 'Elephant Lagoon!' he exclaimed.

Big Daniel boomed with excited laughter. 'He scented the treasure from the Dutch galleons and he thought our Negro lads could lead him to it.'

'How far are we from Elephant Lagoon?' Aboli asked.

'By my reckoning, three hundred sea miles.' The immensity of the distance silenced them.

'It's a long tack,' said Daniel, 'without powder to defend ourselves on the way or with which to fight the Buzzard if we get there.'

Aboli did not reply, but looked at Hal. 'How long will the journey take us, Gundwane?'

'If we can make good ten miles a day, which I doubt, perhaps a little over a month.'

'Will the Buzzard still be there when we arrive, or will he have given up his search and sailed away?' Aboli thought aloud.

'Aye!' Daniel muttered. 'And if he has gone what will become of us then? We'd be marooned there for ever.'

'Do you prefer to be marooned here, Master Daniel? Do you want to die of cold and starvation on this God-forsaken mountain when winter comes round again?'

They were quiet again. Then Aboli said, 'I am ready to leave now. There is no other path open to us.'

'But what of Sir Henry's leg? Is it strong enough yet?'

'Give me another week, lads, and I'll walk the hind legs off all of you.'

'What do we do if we find the Buzzard still roosting at Elephant Lagoon?' Daniel was not ready to agree so easily. 'He has a crew of a hundred well-armed ruffians and, if all of us survive the journey, we will be a dozen armed with swords alone.'

'That's fine odds!' Hal laughed at him. 'I've seen you take on much worse. Powder or no powder, we're off to find the Buzzard. Are you with us or not, Master Daniel?'

'Of course, I'm with you, Captain.' Big Daniel was affronted. 'What made you think I was not?'

That night, around the council fire, Hal explained the plan to the others. When he had finished he looked at their sombre faces in the firelight. 'I will prevail on no man to come with us. Aboli, Daniel and I are determined to go, but if any amongst you wishes to remain here in the mountains we will leave half the store of weapons with you, including half the remaining gunpowder, and we will think no ill of you. Are there any of you who wish to speak?'

'Yes,' said Sukeena, without looking up from the food she was cooking. 'I go wherever you go.'

'Bravely spoken, Princess,' grinned Ned Tyler. 'And I go also.'

'Aye!' said the other seamen in unison. 'We are all with you.'

Hal nodded his thanks to them, and then looked at Althuda. 'You have a woman and your son to think of, Althuda. What say you?'

He could see the distress on the face of little Zwaantie as she suckled the baby at her breast. Her dark eyes were filled with doubts and misgivings. Althuda lifted her to her feet and led her away into the darkness.

When they were gone Sabah spoke for all his band. 'Althuda is our leader. He brought us out of captivity, and we cannot leave him and Zwaantie alone in the wilderness to perish with the baby of cold and hunger. If Althuda goes we go, but if he stays we must stay with him.'

'I admire your resolve and your loyalty, Sabah,' said Hal.

They waited in silence, hearing Zwaantie weeping with fear and indecision in the darkness. Then, after a long while, Althuda led her back to the fire, his arm around her shoulders, and they took their places in the circle.

'Zwaantie fears not for herself but for the baby,' he said. 'But she knows that our best chance will be with you, Sir Hal. We will come with you.'

'I would have mourned if your decision had been different, Althuda.' Hal smiled with genuine pleasure. 'Together our chances are much increased. Now we must make our preparations and agree on the time when we will set out.'

Sukeena came from the fire to sit beside Hal, and spoke out firmly: 'Your leg will not be healed for at least another five days. I will not allow you to march upon it before then.'

'When the Princess speaks,' Aboli declared, in his deep voice, 'only a foolish man does not listen.'

During those last days Hal and Sukeena foraged for the herbs and plants that she would use for medicine and food. The last of the infection in Hal's wounds yielded to her treatment, while climbing and descending the steep and rugged slopes of the mountains rapidly strengthened his injured limb.

On the day before the journey was due to commence, the two stopped at midday to bathe and rest and make love in the soft grass beside the stream. This was a branch of the river that they had not visited on their previous forays, and while Hal lay surfeited with passion in the warm sunlight, Sukeena stood up naked and moved away up the ravine a short distance to ease herself.

Hal watched her squat behind a patch of low bush, lay back and closed his eyes, drifting lazily to the edge of sleep. He was roused by the familiar sound of Sukeena's sharp pointed digging stick pounding into the earth. A few minutes later she returned, still naked, but with a crumbling lump of yellow earth in her hand.

'Flower crystals! The first I have found in these mountains.' She looked delighted with her discovery, and emptied some of the less valuable herbs from her basket to make place for the lumps of friable earth. 'Part of these mountains must once have been volcanoes for the flower crystals are spewed up from the earth in the lava.'

Hal watched her work, more interested in the way her naked body gleamed in the sunlight, like molten gold, and the way her small breasts changed shape as she wielded the stick vigorously, than in the crystalline lumps of yellow earth she was prising from the bank of the ravine.

'What do you use this earth for?' he asked, without rising from his grassy nest.

'It has many uses. It is a sovereign cure for headaches and colic. If I mix it with the juice of the verbena berry it will soothe palpitations of the heart and ease a woman's monthly courses . . .' She reeled off a list of the ailments that she could treat with it, but to Hal it did not seem to have any special virtue, and looked like any other clod of dry earth. The basket was so heavy by now that, on their return to camp, Hal had to take it from her.

That night while the band sat around the fire and held their final council before beginning the long journey east, Sukeena pounded the clods of earth in the crude stone mortar she had made and mixed the powder into a pot of water. She heated this over the fire, then came to sit beside Hal as he went over the order of march for the following day. He was allocating weapons and loads to the men. The weight and bulk of each load would be dictated by the age and strength of the man carrying it.

Suddenly Hal broke off and sniffed the air. 'Sweet heaven and all the apostles!' he cried. 'What have you in this pot, Sukeena?'

'I told you, Gundwane. 'Tis the yellow flowers.' She looked alarmed as he rushed back to her, picked her up in his arms, tossed her high in the air and caught her as she came down, skirts fluttering around her.

''Tis not any type of flower at all! I would know that smell in hell itself where it truly belongs!' He kissed her until she pushed his face away.

'Are you mad?' She laughed and gasped for breath.

'Mad with love for you!' he said, and turned her to face the men who had watched this display in amazement. 'Lads, the Princess has created the miracle which will save us all!'

'You speak in riddles!' said Aboli.

'Yes!' the others cried. 'Speak plain, Captain.'

'I'll speak plain enough so even the slowest-witted of you sea-rats will understand my words.' Hal laughed at their confusion. 'Her pot is filled with brimstone! Magical yellow brimstone!'

It was Ned Tyler who understood first, for he was the master gunner.

He also leaped to his feet, rushed to kneel over the pot and inhaled the fumes as though they were the smoke of an opium pipe.

'The captain's right, lads,' he howled with glee. 'It's brimstone sulphur, sure enough.'

Sukeena led a party, headed by Aboli and Big Daniel, back to the ravine in which she had discovered the sulphur deposit, and they returned to camp staggering under their loads of the yellow earth, packed into baskets or sewn into sacks made of animal skins.

While Sukeena supervised the boiling and leaching of the sulphur crystals from the ore, one-eyed Johannes and Zwaantie tended the slow fires, banked with earth, in which the baulks of cedarwood were being gradually reduced to pure black nuggets of charcoal.

Hal and Sabah's band climbed the steep mountainside above the camp to reach the cliffs in which the multitudes of rock rabbits had their colonies. Sabah's men clung to the precipice like flies to the wall as they scraped away the amber coloured crystals of dried urine. The little animals defecated in communal middens, and while the round pellets of dung rolled away, the urine dribbled down and soaked the rock face. They discovered that, in some places, this coating was several feet thick.

They lowered skin sacks of these odoriferous deposits to the foot of the cliff, then lugged them down to the camp. They worked in shifts to keep the fires burning all day and night under the clay pots, extracting the sulphur from the powdered earth and the saltpetre from the animal excreta.

Ned Tyler and Hal, the two gunners, hovered over these steaming pots like a pair of alchemists, straining the liquid and reducing it with heat. Finally they dried the thick residual pastes in the sun. From the first brewing of the stinking compounds they were left with a store of dried crystalline powders that filled three large pots.

When crushed the charcoal was a smooth black powder, while the saltpetre was pale brown and fine as sea salt. When Hal placed a small pinch of it on his tongue it was indeed as pungent and salty as the sea. The flowers of sulphur were daffodil yellow and almost odourless.

The entire band of fugitives gathered round to watch when, at last, Hal started to mix the three constituents in Sukeena's stone mortar. He measured the proportions and first ground together the charcoal and the sulphur, for without the final vital ingredient these were inert and harmless. Then he added the saltpetre and gingerly combined it with

377

the dark grey primary powder until he had a flask filled with what looked and smelt like veritable gunpowder.

Aboli handed him one of the muskets and he measured a charge, dribbled it down the barrel, stuffed a wad of fibrous dried bark on top of it and rodded home a round pebble he had selected from the sandbank of the stream. He would not waste a lead ball in this experiment.

Meanwhile, Big Daniel had set up a wooden target on the opposite bank. While Hal squatted and took his aim the rest spread out on either side of him and plugged their ears with their fingers. An expectant silence fell as he took aim and pressed the trigger.

There was a thunderous report and a blinding cloud of smoke. The wooden target shattered and toppled down the bank into the water. An exultant cheer went up from everyone, and they pounded each other upon the back and danced delirious jigs of triumph in the sunlight.

'It's as fine a grade of powder as any you can find in the naval stores in Greenwich,' Ned Tyler opined, 'but it will have to be properly caked afore we can bag it and carry it away.'

To this end Hal ordered a large clay pot to be placed behind a grass screen at the edge of the camp, and all were strictly enjoined to make use of it on every possible occasion. Even the two women went behind the screen to make their demure contributions. Once the pot was filled, the gunpowder was moistened into paste with the urine, then formed into briquettes, which dried hard in the sun. These were packed into reed baskets for ease of transporting.

'We will grind the cakes as we need them,' Hal explained to Sukeena. 'Now we do not have to carry such a weight of dried fish and meat for we will hunt as we travel. If there is such an abundance of game, as Sabah tells us there is, we will not go short of fresh meat.'

Ten days later than they had first intended, the band was ready to set out into the east. Hal, as the navigator, and Sabah, who had travelled that route before, led the column; Althuda and the three musketeers were in the centre to guard the women and little Bobby, while Aboli and Big Daniel brought up the rear under their ponderous burdens.

They travelled with the grain and run of the range, not attempting to scale the high ground but following the valleys and crossing only through the passes between the high peaks. Hal estimated the distances travelled by eye and time, and the direction with the leather-cased compass. These he marked on his charts every evening before the light faded.

At night they camped in the open, for the weather was mild and they were too tired to build a shelter. When they woke each dawn, their skin blankets, that Sabah called karosses, were soaked with dew.

As Sabah had warned, it was six days of hard travel through the labyrinth of valleys before they reached the steep eastern escarpment and looked down from its crest on the lower ground.

Far out to their right they could make out the blue stain of the ocean merging with the paler heron's-egg blue of the sky, but below the land was not the true plains that Hal had expected but was broken up with hillocks, undulating grassy glades and streaks of dark green forest that seemed to follow the courses of the many small rivers that criss-crossed the littoral as they meandered down to the sea.

To their left, another range of jagged blue mountains marched parallel to the sea, forming a rampart that guarded the mysterious hinterland of the continent. Hal's sharp eyesight picked out the dark stains on the golden grassy plains, moving like cloud shadows when there were no clouds in the sky. He saw the haze of dust that followed the moving herds of wild game, and now and then he spotted the reflection of sunlight from tusks of ivory or from a polished horn.

'This land swarms with life,' he murmured to Sukeena, who stood at his shoulder. 'There may be strange beasts down there that man has never before laid eyes upon. Perhaps even fire-breathing dragons and unicorns and griffons.' Sukeena shivered and hugged her shoulders, even though the sun was high and warm.

'I saw such creatures drawn on the charts I brought for you,' she agreed.

There was a path before them, beaten by the great round pads of elephant and signposted by piles of their fibrous yellow dung, that wound down the slope, picking the most favourable gradient, skirting the deep ravines and dangerous gorges, and Hal followed it.

As they descended, the features of the landscape below became more apparent. Hal could even recognize some of the creatures that moved upon it. The black mass of bovine animals surmounted by a golden haze of dust and a cloud of hovering tick birds, sparkling white in the sunlight, must be the wild buffalo that Aboli had spoken of. *Nyati*, he had called them, when he had warned Hal of their ferocity. There must be several hundred of these beasts in each of the three separate herds that he had under his eye.

Beyond the nearest herd of buffalo was a small gathering of elephants. Hal remembered them well from his previous sightings long ago on the shores of the lagoon. But he had never before seen them in such numbers. At the very least there were twenty great grey cows each with a small calf, like a piglet, at her heels. Dotted upon the plain like hillocks of grey granite were three or four solitary bulls: he could barely credit the size of these patriarchs or the length and girth of their gleaming yellow ivory tusks.

There were other creatures, not as large as the elephant bulls, but massive and grey none the less, which at first he took for elephant also, but as they descended towards the low ground he was able to make out the black horns, some as long as a man is tall, that decorated their great creased grey snouts. He remembered then what Sabah had told him of these savage beasts, one of which had speared and killed Johannes' woman with its deadly horn. These 'rhenosters', which was Sabah's name for them, seemed solitary in nature for they stood apart from others of the same kind, each in the shade of its own tree.

As Hal strode along at the head of the tiny column, he heard the light tread of feet coming up behind him, footsteps that he had come to know and love so well. Sukeena had left her place at in the centre of the line, as she often did when she found some excuse to walk with him for a while.

She slipped her hand into his and kept pace with him. 'I did not want to go alone into this new land. I wanted to walk beside you,' she said softly, then looked up at the sky. 'See the way the wind veers into the south and the clouds crouch on the mountain tops like a pack of wild beasts in ambush? There is a storm coming.'

Her warning proved timely. Hal was able to lead them to a cave in the mountainside to shelter before the storm struck. They lay up there for three long days and nights while the storm raged without, but when they emerged at last, the land was washed clean and the sky was bright and burning blue.

B efore the *Golden Bough* had made her offing from Good Hope and come onto her true course to round the Cape, Captain Christopher Llewellyn was already regretting having taken on board his paying passenger.

He had found out soon enough that Colonel Cornelius Schreuder was a difficult man to like, arrogant, outspoken and highly opinionated. He held firm and unwavering views on every subject that was raised, and was never diffident in giving expression to these. 'He picks up enemies as a dog picks up fleas,' Llewellyn told his mate.

The second day out from Table Bay, Llewellyn had invited Schreuder to dine with him and some of his officers in the stern cabin. He was a cultured man, and maintained a grand style even at sea. With the prize money that he had won in the recent Dutch war, he could afford to indulge his taste for fine things.

The *Golden Bough* had cost almost two thousand pounds to build and launch, but she was probably the finest vessel of her class and burden afloat. Her culverins were newly cast and her sails were of the finest canvas. The captain's quarters were fitted out with a taste and discrimination unparalleled in any navy, but her qualities as a fighting ship had not been sacrificed for luxury.

During the voyage down the Atlantic, Llewellyn had found, to his delight, that her sea-keeping qualities were all he had hoped. On a broad reach, with her sails full and the wind free, her hull sliced through the water like a blade, and she could point so high into the wind that it made his heart sing to feel her deck heel under his feet.

Most of his officers and petty-officers had served with him during the war and had proved their quality and courage, but he had on board one younger officer, the fourth son of George, Viscount Winterton.

Lord Winterton was the Master Navigator of the Order, one of the richest and most powerful men in England. He owned a fleet of privateers and trading ships. The Honourable Vincent Winterton was on his first privateering voyage, placed by his father under Llewellyn's tutelage. He was a comely youth, not yet twenty years of age but well educated, with a frank and winning manner that made him popular with both the seamen and his brother officers alike. He was one of the other guests at Llewellyn's dinner table that second night out from Good Hope.

The dinner started out gay and lively, for all the Englishmen were merry, with a fine ship under them and the promise of glory and gold ahead. Schreuder, however, was aloof and gloomy. With the second glass of wine warming them all, Llewellyn called across the cabin, 'Vincent, my lad, will you not give us a tune?'

'Could you bear to listen, yet again, to my caterwauling, sir?' The young man laughed modestly, but the rest of the company urged him on. 'Come on, Vinny! Sing for us, man!'

Vincent Winterton stood up and went to the small clavichord that was fastened with heavy brass screws to one of the main frames of the ship. He sat down, tossed back his long thick curling locks and struck a soft, silvery chord from the keyboard. 'What would you have me sing?'

'"Greensleeves"!' suggested someone, but Vincent pulled a face. 'You've heard that a hundred times and more since we sailed from home.'

'"Mother Mine"!' cried another. This time Vincent nodded, threw back his head and sang in a strong, true voice that transformed the mawkish lyrics and brought tears to the eyes of many of the company as they tapped their feet in time to the song.

Schreuder had taken an immediate and unreasoned dislike to the attractive youth, so comely and popular with his peers, so sure of himself and serene in his high rank and privileged birth. Schreuder, in comparison, felt himself ageing and overlooked. He had never attracted the natural admiration and affection of those about him, as this young man so obviously did.

He sat stiffly in a corner, ignored by these men who, not so long ago, had been his deadly enemies, and who, he knew, despised him as a dull foreigner and a foot soldier, not one of their élite brotherhood of the ocean. He found his dislike turning to active hatred of the young man, whose fine features were clear and unlined and whose voice had the timbre and tonal colour of a temple bell.

When the song ended, there was a moment of silence, attentive and awed. Then they all burst out clapping and applauding. 'Oh, well done, lad!' and 'Bravo, Vinny!' Schreuder felt his irritation become unbearable.

The applause went on too long for the liking of the singer, and Vincent rose from the clavichord with a deprecating wave of the hand that begged them to desist.

In the silence that followed, Schreuder said, softly but distinctly, 'Caterwauling? No, sir, that was an insult to the feline species.'

There was a shocked silence in the small cabin. The young man flushed and his hand dropped instinctively to the hilt of the short-bladed dirk that he wore at his jewelled belt, but Llewellyn said sharply, 'Vincent!' and shook his head. Reluctantly he dropped his hand from the weapon and forced himself to smile and bow slightly. 'You have a perceptive ear, sir. I commend your discerning taste.'

He resumed his seat at the board and turned away from Schreuder to engage his neighbour in light-hearted repartee. The awkward moment passed, and the other guests relaxed, smiled and joined in the conversation, which pointedly excluded the Colonel.

Llewellyn's cook had come with him from home, and the ship had been provisioned at Good Hope with fresh meat and vegetables. The meal was as good as any that might be served in the coffee shops and ale-houses of Fleet Street, the conversation as pleasing and the banter nimble and amusing, larded with clever puns, double meanings and fashionable slang. Most of this was above Schreuder's grasp of the language and his resentment built up like the brewing of a tropical typhoon.

He made one contribution to the conversation, a stinging reference to the Dutch victory in the Thames River and the capture of the *Royal Charles*, the pride of the English navy and the namesake of their beloved sovereign. The conversation froze into silence once more, and the company fixed him with chilly scrutiny, before continuing their conversation as though he had not spoken.

Schreuder consoled himself with the claret, and when the bottle in front of him was exhausted, he reached down the table for a flagon of brandy. His head for liquor was as adamantine as his pride, but today it seemed only to make him more truculent and angry. By the end of the meal he was spoiling for trouble, and prospecting for some way in which to ease the terrible sense of rejection and hopelessness that overpowered him.

At last Llewellyn stood up to propose the loyal toast. 'Here's health and a long life to the Black Boy!' Everyone rose enthusiastically to their feet, stooping under the low deck timbers overhead, but Schreuder stayed seated.

Llewellyn knocked on the table. 'If you please, Colonel, come to your feet. We are drinking the health of the King of England.'

'I am no longer thirsty, thank you, Captain.' Schreuder folded his arms.

The men growled, and one said loudly, 'Let me at him, Captain.'

'Colonel Schreuder is a guest aboard this ship,' Llewellyn said ominously, 'and none of you will offer him any discourtesy, no matter if he behaves like a pig himself and transgresses all the conventions of decent society.' Then he turned back to Schreuder. 'Colonel, I am asking you for the last time to join the loyal toast. If you do not, we are still within easy range of Good Hope. I will give the orders immediately for this ship to go about and sail back to Table Bay. There I will return your fare money to you, and have you deposited on the beach like a bucketful of kitchen slops.'

Schreuder sobered instantly. This was a threat he had not anticipated. He had hoped to provoke one of these English oafs into a duel. He would then have given them a display of swordsmanship that would have opened their cold-fish eyes and wiped those superior smirks from their faces, but the thought of being taken back to the scene of his crime and delivered into the vengeful hands of Governor van de Velde made his lips go numb and his fingers tingle with dread. He rose slowly to his feet with his glass in his hand. Llewellyn relaxed slightly, they all drank the toast and sat down again in a hubbub of laughter and talk.

'Does anybody fancy a few throws of the dice?' Vincent Winterton suggested, and there was general agreement.

'But not if you wish to play for shilling stakes again,' one of the older officers demurred. 'Last time I lost almost twenty pounds, all the prize money I won when we captured the *Buurman*.'

'Farthing stakes and a shilling limit,' another suggested, and they nodded and felt for their purses.

'Mr Winterton, sir,' Schreuder broke in, 'I will oblige you with whatever stakes your stomach will hold and not puke up again.' He was pale and sweat sheened his forehead, but that was the only visible effect the liquor had upon him.

Once again a silence fell on the table as Schreuder groped under his tunic and brought out a pigskin purse. He dropped it nonchalantly on the table and it clinked with the unmistakable music of gold. Every man at the table stiffened.

'We play in sport and in good fellowship here,' Llewellyn growled.

But Vincent Winterton said lightly, 'How much is in that purse, Colonel?'

Schreuder loosened the drawstring and, with a flourish, poured the coins into a heavy heap in the centre of the table where they sparkled in the lamplight. Triumphantly he looked around the circle of their faces.

They will not take me so lightly now! he thought, but aloud he said, 'Twenty thousand Dutch guilders. That is over two hundred of your English pounds.' It was his entire fortune, but there was a reckless, self-destructive pounding in his heart. He found himself driven on to folly as though he might wipe away the guilt of his terrible murder with gold.

The company was silenced by the size of his purse. It was an enormous sum, more than most of these officers might expect to accumulate in a lifetime of dangerous endeavour.

Vincent Winterton smiled graciously. 'I see you are indeed a sports-man, sir.'

'Ah! So!' Schreuder smiled coldly. 'The stakes are too high, are they?' And he swept the golden coins back into his purse and made as if to rise from the table.

'Hold hard, Colonel.' Vincent stopped him, and Schreuder sank back into his seat. 'I came unprepared, but if you will afford me a few minutes of your time?' He rose, bowed and left the cabin. They all sat in silence until he returned and placed a small teak chest in front of him on the table.

'Three hundred, was it?' He began to count out the coins from the chest. They made a splendid profusion in the centre of the table.

'Will you be kind enough to hold the stakes, Captain?' Vincent asked politely. 'That is, if the colonel agrees?'

'I have no objection.' Schreuder nodded stiffly and passed his purse to Llewellyn. Inwardly the first regrets were assailing him. He had not expected any of them to take up his challenge. A loss of such magnitude must beggar most men, as indeed it would beggar him.

Llewellyn received both purses, and placed them before him. Then Vincent took up the leather dice cup and passed it across to Schreuder.

'We usually play with these, sir,' Vincent said easily. 'Would you care to examine them? If they are not to your liking, perhaps we may be able to find others that suit you better.'

Schreuder shook the dice out of the cup and rolled them across the table. Then he picked up each ivory cube and held it to the lamplight. 'I can see no blemish,' he said, and replaced them in the cup. 'It remains only to agree on the game. Will it be Hazard?'

'English Hazard,' Vincent agreed. 'What else?'

'What limit on each coup?' Schreuder wanted to know. 'Will it be a pound or five?'

'A single coup only,' said Vincent. 'The shooter to be decided by high dice, and then two hundred pounds on his Hazard.'

Schreuder was stunned by the proposal. He had expected to make his wagers in small increments, which would allow him the possibility of withdrawing with some semblance of grace if the run of the dice turned against him. He had never heard of such an immense sum staked on a single throw of the dice.

One of Vincent's friends chortled delightedly. 'By God's truth, Vinny! That will show up the colour of the cheese-head's liver.'

Schreuder glared at him, but he knew he was trapped. For a moment longer he sought some escape, but Vincent murmured, 'I do hope I have not embarrassed you, Colonel. I mistook you for a sport. Would you rather call off the whole affair?'

'I assure you,' he said coldly, 'that it suits me very well. One hazard for two hundred pounds. I agree.'

Llewellyn placed one of the dice in the cup and passed it to Schreuder. 'One die to decide the shooter. High shoots. Is that your agreement, gentlemen?' Both men nodded.

Schreuder rolled the single die, 'Three!' said Llewellyn, and replaced it in the leather cup.

'Your throw, Mr Winterton.' He placed the cup in front of Vincent, who swept it up and threw in the same motion.

'Five!' said Llewellyn. 'Mr Winterton is the shooter at one coup of English Hazard for a purse of two hundred pounds.' This time he placed both dice in the cup. 'The shooter will throw to decide the main point. If you please, Mr Winterton.'

Vincent took up the cup and rolled it out. Llewellyn read the dice. 'The Main is seven.'

Schreuder's soul quailed. Seven was the easiest Main to duplicate. Many combinations of the dice would yield it. The odds had swung against him, and this realization was reflected on the gloating face of every one of the watchers. If Vincent threw another seven or an eleven

385

he would win, which was likely. If he threw the 'crabs' one and one or one and two, or if he threw twelve then he lost. Any other number would become his Chance, and he would have to keep throwing until he repeated it or threw one of the losing combinations.

Schreuder leaned back and folded his arms as though to defend himself from a brutal attack. Vincent threw.

'Four!' said Llewellyn. 'The Chance is now four.' There was a simultaneous release of breath from every person at the table except Vincent. He had given himself the most difficult Main to achieve. The odds had swung back overwhelmingly in Schreuder's favour. Vincent must now throw a Chance four to win, or a Main seven to lose. Only two combinations could total four, whereas there were many others that would yield a losing seven.

'You have my sympathy, sir.' Schreuder smiled cruelly. 'Four is the devil's own number to make.'

'The angels favour the virtuous.' Vincent waved his hand lightly, and smiled. 'Would you care to increase your stake. I will give you even money for another hundred pounds?' It was a foolhardy offer, with the odds stacked heavily against him, but Schreuder had not another guilder to avail himself of it.

He shook his head curtly. 'I would not take advantage of a man who is on his knees.'

'How gallant you are, Colonel,' Vincent said, and threw again.

'Ten!' said Llewellyn. It was a neutral number.

Vincent picked up the dice and rattled them in the cup and threw again.

'Six!' Another neutral number and, though Schreuder sat still as a corpse, his colour was waxen and he could feel droplets of sweat crawling through his chest hairs like slimy garden slugs.

'This one is for all the pretty girls we left behind us,' said Vincent and the dice clattered on the walnut tabletop as he threw again. For a long terrible moment no man moved or spoke. Then a howl went up from every English throat that must have alarmed the watch on the deck above and reached to the lookout at the top of the mainmast.

'Mary and Joseph! Two pairs of titties! As sweet a little four as I have ever seen!'

'Mr Winterton has thrown his Chance,' intoned Llewellyn, and placed both heavy purses in front of him. 'Mr Winterton wins.' But his voice was almost drowned by the uproar of laughter and congratulation. It went on for several minutes while Schreuder sat immobile as a fallen forest log, his face grey and sweating.

At last Winterton waved away any further chaff and congratulation.

He stood up, leaned over the table towards Schreuder, and said seriously, 'I salute you, sir. You are a gentleman of iron nerve, and a sportsman of the first water. I offer you the hand of friendship.' He stretched out his right hand with the palm open. Schreuder looked at it disdainfully, still not moving, and the smiles faded away. Another charged silence fell over the little cabin.

Schreuder spoke out clearly: 'I should have examined those dice of *yours* more closely while I had the chance.' He placed a heavy emphasis on the possessive pronoun. 'I hope you will forgive me, sir, but I make it a rule never to shake hands with cheats.' Vincent recoiled sharply and stared at Schreuder in disbelief, while the others gasped and gaped.

It took Vincent a long moment to recover from the shock of the unexpected insult, and his handsome young face had paled under his sea- and salt-tanned skin as he replied, 'I would be deeply obliged if you could see fit to accord me satisfaction for that remark, Colonel Schreuder.'

'With the greatest of pleasure.' Schreuder rose to his feet, smiling with triumph. He had been challenged so the choice of weapons was his. There would be no aping about with pistols. It would be the steel and this English puppy would have the pleasure of a yard of the Neptune sword in his belly. Schreuder turned to Llewellyn. 'Would you do me the honour of acting as my second in this matter?' he asked.

'Not I!' Llewellyn shook his head firmly. 'I will not allow duelling on board any ship of mine. You will have to find yourself another person to act for you, and you will have to check your temper until we reach port. Then you can go ashore to settle this matter.'

Schreuder looked back at Vincent. 'I will inform you of the name of my second at the first opportunity,' he said. 'I promise you satisfaction as soon as we reach port.' He stood up and marched out of the cabin. He could hear their voices behind him, raised in comment and conjecture, but the brandy fumes rose to mingle with his rage until he feared the veins beating in his temples might burst with the strength of it.

The following day Schreuder kept to his own kennel of a cabin where a servant brought him his meals as he lay on his bunk like a battle casualty, nursing the terrible wounds to his pride and the unbearable pain caused by the loss of his entire worldly wealth. On the second day he came on deck while the *Golden Bough* was on a larboard tack and making good her course of west-north-west along the bulging coastline of southern Africa.

As soon as his head appeared above the coaming of the companion-way, the officer of the watch turned away and busied himself with the pegs on the traverse board, while Captain Llewellyn raised his telescope and studied the blue mountains that loomed on the horizon to the north. Schreuder paced along the lee rail of the ship while the officers studiously ignored his presence. The servant who had waited at the Captain's dinner party had spread the news of the impending duel through all the ship, and the crew eyed him curiously and kept well out of his path.

After half an hour Schreuder stopped abruptly in front of the officer of the watch and, without preamble, asked, 'Mr Fowler, will you act as my second?'

'I beg your pardon, Colonel, Mr Winterton is a friend of mine. Will you excuse me, please?'

During the days that followed Schreuder approached every officer aboard to act for him, but in each case he was received with frigid refusals. Ostracized and humiliated, he prowled the open deck like a night-stalking leopard. His thoughts swung like a pendulum between remorse and agony over Katinka's death, and resentment of the treatment meted out to him by the captain and officers of the ship. His rage swelled until he could barely support it.

On the morning of the fifth day, as he paced the lee rail, a hail from the masthead aroused him from this black mist of suffering. When Captain Llewellyn strode to the windward rail and stared into the south-west, Schreuder followed him across the deck and stood at his shoulder.

For some moments he doubted his own eyesight as he stared at the mountainous range of menacing dark cloud that stretched from the horizon to the heavens and which bore down upon them with such speed that it made him think again of the avalanche sweeping down the dark gorge.

'You had best go below, Colonel,' Llewellyn warned him. 'We're in for a bit of a blow.'

Schreuder ignored the warning and stood by the rail, filled with awe as he watched the clouds roll down upon them. All around him the ship was in turmoil as the crew rushed to get the sails furled and to bring the bows around, so that the Golden Bough faced into the racing storm. The wind came on so swiftly that it caught her with her royals and jib still set and sheeted home.

The storm hurled itself upon the Golden Bough, howling with fury, and laid her over so that the lee rail went under and green water piled aboard to sweep the deck waist deep. Schreuder was borne away on this

388

flood and might have been washed overboard had he not grabbed hold of the main shrouds.

The *Golden Bough*'s jib and royals burst as though they were wet parchment and for a long minute she wallowed half under as the gale pinned her down. The sea poured into her open hatches, and from below there was the crash and thunder as some of her bulkheads burst and her cargo shifted. Men screamed as they were crushed by a culverin that had broken its breeching tackle and was running amok on the gundeck. Other sailors cried like lost souls falling into the pit as they were carried over the side by the racing green waters. The air turned white with spray so that Schreuder felt himself drowning, even though his face was clear of the water, and the white fog blinded him.

Slowly the *Golden Bough* righted herself as her lead-weighted keel levered her upright, but her spars and rigging were in tatters, snapping and lashing in the gale. Some of her yards were broken away and they clattered, banged and battered the standing masts. Listing heavily with the seawater she had taken in the *Golden Bough* was driven out of control before the wind.

Gasping and choking, half-drowned and doused to the skin, Schreuder dragged himself across the deck to the shelter of the companionway. From there he watched in dread and fascination as the world around him dissolved in silver spray and maddened green waves streaked with long pathways of foam.

For two days the wind never ceased its assault upon them, and the seas grew taller and wilder with every hour until they seemed to tower higher than the mainmast as they rushed down upon them. Half-swamped, the *Golden Bough* was slow to lift to meet them, and as they struck her they burst into foam and tumbled green across her decks. Two helmsmen, lashed to the whipstaff, battled to keep her pointing with the gale, but each wave that came aboard burst over their heads. By the second day all aboard were exhausted and nearing the limits of their endurance. There was no chance of sleep and only hard biscuit to eat.

Llewellyn had lashed himself to the mainmast and from there he directed the efforts of his officers and men to keep the ship alive. No man could stand unsupported upon the open deck, so Llewellyn could not order them to man the main pumps, but on the gundeck teams of seamen worked in a frenzy at the auxiliary pumps to try to clear the six feet of water in her bilges. As fast as they pumped it out the sea poured back through the shattered gunports and the cracked hatch covers.

Always the land loomed closer in their lee as the storm drove them onwards under bare masts, and though the helmsmen strained muscle and heart to hold her off, the *Golden Bough* edged in towards the land. That night they heard the surf break and boom like a barrage of cannon out there in the darkness, growing every hour more tumultuous as they were driven towards the rocks.

When dawn broke on the third day they could see, through the fog and spume, the dark, threatening shape of the land, the cliffs and jagged headlands only a league away across the marching mountains of grey and furious waters.

Schreuder dragged himself across the deck, clinging to mast and shroud and backstay as each wave came aboard. Seawater streamed from his hair down his face, filling his mouth and nostrils, as he gasped at Llewellyn, 'I know this coast. I recognize that headland coming up ahead of us.'

'We'll need God's blessing to weather it on this course,' Llewellyn shouted. 'The wind has us in its teeth.'

'Then pray to the Almighty with all your heart, Captain, for our salvation lies not five leagues beyond,' Schreuder bellowed, blinking the salt water from his eyes.

'How can you be certain of that?'

'I have been ashore here and marched through the country. I know every wrinkle of the land. There is a bay beyond that cape, which we named Buffalo Bay. Once she is into it, the ship should be sheltered from the full force of the wind, and on the far side there stand a pair of rocky heads that guard the entrance to a wide and calm lagoon. In there we would be safe from even such a storm as this.'

'There is no lagoon marked on my charts.' Llewellyn's expression was riven with hope and doubt.

'Sweet Jesus, Captain, you must believe me!' Schreuder shouted. On the sea he was out of his natural element and for once even he was afraid.

'First we must weather those rocks, and after that we can prove the quality of your memory.'

Schreuder was silenced and clung desperately to the mast beside Llewellyn. He stared ahead in horror as he watched the sea open her snarling lips of white foam and bare fangs of black rock. The *Golden Bough* drove on helplessly into her jaws.

One of the helmsmen screamed, 'Oh, holy Mother of God, save our mortal souls! We're going to strike!'

'Hold your helm hard over!' Llewellyn roared at him. Close alongside, the sea opened viciously and the reef burst out like a blowing whale. Claws of stone seemed to reach out towards the frail planks of the little ship, and they were so near that Schreuder could see the masses of shellfish and weed that cloaked the rocks. Another wave, larger than the rest, lifted and flung them at the reef, but the rocks disappeared below the boiling surface and the *Golden Bough* rose up like a hunter at a fence and shot high over it.

Her keel touched the rock and she checked with such force that Schreuder's grip on the mast was broken and he was hurled to the deck, but the ship shook herself free, surged onwards, carried on the crest of that mighty wave, and slid off the reef into the deeper water beyond. She charged forward, the point of the headland dropping away behind her and the bay opening ahead. Schreuder dragged himself upright and felt at once that the dreadful might of the gale had been broken by the sprit of land. Though the ship still hurtled on wildly, she was coming back under control and Schreuder could feel her respond to the urging of her rudder.

'There!' he screamed in Llewellyn's ear. 'There! Dead ahead!'

'Sweet heaven! You were right.' Through the spume and seafret Llewellyn picked out the shape of the twin heads over the ship's bows. He rounded on his helmsmen. 'Let her fall off a point!' Though their terrified expressions showed how they hated to obey, they let her come down across the wind and point towards the next pier of black rock and surf.

'Hold her at that!' Llewellyn checked them, and the *Golden Bough* tore headlong across the bay.

'Mr Winterton!' he roared at Vincent, who crouched below the hatch-coaming close at hand with a half-dozen sailors sheltering on the companion behind him. 'We must shake out a reef on the main topgallant sail to give her steerage. Can you do it?'

He made the order a request, for it was the next thing to murder to send a man to the top of the mainmast in this gale. An officer must lead the way, and Vincent was the strongest and boldest amongst them.

'Come on, lads!' Vincent shouted at his men without hesitation. 'There's a golden guinea for any man who can beat me to the main topgallant yard.' He leapt to his feet and darted across the deck to the mainmast shrouds and went flying up them hand over hand with his men in pursuit.

The *Golden Bough* tore across Buffalo Bay like a runaway horse. Suddenly Schreuder shouted again, 'Look there!' and pointed to where the entrance to the lagoon began to open to their view between the heads that towered on either hand.

Llewellyn threw back his head and gazed up the mainmast at the tiny figures that spread out along the high yard and wrestled with the reefed

391

canvas. He recognized Vincent easily by his lean athletic form and his dark hair whipping in the wind.

'Bravely done thus far,' Llewellyn whispered, 'but hurry, lad. Give me a scrap of canvas to steer her by.'

As he said it the studding-sail flew out and filled with a crack like a musket shot. For a dreadful moment Llewellyn thought the canvas might be shredded in the gale, but it filled and held and immediately he felt the ship's motion change.

'Sweet Mother Mary! We might make it yet!' he croaked, through a throat scoured and rough with salt. 'Hard over!' he called to the helm, and the *Golden Bough* answered willingly and put her bows across the wind.

Like an arrow from a longbow, she drove straight at the western headland as though to hurl herself ashore, but her hull slid away through the water and the angle of her bows altered. The passage opened full before her, and as she passed into the lee of the land she steadied, darted between the heads, caught the tide, which was at full flow, and sped upon it through the channel into the quiet lagoon where she was protected from the full force of the storm.

Llewellyn gazed at the green forested shores in wonder and relief. Then he started and pointed ahead. 'There's another ship at anchor here already!'

Beside him Schreuder shaded his eyes from the slashing gusts of wind that eddied around the cliffs.

'I know that vessel!' he cried. 'I know her well. 'Tis Lord Cumbrae's ship. 'Tis the *Gull of Moray*!'

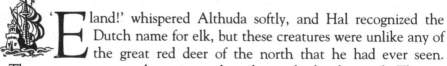

'Eland!' whispered Althuda softly, and Hal recognized the Dutch name for elk, but these creatures were unlike any of the great red deer of the north that he had ever seen. They were enormous, larger even than the cattle that his uncle Thomas had raised on the High Weald estate.

The three of them, Hal, Althuda and Aboli, lay belly down in a small hollow filled with rank grass. The herd was strung out among the open grove of sweet-thorn trees ahead. Hal counted fifty-two bulls, cows and calves together. The bulls were ponderous and fat so that, as they walked, their dewlaps swung from side to side and the flesh on their bellies and quarters quivered like that of a jellyfish. At each pace there came a strange clicking sound like breaking twigs.

'It is their knees that make that noise,' Aboli explained in Hal's ear.

'The Nkulu Kulu, the great god of all things, punished them when they boasted of being the greatest of all the antelope. He gave them this affliction so that the hunter would always hear them from afar.'

Hal smiled at the quaint belief, but then Aboli told him something else that turned off that smile. 'I know these creatures, they were highly prized by the hunters of my tribe, for a bull such as that one at the front of the herd carries a mass of white fat around his heart that two men cannot carry.' For months now none of them had tasted fat, for all the game they had managed to kill was devoid of it. They all craved it, and Sukeena had warned Hal that for lack of it they must soon sicken and fall prey to disease.

Hal studied the herd bull as he browsed on one of the sweet-thorn trees, hooking down the higher branches with his massive spiralling horns. Unlike his cows, who were a soft and velvet brown, striped with white across their shoulders, the bull had turned grey-blue with age and there was a tuft of darker hair on his forehead between the bases of his great horns.

'Leave the bull,' Aboli told Hal. 'His flesh will be coarse and tough. See that cow behind him? She will be sweet and tender as a virgin, and her fat will turn to honey in your mouth.' Against Aboli's advice, which Hal knew was always the best available, he felt the urge of the hunter attract him to the great bull.

'If we are to cross the river safely, then we need as much meat as we can carry. Each of us will fire at his own animal,' he decided. 'I will take the bull, you and Althuda pick younger animals.' He began to snake forward on his belly, and the other two followed him.

In these last days since they had descended the escarpment they had found that the game upon these plains had little fear of man. It seemed that the dreaded upright bipod silhouette he presented had no especial terrors for them, and they allowed the hunters to approach within certain musket shot before moving away.

Thus it must have been in Eden before the Fall, Hal thought, as he closed with the herd bull. The soft breeze favoured him, and the tendrils of blue smoke from their slow-match drifted away from the herd.

He was so close now that he could make out the individual eyelashes that framed the huge liquid dark eyes of the bull, and the red and gold legs of the ticks that clung in bunches to the soft skin between his forelegs. The bull fed, delicately wiping the young green leaves from the twigs between the thorns with its blue tongue.

On each side of him two of his young cows fed from the same thorn tree. One had a calf at heel while the other was full-bellied and gravid. Hal turned his head slowly and looked at the men who lay beside him.

He indicated the cows to them with a slow movement of his eyes, and Aboli nodded and raised his musket.

Once more Hal concentrated all his attention on the great bull, and traced the line of the scapula beneath the skin that covered the shoulder, fixing a spot in all that broad expanse of smooth blue-grey hide at which to aim. He raised the musket and held the butt into the notch of his shoulder, sensing the men on either side of him do the same.

As the bull took another pace forward he held his fire. It stopped again and raised its head, on the thick dewlapped neck, to full stretch, laying the massive twisted horns across its back, reaching up over two fathoms high to the topmost sprigs of the thorn tree where the sweetest bunches of lacy green leaves grew.

Hal fired, and heard the detonation of the other muskets on either side of him blend with the concussion of his own weapon. A swirling screen of white gunsmoke blotted out his forward view. He let the musket drop, sprang to his feet and raced out to his side to get a clear view around the smoke bank. He saw that one of the cows was down, kicking and struggling as her lifeblood spurted from the wound in her throat, while the other was staggering away, her near front leg swinging loosely from the broken bone. Already Aboli was running after her, his drawn cutlass in his right hand.

The rest of the herd was rushing away in a tight brown mass down the valley, the calves falling behind their dams. However, the bull had left the herd, sure sign that the lead ball had struck him grievously. He was striding away up the gentle slope of the low, grass-covered hillock ahead. But his gait was short and hampered, and as he changed direction, exposing his great shoulder to Hal's view, the blood that poured down his flank was red as a banner in the sunlight and bubbling with the air from his punctured lungs.

Hal started to run, speeding away over the tussocked grass. The injury to his leg was by now only a perfectly healed scar, glossy blue and ridged. The long trek over the mountains and plains had strengthened that limb so that his stride was full and lithe. A cable's length or more ahead, the bull was drawing away from him, leaving a haze of fine red dust hanging in the air, but then its wound began to tell and the spilling blood painted a glistening trail on the silver grass to mark his passing.

Hal closed the gap until he was only a dozen strides behind the mountainous beast. It sensed his pursuit and turned at bay. Hal expected a furious charge, a lowering of the great tufted head and a levelling of those spiral horns. He came up short, facing the antelope, and whipped his cutlass from the scabbard, prepared to defend himself.

The bull looked at him with huge puzzled eyes, dark and swimming with the agony of its approaching death. Blood dripped from its nostrils and the soft blue tongue lolled from the side of its mouth. It made no move to attack him, or to defend itself, and Hal saw no malice or anger in its gaze.

'Forgive me,' he whispered, as he circled the beast, waiting for an opening, and felt the slow, sad waves of remorse break over his heart to watch the agony he had inflicted upon this magnificent animal. Suddenly he rushed forward and thrust with the steel. The stroke of the expert swordsman buried the blade full length in the bull's flesh, and it bucked and whirled away, snatching the hilt out of Hal's hand. But the steel had found the heart and, its legs folded gently under it, the bull sagged wearily onto its knees. With one low groan it toppled over onto its side and died.

Hal took hold of the cutlass hilt and withdrew the long, smeared blade, then chose a rock near the carcass and went to sit there. He felt sad yet strangely elated. He was puzzled and confused by these contrary emotions, and he dwelt on the beauty and majesty of the beast that he had reduced to this sad heap of dead flesh in the grass.

A hand was laid on his shoulder, and Aboli rumbled softly, 'Only the true hunter knows this anguish of the kill, Gundwane. That is why my tribe, who are hunters, sing and dance to give thanks to propitiate the spirits of the game they have slain.'

'Teach me to sing me this song and to dance this dance, Aboli,' Hal said, and Aboli began to chant in his deep and beautiful voice. When he had picked up the rhythm Hal joined in the repetitive chorus, praising the beauty and the grace of the prey and thanking it for dying so that the hunter and his tribe might live.

Aboli began to dance, shuffling, stamping and singing in a circle about the great carcass, and Hal danced with him. His chest was choked and his eyes were blurred when, at last, the song ended and they sat together in the slanting yellow sunlight to watch the tiny column of fugitives, led by Sukeena, coming towards them from far across the plain.

Before darkness fell Hal set them to building the stockade, and he checked carefully to make certain that the gaps in the breastwork were closed with branches of sweet-thorn.

They carried the quarters and shoulders of eland meat and stacked them in the stockade where scavengers could not plunder them. They left only the scraps and the offal, the severed hoofs and heads, the mounds of guts and intestines stuffed with the pulp of half-digested leaves and grass. As they moved away the vultures hopped in or sailed down on great pinions, and the hyena and jackal rushed forward to gobble and howl and squabble over this charnel array.

After they had all eaten their fill of succulent eland steaks, Hal allocated to Sukeena and himself the middle watch that started at midnight. Though it was the most onerous, for it was the time when man's vitality was at its lowest ebb, they loved to have the night to themselves.

While the rest of their band slept, they huddled at the entrance to the stockade under a single fur kaross, with a musket laid close to Hal's right hand. After they had made soft and silent love so as not to disturb the others, they watched the sky and spoke in whispers as the stars made their remote and ancient circuits high above.

'Tell me true, my love, what have you read in those stars? What lies ahead for you and me? How many sons will you bear me?' Her hand, cupped in his, lay still, and he felt her whole body stiffen. She did not reply and he had to ask her again. 'Why will you never tell me what you see in the future? I know you have drawn our horoscopes, for often when you thought I was sleeping I have seen you studying and writing in your little blue book.'

She laid her fingers on his lips. 'Be quiet, my lord. There are many things in this existence that are best hidden from us. For this night and tomorrow let us love each other with all our hearts and all our strength. Let us draw the most from every day that God grants us.'

'You trouble me, my sweet. Will there be no sons, then?'

She was silent again as they watched a shooting star leave its brief fiery trail though the heavens and at last perish before their eyes. Then she sighed, and whispered, 'Yes, I will give you a son but—' She bit off the other words that rose to her tongue.

'There is great sadness in your voice.' His tone was disquieted. 'And, yet, the thought that you will bear my son gives me joy.'

'The stars can be malevolent,' she whispered. 'Sometimes they fulfil their promises in a manner that we do not expect, or relish. Of one thing alone I am certain, that the fates have selected for you a labour of great consequence. It has been ordained thus from the day of your birth.'

'My father spoke to me of this same task.' Hal brooded on the old prophecy. 'I am willing to face my destiny, but I need you to help and sustain me as you have done so often already.'

She did not answer his plea, but said, 'The task they have set for you involves a vow and a talisman of mystery and power.'

'Will you be with me, you and our son?' he insisted.

'If I can guide you in the direction you must go, I will do so with all my heart and all my strength.'

'But will you come with me?' he pleaded.

'I will come with you as far as the stars will permit it,' she promised. 'More than that I do not know and cannot say.'

'But—' he started, but she reached up with her mouth and covered his lips with her own to stop him speaking.

'No more! You must ask no more,' she warned him. 'Now join your body with mine once again and leave the business of the stars to the stars alone.'

Towards the end of their watch, when the Seven Sisters had sunk below the hills and the Bull stood high and proud, they lay in each other's arms, still talking softly to fight off the drowsiness that crept upon them. They had become accustomed to the night sounds of the wilderness, from the liquid warble of night birds and the yapping, yodelling chorus of the little red jackals to the hideous shrieking and cackling of the hyena packs at the remains of the carcasses, but suddenly there came a sound that chilled them to the depths of their souls.

It was the sound of all the devils of hell, a monstrous roaring and grunting that stilled all lesser creation, rolled against the hills and came back to them in a hundred echoes. Involuntarily Sukeena clung to him and cried aloud, 'Oh, Gundwane, what terrible creature is that?'

She was not alone in her terror for all the camp was suddenly awake. Zwaantie screamed, and the baby echoed her terror. Even the men sprang to their feet and cried out to God.

Aboli appeared beside them like a dark moonshadow and calmed Sukeena with a hand on her trembling shoulder. 'It is no phantom, but a creature of this world,' he told them. 'They say that even the bravest hunter is frightened three times by the lion. Once when he sees its tracks, twice when he hears its voice, and the third time when he confronts the beast face to face.'

Hal sprang up, and called to the others, 'Throw fresh logs on the fire. Light the slow-match on all the muskets. Place the women and the child in the centre of the stockade.'

They crouched in a tight circle behind its flimsy walls, and for a while all was quiet, quieter than it had been all that night for now even the scavengers has been silenced by the mighty voice that had spoken from out of the darkness.

They waited, their weapons held ready, and stared out into the night where the yellow light of the flames could not reach. It seemed to Hal that the flickering firelight played tricks with his eyes, for all at once he thought he saw a ghostly shape glide silently through the shadows. Then Sukeena gripped his arm, digging her fingernails into his flesh, and he knew that she had seen it also.

Abruptly that gale of terrifying noise broke over them again, raising the hair on their scalps. The women shrieked and the men quaked and tightened their grip on the weapons that now seemed so frail and inadequate in their hands.

'There!' whispered Zwaantie, and this time there could be no doubt that what they saw was real. It was a monstrous feline shape that seemed as tall as a man's shoulder, which passed before their gaze on noiseless pads. The flames lit upon its brazen glossy hide, turning its eyes to glaring emeralds like those in the crown of Satan himself. Another came and then another, passing in swift and menacing parade before them, then disappearing into the night once more.

'They gather their courage and resolve,' Aboli said. 'They smell the blood and the dead flesh and they are hunting us.'

'Should we flee from the stockade, then?' Hal asked.

'No!' Aboli shook his head. 'The darkness is their domain. They are able to see when the night stops up our eyes. The darkness makes them bold. We must stay here where we can see them when they come.'

Then, from out of the night, came such a creature as to dwarf the others they had seen. He strode towards them with a majestic swinging gait, and a mane of black and golden hair covered his head and shoulders and made him seem as huge as a haystack. 'Shall I fire upon him?' Hal whispered to Aboli.

'A wound will madden him,' Aboli replied. 'Unless you can kill cleanly, do not fire.'

The lion stopped in the full glare of the firelight. He placed his forepaws apart and lowered his head. The dark hair of his mane came erect, swelling before their horrified gaze, seeming to double his bulk. He opened his jaws, and they saw the ivory fangs gleam, the red tongue curl out between them, and he roared again.

The sound struck them with a physical force, like a storm-driven wave. It stunned their ear-drums and startled their senses. The beast was so close that Hal could feel the breath from its mighty lungs blow into his face. It smelt of corpses and carrion long dead.

'Quietly now!' Hal urged them. 'Make no sound and do not move, lest you provoke him to attack.' Even the women and the child obeyed. They stifled their cries and sat rigid with the terror of it. It seemed an eternity that they remained thus, the lion eyeing them, until little one-eyed Johannes could bear it no longer. He screamed, flung up his musket and fired wildly.

In the instant before the gunsmoke blinded them Hal saw that the ball had missed the beast and had struck the dirt between its forelegs. Then the smoke billowed over them in a cloud, and from its depths came the grunts of the angry lion. Now both women screamed and the men barged into each other in their haste to run deeper into the stockade. Only Hal and Aboli stood their ground, muskets levelled, and aimed into the bank of smoke. Little Sukeena shrank against Hal's flank but did not run.

Then the lion burst in full charge out of the mist of gunsmoke. Hal pressed the trigger and his musket misfired. Aboli's weapon roared deafeningly, but the beast was a blur of movement so swift, in the smoke and the darkness, that it cheated the eye. Aboli's shot must have flown wide for it had no effect upon the lion, which swept into the stockade, roaring horribly. Hal flung himself down on Sukeena, covering her with his own body and the lion leapt over him.

It seemed to pick out Johannes from the huddle of terrified humanity. Its great jaws closed in the small of the man's back and it lifted him as a cat might carry a mouse. With one more bound it cleared the rear wall of the stockade and disappeared into the night.

They heard Johannes screaming in the darkness, but the lion did not carry him far. Just beyond the firelight it began to devour him while he still lived. They heard his bones crack as the beast bit into them, then the rending of his flesh as it tore out a mouthful. There was more roaring and growling as the lionesses rushed in to share the prey, and while Johannes still shrieked and sobbed they tore him to pieces. Gradually his cries became weaker until they faded away entirely and from the darkness there were only the grisly sounds of the feast.

The women were hysterical and Bobby wailed and beat his little fists in terror against Althuda's chest. Hal quieted Sukeena, who responded swiftly to the feel of his arm around her shoulder. 'Do not run. Move quietly. Sit in a circle. The women in the centre. Reload the muskets, but do not fire until I give the word.' Hal rallied them, then looked at Daniel and Aboli.

'It is our store of meat that draws them. When they have finished with Johannes they will charge the stockade again for more.'

'You are right, Gundwane.'

'Then we will give them eland meat to distract them from us,' Hal said. 'Help me.'

Between the three of them they seized one of the huge hindquarters of raw eland flesh and staggered with it to the edge of the firelight. They threw it down in the dust.

'Do not run,' Hal cautioned them again, 'for as the cat pursues the

399

mouse, they will come after us if we do.' They backed into the stockade. Almost immediately a lioness rushed out, seized the bloody hindquarter and dragged it away into the night. They could hear the commotion as the others fought her for the prize, and then the sounds as they all settled down to feed, snarling and growling and spitting at each other.

That hunk of raw meat was sufficient to keep even that voracious pride of the great cats feeding and squabbling for an hour, but when once more they began to prowl at the edge of the firelight and make short mock charges at the huddle of terrified humans Hal said, 'We must feed them again.' It soon became clear that the lions would accept these offerings in preference to rushing the camp, for when the three men dragged out another hindquarter from the stockade, the beasts waited for them to retire before a lioness slunk out of the night to haul it away.

'Always it is the female who is boldest,' Hal said, to distract the others.

Aboli agreed with him. 'And the greediest!'

'It is not our fault that you males lack courage and the sense to help yourselves,' Sukeena told them tartly, and most of them laughed, but breathlessly and without conviction. Twice more during the night Hal had them carry out legs of eland meat to feed the pride. At last as the dawn started to define the tops of the thorn trees against the paling sky the lions seemed to have assuaged their appetites. They heard the roaring of the black-maned male fading with distance as he wandered away. He roared for the last time a league off, just as the sun pushed its flaming golden rim above the jagged tops of the mountain range that ran parallel with the route of their march.

Hal and Althuda went out to find what remained of poor Johannes. Strangely the lions had left his hands and his head untouched, but had consumed the rest of him. Hal closed the staring eyes and Sukeena wrapped these pathetic remnants in a scrap of cloth and prayed over the grave they dug. Hal placed slabs of rock over the fresh-turned earth to deter the hyenas from digging it up.

'We can spend no more time here.' He lifted Sukeena to her feet. 'We must start out immediately if we are to reach the river today. Fortunately, there is still enough meat left for our purpose.'

They slung the remaining legs of eland meat on carrying poles, and with a man at each end staggered with them over the rolling hills and grasslands. It was late afternoon when they reached the river and, from the high bluff, looked down onto its broad green expanse, which had already proved such a barrier to their march.

The *Golden Bough* dropped her anchor at the head of the channel in Elephant Lagoon, and at once Llewellyn set his crew to work, pumping out the bilges and repairing the storm damage to the hull and the rigging. A full gale still raged overhead, but though the surface of the lagoon was whipped into a froth of white wavelets the high ground of the heads broke its main force.

Cornelius Schreuder fretted to go ashore. He was desperate to get off the *Golden Bough* and rid himself of this company of Englishmen whom he had come to detest so bitterly. He looked upon Lord Cumbrae as a friend and an ally and was anxious to join him and ask him to act as his second in the affair of honour with Vincent Winterton. In his tiny cabin he packed his chests hurriedly and, when a man could not be spared to help him, lugged them up onto the deck himself. He stood with the pile of his possessions at the entryport, staring out across the lagoon to Cumbrae's shore base.

The Buzzard had set up his camp on the same site as Sir Francis Courteney's, which Schreuder had attacked with his green-jackets. A great deal of activity was taking place amongst the trees. It seemed to Schreuder that Cumbrae must be digging trenches and other fortifications and he was puzzled by this: he saw no sense in throwing up earthworks against an enemy that did not exist.

Llewellyn would not leave his ship until he was certain that the repairs to her were well afoot and that, in all other respects, she was snugged down and secure. Eventually he placed his first mate, Arnold Fowler, in charge of the deck and ordered one of his longboats made ready.

'Captain Llewellyn!' Schreuder accosted him, as he came to the ship's side. 'I have decided that, with Lord Cumbrae's agreement, I will leave your ship and transfer to the *Gull of Moray*.'

Llewellyn nodded. 'I understood that was your intention and, in all truth, Colonel, I doubt there will be many tears shed on board the *Golden Bough* when you depart. I am going ashore now to find where we can refill the water casks that have been contaminated with seawater during the gale. I will convey you and your possessions to Cumbrae's camp, and I have here the fare money which you paid to me for your passage. To save myself further unpleasantness and acrimonious argument, I am repaying this to you in full.'

Schreuder would have dearly loved to give himself the pleasure of disdainfully refusing the offer, but those few guineas were all his wealth in the world and he took the thin purse that Llewellyn handed him, and muttered reluctantly, 'In that, at least, you act like a gentleman, sir. I am indebted to you.'

They went down into the longboat, and Llewellyn sat in the stern sheets while Schreuder found a seat in the bows and ignored the grinning faces of the crew and the ironical salutes from the ship's officers on the quarterdeck as they pulled away. They were only half-way to the beach when a familiar figure wearing a plaid and a beribboned bonnet sauntered out from amongst the trees, his red beard and tangled locks blazing in the sunlight, and watched them approach with both hands on his hips.

'Colonel Schreuder, by the devil's steaming turds!' Cumbrae roared as he recognized him. 'It gladdens my heart to behold your smiling countenance.' As soon as the bows touched the beach Schreuder leapt ashore and seized the Buzzard's outthrust hand.

'I am surprised but overjoyed to find you here, my lord.'

The Buzzard looked over Schreuder's shoulder, and grinned widely. 'Och! And if it's not my beloved brother of the Temple, Christopher Llewellyn! Well met, cousin, and God's benevolence upon you.'

Llewellyn did not smile, and showed little eagerness to take the hand that Cumbrae thrust at him as soon as his feet touched the sand. 'How d'ye do, Cumbrae? Our last discourse in the Bay of Trincomalee was interrupted at a crucial point when you left in some disarray.'

'Ah, but that was in another land and long ago, cousin, and I'm sure we can both be magnanimous enough to forgive and forget such a trifling and silly matter.'

'Five hundred pounds and the lives of twenty of my men is not a trifling and silly matter in my counting house. And I'll remind you that I'm no cousin nor any kin of yours,' Llewellyn snapped, and his legs were stiff with the memory of his old outrage.

But Cumbrae placed one arm around his shoulder and said softly, 'In Arcadia habito.'

Llewellyn was obviously struggling with himself, but he could not deny his knightly oath, and at last he gritted the response, 'Flumen sacrum bene cognosco.'

'There you are.' The Buzzard boomed with laughter. 'That was not so bad, was it? If not cousins, then we are still brothers in Christ, are we not?'

'I would feel more brotherly towards you, sir, if I had my five hundred pounds back in my purse.'

'I could set off that debt against the grievous injury that you inflicted on my sweet Gull and my own person.' The Buzzard pulled back his cloak to display the bright scar across his upper arm. 'But I'm a forgiving man with a loving heart, Christopher, and so you shall have it. I give you my word on it. Every farthing of your five hundred pounds, and the interest to boot.'

Llewellyn smiled at him coldly. 'I will delay my thanks until I feel the weight of your purse in my hands.' Cumbrae saw the purpose in his level gaze and, without another look at the *Golden Bough*'s row of gunports and the handy businesslike lines of her hull, he knew that they were evenly matched and it would be hard pounding if it came to a fight between the two ships, just as it had been four years previously in the Bay of Trincomalee.

'I don't blame you for trusting no man in this naughty world of ours, but dine with me today, here ashore, and I will place the purse in your hands, I swear it to you.'

Llewellyn nodded grimly. 'Thank you for that offer of hospitality, sir, but I well remember the last time I availed myself of one of your invitations. I have a fine cook on board my own ship who can provide me with a meal more to my taste. However, I will return at dusk to fetch the purse you have promised me.' Llewellyn bowed and returned to his longboat.

The Buzzard watched him go, with a calculating look in his eyes. The longboat headed up the lagoon towards the stream of fresh water that flowed into its upper end. 'That dandy bastard has a nasty temper,' he growled and, beside him, Schreuder nodded.

'I have never been so pleased to be rid of somebody unpleasant and to be standing here on this beach and appealing to your friendship, as I am now.'

Cumbrae looked at him shrewdly. 'You have me at a disadvantage, sir,' he said. 'What indeed are you doing here, and what is it that I can do for you in good friendship?'

'Where can we talk?' Schreuder asked.

Cumbrae replied, 'This way, my old friend and companion in arms,' led Schreuder to his hut in the grove and poured him half a mug of whisky. 'Now, tell me. Why are you no longer in command of the garrison at Good Hope?'

'To be frank with you, my lord, I am in the devil's own fix. I stand accused by Governor van de Velde of a crime that I did not commit. You know well how bitterly he was obsessed by envy and ill-will towards me,' Schreuder explained, and Cumbrae nodded cautiously without committing himself.

'Please go on.'

'Ten days ago the Governor's wife was murdered in a fit of lust and bestial passion by the gardener and executioner of the Company.'

'Sweet heavens!' Cumbrae exclaimed. 'Slow John! I knew he was a madman. I could see it in his eyes. A blethering maniac! I am sorry to hear about the woman, though. She was a delicious little muffin. Fair put a bone in my breeches just to look at those titties of hers, she did.'

'Van de Velde has falsely accused me of this foul murder. I was forced to flee on the first available ship before he had me imprisoned and placed on the rack. Llewellyn offered me passage to the Orient where I had determined to enlist in the war that is afoot in the Horn of Africa between the Prester and the Great Mogul.'

Cumbrae's eyes lit up and he leaned forward on his stool at the mention of war, like a hyena scenting the blood of a battlefield. By this time he was heartily bored with digging for Franky Courteney's elusive treasure, and the promise of an easier way to fill his holds with riches had all of his attention. But he would not show this posturing braggart just how eager he was, so he left the subject for another time and said, with feeling and understanding, 'You have my deepest sympathy and my assurances of any aid I am able to render.' His mind was seething with ideas. He sensed that Schreuder was guilty of the murder he denied so vehemently but, guilty or not, he was now an outlaw and he was placing himself at Cumbrae's mercy.

The Buzzard had been given ample demonstration of Schreuder's qualities as a warrior. An excellent man to have serve under him, especially as he would be completely under Cumbrae's control by virtue of his guilt and the blood on his hands. As a fugitive and a murderer, the Dutchman could no longer afford to be too finicky in matters of morality.

Once a maid has lost her virginity she lifts her skirts and lies down in the hay with more alacrity the second time, the Buzzard told himself happily, but reached out and clasped Schreuder's arm with a firm and friendly grip. 'You can rely on me, my friend,' he said. 'How may I help you?'

'I wish to throw in my lot with you. I will become your man.'

'And heartily welcome you will be.' Cumbrae grinned through his red whiskers with unfeigned delight. He had just found himself a hunting hound, one perhaps not carrying a great cargo of intelligence but, none the less, fierce and totally without fear.

'I ask only one favour in return,' Schreuder said. The Buzzard let the friendly hand drop from his shoulder, and his eyes became guarded. He might have known that such a handsome gift would have a price written on the underside.

'A favour?' he asked.

'On board the *Golden Bough* I was treated in the most shabby and scurvy fashion. I was cheated out of a great deal of money at Hazard by one of the ship's officers, and insulted and reviled by Captain Llewellyn and his men. To cap it all, the person who cheated me challenged me to a duel. I could find no person on board willing to act as my second, and Llewellyn forbade this matter of honour to be pursued until we reached port.'

'Go on, please.' Cumbrae's suspicions were beginning to evaporate as he realized where the conversation was heading.

'I would be most grateful and honoured if you could consent to act as my second in this affair, my lord.'

'That is all you require of me?' He could hardly credit that it would be so easy. Already he could see the profits that might be reaped from this affair. He had promised Llewellyn his five hundred pounds, and he would give it to him, but only when he was certain that he would be able to get the money back from him, together with any other profit that he could lay hands upon.

He glanced out over the waters of the lagoon. There lay the *Golden Bough*, a powerful, warlike vessel. If he were able to add her to his flotilla, he would command a force in the oriental oceans that few could match. If he appeared off the Great Horn of Africa with these two vessels, in the midst of the war that Schreuder had assured him was raging, what spoils might there be for the picking?

'It will be my honour and my pleasure to act for you,' he told Schreuder. 'Give me the name of the dastard who has challenged you, and I will see to it that you obtain immediate satisfaction from him.'

When Llewellyn came ashore again for dinner, he was accompanied by two of his officers and a dozen of his seamen, carrying cutlass and pistols. Cumbrae was on the beach to welcome him. 'I have the purse I promised you, my dear Christopher. Come with me to my poor lodgings and take a dram with me for loving friendship and for the memory of convivial days we passed in former times in each other's company. But first will ye no' introduce me to these two fine gentlemen of yours?'

'Mr Arnold Fowler, first mate of my ship.' The two men nodded at each other. 'And this is my third officer, Vincent Winterton, son of my patron, Viscount Winterton.'

'Also, so I am informed, a paragon at Hazard, and a mean hand with the dice.' Cumbrae grinned at Vincent and the young man withdrew the hand he was on the point of proffering.

'I beg your pardon, sir, but what do you mean by that remark?' Vincent enquired stiffly.

'Only that Colonel Schreuder has asked me to act for him. Would you be good enough to inform me as to who is your own second?'

Llewellyn cut in quickly, 'I have the honour to act for Mr Winterton.'

'Indeed, then, we have much to discuss, my dear Christopher. Please

405

follow me, but as it is Mr Winterton's affairs we will be discussing, it might be as well if he remained here on the beach.'

Llewellyn followed the Buzzard to his hut, and took the stool that he was offered. 'A dram of the water of life?'

Llewellyn shook his head. 'Thank you, no. Let us come to the matters at hand.'

'You were always impatient and headstrong.' The Buzzard filled his own mug and took a mouthful. He smacked his lips and wiped his whiskers on the back of his hand. 'You'll never know what you're missing. 'Tis the finest whisky in all the islands. But, here, this is for you.' He slid the heavy purse across the keg that served him for a table. Llewellyn picked it up and weighed it thoughtfully in his hand.

'Count it if you will,' the Buzzard invited him. 'I'll take no offence.' He sat back and watched with a grin on his face, sipping at his mug, while Llewellyn arranged the golden coins in neat stacks on the top of the keg.

'Five hundred it is, and fifty for the interest. I am obliged to you, sir.' Llewellyn's expression had softened.

'It's a small price to pay for your love and friendship, Christopher,' Cumbrae told him. 'But now to this other matter. As I told you, I act for Colonel Schreuder.'

'And I act for Mr Winterton.' Llewellyn nodded. 'My principal will be satisfied with an apology from Schreuder.'

'You know full well, Christopher, that my lad will no' give him one. I am afraid that the two young puppies will have to fight it out.'

'The choice of weapons lies with your side,' said Llewellyn. 'Shall we say pistols at twenty paces?'

'We will say no such thing. My man wants swords.'

'Then we must agree. What time and place will suit you?'

'I leave that decision to you.'

'I have repairs to make to my rigging and hull. Damage we sustained in the gale. I need Mr Winterton on board to help with these. May I suggest three days hence, on the beach at sunrise?'

The Buzzard tugged at his beard as he considered this proposal. He would need a few days to make the arrangements he had in mind. Three days' delay would suit him perfectly.

'Agreed!' he said, and Llewellyn rose to his feet immediately and placed the purse in the pocket of his tunic.

'Will you not take that dram I offered you now, Christopher?' Cumbrae suggested, but again Llewellyn declined.

'As I told you, sir, I have much to do on board my ship.'

The Buzzard watched him go down to the beach and step into his longboat. As they were rowed back to where the *Golden Bough* was anchored, Llewellyn and Winterton were in deep and earnest conversation.

'Young Winterton is in for a surprise. He can never have seen the Dutchman with a sword in his hand to have agreed so lightly to the choice of weapons.' He swigged back the few drops of whisky that remained in his mug, and grinned again. 'We shall see if we cannot arrange a little surprise for Christopher Llewellyn also.' He banged the mug onto the keg top, and bellowed, 'Send Mr Bowles to me, and be quick about it.'

Sam Bowles came smarming in, wriggling his whole body like a whipped dog to ingratiate himself with his captain. But his eyes were cold and shrewd.

'Sammy, me boy.' Cumbrae gave him a slap on the arm that stung like a wasp, but did not upset the smile on the man's lips. 'I have something for you, that should be much to your taste. Listen well.'

Sam Bowles sat opposite him and cocked his head so as not to miss a word of his instructions. Once or twice he asked a question or chortled with glee and admiration as Cumbrae unfolded his plans.

'You have always wanted the command of your own ship, Sammy me laddy. This is your chance. Serve me well, and you shall have it. Captain Samuel Bowles. How does that sound to you?'

'I like the sound of it powerful well, your grace!' Sam Bowles bobbed his head. 'And I'll not let you down.'

'That you won't!' Cumbrae agreed. 'Or not more than once, you won't. For if you do, you'll dance me a merry hornpipe while you dangle from the main yard of my *Gull*.'

The riverbanks were lined with wild willow and dark green acacia trees, which were covered with a mantle of yellow blossom. The river ran broad and deep, slow and green between its rocky piers. The sandbanks were exposed and, as they looked down upon them from the steep slopes of the valley, Sukeena shuddered and whispered, 'Oh, what foul and ugly creatures! Surely these are the very dragons we spoke of?'

'They are dragons indeed,' Hal agreed, as they gazed down on the crocodiles that lay sunning on the white beach. There were dozens of them, some not much larger than lizards and other brutes with the beam and length of a ship's boat, massive grey monsters, which surely could swallow a man whole. They had found out how ferocious these creatures

407

were on their first attempt to ford the river, when Billy Rogers had been seized by one and dragged beneath the surface. They had not recovered any part of his body.

'I tremble at the thought of trying to cross again, with these creatures still guarding the river,' Sukeena whispered tremulously.

'Aboli knows them from his own land to the north, and his tribe have a way of dealing with them.'

On the rocky bluff, high above the river where the crocodiles could not reach, they stacked the piles of eland meat, which were already beginning to stink, in the hot sunlight. Then Hal sent some of the men to search the forest floor for dried logs that would float high in the water. Under Ned Tyler's instruction they shaped them with the cutlasses, although Hal hated to see the fine steel edges dulled and chipped. While this was being done Althuda, with Sukeena helping him, carefully slit the wet eland hides into long tough ropes as thick as her little finger.

Aboli sought out the species of tree he needed, and then chopped short supple stakes from its branches and carried bundles of these back to where the others were working. Big Daniel helped him to sharpen both ends of these short, resilient pieces of green wood into spear points, and harden them in the fire. Then, using a log of the correct circumference as a template, the two powerful men bent each stake around the log until it formed a circle, the sharpened points overlapping. While they held them in place, Hal lashed the ends together with strips of the raw eland hide. When they gingerly released the tension the coiled stakes were like the loaded steel springs of a musket lock, ready to fly open if the retaining strip of hide was severed. By sundown they had finished work on a pile of these snares.

They had learned from their encounter with the lion pride, and on this night they hoisted the legs of eland meat high into the top branches of one of the tallest trees that grew along the banks of the broad river. They built their stockade well downstream from this cache of meat, and made certain that the walls were of sturdy logs, and that the entrance was blocked with freshly cut thorn branches.

Though they slept little that night, lying and listening to the hyena and the jackal howling and gibbering below the tree where the meat hung, the lions did not trouble them again. In the dawn they left the stockade to begin work once more on their preparations for the river crossing.

Ned Tyler finished the construction of the raft by lashing the poles together with rawhide rope.

''Tis a rickety vessel.' Sukeena eyed it with obvious misgivings. 'One of those great river dragons could overturn it with a flick of its tail.'

'That is why Aboli has prepared his snares for them.'

They went back up the slope to where Althuda and Zwaantie were helping Aboli wrap the coiled green-wood circlets with a thick covering of half-putrid eland meat.

'The crocodile cannot chew his food,' Aboli explained to them as he worked. 'Each of these lumps of meat is the right size for one of the monsters to swallow whole.'

When all the baits had been prepared, they carried them down to the water's edge. As they approached the sandbank where the great saurians lay like stranded logs, they shouted clapped their hands and fired off the muskets, creating a commotion that alarmed even these huge beasts.

They raised their massive bulks on short stubby legs and lumbered to the shelter of their natural element, sliding into the deep green pools with mighty splashes and setting up waves that broke upon the far bank. As soon as the sandbank was clear, the men rushed out and placed the lumps of stinking meat along the water's edge. Then they hurried back and climbed up to where the women waited on the safety of the high bluff above the river.

After a while, the eye knuckles of the crocodiles began to pop up everywhere over the surface of the pool, and then to move in slowly towards the sandbank.

'They are cowardly, sneaking beasts,' Aboli said, with hatred in his tone and revulsion in his expression, 'but soon, when they smell the meat, their greed will overcome their fear.'

As he spoke one of the largest reptiles lifted itself out of the shallows at the edge and waddled cautiously out on to the sandbank, its massive crested tail ploughing a furrow behind it. Suddenly, with surprising speed and agility, it darted forward and seized one of the lumps of eland meat. It opened its jaws to their full stretch as it strained to swallow. From the bluff they watched in awe as the huge lump of meat slid down into its maw, bulging the soft white scales on the outside of its throat. It turned and rushed back into the pool, but immediately another of the scaly reptiles emerged and gobbled a bait. There followed a general mêlée of long slithering bodies, shining wet in the sunlight, that hissed and snapped and tumbled over each other as they fought for the meat.

Once every bait had been consumed, some crocodiles splashed back into the pool, but many settled down again in the sun-warmed sand from where they had been disturbed. Peace fell over the riverbank again, and the kingfishers darted and hovered over the green waters. A great grey hippopotamus thrust out his head on the far side of the pool and gave vent to a raucous grunt of laughter. His cows clustered around him, their backs like a pile of shiny black boulders.

409

'Your plan has not worked,' said Sabah in Dutch. 'The crocodiles are unharmed and still ready to fall upon any of us who goes near the water.'

'Be patient, Sabah,' Aboli told him. 'It will take a while for the juices of their stomach to eat through the rawhide. But when they do the sticks will spring open and the sharpened ends will pierce their guts and stab through their vitals.'

As he finished speaking, one of the largest reptiles, the first to take the bait, suddenly let out a thunderous roar and arched its back until the coxcombed tail flapped over its head. It roared again, and spun round to snap with mighty jaws at its own flank, its spiked yellow fangs tearing through the armoured scales, ripping out lumps of its own flesh.

'See there!' Aboli sprang to his feet and pointed. 'The sharp end of the stake has cut right through his belly.' Then they saw the fire-blackened point of sharpened green wood protruding a hand's breadth through the scaly hide. As the bull crocodile writhed and hissed in his hideous death throes, a second reptile began to thrash about in gargantuan convulsions, and then another and another, until the pool was turned to white foam, and their terrible stricken cries and roars echoed along the bluffs of the river, startling the eagles and vultures from their nesting platforms high on the cliffs.

'Bravely done, Aboli! You have cleared the way for us.' Hal leaped to his feet.

'Yes! We can cross now,' Aboli agreed. 'But be swift and do not linger in the water or near the edge for there may still be some of the *ngwenya* who have not felt the spikes in their bellies.'

They heeded his advice. Lifting the clumsy raft between them they rushed it down the bank, and as soon as it was afloat they flung aboard the baskets of provisions, the saddle-bags and the bags of gunpowder, then urged the two women and little Bobby onto the frail craft. The men were stripped to their petticoats, and swam the craft across the sluggish current. As soon as they reached the opposite bank they seized their possessions and scampered in haste up the rocky slope until they were well clear of the riverbank.

High above the water they could at last fall upon each other with laughter and congratulation. They camped there that night, and in the dawn Aboli asked Hal quietly, 'How far now to Elephant Lagoon?'

Hal unrolled his chart and pointed out his estimate of their position. 'Here, we are five leagues inland from the seashore and not more than fifty leagues from the lagoon. Unless there is another river as wide as this to bar our way, we should be there in five more days of hard marching.'

'Then let us march hard,' said Aboli, and roused the rest of the

410

depleted band. At his urging, they took up their loads and, with the rays of the rising sun beating full into their faces, fell once more into the order of march that they had maintained through all the long journey.

The four longboats from the *Golden Bough* were crowded with seamen as they rowed ashore in that dark hour before the dawn. A sailor in the bow of each boat held high a lantern to light their way, and the reflections danced like fireflies on the calm black surface of the lagoon.

'Llewellyn is bringing half his crew ashore with him!' the Buzzard gloated, as he watched the little fleet head in towards the beach.

'He suspects treachery,' Sam Bowles laughed delightedly, 'so he comes in force.'

'What a churlish guest, to suspect us of villainy.' The Buzzard shook his head sadly. 'He deserves whatever Fate has in store for him.'

'He has split his force. There are at least fifty men in those boats,' Sam estimated. 'He makes it easier for us. From here it should all be plane sailing and a following wind.'

'Let us hope so, Mr Bowles,' the Buzzard grunted. 'I go now to meet our guests. Remember, the signal is a red Chinese rocket. Wait until you see it burn.'

'Aye, Captain!' Sam knuckled his forehead and slipped away into the shadows. Cumbrae strode down the sand to meet the leading boat. As it came in to the beach he could see in the lamplight that Llewellyn and Vincent Winterton were sitting together in the stern sheets. Vincent wore a dark woollen cloak against the dawn chill, but his head was bare. He had braided his hair into a thick pigtail down his back. He followed his captain ashore.

'Good morrow, gentlemen,' Cumbrae greeted them. 'I commend you for your punctuality.'

Llewellyn nodded a greeting. 'Mr Winterton is ready to begin.'

The Buzzard waggled his beard. 'Colonel Schreuder is waiting. This way, if you please.' They strode abreast along the beach, the seamen from the boats following in an orderly column. 'It is unusual to have such a crowd of ruffians to witness an affair of honour,' he remarked.

'There are but a few conventions out here beyond the Line,' Llewellyn retorted, 'but one is to keep your back well covered.'

'I take your point.' Cumbrae chuckled. 'But to demonstrate my good faith, I will not invite any of my own lads to join us. I am unarmed.' He showed his hands, then opened the front of his tunic to demonstrate the fact. Making a comforting lump in the small of his back, where it was tucked into his belt, was one of the new-fangled wheel-lock pistols, made by Fallon of Glasgow. It was a marvellous invention but prohibitively expensive, which was the main reason why it was not more widely employed. On pressing the trigger the spring-loaded wheel of the lock spun and the iron pyrites striker sent a shower of sparks into the pan to detonate the charge. The weapon had cost him well over twenty pounds but was worth the price for there was no burning match to betray its presence.

'To demonstrate your own good faith, my dear Christopher, will you kindly keep your men together at your side of the square and under your direct control?'

A short way down the beach, they came to the area where the sand had been levelled and a square roped off. A water cask had been set up at each of the four corners. 'Twenty paces each side,' Cumbrae told Llewellyn. 'Will that give your man enough searoom in which to work?'

Winterton surveyed the square then nodded briefly. 'It will suit us well enough.' Llewellyn spoke for him.

'We will have some time to wait for the light to strengthen,' Cumbrae said. 'My cook has prepared a breakfast of hot biscuit and spiced wine. Will you partake?'

'Thank you, my lord. A cup of wine would be welcome.' A steward brought the steaming cups to them, and Cumbrae said, 'If you will excuse me, I will attend my principal.' He bowed and went up the path into the trees, to return minutes later leading Colonel Schreuder.

They stood together at the far side of the roped square, talking quietly. At last Cumbrae looked up at the sky, said something to Schreuder, then nodded and came to where Llewellyn and Vincent waited. 'I think the light is good enough now. Do you gentlemen agree?'

'We can begin.' Llewellyn nodded stiffly.

'My principal offers his weapon for your examination,' Cumbrae said, and proffered the Neptune sword hilt first. Llewellyn took it and held the gold-inlaid blade up to the morning light.

'A fancy piece of work,' he murmured disparagingly. 'These naked females would not be out of place in a whorehouse.' He touched the gold engravings of sea nymphs. 'But at least the point is not poisoned and the length matches that of my principal's blade.' He held the two swords side by side to compare them, and then passed Vincent's sword to Cumbrae for inspection.

'A fair match,' he agreed, and passed it back.

'Five-minute rounds and first blood?' Llewellyn asked, drawing his gold timepiece from the pocket of his waistcoat.

'I am afraid we cannot agree to that.' Cumbrae shook his head. 'My man wishes to fight without pause until one of them cries for quarter or is dead.'

'By God, sir!' Llewellyn burst out. 'Those rules are murderous.'

'If your man pisses like a puppy, then he should not aspire to howl with the wolves.' Cumbrae shrugged.

'I agree!' Vincent interjected. 'We will fight to the death, if that's the way the Dutchman wants it.'

'That, sir, is exactly how he wants it,' Cumbrae assured him. 'We are ready to begin when you are. Will you give the signal, Captain Llewellyn?'

The Buzzard went back and, in a few terse sentences, explained the rules to Schreuder, who nodded and ducked under the rope of the barrier. He wore a thin shirt open at the throat so that it was clear that he wore no body armour beneath it. Traditionally, the brilliant white cotton would give his opponent a fair aiming mark, and show up the blood from a hit.

On the opposite side of the square Vincent loosened the clasp of his cloak and let it drop into the sand. He was dressed in a similar white shirt. With his sword in his hand, he vaulted lightly over the rope barrier and faced Schreuder across the swept beach sand. Both men began to limber up with a series of practice cuts and thrusts that made their blades sing and glitter in the early light.

'Are you ready, Colonel Schreuder?' After a few minutes, Llewellyn called from the side-line as he held on high a red silk scarf.

'Ready!'

'Are you ready, Mr Winterton?'

'Ready!'

Llewellyn let the scarf drop, and a growl went up from the *Gull's* seamen at the far side of the square. The two swordsmen circled each other, closing in cautiously with their blades extended and their points circling and dipping. Suddenly Vincent sprang forward, and feinted for Schreuder's throat, but Schreuder met him easily and locked his blade. For a long moment they strained silently, staring into each other's eyes. Perhaps Vincent saw death in the other man's implacable gaze, and felt the steel in his wrist, for he broke first. As he recoiled Schreuder came after him with a series of lightning ripostes that made his blade glint and glitter like a sunbeam.

It was a dazzling display that drove Vincent, desperately parrying and retreating, against one of the water kegs that marked a corner of the square. Pinned there, he was at Schreuder's mercy. Abruptly Schreuder broke off the assault, turned his back contemptuously on the younger

413

man and strode back into the centre. There, he took up his guard again and, blade poised, waited for Vincent to engage him once more.

All the watchers, except Cumbrae, were stunned by the Dutchman's virtuosity. Clearly Vincent Winterton was a swordsman of superior ability but he had been forced to call upon all his skill to survive that first blazing attack. In his heart Llewellyn knew that Vincent had survived not because of his skill but because Schreuder had wanted it that way. Already the young Englishman had been touched three times, two light cuts on the chest and another deeper wound on the upper left arm. His shirt was slashed in three irregular tears and was turning red and sodden as the wounds began to weep profusely.

Vincent glanced down at them, and his expression mirrored the despair he felt as he faced the knowledge that he was no match for the Dutchman. He lifted his head and looked across to where Schreuder waited for him, his stance classical and arrogant, his expression grave and intent as he studied his adversary over the weaving point of the Neptune sword.

Vincent straightened his spine and took his guard, trying to smile carelessly as he steeled himself to go forward to his certain death. The rough seamen who watched might have bayed and bellowed at the spectacle of a bull-baiting or a cockfight, but even they had fallen silent, awed by the terrible tragedy they saw unfolding. Llewellyn could not let it happen.

'Hold hard!' he cried, and vaulted over the rope. He strode between the two men, his right hand raised. 'Colonel Schreuder, sir. You have given us every reason to admire your swordsmanship. You have drawn first blood. Will you not give us good reason to respect you by declaring that your honour is satisfied?'

'Let the English coward apologize to me in front of all the present company, and then I will be satisfied,' said Schreuder, and Llewellyn turned to appeal to Vincent. 'Will you do what the colonel asks? Please, Vincent, for my sake and the trust I pledged to your father.'

Vincent's face was deathly pale but the blood that stained his shirt was bright crimson, as full blown June roses on the bush. 'Colonel Schreuder has this moment called me a coward. Forgive me, Captain, but you know I cannot accede to such conditions.'

Llewellyn looked sadly upon his young protégé. 'He intends to kill you, Vincent. It is such a shameful waste of a fine young life.'

'And I intend to kill him.' Vincent was able to smile now that it was decided. It was a gay, reckless smile. 'Please stand aside, Captain.' Hopelessly Llewellyn turned back to the sidelines.

'On guard, sir!' Vincent called, and charged with the white sand

414

spurting from under his boots, thrust and parry for very life. The Neptune sword was an impenetrable wall of steel before him, meeting and turning his own blade with an ease that made all his bravest efforts seem those of a child. Schreuder's grave expression never faltered, and when at last Vincent fell back, panting and gasping, sweat diluting his streaming blood to pink, he was wounded twice more. There was black despair in his eyes.

Now, at last, the seamen from the *Golden Bough* had found their voices. 'Quarter! You bloody murdering cheese-head!' they howled, and 'Fair shakes, man. Let the lad live!'

'They'll get no mercy from Colonel Cornelius,' Cumbrae smiled grimly, 'but the din they're making will help Sam to do his job.' He glanced across the lagoon to where the *Golden Bough* lay in the channel. Every man still aboard her was crowded along the near rail, straining his eyes for a glimpse of the duel. Even the lookout at her main top had trained his telescope on the beach. Not one was aware of the boats that were speeding out from amongst the mangroves on the far shore. He recognized Sam Bowles in the leading boat, as it raced in under the *Golden Bough*'s tumble home and was hidden from his view by the ship's hull. *Sweet Mary, Sam will take her without a shot fired!* Cumbrae thought exultantly, and looked back at the arena.

'You have had your turn, sir,' said Schreuder quietly. 'Now it is mine. On guard, if you please.' With three swift strides he had covered the gap that separated them. The younger man met his first thrust, and then the second with a high parry and block, but the Neptune blade was swift and elusive as an enraged cobra. It seemed to mesmerize him with its deadly shining dance and, darting and striking, slowly forced him to yield ground. Each time he parried and retreated, he lost position and balance.

Then suddenly Schreuder executed a coup that few swordsmen would dare attempt outside the practice field. He caught up both blades in the classical prolonged engagement, swirling the two swords together so that the steel edges shrilled with a sound that grated across the nerve endings of the watchers. Once committed neither man dared break off the engagement, for to do so was to concede an opening. Around in a deadly glittering circle the two swords revolved. It became a trial of strength and endurance. Vincent's arm turned leaden and the sweat dripped from his chin. His eyes were desperate and his wrist began to tremble and bend under the strain.

Then Schreuder froze the fatal circle. He did not break away but simply clamped Vincent's sword in a vice of steel. It was a display of such strength and control that even Cumbrae gaped with amazement.

415

For a moment the duellists remained unmoving, then slowly Schreuder began to force both points upward, until they were aimed skywards at full stretch of their arms. Vincent was helpless. He tried to hold the other blade but his arm began to shudder and his muscles quivered. He bit down on his own tongue with the effort until a spot of blood appeared at the corner of his mouth.

It could not last longer, and Llewellyn cried out in despair as he saw that the young man had reached the furthest limits of his strength and endurance. 'Hold hard, Vincent!' It was in vain. Vincent broke. He disengaged with his right arm at full reach above his head, and his chest wide open.

'Ha!' shouted Schreuder, and his thrust was a blur, fast as the release of a bolt from a crossbow. He drove in his point an inch below Vincent's sternum, clear through his body and a foot out of his back. For a long moment Vincent froze like a figure carved from a block of marble. Then his legs melted under him and he toppled into the sand.

'Murder!' cried Llewellyn. He sprang into the square and knelt beside the dying youth. He took him in his arms, and looked up again at Schreuder. 'Bloody murder!' he cried again.

'I must take that as request.' Cumbrae smiled and came up behind the kneeling man. 'And I am happy to oblige you, cousin!' he said, and brought the wheel-lock pistol out from behind his back. He thrust the muzzle into the back of Llewellyn's head and pulled the trigger. There was a bright flare of sparks and then the pistol roared and leaped in the Buzzard's fist. At such close range the load of lead pellets drove clean through Llewellyn's skull and blew half of his face away in red tatters. He flopped forwards with Vincent's body still in his arms.

The Buzzard looked around quickly, and saw that from the dark grove the red rocket was already soaring upwards, leaving a parabola of silver smoke arched against the fragile blue of the early-morning sky, the signal to Sam Bowles and his boarding party to storm the decks of the *Golden Bough*.

Meanwhile, above the beach, the gunners hidden among the trees were dragging away the branches that covered their culverins. The Buzzard had sited the battery himself and laid them to cover all the far side of the square where the seamen from the *Golden Bough* stood in a row four deep. The culverins enfiladed the group, and each was loaded with a full charge of grape shot.

Even though they were unaware of the hidden battery, the seamen from the *Golden Bough* were swiftly recovering from the shock of seeing their officers slaughtered before their horrified gaze. A hum of fury and wild cries of outrage went up from their midst, but there was no officer to give the order, and though they drew their cutlasses, yet instinctively they hesitated and hung back.

The Buzzard seized Colonel Schreuder's free arm and grated in his ear. 'Come on! Hurry! Clear the range.' He dragged him from the roped ring.

'By God, sir, you have murdered Llewellyn!' Schreuder protested. He was stunned by the act. 'He was unarmed! Defenceless!'

'We will debate the niceties of it later,' Cumbrae promised, and stuck out one booted foot, hooking Schreuder's ankle at the same time shoving him forward. The two men sprawled headlong into the shallow trench in the sand that Cumbrae had dug specially for this purpose, just as the seamen from the *Golden Bough* burst through the ropes of the ring behind them.

'What are you doing?' Schreuder bellowed. 'Release me at once.'

'I am saving your life, you blethering idiot,' Cumbrae shouted in his ear, and held his head down below the lip of the trench as the first salvo of grape shot thundered from out of the grove and swept the beach.

The Buzzard had calculated the range with care so that the pattern of shot spread to its most deadly arc. It caught the phalanx of sailors squarely, raked the sand of the beach into a blinding white storm, and went on to tear across the surface of the quiet lagoon waters like a gale. Most of the *Golden Bough*'s men were struck down instantly, but a few stayed on their feet, bewildered and stunned, staggering like drunkards from their wounds and from the turmoil of grape shot and the blast of disrupted air.

Cumbrae seized his claymore from the bottom of the pit, where he had buried it under a light coating of sand, and leaped to his feet. He rushed on these few survivors, the great sword gripped in both hands. He struck the head clean from the torso of the first man in his path, just as his own sailors came charging out of the gunsmoke, yelling like demons and brandishing their cutlasses.

They fell upon the decimated shore party and hacked them down, even when Cumbrae bellowed, 'Enough! Give quarter to those who yield!' They took no heed of his order, and swung the cutlasses until the thrown blood drops wet them to the elbows and speckled their grinning faces. Cumbrae had to lay about him with his fists and the flat of his sword.

'Avast! We need men to sail the *Golden Bough*. Spare me a dozen, you bloody ruffians.' They gave him less than he demanded. When the carnage was over there were only nine, trussed ankle and wrist and lying belly down in the sand like porkers in the marketplace.

'This way!' the Buzzard bellowed again, and led his crew sprinting down the beach to where the longboats from the *Golden Bough* were drawn up. They piled into them and seized the oars. With Cumbrae roaring in the bows like a wounded animal they pulled for the *Golden Bough,* hooked onto her sides and went swarming up onto her deck with cutlass bared and pistols cocked.

There, help was not needed. Sam Bowles's men had taken the *Golden Bough* by surprise and storm. The deck was slippery with blood and corpses were strewn across it and huddled in the scuppers. Under the forecastle a small band of Llewellyn's men were hanging on desperately, surrounded by Sam's gang of boarders, but when they saw the Buzzard and his gang storm up onto the deck they threw down their cutlasses. Those few who could swim raced to the ship's side and dived into the lagoon while the others fell to their knees and pleaded for quarter.

'Spare them, Mr Bowles,' Cumbrae shouted. 'I need sailors!' He did not wait to see the order obeyed but snatched a musket from the hands of the man beside him and ran to the rail. The escaping sailors were splashing their way towards the mangrove trees. He took careful aim at the head of one, whose pink scalp showed through his wet grey hair. It was a lucky shot, and the man threw up both hands and sank, leaving a pink stain on the surface. The men around Cumbrae hooted with glee and joined in the sport, calling their targets and laying wagers on their marksmanship. 'Who'll give me fives in shillings on that rogue with the blond pigtail?' They shot the swimming men like wounded ducks.

Sam Bowles came grinning and bobbing to meet Cumbrae. 'The ship is yours, your grace.'

'Well done, Mr Bowles.' Cumbrae gave him such a hearty blow of commendation as to knock him almost off his feet. 'There will be some hiding below decks. Winkle them out! Try to take them alive. Put a boat in the water and drag those out also!' He pointed at the few survivors still splashing and swimming towards the mangroves. 'I am going down to Llewellyn's cabin to find the ship's papers. Call me when you have all the prisoners trussed up in the waist of the ship.'

He kicked open the locked door to Llewellyn's cabin, and paused to survey the interior. It was beautifully appointed, the furniture carved and polished and the drapery of fine velvet.

In the writing desk he found the keys to the iron strong-box that was bolted to the deck below the comfortable bunk. As soon as he opened it he recognized the purse he had given Llewellyn. 'I am much obliged to you, Christopher. You'll not be needing this where you're going,' he murmured as he slipped it into his pocket. Under it was a second purse, which he carried to the desk. He spilled the golden coins out onto the tabletop. 'Two hundred and sixteen pounds five shillings and twopence,' he counted. 'This will be the money for the running of the ship. Very parsimonious, but I am grateful for any contribution.'

Then his eyes lit on a small wooden chest in the bottom of the box. He lifted it out and inspected the name carved into the lid. 'The Hon. Vincent Winterton'. The chest was locked but it yielded readily to the blade of his dirk. He smiled as he saw what it contained, and let a handful of coins run through his fingers. 'No doubt the gambling losses of the good Colonel Schreuder are in here but he need never be tempted to wager them again. I will take care of them for him.'

He poured a mug of French brandy from the captain's stores and seated himself at the desk while he ran through the ship's books and documents. The log-book would make interesting reading at a later date. He set it aside. He glanced through a letter of partnership agreement with Lord Winterton who, it seemed, owned the *Golden Bough*. 'No longer, your lordship.' He grinned. 'I regret to inform you that she is all mine now.'

The cargo manifest was disappointing. The *Golden Bough* was carrying mostly cheap trade goods, knives and axes, cloth, beads and copper rings. However, there were also five hundred muskets and a goodly store of blackpowder in her holds.

'Och! So you were going to do a spot of gun smuggling. Shame on you, my dear Christopher.' He tutted disapprovingly. 'I'll have to find something better to fill her holds on the return voyage,' he promised himself, and took a pull at the brandy.

He went on sorting through the other documents. There was a second letter from Winterton, agreeing to the *Golden Bough*'s commission as a warship in the service of the Prester John, and a flowery letter of introduction to him signed by the Chancellor of England, the Earl of Clarendon, under the Great Seal, commending Christopher Llewellyn to the ruler of Ethiopia in the highest terms.

'Ah! That is of more value. With some small alteration to the name, even I would fall for that!' He folded it carefully and replaced the chest, the purses, the books and documents in the strong-box, and hung the key on a ribbon around his neck. While he finished the rest of the brandy he considered the courses of action that were now open to him.

This war in the Great Horn intrigued him. Soon the south-east trade winds would begin to blow across the Ocean of the Indies. On their benevolent wings the Great Mogul would be sending his dhows laden with troops and treasure from his empire on the mainland of India and Further India to his *entrepôts* on the African coast. There would also be the annual pilgrimage of the faithful of Islam taking advantage of the same fair wind to sail up the Arabian Sea on their journey to the birthplace of the Prophet of God. Potentates and princes, ministers of state and rich merchants from every corner of the Orient, they would carry with them such riches as he could only guess at, to lay as offerings in the holy mosques and temples of Mecca and Medina.

Cumbrae allowed himself a few minutes to dream of pigeon's-blood rubies and cornflower sapphires the size of his fist, and elephant-loads of silver and gold bullion. 'With the *Gull* and the *Golden Bough* sailing together, there ain't no black heathen prince who will be able to deny me. I will fill my holds with the best of it. Franky Courteney's miserly little treasure pales beside such abundance,' he consoled himself. It still rankled sorely that he had not been able to find Franky's hiding place, and he scowled. 'When I sail from this lagoon, I will leave the bones of Jiri and those other lying blackamoors as signposts to mark my passing,' he promised himself.

Sam Bowles interrupted his thoughts by sticking his head into the cabin. 'Begging your pardon, your grace, we've rounded up all the prisoners. It was a clean sweep. Not one of them got away.'

The Buzzard heaved himself to his feet, glad to have a distraction from these niggling regrets. 'Let's see what you've got for me, then.'

The prisoners were bound and squatting in three files in the ship's waist. 'Forty-two hardened salt-water men,' said Sam proudly, 'sound in wind and limb.'

'None of them wounded?' the Buzzard asked incredulously.

Sam answered in a whisper, 'I knew you wouldn't want to be bothered to play nursemaid to such. We held their heads under water to help them on their way into the bosom of Jesus. For most of them it was a mercy.'

'I'm amazed at your compassion, Mr Bowles,' Cumbrae grunted, 'but in future spare me such details. You know I'm a man of gentle persuasion.' He put that matter out of his mind and contemplated his prisoners. Despite Sam's assurance, many had been heavily beaten, their eyes were blackened and their lips cut and swollen. They hung their heads and none would look at him.

He walked slowly down the squatting ranks, now and then seizing a handful of hair and lifting the man's face to study it. When he reached the end of the line he came back and addressed them jovially: 'Hear me, my bully lads, I have a berth for all of you. Sail with me and you shall have a shilling a month and a fair share of the prize money and, as sure as my name is Angus Cochran, there'll be sackloads of gold and silver to share.'

None replied, and he frowned. 'Are you deaf or has the devil got your tongues? Who will sail with Cochran of Cumbrae?' The silence hung heavily over the deck. He strode forward and picked out one of the most intelligent-looking of his prisoners. 'What's your name, lad?'

'Davey Morgan.'

'Will you sail with me, Davey?'

Slowly the man lifted his head and stared at the Buzzard. 'I saw young Mr Winterton slaughtered and the captain shot down in cold blood on the beach. I'll not sail with any murdering pirate.'

'Pirate!' the Buzzard screamed. 'You dare to call me pirate, you lump of stinking offal? You were born to feed the seagulls, and that's what you shall do!' The great claymore rasped from its scabbard, and he swung it down to cleave Davey Morgan's head, through the teeth as far as his shoulders. With the bloody sword in his hand he strode down the line of prisoners.

'Is there another amongst you who would dare to call me pirate to my face?' No man spoke out, and at last Cumbrae rounded on Sam Bowles. 'Lock them all in the *Golden Bough*'s hold. Feed them on half a pint of water and a biscuit a day. Let them think about my offer more seriously. In a few days' time I'll speak to these lovelies again, and we shall see if they have better manners then.'

He took Sam aside and spoke in a quieter tone. 'There is still some storm damage that needs repair.' He pointed up at the rigging. 'She's your ship now, to sail and command. Make all good at once. I want to leave this godforsaken anchorage as soon as I can. Do you hear me, Captain Bowles?'

Sam Bowles's face lit with pleasure at the title. 'You can rely on me, your grace.'

Cumbrae strode to the entryport and slid down into one of the longboats. 'Take me back to the beach, varlets.' He jumped over the side before they touched the sand and waded knee-deep to the shore where Colonel Schreuder was waiting for him.

'My lord, I must speak to you,' he said, and the Buzzard smiled at him engagingly.

'Your discourse always gives me pleasure, sir. Come with me. We can talk while I go about my affairs.' He led the way across the beach, and into the grove.

'Captain Llewellyn was—' Schreuder began, but the Buzzard cut him off.

'Llewellyn was a bloody pirate. I was defending myself from his treachery.' He stopped abruptly and faced Schreuder, hauling up his sleeve to display the ridged purple scar that disfigured his shoulder. 'Do you see that? That's what I got for trusting Llewellyn once before. If I had not forestalled him, his desperadoes would have fallen on us and slaughtered us where we stood. I am sure that you understand and that you are grateful for my intervention. It could have been you going that way.'

He pointed at the group of his men who were staggering up from the beach, dragging the corpses of Llewellyn and Vincent Winterton by their legs. Llewellyn's shattered head left a red drag mark through the sand.

Schreuder stared aghast at the burial party. He recognized in Cumbrae's words both a warning and a threat. Beyond the first line of trees was a series of deep trenches that had been freshly dug all over the area where once Sir Francis Courteney's encampment had stood. His hut was gone but in its place was a pit twenty feet deep, its bottom filled with seepage of brackish lagoon water. There was another extensive excavation on the site of the old spice godown. It looked as though an army of miners had been at work amongst the trees. The Buzzard's men dragged the corpses to the nearest of these pits and dumped them unceremoniously into it. The bodies slid down the steep side and splashed into the puddle at the bottom.

Schreuder looked troubled and uncertain. 'I find it difficult to believe that Llewellyn was such a person.' But Cumbrae would not let him finish.

'By God, Schreuder, do you doubt my word? What of your assurance that you wanted to throw in your lot with me? If my actions offend you then it's better that we part now. I will give you one of the pinnaces from the *Golden Bough*, and a crew of Llewellyn's pirates to help you make your own way back to Good Hope. You can explain your fine scruples to Governor van de Velde. Is that more to your liking?'

'No, sir, it is not,' said Schreuder hurriedly. 'You know I cannot return to Good Hope.'

'Well, then, Colonel, are you still with me?'

Schreuder hesitated, watching the grisly labours of the burial teams. He knew that if he crossed Cumbrae he would probably end up in the pit with Llewellyn and the sailors from the *Golden Bough*. He was trapped.

'I am still with you,' he said at last.

The Buzzard nodded. 'Here's my hand on it, then.' He thrust out his huge freckled fist covered with wiry ginger hair. Slowly Schreuder reached out and took it. Cumbrae could see in his eyes the realization dawning that from now onwards he would be beyond the pale and was content that he could trust Schreuder at last. By accepting and condoning the massacre of the officers and crew of the *Golden Bough* he had made himself a pirate and an outlaw. He was, in every sense, the Buzzard's man.

'Come along with me, sir. Let me show you what we have done here.' Cumbrae changed the subject easily, and led Schreuder past the mass grave without another glance at the pile of corpses. 'You see, I knew Francis Courteney well – we were like brothers. I am still certain that his fortune is hidden hereabouts. He has what he took from the *Standvastigheid* and that from the *Heerlycke Nacht*. By the blood of all the saints, there must be twenty thousand pounds buried somewhere under these sands.'

At that they came to the long, deep trench where forty of Cumbrae's men were already back at work with spades. Amongst them were the three black seamen he had bought on the slave block at Good Hope.

'Jiri!' the Buzzard bellowed. 'Matesi! Kimatti!' The slaves jumped, threw down their spades and scrambled out of the ditch in trepidation to face their master.

'Look at these great beauties, sir. I paid five hundred florins for each. It was the worst bargain I ever struck. Here before your eyes you have living proof that there are only three things a blackamoor can do well. He can prevaricate, thieve and swive.' The Buzzard let fly a guffaw. 'Isn't that the truth, Jiri?'

'Yes, lordy.' Jiri grinned and agreed. 'It's God's own truth.'

The Buzzard stopped laughing as suddenly as he had begun. 'What do you know about God, you heathen?' he roared and, with a mighty swing of his fist, he knocked Jiri back into the ditch. 'Get back to work all three of you!'

They seized their spades and attacked the bottom of the ditch in a frenzy, sending earth flying over the parapet in a cloud. Cumbrae stood above them, his hands on his hips. 'Listen to me, you sons of midnight. You tell me that the treasure I seek is buried here. Well, then, find it for me or you won't be coming with me when I sail away. I'll bury all three of you in this grave that you're digging with your own sooty paws. Do you hear me?'

'We hear you, lordy,' they answered in chorus.

He took Schreuder's arm in a companionable grip and led him away. 'I have come to accept the sad fact that they never truly knew the whereabouts of Franky's hoard. They've been jollying me along all these months. My rascals and I have had just about a bellyful of playing at moles. Let me offer you the hospitality of my humble abode and a mug of whisky, and you can tell me all you know about this pretty little war that's a-going on between the great Mogul and the Prester. Methinks, you and I might well find better occupation and more profit elsewhere than here at Elephant Lagoon.'

In the firelight Hal studied his band as they ate, with ravenous appetite, their dinner of smoked meat. The hunting had been poor in these last days and most of them were tired. His own seamen had never been slaves. Their labour on the walls of the castle of Good Hope had not broken or cowed them. Rather it had hardened them, and now the long march had put a temper on them. He could want no more from them: they were tough and tried warriors. Althuda he liked and trusted, but he had been a slave from childhood and some of his men would never be fighters. Sabah was a disappointment. He had not fulfilled Hal's expectation of him. He had become sullen and obstructive. He shirked his duties and protested at the orders Hal gave him. His favourite cry had become, 'I am a slave no longer! No man has the right to command me!'

Sabah would not fare well if matched against the likes of the Buzzard's seamen, Hal thought, but he looked up and smiled as Sukeena came to sit beside him.

'Do not make an enemy of Sabah,' she whispered quietly.

'I do not wish that,' he replied, 'but every man amongst us must do his part.' He looked down at her tenderly. 'You are the worth of ten men like Sabah, but today I saw you stumble more than once and when you thought I was not watching you there was pain in your eyes. Are you sickening, my sweetheart? Am I truly setting too hard a pace?'

'You are too fond, Gundwane.' She smiled up at him. 'I will walk with you to the very gates of hell and not complain.'

'I know you would, and it worries me. If you do not complain, how will I ever know what ails you?'

'Nothing ails me,' she assured him.

'Swear it to me,' he insisted. 'You are not hiding any illness from me.'

'I swear it to you, with this kiss.' She gave him her lips. 'All is as well as God ever intended. And I will prove it to you.' She took his hand and led him to the dark corner of the stockade where she had laid out their bed.

Though her body melted into his as sweetly as before, there was a softness and languor in her loving that was strange and, though it delighted him while his passion was in white heat, afterwards it left him with a sense of disquiet and puzzlement. He was aware that something had changed but he was at a loss as to exactly what was different.

424

The next day he watched her carefully during the long march, and it seemed to him that on the steeper ground her step was not as spry as it had been. Then, when the heat was fiercest, she lost her place in the column and began to fall back. Zwaantie went to help her over a rough place in the elephant path that they were following but Sukeena said something sharply to her and thrust away her hand. Hal slowed the pace, almost imperceptibly, to give her respite, and called the midday halt earlier than he had on the preceding days.

Sukeena slept beside him that night with a deathlike stillness while Hal lay awake. By now he was convinced that she was not well, and that she was trying to hide her weakness from him. As she slept her breathing was so light that he had to place his ear to her lips to reassure himself. He held her close and her body seemed heated. Once, just before dawn, she groaned so pitifully that he felt his heart swell with love and concern for her. At last he also fell into a deep dreamless sleep. When he woke with a start and reached out for her, he found her gone.

He lifted himself on one elbow and looked around the stockade. The fire had died down to a puddle of embers, but the full moon, even though it was low in the west, threw enough light for him to see that she was not there. He could make out the dark shape of Aboli: the morning star was almost washed out by the more brilliant light of the moon, but it burned just above his head as he sat his watch at the entrance. Aboli was awake, for Hal heard him cough softly and then saw him draw his fur blanket closer around his shoulders.

Hal threw back his own kaross, and went to squat beside him. 'Where is Sukeena?' he whispered.

'She went out a short while ago.'

'Which way?'

'Down towards the stream.'

'You did not stop her?'

'She was going about her private business.' Aboli turned to look at him curiously. 'Why would I stop her?'

'I am sorry,' Hal whispered back. 'I meant no rebuke. She worries me. She is not well. Have you not noticed?'

Aboli hesitated. 'Perhaps.' He nodded. 'Women are children of the moon, which lacks but a few nights of full, so perhaps her courses are in flood.'

'I am going after her.' Hal stood up and went down the rough path towards the shallow pool where they had bathed the previous evening. He was about to call her name when he heard a sound that silenced and alarmed him. He stopped and listened anxiously. The sound came again, the sound of pain and distress. He started forward and saw her on the

425

sandbank kneeling beside the pool. She had thrown aside her blanket, and the moonlight shone on her bare skin, imparting to it the patina of polished ivory. She was doubled up in a convulsion of pain and sickness. As he watched in distress, she retched and vomited into the sand.

He ran down to her and dropped on his knees beside her. She looked up at him in despair. 'You should not see me thus,' she whispered hoarsely, then turned her head away and vomited again. He put his arm around her bare shoulders. She was cold and shivering.

'You are sick,' he breathed. 'Oh, my love, why did you not answer me straight? Why did you try to hide it from me?'

She wiped her mouth with the back of her hand. 'You should not have followed,' she said. 'I did not want you to know.'

'If you are sick, then I must know. You should trust me enough to tell me.'

'I did not want to be a burden to you. I did not want you to delay the march because of me.'

He hugged her to him. 'You will never be a burden to me. You are the breath in my lungs and the blood in my veins. Tell me now truthfully what ails you, my darling.'

She sighed and shivered against him. 'Oh, Hal, forgive me. I did not want this to happen yet. I have taken all the medicines that I know of to prevent it.'

'What is it?' He was confused and dismayed. 'Please tell me.'

'I am carrying your child in my womb.' He stared at her in astonishment and could neither move nor speak. 'Why are you silent? Why do you look at me so? Please don't be angry with me.'

Suddenly he clasped her to his chest with all his strength. 'It is not anger that stops up my mouth. It is joy. Joy for our love. Joy for the son you promised me.'

That day Hal changed the order of march and took Sukeena to walk with him at the head of the column. Though she protested laughingly, he took her basket from her and added it to his own load. Thus relieved she was able to step out lightly and stay beside him without difficulty. Still he took her hand on the difficult places, and she did not demur when she saw what pleasure it gave him to protect and cherish her thus.

'You must not tell the others,' she murmured, 'else they will want to slow the march on my behalf.'

'You are as strong as Aboli and Big Daniel,' he assured her staunchly, 'but I will not tell them.'

So they kept their secret, walking hand in hand and smiling at each other in such obvious happiness that even if Zwaantie had not told

426

Althuda and he had not told Aboli, they must have guessed. Aboli grinned as if he were the father and showed Sukeena such special favour and attention that even Sabah, in the end, fathomed the reason for this new mood that had come over the band.

The land through which they were passing now became more heavily wooded. Some of the trees were monstrous and seemed, like great arrows, to pierce the very heavens. 'These must have been old when Christ the Saviour was born upon this earth!' Hal marvelled.

With Aboli's wise counsel and guidance they were coming to terms with this savage terrain, and the great animals that abounded in it. Fear was no longer their constant companion, and Hal and Sukeena had learned to take pleasure in the strangeness and beauty all around them. They would pause on a hilltop to watch an eagle sail on the high wind with motionless wings, or to take pleasure in a tiny gleaming metallic bird, no bigger than Sukeena's thumb, as it hung suspended from a flower while it sipped the nectar with a curved beak that seemed as long as its body.

The grassland teemed with a plethora of strange beasts that challenged their imagination. There were herds of the same blue buck that they had first encountered below the mountains, and wild horses barred with stark stripes of cream, russet and black. Often they saw ahead of them amongst the trees the dark mountainous shapes of the double-horned rhinoceros, but they had learned that this fearsome beast was almost blind and that they could avoid its wild, snorting charge by making a short detour from the path.

On the open lands, beyond the forest, there were flocks of small cinnamon-coloured gazelles, so numerous that they moved like smoke across the hills. Their flanks were slashed with a horizontal chocolate stripe, and lyre-shaped horns crowned their dainty heads. When alarmed by the sight of the human figures, they pranced with astonishing lightness of hoof, leaping high in the air and flashing a snowy plume upon their backs. Each ewe was followed by a tiny lamb, and Sukeena clapped her hands with delight and exclaimed to see the young animals nudging the udder or cavorting with their peers. Hal watched her fondly, knowing now that she also carried a child within her, sharing her joy in the young of another species and revelling with her in the secret they thought they had kept from the others.

He read the angle of the noon sun, and everyone in the band gathered around him to watch him mark their position on the chart. The string of dots on the heavy parchment sheet crept slowly towards the indentation on the coastline, which was marked on the Dutch chart as Buffels Baai or the Bay of the Buffaloes.

427

'We are not more than five leagues from the lagoon now.' Hal looked up from the chart.

Aboli agreed. 'While we were out hunting this morning I recognized the hills ahead. From the high ground I saw the line of low cloud that marks the coast. We are very close.'

Hal nodded. 'We must advance with caution. There is the danger that we might run into foraging parties from the *Gull*. This is a favourable place to set up a more permanent camp. There is an abundance of water and firewood and a good lookout from this hill. In the morning, Aboli and I will leave the rest of you here while we go on ahead to discover if the *Gull* is truly lying in Elephant Lagoon.'

An hour before dawn, Hal took Big Daniel aside and committed Sukeena to his care. 'Guard her well, Master Daniel. Never let her out of your sight.'

'Have no fear, Captain. She'll be safe with me.'

As soon as it was light enough to see the track that led eastwards Hal and Aboli left the camp, Sukeena walked a short distance with them.

'God speed, Aboli.' Sukeena embraced him. 'Watch over my man.'

'I will watch over him, even as you watch over his son.'

'You monstrous rogue, Aboli!' She struck him a playful blow on his great broad chest. 'How do you know everything? We were so sure we had kept it a secret even from you.' She turned laughing to Hal. 'He knows!'

'Then all is lost.' Hal shook his head. 'For on the day it is born this rascal will take it as his own, even as he did with me.'

She watched them climb the hill and wave from the crest. But as they disappeared the smile shrivelled on her lips and a single tear traced its way down her cheek. On her way back, she stopped beside the stream and washed it away. When she entered the camp again, Althuda looked up at her from the sword blade he was burnishing and smiled at her, unsuspecting of her distress. He marvelled at how beautiful and fresh she looked, even after all these months of hard travel in the wilderness.

When last they had been here, Hal and Aboli had hunted and explored these hills above the lagoon. They knew the run of the river, and they entered the deep gorge a mile above the lagoon, following an elephant path down to a shallow ford that they knew. They did not approach the lagoon from this direction. 'There may be watering parties from the *Gull*,' Aboli cautioned. Hal nodded and led them up the far side of the gorge and in a wide circuit around the back of the hills, out of sight of the lagoon.

They climbed the back slope of the hills until they were a few paces below the skyline. Hal knew that the cave of the ancient rock paintings, where he and Katinka had dallied, lay just over the crest in front of them, and that from the ridge there would be a panoramic view across the lagoon to the rocky heads and the ocean beyond.

'Use those trees to break your shape on the skyline,' Aboli told him quietly.

Hal smiled. 'You taught me well. I have not forgotten.' He inched his way up the last few yards, followed by Aboli, and, gradually, the view down the far side opened to his gaze. He had not had sight of the sea for weeks now, and he felt his heart leap and his spirits soar as he looked upon its serene blue expanse, flecked with the white horses that pranced before the south-easter. It was the element that ruled his life and he had missed it sorely.

'Oh, for a ship!' he whispered. 'Please, God, let there be a ship!'

As he moved up, there before his eyes appeared the great grey castles of the heads, the bastions that guarded the entrance to the lagoon. He paused before taking another step, steeling himself for the terrible disappointment of finding the anchorage deserted. Like a gambler at Hazard, he had staked his life on this coup of the dice of Fate. He forced himself to take another slow step up the slope, then gasped, seized Aboli's arm and dug his fingers into the knotted muscles.

'The *Gull*!' he muttered, as though it were a prayer of thanks. 'And not alone! There is another fine ship with her.'

For a long while neither spoke again, until Aboli said softly, 'You have found the ship you promised them. If you can seize it, you will be a captain at last, Gundwane.'

They crept forward and, on the crest of the hill, sank on their bellies and gazed down upon the wide lagoon below.

'What ship is that with the *Gull*?' Hal asked. 'I cannot make out her name from here.'

'She is an Englishman,' said Aboli, with certainty. 'No other would cross her mizzen topgallant yard in that fashion.'

'A Welshman, perhaps? She has a rake to her bows and a racy style to her sheer. They build them that way on the west coast.'

'It is possible, but whoever she is, she's a fighting ship. Look at those guns. There would be few to match her in her class,' Aboli murmured thoughtfully.

'Better than the *Gull*, even?' Hal looked at her with longing eyes.

Aboli shook his head. 'You dare not try to take her, Gundwane. Surely she belongs to an honest English sea captain. If you lay hands upon her you turn all of us into pirates. Better we try for the *Gull.*'

For another hour they lay on the hilltop, talking and planning quietly while they studied the two ships and the encampment amongst the trees on the near shore of the lagoon.

'By heavens!' Hal exclaimed abruptly. 'There is the Buzzard himself. I would know that bush of fiery hair anywhere.' His voice was sharp with hatred and anger. 'He is going out to the other ship. See him climb the ladder without a by-your-leave, as if he owns it.'

'Who is that greeting him at the companionway?' Aboli asked. 'I swear I know that walk, and the bald scalp shining in the sunlight.'

'It cannot be Sam Bowles aboard that frigate . . . but it is,' Hal marvelled. 'There is something very strange afoot here, Aboli. How may we find out what it is?'

While they watched the sun begin to slide down the western sky, Hal tried to keep his rage under control. Down there were the two men responsible for his father's terrible death. He relived every detail of his agony and he hated Sam Bowles and the Buzzard to the point where he knew that his emotions might override his reason. His strong instinct was to throw all else aside, go down to confront them and seek retribution for his father's agony and death.

I must not let it happen, he told himself. I must think first of Sukeena and the son that she carries for me.

Aboli touched his arm and pointed down the hill. The rays of the sinking sun had changed the angle of the shadows of the trees of the forest, so that they could see down more clearly through them into the encampment.

'The Buzzard is digging fortifications down there.' Aboli was puzzled. 'But there is no plan to them. His trenches are all higgledy-piggledy.'

'Yet all his men seem to be at work in the diggings. There must be some plan—' Hal broke off and laughed. 'Of course! This is why he came back to the lagoon! He is still searching for my father's hoard.'

'He is a long way off course.' Aboli chuckled. 'Perhaps Jiri and Matesi have deliberately misled him.'

'Sweet Mary, of course those rascals have played the fool with him. Cumbrae bought more than he bargained for in the slave market. They will tweak his nose while they pretend to grovel and call him Lordy.' He smiled at the thought, then became serious again. 'Do you think they may still be down there, or has the Buzzard murdered them already?'

'No, he will keep them alive as long as he thinks they are of value to him. He is digging, so he is still hoping. My guess is that they are still alive.'

'We must watch for them.' For another hour they lay on the hilltop in silence, then Hal said, 'The tide is turning. The strange frigate is swinging on her moorings.' They watched her bow and curtsy to the ebb with a stately grace, and then Hal spoke again. 'Now I can see the name on her transom, but it is difficult to read. Is it the *Golden Swan*? The *Golden Hart*? No, I think not. 'Tis the *Golden Bough*!'

'A fine name for a fine ship,' said Aboli, and then he started, and pointed excitedly down at the network of trenches and pits amongst the trees. 'There are black men coming out of that ditch, three of them. Is that Jiri? Your eyes are sharper than mine.'

'By heavens! So it is, and Matesi and Kimatti behind him.'

'They are taking them to a hut near the water's edge. That must be where they lock them up at night.'

'Aboli, we must speak to them. I will go down as soon as it's dark and try to reach their hut. What time will the moon rise?'

'An hour after midnight,' Aboli answered him. 'But I will not let you go. I made a promise to Sukeena. Besides your white skin shines like a mirror. I will go.'

Stripped naked, Aboli waded out from the far shore until the water reached his chin and struck out in a dog-paddle that made no splash and left only a silent oily wake behind his head. When he reached the far shore, he lay in the shallows until he was certain the beach was clear. Then he crawled swiftly across the open sand and huddled against the bole of the first tree.

One or two camp fires were burning in the grove, and from around them he heard the sound of men's voices and an occasional snatch of song or a shout of laughter. The flames gave him enough light to discern the hut where the slaves where imprisoned. Near the front of it he picked out the glow of a burning match on the lock of a musket, and from this he placed the single sentry, who sat with his back to a tree covering the door of the hut.

They are careless, he thought. Only one guard, and he seems to be asleep.

He crept forward on hands and knees, but before he reached the back wall of the hut he heard footsteps and moved quickly to the shelter of another tree-trunk and crouched there. Two of the Buzzard's sailors came sauntering through the grove towards him. They were arguing loudly.

431

'I'll no' sail with that little weasel,' one declared. 'He would cut a throat for the fun of it.'

'So would you, Willy MacGregor.'

'Aye, but I'd no' be using a pizened blade, like Sam Bowles would.'

'You'll sail with whoever the Buzzard says you will, and that's an end to your carping,' his mate announced and paused beside the tree where Aboli crouched. He lifted his petticoats and urinated noisily against the trunk. 'By the devil's nuggets, even with Sam Bowles as captain I'll be happy enough to get away from this place. I left bonnie Scotland to escape the coal pit, and here I am digging holes again.' He shook the droplets vigorously from himself and the two walked on.

Aboli waited until they were well clear, and then crawled to the rear wall of the hut. He found that it was plastered with unburnt clay, but that chunks of this were falling from the framework of woven branches beneath. He crawled slowly along the wall, gently probing each crack with a stalk of grass until he found a chink that went right through. He placed his lips to the opening and whispered softly, 'Jiri!'

He heard a startled movement on the far side of the wall, and a moment later a fearful whisper came back. 'Is that the voice of Aboli, or is it his ghost?'

'I am alive. Here feel the warmth of my finger – 'tis not the hand of a dead man.'

They whispered to each other for almost an hour before Aboli left the hut and crawled back down the beach. He slipped into the waters of the lagoon like an otter.

The dawn was painting the eastern sky the colours of lemons and ripe apricots when Aboli climbed the hill again to where he had left Hal. Hal was not in the cave, but when Aboli gave a soft warbling bird-call, he stepped out from behind the hanging vines that screened the entrance, his cutlass in his hand.

'I have news,' said Aboli. 'For once the gods have been kind.'

'Tell me!' Hal commanded eagerly, as he sheathed the blade. They sat side by side in the entrance to the cave from where they could keep the full sweep of the lagoon under their eyes, while Aboli related in detail everything that Jiri had been able to tell him.

Hal exclaimed when Aboli described the massacre of the captain and men of the *Golden Bough*, and the way in which Sam Bowles had drowned the wounded like unwanted kittens in the shallows of the lagoon. 'Even for the Buzzard that is a deed that reeks of hell itself.'

'Not all were killed,' Aboli told him. 'Jiri says that a large number of the survivors are locked up in the main hold of the *Golden Bough*.' Hal

432

nodded thoughtfully. 'He says too that the Buzzard has given the command of the *Golden Bough* to Sam Bowles.'

'By heaven, that rogue has come up in the world,' Hal exclaimed. 'But all this could work to our advantage. The *Golden Bough* has become a pirate ship, and is now fair game for us. However, it will be a dangerous enterprise to hunt the Buzzard in his own nest.' He lapsed into a long silence, and Aboli did not disturb him.

At last Hal looked up and it was clear he had reached some decision. 'I swore an oath to my father never to reveal that which I am now to show you. But circumstances have changed. He would forgive me, I know. Come with me, Aboli.'

Hal led him down the back slope of the hill, and then turned towards the gorge of the river. They found a trail made by the baboons and scrambled down the steep side to the bottom. There Hal turned upstream, and the cliffs became higher and steeper as they went. At places they were forced to enter the water and wade alongside the cliff. Every few hundred yards Hal paused to take his bearings, until at last he grunted with satisfaction as he marked the dead tree. He waded along the lip of the bank until he reached it, then scrambled ashore and began to climb.

'Where are you going, Gundwane?' Aboli called after him.

'Follow me,' Hal answered, and Aboli shrugged and began to climb after him. He chuckled when Hal suddenly reached down and gave him a hand onto the narrow ledge that he had not been able to see from below. 'This has the smell of Captain Franky's lair to it,' he said. 'The Buzzard would have saved himself a lot of work by searching here instead of digging holes in the grove, am I right?'

'This way.' Hal shuffled along the ledge with his back to the cliff, and the hundred-foot drop that opened under his toes. When he reached the place where the ledge widened and the cleft split the face, he paused to examine the rocks that blocked the entrance.

'There have been no visitors, not even the apes,' he said, with relief, and began to move the rocks out of the opening. When there was space to pass he crept through and groped in the darkness for the flint and steel box and the candle that his father had placed on the ledge above head level. The tinder flared at the third stroke of the steel on the flint, and he lit the candle stub and held it high.

Aboli laughed in the yellow light as he looked upon the array of canvas sacks and chests. 'You are a rich man, Gundwane. But what use is all this gold and silver to you now? It will not buy you a mouthful of food or a ship to carry it all away.'

Hal crossed to the nearest chest and opened the lid. The gold bars glinted in the candle-light. 'My father died to leave me this legacy. I would rather have had him alive and me a beggar.' He slammed the lid, and looked back at Aboli. 'Despite what you may think, I did not come here for the gold,' he said. 'I came for this.' He kicked the powder keg beside him. 'And those!' He pointed to the piles of muskets and swords that were stacked against the far wall of the cave. 'And these also!' He crossed to where the sheaves and gantry were piled in a heap and picked up one of the coils of manila rope that he and his father had used. He tried the strength of the line by stretching a length of it over his back and straining to break it with his arms and shoulders.

'It is still strong, and has not rotted,' he dropped the coil, 'so we have all we need here.'

Aboli came to sit on the chest beside him. 'So you have a plan. Then share it with me, Gundwane.' He listened quietly as Hal laid it out for him, and once or twice he nodded or made a suggestion.

That same morning they set off for the base camp and by travelling fast, trotting and running most of the way, they reached it shortly after noon. Sukeena saw them climbing the hill and came running down to meet them. Hal seized her and swung her high in the air, then checked himself and set her down with great care as though she were woven of gossamer and might easily tear. 'Forgive me, I treat you roughly.'

'I am yours to treat as you will, and I will be happier for it.' She clung to him and kissed him. 'Tell me what you have found. Is there a ship in the lagoon?'

'A ship. A fine ship. A beautiful ship, but not half as lovely as you.'

With Hal urging them they broke the camp and moved out at once. He and Aboli scouted ahead to clear the path and to lead the band on towards the lagoon.

When they reached the river and climbed down the gorge Hal left Big Daniel there and all the other seamen but Ned Tyler. They were unaware that the treasure cave was only a cable's length upstream. 'Wait for me here, Master Daniel. I must take the others to a safe place. Hide yourselves well. I will return after dark.'

Aboli went with them, as Hal led the rest of the party up the far side of the gorge, then took them round the far side of the hills. They approached the sandbanks that separated the mainland from the island, on which they had built the fireships.

By this time it was late afternoon, and Hal allowed them to rest there until nightfall. As soon as it was dark they all waded across the shallows, Hal carrying Sukeena on his back. As soon as they reached the island they hurried deep into the thick bush, where they were safe from observation from the pirate encampment.

'No fires!' Hal cautioned them. 'Speak only in whispers. Zwaantie, keep little Bobby from crying. No one to wander away. Keep close. Ned is in command when I am not here. Obey him.'

Hal and Aboli went on across the island, through the bush to the beach facing the lagoon. In the area where they had built the fireships the undergrowth had sprung up again thickly. They groped and searched beneath it until they located the two abandoned double-hulled vessels that had not been used on the attack on the *Gull*, and dragged them closer to the beach.

'Will they still float?' Aboli asked dubiously.

'Ned made a good job of them, and they seem sturdy enough,' Hal told him. 'If we unload the combustibles, then they will float higher in the water.'

They stripped the ships of their cargo of dry tar-soaked wooden faggots. 'That's better,' Hal said, with satisfaction. 'They will be lighter and easier to handle now.' They concealed them again, covering them with branches.

'There is still much to do before daylight.' Hal led Aboli back to where most of Althuda's party were already asleep. 'Do not wake Sukeena,' he warned her brother. 'She is exhausted and must rest.'

'Where are you going?' Althuda asked.

'There is no time to explain. We will return before dawn.'

Hal and Aboli crossed the channel to the mainland and then hurried back through the forest in the darkness, but when they reached the line of hills Hal stopped and said, 'There is something I have to find.'

He turned back towards the flickering lights of the pirate camp, moving slowly and pausing often to get his bearings, until at last he stopped at the base of a tall tree.

'This is the one.' With the point of his cutlass he probed the soft loamy earth around the roots. He felt it strike metal, and fell to his knees. He dug with his bare hands, then lifted the golden chain and held it to catch the starlight.

''Tis your father's Nautonnier seal.' Aboli recognized it at once.

'The ring also. And the locket with its portrait of my mother.' Hal stood up and wiped the damp earth from the glass that had protected the miniature. 'With these in my hands, I feel a whole man again.' He dropped the treasures into his leather pouch.

435

'Let us go on, before we are discovered.'

It was after midnight when, once again, they scrambled down the side of the gorge and Big Daniel challenged them softly as they reached the riverbank.

"Tis me,' Hal reassured him, and the others emerged from where they were hidden.

'Stay here,' Hal ordered. 'Aboli and I will return shortly.'

The two set off upstream. Hal led the climb to the ledge and groped his way into the blackness of the cave. Working in the candle's feeble light, they tied the cutlasses into bundles of ten, then stacked them at the entrance. Hal emptied one of the chests of its precious contents, piling the gold bars disdainfully in a corner of the cave, and packed twenty pistols into the empty chest.

Then they rolled the kegs of gunpowder, with the slow-match, out onto the narrow ledge, and set up the gantry and sheave blocks with the rope rove through. Hal scrambled back down the cliff. When he reached the riverbank he whistled softly. Aboli lowered the bundles of weapons and the kegs down to him.

It was heavy work, but Aboli's great muscles made light of it. When they had finished Aboli climbed down to join Hal, and they began the weary porterage of the goods down to where Big Daniel and the other seamen waited.

'I recognize these,' Big Daniel chuckled, as he ran his hands over a bundle of cutlasses then examined them in the moonlight.

'Here is something else you will recognize,' Hal told him, and gave him two of the heavy powder kegs to carry.

All of them carrying as much as their backs would bear, they toiled up the side of the gorge, dumped their burdens and then scrambled down again to bring up the next load. At last fully laden they struck out through the forest. Hal made only one detour to cache the two kegs of powder, a bundle of slow-match, and three cutlasses in the cave of the rock paintings. Then they went on again.

It was almost morning when at last they joined Althuda and his band on the island. They ate the cold smoked venison that Sukeena and Zwaantie had ready for them. Then, when the others rolled in their karosses, Hal took Sukeena aside and showed her the great seal of the Nautonnier and the locket.

'Where did you find these, Gundwane?'

'I hid them in the forest on the day we were captured.'

'Who is the woman?' She studied the portrait.

'Edwina Courteney, my mother.'

'Oh, Hal, she is beautiful. You have her eyes.'

436

'Give my son those same eyes.'

'I will try. With all my heart I will try.'

In the late afternoon Hal roused the others and assigned their duties to them.

'Sabah, take the pistols out of the chest and draw the loads. Reload them, then pack them back into the chest to keep them dry.' The other man set to work at once.

'Big Daniel will help me load the boats. Ned, you take the women down to the beach and explain to them how to help you launch the second boat when the time comes. They must leave everything else behind. There will be neither space nor time to care for extra baggage.'

'Even my bags?' Sukeena asked.

Hal hesitated then nodded firmly. 'Even your bags,' he said, and she did not argue, merely gave him a demure look from under her lashes before she and Zwaantie, carrying Bobby strapped to her back, followed Ned away through the trees.

'Come with me, Aboli.' Hal took his arm and they moved silently to the top end of the island. Then they crept forward on hands and knees until they could lie and look across the open stretch of water at the beach where the boats from the *Gull* and the *Golden Bough* were drawn up below the encampment.

While they kept watch Hal explained the finer details and small modifications to his original plan. From time to time Aboli's tattooed head nodded. In the end he said, 'It is a good and simple plan, and if the gods are kind, it will work.'

In the sunset they studied the two ships anchored in the channel and watched the activity on the beach. As it grew darker, the teams of men who had worked all day, digging the Buzzard's trenches, were relieved. Some came down to bathe in the lagoon. Others rowed out to their berths on the *Gull*.

Smoke from their cooking fires spiralled up through the trees and spread in a pale blue haze across the waters. Hal and Aboli could smell grilling fish on the smoke. Sound carried clearly across the still water. They could hear men's voices and even make out something of what they were saying, a shouted oath or a boisterous argument. Twice Hal was sure that he recognized the Buzzard's voice but they had no further sight of him.

Just as darkness began to fall a longboat pulled away from the side of the *Golden Bough* and headed in towards the beach.

'That's Sam Bowles in the stern,' Hal said, and his voice was filled with loathing.

'Captain Bowles now, if what Jiri tells me is true,' Aboli corrected him.

'It is almost time to move,' Hal said, as the shapes of the anchored ships began to merge with the dark mass of the forest behind them. 'You know what to do, and God go with you, Aboli.' Hal gripped his arm briefly.

'And with you also, Gundwane.' Aboli rose to his feet and went down into the water. He made no noise as he swam across the channel, but he left a faint phosphorescent trail on the dark surface.

Hal found his way back through the bush to where the others waited by the ungainly shapes of the two fireships. He made them sit in a tight circle around him while he spoke to them softly. At the end he made each repeat his instructions, and corrected them when they erred.

'Now nothing remains but to wait until Aboli has done his work.'

Aboli reached the mainland and left the water quickly. He moved quietly through the forest, and the warm breeze had dried his body before he reached the cave of the paintings. He squatted beside the powder kegs and made his preparations as Hal had instructed him.

He cut two fuses from the slow-match. One was only a fathom in length, but the second was a coil thirty feet long. The time delay was an imprecise calculation and the first might burn for ten minutes, but the second for almost thrice as long.

He worked swiftly, and when both kegs were ready he tied the bundle of three cutlasses on his back, swung a powder keg up onto each shoulder and crept out of the cave. He remembered that the previous night when he had visited the hut in which Jiri and the other slaves were being held, he had observed that the Buzzard's men had become careless. The uneventful months they had been camped here had lulled them into a complacent mood. The sentries were no longer vigilant. Still he was not relying on their sloth.

Stealthily he moved closer to the camp, until he could clearly make out the features of the men sitting around the cooking fires. He recognized many, but there was no sign of either Cumbrae or Sam Bowles. He set up the first keg in a patch of scrub on the perimeter of the camp, as close as he dared approach, and then, without lighting the fuse, moved away until he reached one of the trenches where the Buzzard's men had been digging for treasure.

He placed the keg with the longest fuse on the lip of the trench and covered it with sand and debris from the excavation. Then he paid out the coiled fuse and took the end of it down into the trench. He crouched there and shielded the flint and steel with his body so the flare of sparks would not alert the men in the camp as he lit the slow-match. When it was glowing evenly he lit the fuse from it and watched it for a minute to make certain that it was also burning well. Then he climbed out of the trench and moved swiftly and silently back to the first keg. From the slow match in his hand he lit the shorter fuse.

'The first explosion will bring them running,' Hal had explained. 'Then the second keg will go off in their faces.'

Still carrying the bundle of cutlasses, Aboli moved away swiftly. There was always the danger that the flame of one of the fuses might jump ahead and set off the keg prematurely. Once he was clear, and moving with more caution, he found the path that ran down towards the beach. Twice he was forced to leave the path as other figures came towards him out of the darkness. Once he was not quick enough but he brazened it out, exchanging a gruff 'Good night!' with the pirate who brushed past him.

He picked out the mud hut against the glow of the campfires and crept up to the back wall. Jiri responded immediately to his whisper. 'We are ready, brother.' His tone was crisp and fierce, no longer the cringing whine of the slave.

Aboli laid down the bundle of weapons and, with his own cutlass, severed the twine that held them. 'Here!' he whispered, and Jiri's hand came out through the crack in the mud wall. Aboli passed the cutlasses through to him.

'Wait until the first keg blows,' he told him, through the hole in the wall.

'I hear you, Aboli.'

Aboli crept to the corner of the hut and glanced round it. The guard sat in his usual position in front of the door. Tonight he was awake, smoking a long-stemmed clay pipe. Aboli saw the burning tobacco glow in the bowl as he drew upon it. He squatted behind the corner of the wall and waited.

The time passed so slowly that he began to fear that the fuse on the first keg had been faulty and had burned out before reaching it. He decided that he would have to go back to check it, but as he began to rise to his feet the blast swept through the camp.

It tore branches from the trees and sent clouds of burning ash and sparks swirling from campfires. It struck the mud hut, knocking down half the front wall and ripping the thatch from the roof. It hit the guard by the front door and hurled him over backwards. He floundered about on his back, trying to sit up, but his big belly made him ungainly. While he struggled Aboli stood over him, placed one foot on his chest, pinning him to the earth, swung the cutlass and felt the hilt jar in his hand as the edge hacked into the man's neck. His whole body spasmed and then lay still. Aboli leaped away from him and grabbed the rope handle of the rough-hewn door to the hut. As he heaved at it the three men inside hurled their combined weight upon it from the far side, and it burst open.

'This way, brethren.' Aboli led them down towards the beach.

The camp was in uproar. The darkness was full of men blundering about, swearing, shouting orders and alarms.

'To arms! We are attacked.'

'Stand to here,' they heard the Buzzard roar. 'Have at them, lads!'

'Petey! Where are you, me darling boy?' a wounded man screamed for his shipwife. 'I am killed. Come to me, Petey.'

Burning brands from the campfires had been carried into the scrub and the flames were taking hold in the forest. They gave the scene a hellish illumination, and men's shadows made monsters of them as they rushed about, startling each other. Someone fired a musket, and immediately there was a wild fusillade as panic-stricken sailors fired at shadows and at one another. More screams and cries as the flying musket balls took their toll amongst the scurrying figures.

'The bastards are in the forest behind us!' It was the Buzzard's voice again. 'This way, my brave boys!' He was rallying them, and men came rushing up from the beach to join the defence. They ran full into the musket fire of their nervous fellows amongst the trees and fired back at them.

When Aboli reached the beach he found longboats drawn up, abandoned by their crews who had rushed away to answer the Buzzard's call to arms.

'Where do they keep their tools?' Aboli snapped at Jiri.

'There is a store over there.' Jiri led him to it at a run. The spades, axes and iron bars were stacked under an open lean-to shed. Aboli sheathed his cutlass and seized a heavy iron bar. The other three followed his example, then ran back to the beach, and fell upon the boats lying there.

With a few hefty blows they knocked in their bottom timbers, leaving only one unscathed.

'Come on! Waste no more time!' Aboli urged, and they threw down the tools and ran to the single undamaged boat. They thrust it out into

440

the lagoon and tumbled aboard, grabbed an oar each and began to pull for the dark shape of the frigate, which was now emerging from the darkness as the flames of the burning forest lit her.

While they were still only a few oar strokes off the beach a mob of pirates poured out from the grove.

'Stop! Come back!' one shouted.

'It's those black apes. They're stealing one of the boats.'

'Don't let them get away!' A musket banged and a ball hummed over the heads of the men at the oars. They ducked and rowed the harder, putting all their weight into their strokes. Now all the pirates were firing and balls kicked spray off the water close at hand, or thumped into the timbers of the longboat.

Some of the pirates ran to the boats at the water's edge and swarmed into them. They pushed off in pursuit, but almost immediately there were howls of dismay as the water poured in through the shattered floorboards and the boats swamped and overturned. Few could swim, and the yells of rage turned to piteous cries for help as they splashed and floundered in the dark water.

At that moment the second explosion swept through the camp. It did even more damage than the first for, in response to his bellowed orders, the Buzzard's men were charging straight into the blast when it struck them.

'There's something to keep them busy for a while,' Aboli grunted. 'Pull for the frigate, lads, and leave the Buzzard to his kinsman the devil.'

Hal had not waited for the first explosion to shatter the night before he launched the fireship. With all the men in the party helping, they dragged the hull down the beach. Relieved of her cargo, she was a great deal lighter to handle. They piled into her the bundles of cutlasses and the chest filled with loaded pistols.

They left Sabah to hold her and ran back to fetch the second vessel. The women ran beside them as they dragged it down to the water's edge and scrambled on board. Big Daniel carried little Bobby and handed him to Zwaantie when she was safely seated on the floorboards. Hal lifted Sukeena in and placed her gently in the stern sheets. He gave her one last kiss.

'Keep out of danger until we have secured the ship. Listen to Ned. He knows what to do.'

He left her and ran back to take command of the first boat. Big Daniel and the two birds, Sparrow and Finch, were with him, as were Althuda and Sabah. They would need every fighting man on the deck of the frigate if they were to take her.

They pushed the boat out into the channel and as their feet lost the bottom they began to swim and steered her for the anchored frigate. The tide was at high slack: soon it would turn and give them its help as they ran the frigate for the deep channel between the heads.

But first we have to make her ours! Hal told himself as he kicked out strongly, clinging to the gunwale.

A cable's length from the *Golden Bough* Hal whispered, 'Avast, lads. We don't want to arrive before we're welcome.' They hung in the water as the boat drifted aimlessly in the slack of the tide.

The night was quiet, so quiet that they could hear the voices of the men on the beach and the tap and clatter of the frigate's rigging as she snubbed her anchor and her bare masts rolled, almost imperceptibly, against the blaze of the stars.

'Maybe Aboli has run into trouble,' Big Daniel muttered at last. 'We might have to board her without any diversion.'

'Wait!' Hal replied. 'Aboli will never let us down.'

They hung in the water, their nerves stretched to breaking point. Then came the sound of a soft splash behind them, and Hal turned his head. The shape of the second boat crept towards them from the island.

'Ned is over-eager,' Big Daniel said.

'He's only following my orders, but he must not get ahead of us.'

'How can we stop him?'

'I will swim across to speak to him,' Hal answered, and let go his hold on the gunwale. He struck out towards the other boat in a silent breaststroke that did not break the surface. Close alongside he trod water and called softly, 'Ned!'

'Aye, Captain!' Ned answered as softly.

'There is some delay. Wait here and do not get ahead of us. Wait until you hear the first explosion. Then take her in and latch on to the frigate's anchor cable.'

'Aye, Captain,' Ned replied, and looking up at the black hull Hal saw a head peering down at him over the side. The starlight glowed on Sukeena's honey-gold skin, and he knew he must not speak to her again or swim closer lest his concern for her affect his judgement – lest his love for her quench the fighting fire in his blood. He turned and swam back towards the other boat.

As he reached its side and lifted his hand to grip the gunwale, the quiet night was shattered by thunder and the echoes that burst against the hills swept over the lagoon. From the dark grove, flames shot up into the night sky and, for a brief moment, lit the scene like dawn. In that illumination Hal saw every sheet and spar of the frigate's rigging, but there was no sign of an anchor watch or other human presence aboard her.

'All together now, lads,' Hal said, and they struck out again with new heart. It took them only minutes to close the gap. But in that time the night was transformed. They could hear the shouting and musket fire from the beach and the flames of the burning forest danced and glimmered on the surface around them. Hal was afraid that they might be lit brightly enough to be spotted by a vigilant sentry on the frigate's deck.

With relief they swam the awkward craft into the shadow cast by the frigate's tall hull. He glanced back and saw Ned Tyler bringing the other boat close behind them. As Hal watched they reached the frigate's drooping anchor line and he saw Sukeena stand up in the bows and take hold of the cable. He felt a lift of relief. His orders to Ned were to keep the women safely out of the way until they had control of the frigate's deck.

He saw with satisfaction that a skiff was moored alongside the *Golden Bough*, a rope ladder dangling into her from the deck above. Even more fortunately, it was empty, and no heads showed above the frigate's rail. However, he could hear a babble of voices above. The crew must be lining the frigate's far rail facing the beach, staring across in alarm and consternation at the flames, watching the running figures and the flashes of musket fire in bewilderment.

They pushed the fireship the last few feet and bumped softly against the side of the empty skiff. Immediately Hal hauled himself out of the water over her side, leaving the others to secure her, and swarmed up the rope ladder to the deck.

As he had hoped, the skeleton crew of the frigate were all watching the disturbance, but he was dismayed at their numbers. There must be fifty of them at least. However, they were absorbed in what was happening ashore, and as Hal gathered himself to climb out onto the deck there was another mighty detonation from out of the forest.

'By God, will you no' look at that?' one of Sam Bowles's pirates shouted.

'There's a bloody great battle going on out there.'

'Our shipmates are in trouble. They need our help.'

'I owe no favours to any of them. They'll get no help from me.'

'Shamus is right. Let the Buzzard fight his own battles.'

443

Hal swung himself onto the deck and, with half a dozen quick steps, he had reached the shelter of the break in the forecastle. He crouched there and surveyed the deck. Jiri had told Aboli they were holding the frigate's loyal crew in the main hold. But the hatch was in full view of Sam Bowles's men at the far rail.

He glanced back, and saw Big Daniel's head appear at the entryport. He could not delay. He jumped up, ran out to the main hatch coaming and dropped on his knees behind it. There was a mallet lying beside the hatch, but he dared not use it to hammer out the wedges. The pirates would hear him and be upon him in an instant.

He knocked softly on the timbers with the hilt of his cutlass and spoke in a quiet voice. 'Ahoy there, *Golden Bough*. Do you hear me?'

A muffled voice from beneath the hatch cover answered immediately, in a lilting Celtic accent. 'We hear you. Who are you?'

'An honest Englishman, come to set you free. Will you fight with us against the Buzzard?'

'God love you, honest Englishman! We beg you for a taste of his mongrel blood.'

Hal glanced round. Big Daniel had brought up a bundle of cutlasses, and both Wally Finch and Stan Sparrow carried others. Althuda had the chest of loaded pistols. He lowered it to the deck and opened the lid. At first glance the weapons within seemed dry and ready to fire.

'We have weapons for you,' Hal whispered to the man under the hatch. 'Lend a hand to throw back the hatch when I knock out the wedges, then come out fighting like terriers but call your ship's name, so we will know you and you us.'

He nodded to Daniel and hefted the heavy mallet. Big Daniel seized the lip of the hatch and put all his weight under it. Hal swung the mallet, and with a resounding crack the first wedge flew across the deck. He leaped across the hatch and with another two more full-blooded swings of the mallet sent the remaining wedges clattering to the deck. With Big Daniel straining above and the trapped crew of the *Golden Bough* heaving underneath the coaming cover flew back with a crash and the prisoners came boiling out like angry wasps.

At this sudden uproar behind them, Sam Bowles's men turned and gaped. It took them a long moment to realize that they had been boarded and that their prisoners were free. But by that time Hal and Daniel faced them across the firelit deck, cutlass in hand.

Behind them Althuda was striking sparks from flint and steel as he hurried to light the slow-match on the locks of the pistols, and Wally and Stan were tossing cutlasses to the liberated seamen as they stormed out of the hold.

With a wild shout a pack of pirates led by Sam Bowles charged across the deck. They were twenty against two, and their first rush drove Daniel and Hal back, steel ringing and rasping against steel as they gave ground slowly. But the pair held them long enough for the seamen of the *Golden Bough* to dash into the fight.

Within minutes the deck was thronged with struggling men, and they were so mingled that only their shouted war-cries identified foe from new-made friend.

'Cochran of Cumbrae!' Sam Bowles howled, and Hal's men roared back, 'Sir Hal and the *Golden Bough*!'

The frigate's freed sailors were mad for vengeance – not merely for their own imprisonment but for the massacre of their officers and the drowning of their wounded mates. Hal and his men had a thousand better reasons for their rage, and they had waited infinitely longer to pay off this score.

Sam Bowles's crew were cornered animals. They knew they could expect no help from their fellows on the shore. Nor would they receive mercy or quarter from the avengers who confronted them.

The two sides were almost evenly matched in numbers, but perhaps the crew of the frigate had been weakened by their long confinement in the dark and airless hold. In the forefront of the fight Hal became aware that it was swinging against them. His men were being forced to yield more of the deck and retreat towards the bows.

From the corner of his eye he saw Sabah break and run, throwing aside his sword and scurrying for the hatch to hide below decks. Hal hated him for it. It takes but one coward to start a rout. But Sabah never reached the hatch. A tall black-bearded pirate sent a thrust through the small of his back that came out through his belly-button.

Another hour on the practice field might have saved him, Hal thought fleetingly, then concentrated all his mind and strength on the four men who crowded forward, yammering like hyenas around their bleeding prey, to engage him.

Hal killed one with a thrust under his raised arm into his heart and disarmed another with a neat slash across his wrist that severed his straining sinews. The sword dropped from the man's fingers and he ran screaming across the deck and threw himself, bleeding, overboard. Hal's other two attackers drew back in fear, and in the respite he looked around in the mêlée for Sam Bowles.

He saw him in the back of the horde, keeping carefully out of the worst of it, screaming orders and threats at his men, his ferrety features twisted with malice.

'Sam Bowles!' Hal shouted at him. 'I have you in my eye.' Over the

445

heads of the men between them, Sam looked across at him and there was sudden terror in his pale, close-set eyes.

'I am coming for you now!' Hal roared, and bounded forward, but three men were in his way. In the seconds it took him to beat them aside and clear a path for himself, Sam had darted away and hidden himself in the throng.

Now the pirates clamoured about Hal like jackals around a lion. For a moment he fought side by side with Daniel and saw with amazement that the big man was wounded in a dozen places. Then he felt the hilt of the cutlass sticky in his hand as though he had scooped honey from a jar with his fingers. He realized that it was not honey but his own blood. He, too, was wounded, but in the heat of it all he felt no pain and fought on.

'Beware, Sir Hal!' Big Daniel roared, close beside him in the confusion. 'The stern!'

Hal jumped back, disengaging from the fight, and looked back. Daniel's warning had come just in time to save him.

Sam Bowles was at the rail of the stern overlooking the lower deck. There was a heavy bronze murderer in the slot of the rail and Sam had a lighted match in his hand as he swivelled and aimed the small hand cannon. He had picked out Hal from the press of fighting men and the murderer was aimed at him. Sam touched the match to the pan of the cannon.

In the instant before it fired Hal leaped forward, seized the pirate in front of him around his waist and lifted him off his feet. The man yelled with surprise as Hal held him like a shield, just as the murderer fired and a gale of lead shot swept the deck. Hal felt the body of the man in his arms jump as half a dozen heavy pellets smashed into him. He was dead even before Hal dropped him to the deck.

But the shot had done fearful slaughter amongst the crew of the *Golden Bough*, who were grouped close around where Hal stood. Three were down and kicking in their own blood while another two or three had been struck and were struggling to stay on their feet.

The pirates saw that this sudden onslaught had tipped the balance in their favour and surged forward in a pack, Sam urging them on with excited cries. Like a cracked dam Hal's men started to give way. They were seconds from total rout – when from over the rail behind the raging rabble of pirates rose a great black tattooed face.

Aboli let out a bellow that froze them all where they stood, and as he sprang over the rail he was followed closely by three other huge shapes, each with cutlass in hand. They had killed five men before the pirates had gathered themselves to face this fresh onslaught.

Those around Hal were given new heart: they rallied to Hal's hoarse shouts and, with Big Daniel leading them, rushed back into the fight. Caught between Aboli with his savages and the rejuvenated seamen, the pirates wailed with despair and fled. Those unable to swim scuttled down the hatchways into the bowels of the frigate while the others rushed to the rail and jumped overboard.

The fight was over and the frigate was theirs. 'Where is Sam Bowles?' Hal shouted across at Daniel.

'I saw him run below.'

Hal hesitated a moment, fighting the temptation to rush after him and have his revenge. Then, with an effort, he thrust it aside and turned to his duty.

'There will be time for him later.' He strode to the captain's place on the quarterdeck and surveyed his ship. Some of his men were firing their pistols over the side at the men splashing and swimming towards the beach. 'Avast that nonsense!' he shouted at them. 'Stand by to get the ship under way. The Buzzard will be upon us at any moment now.'

Even the strangers he had released from the hold rushed to obey his command, for they recognized the tone of authority.

Then Hal dropped his voice. 'Aboli and Master Daniel, get the women on board. As quick as you can.' While they ran to the entryport, he turned his full attention to the management of the frigate.

The topmast men were already half-way up the shrouds, and another gang was manning the capstan to weigh the anchor.

'No time for that,' Hal told them. 'Take an axe to the anchor cable and cut us free.' He heard the clunk of the axe into the timbers at the bows, and felt the ship pay off and swing to the ebb.

He glanced towards the entryport and saw Aboli lift Sukeena onto the deck. Big Daniel had little Bobby weeping on his chest and Zwaantie on his other arm.

The main sail blossomed out high above Hal's head, flapped lazily and filled with the gentle night breeze. Hal turned to the helm and felt another great lift of his heart as he saw that Ned Tyler was already at the whipstaff.

'Full and by, Mr Tyler,' he said.

'Full and by it is, Captain.'

'Steer for the main channel!'

'Aye, Captain!' Ned could not suppress his grin, and Hal grinned back at him.

'Will this ship do you, Mr Tyler?'

'It will do me well enough,' Ned said, and his eyes sparkled.

Hal seized the speaking trumpet from its peg and pointed to the sky as he called the order for the top sails to be set above the courses. He felt the ship start under his feet and begin to fly.

'Oh, sweet!' he whispered. 'She is a bird, and the wind is her lover.'

He strode across to where Sukeena was already kneeling beside one of the wounded seamen.

'I told you to leave those bags ashore, did I not?'

'Yes, my lord.' She smiled sweetly up at him. 'But I knew that you were jesting.' Then her expression changed to dismay. 'You are hurt!' She sprang to her feet. 'Let me attend to your injuries.'

'I am scratched, not hurt. This man needs your skills more than I do.' Hal turned from her, strode to the rail and looked across to the beach. The fire had taken fierce hold on the forest, and now the scene was lit like the dawn. He could clearly make out the features of the horde of men at the waterside. They were dancing with rage and frustration for they had realized at last that the frigate was being cut out under their noses.

Hal picked out the giant figure of Cumbrae in the front of the press of men. He was waving his claymore and his face was so swollen with rage that it seemed it might burst open like an overripe tomato. Hal laughed at him and the Buzzard's fury was magnified a hundredfold. His voice carried over the hubbub that his men were making. 'There is no ocean wide enough to hide you, Courteney. I will find you if it takes fifty years.'

Then Hal stopped laughing as he recognized the man who stood a little higher up the beach. At first he doubted his own eyesight, but the flames lit him so clearly that there could be no mistake. In contrast to the Buzzard's antics and transparent rage, Cornelius Schreuder stood, arms folded, staring across at Hal with a cold gaze that placed a sudden chill on Hal's heart. Their eyes locked, and it was as though they confronted each other upon the duelling field.

The *Golden Bough* heeled slightly as a stronger eddy of wind over the heads caught her, and the water began to gurgle under her forefoot like a happy infant. The deck trembled and she drew away from the beach. Hal gave all his attention to the con of the ship, lining her up for the run through the dangerous channel into the sea. It was long minutes before he could look back again towards the shore.

Only two figures remained on the beach. The two men whom Hal hated most in all the world, both his implacable enemies. The Buzzard had waded out waist-deep into the lagoon, as though to remain as close as he could. Schreuder still stood where Hal had last seen him. He had not moved and his reptilian stillness was every bit as chilling as Cumbrae's wild histrionics.

'The day will come when you will have to kill both of them,' said a deep voice beside him, and he glanced at Aboli.

'I dream of that day.'

Beneath his feet he felt the first thrust of the sea coming in through the heads. The flames had destroyed his night vision, and ahead lay utter darkness. He must grope his way through the treacherous channel like a blind man.

'Douse the lanterns!' he ordered. Their feeble light would not penetrate the darkness ahead and would serve only to dazzle him.

'Bring her up a point to larboard,' he ordered Ned Tyler quietly.

'A point to larboard!'

'Meet her!'

He felt rather than saw the loom of the cliff ahead, and heard the surge and break of the waves on the reef at the entrance. He judged his turn by the sounds of the sea, the feel of the wind on his chest and the deck beneath his feet.

After all the shouting and pistol fire, the ship was deathly quiet. Every seaman aboard her knew that Hal was leading them against an ancient enemy far more dangerous than the Buzzard or any man alive.

'Harden up your main and mizzen courses,' he called to the men on the sheets. 'Stand ready to let your topgallants fly.'

An almost palpable fear lay upon the *Golden Bough* for the ebb had her by the throat and there was no manner in which the crew could slow the ship's headlong rush towards the unseen cliffs in the aching blackness.

The moment came. Hal felt the back surge from the breaking reef push across the bows, and the puff of wind on his cheek coming from a new direction as the ship ran on into the maw of rock.

'Starboard your helm!' he said sharply. 'Hard over. Let your topgallants fly.'

The *Golden Bough* spun on her heel and her top sails flapped in the wind, like the wings of a vulture scenting death. The ship rushed on into the darkness and every man on the deck braced himself for the terrible crash as the belly was ripped out of her by the fangs of the reef.

Hal stepped to the rail and peered up into the sky. His eyes were adjusting to the darkness. He saw the line; high above, where the stars were extinguished by the loom of the rocky head.

'Midship your helm, Mr Tyler. Hold her at that.'

The ship steadied on her new course into the night, and Hal's heart beat fast to the echo of booming surf from the cliff close at hand. He clenched his fists at his sides in anticipation of the strike into the reef.

Instead he felt the scend of the open sea hump up under her, and the *Golden Bough* meet it with the passion thrust of a lover.

'Harden up your topgallants.' He raised his voice to carry on high. The flapping of sails ceased and he heard once again the thrumming of tight canvas.

The *Golden Bough* threw up her bows as the first ocean roller slid under her and for a moment no man dared believe that Hal had led them through the maelstrom to safety.

'Light the lanterns,' Hal said quietly. 'Mr Tyler, come around to due south. We will make a good offing.'

The silence persisted, then a voice from the main yard yelled down, 'Lord love you, Captain! We're through.' Then the cheering swept down the deck.

'For Sir Hal and the *Golden Bough*.' They cheered him until their throats ached, and Hal heard strange voices calling his name. The seamen he had released from the hold were cheering him as loudly as the others.

He felt a small warm hand creep into his and looked down to see Sukeena's sweet face glow in the lantern light beside the binnacle.

'Already they love you almost as much as I do.' She tugged softly on his hand. 'Will you not come away to where I can see to your wounds?'

But he did not want to leave his quarterdeck. He wanted to revel longer in the sounds and the feel of his new ship and the sea under her. So he kept Sukeena close beside him as the *Golden Bough* ran on into the night and the stars blazed down from above.

Big Daniel came to them at last, dragging with him an abject figure. For a moment Hal did not recognize the creature but then the whining voice made his skin crawl with loathing and the fine hairs at the back of his neck rise.

'Sweet Sir Henry, I pray you to have mercy on an old shipmate.'

'Sam Bowles.' Hal tried to keep his voice level. 'You have enough innocent blood on your conscience to float a frigate.'

'You do me injustice, good Sir Henry. I am a poor wretch driven by the storms and gales of life, noble Sir Henry. I never wanted to do no man harm.'

'I will deal with him in the morning. Chain him to the mainmast and put two good men to guard him,' Hal ordered Big Daniel. 'Make sure that this time he does not eel his way out of our hands and cheat us once again of the vengeance that we so richly deserve.'

He watched in the lantern light as they shackled Sam Bowles to the foot of the mainmast and two of the crew stood over him with drawn cutlasses.

'My little brother Peter was one of those you drowned,' the older of the two guards told Sam Bowles. 'I beg you for any excuse to stick this blade through your belly.'

Hal left Daniel in charge of the deck and, taking Sukeena with him, went below to the main cabin. She would not rest until she had bathed and bandaged his cuts and wounds, although none were serious enough to cause her alarm. When she had finished, Hal led her through into the small cabin next door. 'You will be able to rest here undisturbed,' he told her, lifted her onto the bunk and, though she protested, covered her with a woollen blanket.

'There are wounded men that need my help,' she said.

'Your unborn son and I need you more,' he told her firmly, and pushed her head down gently. She sighed and was almost immediately asleep.

He returned to the main cabin and sat down at Llewellyn's desk. In the centre of the mahogany top lay a great black leather-covered Bible. During all his captivity Hal had been denied access to the book. He opened the front cover, and read the inscription, written in a bold sloping hand: 'Christopher Llewellyn esq; Born 16th October in the year of grace 1621.'

Below it was another, fresher inscription: 'Consecrated as a Nautonnier Knight of the Temple of the Order of St George and the Holy Grail 2nd August 1643.'

Knowing that the man who had captained this ship before him was a brother Knight gave Hal a deep purpose and pleasure. For an hour he turned the pages of the Bible and reread the familiar and inspiring passages by which his father had taught him to steer his course through life. At last he closed it, stood up and began to search the cabin for the ship's books and documents. He soon discovered the iron strong-box below the bunk. When he could not find the key he called Aboli to help him. They forced open the lid and Hal sent Aboli away. He sat the rest of the night at Llewellyn's desk, studying the ship's books and papers in the lantern light. He was so absorbed by his reading that when Aboli came down to fetch him, an hour after the sun had risen, he looked up in surprise. 'What time is it, Aboli?'

'Two bells in the morning watch. The men are asking to see you, Captain.'

Hal stood up from the desk, stretching and rubbing his eyes, then crossed to the door of the cabin where Sukeena still slept.

'It would be best if you spoke to the new men as soon as you can, Gundwane,' Aboli said, behind him.

'Yes, you are right.' Hal turned back to him.

'Daniel and I have already told them who you are, but you must

451

convince them now to sail under your command. If they refuse to accept you as their new captain, there is little we can do. There are thirty-four of them, and only six of us.'

Hal went to the small mirror on the bulkhead above the jug and basin of the toilet stand. When he saw his reflection he started with amazement. 'Sweet heavens, Aboli, I look such a pirate that I do not even trust myself.'

Sukeena must have been listening, for she appeared suddenly in the doorway with the blanket draped over her shoulders.

'Tell them we will come in a minute, Aboli, when I have made the best of his appearance,' she said.

When Hal and Sukeena stepped out onto the deck together, the men gathered in the ship's waist stared at them with astonishment. The transformation was extraordinary. Hal was freshly shaved and dressed in simple but clean clothing from Llewellyn's locker. Sukeena's hair was combed, oiled and plaited and she had fashioned a long skirt from one of the cabin's velvet drapes and wrapped it around her girlish waist and hips. They made an extraordinary couple, the tall young Englishman and the oriental beauty.

Hal left Sukeena at the companionway and strode out in front of the men. 'I am Henry Courteney. I am an Englishman, as you are. I am a sailor, as you are.'

'Aye, that you are, Captain,' one said loudly. 'We watched you take a strange ship out through the heads in darkness. You're enough sailor to fill my tankard and give me a warm feel in the guts.'

Another called out, 'I sailed with your father, Sir Francis, on the old *Lady Edwina*. He was a seaman and fighter, and an honest man to boot.'

Then another cried, 'Last night, by my count, you took down seven of the Buzzard's scum with your own blade. The pup is well bred from the old dog.'

They all began to cheer him so he could not speak for a long while, but at last he held up his hand. 'I tell you straight that I have read Captain Llewellyn's log. I have read the charter he had with the ship's owner, and I know whither the *Golden Bough* was bound and what was her purpose.' He paused, and looked at their honest, weather-beaten faces. 'We have a choice, you and I. We can say we were beaten by the Buzzard before we began and sail back home to England.'

They groaned and shouted protests until he held up his hand again. 'Or I can take over Captain Llewellyn's charter and his agreement with the owners of the *Golden Bough*. On your side, you can sign on with me on the same terms and with the same share of the prize you agreed before. Before you answer me, remember that if you come with me the

452

chances are strong that we will run in with the Buzzard again, and you will have to fight him once more.'

'Lead us to him now, Captain,' one yelled. 'We'll fight him this very day.'

'Nay, lad. We're short-handed and I need to learn to con this ship before we meet the Buzzard again. We will fight the *Gull* on the day and at the place of my own choosing,' Hal told them grimly. 'On that day we will hoist the Buzzard's head to our masthead and divide up his booty.'

'I'm with you, Captain,' shouted a lanky fair-headed sailor. 'I cannot write my name, but bring me the book and I'll mark a cross so big and black it will fright the devil himself.' They all roared with fierce laughter.

'Bring the book and let us sign.'

'We're with you. My oath and my mark on it.'

Hal stopped them again. 'You will come one at a time to my cabin, so that I can learn each of your names and shake you by the hand.'

He turned to the rail and pointed back over their stern. 'We have made good our offing.' The African coast lay low and blue along the horizon. 'Get aloft now to make sail and bring the ship around onto her true course for the Great Horn of Africa.'

They swarmed up the shrouds and out along the yards and the canvas billowed out until it shone in the sunlight like a soaring thunderhead.

'What course, Captain?' Ned Tyler called from the helm.

'East by north, Mr Tyler,' Hal replied, and felt the ship surge forward under him, as he turned to watch the wake furrow the blue rollers with a line of flashing foam.

Whenever one of the crew passed the foot of the mainmast where Sam Bowles crouched, shackled at hand and foot like a captive ape, they paused to gather saliva and spit at him.

Aboli came to Hal in the forenoon watch. 'You must deal with Sam Bowles now. The men are becoming impatient. One of them is going to cheat the rope and stick a knife between his ribs.'

'That will save me a deal of bother.' Hal looked up from the bundle of charts and the book of sailing directions that he had found in Christopher Llewellyn's chest. He knew that his crew would demand a savage revenge on Sam Bowles, and he did not relish what had to be done.

'I will come on deck at once.' He sighed, surrendering at last to Aboli's ruthless persuasion. 'Have the men assembled in the waist.'

He had thought that Sukeena was still in the small cabin that adjoined the powder magazine, which she had turned into a sickbay and in which two of the wounded men still teetered on the edge of life. He hoped that she would stay there, but as he stepped out onto the deck she came to meet him.

'You should go below, Princess,' he told her softly. 'It will not be a sight fitting to your eyes.'

'What concerns you is my concern also. Your father was part of you, so his death touches upon me. I lost my own father in terrible circumstances, but I avenged him. I will stay to see that you avenge your father's death.'

'Very well.' Hal nodded, and called across the deck. 'Bring the prisoner!'

They were forced to drag Sam Bowles to face his accusers, for his legs could barely support him and his tears ran down to mingle with the spittle that the men had ejected into his face.

'I meant no ill,' he pleaded. 'Hear me, shipmates. 'Twas that devil Cumbrae that drove me to it.'

'You laughed as you held my brother's head under the waters of the lagoon,' shouted one of the seamen.

As they dragged him past where Aboli stood with his arms folded across his chest, he stared at Sam with eyes that glittered strangely.

'Remember Francis Courteney!' Aboli rumbled. 'Remember what you did to the finest man who ever sailed the oceans.'

Hal had prepared a list of the crimes for which Sam Bowles must answer. As he read aloud each charge, the men howled for vengeance.

Finally Hal came to the last item of the dreadful recital: 'That you, Samuel Bowles, in the sight of their comrades and shipmates, did murder the wounded seamen from the *Golden Bough*, who had survived your treacherous ambush, by causing them to be drowned.'

He folded the document, and demanded sternly, 'You have heard the charges against you, Samuel Bowles. What have you to say in your defence?'

'It was not my own fault! I swear I would not have done it but I was in terror of my life.'

The crew shouted him down, and it was some minutes until Hal could quieten them. Then he asked, 'So you do not deny the charges against you?'

'What use denying it?' one of the men shouted. 'We all saw it with our own eyes.'

Sam Bowles was weeping loudly now. 'For the love of sweet Jesus have mercy, Sir Henry. I know I have erred, but give me a chance and you will find no more trusty and loving creature to serve you all the days of your life.'

The sight of Bowles disgusted Hal so deeply that he wanted to wash the foul taste of it from his mouth. Suddenly an image appeared in the eye of his mind. It was of his father lying on the litter, being borne away to the scaffold, his body broken and twisted from the rack. He began to tremble.

Beside him, Sukeena sensed his distress. She laid her hand softly on his arm to steady him. He drew a deep, slow breath and fought back the black waves of sorrow that threatened to overwhelm him. 'Samuel Bowles, you have admitted your guilt to all the charges brought against you. Is there anything that you wish to say before I pronounce sentence upon you?' Grimly he stared into Sam's flooded eyes, and watched a strange transformation take place. He realized that the tears were a device that Sam could call upon at will. Something else burned out from a deep and hidden part of his soul, a nimbus so feral and evil that he doubted he still looked into the eyes of a human being and not those of a wild beast standing at bay.

'You think you hate me, Henry Courteney? You do not know what hatred truly is. I glory in the thought of your father screaming on the rack. Sam Bowles did that. Remember it every day you live. Sam Bowles might be dead but Sam Bowles did that!' His voice rose to a scream, and spittle foamed on his lips. His own evil overwhelmed him and his shrieks were barely coherent. 'This is my ship, my own ship. I would have been Captain Samuel Bowles, and you took it from me. May the devil drink your blood in hell. May he dance on your father's twisted and rotting corpse, Henry Courteney.'

Hal turned away from the revolting spectacle, trying to close his ears to the stream of invective.

'Mr Tyler.' He spoke loudly enough for all the crew to hear above Sam Bowles's screams. 'We will waste no more of the ship's time with this matter. The prisoner is to be hanged immediately. Reeve a rope to the main yard—'

'Gundwane!' Aboli roared a warning. 'Behind you!' And he started forward too late to intervene. Sam Bowles had reached under his petticoats. Strapped to the inside of his thigh was a leather sheath. He was as swift as a striking adder. In his hand the blade of the stiletto sparkled like a sliver of crystal, pretty as a maiden's bauble. He threw it with a snap of his wrist.

Hal had begun to turn to Aboli's warning, but Sam was swifter. The

455

dagger flitted across the space that separated them, and Hal winced in anticipation of the sting of the razor-edged blade burying itself in his flesh. For an instant he doubted his own senses, for he felt no blow.

He looked down and saw that Sukeena had flung out one slim bare arm to block the throw. The silver blade had struck an inch below her elbow and buried itself to the haft.

'Sweet Jesus, shield her!' Hal blurted, seized her in his arms and hugged her to him. Both of them stared down at the hilt of the dagger protruding from her flesh.

Aboli reached Sam Bowles the instant after the stiletto had flown from his fingers and sent him crashing to the deck with a blow of his bunched fist. Ned Tyler and a dozen men leapt forward to seize him, and drag him to his feet. Sam shook his head blearily for Aboli's fist had stunned him. Blood dribbled from the side of his mouth.

'Reeve a rope through the main yard block,' Ned Tyler shouted, and a man raced up the shrouds to obey. He ran out along the main yard, and a minute later the rope fell down through the sheave and its tail flopped onto the deck.

'The blade has gone deep,' Hal whispered, as he held Sukeena against his chest and tenderly lifted her wounded arm.

'It is thin and sharp.' Sukeena smiled bravely up at him. 'So sharp I hardly felt it. Draw the blade swiftly, my darling, and it will heal cleanly.'

'Help me here! Hold her arm,' Hal called to Aboli, who sprang to his side, grasped the slim engraved hilt and, with one swift motion, plucked the blade from Sukeena's flesh. It came away with surprising ease.

She said softly, 'There is little harm done,' but her cheeks had paled and tears trembled on her lower eyelids. Hal lifted her in his arms and started towards the companionway of the stern. A wild scream stopped him.

Sam Bowles stood beneath the dangling rope. Ned Tyler was snugging the noose down under his ear. Four men waited ready with the tail of the rope in their hands.

'Your bitch is dead, Henry Courteney. She is dead just like your bastard sire. Sam Bowles killed both of them. Glory be, Captain Bloody Courteney, remember me in your prayers. I am the man you will never forget!'

''Tis a little cut. The Princess is a strong, brave girl. She will live on,' Ned muttered grimly in Sam Bowles's ear. 'You are the one who is dead, Sam Bowles.' He stepped back and nodded to the men on the rope's end, who walked away with it, slapping their bare feet on the deck timbers in unison.

The instant before the rope came up tight and stopped his breath,

Sam screamed again, 'Look well at the blade that cut your whore, Captain. Think on Sam Bowles when you try the point.' The rope bit into his throat and yanked him off his feet, throttling the next word before it reached his lips.

The crew howled with wolflike glee as Sam Bowles rose spiralling in the air, swinging on the rope's end as the *Golden Bough* rolled under him. His legs kicked and danced so that the chains on his ankles tinkled like sleigh bells.

He was still twitching and gurgling when his neck jammed up tight against the sheave block at the end of the main yard high above the deck.

'Let him hang there all night,' Ned Tyler ordered. 'We'll cut him down in the morning and throw him to the sharks.' Then he stooped and picked up the stiletto from the deck where Hal had flung it. He studied the blood-smeared blade and his tanned face turned yellow grey. 'Sweet Mary, let it not be so!' He looked up again at Sam Bowles's corpse swaying to the ship's motion high above him.

'Your death was too easy. If it were in my power, I would kill you a hundred times over, and each time more painfully than the last.'

Hal laid Sukeena on the bunk in the main cabin. 'I should cauterize the wound but the hot iron would leave a scar.' He knelt beside the bunk and examined it closely. 'It is deep but there is almost no bleeding.' He wrapped her arm in a fold of white linen that Aboli brought him from the sea-chest at the foot of the bunk.

'Bring me my bag,' Sukeena ordered, and Aboli went immediately.

As soon as they were alone, Hal bent over her and kissed her pale cheek. 'You took Sam's throw to save me,' he murmured, his face pressed to hers. 'You risked your own life and the life of the child in your womb for me. It was a bad bargain, my love.'

'I would strike the same bargain—' She broke off and he felt her stiffen in his arms and gasp.

'What is it that ails you, my sweetheart?' He drew back and stared into her face. Before his eyes, tiny beads of perspiration welled up out of the pores of her skin, like the dew on the petals of a yellow rose. 'You are in pain?'

'It burns,' she whispered. 'It burns worse than the hot iron you spoke of.'

Swiftly he unwrapped her arm and stared at the change in the wound

457

that had taken place as they embraced. The arm was swelling before his eyes, like one of the Toby fish of the coral reef that could puff itself up to many times its original size when threatened by a predator.

Sukeena lifted the arm and nursed it to her bosom. She whimpered involuntarily as the pain flowed up from the wound to fill her chest like glowing molten lead.

'I do not understand what is happening.' She began to writhe upon the bunk. 'This is not natural. Look how it changes colour.'

Hal stared helplessly as the lovely limb slowly bloated and discoloured with lines of crimson and vivid purple, that ran up from the elbow to her shoulder. The wound began to weep a viscous yellow fluid.

'What can I do?' he blurted.

'I do not know,' she said desperately. 'This is something beyond my understanding.' A spasm of agony seized her in a vice, and her back arched. Then it passed and she pleaded, 'I must have my bag. I cannot endure this pain. I have a powder made from the opium poppy.'

Hal sprang to his feet and bounded across the cabin. 'Aboli, where are you?' he bellowed. 'Bring the bag, and swiftly!'

Ned Tyler stood upon the threshold of the door. He held something in his hand and there was a strange expression on his face. 'Captain, there is something I must show you.'

'Not now, man, not now.' Hal raised his voice again. 'Aboli, come quickly.'

Aboli came down the companionway in a rush, carrying the saddlebags. 'What is it, Gundwane?'

'Sukeena! There is something happening to her. She needs the medicine—'

'Captain!' Ned Tyler forced his way past Aboli's bulk into the cabin and seized Hal's arm urgently. 'This cannot wait. Look at the dagger. Look at the point!' He held up the stiletto, and the others stared at it.

'In God's name!' Hal whispered. 'Let it not be so.'

A narrow groove down the length of the blade was filled with a black, tarry paste that had dried hard and shiny.

'It is an assassin's blade,' Ned said quietly. 'The groove is filled with poison.'

Hal felt the deck sway under his feet as though the *Golden Bough* had been struck by a tall wave. His vision went dark. 'It cannot be,' he said. 'Aboli, tell me it cannot be.'

'Be strong,' Aboli muttered. 'Be strong for her, Gundwane.' He gripped Hal's arm.

The hand steadied Hal and his vision brightened, but when he tried to draw breath the leaden hand of dread crushed in his ribs. 'I cannot live without her,' he said, like a confused child.

'Do not let her know,' Aboli said. 'Do not make the parting harder for her than it need be.'

Hal stared at him uncomprehendingly. Then he began to understand the finality, the significance of that tiny groove in the steel blade, and of the fatal threats that Sam Bowles had shouted at him with the hangman's noose around his neck.

'Sukeena is going to die,' he said, in a tone of bewilderment.

'This will be harder for you than any fight you have ever fought before, Gundwane.'

With an enormous effort Hal fought to regain control of himself. 'Do not show her the dagger,' he said to Ned Tyler. 'Go! Hurl the cursed thing overboard.'

When he got back to Sukeena he tried to conceal the black despair in his heart. 'Aboli has brought your bags.' He knelt beside her again. 'Tell me how to prepare the potion.'

'Oh, do it swiftly,' she pleaded as another spasm gripped her. 'The blue flask. Two measures in a mug of hot water. No more than that, for it is powerful.'

Her hand shook violently as she tried to take the mug from him. She had only the use of the one hand now: her wounded arm was swollen and purpled, the once dainty fingers so bloated that the skin threatened to burst open. She had difficulty holding the mug and Hal lifted it to her lips while she gulped down the potion with pathetic urgency.

She fell back with the effort and writhed on the bunk, drenching the bedclothes with the sweat of agony. Hal lay beside her and held her to his chest, trying to comfort her but knowing too well how futile were his efforts.

After a while the poppy flower seemed to have its effect. She clung to him and pressed her face into his neck. 'I am dying, Gundwane.'

'Do not say so,' he begged her.

'I have known it these many months. I saw it in the stars. That was why I could not answer your question.'

'Sukeena, my love, I will die with you.'

'No.' Her voice was a little stronger. 'You will go on. I have travelled with you as far as I am permitted. But for you the Fates have reserved a special destiny.' She rested a while, and he thought that she had fallen into a coma, but then she spoke again. 'You will live on. You will have many strong sons and their descendants will flourish in this land of Africa, and make it their own.'

'I want no son but yours,' he said. 'You promised me a son.'

'Hush, my love, for the son I give you will break your heart.' Another terrible convulsion took her, and she screamed in the agony of it. At last, when it seemed she could bear no more, she fell back trembling and wept. He held her and could find no words to tell her of his grief.

The hours passed, and twice he heard the ship's bell announce the watch changes. He felt her grow weaker and sink away from him. Then a series of powerful convulsions racked her body. When she fell back in his arms, she whispered, 'Your son, the son I promised you, has been born.' Her eyes were tightly closed, tears squeezing out between the lids.

For a long minute he did not understand her words. Then, fearfully, he drew back the blanket.

Between her bloody thighs lay a tiny pink mannikin, glistening wet and bound to her still by a tangle of fleshy cord. The little head was only half formed, the eyes would never open and the mouth would never take suck, nor cry, nor laugh. But he saw that it was, indeed, a boy.

He took her again in his arms and she opened her eyes and smiled softly. 'I am sorry, my love. I have to go now. If you forget all else, remember only this, that I loved you as no other woman will ever be able to love you.'

She closed her eyes and he felt the life go out of her, the great stillness descend.

He waited with them, his woman and his son, until midnight. Then Althuda brought down a bolt of canvas and sailmaker's needle, thread and palm. Hal placed the stillborn child in Sukeena's arms and bound him there with a linen winding sheet. Then he and Althuda sewed them into a shroud of bright new canvas, a cannonball at Sukeena's feet.

At midnight Hal carried the woman and child in his arms up onto the open deck. Under the bright African moon he gave them both up to the sea. They went below the dark surface and left barely a ripple in the ship's wake at their passing.

'Goodbye, my love,' he whispered. 'Goodbye, my two darlings.'

Then he went down to the cabin in the stern. He opened Llewellyn's Bible and looked for comfort and solace between its black-leather covers, but found none.

For six long days he sat alone by his cabin window. He ate none of the food that Aboli brought him. Sometimes he read from the Bible, but mostly he stared back along the ship's wake. He came up on deck at noon each day, gaunt and haggard, and sighted the sun. He made his calculations of the ship's position and gave his orders to the helm. Then he went back to be alone with his grief.

At dawn on the seventh day Aboli came to him. 'Grief is natural, Gundwane, but this is indulgence. You forsake your duty and those of us who have placed our trust in you. It is enough.'

'It will never be enough.' Hal looked at him. 'I will mourn her all the days of my life.' He stood up and the cabin swam around him, for he was weak with grief and lack of food. He waited for his head to steady and clear. 'You are right, Aboli. Bring me a bowl of food and a mug of small beer.'

After he had eaten, he felt stronger. He washed and shaved, changed his shirt and combed his hair back into a thick plait down his back. He saw that there were strands of pure white in the sable locks. When he looked in the mirror, he barely recognized the darkly tanned face that stared back at him, the nose as beaky as that of an eagle, and there was no spare flesh to cover the high-ridged cheek-bones or the unforgiving line of the jaw. His eyes were green as emeralds, and with that stone's adamantine glitter.

I am barely twenty years of age, he thought, with amazement, and yet I look twice that already.

He picked up his sword from the desk top and slipped it into the scabbard. 'Very well, Aboli. I am ready to take up my duty again,' he said, and Aboli followed him up onto the deck.

The boatswain at the helm knuckled his forehead, and the watch on deck nudged each other. Every man was intensely aware of his presence, but none looked in his direction. Hal stood for a while at the rail, his eyes darting keenly about the deck and rigging.

'Boatswain, hold your luff, damn your eyes!' he snapped at the helmsman.

The leech of the main sail was barely trembling as it spilled the wind, but Hal had noticed it and the watch, squatting at the foot of the mainmast, grinned at each other surreptitiously. The captain was in command again.

At first they did not understand what this presaged. However, they were soon to learn the breadth and extent of it. Hal started by speaking to every man of the crew alone in his cabin. After he had asked their names and the village or town of their birth, he questioned them shrewdly as to their service. Meanwhile he was studying each and assessing his worth.

Three stood out above the others; they had all been watchkeepers under Llewellyn's command. The boatswain, John Lovell, was the man who had served under Hal's father.

'You'll keep your old rating, boatswain,' Hal told him, and John grinned.

'It will be a pleasure to serve under you, Captain.'

'I hope you feel the same way in a month from now,' Hal replied grimly.

The other two were William Stanley and Robert Moone, both coxswains. Hal liked the look of them: Llewellyn had a good eye for judging men, he thought, and shook their hands.

Big Daniel was his other boatswain, and Ned Tyler, who could both read and write, was mate. Althuda, one of the few other literates aboard, became the ship's writer, in charge of all the documents and keeping them up to date. He was Hal's closest remaining link with Sukeena, and Hal felt the greatest affection for him and wished to keep him near at hand. They could share each other's grief.

John Lovell and Ned Tyler went through the ship's roster with Hal and helped him draw up the watch-bill, the nominal list by which every man knew to which watch he was quartered and his station for every purpose.

As soon as this was done Hal inspected the ship. He started on the main deck and then, with his two boatswains, opened every hatch. He climbed and sometimes crawled into every part of the hull, from her bilges to her maintop. In her magazine he opened three kegs, chosen at random, and assessed the quality of her gunpowder and slow-match.

He checked off her cargo against the manifest, and was surprised and pleased to find the amount of muskets and lead shot she carried, together with great quantities of trade goods.

Then he ordered the ship hove to, and a longboat lowered. He had himself rowed around the ship so he could judge her trim. He moved some of the culverins to gunports further aft, and ordered the cargo swung out on deck and repacked to establish the trim he favoured. Then he exercised the ship's company in sail setting and altering, sailing the *Golden Bough* through every point of the compass and at every attitude to the wind. This went on for almost a week, as he called out the watch below at noon or in the middle of the night to shorten or increase sail and push the ship to the limits of her speed.

Soon he knew the *Golden Bough* as intimately as a lover. He found out how close he could take her to the wind, and how she loved to run before it with all her canvas spread. He had a bucket crew wet down her sails so they would better hold the wind, and then, when she was in full flight, took her speed through the water with glass and log timed from bow to stern. He found out how to coax the last yard of speed out of her, and how to have her respond to the helm like a fine hunter to the reins.

The crew worked without complaint, and Aboli heard them talking amongst themselves in the forecastle. Far from complaining, they seemed to be enjoying the change from Llewellyn's more complacent command.

'The young 'un is a sailor. The ship loves him. He can drive the *Bough* to her limit, and make her fly through the water, he can.'

'He's happy to drive us to the limit, also,' another opined.

'Cheer up, all you lazy layabouts, I reckon there'll be prize money galore at the end of this voyage.'

Then Hal worked them at the guns, running them out then in again, until the men sweated, strained and grinned as they cursed him for a tyrant. Then he had the guncrews fire at a floating keg, and cheered with the best of them as the target shattered to the shot.

In between times, he exercised them with the cutlass and the pike, and he fought alongside them, stripped to the waist and matching himself against Aboli, Big Daniel or John Lovell, who was the best swordsman of the new crew.

The *Golden Bough* sailed on around the bulge of the southern African continent and Hal headed her up into the north. Now with every league they sailed the sea changed its character. The waters took on a vivid indigo hue that stained the sky the same colour. They were so clear that, leaning over the bows, Hal could see the pods of porpoises four fathoms down, racing ahead of the bows and frolicking like a pack of boisterous spaniels until they arched up to the surface. As they broke through it he could see the nostril on top of their head open to breathe, and they looked up at him with a merry eye and a knowing grin.

The flying fish were their outriders, sailing ahead of them on flashing silver wings, and the mountains of towering cumulus clouds were the beacons that beckoned them ever northwards.

When they sailed into the great calms he would not let his crew rest, but lowered the boats and raced watch against watch, the oars churning the water white. Then at the end of the course he had them board the *Golden Bough* as though she were an enemy, while he and Aboli and Big Daniel opposed them and made them fight for a footing on the deck.

In the windless heat of the tropics, while the *Bough* rolled gently on the sluggish swells and the empty sails slatted and lolled, he raced the hands in relay teams to the top of the mainmast and down, with an extra tot of rum as the prize.

Within weeks the men were fit and lean and bursting with high spirits, spoiling for a fight. Hal, however, was plagued by a nagging worry that he shared with nobody, not even Aboli. Night after night he sat at his desk in the main cabin, not daring to sleep, for he knew that the grief and the memories of the woman and the child he had lost would haunt his dreams, and he studied the charts and tried to puzzle out a solution.

He had barely forty men under his command, only just sufficient to work the ship, but too few by far to fight her. If they met again, the Buzzard would be able to send a hundred men onto the *Golden Bough's* deck. If they were to be able to defend themselves, let alone seek employment in the service of the Prester, then Hal must find seamen.

When he perused the charts he could find few ports where he might enlist trained seamen. Most were under the control of the Portuguese and the Dutch, and they would not welcome an English frigate, especially one whose captain was intent on seducing their sailors into his service.

The English had not penetrated this far ocean in any force. A few traders had factories on the Indian continent, but they were under the thrall of the Great Mogul, and, besides, to reach them would mean a voyage of several thousand miles out of his intended course.

Hal knew that on the south-east shore of the long island of St Lawrence, which was also called Madagascar, the French Knights of the Order of the Holy Grail had a safe harbour which they called Fort Dauphin. If he called in there, as an English Knight of the Order he could expect a welcome but little else for his comfort, unless some rare circumstance such as a cyclone had caused a wreck and left sailors in the port without ship. However, he decided that he must take that chance and make Fort Dauphin his first call, and laid his course for the island.

As he sailed on northwards, with Madagascar as his goal, Africa was always there off the larboard beam. At times the land dreamed in the blue distance, and at other times it was so close that they could smell its peculiar aroma. It was the peppery scent of spice and the rich dark odour of the earth, like new-baked biscuit hot from the oven.

Often Jiri, Matesi and Kimatti clustered at the rail, pointing at the green hills and the lacy lines of surf, and talking together quietly in the language of the forests. When there was a quiet hour, Aboli would climb to the masthead and stare across at the land. When he descended his expression was sad and lonely.

464

Day after day they saw no sign of other men. There were no towns or ports along the shore that they could spy out, and no sail upon the sea, not even a canoe or coasting dhow.

It was not until they were less than a hundred leagues south of Cap St Marie, the southernmost point of the island, that they raised another sail. Hal stood the ship to quarters and had the culverin loaded with grape and the slow-match lit, for out here beyond the Line he dared take no ship on trust.

When they were almost within hail of the other ship, it broke out its colours. Hal was delighted to see the Union flag and the *croix patté* of the Order streaming from her masthead. He replied with the same show of cloth and both ships hove to within hail of each other.

'What ship?' Hal asked, and the reply came back across the blue swells, 'The *Rose of Durham*. Captain Welles.' She was an armed trader, a caravel with twelve guns a side.

Hal lowered a longboat and had himself rowed across. He was greeted at the entryport by a spry, elfin captain of middle years. '*In Arcadia habito.*'

'*Flumen sacrum bene cognosco*,' Hal replied, and they clasped hands in the recognition grip of the Temple.

Captain Welles invited Hal down to his cabin where they drank a tankard of cider together and exchanged news avidly. Welles had sailed four weeks previously from the English factory of St George near Madras on the east coast of Further India with a cargo of trade cloth. He intended to exchange this for slaves on the Gambian coast of West Africa, and then sail on across the Atlantic to the Caribbean where he would barter his slaves for sugar, and so back home to England.

Hal questioned him on the availability of seamen from the English factories on the Carnatic, that stretch of the shore of Further India from East Ghats down to the Coromandel coast, but Welles shook his head. 'You'll be wanting to give the whole of that coast a wide berth. When I left the cholera was raging in every village and factory. Any man you take aboard might bring death with him as a companion.'

Hal chilled at the thought of the havoc that this plague would wreak among his already depleted crew, should it take hold on the *Golden Bough*. He dared not risk a visit to those fever ports.

Over a second mug of cider, Welles gave Hal his first reliable account of the conflict raging in the Great Horn of Africa. 'The younger brother of the Great Mogul, Sadiq Khan Jahan, has arrived off the coast of the Horn with a great fleet. He has joined forces with Ahmed El Grang, who they call the Left-handed, the king of the Omani Arabs who holds sway over the lands bordering the Prester's empire. These two have declared

465

jihad, holy war, and together they have swept down like a raging gale upon the Christians. They have taken by storm and sacked the ports and towns of the coast, burning the churches and despoiling the monasteries, massacring the monks and the holy men.'

'I intend sailing to offer my services to the Prester to help him resist the pagan,' Hal told him.

'It is another crusade, and yours is a noble inspiration,' Welles applauded him. 'Many of the most sacred relics of Christendom are held by the holy fathers in the Ethiopian city of Aksum and in the monasteries in secret places in the mountains. If they were to fall into the hands of the pagan, it would be a sad day for all Christendom.'

'If you cannot yourself go upon this sacred venture, will you not spare me a dozen of your men, for I am sore pressed for the lack of good sailors?' Hal asked.

Welles looked away. 'I have a long voyage ahead of me, and there are bound to be heavy losses amongst my crew when we visit the fever coast of the Gambia and make the middle passage of the Atlantic,' he mumbled.

'Think on your vows,' Hal urged him.

Welles hesitated, then shrugged. 'I will muster my crew, and you may appeal to them and call for volunteers to join your venture.'

Hal thanked him, knowing that Welles was on a certain wager. Few seamen at the end of a two-year voyage would forgo their share of profits and the prospect of a swift return home, in favour of a call to arms to aid a foreign potentate, even if he were a Christian. Only two men responded to Hal's appeal, and Welles looked relieved to be shot of them. Hal guessed that they were trouble-makers and malcontents, but he could not afford to be finicky.

Before they parted, Hal handed over to Welles two packets of letters, stitched in canvas covers with the address boldly written on each. One was addressed to Viscount Winterton, and in the long letter Hal had penned to him he set out the circumstances of Captain Llewellyn's murder, and his own acquisition of the *Golden Bough*. He gave an undertaking to sail the ship in accordance with the original charter.

The second letter was addressed to his uncle, Thomas Courteney, at High Weald, to inform him of the death of his father and his own inheritance of the title. He asked his uncle to continue to run the estate on his behalf.

When at last he took leave of Welles, the two seamen he had acquired went with him back to the *Golden Bough*. From his quarterdeck Hal watched the top sails of the *Rose of Durham* drop below the southern horizon, and days afterwards the hills of Madagascar rise before him out of the north.

That night Hal, as had become his wont, came up on deck at the end of the second dog watch to read the traverse board and speak to the helmsman. Three dark shadows waited for him at the foot of the mainmast.

'Jiri and the others wish to speak to you, Gundwane,' Aboli told him.

They clustered about him as he stood by the windward rail. Jiri spoke first in the language of the forests. 'I was a man when the slavers took me from my home,' he told Hal quietly. 'I was old enough to remember much more of the land of my birth than these others.' He indicated Aboli, Kimatti and Matesi, and all three nodded agreement.

'We were children,' said Aboli.

'In these last days,' Jiri went on, 'when I smelled the land and saw again the green hills, old memories long forgotten came back to me. I am sure now, in my deepest heart, that I can find my way back to the great river along the banks of which my tribe lived when I was a child.'

Hal was silent for a while, and then he asked, 'Why do you tell me these things, Jiri? Do you wish to return to your own people?'

Jiri hesitated. 'It was so long ago. My father and my mother are dead, killed by the slavers. My brothers and the friends of my childhood are gone also, taken away in the chains of the slavers.' He was silent awhile, but then he went on, 'No, Captain, I cannot return, for you are now my chief as your father was before you, and these are my brothers.' He indicated Aboli and the others who stood around him.

Aboli took up the tale. 'If Jiri can lead us back to the great river, if we can find our lost tribe, it may well be that we can find also a hundred warriors amongst them to fill the watch-bill of this ship.'

Hal stared at him in astonishment. 'A hundred men? Men who can fight like you four rascals? Then, indeed, the stars are smiling upon me again.'

He took all four down to the stern cabin, lit the lanterns and spread his charts upon the deck. They squatted around them in a circle, and the black men prodded the parchment sheets with their forefingers and argued softly in their sonorous voices, while Hal explained the lines on the charts to the three who, unlike Aboli, could not read.

When the ship's bell tolled the beginning of the morning watch, Hal went on deck and called Ned Tyler to him. 'New course, Mr Tyler. Due south. Mark it on the traverse board.'

Ned was clearly astounded at the order to turn back, but he asked no question. 'Due south it is.'

Hal took pity on him, for it was evident that curiosity itched him like a burr in his breeches. 'We're closing the African mainland again.'

They crossed the broad channel that separated Madagascar from the African continent. The mainland came up as a low blue smudge on the horizon and, at a good offing, they turned and sailed southwards once more along the coast.

Aboli and Jiri spent most of the hours of daylight at the masthead, peering at the land. Twice Jiri came down and asked Hal to stand inshore to investigate what appeared to be the mouth of a large river. Once it turned out to be a false channel and the second time Jiri did not recognize it when they anchored off the mouth. 'It is too small. The river I seek has four mouths.'

They weighed anchor and worked out to sea again, then went on southwards. Hal was beginning to doubt Jiri's memory but he persevered. Several days later he noticed the patent excitement of the two men at the masthead as they stared at the land and gesticulated to each other. Matesi and Kimatti, who as part of the off-duty watch had been lazing on the forecastle, scrambled to their feet and flew up the shrouds to hang in the rigging and stare avidly at the land.

Hal strode to the rail and raised Llewellyn's brass-bound telescope to his eye. He saw the delta of a great river spread before them. The waters that spilled out from the multiple mouths were discoloured and carried with them the detritus of the swamps and the unknown lands that must lie at the source of this mighty river. Squadrons of sharks were feeding on this waste, and their tall, triangular fins zigzagged across the current.

Hal called Jiri down to him and asked, 'What do your tribe call this river?'

'There are many names for it, for the one river comes to the sea as many rivers. They are called Muselo and Inhamessingo and Chinde. But the chief of them is Zambere.'

'They all have a noble ring to them,' Hal conceded. 'But are you certain this is the river serpent with four mouths?'

'On the head of my dead father I swear it is.'

Hal had two men in the bows taking soundings as he crept inshore, and as soon as the bottom began to shelve steeply he dropped anchor in twelve fathoms. He would not risk the ship in the narrow inland waters and the convoluted channels of the delta. But there was another risk he was unwilling to face.

He knew from his father that these tropical deltas were dangerous to the health of his crew. If they breathed the night airs of the swamp, they would soon fall prey to the deadly fevers that were borne upon them, aptly named the malaria, the bad airs.

Sukeena's saddle-bags, which with her mother's jade brooch were her only legacy to Hal, contained a goodly store of the Jesuit's powder, the extract of the bark of the Cinchona tree. He had also discovered a large jar of the same precious substance amongst Llewellyn's stores. It was the only remedy against the malaria, a disease that mariners encountered in every known area of the oceans, from the jungles of Batavia and Further India to the canals of Venice, the swamps of Virginia and the Caribbean in the New World.

Hal would not risk his entire crew to its ravages. He ordered the two pinnaces swung up from the hold and assembled. Then he chose the crews for these vessels, which naturally included the four Africans and Big Daniel. He placed a falconet in the bows of each and had a pair of murderers mounted in the sterns.

All the men in the expedition were heavily armed, and Hal placed three heavy chests of trade goods in each boat, knives and scissors and small hand mirrors, rolls of copper wire and Venetian glass beads.

He left Ned Tyler in charge of the Golden Bough with Althuda, and ordered them to remain anchored well offshore, and await his return. The distress signal would be a red Chinese rocket: only if he saw it was Ned to send the longboats in to find them.

'We may be many days, weeks even,' Hal warned. 'Do not lose patience. Stay on your station as long as you do not have word of us.'

Hal took command of the leading boat. He had Aboli and the other Africans in his crew. Big Daniel followed in the second.

Hal explored each of the four mouths. The water levels seemed low, and some of the entrances were almost sealed by their sand bars. He knew of the danger of crocodiles and would not risk sending men over the side to drag the boats over the bar. In the end he chose the river mouth with the greatest volume of water pouring through it. With the onshore morning breeze filling the lug sail and all hands at the oars they forced their way over the bar into the hot, hushed world of the swamps.

Tall papyrus plants and stands of mangroves formed a high wall down each side of the channel so that their vision was limited and the wind was blanketed from them. They rowed on steadily, following the twists of the channel. Each turn opened the same dreary view. Hal realized almost at once how easy it would be to lose his way in this maze and he marked each branch of the channel with strips of canvas tied to the top branches of mangrove.

For two days they groped their way westwards, guided only by the compass and the flow of the waters. In the pools wallowed herds of the great grey river-cows which opened cavernous pink jaws and honked at them with wild laughter as they approached. At first they steered well

469

clear of them, but once they became more familiar with them Hal began to ignore their warning cries and displays of rage, and pushed on recklessly.

His bravado at first seemed justified and the animals submerged when he drove straight at them. Then they came round another bend into a large green pool. In the centre was a mud-bank, and on it stood a huge female hippopotamus and at her flank a new-born calf not much bigger than a pig. The cow bellowed at them threateningly as they rowed towards her, but the men laughed with derision and Hal shouted from the bows, 'Stand aside, old lady, we mean you no harm, but we intend to pass.'

The great beast lowered her head and, grunting belligerently, charged across the mud in a wild, ungainly gallop that hurled up clods of mud. As soon as he realized that the brute was in earnest Hal snatched up the slow-match from the tub at his feet. 'By heavens, she means to attack us.'

He grabbed the iron handle of the falconet and swung it to aim ahead, but the hippopotamus reached the water and plunged into it at full tilt, sending up a sheet of spray and disappearing beneath the surface. Hal swung the barrel of the falconet from side to side, seeking a chance to fire, but he saw only a ripple on the surface as the animal swam deep below it.

'It is coming straight for us!' Aboli shouted. 'Wait until you get a clear shot, Gundwane!'

Hal peered down, the burning match held ready, and through the clear green water he saw a remarkable sight. The hippo was moving along the bottom in a slow dreamlike gallop, clouds of mud boiling up under her hoofs with each stride. But she was still a fathom deep and his shot could never reach her.

'She has gone beneath us!' he shouted at Aboli.

'Get ready!' Aboli warned. 'This is how they destroy the canoes of my people.' The words had barely left his lips when beneath their feet came a resounding crack as the beast reared up under them, and the heavy boat with its full complement of ten rowers was lifted high out of the water.

They were hurled from their benches, and Hal might have been thrown overboard if he had not grabbed the thwart. The boat crashed back to the surface and Hal again seized the tail of the falconet.

The animal's charge would have stove in the hull of any lesser craft, and would certainly have splintered a native dugout canoe, but the pinnace was robustly constructed to withstand the ravages of the North Sea.

Close alongside, the huge grey head burst through the surface, and the mouth opened like a pink cavern lined with fangs of yellow ivory as long as a man's forearm. With a bellow that shocked the crew with its ferocity the hippopotamus rushed at them with gaping jaws to tear the timbers out of the boat's side.

Hal swung the falconet until it was almost touching the onrushing head. He fired. Smoke and flame shot straight down the gaping throat and the jaws clashed shut. The beast disappeared in a swirl, to surface seconds later half-way back to the mud-bank on which her calf stood, forlorn and bewildered.

The huge rotund body reared half out of the water in a gargantuan convulsion then collapsed back and sank away in death, leaving a long wake of crimson to mark the green waters with its passing.

The rowers wielded their oars with renewed vigour and the boat shot round the next bend, with Big Daniel's boat close astern. The hull of Hal's vessel was leaking fairly heavily, but with one man bailing they could keep her dry until they had an opportunity to beach her and turn her over to repair the damage. They pressed on up the channel.

Clouds of waterfowl rose from the dense stands of papyrus around them or perched in the branches of the mangroves. There were herons, duck and geese that they recognized, together with dozens of other birds that they had never seen before. Several times they caught glimpses of a strange antelope with a shaggy brown coat and spiral horns with pale tips, which seemed to make the deep swamps its home. At dusk they surprised one as it stood on the edge of the papyrus. With a long and lucky musket shot, Hal brought it down. They were astonished to find that its hoofs were deformed, enormously elongated. Such feet would act like the fins of a fish in the water, Hal reasoned, and give it purchase on the soft footing of mud and reeds. The antelope's flesh was sweet and tender and the men, long starved of fresh food, ate it with relish.

The nights, when they slept on the bare deck, were murmurous, troubled by great clouds of stinging insects, and in the dawn their faces were swollen and bloated with red lumps.

On the third day the papyrus began to give way to open flood plains. The breeze could reach them now, and blew away the clouds of insects and filled the lug sail they set. They went on at better speed and came to where the other branches of the river all joined up to form one great flow almost three cables' length in width.

The flood plains on each bank of this mighty river were verdant with a knee-high growth of rich grasses, grazed by huge herds of buffalo. Their numbers were uncountable, and they formed a moving carpet as far as

Hal could see, even when he shinned up the pinnace's mast. They stood so densely upon the plain that large areas of the grasslands were obscured by their multitudes. They were tarry lakes and running rivers of bovine flesh.

The outer fringes of these herds lined the banks of the river and stared across the water at them, their drooling muzzles lifted high and their bossed heads heavy with drooping horns. Hal steered the boat in closer and fired the falconet into the thick of them. With that single discharge he brought down two young cows. That night, for the first time, they camped ashore and feasted on buffalo steaks roasted on the coals.

For many days, they went on following the stately green flow, and the flood plains on either hand gradually gave way to forests and glades. The river narrowed, became deeper and stronger and their progress was slower against the current. On the eighth evening after leaving the ship, they went ashore to camp in a grove of tall wild fig trees.

Almost immediately they came upon signs of human habitation. It was a decaying stockade, built of heavy logs. Within its wooden walls were pens that Hal thought must have been for enclosing cattle or other beasts.

'Slavers!' said Aboli bitterly. 'This is where they have chained my people like animals. In one of these *bomas*, perhaps this very one, my mother died under the weight of her sorrow.'

The stockade had been long abandoned but Hal could not bring himself to camp on the site of so much human misery. They moved a league upstream and found a small island on which to bivouac. The next morning they went on along the river through forest and grassland innocent of any further evidence of man. 'The slavers have swept the wilderness with their net,' Aboli said sorrowfully. 'That is why they have abandoned their factory and sailed away. It seems that there are no men or women of our tribe who have survived their ravages. We must abandon the search, Gundwane, and turn back.'

'No, Aboli. We go on.'

'All around us is the ancient memory of despair and death,' Aboli pleaded. 'These forests are inhabited only by the ghosts of my people.'

'I will decide when we turn back, and that time is not yet come,' Hal told him, for in truth he was becoming fascinated by this strange new land and the plethora of wild creatures with which it abounded. He felt a powerful urge to travel on and on, to follow the great river to its source.

The next day, from the bows, Hal spied a range of low hillocks a short distance north of the river. He ordered them to beach the boats and left Big Daniel and his seamen to repair the leaks in the hull of the first caused by the hippopotamus attack. He took Aboli with him and they set off to climb the hills for a better view of the country ahead. They were further off than they had appeared to be, for distances are deceptive in the clear air and under the bright light of the African sun. It was late afternoon when they stepped out onto the crest and gazed down upon the limitless distances where forests and hills replicated themselves, rank upon rank and range upon range, like images of infinity in mirrors of shaded blue.

They sat in silence, awed by the immensity of this wild land. At last Hal stood up reluctantly. 'You are right, Aboli. There are no men here. We must return to the ship.'

Yet he felt deep within him a strange reluctance to turn his back upon this tremendous land. More than ever, he felt drawn to its mystery and the romance of its vast spaces.

'You will have many strong sons,' Sukeena had prophesied. 'Their descendants will flourish in this land of Africa and make it their own.'

He did not yet love this land. It was too strange and barbaric, too alien from all he had known in the gentler climes of the north, but deeply he felt the magic of it in his blood. The silence of dusk fell upon the hills, that moment when all creation held its breath before the insidious advance of the night. He took one last look, sweeping the horizon where, like monstrous chameleons, the hills changed colour. Before his eyes they turned sapphire, azure, and the blue of a kingfisher's back. Suddenly he stiffened.

He grasped Aboli's arm and pointed. 'Look!' he said softly. From the foot of the next range a single thin plume of smoke rose out of the forest and climbed up into the violet evening air.

'Men!' Aboli whispered. 'You were right not to turn back so soon, Gundwane.'

They went down the hill in darkness and moved through the forest like shadows. Hal guided them by the stars, fixing his eye upon the great shining Southern Cross that hung above the hill at the foot of which they had marked the column of smoke. After midnight, as they crept forward with increasing caution, Aboli stopped so abruptly that Hal almost ran into him in the darkness.

'Listen!' he said. They stood in silence for minute after minute.

Then Hal said, 'I hear nothing.'

'Wait!' Aboli insisted, and then Hal heard it. It was a sound once so commonplace, but one that he had not heard since he had left Good Hope. It was the mournful lowing of a cow.

'My people are herders,' Aboli whispered. 'Their cattle are their most treasured possessions.' He led Hal forward cautiously until they could smell the woodsmoke and the familiar bovine odour of the cattle pen. Hal picked out the puddle of faintly glowing ash that marked the campfire. Silhouetted against it was the outline of a sitting man, wrapped in a kaross.

They lay and waited for the dawn. However, long before first light the camp began to stir. The watchman stood up, stretched, coughed and spat in the dead coals. Then he threw fresh wood upon the fire, and knelt to blow it. The flames flared and, by their light, Hal saw that he was but a boy. Naked except for a loincloth, the lad left the fire and came close to where they were hidden. He lifted his loincloth and peed into the grass, playing games with his urine stream, aiming at fallen leaves and twigs and chuckling as he tried to drown a scurrying scarab beetle.

Then he went back to the fire and called out towards the lean-to of branches and thatch, 'The dawn comes. It is time to let out the herd.'

His voice was high and unbroken, but Hal was delighted to find that he understood every word the boy had said. It was the language of the forests that Aboli had taught him.

Two other lads of the same age crawled out of the hut, shivering, muttering and scratching, and all three went to the cattle pen. They spoke to the beasts as though they, too, were children, rubbed their heads and patted their flanks.

As the light strengthened Hal saw that these cattle were far different from those he had known on High Weald. They were taller and rangier, with huge humps over their shoulders, and the span of their horns was so wide as to appear grotesque, the weight almost too much for even their heavy frames to support.

The boys picked out a cow and pushed her calf away from the udder. Then one knelt under her belly and milked her, sending purring jets into a calabash gourd. Meanwhile, the other two seized a young bullock and passed a leather thong around its neck. They drew this tight and when the restricted blood vessels stood proud beneath the black skin, one pricked a vein with the sharp point of an arrow head. The first child came running with the gourd half-filled with milk and held the mouth of it under the stream of bright red blood that spurted from the punctured vein.

When the gourd was full, one staunched the small wound in the

474

bullock's neck with a handful of dust, and turned it loose. The beast wandered away, none the worse for the bleeding. The boys shook the gourd vigorously, then passed it from one to the other, each drinking deeply from the mixture of milk and blood as his turn came, smacking his lips and sighing with pleasure.

So engrossed were they with their breakfast that none noticed Aboli or Hal until they were grabbed from behind and hoisted kicking and shrieking in the air.

'Be quiet, you little baboon,' Aboli ordered.

'Slavers!' wailed the eldest child, as he saw Hal's white face. 'We are taken by slavers!'

'They will eat us,' squeaked the youngest.

'We are not slavers!' Hal told them. 'And we will not harm you.'

This assurance merely sent the trio into fresh paroxysms of terror. 'He is a devil who can speak the language of heaven.'

'He understands all we say. He is an albino devil.'

'He will surely eat us as my mother warned me.'

Aboli held the eldest at arm's length and glared at him. 'What is your name, little monkey?'

'See his tattoos.' The boy howled in dread and confusion. 'He is tattooed like the Monomatapa, the chosen of heaven.'

'He is a great Mambo!'

'Or the ghost of the Monomatapa who died long ago.'

'I am indeed a great chief,' Aboli agreed. 'And you will tell me your name.'

'My name is Tweti – oh, Monomatapa, spare me for I am but little. I will be only a single mouthful for your mighty jaws.'

'Take me to your village, Tweti, and I will spare you and your brothers.'

After a while the children began to believe that they would neither be eaten nor turned into slaves, and they started to smile shyly at Hal's overtures. From there it was not long before they were giggling delightedly to have been chosen by the great tattooed chief and the strange albino to lead them to the village.

Driving the cattle herd before them, they took a track through the hills and came out suddenly in a small village surrounded by rudimentary fields of cultivation, in which a few straggling millet plants grew. The huts were shaped like bee-hives and beautifully thatched, but they were deserted. Clay pots stood on the cooking fires before each hut and there were calves in the pens and woven baskets, weapons and accoutrements scattered where they had been dropped when the villagers fled.

The three boys squeaked reassurances into the surrounding bush. 'Come out! Come and see! It is a great Mambo of our tribe come back from death to visit us!'

An old crone was the first to emerge timidly from a thicket of elephant grass. She wore only a greasy leather skirt, and her one eye socket was empty. She had but a single yellow tooth in the front of her mouth. Her dangling dugs flapped against her wrinkled belly, which was scarified with ritual tattoos.

She took one look at Aboli's face, then ran to prostrate herself before him. She lifted one of his feet and placed it on her head. 'Mighty Monomatapa,' she keened, 'you are the chosen of heaven. I am a useless insect, a dung beetle, before your glory.'

In singles and pairs, and then in greater numbers, the other villagers emerged from their hiding places and gathered before Aboli to kneel in obeisance and pour dust and ashes on their heads in reverence.

'Do not let this adulation turn your head, oh Chosen One,' Hal told him sourly in English.

'I give you royal dispensation,' Aboli replied, without smiling. 'You need not kneel in my presence, nor pour dust on your head.'

The villagers brought Aboli and Hal carved wooden stools to sit upon, and offered them gourds of soured milk mixed with fresh blood, porridge of millet, grilled wild birds, roasted termites and caterpillars seared on the coals so that their hairy coverings were burnt off.

'You must eat a little of everything they offer you,' Aboli warned Hal, 'or else you will give great offence.'

Hal gagged down a few mouthfuls of the blood and milk mixture, while Aboli swigged back a full gourd. Hal found the other delicacies a little more palatable, the caterpillars tasted like fresh grass juice and the termites were crisp and delicious as roasted chestnuts.

When they had eaten, the village headman came forward on hands and knees to answer Aboli's questions.

'Where is the town of the Monomatapa?'

'It is two days' march in the direction of the setting sun.'

'I need ten good men to guide me.'

'As you command, O Mambo.'

The ten men were ready within the hour, and little Tweti and his companions wept bitterly that they were not chosen for this honour but were instead sent back to the lowly task of cattle-herding.

The trail they followed towards the west led through open forests of tall, graceful trees interspersed with wide expanses of savannah grasslands. They began to encounter more herds of the humped cattle herded by small naked boys. The cattle grazed in close and unlikely truce with

476

herds of wild antelope. Some of the game were almost equine, but with coats of strawberry roan or midnight sable, and horns that swept back like Oriental scimitars to touch their flanks.

Several times in the forests they saw elephants, small breeding herds of cows and calves. Once they passed within a cable's length of a gaunt bull standing under a flat-topped thorn tree in the middle of the open savannah. This patriarch showed little fear of them but spread his tattered ears like battle standards and raised his curved tusks high to peer at them with small eyes.

'It would take two strong men to carry one of those tusks,' Aboli said, 'and in the markets of Zanzibar they would fetch thirty English pounds apiece.'

They passed many small villages of thatched bee-hive huts, similar to the one in which Tweti lived. Obviously, the news of their arrival had gone ahead of them for the inhabitants came out to stare in awe at Aboli's tattoos and then to prostrate themselves before him and cover themselves with dust.

Each of the local chieftains pleaded with Aboli to honour his village by spending the night in the new hut his people had built especially for him as soon as they had heard of his coming. They offered food and drink, calabashes of the blood and milk mixture and bubbling clay pots of millet beer.

They presented gifts, iron spear- and axe-heads, a small elephant tusk, tanned leather cloaks and bags. Aboli touched each of these to signal his acceptance then returned them to the giver.

They brought him girls to choose from, pretty little nymphs with copper-wire bangles on their wrists and ankles, and tiny aprons of coloured trade beads that barely concealed their pudenda. The girls giggled and covered their mouths with dainty pink-palmed hands and ogled Aboli with huge dark eyes, liquid with awe. Their plump pubescent breasts were shining with cow fat and red clay, and their buttocks were bare and round and joggled with each disappointed pace as Aboli sent them away. They looked back at him over a bare shoulder with longing and reverence. What prestige they would have enjoyed if they had been chosen by the Monomatapa.

On the second day they approached another range of hills, but these were more rugged and their sides were sheer granite. As they drew closer they saw that the summit of each hill was fortified with stone walls.

'Yonder is the great town of the Monomatapa. It is built upon the hill tops to resist the attacks of the slavers, and his regiments of warriors are always at the ready to repel them.'

A throng of people came down to welcome them, hundreds of men and women wearing all their finery of beads and carved ivory jewellery. The elders wore head-dresses of ostrich feathers and skirts of cow tails. All the men were armed with spears, and war bows were slung upon their backs. They groaned with awe as they saw Aboli's face and flung themselves down before him so that he could tread upon their quivering bodies.

Borne along by this throng, they slowly ascended the pathway to the summit of the highest hill, passing through a series of gateways. At each gate part of the crowd about them fell back until, as they approached the final glacis before the fortress that crowned the summit, they were accompanied only by a handful of chieftains, warriors and councillors of the highest rank, wearing all the regalia and finery of their office.

Even these paused at the final gateway, and one noble ancient with silver hair and aquiline eye took Aboli by the hand and led him into the inner courtyard. Hal shrugged off the councillors who sought to restrain him and strode into the inner courtyard at Aboli's side.

The floor was of clay that had been mixed with blood and cow dung and then screeded until it dried like polished red marble. Huts surrounded this courtyard, but many times larger than Hal had seen before, and the thatching was of new golden grass, intricate and splendid. The doorway of each hut was decorated by what seemed, at first glance, to be orbs of ivory, and it was only when they were half-way across the courtyard that Hal realized they were human skulls, and that tall pyramids formed of hundreds stood at spaced intervals around the perimeter.

Beside each skull pyramid was planted a tall pole and on the sharpened point of these stakes a man or woman had been impaled through the anus. Most of these victims were long dead and stank, but one or two still twitched or groaned pitifully.

The old man stopped them in the centre of the courtyard. Hal and Aboli stood in silence for a while, until a weird cacophony of primitive musical instruments and discordant human voices issued from the largest and most imposing hut facing them. A procession of creatures came forth into the sunlight. They crawled and wriggled like insects on the polished clay surface, and their bodies and faces were daubed with coloured clay and painted in fantastic patterns. They were hung with charms, amulets and magical fetishes, skins of reptiles, bones and skulls of man and animal, and all the gruesome paraphernalia of the wizard and the witch. They whined and howled and gibbered, and rolled their eyes and chattered their teeth, and beat on drums and twanged single-stringed harps.

Two women followed them. Both were stark naked, the first a mature female with full and bountiful breast, her belly marked with the stria of childbearing. The other was a girl, slim and graceful with a sweet moon face and startlingly white teeth behind full lips. She was the loveliest of any that Hal had laid eyes upon since they had entered the land of the Monomatapa. Her waist was narrow and her hips full and her skin was like black satin. She knelt on hands and knees with her buttocks turned towards them. Hal shifted uneasily as the deepest folds of her privy parts were exposed to his gaze. Even in these circumstances of danger and uncertainty he found himself aroused by her nubility.

'Show no emotion,' Aboli warned him softly, without moving his lips. 'As you love life, remain unmoved.'

The wizards fell silent and for a space everyone was still. Then, out of the hut stooped a massively corpulent figure clad in a leopardskin cloak. Upon his head was a tall hat of the same dappled fur, which exaggerated his already magisterial height.

He paused in the doorway and glared at them. All the company of wizards and witches crouching at his feet moaned with amazement and covered their eyes, as if his beauty and majesty had blinded them.

Hal stared back at him. It was difficult to follow Aboli's advice to remain expressionless, for the features of the Monomatapa were tattooed in exactly the same pattern and style as the face he had known from childhood, the great round face of Aboli.

Aboli broke the silence. 'I see you, great Mambo. I see you, my brother. I see you, N'Pofho, son of my father.'

The Monomatapa's eyes narrowed slightly, but his patterned features remained as if carved in ebony. With slow and stately stride he crossed to where the naked girl knelt and seated himself upon her arched back as though she were a stool. He continued to glare at Aboli and Hal, and the silence drew out.

Suddenly he made an impatient gesture to the woman who stood beside him. She took one of her own breasts in her hand and, placing the engorged nipple between his thick lips, gave him suck. He drank from her, his throat bobbing, then pushed her away and wiped his mouth with the palm of his hand. Refreshed by this warm draught, he looked to his principal soothsayer. 'Speak to me of these strangers, Sweswe!' he commanded. 'Make me a prophecy, O beloved of the dark spirits!'

The oldest and ugliest of the wizards sprang to his feet and began a wild gyrating, whirling dance. He shrieked and leaped high in the air, shaking the rattle in his hand. 'Treason!' he screamed, and frothy spittle splattered from his lips. 'Sacrilege! Who dares claim blood ties with the Son of the Heavens?' He pranced in front of Aboli like a wizened ape on skinny shanks. 'I smell the stink of treachery!' He hurled his rattle at Aboli's feet and snatched a cow's-tail whisk from his belt. 'I smell sedition!' He brandished the whisk, and began to tremble in every muscle. 'What devil is this who dares to imitate the sacred Tattoo?' His eyes rolled back in his skull until only the whites showed. 'Beware! For the ghost of your father, the great Holomima, demands the blood sacrifice!' he shrieked, and gathered himself to spring full at Aboli's face to strike him with the magician's whisk.

Aboli was faster. The cutlass sprang from the scabbard on his belt as though it were a living thing. It flashed in the sunlight as he cut back-handed. The wizard's head was severed cleanly from his trunk and rolled down his back. It lay on the polished clay gazing with wide astonished eyes at the sky, and the lips writhing and twitching as they tried to utter the next wild denunciation.

The headless body stood, for a moment, on trembling legs. A fountain of blood from the severed neck spouted high in the air, the whisk fell from the hand and the body collapsed slowly on top of its own head.

'The ghost of our father Holomima demands the blood sacrifice,' said Aboli softly. 'And lo! I, Aboli his son, have given it to him.'

No person in the royal enclosure spoke or moved for what seemed half a lifetime to Hal. Then the Monomatapa began to shake all over. His belly began to wobble and his tattooed jowls danced and shook. His face contorted in what seemed a berserker's fury.

Hal placed his hand on the hilt of his cutlass. 'If he is truly your brother, then I will kill him for you,' he whispered to Aboli. 'You cover my back and we will fight our way out of here.'

But the Monomatapa opened his mouth wide and let fly a huge shout of laughter. 'The tattooed one has made the blood sacrifice that Sweswe demanded!' he bellowed. Then mirth overcame him and for a long while he could not speak again. He shook with laughter, gasped for breath, hugged himself then hooted again.

'Did you see him stand there with no head while his mouth tried still to speak?' he roared, and tears of laughter rolled down his cheeks.

The grovelling band of magicians burst out in squeaks and shrieks of sympathetic glee. 'The heavens laugh!' they whined. 'And all men are happy.'

Suddenly the Monomatapa stopped laughing. 'Bring me Sweswe's stupid head!' he commanded, and the councillor who had led them here bounded forward to obey. He retrieved it and knelt before the king to hand it to him.

The Monomatapa held the head by its matted plaits of kinky hair and stared into the wide blank eyes. He began to laugh again. 'What stupidity not to recognize the blood of kings. How could you not know my brother Aboli by his majestic bearing and the fury of his temper?'

He flung the dripping head at the other magicians, who scattered. 'Learn from the stupidity of Sweswe,' he admonished them. 'Make no more false prophecy! Tell me no more falsehoods! Begone, all of you! Or I will ask my brother to make another blood sacrifice.'

They fled in pandemonium, and the Monomatapa rose from his live throne and advanced upon Aboli, a huge and happy grin splitting his fat, tattooed face. 'Aboli,' he said, 'my brother who was long dead and who now lives!' and he embraced him.

One of the elaborately thatched huts on the perimeter of the courtyard was placed at their disposal, and a procession of maidens was sent to them, bearing clay pots of hot water balanced upon their heads for the two men to bathe. Still other girls carried trays on which was piled fine raiment to replace their travel-stained clothing, beaded loincloths of tanned leather and cloaks of fur and feathers.

When they had washed and changed into this finery, another file of girls came bearing gourds of beer, a type of mead fermented from wild honey, and the blended blood and milk. Others brought platters of hot food.

When they had eaten, the silver-headed councillor who had taken them into the presence of the Monomatapa came to them. With great civility and every mark of respect he squatted at Aboli's feet. 'Though you were far too young when last you saw me to remember me now, my name is Zama. I was the Induna of your father, the great Monomatapa Holomima.'

'It grieves me, Zama, but I remember almost nothing of those days. I remember my brother N'Pofho. I remember the pain of the tattoo knife and the cut of our circumcision that we underwent together. I remember that he squealed louder than I.'

Zama looked worried and shook his head as if to warn Aboli against such levity when speaking of the King, but his voice was level and calm. 'All this is true, except only that the Monomatapa never squealed. I was present at the ceremony of the knife, and it was I who held your head while the hot iron seared your cheeks and trimmed the hood from your penis.'

'Dimly now I think that I can remember your hands and your words of comfort. I thank you for them, Zama.'

481

'You and N'Pofho were twins, born in the same hour. Thus it was that your father commanded that both of you were to bear the royal tattoo. It was new to custom. Never before had two royal sons been tattooed in the same ceremony.'

'I remember little of my father, except how tall he was and strong. I remember how afraid I was at first of the tattoos on his face.'

'He was a mighty man and fearsome,' Zama agreed.

'I remember the night he died. I remember the shouting and the firing of muskets and the terrible flames in the night.'

'I was there when the slavemasters came with their chains of sorrow.' Tears filled the old man's eyes. 'You were so young, Aboli. I marvel that you remember these things.'

'Tell me about that night.'

'As was my custom and my duty, I slept at the portal of your father's hut. I was at his side when he was struck by a ball from the slavers' muskets.' Zama fell silent at the memory, and then he looked up again. 'As he lay dying he said to me, "Zama, leave me. Save my sons. Save the Monomatapa!" and I hurried to obey.'

'You came to save me?' Aboli asked.

'I ran to the hut where you and your brother slept with your mother. I tried to take you from her, but your mother would not hand you to me. "Take N'Pofho!" she commanded me, for you were always her favourite. So I seized your brother and we ran together into the night. Your mother and I were separated in the darkness. I heard her screams but I had the other child in my arms, and to turn back would have meant slavery for all of us and the extinction of the royal line. Forgive me now, Aboli, but I left you and your mother and I ran on, and with N'Pofho escaped into the hills.'

'There is no blame in what you did,' Aboli absolved him.

Zama looked around the hut carefully, and then his lips moved but he uttered no sound. 'It was the wrong choice. I should have taken you.' His expression changed, and he leaned closer to Aboli as if to say something more. Then he drew back reluctantly, as though he had not the courage to make some dangerous gamble.

He rose slowly to his feet. 'Forgive me, Aboli, son of Holomima, but I must leave you now.'

'I forgive you everything,' Aboli said softly. 'I know what is in your heart. Think on this, Zama. Another lion roars on the hill top that once might have been mine. My life now is linked to a new destiny.'

'You are right, Aboli, and I am an old man. I no longer have the strength or the desire to change what cannot be changed.' He drew himself up. 'The Monomatapa will grant you another audience tomorrow morning. I will come for you.' He lowered his voice slightly. 'Please do not try to leave the royal enclosure without the permission of the King.'

When he was gone, Aboli smiled. 'Zama has asked us not to leave. It would be difficult to do so. Have you seen the guards that have been placed at every entrance?'

'Yes, they are not easy to overlook.' Hal stood up from the carved ebony stool and crossed to the low doorway of the hut. He counted twenty men at the gate. They were all magnificent warriors, tall and well muscled, and each was armed with spear and war axe. They carried tall shields of dappled black and white ox hide, and their head-dresses were of cranes' feathers.

'It will be more difficult to leave this place than it was to enter,' Aboli said grimly.

At sunset there came another procession of young girls bearing the evening meal. 'I can see why your royal brother carries such a goodly cargo of fat,' Hal remarked, as he surveyed this superabundance of food.

Once they declared their hunger satisfied, the girls retired with the platters and pots, and Zama came back. This time he led two maidens, one by each hand. The girls knelt before Hal and Aboli. Hal recognized the prettiest and pertest of the two as the girl who had been the live throne of the Monomatapa.

'The Monomatapa sends these females to you to sweeten your dreams with the honey of their loins,' said Zama and retired.

In consternation Hal watched the pretty one raise her head and smile at him shyly. She had a calm sweet face with full lips and huge dark eyes. Her hair had been twisted and braided with beads so that the tresses hung to her shoulders. Her body was plump and glossy. Her breasts and buttocks were naked, only now she wore a tiny beaded apron in front.

'I see you, Great Lord,' she whispered, 'and my eyes are dimmed by the splendour of your presence.' She crept forward like a kitten and laid her head upon his lap.

'You cannot stay here.' Hal sprang to his feet. 'You must go away at once.'

The girl stared up at him in dismay, and tears filled her dark eyes. 'Do I not please you, Great One?' she murmured.

'You are very pretty,' Hal blurted, 'but—' How could he tell her that he was married to a golden memory?

'Let me stay with you, lord,' the girl pleaded pathetically. 'If you reject me, I will be sent to the executioner. I will die with the sharp stake

483

thrust up through the secret opening of my body to pierce my bowels. Please let me live, O Great One. Have mercy on this unworthy female, O Glorious White Face.'

Hal turned to Aboli. 'What can I do?'

'Send her away.' Aboli shrugged. 'As she says, she is worthless. You can stop up your ears so that you do not have to listen to her screaming on the stake.'

'Do not mock me, Aboli. You know I cannot betray the memory of the woman I love.'

'Sukeena is dead, Gundwane. I also loved her, as a brother, but she is dead. This child is alive, but she will not be so by sunset tomorrow unless you take pity upon her. Your vow was not anything that Sukeena demanded of you.'

Aboli stooped over the other girl, took her hand and lifted her to her feet.

'I cannot give you any further help, Gundwane. You are a man and Sukeena knew that. Now that she has gone, she might deem it fitting that you live the rest of your life like one.'

He led his own girl to the rear of the hut, where a pile of soft karosses was laid and a pair of carved wooden head rests stood side by side. He laid her down and dropped the leather curtain that screened them.

'What is your name?' Hal asked the girl who crouched at his feet.

'My name is Inyosi, Honey-bee,' she answered. 'Please do not send me to die.' She crawled to him, clasped his legs and pressed her face to his lower body.

'I cannot,' he mumbled. 'I belong to another.' But he wore only the beaded loincloth and her breath was warm and soft on his belly and her hands stroked the backs of his legs.

'I cannot,' he repeated desperately, but one of Inyosi's little hands crept up under his loincloth.

'Your mouth tells me one thing, Mighty Lord,' she purred, 'but the great spear of your manhood tells me another.'

Hal let out a smothered groan, picked her up in his arms and ran with her across the floor to where his own pallet of furs had been laid out.

At first Inyosi was startled by the fury of his passion, but then she let out a joyous cry and matched him kiss for kiss and thrust for thrust.

In the dawn, as she prepared to leave him, she whispered, 'You have saved my worthless life. In return I must attempt to save your illustrious one.' She kissed him one last time, then murmured with her lips against his, 'I heard the Monomatapa speak to Zama while he bestrode my back. He believes that Aboli has returned to claim the Seat of Heaven from him. Tomorrow, during the audience to which he has commanded you and Aboli, he will give the order for his bodyguard to seize you and hurl you from the cliff top onto the rocks below, where the hyenas and the vultures wait to devour your corpses.' Inyosi snuggled against his chest. 'I do not want you to die, my lord. You are too beautiful.'

Then she rose from the pallet and slipped away silently into the darkness. Hal crossed to the hearth and threw a faggot of firewood upon it. The smoke rose up through the hole in the centre of the domed roof and the flames lit the interior with flickering yellow light.

'Aboli? Are you alone? We must talk at once,' he called, and Aboli came out from behind the curtain.

'The girl is asleep, but speak in English.'

'Your brother intends to have both of us killed during the audience.'

'The girl told you this?' Aboli asked, and Hal nodded guiltily at the mention of his infidelity.

Aboli smiled in sympathy. 'So the little Honey-bee saves your life. Sukeena would rejoice for that. You need feel no guilt.'

'If we attempt to escape, your brother would send an army to pursue us. We would never reach the river again.'

'So, do you have a plan, Gundwane?'

Zama came to lead them to the royal audience. They stepped out of the gloom of the great hut into the brilliant African sunlight, and Hal paused to gaze around the concourse of the Monomatapa.

He could only estimate their numbers, but a full regiment of the royal bodyguard ringed the open space, perhaps a thousand tall warriors with the high head-dresses of cranes' feathers turning each into a giant. The light morning breeze tossed and tumbled the feathers, and the sunlight glinted on their broad-bladed spears.

Beyond them the nobles of the tribe filled every space and lined the top of the wall of granite blocks that surrounded the citadel. A hundred royal wives clustered about the door to the King's hut. Some were so fat and loaded with bangles and ornaments that they could not walk unaided and leant heavily on their handmaidens. When they waddled along their buttocks rolled and undulated like soft bladders filled with lard.

Zama led Hal and Aboli to the centre of the courtyard and left them there. A heavy silence fell on the throng and no one moved, until suddenly the captain of the bodyguard blew a blast on a spiral kudu horn and the Monomatapa loomed in the doorway of his hut.

A moaning sigh swept through the gathering and, as one, they threw themselves full length to the earth and covered their faces. Only Hal and Aboli remained standing upright.

The Monomatapa strode to his living throne and sat upon Inyosi's naked back.

'Speak first!' Hal breathed from the side of his mouth. 'Don't let him give the order for our execution.'

'I see you, my brother!' Aboli greeted him, and the courtiers moaned with horror at this breach of protocol. 'I see you, Great Lord of the Heavens!'

The Monomatapa showed no sign of having heard.

'I bring you greetings from the ghost of our father, Holomima, who was the Monomatapa before you.'

Aboli's brother recoiled visibly, as though a cobra had reared up before his face. 'You speak with ghosts?' His voice trembled slightly.

'Our father came to me in the night. He was as tall as a great baobab tree, and his face was terrible with eyes of fire. His voice was as the thunder of the heavens. He came to me to issue a dire warning.' The congregation moaned with superstitious dread.

'What was this warning?' croaked the Monomatapa, staring at his brother with awe.

'Our father fears for our lives, yours and mine. Great danger threatens us both.' Some of the fat wives screamed, and one fell to the ground in a fit, frothing at the mouth.

'What danger is this, Aboli?' The King glanced around him fearfully, as if seeking an assassin amongst his courtiers.

'Our father warned me that you and I are joined in life as we were in birth. If one of us prospers, then so does the other.'

The Monomatapa nodded. 'What else did our father say?'

'He said that as we are joined in life, so we will be joined in death. He prophesied that we will die upon the very same day, but that that day is of our own choosing.'

The King's face turned a strange greyish tone and glistened with sweat. The elders shrieked and those nearest to where he sat drew small iron knives and slashed their own chests and arms, sprinkling their blood on the earth to protect him from witchcraft.

'I am deeply troubled by these words that our father uttered,' Aboli went on. 'I wish that I were able to abide with you here in the Land of Heaven, to protect you from this fate. But, alas, my father's shade warned me further that should I stay here another day then I will die and the Monomatapa with me. I must leave at once and never return. That is the only way in which we can both survive the curse.'

486

'So let it be.' The Monomatapa rose to his feet and pointed with a trembling finger. 'This very day you must be gone.'

'Alas, my beloved brother, I cannot leave here without that boon I came to seek from you.'

'Speak, Aboli! What is it that you lack?'

'I must have one hundred and fifty of your finest warriors to protect me, for a dreadful enemy lies in wait for me. Without these soldiers, then I go to certain death, and my death must portend the death of the Monomatapa.'

'Choose!' bellowed the Monomatapa. 'Choose of my finest Amadoda, and take them with you. They are your slaves, do with them as you wish. But then get you gone this very day, before the setting of the sun. Leave my land for ever.'

In the leading pinnace Hal shot the bar and rowed out through the Musela mouth of the delta into the open sea. Big Daniel followed closely, and there lay the *Golden Bough* at her anchor on the ten-fathom shoal where they had left her. Ned Tyler stood the ship to quarters and ran out his guns when he saw them approaching. The pinnaces were so packed with men that they had only an inch or two of freeboard. Riding so low in the water, from afar they resembled war canoes. The glinting spears and waving head-dresses of the Amadoda strengthened this impression and Ned gave the order to fire a warning shot across their bows. As the cannon boomed out and a tall plume of spray erupted from the water half a cable's length ahead of the leading boat, Hal stood up in the bows and waved the *croix patté*.

'Lord love us!' Ned gasped. ''Tis the Captain we're shooting at.'

'I'll not be in a hurry to forget that greeting you gave me, Mr Tyler,' Hal told him sternly, as he came in through the entryport. 'I rate a four-gun salute, not a single gun.'

'Bless you, Captain, I had no idea. I thought you was a bunch of heathen savages, begging your pardon, sir.'

'That we are, Mr Tyler. That we are!' And Hal grinned at Ned's confusion as a horde of magnificent warriors swarmed onto the *Golden Bough*'s deck. 'Think you'll be able to make seamen of them, Mr Tyler?'

As soon as he had made his offing, Hal turned the bows into the north once more and sailed up the inland channel between Madagascar and the mainland. He was heading for Zanzibar, the centre of all trade on this coast. There he hoped to have further news of the progress of the Holy War on the Horn and, if he were fortunate, to learn something of the movements of the *Gull of Moray*.

This was a settling-in time for the Amadoda. Everything aboard the *Golden Bough* was strange to them. None had ever seen the sea. They had believed the pinnaces to be the largest canoes ever conceived by man, and were overawed by the size of the ship, the height of her masts and the spread of her sails.

Most were immediately smitten by seasickness, and it took many days for them to find their sea-legs. Their bowels were in a turmoil induced by the diet of biscuit and pickled meat. They hungered for their pots of millet porridge and their gourds of blood and milk. They had never been confined in such a small space and they pined for the wide savannah.

They suffered from the cold, for even in this tropical sea the trade winds were cool and the warm Mozambique current many degrees below the temperature of the sun-scorched plains of the savannah. Hal ordered Althuda, who was in charge of the ship's stores, to issue bolts of sail canvas to them and Aboli showed them how to stitch petticoats and tarpaulin jackets for themselves.

They soon forgot these tribulations when Aboli ordered a platoon of men to follow Jiri and Matesi and Kimatti aloft to set and reef sail. A hundred dizzy feet above the deck and the rushing sea, swinging on the great pendulum of the mainmast, for the first time in their lives these warriors – who had each killed their lion – were overcome by terror.

Aboli climbed up to where they clung helplessly to the shrouds and mocked them: 'Look at these pretty virgins. I thought at first there might be a man among them, but I see they should all squat when they piss.' Then he stood upright on the swaying yard and laughed at them. He ran out to the end of it and there performed a stamping, leaping war dance. One of the Amadoda could abide his mockery no longer: he loosed his death grip on the rigging and shuffled out along the yard to where Aboli stood with hands on hips.

'One man amongst them!' Aboli laughed and embraced him. During the next week three of the Amadoda fell from the rigging while trying to emulate this feat. Two dropped into the sea but before Hal could wear the ship around and go back to pick them up the sharks had taken them. The third man struck the deck and his was the most merciful end. After that there were no more casualties, and the Amadoda, each one accustomed since boyhood to climbing the highest trees for honey and birds' eggs, swiftly became adept topmastmen.

When Hal ordered bundles of pikes to be brought up from the hold and issued to the Amadoda they howled and danced with delight, for they were spearmen born. They delighted in the heavy-shafted pikes with their deadly iron heads. Aboli adapted their tactics and fighting formation to the *Golden Bough*'s cramped deck spaces. He showed them how to form the classical Roman Testudo, their shields overlapping and locked like the scales of an armadillo. With this formation they could sweep the deck of an enemy ship irresistibly.

Hal ordered them to set up a heavy mat of oakum under the forecastle break to act as a butt. Once the Amadoda had learned the weight and balance of the heavy pikes they could hurl them the length of the ship to bury the iron heads full length in the mat of coarse fibres. They plunged into these exercises with such gusto that two of their number were speared to death before Aboli could impress upon them that these were mock battles and should not be fought to the death.

Then it was time to introduce them to the English longbow. Their own bows were short and puny in comparison and they looked askance at this six-foot weapon, dubiously tried the massive draw weight and shook their heads. Hal took the bow out of their hands and nocked an arrow. He looked up at the single black and white gull that floated high above the mainmast. 'If I bring down one of those birds will you eat it raw?' he asked, and they roared with laughter at the joke.

'I will eat the feathers as well!' shouted a big cocky one named Ingwe, the Leopard. In a fluid motion Hal drew and loosed. The arrow arced up, its flight curving across the wind, and they shouted with amazement as it pierced the gull's snowy bosom and the wide pinions folded. The bird tumbled down in a tangle of wings and webbed feet, and struck the deck at Hal's feet. An Amadoda snatched it up, and the transfixed carcass was passed from hand to hand amid astonished jabbering.

'Do not ruffle the feathers,' Hal cautioned them. 'You will spoil Ingwe's dinner for him.'

From that moment their love of the longbow was passionate and within days they had developed into archers of the first water. When Hal towed an empty water keg at a full cable's length behind the ship, the Amadoda shot at it, first individually then in massed divisions like English archers. When the keg was heaved back on deck it was bristling like a porcupine's back, and they retrieved seven out of every ten arrows that had been shot.

In one area alone the Amadoda showed no aptitude: at serving the great bronze culverins. Despite all the threats and mockery that Aboli heaped upon them, he could not get them to approach one with anything less than superstitious awe. Each time a broadside boomed they howled, 'It is witchcraft. It is the thunder of the heavens.'

Hal drew up a new watch-bill, in which the battle stations of the crew were rearranged to have the white seamen serving the batteries and the Amadoda handling the sails and making up the boarding-party.

A standing bank of high clouds twenty leagues ahead of their bows marked the island of Zanzibar. A fringe of coconut palms ringed the white beach of the bay, but the massive walls of the fortress were even whiter, dazzling as the ice slopes of a glacier in the sunlight. The citadel had been built a century before by the Portuguese and until only a decade previously it had assured that nation's domination of the trade routes of the entire eastern shores of the African continent.

Later the Omani Arabs, under their warrior king Ahmed El Grang the Left-handed, had sailed in with their war dhows, attacked the Portuguese and had driven out their garrison with great slaughter. This loss had signalled the beginning of the decline of Portuguese influence on the coast, and the Omanis had usurped their place as the foremost trading nation.

Hal examined the fort through the lens of his telescope and noted the banner of Islam flying above the tower, and the serried ranks of cannon along the tops of the walls. Those weapons could hurl heated shot onto any hostile vessel that attempted to enter the bay.

He felt a thrill of foreboding along his spine as he contemplated the fact that if he enlisted with the forces of the Prester, he would become the enemy of Ahmed El Grang. One day those huge cannon might be firing upon the *Golden Bough*. In the meantime he must make the most of this last opportunity to enter the Omani camp as a neutral and to gather all the intelligence that came his way.

The harbour was crowded with small craft, mostly the dhows of the Mussulmen from India, Arabia and Muscat. There were two tall ships amongst this multitude: one flew a Spanish flag and the other was French, but Hal recognized neither.

All these traders were drawn to Zanzibar by the riches of Africa, the gold of Sofala, the gum arabic, ivory, and the endless flood of humanity into its slave market. This was where seven thousand men, women and children were offered for sale each season when the trade winds brought the barques in from around the Cape of Good Hope and from all the vast basin of the Indian Ocean.

Hal dipped his ensign in courtesy to the fortress, then conned the *Golden Bough* towards the anchorage under top sails. At his order the anchor splashed into the clear water and the tiny sliver of canvas was whipped off her and furled by Aboli's exuberant Amadoda. Almost immediately the ship was besieged by a fleet of little boats, selling every conceivable commodity from fresh fruit and water to small boys. These last were ordered by their masters to bend over the thwarts, lift their robes and display their small brown buttocks for the delectation of the seamen at the *Golden Bough*'s rail.

'Pretty jig-jig boys,' the whoremasters crooned in pidgin English. 'Sweet bums like ripe mangoes.'

'Mr Tyler, have a boat lowered,' Hal ordered. 'I'm going ashore. I will take Althuda and Master Daniel with me and ten of your best men.'

They rowed across to the stone landing steps below the fortress walls, and Big Daniel went ashore first to plough open a passage through the throng of merchants, who swarmed down to the water's edge to offer their wares. On their last visit he had escorted Sir Francis ashore so he led the way. His seamen formed in a phalanx around Hal and they marched through the narrow streets.

They passed through bazaars and crowded souks where the merchants displayed their stocks. Traders and seamen from the other vessels in the harbour picked over the piles of elephant tusks, and cakes of fragrant golden gum arabic, bunches of ostrich feathers and rhinoceros horns. They haggled over the price of the carpets from Muscat and the stoppered porcupine quills filled with grains of alluvial gold from Sofala and the rivers of the African interior. The slavemasters paraded files of human beings for potential buyers to examine their teeth, and palpate the muscles of the males or lift the aprons of the young females to consider their sweets.

From this area of commerce, Big Daniel led them into a sector of the town where the buildings on each side of the lanes almost touched each other overhead and blocked out the light of day. The stench of human faeces from the open sewers, which ran down to the harbour, almost suffocated them.

Big Daniel stopped abruptly in front of an arched mahogany door, carved with intricate Islamic motifs and studded with iron spikes, and heaved on the dangling bell-rope. Within minutes they heard the bolts on the far side being pulled back and the huge door creaked open. Half a dozen small brown faces peered out at them, boys and girls of mixed blood and of all ages between five and ten years.

'Welcome! Welcome!' they chirruped in quaintly accented English. 'The blessing of Allah the All Merciful be upon you, English milord. May all your days be golden and scented with wild jasmine.'

A little girl seized Hal by the hand and led him through into the interior courtyard. A fountain tinkled in the centre and the air was filled with the scent of frangi-pani and yellow tamarind flowers. A tall figure, clad in flowing white robes and gold-corded Arabian head-dress, rose from the pile of silk carpets where he had been reclining.

'Indeed, I add a thousand welcomes to those of my children, my good Captain, and may Allah shower you with riches and blessing,' he said, in a familiar and comforting Yorkshire accent. 'I watched your fine ship anchor in the bay, and I knew you would soon call upon me.' He clapped his hands, and from the back of the house emerged a line of slaves each bearing trays that contained coloured glasses of sherbet and coconut milk and little bowls of sweetmeats and roasted nuts.

The consul sent Big Daniel and his seamen through to the servants' quarters at the rear of the house. 'They will be given refreshment,' he said.

Hal cast Big Daniel a significant look, which the boatswain interpreted accurately. There would be no liquor in this Islamic household, but there would be women and the seamen had to be protected from themselves. Hal kept Althuda beside him. There might be call for him to draw up documents or to take down notes.

The consul led them to a secluded corner of the courtyard. 'Now, let me introduce myself, I am William Grey, His Majesty's consul to the Sultanate of Zanzibar.'

'Henry Courteney, at your service, sir.'

'I knew a Sir Francis Courteney. Are you by chance related?'

'My father, sir.'

'Ah! An honourable man. Please give him my respects when next you meet.'

'Tragically he was killed in the Dutch war.'

'My condolences, Sir Henry. Please be seated.' A pile of beautifully patterned silk carpets had been set close at hand for Hal. The consul sat opposite him. Once he was comfortable, a slave brought Grey a water-pipe. 'A pipeful of *bhang* is a sovereign remedy for distempers of the liver and for the malaria which is a plague in these climes. Will you join me, sir?'

Hal refused this offer, for he knew of the tricks the Indian hemp flowers played upon the mind, and the dreams and trances with which it could ensnare the smoker.

While he puffed at his pipe, Grey questioned him cunningly as to his recent movements and his future plans, and Hal was polite but evasive. Like a pair of duellists, they sparred and waited for an opening. As the water bubbled in the tall glass bowl of the pipe and the fragrant smoke drifted across the courtyard Grey became more affable and expansive.

'You live in the style of a great sheikh.' Hal tried a little flattery and Grey responded with gratification.

'Would you find it difficult to believe that fifteen years ago I was merely a lowly clerk in the employment of the English East India Company? When my ship was wrecked on the corals of Sofala, I came ashore here as a castaway.' He shrugged and made a gesture that was more Oriental than English. 'As you say, Allah has smiled on me.'

'You have embraced Islam?' Hal did not allow his expression to show the repugnance he felt for the apostate.

'I am a true believer in the one God, and in Muhammad his Prophet.' Grey nodded. Hal wondered how much his decision to convert had rested on political and practical considerations. Grey, the Christian, would not have prospered in Zanzibar as Grey, the Mussulman, so obviously had.

'Most Englishmen who call at Zanzibar have one thing in mind,' Grey went on. 'They have come here for trade, and usually to acquire a cargo of slaves. I regret that this is not the best season for slaving. The trade winds have brought in the dhows from Further India and beyond. They have already carried away the best specimens, and what is now left in the market is the dregs. However, in my own barracoon I have two hundred prime creatures, the best you will find in a thousand miles of sailing.'

'Thank you, sir, but I am not interested in slaving,' Hal declined.

'That, sir, is a regrettable decision. I assure you there are great fortunes still to be made in the trade. The Brazilians and the Caribbean sugar planters are crying out for labour to work their fields.'

'Thank you again. I am not in the market.' Now it was clear to Hal how Grey had made his own fortune. The post of consul was secondary to that of agent and middleman to European traders calling in at Zanzibar.

'Then there is another highly profitable area in which I could be of assistance to you.' Grey paused delicately. 'I observed your ship from my rooftop when you anchored and could not but notice that she is well armed. One might be forgiven for believing her to be a man-of-war.' Hal nodded noncommittally, and Grey continued, 'You may not know that the Sultan of Oman, Beloved of Allah, Ahmed El Grang, is at war with the Emperor of Ethiopia.'

'I had heard so.'

'A war is raging on land and sea. The Sultan has issued Letters of Marque to ships who wish to join his forces. These commissions have been, in the main, restricted to Mussulman captains. However, I have great influence at the Sultan's court. I may be able to obtain a commission for you. Of course, such a boon does not come cheaply. It would cost two hundred pounds for me to obtain an Omani Letter of Marque for you, sir.'

Hal was about to refuse with indignation this offer to join the pagan in the war against Christ and his followers, but instinct warned him not to repudiate it out of hand. 'There might be profits to be made, then, sir?' he asked thoughtfully.

'Indeed. There are vast riches to be snapped up. The empire of the Prester is one of the most ancient citadels of the Christian faith. For well over a thousand years the gold and offerings of the pilgrims and worshippers have been piling up in the treasure houses of the churches and monasteries. The Prester himself is as rich as any European sovereign. They say there is over twenty tons of gold in his treasury at Aksum.' Grey was breathing heavily with avarice at the picture he had conjured up in his own mind.

'You would be able to obtain a commission for me from the Sultan?' Hal leaned forward with assumed eagerness.

'Indeed, sir. Not a month past I was able to obtain a commission for a Scotsman.' A sudden thought occurred to Grey, and his face lit up. 'If I did the same for you, perhaps you could join forces with him. With two fighting ships such as yours you would be a squadron powerful enough to take on anything the navy of the Prester could send against you.'

'The thought excites me.' Hal smiled encouragingly, trying not to show too much interest. He had guessed who the Scotsman must be. 'But tell me, who is this man of whom you speak?'

'A fine gentleman and a great mariner,' Grey replied enthusiastically. 'He sailed from Zanzibar not five weeks back, bound for the Horn.'

'Then I may be able to come up with him and join my ship to his,' Hal mused aloud. 'Give me his name and station, sir.'

Grey glanced around the courtyard in a conspiratorial fashion, then lowered his voice. 'He is a nobleman of high rank, the Earl of Cumbrae.' Grey leaned back and slapped his knees to emphasize the enormity of his disclosure. 'There, sir! And what do you think of that?'

'I am greatly amazed!' Hal did not have to cover his excitement. 'But do you truly believe that you can obtain a commission for me also? And, if so, how long will the business take?'

'Things are never swiftly done in Arabia.' Grey became evasive again. 'But they can always be speeded up with a little *baksheesh*. Say an extra two hundred pounds, that is four hundred in all, and I should be able to place the commission in your hands by tomorrow evening. Naturally, I would need to have your payment in advance.'

'It is a great deal of money.' Hal frowned. Now that he knew where the Buzzard was headed, he wanted to rush back to the *Golden Bough* immediately and set off in pursuit. But he restrained the impulse. He must gather every scrap of information from Grey.

'Yes, it is,' Grey agreed. 'But think on the return it will bring. Twenty tons of pure gold for the man bold enough to seize it from the Prester's treasury. And that's not all. There are also the jewels and other treasures sent in tribute to the empire over a thousand years, the treasures of the Coptic churches – the relics of Jesus Christ and the Virgin, of the apostles and the saints. The ransom they could command is without limit.' Grey's eyes shone with greed. 'They say—' He broke off and lowered his voice again. 'They do say, that the Prester John is the guardian of the Holy Grail itself.'

'The Holy Grail.' Hal went pale with awe, and Grey was delighted to see the reaction he had evoked.

'Yes! Yes! The Holy Grail! The precious cup for which Christians have searched since the Crucifixion.' Hal shook his head and stared at Grey in unfeigned amazement. He was moved by a strange sense of *déjà vu* that rendered him speechless. The prophecies of both his father and Sukeena flashed across his mind. He knew, deep in his heart, that this was part of the destiny they had foretold for him.

Grey took his silence and the shake of his head for scepticism. 'I assure you, sir, that the Holy Grail is the most poignant reason that the Great Mogul and Ahmed El Grang have attacked the empire of Ethiopia. I have had this from the Sultan's own lips. He also is convinced that the relic is in the care of the Prester. One of the mightiest ayatollahs of Islam has prophesied this and has given him the word of Allah that if he can wrest the Grail from the Prester his dynasty will be invested with power untold, and will herald the triumph of Islam over all the false religions of the world.'

Hal stared at him aghast. His thoughts were in wild confusion and he was no longer certain of himself or of anything around him. It took a vast effort to put aside such a terrible prospect as the subjugation of Christianity and to reassemble his thoughts.

'Where is this relic kept hidden?' he asked huskily.

'Nobody but the Prester and his monks know for certain. Some say at Aksum or at Gonder, and others say that it is secreted in a monastery in the high mountains.'

'Perhaps it has already fallen into the hands of El Grang or the Mogul? Perhaps the war is already lost and won?' Hal suggested.

'No! No!' Grey was vehement. 'A dhow arrived from the Gulf of Aden this very morning. The news it brings is less than eight days old.

It seems that the victorious armies of Islam have been checked at Mitsiwa. There has arisen within the Christian ranks a mighty general. They call this warrior Nazet, and though he is but a stripling the armies of Tigre and Galla flock to his standard.' It seemed to Hal, from the relish with which Grey recounted these setbacks to the cause of Islam, that the consul was backing both horses. 'Nazet has driven back the armies of El Grang and the Mogul. They confront each other before Mitsiwa, gathering themselves for the final battle, which will decide the war. It is far from over yet. I earnestly counsel you, my young friend, that once you have in your hand the Letter of Marque that I shall procure for you, you should make all haste to sail to Mitsiwa in time to share the spoils.'

'I must think on all you have told me.' Hal rose from the pile of carpets. 'If I decide to avail myself of your generous offer, I will return tomorrow with the four hundred pounds to purchase my commission from the Sultan.'

'You will always be welcome in my home,' Grey assured him.

'Get me back to the ship as fast as you like,' Hal snapped at Big Daniel, the moment the tall carved doors closed behind them. 'I want to sail on this evening's tide.'

They had not reached the first bazaar when Althuda caught at Hal's arm. 'I must go back. I have left my journal in the courtyard.'

'I am in desperate haste, Althuda. The Buzzard is already more than a month ahead of us, but I know now for certain where I must search for him.'

'I must retrieve my journal. Go on ahead to the ship. I will not be long behind you. Send the boat back for me, and have them wait at the harbour steps. I will be there before you sail.'

'Do not fail me, Althuda. I cannot delay.'

Reluctantly Hal let him go, and hurried on after Big Daniel. As soon as he reached the *Golden Bough*, he sent the longboat to wait for Althuda at the landing, and gave the orders to ready the ship for sea. Then he went down to his cabin and spread on his desk under the stern windows those charts and sailing directions for the Gulf of Aden and the Red Sea that he had inherited from Llewellyn.

He had studied these almost daily ever since he had been aboard the *Golden Bough*, so he had no difficulty in placing all the names Grey had mentioned in his discourse. He plotted his course to round the tip of the Great Horn and sail down the Gulf of Aden, through the narrows of the

496

Bab El Mandeb and into the southern reaches of the Red Sea. There were hundreds of tiny islands scattered off the Ethiopian coast, perfect lairs for the privateer and the corsair.

He would have to avoid the fleets of the Mogul and the Omani until he had reached the Christian court of the Prester and obtained his commission from him. He could not attack the Mussulmen before he had that document in his hands or he risked the same fate as his father, of being accused of piracy on the high seas.

Perhaps he would be able to link up with the Christian army commander General Nazet, of whom Grey had spoken, and place the *Golden Bough* at his disposal. In any event, he reasoned that the transport fleet of the Mussulman army would be gathered in these crowded seas in huge numbers, and they would fall easy prey to a swift frigate boldly handled. Grey was right in one respect: there would be fortune and glory to be won in the days ahead.

He heard the bell sound the end of the watch, left his charts and went up on deck. He saw at a glance, from the ship's changed attitude to the tide, that the ebb had set in.

Then he looked across the harbour and, even at that distance, recognized the figure of Althuda at the head of the landing steps. He was in deep conversation with Stan Sparrow, who had taken the longboat back to wait for him.

'Damn him,' Hal muttered. 'He is wasting time in idle chatter.' He turned all his attention to the affairs of the ship, and watched his topmastmen going aloft, quick and surefooted, to set the sails. When he looked back at the shore again he saw that the longboat was coming in against the ship's side below where he stood.

As soon as it touched, Althuda came up the ladder. He stood in front of Hal and said with a serious expression, 'I have come to fetch Zwaantie and my son,' he said solemnly. 'And to bid you farewell.'

'I do not understand.' Hal was aghast.

'Consul Grey has taken me into his service as a writer. I intend to remain with my family here in Zanzibar,' Althuda replied.

'But why, Althuda? Why?'

'As you know well, both Sukeena and I were raised by our mother as followers of Muhammad, the Prophet of Allah. You are intent on waging war on the armies of Islam in the name of the Christian God. I can no longer follow you.' Althuda turned away and went to the forecastle. He returned a few minutes later leading Zwaantie and carrying little Bobby. Zwaantie was weeping silently, but she did not look at Hal. Althuda stopped at the head of the ladder and gazed at him.

'I regret this parting, but I cherish the memory of the love you bore my sister. I call down the blessing of Allah upon you,' he said, then followed Zwaantie down into the longboat. Hal watched them row across to the quay and climb the stone steps. Althuda never looked back, and he and his little family disappeared in the throng of white-robed merchants and their slaves.

Hal felt so saddened that he did not realize that the longboat had returned until, with a start, he saw that it had already been hoisted aboard and that Ned Tyler waited by the whipstaff for his orders.

'Up anchor, if you please, Mr Tyler. Set the top sails and steer for the channel.'

Hal took one last look back at the land. He felt bereaved, for Althuda had severed his last tenuous link to Sukeena. 'She is gone,' he whispered. 'Now she is truly gone.'

Resolutely he turned his back on the white citadel and looked ahead to where the Usambara mountains on the African mainland lay low and blue upon the horizon.

'Lay the ship on the larboard tack, Mr Tyler. Set all plain sail. Course is north by east to clear Pemba Island. Mark it on the traverse board.'

The wind held fair, and twelve days later they cleared Cape Guardafui, at the tip of the great rhino horn of Africa, and before them opened the Gulf of Aden. Hal ordered the change of course and they steered down into the west.

The harsh red rock cliffs and hills of the Gulf of Aden were the jaws of Africa. They sailed into them with the last breezes of the trades filling their canvas. The heat was breathtaking, and without the wind would have been insupportable. The sea was a peculiarly vivid blue, which reflected off the snowy bellies of the terns that wheeled across the wake.

Ahead the rocky shores constricted into the throat of the Bab El Mandeb. In daylight they passed through the rock-bound narrows into the maw of the Red Sea and Hal shortened sail, for these were treacherous waters, dotted with hundreds of islands and sown with reefs of fanged coral. To the east lay the hot lands of Arabia, and to the west the shores of Ethiopia and the empire of the Prester.

They began to encounter other shipping in these congested waters. Each time the lookout hailed the quarterdeck, Hal went aloft himself, longing to see the top sails of a square-rigged ship come up over the horizon, and to recognize the set of the *Gull of Moray*. But each time he was disappointed. They were all dhows that fled from their tall and ominous profile, seeking shelter in the sanctuary of the shoal waters where the *Golden Bough* dared not follow.

Swiftly Hal learned how inaccurate were the charts that he had found in Llewellyn's desk. Some of the islands they passed were not shown and others were depicted leagues off their true position. The marked soundings were mere fictions of the cartographer's imagination. The nights were moonless and Hal dared not press on amongst these reefs and islands in the darkness. At dusk he anchored for the night in the lee of one of the larger islands.

'No lights,' he warned Ned Tyler, 'and keep the hands quiet.'

'There is no keeping Aboli's men quiet, Captain. They gabble like geese being ate by a fox.'

Hal grinned. 'I will speak to Aboli.'

When he came up on deck again at the beginning of the first dog watch, the ship was silent and dark. He made his rounds, stopping for a few minutes to speak to Aboli who was the watch-keeper. Then he went to stand alone by the rail, gazing up at the heavens, lost in wonder at the glory of the stars.

Suddenly he heard an alien sound and, for a moment, thought that it came from the ship. Then he realized that it was human voices speaking a language that he did not know. He moved swiftly to the stern and the sounds were closer and clearer. He heard the creak of rigging and the squeak and splash of oars.

He ran forward again and found Aboli. 'Assemble an armed boarding-party. Ten men,' he whispered. 'No noise. Launch the longboat.'

It took only minutes for Aboli to carry out the order. As the boat touched the water they dropped into it and pulled away. Hal was at the tiller and steered into the darkness, groping towards the unseen island.

After several minutes he whispered, 'Avast heaving!' and the rowers rested on their oars. The minutes drifted by, then suddenly close at hand they heard something clatter on a wooden deck, and an exclamation of pain or annoyance. Hal strained his eyes in that direction and saw the pale set of a small lateen sail against the starlight.

'All together. Give way!' he whispered, and the boat shot forward. Aboli stood in the bows with a grappling hook and line. The small dhow that emerged abruptly out of the darkness dead ahead was not much taller at the rail than the longboat. Aboli hurled the hook over her side and leaned back on the line.

'Secured!' he grunted. 'Away you go, lads.'

The crew dropped the oars and, with a bloodcurdling chorus of yells, swarmed up onto the deck of the strange craft. They were met by pathetic cries of dismay and terror. Hal lashed the tiller over, seized the hooded lantern and rushed up after his men to restrain their belligerence. When he opened the shutter of the lantern and flashed it around he found that the crew of the dhow had already been subdued, and were spreadeagled on the deck. There were a dozen or so half-naked dark-skinned sailors, but amongst them an elderly man dressed in a full-length robe whom Hal at first took to be the captain.

'Bring that one here,' he ordered. When they dragged the captive to him, Hal saw that he had a flowing beard, which reached almost to his knees, and a cluster of Coptic crosses and rosaries dangling down onto his chest. The square mitre on his head was embroidered with gold and silver thread.

'All right!' he cautioned the men who held him. 'Treat him gently. He's a priest.' They released their prisoner with alacrity. The priest rearranged his robes and brushed out his beard with his fingertips, then drew himself up to his full height and regarded Hal with frosty dignity.

'Do you speak English, Father?' Hal asked. The man stared back at him. Even in the uncertain lantern light, his gaze was cold and piercing. He showed no sign of having understood.

Hal switched into Latin. 'Who are you, Father?'

'I am Fasilides, Bishop of Aksum, confessor to his Christian Majesty Iyasu, Emperor of Ethiopia,' he replied, in fluent, scholarly Latin.

'I humbly beg your forgiveness, your grace. I mistook this ship for an Islamic marauder. I crave your blessing.' Hal went down on one knee. Perhaps I am pouring too much oil, he thought, but the Bishop seemed to accept this as his due. He made the sign of the cross over Hal's head, then laid two fingers on his brow.

'*In nomine patris, et filio et spiritu sancto,*' he intoned and gave Hal his ring to kiss. He seemed sufficiently mollified for Hal to press the advantage.

'This is a most providential encounter, your grace.' Hal rose to his feet again, 'I am a Knight of the Temple of the Order of St George and the Holy Grail. I am on a voyage to place my ship and its company at the disposal of the Prester John, the Most Christian Emperor of Ethiopia, in his holy war against the forces of Islam. As His Majesty's confessor, perhaps you could lead me to his court.'

'It may be possible to arrange an audience,' said Fasilides importantly.

However, his aplomb was shaken and his manner much improved when the dawn light revealed the power and magnificence of the *Golden Bough*, and he became even more amenable when Hal invited him aboard and offered to convey him on the rest of his journey.

Hal could only guess at why the Bishop of Aksum should be creeping around the islands at midnight in a small, smelly fishing dhow, and

Fasilides became remote and haughty again when questioned. 'I am not at liberty to discuss affairs of state, either temporal or spiritual.'

Fasilides brought his two servants aboard with him, and one of the fishermen from the dhow to act as a pilot for Hal. Once on board the *Golden Bough*, he settled comfortably into the small cabin adjoining Hal's. With a local pilot on board Hal was able to head on towards Mitsiwa with all dispatch, not even deigning to shorten sail when the sun set that evening.

He invited Fasilides to dine with him and the good Bishop showed a deep affinity for Llewellyn's wine and brandy. Hal kept his glass filled to the brim, a feat that called for sleight-of-hand. Fasilides' dignity lowered in proportion to the level in the brandy decanter, and he answered Hal's questions with less and less reserve. 'The Emperor is with General Nazet at the monastery of St Luke on the hills above Mitsiwa. I go to meet him there,' he explained.

'I have heard that the Emperor has won a great victory over the pagan at Mitsiwa?' Hal prompted him.

'A great and wonderful victory!' Fasilides enthused. 'In the Easter season, the pagan crossed the narrows of the Bab El Mandeb with a mighty army, then drove northwards up the coast seizing all the ports and forts. Our Emperor Caleb, father of Iyasu, fell in battle and much of our army was scattered and destroyed. The war dhows of El Grang fell upon our fleet in Adulis Bay and captured or burned twenty of our finest ships. Then when the pagan arrayed a hundred thousand men before Mitsiwa it seemed that God had forsaken Ethiopia.' Fasilides' eyes filled with tears and he had to take a deep draught of the good brandy to steady himself. 'But He is the one God and true to his people, and he sent us a warrior to lead our shattered army. Nazet came down from the mountains, bringing the army of the Amhara to join our forces here on the coast, and bearing in the vanguard the sacred Tabernacle of Mary Mother of God. This talisman is like a thunderbolt in Nazet's hand. Before its advance the pagan was hurled back in confusion.'

'What is this talisman of which you speak, your grace? Is it a sacred relic?' Hal asked.

The bishop lowered his voice and reached across the table to grip Hal's hand and stare into his eyes. 'It is a relic of Jesus Christ, the most powerful in all Christendom.' He stared into Hal's face with a fanatical fervour so intense that Hal felt his skin crawl with religious awe. 'The Tabernacle of Mary contains the Cup of Life, the Holy Grail that Christ used at the Last Supper. The same chalice in which Joseph of Arimathea collected the blood of the Saviour as he hung upon the Cross.'

'Where is the Tabernacle now?' Hal's voice was husky, and he returned Fasilides' grip with such strength that the old man winced. 'Have you seen it? Does it truly exist?'

'I have prayed over the Tabernacle that contains the sacred chalice, although none may view or lay hands upon the chalice itself.'

'Where is this holy thing?' Hal's voice rose with excitement. 'I have heard of it all my life. The chivalric order of which I am a Knight is based upon this fabulous cup. Where may I find it and worship before it?'

Fasilides seemed to sober at Hal's excitement, and he drew back, freeing his hand from Hal's grip. 'There are things which cannot be disclosed.' Once again he became remote and unapproachable. Hal realized that it would be unwise to pursue the subject further, and he sought some other topic to thaw the Bishop's frozen features.

'Tell me of the fleet engagement at Adulis Bay,' Hal suggested. 'As a sailor, my concerns lie heavily upon the seas. Was there a tall ship similar to this one fighting with the squadrons of Islam?'

The Bishop unbent a little. 'There were many ships on both sides. Great storms of gunfire and terrible slaughter.'

'A square-rigged ship, flying the red *croix patté*?' Hal insisted. 'Did you have report of such a one?' But it was clear that the Bishop did not know a frigate from a quinquereme.

He shrugged. 'Perhaps the admirals and the generals will be able to answer these questions when we reach the monastery of St Luke,' he suggested.

The following afternoon they sailed past the entrance to Adulis Bay, steering inshore of the island of Dahlak at the mouth of the bay. In this much Fasilides had been accurate in his report. The roads were crowded with shipping. A forest of mast and rigging was outlined against the brooding red hills that ringed the bay. From each masthead flew the banners of Islam and the pennants of Omani and the Great Mogul.

Hal ordered the *Golden Bough* hove to, and he climbed to the main yard and sat there for an hour with the telescope held to his eye. It was not possible to count the number of ships at anchor in the bay, and the waters seethed with small boats ferrying the stores and provisions of a great army to the shore. Of one thing only Hal was certain, when he returned to the deck and ordered sail to be set once more: there was no square-rigged ship in Adulis Bay.

The shattered remnants of the Emperor Iyasu's fleet lay off Mitsiwa. Hal anchored well clear of these burned and battered hulks, and Fasilides sent one of his servants ashore in the longboat. 'He must find out if Nazet's headquarters are still at the monastery, and if they are we must arrange horses for us to travel there.'

While they waited for the servant to return, Hal made arrangements for his temporary absence from the *Golden Bough*. He decided to take only Aboli with him, and to leave command of the ship to Ned Tyler.

'Do not remain at anchor, for this is a lee shore, and you will be vulnerable if the Buzzard should find you here,' he warned Ned. 'Patrol well off the coast, and look upon every sail as that of an enemy. If you should encounter the *Gull of Moray* you are, under no circumstances, to offer battle. I shall return as swiftly as I am able. My signal will be a red Chinese rocket. When you see that, send a boat to pick me up from the shore.'

Hal fretted out the rest of that day and night but at first light the masthead hailed the deck. 'Small dhow coming out from the bay. Heading this way.'

Hal heard the cry in his cabin and hurried on deck. Even without his telescope he recognized Fasilides' servant standing on the open deck of the small craft. He sent for the Bishop. When Fasilides came on deck he was showing the effects of the previous evening's tippling, but he and the servant spoke rapidly in the Geez language. He turned to Hal. 'The Emperor and General Nazet are still at the monastery. Horses are waiting for us on the beach. We can be there by noon. My servant has brought clothing for you and your servant that will make you less conspicuous.'

In his cabin Hal donned the breeches of fine cotton that were cut full as petticoats and taken in at the ankles. The boots were of soft leather with pointed upturned toes. Over the cotton shirt he wore an embroidered dolman tunic that reached half-way down his thighs. The Bishop's servant showed him how to wind the long white cloth around his head to form the ha'ik turban. Over the headcloth he fitted the burnished steel onion-shaped helmet, spiked on top and engraved and inlaid with Coptic crosses.

When he and Aboli came back on deck the crew gawked at them, and Fasilides nodded approval. 'Now none will recognize you as a Frank.'

The longboat deposited them on the beach below the cliffs, where an armed escort was waiting for them. The horses were Arabians with long flowing manes and tails, the large nostrils and fine eyes of the breed. The saddles were carved from a single block of wood and decorated with brass and silver, the saddle-cloths and reins stiff with metal-thread embroidery.

'It is a long ride to the monastery,' Fasilides warned them. 'We must waste no time.'

They climbed the cliff path and came out onto the level ground that lay before Mitsiwa.

'This is the field of our victory!' Fasilides crowed, and stood in his

503

stirrups to make a sweeping gesture that encompassed the grisly plain. Although the battle had taken place weeks before, the carrion birds still hovered over the field like a dark cloud, and the jackals and pariah dogs snarled over piles of bones and chewed at the sun-blackened flesh that still clung to them. The flies were blue in the air like swarming bees. They crawled on Hal's face and tried to drink from his eyes and tickled his nostrils. Their white maggots swarmed and wriggled so thickly in the rotting corpses that they appeared to move as though they still lived.

The human scavengers were also at work across the wide battlefield, women and their children in long dusty robes, their mouths and noses covered against the stench. Each carried a basket to hold their gleanings of buttons, small coins, jewellery, daggers and the rings they tore from the skeletal fingers of the corpses.

'Ten thousand enemy dead!' Fasilides said triumphantly, and led them on a track that left the battlefield and skirted the walled town of Mitsiwa. 'Nazet is too much a warrior to have our army bottled up behind those walls,' he said. 'From those heights Nazet commands the terrain.' He pointed ahead to the first folds and peaks of the highlands.

Beyond the town on the open ground below the bleak hills the victorious army of Emperor Iyasu was encamped. It was a sprawling city of leather tents and hastily built huts and lean-tos of stone and thatch that stretched five leagues from the sea to the hills. The horses, camels and bullocks stood in great herds amongst the rude dwellings, and a cloud of shifting dust and blue smoke from the fires of dried dung blotted out the blue of the sky. The ammoniacal stink of the animal lines, the smoke and the stench of rubbish dumps rotting in the sun, the dunghills and the latrine pits, the ripe odour of carrion and unwashed humanity under the desert sun rivalled the effusions of the battlefield.

They passed squadrons of cavalry on magnificent chargers with trailing manes and proudly arched tail plumes. The riders were clad in weird armour and fanciful costume of rainbow colours. They were armed with bow and lance and long-barrelled jezails with curved and jewelled butts.

The artillery parks were scattered over a league of sand and rock, and there were hundreds of cannon. Some of the colossal siege guns were shaped like dolphins and dragons on carriages drawn by a hundred bullocks each. The ammunition wagons, loaded with kegs of blackpowder, were drawn up in massed squares.

Regiments of foot-soldiers marched and counter-marched. They had added to their own diverse and exotic uniforms the plunder of the battlefield so that no two men were dressed alike. Their shields and bucklers were square, round and oblong, made from brass, wood or rawhide. Their faces were hawklike and dark, and their beards were silver as beach sand, or sable as the wings of the carrion crows that soared above the camp.

'Sixty thousand men,' said Fasilides. 'With the Tabernacle and Nazet at their head, no enemy can stand before them.'

The whores and camp-followers who were not busy scavenging the battlefield were almost as numerous as the men. They tended the cooking fires or lolled in the sparse shade of the baggage wagons. The Somali women were tall and mysteriously veiled, the Galla girls bare-breasted and bold-eyed. Some picked out Hal's virile broad-shouldered figure and shouted unintelligible invitations to him, making their meanings plain by the lewd gestures that accompanied them.

'No, Gundwane,' Aboli muttered in his ear. 'Do not even think about it, for the Galla circumcise their women. Where you might expect a moist and oleaginous welcome, you would find only a dry, scarred pit.'

So dense was this array of men, women and beasts that their progress was reduced to a walk. When the faithful recognized the Bishop, they flocked to him and fell to their knees in the path of his horse to beg his blessing.

At last they forged their way out of this morass of humanity, and spurred up the steep track into the hills. Fasilides led them at a gallop, his robes swirling about his wiry figure and his beard streaming out over his shoulder. At the crest he reined in his steed and pointed to the south. 'There!' he cried. 'There is Adulis Bay, and there before the port of Zulla lies the army of Islam.' Hal shaded his eyes against the desert glare, and saw that the dun cloud of smoke and dust was shot through with sparks of reflected sunlight from the artillery trains and the weapons of another vast army.

'How many men does El Grang command in his legions?'

'That was my mission when you found me – to find the answer to that question from our spies.'

'How many, then?' Hal persisted, and Fasilides laughed.

'The answer to that question is for the ears of General Nazet alone,' he said, and spurred his horse. They climbed higher along the rough track, and came up onto the next ridge.

'There!' Fasilides pointed ahead. 'There stands the monastery of St Luke.'

It clung to a rugged hill top. The walls were high and their harsh square outline unrelieved by ornament, column or architrave. One of the Bishop's outriders blew a blast on a ram's horn, and the single

505

massive wooden gate swung open before them. They galloped through into the courtyard, and dismounted before the keep. Grooms ran forward to take their horses and lead them away.

'This way!' Fasilides ordered, and strode through a narrow doorway into the warren of passageways and staircases beyond. Their boots clattered on the stone paving and echoed in the corridors and smoky halls.

Abruptly they found themselves in a dark, cavernous chapel, whose domed ceiling was lost in the gloom high overhead. Hundreds of flickering candles and the glow from suspended incense burners illuminated the hanging tapestries of saints and martyrs, the tattered banners of the monastic orders and the painted and bejewelled icons.

Fasilides knelt at the altar, on which stood a silver Coptic cross, six feet tall. Hal knelt beside him but Aboli stood behind them, his arms folded over his chest.

'God of our fathers, Lord of hosts!' the Bishop prayed, in Latin for Hal's benefit. 'We give thanks for your bounty and for the mighty victory over the pagan which you have vouchsafed us. We commend this your servant, Henry Courteney, to your care. May he prosper in the service of the one true God, and may his arms prevail against the unbelievers.'

Hal had barely time to complete his genuflections and his amens before the Bishop was up and away again, leading him to a smaller shrine off the nave.

'Wait here!' he said. He went directly to the vividly coloured woollen wall-hanging behind the smaller altar and drew it aside to reveal a low, narrow doorway. Then he stooped through the opening and disappeared.

When Hal looked around the shrine, he saw that it was more richly furnished than the bleak, gloomy chapel. The small altar was covered with foil of yellow metal that might have been brass but which shone like pure gold in the candle-light. The cross was decorated with large coloured stones. Perhaps these were merely glass, but it seemed to Hal that they had the lustre of emerald, ruby and diamond. The shelves that rose to the vaulted roof were loaded with offerings from wealthy and noble penitents and supplicants. Some must have stood untouched for centuries for they were thickly coated with dust and cobwebs so that their true nature was hidden. Five monks in grubby, ragged habits knelt at prayer before the statue of a black-featured Virgin Mary with a little black Jesus in her arms. They did not look up from their devotions at his intrusion.

Hal and Aboli stood together, leaning against a stone column at the back of the shrine, and time stretched out. The air was heavy and oppressive with incense and antiquity. The soft chanting of the monks was hypnotic. Hal felt sleep coming over him in waves and it was an effort to fight it off and keep his eyes from closing.

Suddenly there came the patter of running feet from beyond the wall-hanging. Hal straightened as a small boy appeared from under the curtain and, with all the exuberance of a puppy, rushed into the shrine. He skidded to a halt on the paving. He was four or five years of age, dressed in a plain white cotton shift and his feet were bare. His head was covered with shining black curls that danced as he looked about the shrine eagerly. His eyes were dark, and as large as those of the saints pictured in the stylized portraits that hung on the stone walls behind him.

He saw Hal, ran to where he stood and stopped in front of him. He stared at Hal with such solemnity that Hal was enchanted by the pretty elf, and went down on one knee so that they could study each other at the same level.

The boy said something in the language that Hal could now recognize as Geez. It was obviously a request but Hal could not even guess at the substance of it. 'You too!' Hal laughed, but the child was serious and asked the question again. Hal shrugged, and the boy stamped his foot and asked the third time.

'Yes!' Hal nodded vigorously. The boy laughed delightedly and clapped his hands. Hal straightened up but the child opened his arms and gave a command that could mean only one thing. 'You want to be picked up!' Hal stooped and gathered him in his arms where the boy stared into his eyes then spoke again, pointing so passionately at Hal's face that he almost impaled one eye with his little finger.

'I cannot understand what you're saying, little one,' Hal said gently.

Fasilides had come up silently behind him and now said solemnly, 'His Most Christian Majesty, Iyasu, King of Kings, Ruler of Galla and Amhara, Defender of the Faith of Christ Crucified, remarks that your eyes are of a strange green colour unlike any he has seen before.'

Hal stared into the angelic features of the imp he held in his arms. 'This is the Prester John?' he asked in awe.

'Indeed,' replied the bishop. 'You have also promised to take him for a sail on your tall ship, which I have described to him.'

'Would you inform the Emperor that I would be deeply honoured to have him as a guest aboard the Golden Bough?'

Suddenly Iyasu wriggled down from Hal's arms, seized his hand and dragged him towards the concealed doorway. Beyond the opening they went down a long passageway lit with torches in iron brackets on the stone walls. At the end of the passage were two armed guards, but the Emperor squeaked an order and they stood aside and saluted His tiny Majesty. Iyasu led Hal into a long chamber.

Narrow embrasures were set high up in the walls, and through these the brilliant desert sunlight beamed down in solid golden shafts. A long table ran the length of the chamber, and seated at it were five men. They stood up and bowed deeply to Iyasu, then looked keenly at Hal.

They were all warriors – that much was clear from their bearing and their attire: they wore chain-mail and cuirass, and some had steel helmets on their heads, and tunics over the armour, which were emblazoned with crosses or other heraldic devices.

At the far end of the table stood the youngest and most simply dressed yet the most impressive and commanding of all. Hal's eye was drawn immediately to this slim, graceful figure.

Iyasu drew Hal impatiently towards him, chattering in Geez, and the warrior watched them with a steady, frank gaze. Although he gave the illusion of height, he was in fact a head shorter than Hal. A shaft of sunlight from one of the high embrasures backlit him, surrounding him with a golden aura in which the dust motes danced and swirled.

'Are you General Nazet?' Hal asked in Latin, and the General nodded. Around his head was a huge bush of crisp curls, like a dark crown or a halo. He wore a white tunic over the shirt of chain-mail, but even under that bulky covering his waist was narrow and his back straight and supple.

'I am indeed General Nazet.' His voice was low and husky, yet strangely musical to the ear. Hal realized with a shock how young he was. His skin was flawless, the dark translucent amber of gum arabic. No trace of beard or moustache marred his sleek jawline or the proud curl of his full lips. His nose was straight and narrow, the nostrils finely chiselled.

'I am Henry Courteney,' said Hal, 'the English Captain of the *Golden Bough.*'

'Bishop Fasilides has told me this,' said the General. 'Perhaps you would prefer to speak your own language.' Nazet switched into English. 'I must admit that my Latin is not as fluent as yours, Captain.'

Hal gaped at him, for the moment at a loss, and Nazet smiled. 'My father was ambassador to the palace of the Doge in Venice. I spent much of my childhood in your northern latitudes and learned the languages of diplomacy, French, Italian and English.'

'You astound me, General,' Hal admitted, and while he gathered his wits, he noticed that Nazet's eyes were the colour of honey and his lashes long, thick and curled as those of a girl. He had never felt sexually attracted to another male before. Now, however, as he looked on those regal features and fine golden skin, and stared into those lustrous eyes, he became aware of a pressure in his chest that made it difficult for him to draw the next breath.

'Please be seated, Captain.' Nazet indicated the stool beside him. They sat so close together that he could smell the odour of the other man's body. Nazet wore no perfume, and it was a natural, warm, musky smell that Hal found himself savouring deeply. Guiltily, he acknowledged how unnatural was this sinful attraction he felt, and drew back from the General as far as the hard, low stool would allow him.

The Emperor scrambled into General Nazet's lap and patted his smooth golden cheek, gabbling something in a high, childish voice at which the General laughed softly and replied in Geez, without taking his eyes off Hal's face.

'Fasilides tells me that you have come to Ethiopia to offer your services in the cause of the Most Christian Emperor.'

'That is so. I have come to petition His Majesty to grant me a Letter of Marque, so that I may employ my ship against the enemies of Christ.'

'You have arrived at a most propitious time.' Nazet nodded. 'Has Fasilides told you of the defeat that our navy suffered at Adulis Bay?'

'He has also told me of your magnificent victory at Mitsiwa.'

Nazet showed no false pride at the compliment. 'The one counterbalances the other,' he said. 'If El Grang commands the sea, he can bring in endless reinforcements and stores from Arabia and the territory of the Mogul to replenish his wasted army. Already he has made good all the losses I inflicted upon him at Mitsiwa. I am waiting for reinforcements to arrive from the mountains, so I am not ready to attack him again where he lies at Zulla. Every day he is fed from the sea and grows stronger.'

Hal inclined his head. 'I understand your predicament.' There was something about the General's voice that troubled him: as Nazet became more agitated its timbre altered. Hal had to make an effort to consider the words and not the speaker.

'A new menace now besets me,' Nazet went on. 'El Grang has taken into his service a foreign ship of greater force than any we can send out to meet it.' Hal felt a prickle of anticipation run down the back of his neck and the hairs rise upon his forearms.

'What manner of ship is this?' he asked softly.

'I am no sailor, but my admirals tell me that it is a square-rigged ship of the frigate class.' Nazet looked keenly at Hal. 'It must be similar to your own vessel.'

'Do you know the name of the captain?' Hal demanded, but Nazet shook his head.

'I know only that he is inflicting terrible losses on our transport dhows that I rely on to bring supplies down from the north.'

'What flag does he fly?' Hal persisted.

Nazet spoke rapidly to one of the officers in Geez, then turned back to him. 'This ship flies the pennant of Omani, but also a red cross of unusual shape on a white ground.'

'I think I know this marauder,' said Hal grimly, 'and I will pit my own vessel against his at the first opportunity – that is, if His Most Christian Majesty will grant me a commission to serve as a privateer in his navy.'

'At Fasilides' urging, I have already ordered the court scribes to draft your commission. We need only agree the terms and I shall sign it on the Emperor's behalf.' Nazet rose from the stool. 'But come, let me show you in detail the position of our forces and those of El Grang.' He led the way to the far side of the chamber, and the other senior officers rose with him. They surrounded the circular table on which, Hal saw, had been built a clay model of the Red Sea and the surrounding territories. It was executed in graphic detail, and realistically painted. Each town and port was clearly shown; tiny carved ships sailed upon the blue waters while regiments of cavalry and foot were represented by model figures carved in ivory and painted in splendid uniform.

As they studied this soberly, the Emperor dragged up a stool and climbed onto it so that he could reach the models. With squeals of glee and the childish imitations of neighing horses and firing cannon, he began to move the figures about the board. Nazet reached out to restrain him, and Hal stared at the hand. It was slim and smooth and dainty, with long, tapered fingers, the nails pearly pink. Suddenly the truth dawned on him and, before he could prevent himself, he blurted out in English, 'Mother Mary, you're a woman!'

Nazet glanced up at him, and her amber cheeks darkened with annoyance. 'I advise you not to disparage me on account of my gender, Captain. As an Englishman, you might remember the military lesson a woman handed out to you at Orléans.'

The retort rose to Hal's lips, 'Yes, but that was more than two hundred years ago and we burned her for her troubles!' but he managed to stop himself and instead tried to make his tone placatory.

'I meant no offence, General. It only enhances the admiration I had already conceived for your powers of leadership.'

Nazet was not so easily mollified and her manner became brisk and businesslike as she explained the tactical and strategic positions of the two armies and pointed out to him where he might best employ the *Golden Bough*. She no longer looked at him directly, and the line of those full soft lips had hardened. 'I will expect you to place yourself

510

under my direct command, and to that end I have ordered Admiral Senec to draw up a simple set of signals, rockets and lanterns by night and flags and smoke by day, through which I can pass my orders from the shore to you at sea. Do you have any objection to that?'

'No, General, I do not.'

'As to your share of the prize money, two-thirds will accrue to the Imperial exchequer, and the balance to you and your crew.'

'It is customary for the ship to retain half of the prize,' Hal demurred.

'Captain,' said Nazet coldly, 'in these seas the custom is set by His Most Christian Majesty.'

'Then I must concur.' Hal smiled ironically, but received no encouragement to further levity from Nazet.

'Any warlike stores or provisions you may capture will be purchased by the exchequer, and likewise any enemy vessels will be purchased by the navy.'

She looked away from him as a scribe entered the chamber and bowed before handing her a document written on stiff yellow parchment. Nazet glanced swiftly through it then took up the quill that the scribe handed her, filled in the blanks in the script and signed at the foot, 'Judith Nazet', and added a cross behind her name.

As she sanded the wet ink she said, 'It is written in Geez, but I will have a translation prepared for you when next we meet. In the meantime, I give you my assurance that this letter sets out exactly the terms we have discussed.' She rolled the document, secured it with a ribbon and handed it to Hal.

'Your assurance is sufficient for me.' Hal slipped the rolled document into the sleeve of his tunic.

'I am certain you are eager to rejoin your ship, Captain. I will detain you no longer.' With that dismissal, she seemed to forget his existence and turned her full attention back to her commanders and the clay panorama of the battlefield on the tabletop in front of her.

'You spoke of a series of signals, General.' Despite her uncompromising manner, Hal found himself strangely reluctant to leave her presence. He was drawn to her in the way a compass needle seeks the north.

She did not look up at him again but said, 'Admiral Senec will have a signal book sent out to your ship before you sail. Bishop Fasilides will see you to where your horses are waiting. Farewell, Captain.'

As Hal strode down the long stone passageway alongside the Bishop he said quietly, 'The Tabernacle of Mary is here in this monastery. Am I right in believing that?'

Fasilides stopped dead in his tracks and stared at him. 'How did you know? Who told you?'

'As a devout Christian I should like to look upon such a sacred object,' said Hal. 'Can you grant me that wish?'

Fasilides tugged nervously at his beard. 'Perhaps. We shall see. Come with me.' He led Hal to where Aboli still waited and then both of them followed him through another maze of stairways and passages, then stopped before a doorway guarded by four priests in robes and turbans.

'Is this man of yours a Christian?' he asked as he looked at Aboli, and Hal shook his head. 'Then he must remain here.'

The Bishop took Hal's arm and led him to the door. He spoke softly in Geez to one of the priests, and the old man took a huge black key from under his robe and turned the lock. Fasilides drew Hal into the crypt beyond.

Surrounded by a forest of burning candles in tall, many-branched brass holders, the Tabernacle stood in the centre of the paved floor.

Hal felt an overwhelming sense of awe and grace come upon him. He knew that this was one of the supreme moments of his life, perhaps even the reason for his birth and existence.

The Tabernacle was a small chest that stood on four legs, carved like the paws of a lion. There were four carrying handles. Its square body was covered with a tapestry of silver and gold embroidery that had the patina of great age upon it. On each end of the lid knelt a miniature golden statue of an angel, with head bowed and hands clasped in prayer. It was a thing of exquisite beauty.

Hal fell to his knees in the same attitude as the golden angels. 'Lord God of Hosts, I have come to do your bidding, as you commanded,' he began to pray aloud. After a long while, he crossed himself and rose to his feet.

'May I see the chalice?' he asked deferentially, but Fasilides shook his head.

'Not even I have seen it. It is too holy for the eyes of mortal man. It would blind you.'

The Ethiopian pilot guided the *Golden Bough* southwards in the night under top sails alone. With a leadsman taking soundings they crept up into the lee of Dahlak Island off the mouth of Adulis Bay.

Anxiously Hal listened in the darkness to the chant of the leadsman, 'No bottom with this line!' and minutes later, 'No bottom with this line!' and then the plop of the lead as it was swung out ahead of the bows and hit the surface. Suddenly the chant altered and the leadsman's voice took on a sharper tone. 'By the deep, twenty!'

'Mr Tyler!' Hal barked. 'Take another reef in your top sails. Stand by to let the anchor go!'

'By the mark, ten!' The leadsman's next cry was sharper still.

'Furl all your canvas. Let go your anchor!'

The anchor went down and the *Golden Bough* glided on a short distance before she snubbed up on the cable.

'Take the deck, Mr Tyler,' Hal said. 'I am going aloft.'

He went up the shrouds from deck to the top of the mainmast without a pause, and was pleased that his breathing was merely deep and even when he reached the canvas crow's nest.

'I see you, Gundwane!' Aboli greeted him, and made room for him in the canvas nest. Hal settled beside him and looked first to the land. Dahlak Island was a darker mass in the dark night, but they were a full cable's length clear of her rocks. Then he looked to the west and saw the sweep of Adulis Bay, clearly outlined by the fires of El Grang's army encamped along the shoreline around the little port of Zulla. The waters of the bay sparkled with the riding lanterns of the anchored fleet of Islam. He tried to count those lights but gave up when the tally reached sixty-four. He wondered if one of those was the *Gull of Moray*, and felt his guts contract at the thought.

He turned to look into the east and saw the first pale promise of the dawn silhouette the rugged peaks of Arabia, from which came El Grang's transport dhows laden with men, horses and provisions to swell his legions.

Then, below the dawn on the dark sea, he saw the riding lanterns of other ships winking like fireflies as they sailed in on the night breeze towards Adulis Bay.

'Can you count them, Aboli?' he asked, and Aboli chuckled.

'My eyes are not as sharp as yours, Gundwane. Let us say merely that there are many, and wait for the dawn to disclose their true numbers,' he murmured.

They waited in the silence of old companions, and both felt the chill of the coming dawn warmed away by the promise of battle that the day must bring, for this narrow sea swarmed with the ships of the enemy.

The eastern sky began to glow like an ironsmith's forge. The rocks of the island close at hand showed pale through the gloom, painted white by the dung of the sea birds that for centuries had roosted upon them. From their rocky perches the birds launched into flight. In staggered arrowhead formations they flew across the red dawn sky uttering wild, haunting cries. Looking up at them Hal felt the morning wind brush his

513

cheek with cool fingers. It was blowing out of the west as he had relied upon it to do. He had the flotilla of small dhows under his lee, and at his mercy.

The rising sun flared upon the mountain tops and set them aflame. Far out beyond the low rocks of the island a sail glinted on the darkling waters, and then another and, as the circle of their vision expanded, a dozen more.

Hal slapped Aboli lightly on the shoulder. 'It is time to go to work, old friend,' he said, and slid down the shrouds. As his feet hit the deck he called to the helm, 'Up anchor, Mr Tyler. All hands aloft to set sail.'

Released from restraint the *Golden Bough* spread her canvas and wheeled away. The waters rustling under her bows and her wake creaming behind her, she sped out from her ambush behind Dahlak Island.

The light was bright enough by now for Hal to make out clearly his quarry scattered across the wind-flecked waters ahead. He looked eagerly for the piled canvas of a tall ship amongst them, but saw only the single lateen sails of the Arabian dhows.

The closest of these vessels seemed unalarmed by the *Golden Bough*'s appearance, her high pyramid of sails standing right across the entrance to Adulis Bay. They held their course and, as the frigate bore down upon the nearest of them, Hal saw the crew and passengers lining the dhow's side and peering across at them. Some had scampered up the stubby mast and were waving a greeting.

Hal stopped beside the helm and said to Ned Tyler, "Tis likely that they have seen only one other ship like ours in these waters and that's the *Gull*. They take us for an ally.' He looked up to where his topmastmen hung in the rigging, ready to handle the great mass of canvas. Then he looked back along the deck, where the gunners were fussing over the culverins and the powder boys were scurrying up from below decks with their deadly burdens.

'Mr Fisher!' he called. 'Load one battery on each side with ball, all the others with chain and grape, if you please.' Big Daniel grinned, with black and rotten teeth, and knuckled his brow. Hal wanted simply to disable the enemy vessels, not sink or burn them. Even the smallest and poorest of those craft must be worth a great deal to the exchequer of His Most Christian Majesty, if he could capture them and deliver them to Admiral Senec at Mitsiwa. The battery on each side loaded with ball would be held in reserve.

The first dhow was so close ahead that Hal could see the expressions on the faces of her crew. They were a dozen or so sailors, dressed in

514

ragged and faded robes and ha'ik turbans. Most were still smiling and waving but the old man at the tiller in the stern was looking about wildly, as if to seek some providential escape from the tall hull that was racing down upon his little vessel.

'Break out our colours, if you please, Mr Tyler,' Hal ordered, and watched the *croix patté* unfurl alongside the white Coptic cross of the Empire on its royal blue ground. The dismay on the faces of the dhow's crew as they saw the cross of their doom spread before their eyes was pathetic to behold and Hal gave his next order. 'Run out your guns, Master Daniel!' The *Golden Bough*'s gunports crashed back and the hull reverberated to the rumble of the guns as the culverins poked out their bronze muzzles.

'I'll pass the chase close to starboard. Fire as you bear, Master Daniel!' Big Daniel raced to the bows and took command of the number-one starboard battery. Hal saw him move swiftly from gun to gun to check their laying, inserting the wedges to lower the aim. They would be firing almost directly down into the dhow as they swept past her.

The *Golden Bough* rushed down silently upon the little craft, and Hal said quietly to the helm, 'Slowly bring her up a point to larboard.'

As they realized the menace of the gaping guns, the crew of the dhow fled from the rail and flung themselves down behind the stubby little mast or crouched behind the bales and casks that cluttered her deck.

The first battery fired together in one smoking, thunderous discharge and every shot struck home. The base of the mast was blown away in a storm of white wood splinters and her rigging crashed down to hang overside in an untidy tangle of rope and canvas. The old man at the tiller disappeared, as though turned to air by a wizard's spell. He left only a red smear on the torn planking.

'Avast firing!' Hal bellowed, to make himself heard in the ear-numbing aftermath of the gunfire. The dhow was crippled: her bows were already swinging away before the wind, the tiller shot away and her mast gone overboard. The *Golden Bough* left her rolling in her wake.

'Hold your course, Mr Tyler.' The *Golden Bough* tore straight at the flotilla of small craft strewn across the blue waters ahead. These had seen the merciless treatment of the first dhow and the Imperial colours flying at the frigate's masthead, and now every one put his helm hard up and came around before the wind. Goose-winged, they fled before the *Golden Bough*'s charge.

'Steer for the vessel dead ahead!' said Hal quietly, and Ned Tyler brought the frigate around a point. The dhow Hal had chosen was one of the largest in sight, and its open deck was crowded with men. There must be at least three hundred packed into her, Hal estimated. It was a short voyage across the narrow sea, and her captain had taken a risk: she was carrying far more troops than was prudent.

A thin shout of defiance reached Hal's ears as they closed the range: 'Allah Akbar! God is great!' Steel war helmets glinted on the heads of the Omani troops, and they brandished their long, curved scimitars. There came an untidy volley of musket fire, aimed at the frigate, the popping of the jezails and puffs of gunsmoke along the dhow's side. A lead ball thudded into the mast above Hal's head.

'Every man aboard her is a soldier,' Hal said aloud. He did not have to add that if they were allowed to reach the western shore of the sea they would march against Judith Nazet. 'Give her a volley of ball. Sink her, Master Daniel!'

The heavy iron cannonballs raked the troopship from deck to keel and split her like kindling under the axe. The sea rushed in through her torn belly. She capsized and the water was suddenly filled with the bobbing heads of struggling, drowning men.

'Steer for that vessel with the silver pennant.' Hal did not look back but tore through the fleet like a barracuda into a shoal of flying fish. Not one could outrun him. With her mountain of white sails driving her, the *Golden Bough* flew upon them as if they were at anchor, and her guns crashed out in flame and smoke. Some of the little ships burst open and sank, others were left in the frigate's wake with mast snapped away and sails dragging alongside. Some of the sailors threw themselves overboard at the moment that the culverins came to bear upon them. They preferred the sharks to the blast of guns.

Several ran for the nearest island and tried to anchor in the shoal waters where the *Golden Bough* could not follow. Others deliberately ran aground, and their crews dived overboard to swim and wade to the beach.

Only those ships furthest to the east and closest to the Arabian coast had the head start to run from the frigate's charge. Hal looked astern and saw the water behind him dotted with the floundering hulls of those he had overtaken. Every mile he chased the survivors eastwards was a mile further from Mitsiwa.

'None of those will come back in a hurry!' he said grimly, as he watched them fly in confusion. 'Mr Tyler, please be good enough to wear the ship around and lay her close hauled on the starboard tack.'

This was the *Golden Bough*'s best point of sailing. 'There is no dhow built in all Arabia that can point higher into the wind than my darling can,' Hal said aloud, as he saw twenty sail to windward trying to escape by beating up into the west. The *Golden Bough* tore back into the scattered fleet, and now some of the dhows dropped their wide triangular main sail as they saw him coming and screamed to Allah for mercy.

Hal checked the frigate as he came alongside each of these, bringing her head to the wind as he launched a boat and sent a prize crew, comprising one white seaman and six of his Amadoda, to board the surrendered ship. 'If there is nothing of value in her cargo, take off her crew and put a torch to her.'

By late that afternoon, Hal had five large dhows on tow behind the *Golden Bough*, and another seven sailing in company with him, under jury-rigging and with his prize crews aboard, as they headed back towards Mitsiwa. Every one of the captured vessels was heavily laden with vital provisions of war. Behind him, the sky was dulled with the smoke of the burning hulls and the sea was littered with the wreckage.

General Nazet sat on her black Arabian stallion and watched from the cliff tops as this untidy flotilla straggled into Mitsiwa Roads. At last she closed her telescope and remarked to Admiral Senec beside her, 'I see why you call him El Tazar! This Englishman is a barracuda, indeed.' Then she turned away her face so that he could not see the thoughtful smile that softened her handsome features. El Tazar. It is a good name for him, she thought, and then, irrelevantly, another notion occurred to her. I wonder if he is as fierce a lover as he is a warrior. It was the first time since God had chosen her to lead his legions against the pagan that she had looked at any man through a woman's eyes.

Colonel Cornelius Schreuder dismounted in front of the spreading tent of shimmering red and yellow silk. A groom took his horse and he paused to look around the encampment. The royal tent stood on a small knoll overlooking Adulis Bay. Up here the sea breeze cooled the air and made it possible to breathe. On the plain below, where the army of Islam was bivouacked around the port of Zulla, the stones crackled in the heat and shimmered in the mirage.

The bay was crowded with shipping, but the tall masts of the *Gull of Moray* dominated all others. The Earl of Cumbrae's ship had come in during the night, and now Schreuder heard his voice raised in argument within the silken tent. His lips twitched in a smile that lacked humour, and he adjusted the hang of the golden sword at his side before he strode to the flap of the tent. A tall subahdar bowed to him. All the troops of Islam had come to know him well: in the short time he had served with them, Schreuder's feats of daring had become legend in the Mogul's army. The officer ushered him into the royal presence.

517

The interior of the tent was commodious and sumptuously furnished. The entire floor was thickly covered with gorgeously coloured silk carpets and silken draperies formed a double skin that kept out the sun's heat. The low tables were of ivory and rare wood, and the vessels upon them were of solid gold.

The Great Mogul's brother, the Maharajah Sadiq Khan Jahan, sat in the centre on a pile of silk cushions. He wore a tunic of padded yellow silk and striped pantaloons of red and gold. The slippers on his feet were scarlet with long, curling toes and buckles of gold. His turban was yellow and secured above his brow by an emerald the size of a walnut. He was close-shaven, with only a kohl line of fine moustache upon his petulant upper lip. Across his lap was a scimitar in a scabbard so richly encrusted with jewels that the sparkle of them pricked the eye. On one gloved hand he held a falcon, a magnificent Saker of the desert. He lifted the bird and kissed its beak as tenderly as if it had been a beautiful woman – or rather, Schreuder thought bleakly, as if it were one of his pretty dancing boys.

A little behind him, on another pile of cushions, sat Ahmed El Grang, the Left Hand of Allah. He was so wide-shouldered as to seem deformed, and his neck was thick and corded with muscle. He wore a steel war helmet and his beard was dyed with henna, red as that of the Prophet. His massive chest was covered with a steel cuirass, and there were bracelets of steel upon his wrists. His brows beetled and his eyes were as cold and implacable as those of an eagle.

Behind this ill-matched pair sat a host of courtiers and officers, all richly dressed. Before the Prince knelt a translator who, his forehead pressed to the ground, was trying to keep up with the Buzzard's flood of invective.

The Buzzard stood before the Prince with his fists bunched on his hips. On his head was his beribboned bonnet, and his beard was more bushy and fiery than the dyed, barbered curls that covered El Grang's chin. He wore half armour above his plaid. He turned with relief when Schreuder entered the tent and made deep and respectful obeisance, first to the Prince and then to El Grang.

'Jesus love you, Colonel. I need you now to talk some sense into these two lovely laddies. This ape—' Cumbrae spurned the grovelling translator with his boot. 'This ape is blethering away, and making a nonsense of what I'm telling them.' He knew that Schreuder had spent many years in the Orient, and that Arabic was one of the languages in which he was fluent.

'Tell them that I came here to take prizes, not to match my *Gull* against a ship of equal force and have her shot away beneath my feet!' the Buzzard instructed him. 'They want me to do battle with the *Golden Bough.*'

'Explain the matter to me more fully,' Schreuder invited. 'That way I may be able to assist you.'

'The *Golden Bough* has arrived in these waters – we must presume under the command of young Courteney,' the Buzzard told him.

Schreuder's face darkened at the name. 'Will we never be rid of him?'

'It seems not.' Cumbrae chuckled. 'In any event, he is flying the white cross of the Empire, and whaling into El Grang's transports with a vengeance. He has sunk and captured twenty-three sail in the last week, and no Mussulman captains will put out to sea while he is in the offing. Single-handed he is blockading the entire coast of Ethiopia.' He shook his head in reluctant admiration. 'From the cliffs above Tenwera, I watched him fall upon a flotilla of El Grang's war dhows. He cut them to pieces. By Jesus, he handles his ship as well as Franky ever could. He sailed circles around those Mussulmen and shot them out of the water. The entire fleet of Allah the All Merciful is all bottled up in port, and El Grang is starved of reinforcements and stores. The Mussulmen call young Courteney *El Tazar*, the Barracuda, and not one will go out to face him.'

Then his grin faded and he looked lugubrious. 'The *Golden Bough* is bright and clean of weed. My *Gull* has been at sea for nigh on three years. Her timbers are riddled with shipworm. I would guess that, even on my best point of sailing, the *Golden Bough* has at least three knots of speed on me.'

'What do you want me to tell his highness?' Schreuder asked scornfully. 'That you are afraid to meet young Courteney?'

'I am afraid of no man living – or dead, for that matter. But there is no profit in it for me. Hal Courteney has nothing I want, but if it comes to a single-ship fight, he could do me and my *Gull* fearful damage. If they want me to fight him they will have to sweeten my cup a little.'

Schreuder turned back to the Prince and explained this to him in carefully chosen diplomatic terms. Sadiq Khan Jahan stroked his falcon as he listened expressionlessly, and the bird ruffled out its feathers and hooded its yellow eyes. When Schreuder had finished, the Prince turned to El Grang. 'What did you say they called this red-bearded braggart?'

'They call him the Buzzard, your highness,' El Grang replied hoarsely.

'A name well chosen, for it seems he prefers to pick out the eyes of the weak and the dying and scavenge the leavings of fiercer creatures rather than to kill for himself. He is no falcon.'

El Grang nodded agreement, and the Prince turned back to Schreuder. 'Ask this noble bird of prey what payment he demands for fighting El Tazar.'

'Tell the pretty boy I want a lakh of rupees in gold coin, and I want it in my hands before I leave port,' Cumbrae replied, and even Schreuder gasped at the audacity. One lakh was a hundred thousand rupees. The Buzzard went on amiably, 'You see, I have got the Prince with his bum in the air and his pantaloons round his ankles. I intend to tup him full length, but not the way he likes it.'

Schreuder listened to the Prince's reply, then turned back to Cumbrae. 'He says that you could build twenty ships like the *Gull* for a lakh.'

'That may be so, but it won't buy me a pair of balls to replace the ones that Hal Courteney shoots away.'

The Prince smiled at this response. 'Tell the Buzzard he must have lost them long ago, but he makes a fine eunuch. I could always find a place for him in my harem.'

The Buzzard guffawed at the insult, but shook his head. 'Tell the pretty pederast, no gold and the Buzzard flies away.'

The Prince and El Grang whispered to each other, gesticulating. At last, they seemed to reach a decision.

'I have another proposition that the bold captain might find more to his taste. The risk he takes will not be so great, but he will receive the lakh he demands.' The Prince rose to his feet, and all his court fell upon their knees and pressed their foreheads to the ground. 'I will leave Sultan Ahmed El Grang to explain this to you in secrecy.'

He retired through the curtains at the back of the tent, and all his retinue went with him, leaving only the two Europeans and the Sultan in the cavern of silk.

El Grang gestured to both men to come closer and to sit in front of him. 'What I have to say is for the ears of no other living soul.' While he arranged his thoughts, he fingered the old lance wound that ran in a ridge of raised scar tissue from below his ear, down under the high collar of his tunic: half his vocal cords had been severed by that old injury. He began to speak, in his hoarse, wheezing voice. 'The Emperor was slain before Suakin and his infant son Iyasu has inherited the crown of Prester John. His armies were in disarray when there arose a female prophet who proclaimed that she had been chosen by the Christian God to lead his armies. She came down from the mountains leading fifty thousand fighting men and carrying before her a religious talisman that they call the Tabernacle of Mary. Her armies, inspired by religious fanaticism, were able to check us at Mitsiwa.'

Both Schreuder and Cochran nodded. This was nothing new. 'Now,

520

Allah has given me the opportunity to seize both this talisman and the person of the infant Emperor.' El Grang sat back and lapsed into silence, watching the faces of the two white men shrewdly.

'With the Tabernacle and the Emperor in your hands, the armies of Nazet would dissolve like snow in the summer sun,' Schreuder said softly.

El Grang nodded. 'A renegade monk has come in to us, and offered to lead a small party commanded by a bold man to the place where both the talisman and the Emperor are hidden. Once the child and the Tabernacle have been captured, I will need a fast, powerful ship to carry them to Muscat before Nazet can make an attempt to rescue them from us.' He turned to Schreuder and said, 'You, Colonel, are the bold man I need. If you succeed, your payment will also be a lakh.'

Then El Grang looked at Cochran. 'Yours is the fast ship to carry them to Muscat. When you deliver them there, there will be another lakh for you.' He smiled coldly. 'This time I will pay you to fly from El Tazar, rather than confront him. Are your balls big and heavy enough for that task, my brave Buzzard?'

The *Golden Bough* ran southwards, her sails glowing in the last rays of the sun, like a tower of gold.

"The *Gull of Moray* lies at anchor in Adulis Bay,' Fasilides' spies had brought the report, 'and her captain is ashore. They say he sits in council with El Grang.' But that intelligence was two days' stale.

'Will the Buzzard still be there?' Hal fretted to himself, and studied his sails. The *Golden Bough* could carry not another stitch of canvas, and every sail was drawing sweetly. The hull sliced through the water, and the deck vibrated beneath his feet like a living creature. If I find her still at anchor, we can board her even in darkness, Hal thought, and strode down the deck, checking the tackle of his guns. The white seamen knuckled their foreheads and grinned at him, while the squatting ranks of Amadoda grinned and crossed their chests with their open right hand in salute. They were like hunting dogs with the scent of the stag in their nostrils. He knew that they would not flinch when he laid the *Golden Bough* alongside the *Gull* and led them onto her deck.

The sun dipped towards the horizon and quenched its flames in the sea. The darkness descended and the outline of the land melted into it.

Moonrise in two hours, Hal thought, as he stopped by the binnacle to check the ship's heading. We will be into Adulis Bay by then. He looked up at Ned Tyler, whose face was lit by the compass lantern.

'Hoist our new canvas,' he ordered, and Ned repeated the order through the speaking trumpet. The new canvas was laid out on the deck, the sheets already reeved into the clews and earing cringles, but it took an hour of hard, dangerous work before her white canvas was brought down and stowed away, and the sails that were daubed with pitch were hoist to the yards and unfurled.

Black was her hull, and black as midnight her canvas. The *Golden Bough* would show no flash in the moonlight when they sailed into Adulis Bay to take unawares the anchored fleet of Islam.

Let the Buzzard be there, Hal prayed silently. Please, God, let him not have sailed.

Slowly the bay opened to them, and they saw the lanterns of the enemy fleet like the lights of a large town. Beyond them the watchfires of El Grang's host reflected off the belly of the low cloud of dust and smoke.

'Lay the ship on the larboard tack, Mr Tyler. Steer into the bay.' The ship came around and bore swiftly towards the anchored fleet.

'Take a reef in your mains. Furl all your top-hamper, please, Mr Tyler.' The ship's rush slowed and the rustle of the bow wave dwindled as they went in under fighting canvas.

Hal walked towards the bows and Aboli stood up out of the darkness. 'Are your archers ready?' Hal asked.

Aboli's teeth flashed in the gloom. 'They are ready, Gundwane.'

Hal made them out now, dark shapes crouched along the ship's rail between the culverins, their bundles of arrows laid out on the deck.

'Keep them under your eye!' Hal cautioned him. If the Amadoda had one fault in battle it was that they could be carried away by their blood lust.

As he went on to Big Daniel's station in the waist, he was checking that all the burning slow-match was concealed in the tubs and that the glowing tips would not alert a watchful enemy. 'Good evening, Master Daniel. Your men have never been in a night battle. Keep a tight rein. Don't let them start firing wildly.'

He went back to the helm, and the ship crept on into the bay, a dark shadow on the dark waters. The moon rose behind them and lit the scene ahead with a silvery radiance, so that Hal could discern the shapes of the enemy fleet. He knew that his own ship was still invisible.

On they glided, and they were close enough now to hear the sounds from the moored vessels ahead, voices singing, praying and arguing. Someone was hammering a wooden mallet, and there was the creak of oars and the slatting of rigging as the dhows rolled gently at anchor.

Hal was straining his eyes to pick out the masts of the *Gull of Moray*, but he knew that if she were in the bay he would not be able to spot her until the first broadside lit the darkness.

'A large dhow dead ahead,' he said quietly to Ned Tyler. 'Steer to pass her close to starboard.'

'Ready, Master Daniel!' He raised his voice. 'On the vessel to starboard, fire as you bear!'

They crept up to the anchored dhow and, as she came fully abeam, the *Golden Bough*'s full broadside lit the darkness like sheet lightning and the thunder of the guns stunned their ear-drums and echoed off the desert hills. In that brief eye-searing illumination Hal saw the masts and hulls of the entire enemy fleet brightly lit, and he felt the lead of disappointment heavy in his guts.

'The *Gull* has gone,' he said aloud. Once again, the Buzzard had eluded him. There will be another time, he consoled himself. Firmly he put the distracting thought from his mind, and turned his full attention back to the battle that was opening like some hellish pageant before him.

The moment that first broadside tore into the quarry, Aboli did not have to wait for an order. The deck was lit by the flare of many bright flames as the Amadoda lit their fire-arrows. On each cane shaft, tied behind the iron arrowhead, was a tuft of unravelled hemp rope that had been soaked in pitch, which spluttered and then burned fiercely when touched with the slow-match.

The archers loosed their arrows, which sailed up in a high, flaming parabola and dropped down to peg into the timbers of an anchored vessel. As the screams of terror and agony rose from the shot-shattered hull, the *Golden Bough* glided on deeper into the mass of shipping.

'Two vessels a point on either side of your bows,' Hal told the helmsman. 'Steer between them.'

As they passed them close on either hand, the ship heeled first to one side and then to the other as her broadsides thundered out in quick succession, and a rain of fire-arrows fell from the sky upon the stricken vessels.

Behind them the first dhow was ablaze, and her flames lit the bay, brilliantly illuminating the quarry to the *Golden Bough*'s gunners as she ran on amongst them.

'El Tazar!' As Hal heard the terrified Arab voices screaming his name from ship to ship, he smiled grimly and watched their panic-stricken efforts to cut their anchor cables and escape his terrible approach. Now five dhows were burning, and drifted out of control into the crowded anchorage.

Some enemy vessels were firing wildly, blazing away without making any attempt to lay their aim on the frigate. Stray cannonballs, aimed too high, howled overhead, while others, aimed too low, skipped across the surface of the water and crashed into the friendly ships anchored alongside them.

The flames jumped from ship to ship and the whole sweep of the bay was bright as day. Once again Hal looked for the *Gull*'s tall masts. If she were here, by this time the Buzzard would have set sails and his silhouette would be unmistakable. But he was nowhere in sight, and Hal turned back angrily to the task of wreaking as much destruction as he could upon the fleet of Islam.

Behind them one of the blazing hulls must have been loaded with several hundred tons of blackpowder for El Grang's artillery. It went up in a vast tower of black smoke, shot through with flaring red flames as though the devil had flung open the doors of hell. The rolling column of smoke went on mounting into the night sky until its top was no longer visible and seemed to have reached into the heavens. The blast swept through the fleet striking down those vessels closest to it and shattering their timbers or rolling them over on their backs.

The wind from the explosion roared over the frigate and, for a moment, her sails were taken aback and she began to lose steerage way. Then the offshore night breeze took over and filled them once more. She bore onwards, deeper into the bay and into the heart of the enemy fleet.

Hal nodded with grim satisfaction each time one of the *Golden Bough*'s salvoes crashed out. They were one sudden shock of thunder and a single flare of red flame as every gun fired at the same instant. Even Aboli's Amadoda launched their flights of arrows in a single flaming cloud. In contrast, there was never such a wild discordant banging of uncontrolled shot as stuttered from the enemy ships.

El Grang's shore batteries began to open up as their sleep-groggy gunners stumbled to their colossal siege guns. Each discharge was like a separate clap of thunder, belittling even the roar of the frigate's massed volleys. Hal smiled each time one of their mighty muzzle flashes tore out from the rock-walled redoubts across the bay. The shore gunners could not possibly pick out the black sails of the *Golden Bough* in the confusion and smoke. They fired into their own fleet and Hal saw at least one enemy ship smashed to planks by a single ball from the shore.

'Stand by to go about!' Hal gave the order in one of the fleeting moments of quiet. The shore was coming up fast, and they would soon be landlocked in the depths of the bay. The topmastmen handled the sails with perfect timing, and the bows swung through a wide arc then steadied as they pointed back towards the open sea.

Hal walked forward in the brilliant light of the burning ships and raised his voice so that the men could hear him: 'I doubt not that El Grang will long remember this night.' They cheered him even as they heaved on the gun tackles and nocked their arrows. 'The *Bough* and Sir Hal!'

Then a single voice sang out, 'El Tazar!' and they all took up the cry so heartily that El Grang and the Prince must have heard them as they stood before the silken tent on the knoll above the bay and looked down upon their shattered fleet.

'El Tazar! El Tazar!'

Hal nodded at the helm. 'Take us out, please, Mr Tyler.'

As they wove their way through the burning hulks and floating wreckage, and drew slowly out towards the entrance a single shot fired from one of the drifting dhows smashed in through the gunwale, and tore across the open deck. Miraculously it passed between one of the guncrews and a group of the half-naked archers without touching them. But Stan Sparrow was standing at the far rail, commanding a gun battery, and the hot iron ball took off both his legs neatly, just above the knees.

Instinctively Hal started forward to succour him, but then he checked himself. As captain, the dead and wounded were not his concern, but he felt the agony of loss. Stan Sparrow had been with him from the beginning. He was a good man and a shipmate.

When they carried Stan away, they passed close by where Hal stood. He saw that Stan's face was ivory pale, and that he was drained of blood. He was sinking fast but he saw Hal and, with a great effort, lifted his hand to touch his forehead. 'They was good times, Captain,' he said, and his hand dropped.

'God speed, Master Stan,' Hal said, and while they carried him below, he turned to look back into the bay, so that in the light of the burning ships no man might see his distress.

Long after they had run out of the bay and turned away northwards towards Mitsiwa, the night skies behind them glowed with the inferno they had created. The captains of divisions came one at a time to make their battle reports. Though Stan Sparrow was the only man killed, three others had been wounded by musket fire from the dhows as they sailed past, and another man's leg had been crushed in the recoil of an overshotted culverin. It was a small price to pay, Hal supposed, and yet, though he knew it to be weakness, he mourned Stan Sparrow.

Although he was exhausted and his head ached from the din of battle and the powder smoke, Hal was too wrought-up for sleep and his mind was in a turmoil of emotion and racing thoughts. He left the helm to

Ned Tyler and went to stand alone in the bows to let the cool night air soothe him.

He was still alone there as the dawn began to break and the *Golden Bough* headed in towards Mitsiwa roads, and the first to see the three red Chinese rockets soar up into the sky from the heights of the cliffs above the bay.

It was a signal from Judith Nazet, an urgent recall. He felt his pulse quicken with dread as he turned and bellowed to Aboli, who had the watch, 'Hoist three red lanterns to the masthead!'

Three red lights was an acknowledgement of her signal.

She has heard the guns and seen the flames, he thought. She wishes to have my report of the battle. Somehow he knew that it was not so but he hoped to quieten the sudden sense of dread that assailed him.

It was fully light as they nosed in towards the shore. Hal was still in the bows and the first to spot the boat that darted out from the beach to meet them. From two cables' length away he recognized the slim figure standing beside the single mast. He felt his heart leap and his sadness fall away, replaced by a sense of eager anticipation.

Judith Nazet's head was bare and the dark halo of her hair framed her face. She wore armour and a sword was buckled at her side, a steel helmet under her arm.

Hal strode back to the quarterdeck and gave his order to the helm: 'Round her up and heave to! Let the boat come alongside.'

Judith Nazet came through the entryport with a lithe and graceful urgency, and Hal saw that her marvellous features were stricken. 'I give thanks to God for bringing you back so swiftly,' she said, in a voice that trembled with some strong emotion. 'A terrible catastrophe has over-taken us. I can hardly find words to describe it to you.'

They had muffled the horses' hoofs with leather boots so they made little sound on the rocky earth. The priest rode close beside him, but Cornelius Schreuder had taken the precaution of securing a light steel chain around the man's waist and the other end around his own wrist. The priest had a shifty eye and a ferrety face that Schreuder trusted not at all.

They rode in double file along the narrow valley, and although the moon had risen an hour before the rocky sides still threw the sun's heat into their faces. Schreuder had selected the fifteen most trustworthy men from his regiment, and all were mounted on fast horses. The tack had been carefully muffled and their weapons wrapped in cloth so they made no sound in the night.

The priest held up his hand suddenly. 'Stop here!' Schreuder repeated the order in a whisper.

'I must go forward to see if the way is clear,' said the priest.

'I will go with you.' Schreuder dismounted and shortened his grip on the chain. They left the rest of the band in the bottom of the wadi and crawled up the steep side.

'There is the monastery.' The priest pointed at the massive square bulk that squatted on the hills above them, blotting out half the stars from the night sky. 'Flash twice and then twice again,' he said.

Schreuder aimed the small lantern towards the walls of the monastery and flipped open the shutter that screened the flame. Twice, and then again, he flashed the signal, and they waited. Nothing happened.

'If you are playing with me, I will hack off your head with the back of my sword,' Schreuder growled, and felt the little priest shiver beside him.

'Flash again!' he pleaded, and Schreuder repeated the signal. Suddenly a weak speck of light glimmered briefly on the top of the wall. Twice it showed, and then was extinguished.

'We can go on,' whispered the priest excitedly, but Schreuder restrained him.

'What have you told those within the monastery who will help us to enter?'

'They have been told that we are spiriting away the Emperor and the Tabernacle to a safe place to save him from an assassination plot by a great noble of the Galla faction who seeks to take the crown of Prester John from him.'

'A good plan,' Schreuder murmured, and urged the priest down the bank to where the horses waited. Their guide led them onwards, and they climbed another deep ravine until they were beneath the massive, looming walls.

'Leave the horses here,' whispered the priest. His voice was tremulous.

Schreuder's men dismounted and handed their reins to two comrades, who had been delegated as horse-holders. Schreuder assembled the raiding party and led them after the priest to the wall. A rope-ladder dangled down from the heights, and in the darkness Schreuder could not see to the top of it.

'I have kept my side of the bargain,' muttered the priest. 'Another will meet you at the top. Do you have the reward that I was promised?'

'You have done well,' Schreuder agreed readily. 'It is in my saddle-bags. One of my men will see you back to the horses and give it to you.'

He passed the end of the chain to his lieutenant. 'Look after him well, Ezekiel,' he said in Arabic, so the priest could understand. 'Give him the reward he has earned.'

Ezekiel led the man away, and Schreuder waited a few minutes until there was a grunt of shock and surprise out of the darkness and the soft rush of air escaping through a severed windpipe. Ezekiel returned silently, wiping his dagger on a fold of his turban.

'That was neatly done,' said Schreuder.

'My knife is sharp,' said Ezekiel, and slid the blade back into its sheath.

Schreuder stepped onto the bottom rung of the ladder and began to climb. Fifty feet up he reached a narrow embrasure cut back into the wall. It was just wide enough to squeeze his shoulders through. Another priest waited for him in the tiny stone cell beyond.

One after the other Schreuder's men followed him up and slid over the lintel, until all of them were crowded into the room.

'Lead us to the infant first!' Schreuder ordered the priest, and placed his hand on his bony shoulder. His men followed along the dark, winding passageways, each gripping the shoulder of the man in front.

They twisted and turned through the dark labyrinth, until at last they descended a spiral staircase and saw a glimmer of light ahead. It grew stronger as they crept towards it until they reached a doorway, on either side of which torches guttered in their brackets. Two guards lay huddled on the threshold, with their weapons laid beside them.

'Kill them!' Schreuder whispered to Ezekiel.

'They are dead already,' said the priest. Schreuder touched one with his foot: the guard's arm flopped over lifelessly and the empty bowl that had held the poisoned mead rolled from his hand.

The priest tapped a signal on the door, and the locking bar was lifted on the far side. The door swung open and a nursemaid stood on the other side with a child in her arms, her eyes huge with terror in the light of the torches.

'Is this the one?' Schreuder lifted the fold of blanket and peered into the child's sweet brown face. His eyes were closed in sleep, and the dark curls were damp with perspiration.

'This is the one,' the priest confirmed.

Schreuder took a firm grip on the nursemaid's arm, and drew her out beside him. 'Now lead me to the other thing,' he said softly.

They went on, deeper into the maze of dark halls and narrow corridors, until they reached another heavy studded door before which lay the bodies of four priests, contorted in the agony of their poisoned deaths. The guide knelt beside one and groped in his robes. When he stood again he had in his hands a massive iron key. He fitted it to the lock and stood back.

Schreuder called Ezekiel to him in a whisper and placed the nursemaid in his hands. 'Guard her well!' Then he stepped up to the door and seized the bronze handle. As it swung open, the traitorous priest and even the band of raiders shrank back from the brilliance of the light that flooded out from the stone-walled crypt. After the darkness the glow of a hundred candles was dazzling.

Schreuder stepped over the threshold, then even he faltered and came to an uncertain halt. He gazed upon the Tabernacle in its suit of radiant tapestry. The angels upon the lid seemed to dance in the wavering light, and he was struck with a sense of religious awe. Instinctively he crossed himself. He tried to step forward to lay hold of one of the handles of the chest but it was as though he had encountered an invisible barrier that held him back. His breathing was hoarse and his chest felt constricted. He was filled with an irrational urge to turn and run, and he recoiled a pace before he could check himself. Slowly he backed out of the crypt.

'Ezekiel!' he said hoarsely. 'I will take care of the woman and the child. With Mustapha to help you, do you take hold of the chest.'

The two Muslims suffered from no religious qualms; they stepped forward eagerly and seized the handles. The Tabernacle was surprisingly light, almost weightless. They bore it effortlessly between them.

'Our horses will be waiting at the main gate,' Schreuder told their guide in Arabic. 'Take us there!'

They moved swiftly through the dark passages. Once they ran unexpectedly into another white-robed priest, who was shuffling around an angle in the corridor towards them. In the uncertain light of the torches he saw the Tabernacle in the hands of the two armed soldiers, screamed with horror at the sacrilege and fell to his knees. Schreuder had the woman's arm in his left hand and the naked Neptune sword in his right. He killed the kneeling priest with a single thrust through his ribs.

They all listened quietly for a while, but there was no outcry.

'Lead on!' Schreuder ordered.

Their guide stopped again suddenly. 'The gate is only a short distance ahead. There are three men in the guardroom beside it.' Schreuder could make out the glow of their lamp falling through the open doorway. 'I must leave you here.'

'Go with God!' said Schreuder ironically, and the man darted away.

'Ezekiel, lay down the chest. Go forward and deal with the guards.' Three of them crept down the passage, while Schreuder kept the nursemaid in his grasp. Ezekiel slipped into the guardroom. There was silence for a moment and then the clatter of something falling to the stone floor.

Schreuder winced, but all was quiet again, and Ezekiel came back. 'It is done!'

'You grow old and clumsy,' Schreuder chided him, and led them to the massive door. It took three of them to lift the great wooden beams that locked it, then Ezekiel wound the handle of the primitive winch wheel and the door trundled open.

'Keep close together now!' Schreuder warned, and led them in a running group across the bridge and out onto the rocky track. He paused in the moonlight and whistled once softly. There was the soft thudding of muffled hoofs, as the horse-holders left the rocks where they had been concealed. Ezekiel lifted the Tabernacle onto the pack saddle of the spare horse, and lashed it securely in place. Then each man seized the reins of his own mount and swung up into the saddle. Schreuder reached down and lifted the sleeping child out of the arms of his nursemaid. The boy squawked drowsily but Schreuder hushed him and settled him firmly on the pommel of his saddle.

'Go!' he ordered the nursemaid. 'You are no longer needed.'

'I cannot leave my baby.' The woman's voice was high and agitated.

Schreuder leaned down again and, with a thrust of the Neptune sword, killed the nursemaid cleanly. He left her lying beside the track and led the raiding party away down the mountainside.

'Two of the priests from the monastery were able to follow the blasphemers when they fled,' Judith Nazet explained to Hal. Even in the face of disaster her lips was firm and her eyes calm and steady. He admired her fortitude, and saw how she had been able to take command of a broken army and turn it victorious.

'Where are they now?' Hal demanded. He was so shaken by the dreadful news that it was difficult to think clearly and logically.

'They rode directly from the monastery to Tenwera. They reached there just before dawn, three hours ago, and there was a great ship waiting for them, anchored in the bay.'

'Did they describe this vessel to you?' Hal demanded.

'Yes, it was the privateer that has the commission of the Mogul. The one we spoke of before, at our last meeting. The same one that has caused such havoc amongst our fleet of transports.'

'The Buzzard!' Hal exclaimed.

'Yes, that is what he is called even by his allies.' Judith nodded.

'While my people watched from the cliffs, a small boat took both the Emperor and the Tabernacle out to where this ship was anchored. As soon as they were aboard the Buzzard weighed anchor and set out to sea.'

'Which direction?'

'When he was out of the bay, he turned south.'

'Yes, of course.' Hal nodded. 'He will have been ordered to take Iyasu and the Tabernacle to Muscat, or even to India, to the realm of the Great Mogul.'

'I have already sent one of our fastest ships to follow him. It was only an hour or so behind him and the wind is light. It is a small dhow and could never attack such a powerful ship as his. But if God is merciful it should still be shadowing him.'

'We must follow at once.' He turned away and called urgently to Ned Tyler. 'Bring her around, and lay her on the opposite tack. Set all sail, every yard of canvas you can cram onto her. Course is south-south-east for the Bab El Mandeb.'

He took Judith's arm, the first time he had ever touched her, and led her down to his cabin. 'You are weary,' he said. 'I can see it in your eyes.'

'No, Captain,' she replied. 'It is not weariness you see, but sorrow. If you cannot save us, then all is lost. A king, a country, a faith.'

'Please sit,' he insisted. 'I will show you what we must do.' He opened the chart in front of her. 'The Buzzard might sail straight across to the western coast of Arabia. If he does that then we have lost. Even in this ship I cannot hope to catch him before he reaches the other shore.'

The early-morning sun shone in through the stern windows, and cruelly showed up the marks of anguish chiselled into her lovely face. It was a terrible thing for Hal to see the pain his words had caused, and he looked down at the chart to spare her.

'However, I do not believe that that is what he will do. If he sails directly to Arabia, the Emperor and the Tabernacle would have a dangerous and difficult overland journey to reach either Muscat or India.' He shook his head. 'No. He will sail south through the Bab El Mandeb.'

Hal placed his finger on the narrow entrance to the Red Sea. 'If we can reach there before he does, then he cannot avoid us. The Bab is too narrow. We must be able to catch him there.'

'God grant it!' Judith prayed.

'I have a long account to settle with the Buzzard,' Hal said grimly. 'I ache in every part of my body and soul to have him under my guns.'

Judith looked up at him in consternation. 'You cannot fire upon his ship.'

'What do you mean?' He stared back at her.

'He has the Emperor and the Tabernacle on board with him. You cannot risk destroying either of those.'

As he realized the truth of what she had said Hal felt his spirits quail. He would have to run down the *Gull of Moray* and close with her while the Buzzard fired his broadsides into the *Golden Bough* and he could make no reply. He could imagine the terrible punishment they would have to endure, the cannonballs ripping through the hull of his ship and the slaughter on her decks, before they could board the *Gull*.

The *Golden Bough* ran on into the south. At the end of the forenoon watch Hal assembled all the men in the waist of the ship and told them of the task he demanded of them. 'I will not hide it from you, lads. The Buzzard will be able to have his way with us, and we will not be able to fire back.' They were silent and sober-faced. 'But think how sweet it will be when we go aboard the *Gull* and take the steel to them.'

They cheered him then, but there was fear in their eyes when he sent them back to trim the sails and coax every inch of speed out of the ship in her flight towards the Bab El Mandeb.

'You promise them death, and they cheer you,' Judith Nazet said softly, when they were alone. 'Yet you call me a leader of men.' He thought he heard more than respect in her tone.

Half-way through the first dog watch there was a hail from the masthead. 'Sail ho! Full on the bow!'

Hal's pulse raced. Could they have caught the Buzzard so soon? He snatched the speaking trumpet from its bracket. 'Masthead! What do you make of her?'

'Lateen rig!' His heart sank. 'A small ship. On the same course as we are.'

Judith said quietly. 'It could be the one I sent to follow the *Gull*.'

Gradually they gained on the other vessel, and within half an hour it was hull up from the deck. Hal handed his telescope to Judith and she studied it carefully. 'Yes. It is my scout.' She lowered the glass. 'Can you fly the white cross to allay their fears, then take me close enough to speak to her?'

They passed her so closely that they could look down onto her single deck. Judith shouted a question in Geez, then listened to the faint reply.

She turned back to Hal, her eyes bright with excitement. 'You were right. They have been following the *Gull* since dawn. Until only a few hours ago they had her top sails in sight but then the wind strengthened and she pulled away from them.'

'What course was she on when last they saw her?'

'The same course she has held all this day,' Judith told him. 'Due south, heading straight for the narrows of the Bab.'

Though he entreated her to go down to his cabin and rest, Judith insisted on staying beside him on the quarterdeck. They spoke little, for both were too tense and fearful, but slowly there came over them a feeling of companionship. They took comfort from each other, and drew on a mutual reserve of strength and determination.

Every few minutes Hal looked up at his funereal black sails, then crossed to the binnacle. There was no order he could give the helm, for Ned Tyler was steering her fine as she could sail.

A charged and poignant silence lay heavy on the ship. No man shouted or laughed. The off-duty watch did not doze in the shade of the main sail as was their usual practice but huddled in small silent groups, alert to every move he made and to every word he uttered.

The sun made its majestic circle of the sky and drooped down to touch the far western hills. Night came upon them as stealthily as an assassin, and the horizon blurred and melded with the darkening sky, then was gone.

In the darkness he felt Judith's hand on his arm. It was smooth and warm, yet strong. 'We have lost them, but it is not your fault,' she said softly. 'No man could have done more.'

'I have not yet failed,' he said. 'Have faith in God and trust in me.'

'But in darkness? Surely the Buzzard would not show a light, and by dawn tomorrow he will be through the Bab and into the open sea.'

He wanted to tell her that all of this had been ordained long ago, that he was sailing south to meet a special destiny. Even though this might seem fanciful to her, he had to tell her. 'Judith,' he said, then paused as he sought the right words.

'Deck!' Aboli's voice boomed out of the darkness high above. It had a timbre and resonance to it that made Hal's skin prickle and the hairs at the back of his neck stand.

'Masthead!' he bellowed back.

'A light dead ahead!'

He placed one arm around Judith's shoulders and she made no move to pull away from him. Instead, she leaned closer.

'There is the answer to your question,' he whispered.

'God has provided for us,' she replied.

'I must go aloft.' Hal dropped his arm from around her shoulders. 'Perhaps we are too hasty, and the devil is playing us tricks.' He strode across to Ned. 'Dark ship, Mr Tyler. I'll keel haul the man who shows a light. Silent ship, no sound or voice.' He went to the mainmast shrouds.

Hal climbed swiftly until he had joined Aboli. 'Where is this light?' He scanned the darkness ahead. 'I see nothing.'

'It has gone, but it was almost dead ahead.'

533

'A star in your eye, Aboli?'

'Wait, Gundwane. It was a small light and far away.'

The minutes passed slowly, and then suddenly Hal saw it. Not even a glimmer, but a soft luminescence, so nebulous that he doubted his eyes, especially as Aboli beside him had shown no sign of seeing it. Hal looked away to rest his eyes then turned back and saw in the darkness that it was still there, too low for a star, a weird unnatural glow.

'Yes, Aboli. I see it now.' As he spoke it became brighter, and Aboli exclaimed also. Then it died away again.

'It could be a strange vessel, not the *Gull*.'

'Surely the Buzzard would not be so careless as to show a running light.'

'A lantern in the stern cabin? The reflection from his binnacle?'

'Or one of his sailors enjoying a quiet pipe?'

'Let us pray that it is one of those. It is where we could expect the Buzzard to be,' said Hal. 'We will keep after it until moonrise.'

They stayed together, peering ahead into the night. Sometimes the strange light showed as a distinct point, at others it was a faint amorphous glow, and often it disappeared. Once it was gone completely for a terrifying half hour, before it shone again perceptibly stronger.

'We are gaining,' Hal dared whisper. 'How far off now, do you reckon?'

'A league,' said Aboli, 'maybe less.'

'Where is the moon?' Hal looked into the east, 'Will it never rise?'

He saw the first iridescence beyond the dark mountains of Arabia and, shyly as a bride, the moon unveiled her face. She laid down a silver path upon the waters, and Hal felt his breath lock in his chest and every sinew of his body drawn tight as a bowstring.

Out of the darkness ahead appeared a lovely apparition, soft as a cloud of opaline mist.

'There she is!' he whispered. He had to draw a deep breath to steady his voice. 'The *Gull of Moray* dead ahead.'

He grasped Aboli's arm. 'Do you go down and warn Ned Tyler and Big Daniel. Stay there until you can see the *Gull* from the deck, then come back.'

When Aboli was gone he watched the shape of the *Gull*'s sails firm and harden in the moonlight, and he felt fear as he had seldom known it in his life, fear not only for himself but for the men who trusted him and the woman on the deck below and the child aboard the other ship. How could he hope to lay the *Golden Bough* alongside the *Gull* while she fired her broadsides into them, and they could make no reply? How many must die in the next hour and who would be among them? He though of Judith Nazet's proud slim body torn by flying grape. 'Do not let it happen, Lord God. You have taken from me already more than I can bear. How much more? How much more will you ask of me?'

He saw the light again on board the other ship. It glowed from the tall windows in her stern. Were there candles burning in there? He stared until his eyes ached, but there was no single source to the emanation of light.

There was a light touch on his arm. He had not heard Aboli climb back to him. 'The *Gull* is in sight from the deck,' he told Hal softly.

Hal could not leave the masthead yet, for he felt a sense of religious dread as he stared at the strange light in the *Gull's* stern.

''Tis no lamp or lantern or candle, Aboli,' he said. ''Tis the Tabernacle of Mary that glows in the darkness. A beacon to guide me to my destiny.'

Aboli shivered beside him. ''Tis true that it is a light not of this world, a fairy light, such as I have never seen before.' His voice shook. 'But how do you know, Gundwane? How can you be so sure that it is the talisman that burns so?'

'Because I know,' said Hal simply, and as he said it the light died away before their eyes, and the *Gull* was dark. Only her moonlit sails towered before them.

'It was a sign,' Aboli murmured.

'Yes, it was a sign,' said Hal, and his voice was strong and serene once again. 'God has given me a sign.'

They climbed down to the deck, and Hal went directly to the helm. 'There she is, Mr Tyler.' They both looked ahead to where the *Gull's* canvas shone in the moonlight.

'Aye, there she is, Captain.'

'Douse the light in the binnacle. Lay me alongside the *Gull*, if you please. Have four spare helmsmen standing by to take the whipstaff when the others are killed.'

'Aye, Sir Hal.'

Hal went forward. Big Daniel's figure emerged out of the darkness. 'Grappling irons, Master Daniel?'

'All ready, Captain. Me and ten of my strongest men will heave them.'

'Nay, Daniel, leave that to John Lovell. I have better work for you and Aboli. Come with me.'

He led Daniel and Aboli back to where Judith Nazet stood at the foot of the mainmast.

'The two of you will go with General Nazet. Take ten of your best seamen. Do not get caught up in the fighting on deck. Swift as you can, get down to the *Gull's* stern cabin. There you will find the Tabernacle and the child. Bring them out. Nothing must turn you aside from that purpose. Do you understand?'

'How do you know where they are holding the Emperor and the Tabernacle?' Judith Nazet asked quietly.

'I know,' Hal said, with such finality that she was silent. He wanted to order her to stay in a safe place until the fight was over, but he knew she would refuse – and besides which there was no safe place when two ships of such force were locked in mortal combat.

'Where will you be, Gundwane?' Aboli asked softly.

'I shall be with the Buzzard,' Hal said, and left them without another word.

He went towards the bows, pausing as he reached each of the divisions who crouched below the gunwale, and speaking softly to their boatswains. 'God love you, Samuel Moone. We might have to take a shot or two before we board her, but think of the pleasure that waits you on the *Gull*'s deck.'

To Jiri he said, 'This will be such a fight as you will boast of to your grandchildren.'

He had a word for each, then stood once more in the bows and looked across at the *Gull*. She was a cable's length ahead now, sailing on serenely under her moon-radiant canvas.

'Lord, keep us hidden from them,' he whispered, and looked up at his own black sails, a tall dark pyramid against the stars.

Slowly, achingly slowly they closed the gap. She cannot elude us now, Hal thought, with grim satisfaction. We are too close.

Suddenly there came a wild scream of terror from the *Gull*'s masthead. 'Sail ho! Dead astern! The *Golden Bough*!'

Then all was shouting and confusion on the other ship's deck. There was the savage beat of a drum calling the Buzzard's crew to battle quarters, and the rush of many feet on her planking. A loud series of crashes as her gunports were flung open, and then the squeal and rumble as the guns were run out. From twenty points along her dark rail came the glow of slow-match burning, and the glint of their reflection from steel.

'Light the battle lamps!' Hal heard the Buzzard's bellows of rage as he drove his panicky crew to their stations, then clearly his order to the helm. 'Hard to larboard! Lay the bastards under our broadside! We'll give them such a good sniff of gunsmoke that they'll fart it in the devil's face when we send them down to hell.'

The *Gull*'s battle lanterns flared, as she lit up to give her gunners light to work. In their yellow glow Hal glimpsed the Buzzard's bush of red hair.

Then the silhouette of the *Gull* altered rapidly as she came around. Hal nodded, the Buzzard had acted instinctively but unwisely. In his position Hal would have stood off and shot the *Golden Bough* to a wreck while she was unable to reply. Now he would have to be fortunate and quick to get off one steady broadside before the *Golden Bough* was upon him.

Hal grinned. The Buzzard was the victim of his own iniquity. Probably it had not even entered his calculations that Hal would hold his fire on account of a child and an ancient relic. If he were in the same position as Hal, the Buzzard would have blazed away with all his cannon.

As the *Gull* came slowly around, the *Golden Bough* flew at her and, for a moment, Hal thought they might be alongside her before her guns could bear.

They closed the last hundred yards and Ned had already given the order to shorten to fighting sail, when the *Gull* turned through the last few degrees of arc and all her guns were aimed straight at where Hal stood.

Looking directly into the *Gull*'s battery, Hal's eyeballs were seared by the brilliant crimson glow as she fired her broadside into the *Golden Bough* at point-blank range.

A tempest of disrupted air struck them so viciously that Hal was hurled backwards and thought that he had been hit by a ball. The deck around him dissolved into a buzzing storm of splinters and the knot of Amadoda nearest him were struck squarely and blown into nothingness. The *Golden Bough* heeled over sharply to the weight of shot that tore through her, and the choking fog of gunsmoke drifted over her shattered hull.

The terrible silence that followed the thunder of the broadside was marred only by the screams and groans of the wounded and the dying. Then the wall of gunsmoke was blown aside, and from across the narrow gap of water came the cheering of the other crew. 'The *Gull* and Cumbrae!' and Hal heard the rumble of the gun trains as they were run in-board to be reloaded.

How many of my lads are dead? he wondered. A quarter? Half? He looked back at his own decks, but the darkness hid from his eyes the torn timbers and the heaps of dead and dying.

From across the water he heard the thudding of ramrods forcing powder and shot down the barrels of the guns. 'Faster!' he whispered. 'Faster, my darling. Close the gap and do not make us face another such blast.'

He heard the squeal of the tackle and the rumble as one of the swiftest guncrews completed loading before the others and ran out its culverin. The two ships were now so close together that Hal saw the monstrous gaping barrel come poking out through its gunport. With the muzzle almost touching the *Golden Bough*'s side it roared again, and timbers shattered and men screamed as the heavy ball tore through them.

Then before any more of the *Gull*'s guns could be run out, the two ships came together with a rending, grinding crash. In the light of the *Gull*'s battle lanterns Hal saw the grappling hooks hurled over her side and heard them clatter on her deck. He did not hesitate but sprang to the gunwale and leaped across the narrow strip of water as the two hulls surged alongside each other. He landed lightly as a cat among the nearest of the Buzzard's guncrews and killed two men before they could draw their cutlasses.

Then a wave of his boarders followed him over her side, led by the Amadoda armed with pike and axe. Within seconds the *Gull*'s upper deck was transformed into a battlefield. Men fought chest to chest and hand to hand, shouting and yelling with rage and terror.

'El Tazar!' roared the men of the *Golden Bough*, to be answered by, 'The *Gull* and Cumbrae!' as they came together.

Hal found himself confronted by four men simultaneously and was driven back to the rail before John Lovell tore into them from behind and killed one with a thrust between the shoulder-blades. Hal killed another as he hesitated and the other two broke and ran. Hal had a moment to look about him. He saw the Buzzard on the far side of the deck, roaring with rage, the great claymore swinging high above his head as he hacked down the men in front of him.

Then from the corner of his eye Hal caught the glint of Judith Nazet's steel helmet and, towering on each side of her, the forms of Aboli and Big Daniel. They drove across the deck and disappeared down the companionway to the stern cabin. That moment of distraction might have cost Hal his life for a man stabbed at him with a pike, and he turned only just in time to avoid the thrust. Then he was in the midst of the fight again as it swayed back and forth across the deck.

He put down another man with a thrust in the belly, then looked about for the Buzzard. He saw him in the waist, and shouted at him, 'Cumbrae, I am coming for you!' But in the uproar the Buzzard did not look round at him, and Hal started towards him cutting a path for himself through the mob of fighting men.

At that moment one of the main shrouds was cut loose by a swinging axe that missed the head at which it was aimed, and the battle lantern that was suspended from it came crashing to the deck at Hal's feet. He sprang back from the blaze of burning oil that roared up into his face then gathered himself and leapt through the flames to reach the Buzzard.

He landed on the far side and looked about him swiftly, but the Buzzard had disappeared and instead two of his sailors charged at Hal. He took them on and slashed through the sinews of an extended sword arm as one lunged at him. Then, in the same movement, he changed cut to thrust and drove his point deeply into the second man's throat.

He recovered and glanced back over his shoulder. The flames from the shattered lantern had taken hold and were lighting the deck brightly. Streamers of fire were running up the dangling shroud towards the rigging. Through the dancing flames he saw Judith Nazet leap out of the entrance to the stern companionway. She was followed closely by Big Daniel carrying the Tabernacle of Mary, balanced easily on his shoulder as though it were light as a down-filled bolster. The golden angels on its lid sparkled in the light of the flames.

A sailor rushed at Judith with his pike, and Hal shouted with horror as the gleaming spearhead struck her full in the side under her raised arm. It tore through the thin cotton of her tunic, but glanced harmlessly off the shirt of steel chain-mail beneath the cloth. Judith whirled like an angry panther, and her blade flashed as she aimed at his face. Such was the fury of her blow that the point came out of the back of the pirate's skull, and the man dropped at her feet.

Judith's fierce dark eyes met Hal's across the teeming deck.

'Iyasu!' she shouted. 'He is gone!'

The flames were leaping up between them, and Hal yelled through them, 'Go with Daniel! Get off this ship! Take the Tabernacle to safety on the *Golden Bough*. I will find Iyasu.'

She neither argued nor hesitated but ran, with Daniel beside her, to the rail and leaped across onto the *Golden Bough*'s deck. Hal started to fight his way towards the companionway to reach the lower decks where the child must be hidden, but a phalanx of Amadoda led by Jiri swept across the deck and cut him off. The black warriors had locked their shields together into the solid carapace of the testudo and, with their pikes thrust through the gaps, the pirates could not stand before their charge.

In every battle there comes a moment when its outcome is decided and as the *Gull*'s sailors scattered before that rush of howling, prancing warriors it had come. The Buzzard's men were beaten.

'I must find Iyasu and get him off the *Gull* before the flames reach the powder magazine,' Hal told himself, and turned towards the break in the forecastle as his easiest access to the lower decks. At that moment a bellow stopped him dead.

The Buzzard stood on high, lit by the dancing yellow light of the flames. 'Courteney!' he roared. 'Is this what you are searching for?'

His head was bared and his tangled red locks tumbled about his face. In his right hand he held his claymore, and in his left he carried Iyasu. The child was screaming with terror as the Buzzard lifted him high. He wore only a thin nightshirt, which had rucked up above his waist, and his slender brown legs kicked frantically in the air.

'Is this what you are looking for?' the Buzzard bellowed again, and lifted the child high above his head. 'Then come and fetch the brat.'

Hal bounded forward, cutting two men out of his way, before he reached the foot of the forecastle ladder. The Buzzard watched him come. He must have known that he was beaten, with his ship in flames and his crew being cut down and hurled overboard by the rush of the pikemen, but he grinned like a gargoyle. 'Let me show you a fine little trick, Sir Henry. It's called catch the bairn on the steel.'

With a sweep of his thick hairy arm he threw the child fifteen feet straight up in the air, and then held the point of the claymore beneath him as he dropped.

'No!' Hal screamed wildly.

At the last instant before the child was impaled on the point the Buzzard flicked aside the sword and Iyasu fell back unscathed into his grasp.

'Parley!' Hal shouted. 'Give me the child unharmed and you can go free, with all your booty.'

'What a bargain! But my ship is burned and my booty with it.'

'Listen to me,' Hal pleaded. 'Let the boy go free.'

'How can I refuse a brother Knight?' the Buzzard asked, still spluttering with laughter. 'You shall have what you ask. There! I set the little black bastard free.' With another mighty swing of his arm he hurled Iyasu far out over the ship's side. The child's shirt fluttered around his little body as he fell. Then, with only a soft splash, the dark sea swallowed him.

Behind him Hal heard Judith Nazet scream. He dropped his sword to the deck and with three running strides reached the rail and dived head first over the side. He struck the water and knifed deep, then turned for the surface.

Looking up from twenty feet deep, the water was clear as mountain air. He could see the weed-fouled bottom of the *Gull* drifting past him, and the reflection of the flames from the burning ship dancing on the surface ripple. Then, between him and the firelight, he saw a small dark shape. The tiny limbs were struggling like a fish in a net and silver bubbles streamed from Iyasu's mouth as he turned end over end in the wake of the hull.

Hal struck out with arms and legs and reached him before he was whirled away. Holding him to his chest he shot to the surface, and lifted the child's face clear.

Iyasu struggled feebly, coughing and choking, then he let out a thin, terrified wail. 'Blow it all out of you,' said Hal, and looked around.

Big Daniel must have recalled his men, then cut the grappling lines to get the *Golden Bough* away from the burning hull. The two ships were drifting apart. The seamen from the *Gull* were leaping over her sides as the heat of the flames washed over them and her main sail caught fire. The *Gull* began to sail with flaming canvas and no hand on her helm. She bore down slowly on where Hal trod water, and he struck out desperately with one hand, dragging Iyasu out of her path.

For a long, dreadful minute it seemed that they would be trodden under, then a fluke of the wind pushed the bows across a point and she passed less than a boat's length from them.

With amazement Hal saw that the Buzzard still stood alone on the break of the forecastle. The flames surrounded him, but he did not seem to feel their heat. His beard began to smoke and blacken, but he looked down at Hal and choked with laughter. He gasped for breath then opened his mouth to shout something to him, but at that moment the *Gull's* foresail sheets burned clean through and the huge spread of canvas came floating down, covering the Buzzard. From under that burning shroud Hal heard one last terrible shriek and then the flames leapt high, and the stricken *Gull* bore away her master on the wind.

Hal watched him go until the swells of the ocean intervened and he lost sight of the burning ship. Then a freak wave lifted him and the child high. The *Gull* was a league off, and at that instant the flames must have reached her powder magazine for she blew up with a devastating roar, and Hal felt the waters constrict his chest as the force of the explosion was transmitted through them. He watched still as burning timbers were hurled high into the night sky then fell to quench in the dark waters. Darkness and silence descended again.

There was neither sight nor sign of the *Golden Bough* in the night. The child was weeping piteously, and Hal had no word of Geez to comfort him, so he held his head clear and spoke to him in English. 'There's a good strong lad. You have to be brave, for you are born an Emperor, and I know for certain that an Emperor never cries.' But Hal's boots and sodden clothing were drawing him down, and he had to swim hard to resist. He kept the two of them afloat for the rest of that long night, but in the dawn he knew that he was near the end of his strength and the child was shivering and whimpering softly in his arms. 'Not long now, Iyasu, and it will be bright day,' he croaked through his salt-scalded throat, but he knew that neither of them could last that long.

'Gundwane!' He heard a well-beloved voice call to him, but he knew it was delirium and he laughed aloud. 'Don't play tricks on me now,' he said, 'I do not have the stomach for it. Let me be in peace.'

Then, out of the darkness, he saw a shape emerge, heard the splash of oars pulling hard towards him, and the voice called again, 'Gundwane!'

'Aboli!' his voice cracked. 'I am here!'

Those great black hands reached down and seized him, lifted him and the child over the side of the longboat. As soon as he was aboard Hal looked about him. With all her lanterns lit, the *Golden Bough* lay hove to half a league across the water but Judith Nazet sat before him in the stern sheets and she took the child from Hal and wrapped him in her cloak. She crooned to Iyasu and spoke soothingly to him in Geez, while the crew pulled back towards the ship. Before they reached the *Golden Bough* Iyasu was asleep in her arms.

'The Tabernacle?' Hal asked Aboli hoarsely. 'Is it safe?'

'It is in your cabin,' Aboli assured him, and then dropped his voice. 'All of this is as your father foretold. At last the stars must set you free, for you have fulfilled the prophecy.'

Hal felt a deep sense of fulfilment come over him, and the desperate weariness slid from his shoulders like a discarded mantle. He felt light and free as though released from some long, onerous penance. He looked across at Judith, who had been watching him. There was something in her dark gaze that he could not fathom, but she dropped her eyes before he could read it clearly. Hal wanted to move closer to her, to touch her, speak to her and tell her about these strange, powerful feelings that possessed him, but four ranks of rowers separated them in the small, crowded boat.

As they approached the *Golden Bough* her crew were in the rigging and they cheered him as the longboat latched onto her chains. Aboli offered Hal a hand to help him climb the ladder to the deck but Hal ignored it and went up alone. He paused as he saw the long line of canvas-shrouded corpses laid out in the waist, and the terrible damage that the *Gull's* gunfire had wrought to his ship. But this was not the time to brood on that, he thought. They would send the dead men overside and mourn them later, but now was the hour of victory. Instead he looked around the grinning faces of his crew. 'Well, you ruffians paid out the Buzzard and his cutthroats in a heavier coin than they bargained for. Mr Tyler, break out the rum barrel and give a double ration to every hand aboard to toast the Buzzard on his way to hell. Then set a course back to Mitsiwa roads.'

He took the child from Judith Nazet's arms and carried him down to the stern cabin. He laid him on the bunk, and turned to Judith who stood close beside him. 'He is a sturdy lad, and has come to little harm. We should let him sleep.'

'Yes,' she said quietly, looking up at him with that same inscrutably dark gaze. Then she took his hand and led him to the curtained alcove where the Tabernacle of Mary stood.

'Will you pray with me, El Tazar?' she asked, and they knelt together.

'We thank you, Lord, for sparing the life of our Emperor, your tiny servant, Iyasu. We thank you for delivering him from the wicked hands of the blasphemer. We ask your blessing upon his arms in the conflict that lies ahead. When the victory is won, we beseech you, Lord, to grant him a long and peaceful reign. Make him a wise and gentle monarch. For thy name's sake, Amen!'

'Amen!' Hal echoed, and made to rise, but she restrained him with a hand on his arm.

'We thank you also, Lord God, for sending to us your good and faithful Henry Courteney, without whose valour and selfless service the godless would have triumphed. May he be fully rewarded by the gratitude of all the people of Ethiopia, and by the love and admiration that your servant, Judith Nazet, has conceived towards him.'

Hal felt the shock of her words reverberate through his whole body and turned to look at her, but her eyes were closed. He thought that he had misheard her, but then her grip on his arm tightened. She stood and drew him up with her.

Still without looking at him she led him out of the main cabin to the small adjoining one, closed the door and bolted it.

'Your clothes are wet,' she said, and, like a handmaiden, began to undress him. Her movements were calm and slow. She touched his chest when it was bared and ran her long brown fingers down his flanks. She knelt before him to loosen his belt and peel down his breeches. When he was completely naked she stared at his manhood with a dark profound gaze, but without touching him there. She rose to her feet, took his hand and led him to the hard wooden bunk. He tried to pull her down beside him, but she pushed away his hands.

Standing before him she began to undress. She unlaced the chain-mail shirt, which fell to the deck around her feet. Beneath the heavy, masculine, warlike garb, her body was a paradox of femininity. Her skin was a translucent amber. Her breasts were small, but the nipples were hard, round and dark red as ripe berries. Her lean hips were sculpted into the sweet sweep of her waist. The bush of curls that covered her mount of Venus was crisp and a lustrous black.

At last she came to where he lay, and stooped over and kissed deeply into his mouth. Then she gave an urgent little cry and with a lithe movement fell upon him. He was astonished by the strength and suppleness of her body as he reached up and cleaved to her.

In the late afternoon of that hot, dreamlike day, they were aroused by the crying of the child in the cabin next door. Judith sighed but rose immediately. While she dressed she watched him as though she wished to remember every detail of his face and body. Then, as she laced her armour she came to stand over him, 'Yes, I do love you. But, in the same fashion as he chose you, God has singled me out for a special task. I must see the boy Emperor safely installed upon the throne of Prester John in Aksum.' She was silent a while longer, then said softly, 'If I kiss you again, I may lose my resolve. Goodbye, Henry Courteney. I wish with all my heart that I were a common maid and that it could have been otherwise.' She strode to the door and went to wait upon her King.

Hal anchored off the beach in Mitsiwa roads and lowered the longboat. Reverently Daniel Fisher placed the Tabernacle of Mary on its floorboards. Judith Nazet, in full armour and war helmet, stood in the bows holding the hand of the little boy beside her. Hal took the tiller and ten seamen rowed them in through the low surf towards the beach.

Bishop Fasilides and fifty war captains waited for them on the red sands. Ten thousand warriors lined the cliffs above. As they recognized their general and their monarch, they began to cheer and the cheering swept away across the plain, until it was carried by fifty thousand voices to echo along the desert hills.

Those regiments that had lost heart and were already on the road back to the mountains and the far interior, believing themselves deserted by their General and their Emperor, heard the sound and turned back. Rank upon rank, column upon column, a mighty confluence, the hoofs of their horses raising a tall cloud of red dust, their weapons sparkling in the sunlight and their voices swelling the triumphant chorus, they came pouring back out of the hills.

Fasilides came forward to greet Iyasu, as he stepped ashore, hand in hand with Judith. The fifty captains knelt in the sand, raised their swords and called down God's blessings upon him. Then they crowded forward and competed fiercely for the honour of bearing the Tabernacle of Mary upon their shoulders. Singing a battle hymn, they wound in procession up the cliff path.

Judith Nazet mounted her black stallion with its golden chest armour and its crest of ostrich feathers. She wheeled the horse and urged him, rearing and prancing, to where Hal stood at the water's edge.

'If the battle goes with us, the pagan will try to escape by sea. Visit the wrath and the vengeance of Almighty God upon him with your fair ship,' she ordered. 'If the battle goes against us, have the *Golden Bough* waiting here at this place to take the Emperor to safety.'

'I will be here waiting for you, General Nazet.' Hal looked up at her and tried to give the words a special emphasis.

She leaned down from the saddle and her eyes were dark and bright behind the steel nose-piece of her helmet, but he could not be sure whether the brightness was warrior ferocity or the tears of the lost lover.

'I will wish all the days of my life that it could have been otherwise, El Tazar.' She straightened up, wheeled the stallion away and went up the cliff path. The Emperor Iyasu turned in Bishop Fasilides' arms and waved back at Hal. He called something in Geez, and his high, piping voice carried down faintly to where Hal stood at the water's edge, but he understood not a word of it.

He waved back and shouted, 'You too, lad! You too!'

The *Golden Bough* put out to sea and, beyond the fifty-fathom line with their heads bared in the stark African sunlight, they committed their dead to the sea. There were forty-three in those canvas shrouds, men of Wales and Devon and the mysterious lands along the Zambere River, all comrades now for ever.

Then Hal ran the ship back into the shallow protected waters where he put every man to work repairing the battle damage and recharging the powder magazine with the munitions that General Nazet sent out from the shore.

On the third morning he woke in the darkness to the sound of the guns. He went on deck immediately. Aboli was standing by the lee rail. 'It has begun, Gundwane. The General has pitted her army against El Grang in the final battle.'

They stood together at the rail and looked towards the dark shore, where the far hills were lit by the hellish flashes of the battlefield and a vast pall of dust and smoke climbed slowly into the windless sky and billowed out into the anvil shape of a tall tropical thunderhead.

'If El Grang is beaten, he will try to escape with all his army across the sea to Arabia,' Hal told Ned Tyler and Aboli, as they listened to the ceaseless pandemonium of the cannon. 'Weigh anchor and put the ship on a southerly course. We will go down to meet the fugitives as they try to escape from Adulis Bay.'

It was past noon when the *Golden Bough* took up her station off the mouth of the bay and shortened sail. The sound of the guns never ceased and Hal climbed to the masthead and focused his telescope on the wide plain beyond Zulla where the two great hosts were locked in the death struggle.

Through the curtains of dust and smoke he could make out the tiny shapes of the horsemen as they charged and counter-charged, wraithlike in the dust of their own hoofs. He saw the long flashes of the great guns, pale red in the sunlight, and the snaking regiments of foot-soldiers winding through the red fog like dying serpents, their spearheads glistening like the reptiles' scales.

Slowly the battle rolled towards the shoreline and Hal saw a charge of cavalry sweep along the top of the cliffs and tear into a loose, untidy formation of infantry. The sabres rose and fell and the foot-soldiers scattered before them. Men began to hurl themselves from the cliffs into the sea below.

'Who are they?' Hal fretted. 'Whose horses are those?' And then through the lens he made out the white cross of Ethiopia at the head of the mass of horsemen as they raced on towards Zulla.

'Nazet has beaten them,' said Aboli. 'El Grang's army is in rout!'

'Put a leadsman to take soundings, Mr Tyler. Take us in closer.'

The *Golden Bough* glided silently into the mouth of the bay, cruising only a cable's length offshore. From the masthead Hal watched the dun clouds of war roll ponderously towards the beach, and the rabble of El Grang's defeated army streaming back before the Ethiopian cavalry squadrons.

They threw down their weapons and stumbled down to the water's edge to find any vessel to take them off. A motley armada of dhows of every size and condition, packed with fugitives, set out from the beaches around the blazing port of Zulla towards the opening of the bay.

'Sweet heavens!' laughed Big Daniel. 'They are so thick upon the water that a man might cross from one side of the bay to the other over their crowded hulls without wetting his feet.'

'Run out your guns, please, Master Daniel, and let us see if we can wet more than their feet for them,' Hal ordered.

The *Golden Bough* ploughed into this vast fleet and the little boats tried to flee, but she overhauled them effortlessly and her guns began to thunder. One after the other they were shattered and capsized, and their cargoes of exhausted, defeated troops hurled into the water. Their armour bore them down swiftly.

It was such a terrible massacre that the gunners no longer cheered as they ran out the guns, but served them in grim silence. Hal walked along the batteries, and spoke to them sternly. 'I know how you feel, lads, but if you spare them now, you may have to fight them again tomorrow, and who can say that they will give you quarter if you ask for it then?'

He, also, was sickened by the slaughter, and longed for the setting of the sun, or any other chance to cease the carnage. That opportunity came from an unlooked-for direction.

Aboli left his station at the starboard battery of cannon and ran back to where Hal paced his quarterdeck. Hal looked up at him sharply, but before he could snap a reprimand, Aboli pointed out over the starboard bow.

'That ship with the red sail. The man in the stern. Do you see him, Gundwane?'

Hal felt the prickle of apprehension on his arms and the cold sweat sliding down his back as he recognized the tall figure standing and leaning back against the tiller arm. He was clean-shaven now, the spiked moustaches were gone. He wore a turban of yellow, and the heavily embroidered dolman of an Islamic grandee over baggy white breeches and soft knee-high boots, but his pale face stood out like a mirror among the dark-bearded men around him. There may have been others with the same wide set of shoulders and tall athletic figure, but none with the same sword upon the hip, in its scabbard of embossed gold.

'Bring the ship about, Mr Tyler. Heave to alongside that dhow with the red sail,' Hal ordered.

Ned looked where he pointed then swore. 'Son of a bawd, that's Schreuder! May the devil damn him to hell.'

The Arab crew ran to the side of the dhow as the tall frigate bore down upon them. They jumped overboard and tried to swim back towards the beach, choosing the sabres of the Ethiopian cavalry rather than the gaping culverins of the *Golden Bough*'s broadside. Schreuder stood alone in the stern and looked up at the frigate with his cold, unrelenting expression. As they drew closer, Hal saw that his face was streaked with dust and powder soot, and that his clothing was torn and soiled with the muck of the battlefield.

Hal strode to the rail and returned his stare. They were so close that Hal had hardly to raise his voice to make himself heard. 'Colonel Schreuder, sir, you have my sword.'

'Then, sir, would you care to come down and take it from me?' Schreuder asked.

'Mr Tyler, you have the con in my absence. Take me closer to the dhow so that I may board her.'

'This is madness, Gundwane,' Aboli said softly.

'Make sure neither you nor any man intervenes, Aboli,' Hal said, and went to the entryport. As the little dhow bobbed close alongside, he slid down the ladder and jumped across the narrow gap of water, landing lightly on her single deck.

He drew his sword and looked to the stern. Schreuder stepped away from the tiller bar and shrugged out of the stiff dolman tunic.

'You are a romantic fool, Henry Courteney,' he murmured, and the blade of the Neptune sword whispered softly from its scabbard.

'To the death?' Hal asked, as he drew his own blade.

'Naturally.' Schreuder nodded gravely. 'For I am going to kill you.'

They came together with the slow grace of two lovers beginning a minuet. Their blades met and flirted as they circled, tap and brush and slither of steel on steel, their feet never still, points held high and eyes locked.

Ned Tyler held the frigate fifty yards off, keeping that interval with deft touches of helm and trim of her shortened sails. The men lined the near rail. They were quiet and attentive. Although few understood the finer points of style and technique, they could not but be aware of the grace and beauty of this deadly ritual.

'An eye for his eyes!' Hal seemed to hear his father's voice in his head. 'Read in them his soul!'

Schreuder's face remained grave, but Hal saw the first shadow in his cold blue eyes. It was not fear, but it was respect. Even with these light touches of their blades, Schreuder had evaluated his man. Remembering their previous encounters, he had not expected to be met with such strength and skill. As for Hal he knew that, if he lived through this, he would never again dance so close to death and smell its breath as he did now.

Hal saw it in his eyes, the moment before Schreuder opened his attack, stepping in lightly and then driving at him with a rapid series of lunges. He moved back, checking each thrust but feeling the power in it. He hardly heard the excited growl of the watchers on the deck of the frigate above them, but he watched Schreuder's eyes and met him with the high point. The Dutchman drove suddenly for his throat, his first serious stroke, and the moment Hal blocked he disengaged fluidly and dropped on bent right knee and cut for Hal's ankle, the Achilles stroke intended to cripple him.

Hal vaulted lightly over the flashing golden blade but felt it tug at the heel of his boot. With both feet in the air he was momentarily out of balance and Schreuder straightened and like a striking cobra turned the angle of his blade and went for Hal's belly. Hal sprang back but felt it touch him, no pain from that razor edge but just a tiny snick. He bounced back off his left foot, and aimed for one of Schreuder's blue eyes. He saw the surprise in that eye, but then Schreuder rolled his head and the point slit his cheek.

They backed and circled, both men bleeding now. Hal felt the warm wetness soaking through the front of his shirt, and a scarlet snake ran slowly down past the corner of Schreuder's thin lips and dripped from his chin.

'First blood was mine, I think, sir?' Schreuder asked.

'It was, sir.' Hal conceded. 'But whose will be the last?' And the words were not past his lips before Schreuder attacked in earnest. While the watchers on the *Golden Bough* howled and danced with excitement, he drove Hal step by step from the stern to the bows of the dhow and pinned him there, with their blades locked, and forced his back against the gunwale. They stood like that with their blades crossed in front of their faces, and their eyes only a hand's span apart. Their breath mingled and Hal watched the drops of sweat form on Schreuder's upper lip as he strained to hold him like that.

Deliberately Hal swayed backwards, and saw the gleam of triumph in the blue eyes so close to his own, but his back was loaded like a longbow taking the weight of the archer's draw. He unleashed and, with the strength of his legs, arms and upper body, hurled Schreuder backwards. With the impetus of that movement Hal went on the attack and, their blades rasping and clashing together, he forced Schreuder back down the open deck to the stern.

With the tiller arm digging into his spine, Schreuder could retreat no further. He caught up Hal's blade and with all the power of his wrist forced him into the prolonged engagement, the ploy with which he had killed Vincent Winterton and a dozen others before him. Their swords swirled and shrilled together, a silver whirlpool of molten sunlight that held them apart yet locked them together.

On it went, and on. The sweat streamed down both their faces, and their breath came in short, urgent grunts. It was death to the first man to break. Their wrists seemed forged from the same steel as their blades, and then Hal saw something in Schreuder's eyes that he had never dreamed of seeing there. Fear.

Schreuder tried to break the circle and lock up the blades as he had with Vincent, but Hal refused and forced him on and on. He felt the first weakness in Schreuder's iron sword arm, and saw the despair in his eyes.

Then Schreuder broke, and Hal was on him in the same instant that his point dropped and his guard opened. He hit him hard in the centre of his chest and felt the point go home, strike bone, and the hilt thrill in his hand.

The roar from the men on the deck of the frigate broke over them like a wave of storm-driven surf. In the moment that Hal felt the surge of triumph and the live feeling of his blade buried deep in his opponent's flesh, Schreuder reared back and raised the gold-inlaid blade of the Neptune sword to the level of his eyes in which the sapphire lights were beginning to fade, and lunged.

The forward movement forced Hal's blade deeper into his body, but as the point of the Neptune sword flashed towards his chest Hal had no defence. He released his grip on the hilt of his own sword, and sprang back, but he could not escape the reach of the golden sword or its gimlet-sharp point.

Hal felt the hit, high in the left side of his chest, and as he reeled back felt the blade slip out of his flesh. With an effort he kept his feet, and the two men confronted each other, both hard hit but Hal disarmed and Schreuder with the Neptune sword still clutched in his right hand.

'I think I have killed you, sir,' Schreuder whispered.

'Perhaps. But I know I have killed you, sir,' Hal answered him.

'Then I will make certain of my side of it,' Schreuder grunted, and took an unsteady pace towards him, but the strength went out of his legs. He sagged forward and fell to the deck.

Painfully Hal went down on one knee beside his body. With his left hand he clutched his own chest wound, but with his right he prised open Schreuder's dead fingers from the hilt of the Neptune sword and with it in his own hand rose to face the towering deck of the *Golden Bough*.

He held the gleaming sword high, and they cheered him wildly. The sound of it echoed weirdly in Hal's ears and he blinked uncertainly as the brilliant African sunlight faded and his eyes were filled with shadows and darkness.

His legs gave way under him and he sat down heavily on the deck of the dhow, bowed forward over the sword in his lap.

He felt but did not see the frigate bump against the dhow as Ned Tyler brought her alongside, and then Aboli's hands were on his shoulders and his voice was deep and close as he lifted Hal in his arms.

'It is over now, Gundwane. All of it is done.'

N ed Tyler took the ship deeper into the bay and anchored her in the calm waters off the port of Zulla where now the white cross of Ethiopia flew above the shot-battered walls.

Hal lay for fourteen days on the bunk in the stern cabin, attended only by Aboli. On the fifteenth day Aboli and Big Daniel lifted him into one of the oak chairs and carried him up onto the deck. The men came to him one at a time with a touch of the forehead and a self-consciously muttered greeting.

Under his eye they made the ship ready for sea. The carpenters replaced the timbers that had been shot away, and the sailmakers resewed the torn sails. Big Daniel plunged overside and swam under the hull to check for damage beneath the waterline. 'She's tight and sweet as a virgin's slit,' he shouted up to the deck as he surfaced on the other side.

There were many visitors from the shore. Governors and nobles and soldiers coming with gifts to thank Hal, and to stare at him in awe. As he grew stronger, Hal was able to greet them standing on his quarterdeck. They brought news as well as gifts.

'General Nazet has borne the Emperor back to Aksum in triumph,' they told him.

Then, many days later, they said, 'Praise God, the Emperor has been crowned in Aksum. Forty thousand people came to his coronation.' Hal stared longingly at the far blue mountains, and that night slept little.

Then in the morning Ned Tyler came to him. 'The ship is ready for sea, Captain.'

'Thank you, Mr Tyler.' Hal turned from him and left him standing without orders.

Before he reached the companionway to the stern cabin, there came a hail from the masthead. 'There is a boat putting out from the port!'

Eagerly Hal strode back to the rail. He scanned the passengers, searching for a slim figure in armour with a dark halo of curls around a beloved amber face. He felt the lead of disappointment weight his limbs when he recognized only Bishop Fasilides' lanky frame and his white beard blowing over his shoulder.

Fasilides came in through the entryport and made the sign of the Cross. 'Bless this fine ship, and all the brave men who sail in her.' The rough seamen bared their heads and went down on their knees. When he had blessed each, Fasilides came to Hal. 'I come as a messenger from the Emperor.'

'God bless him!' Hal answered.

'I bring his greetings and his thanks to you and your men.'

He turned to one of the priests who followed him and took from him the heavy gold chain he carried. 'On the Emperor's behalf I bestow upon you the order of the Golden Lion of Ethiopia.' He placed the chain with its jewelled medallion around Hal's neck. 'I bring with me the prize monies that you have earned from your gallant war upon the pagan, together with the reward that the Emperor personally sends you.'

From the dhow they brought up a single small wooden chest. It was too heavy to be carried up the side, and it took four strong seamen on the block and tackle to lift it to the *Golden Bough*'s deck.

Fasilides lifted the lid of the chest and the sparkle of gold within was dazzling in the sunlight.

'Well, my lads!' Hal called to his men. 'You will have the price of a flagon of beer in your purse when next we dock in Plymouth harbour.'

'When will you sail?' Fasilides wanted to know.

'All is in readiness,' Hal replied. 'But tell me, what news of General Nazet?'

Fasilides looked at him shrewdly. 'No news. After the coronation she disappeared, and the Tabernacle of Mary with her. Some say she has gone back into the mountains, whence she came.'

Hal's face darkened. 'I will sail on tomorrow morning's tide, Father. And I thank you and the Emperor for your charity and your blessings.'

The following morning Hal was on deck two hours before sunrise, and all the ship was awake. The excitement that always attended departure gripped the *Golden Bough*. Only Hal was unaffected by it. The sense of loss and betrayal was heavy upon him. Though she had made no promise, he had hoped with all his heart that Judith Nazet might come. Now, as he made his final tour of inspection of the ship, he steadfastly refrained from looking back towards the shore.

Ned came to him. 'The tide has turned, Captain! And the wind stands fair to weather Dahlak Island on a single tack.'

Hal could delay no longer. 'Up anchor, Mr Tyler. Set all plain sail. Take us south to Elephant Lagoon. We have some unfinished business thereabouts.'

Ned Tyler and Big Daniel grinned at the prospect of reclaiming their share of the treasure that they knew was hidden there.

The canvas billowed out from her yards and the *Golden Bough* shook herself and came awake. Her bows swung round and steadied as they pointed at the entrance to the open sea.

Hal stood, his hands clasped behind his back, and stared straight ahead. Aboli came to him then with a cloak over his arm, and when Hal turned to him he shook it out and lifted it high for his appraisal.

'The *croix patté*, the same as your father wore at the beginning of every voyage.'

'Where did you get that, Aboli?'

'I had it made for you in Zulla while you lay wounded. You have earned the right to wear it.' He spread it over Hal's shoulders, and stood back to appraise him. 'You look like your father did on the first day I saw him.' Those words gave Hal such pleasure as to lighten his sombre mood.

'Deck!' The hail from the lookout rang out of the lightening sky.

'Masthead?' Hal threw his head back and looked up.

'Signal from the shore!'

Hal turned quickly with the cloak swirling about him. Above the walls of Zulla three bright red lights hung in the dawn sky, and as he watched they floated gracefully back to earth.

'Three Chinese rockets!' Aboli said. 'The recall signal.'

'Put the ship about, please, Mr Tyler,' said Hal, and went to the rail as the ship swung round.

'Boat putting out from the port!' came Aboli's hail.

Hal peered ahead and, out of the gloom, saw the shape of a small dhow coming to meet them. As the range closed and the light strengthened, he felt his heart leap and his breath come shorter.

In the bows stood a figure in unfamiliar garb, a woman who wore a blue caftan and a headcloth of the same colour. As the boat drew alongside she lifted the cloth from her head and Hal saw the glorious dark crown of her hair.

He was waiting for her at the entryport. When Judith Nazet stepped onto the deck, he greeted her awkwardly. 'Good morrow, General Nazet.'

'I am a general no longer. Now I am only a common maid named Judith.'

'You are welcome, Judith.'

'I came as soon as I was able.' Her voice was husky and uncertain. 'Now at last Iyasu is crowned, and the Tabernacle has gone back to its resting place in the mountains.'

'I had despaired of you,' he said.

'No, El Tazar. Never do that,' she answered him.

With surprise, Hal saw that the dhow was already on its way back to the shore. It had unloaded no baggage. 'You have brought nothing with you?' he asked.

'Only my heart,' she replied softly.

'I am southward bound,' he said.

'Wherever you go, my lord, I go also.'

553

Hal turned to Ned Tyler. 'Bring the ship round. Lay her on the other tack. Course to clear Dahlak Island, and then south for the Bab El Mandeb. Full and by, Mr Tyler.'

'Full and by it is, Captain.' Ned grinned widely and winked at Big Daniel.

As the *Golden Bough* ran out to meet the dawn, Hal stood tall on her quarterdeck, his left hand resting lightly on the sapphire in the pommel of the Neptune sword. With his other arm he reached out and drew Judith Nazet closer to him. She came willingly.

OCEAN

GULF OF ADEN

CAPE GUARDAFUI

ARABIA

BAB EL MANDEB

DAHLAK
ISLAND

ADULIS BAY

ZULLA
MITSIWA

ETHIOPIA

AKSUM
GONDER
LAKE TANA

PEMBA ISLAND

ZANZIBAR

RED SEA

USAMBARA
MOUNTAINS

SUDAN

NUBIA

CON

BIRDS
OF
PREY